# WHITMAN SERIES

## BOOKS 1-6

### E.A. SHANNIAK

To Brave A Colorado River by E.A. Shanniak – The Complete Whitman Series Western Romances Books 1-6

To Find A Whitman by E.A. Shanniak

To Love A Thief by E.A. Shanniak

To Save A Life by E.A. Shanniak

To Lift A Darkness by E.A. Shanniak

To Veil A Fondness by E.A. Shanniak

To Bind A Heart by E.A. Shanniak

Entire Series Credits

Cover Design – Silver Sage Book Covers: Charlene Raddon

Developmental & Line Editing – Brittany G.

Proof Reading – Leslie L.

Formatting – Keyminor Publishing

Published by Eagle Creek Books LLC of Molalla, Oregon

www.eashanniak.eaglecreekbooks.com

# DEDICATION

To all my readers,

Thank you for following me on this new and amazing adventure into the world of western romance. Thank you for reading, your support and kindness! I hope you have a great adventure in these final series books.

Much Love,
    Ericka

# MORE BY—E.A. SHANNIAK

Fantasy Romance – A Castre World Novel Series Standalones
    Jordie In Charge
    Avalee's Voice
    Calida's Forge
    Irie's Strength
    The Protector
    Devan's Tenacity
    The Search
    The Visitor – coming soon
    Shifting Aramoren – A Castre World Short Story
    Anchoring Nola – A Castre World Short Story

Storming Area 51— A Bayonet Books Anthology (*military science fiction*)
    Stalking Death

Clean & Sweet Western Romance – Whitman Series
    To Find A Whitman
    To Love A Thief
    To Save A Life

To Lift A Darkness
To Veil A Fondness
To Bind A Heart

Urban Fantasy Romance – A Quivleren World Novel Series
Opening Danger – *coming soon*

# I

## TO FIND A WHITMAN

# CHAPTER ONE

The silvery bells on the flower shop door tinkled merrily behind her as Audrey stepped out into the St. Louis sunshine. She frowned, pulling the door hard behind her. It shut with a satisfying thud.

All around her, wagons clattered, merchants called, horses snorted at their drivers urging them on. It was a brilliant day in the bustling midwestern metropolis. Audrey hadn't been to many cities before, never outside her allotted areas to shop, and definitely never unaccompanied. The excitement prickled Audrey's skin. There was an exhilaration in the air, a whisper of promise and possibility, of freedom—something she'd dreamt of all her life, but never acted upon, not until today.

Her father had kept her secluded either in her mansion or finishing schools. He did not want the pretentiousness of society to hinder her heart. Her father wanted her to believe in goodness. However, twelve years was quite a long time to dream about freedom from the cooped-up comfort of a finishing school, or to see the pretentiousness her father tried so hard to protect her from. And sure as sunshine, Audrey wasn't about to spend the next eighteen years cooped up in her aunt's stuffy parlor with her horrendous cousin. *Perish the thought,* she shivered.

For almost a decade, Audrey lived under the malicious rule of her aunt. Nothing she did was ever good enough; from the way she styled her hair to embroidery. While Audrey, in her youth, craved the attention of Georgiana, the only mother-figure she'd known, it was not to come. Growing older taught her a valuable lesson – for so many people, money spoke louder than a voice. And all Georgiana wanted was her father's wealth... at whatever cost.

Now that she was of age, she was summoned to her aunt's estate here in St. Louis to draw up wedding plans to marry her odious cousin Thomas. Audrey's stomach roiled. Being unattached, wealthy, and a woman made any choices she had complicated. There was always someone to tell her no or dictate her path.

Audrey adjusted her skirts. *Not any more,* she thought. *I will not be a peon any longer. Like Jane Eyre, I shall make my own decisions. My aunt shall not control me.*

Aunt Georgiana was comparable to the dastardly characters in old folklore – cold, calculated, and callous. The most atrocious part of Georgiana was her infatuation with Audrey marrying her son, Thomas. Good Lord above, there was no way she would marry him.

A sneaky smile crept across her lips. *What was that penny novel about, again,* Audrey pondered, *wasn't the girl kidnapped?* Audrey's green eyes brightened. *Brilliant!*

Audrey stood patiently. A stage coach rumbled by. She weaved her way across the street to her waiting carriage. She fiddled with the ends of her braided brown hair. Her aunt's gentle carriage driver waited by the door, bowler hat in hand. When he stepped forward, grinning eagerly and eyes alight, she almost regretted her sudden inspiration, but not quite.

"Rafe, I've just been to the flower shop and have ordered a delicious arrangement of dahlias for my aunt. Could you please load it in the carriage when it is finished?"

"Yes, Miz Audrey." The wrinkled older man bowed his head in respect.

"Thank you. You may wait inside the shop, please. It shan't be long, not more than one hour at most, the lady said." When Rafe's face fell, Audrey hurriedly continued, "Plus the shopkeeper has a nice tea set out. It looked delicious. Thank you, Rafe. You are always so dear and kind."

Rafe grinned, ducking his head. "Aw, thank you, Miz Audrey."

"I am sorry about the wait. I do hope it's no trouble."

He flashed a smile. "No trouble at all. I'll just enjoy me some of those little cookies Susan is famous for."

"I shall be in the next store over on the right, Rafe," she said pointing.

"Yes, Miz Audrey."

She wandered over to the lead horse, a beautiful chestnut gelding with a white star on his forehead, and patted his neck for a moment. When she peeked back over her shoulder, Rafe disappeared into the flower shop.

The noise of the city intensified around her. She calmly gathered her skirts in one hand and used the other to jump into the driver's seat. She clambered on, slipping and tripping over her taffeta skirts. With the reins in hand, she threw the brake.

Audrey clucked her tongue the way she'd often done with her horse at school. "Come on now," she encouraged, mimicking Rafe's speech, and giving the reins a slap. "Nice and easy like."

The horses' ears flicked back and forth, taking a couple of hesitant steps. Audrey grinned triumphantly. With firm hands, she guided the horses into the dusty street, hoping to meld into traffic unnoticed. Audrey pulled her bonnet lower to prevent the sun from blinding her or others recognizing her.

*No wonder most wear darker colors. The dust is ridiculous,* she thought, peeking over her shoulder. The horses whinnied, picking up the pace with her not paying attention. Audrey smiled. Most would call what she was doing insane. Audrey considered it survival.

Getting away from the fiscal pulls of society and the entrapment of it all weighed heavily on her mind. She didn't want to be bound to high society, to the balls and galas, or the double toned meanings of statements. Or her aunt's verbal abuse constantly reminding her how dimwitted and worthless she is.

Audrey cocked her head to the side. "I can make it absolutely dramatic," she announced to the horses.

The animals snorted a reply.

"I believe it's a wonderful idea, thank you." She grinned amused with herself.

Goose pimples prickled her skin. Her stomach churned with equal amounts excitement, and uneasiness. Her plan was bold, even for her.

*Goodness,* Audrey thought, *turn right by the large buildings. All right, here we go.*

"Let's turn," Audrey whispered to the horses. "Nice and easy, please."

She navigated her way down the lane following it back going past several other streets. Audrey bit her lip, glancing around her. No one paid her any mind. She let out the breath she was holding. Audrey's smile grew wider than the streets of Philadelphia. An old wooden warehouse stood abandoned on the corner. Rocks and weeds surrounded the exterior of the building. Audrey made for it, slapping the reins on the backs of the animals. The horses shook their heads, manes tossing. Audrey guided them around the back.

The nervousness that roiled in her body, dissipated. The saccharine appeal of freedom was within her grasp.

"Whoa!" she hollered.

In her hurry, the parasol slipped from her hand and fell beneath the carriage wheel with a crunch. *Oh no,* Audrey thought a moment. *Wait... It's perfect!*

Audrey threw the brake. With a less than graceful leap, Audrey stumbled out of the carriage, landing on her feet. She caught herself with a triumphant gleam in her eye. Shaking out her skirts, she gazed around for a brick, a rock, anything hard.

"Ah, here we are," she announced to the horses.

Hefting a rock in her delicately gloved hand, she threw it

against the carriage window. Cracks spread across the window like a spider web. She tried again, putting her weight against it this time. *Krish!* The window shattered.

"It's all right," she cooed to the startled horses.

The horses snorted, lunging against the carriage ties. She murmured assurances to the spooked creatures. Audrey stealthily pulled out a knife from beneath her skirts. She'd spent the last few hours sharpening it in the solitude of her room. She hefted its weight in her right hand while reaching for the carriage door handle with the other.

The carriage door opened easily. Glass crunched under her boots as she stepped inside. She gripped her knife just as she imagined pirates on the open sea must do, and slashed the seats. She laughed a little imagining herself to be aboard Hawkins' Hispaniola.

"No more uncomfortable seats," she panted, slicing the cushions. "No dreary, confining rides to Aunt Coldaire's! No more Thomas's foul-smelling breath on my neck!" Audrey grinned, pulled her arm back for one final blow. "And no more anyone telling me how I should be!"

Audrey wrenched the knife out of the cushion, and was rewarded with a most satisfying rip. Stuffing from the seats exploded out, floating in tufts she swatted away from her face. The carriage looked like three cats with their tails on fire had clawed their way out.

*It looks marvelous. No one will suspect*, Audrey beamed, pulling off a lace glove, considering her pale pink palm and the winking edge of her sharpened knife. Could she do it?

Audrey pursed her lips. *Much too over the top. A lock of hair will have to do.*

She pulled out a lock from her braid and cut it off, leaving the strands behind for evidence of her certain distress. Now anyone finding her carriage would be forced to believe she'd been taken in some desperate manner, perhaps by some hooligan. Then she'd be free to do as she pleased. She giggled a little. That's how it worked in the novels she'd read. Why wouldn't it work for her?

Stepping down from the carriage, Audrey wondered if she could leave any final touches. She did have a ruby bracelet she cared very little for, despite the obvious cost of the jewelry. *A small token of my enduring affection,* her debonair cousin said in the oily way of his, his cold fingers clasping it around her wrist. She gagged on her own spittle, her skin crawling at the thought.

"All for the cause," she said aloud. She yanked it off, dropping it onto the cobblestones, and ground it gleefully under her boot. *Good riddance!*

Turning to the horses, she loosed them both from their traces and gave the brown mare a slap. With a squeal, the horse headed onto the road, presumably toward her stable home. Audrey kept her hand on the chestnut's halter. Audrey spoke soothingly to him stroking his neck. She cut the reins into something manageable and mounted in an easy leap. Riding bareback was most frowned upon, however, Audrey never cared, enjoying the sense of freedom and the bit of rebellion that came with the act. She arranged her skirts then urged the gelding forward. He began to trot, getting the nervousness of earlier out of his system.

Off in the distance, a train whistle blew, echoing down the street she was leaving behind. Audrey paused. The horse beneath her shuddering with the same excitement. Audrey smiled; her animal's ears perked in the same direction. The gelding whinnied.

"Splendid!" Audrey exclaimed, galloping toward freedom.

# CHAPTER TWO

The setting sun painted the countryside in pinked hues, warming the green rolling hills in a golden glow that contrasted with the deep blue sky. The effect was heartwarming and entirely lost on Georgiana Coldaire. Face bathed in the sun's final rays, she stood in the open doorway of her vast mansion home clutching a handkerchief in her fist while working on her sniffles, not that the man in front of her could tell they were fake. The sheriff walked down the long white gravel drive, passing beneath the shadows of precisely shaped magnolia trees. He untied his waiting horse and turned to give her a final reassuring wave. Georgiana gently dabbed her eyes, raising her handkerchief. The sheriff tipped his hat, and took off down the drive back to St. Louis.

Even before the hoofbeats retreated, Georgiana tossed the lace cloth behind her and entered her parlor, sitting down in a chair with a laugh. It was almost too perfect. Never in her wildest dreams had she thought her niece would simply disappear. Grow ill and die maybe—tuberculosis was still happily common these days among the young people—but to go out one day and never return? For such a stroke of luck, one could thank Providence. If one believed so.

Georgiana smiled, leaning back comfortably in the chair. She rang the bell on the table.

Ruth entered the room. The red-headed maid dipped a curtsey. "Yes, ma'am?"

"Get me Thomas immediately."

Ruth hesitated. "With all due respect, ma'am, Master Thomas is not here."

Georgiana spun around. Her eyes narrowed with tight lips. "What part of 'get me Thomas immediately' did not penetrate your head, girl? I do not care where my son is, get him to me!"

"Yes, ma'am." Ruth dipped a curtsey and bolted way.

"Insolent girl!" Georgiana grumbled. In a louder voice, "Able, are you there?"

"Yes, ma'am." The butler, a balding dark-skinned man, gave a slight bow.

"Get me a pen and paper. I need to send an urgent telegram to my brother's lawyer."

Georgiana straightened herself in the chair, awaiting Able's return. She wondered who took the brat and where she was. Hopefully dead, although it did not matter. The sheriff was a bumbling idiot who could not handle much past the drunken bums in the streets. After being attacked in her own carriage, Audrey was good as dead.

Georgiana seethed under her breath. "Time to take what is rightfully mine."

That bubbly, ditz of a girl inherited everything after her father died while she was forced to live on the stipends he provided previous to his tragic passing. Everything, every estate he owned, and hotel, should have been hers. Audrey hadn't the cunning or the smarts for managing so much wealth. Audrey's romantic putz of a head was much to in the clouds, or in a book. Now, her Thomas. He was another story. When he pulled his own head out of the gambling tables, he was cunning and wily. No matter, she would run it all now, as it should have been long ago.

Georgiana's eyes narrowed. *It was MY idea to begin hotels. It was my idea to rise up from poverty and rise I have.* Georgiana hissed under her breath. *My brother borrowed money from my husband to start up his business. It is only fitting I get my investment back, tenfold.*

The door to the parlor opened. She looked over her shoulder. Able strode forth with her requirements on a silver tray. Georgiana scribbled a telegram to Wilfred Darrow, instructing Able to send straight away. Able left, handing off the telegram to another servant.

*I should send a thank you note to whoever disposed of the wretch,* Georgiana mused.

On the other side of the parlor, the door burst open. Thomas ran in, his eyes wild, searching for the woman who was no longer here. Georgiana rolled her eyes. Thomas's love for theatre took a turn for the ludicrous dramatics.

"Mother, I just got back. What seems to be the matter?" Thomas asked trying to catch his breath.

Georgiana motioned for Thomas to sit. "Most grievous news, my dearest son. It seems your marriage is to be postponed. Audrey has gotten herself murdered."

"Indeed, what grievous news." Thomas turned his back on his mother and ran his hands through his hair. "I was looking forward to the nuptials," he said turning around with a malicious upward quirk of his lips.

"Indeed." Georgiana matched his countenance.

He took a seat and pulled out his pipe. Georgiana's lip curled. He struck a match and sucked on his pipe until the flame caught. "I suppose arrangements must be made," he said. "A funeral and all."

"Quite."

"And then, what of her fortune?"

"You mean, our family fortune?"

Thomas inclined his head.

"I suppose it must be passed on to the family, all fortunes must when one passes over to the Golden Shore."

There were times when even poetry and religion spoke to Madame Coldaire's heart. Tonight, was one of those moments. She was in a good mood. Georgiana leaned back in her cushioned seat. A small smile toyed at the edges of her lips. "Dear Audrey. Such a sweet, kind child she was. I am sure nothing would make her happier than to know her fortune passed on to her loving aunt and most attentive cousin. I have sent a note to summon Wilfred Darrow here. Once the lawyer arrives, he shall get all the proper paperwork in order, and dear Audrey's fortune shall be ours."

Thomas clasped his hands together, leaning back in the chair, crossing his legs and exhaling luxuriously, a content grin forming, "Splendid, Mother."

# CHAPTER THREE

E ugene strolled down the cobblestone streets of Philadelphia, his hands in his coat pockets. His broad brimmed hat tipped downward, shading his tanned face from the hot late summer sun. He paused to let a lorry rumble by. Glancing down the busy street, he found what he was looking for. A crowd of bystanders gathered about a salesman like curious flies bumbling around a honeypot.

*Poor fellows falling for the same scandal I had once,* Eugene thought, adjusting the hat on his brown head.

He glanced down at the crumpled paper in his hands while casually glancing over his shoulders, checking to see if anyone matched the rough sketch on the paper. The fellow was a wanted man for conning, robbery and groping a woman. The tip he received from his errand boy was well worth the few hours on foot, tracking him down to get here. Luckily the man hadn't left Philadelphia, just changed streets, and he was standing in the middle of the gathered crowd.

*That's him,* Eugene surmised, tucking the note and sketch away. *After this, I need to get back to the station, and finalize the case.* He paused for a while, looking on at the scene below. The man was building momentum, gaining curious onlookers and potential cons by the moment. A man strolled by with his lady on his arm. Eugene watched the lady lay her head on the man's shoulder when they paused to listen. *I don't want to do this forever,* Eugene decided. *I would like a home with a wife. Someone who will lean on me like that.*

Eugene put his hands back in his pockets, internally shaking his head at the thought and turning his focus back to the wanted man. He grumbled at the thought of returning to the station. He wasn't quite a police officer or a detective. He was a Pinkerton, a free-lance, under respected, underpaid private investigator for officials who deemed themselves too busy to investigate certain cases.

Eugene rolled his eyes. He worked long and hard to get to where he was unlike the upper class with money and mansions being handed to them. To rise from the slums of New York to a free-lance investigator was more than what his family thought capable, God rest their souls. And he thrived in the field he'd chosen, earning money from the aristocrats themselves.

The man on the street corner's voice boomed off the brick buildings. He hollered at the gathered crowd about his miracle soaps. Allegedly, they could clean all surfaces and cure all manner of ills. The delightful scents, the full lather, the guaranteed effica-ciousness of this marvelous soap—the salesman's handlebar mustache trembled in rapture over his soap as he proclaimed all its wonderful benefits.

Eugene joined the mass near the front, wanting to laugh at the man's mustache. He rolled his broad shoulders back, taking in the scene. He was within arm's reach of the man's open suitcase displaying a neatly stacked pyramid of soap, each bar wrapped in brown paper.

The peddler clapped his hands then spreading them wide, "Now, my fine fellows, for only one dollar, you can buy yourself a genuine miracle. You've heard what it has done for me, now try it for yourself—"

"Imagine paying one whole dollar for a single bar of soap," the stout housewife next to Eugene muttered to her companion. "I could buy three cases of it with the money."

"But if it can clean all that he says, isn't it worth the expense?" her friend asked.

"Bollocks to that. To hear him speak of it, his miracle soap cleans stains out of lace, rust off of pots, and leprosy out of skin! Let's go. We've wasted enough time on this foolishness."

As they turned to leave, the women caught the salesman's eye. "But that's not all," he went on, his excitement tipping him up on his toes like a marionette on strings. "In honor of my dear old mum's birthday, which happens to be today, I have hidden a ten-dollar bill within one of these five lucky soaps. Here, sir—try one!"

The housewife stopped to watch the salesman toss a bar of soap to a bystander. Catching it, the man ripped open the paper and crowed with delight, holding up the bill. The crowd buzzed with excitement.

"Two twenty-dollar bills are hidden somewhere in this pile," the peddler said, gesturing to his pyramid. "And, in one lucky, *lucky* bar of soap, I have hidden... a one-hundred-dollar bill." His eyes went heavenward. "All for my dear old mum!"

The honey had been set, and the crowd caught. They swarmed the peddler, all reaching for the purses and pockets to fish out coins, each wanting a bar of soap for themselves. They pushed and shoved their way forward to the man's open suitcase.

To Eugene, the charade went on long enough. "All right, show's over," he hollered, stepping forward.

The peddler grinned broadly, placing his hands on his hips in a way that made Eugene wonder if there was a pistol hiding beneath his coat. "Ah, good sir, there is more than enough to go around, I assure you."

Eugene nodded. "I am certain there is; however, I am afraid I must call out your ploy."

The man chuckled, taking two dollars from a nearby woman and handed her a couple of bars. "I am afraid, good sir, I do not understand what you mean."

Eugene's light cinnamon brown eyes narrowed. "I apologize for the confusion. Your soap selling is a hoax, a con, a ruse. Are any of those terms able to resolve your confusion?"

Two men from the crowd moved toward the front; one, the man who found money in his soap package, the other one of the big men who watched the crowd from the back, Eugene noted. Money-package Man rolled up his sleeves while the other's hands clenched into fists.

The swindler laughed uncomfortably. "Now, now, ladies and gentlemen, this man is simply angry he has not won any money! I assure you, there *is* money inside these marvelously crafted bars of soap."

Eugene spun around and faced the crowd. "Please return to your business. This man is a crook. If you will all check your purchases now, you will find there is no money in the packaging."

The murmurs in the crowd went from disappointment and confusion to outrage. People opened their packets and found nothing but bars of waxy tallow. Some left, but others started demanding their money back. The con artist turned to Eugene, his mustache twitching in rage. Two more men approached from either side, their expressions matching the darkness of their ring leader's. The tallest of them stood on his left. Eugene lowered his head, waiting for the fist he knew was seconds away.

The hustler wasn't done. "I have just two bars left and one must have the hundred-dollar bill," he announced, holding up the packaged soap. "Who wants it? Let's start the bidding at ten dollars!"

"Run along, people," Eugene returned, lifting his head to be heard.

Furious, the crook slammed his suitcase closed, shaking the rickety tripod beneath it. "I've had enough of you! Get 'em, boys!"

The big man, Fist Man, reached Eugene right at that moment, taking a swing at him. Eugene ducked from the heavy-handed throw, coming up with a right hook to the gut. With a *whoof*, the man doubled over. Eugene finished him with a kick to the face. The man to Eugene's right grabbed the collar of his shirt and swung. The blow landed on Eugene's jaw.

Pain radiated through his head. Eugene planted his feet and swung back, hitting the other con man on the right temple, dropping him like a stone. Police whistles sounded from the distance.

Eugene spun around and ran ten steps, grabbing the ringleader before he'd a chance to flee. The panicked man took a less than accurate swing with his suitcase and the case slammed feebly against Eugene's shoulder, popping open and spilling the last two soap bars on the cobblestones. Eugene threw him in a headlock as he awaited the officers rushing toward him.

"Nice work, Turner," Officer Hudson of the Philadelphia police said with a smile.

Eugene shook his hand. "Thank you, John. The tip I received proved well worth my time. Thank you for arriving quickly."

John gave a tight smile. "Think nothing of it. Always a pleasure working with you, Eugene."

"Mr. Turner! Mr. Turner!"

Eugene pivoted to the voice. One of his errand boys rushed toward him waving a yellow paper in his small hands. Eugene strode to him, bending down to his level as the boy approached. The boy stopped, staggering forward, out of breath.

"What's the matter, Sean?" Eugene asked.

The boy huffed, catching his breath. "A telegram, sir. Just came in from Mr. Darrow."

Eugene plucked the message from the boy's hand and read the urgent telegram. He shoved the yellow slip of paper in his coat pocket.

"Good work, Sean," he praised, handing the boy a packet of black licorice and five cents. "That will be all for the day. Run along."

Eugene peered behind him at the officers dragging the reluctant con artists to the paddy wagon. His pocket watch declared it was just past two o'clock. *Should give me enough time to catch the next train to Saint Louis.*

# CHAPTER FOUR

The train shrieked, chugging to a halt at the St. Louis station. Eugene pulled out his pocket watch. He was to meet Darrow at the Coldaire estate at one o'clock. It was already twelve thirty. He grimaced, not liking the possibility of being late.

After disembarking, Eugene hailed a Hansom cab and directed the driver to the Coldaire estate. Settling back into the leather seat, Eugene opened his briefcase, reviewing the report he'd picked up from the local sheriff once again. According to the report, Audrey Whitman died from multiple stab wounds. However, the body of the young woman was yet to be found and there was no blood at the scene. The report went on to detail the destruction of the carriage, the victim's personal items, and the team of horses being cut loose. Ms. Whitman's benefactors, Georgiana Coldaire and her son Thomas, desired to close the case, claiming the death, and subsequent scandal too painful for their small family to endure. Evidently, it was enough for this sheriff to call the case closed.

Eugene rolled his eyes. *How shoddy can an officer of the law get? No body, no blood, no ransom note. No one disappears, for goodness sakes, especially a wealthy young heiress. More than likely, she ran off with a fellow, or perhaps from someone in particular.*

Eugene pulled out the telegram from Wilfred Darrow. He'd the pleasure of working for Darrow previously on a case involving stolen horses. Eugene sighed, raking his fingers through his warm brown hair. *Come to St. Louis forthwith. You shall be investigating a disappearance,* Eugene read thinking about Darrow's slight English accent that dissipated with his immigration to America. Clearly, Darrow believed otherwise also.

Seeing the good lawyer would be beneficial. Darrow might have something for him to help the case. Eugene hoped as much. Missing persons cases were not his favorite.

*After this, home to Philadelphia,* Eugene sighed with anticipation. *Buy a home and find a wife.* He chuckled to himself. *And not necessarily in that order.*

He stuffed the papers back in his briefcase, slamming the lid shut. He gazed out the open Hansom cab, to the rows of manicured hedges and trees leading up to the mansion. Wilfred Darrow waited for him outside, underneath the white marble pillars. The old lawyer dabbed his forehead with a kerchief.

In a few quick strides, Eugene mounted the stairs and shook Darrow's hand.

"Darrow. How goes it with you?" Eugene asked.

Darrow's eyes narrowed, glancing at the open double doors behind him. "Decent enough. Thank you for coming, Eugene. Let's handle this now." His tone and glance at the doors set Eugene on the alert.

Stone-faced, Darrow led the way into the mansion. The butler, a balding man with a benign but keen expression, led them to the parlor, where Mrs. Coldaire sat in a chair looking distraught. She held the posture of a queen in full mourning, her elegantly coiffed coal-black hair streaked with silver, her voluminous black skirts emphasizing one of the smallest waists Eugene had ever seen on an older lady. It couldn't be comfortable. She clutched a kerchief in her right hand, sniffling intermittently and dabbing occasionally at her clear, calculating, dry green eyes. Thomas, her son, stood smoking a pipe by the window, looking handsome, bored, and listless.

Eugene sighed inwardly. *Typical aristocrat.*

"Thank you, gentlemen, for coming to my humble abode on such short notice," Madam Coldaire said. "These are such trying times for the family, and yet we must stir ourselves up to move forward. Much is yet to be done without poor, dear Audrey."

Darrow's lips pressed in a thin line. "Indeed," he said.

"Able," she snapped at the butler. Eugene perked a brow at her momentarily forgotten grief. Mrs. Coldaire pointed a shaky hand at a mirror, "throw the shawl over the hallway mirror. I can't stand to see a mirror when there's been a death in the house." She collapsed into her chair as if suddenly overwhelmed. Eugene suppressed the smirk and eye roll that wanted to come out at the woman's dramatics.

"Please, have a seat," Thomas instructed. "My mother has been sorely vexed. She's waited these past few days for any word about dearest Audrey. Sadly, no one's turned up anything."

"Absolutely nothing, Mrs. Coldaire?" Eugene asked.

Mrs. Coldaire put a hand to her head. "Indeed. The sheriff dropped off the wrecked carriage this morning for you to inspect."

"Mrs. Coldaire, was there a note for ransom or any letters left behind?"

Georgiana shook her head, sniffling, and patting her dry eyes. Thomas relayed there wasn't anything unusual or out of place. Georgiana looked away, putting a hand against her mouth, staring blankly out the window. Thomas pulled on his pipe. Soon a stream of smoke billowed up in lazy waves.

Eugene struggled to remain passive. His fingers strummed on the arm of the chair. *Overly dramatic aunt and a distant, dandy cousin,* Eugene thought. *Clearly, they do not miss her at all.*

A tight line formed on Eugene's lips. He'd not seen so distantly shocking reactions to a death of a person deemed 'beloved by all'. Eugene took a side glance toward Wilfred Darrow whose keen hawk-like gaze hadn't changed during their entire interaction.

*Clearly not buying it either,* Eugene surmised.

"With her father's untimely death when she was naught but twelve, we took her in and cared for her. We developed a fondness for each other," Thomas sighed, shaking his head. Georgiana patted his hand. Woefully, Thomas continued, "Audrey and I decided to marry this fall. She left her finishing school to come here and plan the event with me and my mother. She," Thomas sighed again, shaking his head, "never made it here." Georgiana roused herself up long enough to attest to her delight in seeing her most favorite niece at last.

Eugene consulted his book of notes. Locking eyes with Georgiana, he asked, "she is your *only* niece, is she not?"

Mrs. Coldaire dabbed her eyes. "Quite right, my only niece and the best in all the world!"

Thomas, shifted from foot to foot, giving his pipe another pull.

"Dear Audrey was very excited for the wedding," Georgiana continued, sniffling. "Of course, being such a young lady, she left all the arrangements in my hands—the seamstresses, flowers, invitations and all. Such an expense. I suppose it must all be returned now since the dear child is gone. I shall never get over the heartbreak of it all."

Thomas exhaled smoke through his nostrils in twin streams. "Do not worry, Mother. We will honor her memory forever," his voice hitching at the end.

Eugene glanced to the floor for a moment. *By all that is Holy, I've never seen such... a theatre.*

Georgiana tapped a black-gloved finger to her lips, momentarily lost in thought. "But what shall become of the estate and all of the holdings? My brother's hotels won't run themselves. Shouldn't it all pass to us to take care of? After all, we are the sole family she had."

Wilfred Darrow cleared his throat. "*Has* left, madam. Let us not be hasty. Without a body or any confirmation of her death, we must assume Miss Whitman remains alive. Therefore, there can be no legal change of ownership, and the estate and financial holdings remain in my care. It is why I hired Eugene Turner," Darrow stated, motioning to Eugene, "a Pinkerton, widely respected in his field. He's a highly trained professional and shall investigate the murder or disappearance of Audrey forthwith. Meanwhile, I will return to my work, for you are right. The hotels won't run themselves." Darrow rose. "And so, Eugene, I leave you to it. Good day, Madam Coldaire. Thomas."

Eugene walked over to Darrow and shook his hand. "I will find her."

"See that you do," Darrow said, and the butler saw him out.

Eugene turned to face the two Coldaire's. "I should like to see Audrey's room and the carriage."

Georgiana nodded. "Thomas, show him the carriage."

"Yes, Mother. Eugene, if you'd please."

Eugene followed Thomas out of the room, wondering at the true state of the carriage. Thomas led Eugene on a meandering path through the back of the house. Eugene couldn't help but note how empty the place was. Aside from Able, he caught sight of two other servants, and the halls seemed oddly bare. Large squares of dark-colored paint marred the walls, wooden stands stood empty without vases, and the kitchen was a wreck of hastily constructed meals with no cook to oversee them. Outside, the grounds certainly did not have enough hands to maintain such a large property.

Thomas grunted, the barn doors creaking open. "Blast this infernal building!" Thomas huffed. "Perspiration will certainly ruin my new suit!"

The corner of Eugene's lip twitched. As the dandy continued his complaints, Eugene resisted the urge to check the time. He was quickly losing patience with this man and this case. He did not like searching for missing persons. They were either found, well off and hiding, or dead. In the present case, Audrey was wealthier than Spain or England which could leave her in either situation.

*She had to have been abducted,* Eugene surmised. *More than likely taken west where her ties to society would be far and few between.*

Thomas's whining about his suit gave way to boasts about how the ladies flocked to him. However, the man supposedly devoted his soul to his poor cousin, and no woman could ever come close to her in beauty. And now, here he was, left bereft without his beloved.

"I am telling you, Pinkerton, Audrey is dead," Thomas continued. "You can even ask Rafe."

Eugene whirled around. "Rafe?"

Thomas sighed irritably. "The carriage driver. The last person to see Audrey."

Eugene made a mental note to speak to the man soon. Eugene sized up the wrecked carriage. Its slashed leather reins were the first item to catch his attention. Eugene picked up a leather strap, inspecting the cut. The straps were cut with a downward slash at an angle, and evidently the person sawed through the leather a bit.

Eugene scrutinized the leather, *either the knife wasn't sharp or their wrists were weak. Perhaps a bit of both.*

He moved around to the right side of the carriage. The glass was smashed out of the windows, but for what purpose? None he could discern seeing the door lock intact and easily unlatched.

"See?" Thomas said, stroking his ridiculous mustache. "It is as the sheriff said. My poor cousin is lost to us forever."

Eugene ignored his voice like the buzzing of a gnat and turned his interest to the inside of the carriage. His shoes crunched on glass as he stepped inside. Someone had taken a knife to the carriage seat. It was completely destroyed along with the cushion of the backrest. Stuffing from inside littered the carriage floor. The person, or persons, who made these vigorous stabbing and slash marks was in a hurry; the slashes seemed random and for no particular reason.

*A great deal of energy went into making a scene like this*, Eugene thought.

However, he couldn't detect any sign of blood. The only damage received was to the carriage itself. There may have been a struggle, *although with the randomness of the slash marks, I'd imagine she would've been hit by the knife at some point.* With the lack of blood on the carriage material and no sign of a body, he could now assume the girl was, most likely, alive. *Something more is going on than a simple kidnapping.*

"I should like to see her room, if I may," Eugene announced.

Thomas gave an impatient jerk of his head. "If you must. I don't quite see what good it will do, seeing it is plain the girl was attacked, quite violently, and now is gone. It's not like Mother to give up hope, the woman's a stubborn old bird, but even she can tell the situation's hopeless. What more do you need to see, to know, dear Audrey, is woefully dead?"

"It is for me to decide in the course of my investigation," Eugene said pointedly. "I shall find your beloved cousin dead or alive. If dead, I shall return with the body. And, if this is the case, as you assume, in a few days her body shall be quite odorous and the pungency of her remains will, without question, affect the quality of your attire. Observing how enamored you are with Miss. Whitman, it should not be a hindrance though. If anything, having a type of closure will be a relief."

Thomas blinked. "This way, if you will," he harrumphed, turning on his heel.

Eugene curbed the smirk twitching on the edges of his lips. Thomas led him back toward the Coldaire Estate. A man approached from a side path, his dusty bowler hat in his caramel hands. Thomas sighed again, seemingly more irritated at the delay.

"'Evenin'. I'm Rafe the driver," the man said, sticking out his hand.

Eugene took it. "Pleasure. Eugene Turner, Pinkerton. I hear you can you tell me what happened?"

Rafe nodded. "We stopped in St. Louis. Miz Audrey asked to stop at a flower shop and ordered a passel of flowers for Madam Coldaire."

Eugene whipped out his notepad and scribbled it down. "Flowers?"

"Yep. Dahlias, Miz Audrey said. Said the arrangement would take an hour to put together. Wanted me to wait for 'em while they're being made."

"What else happened?"

"So's, I went into the store like she asked me to, while she went next door to shop."

"What else?"

Rafe sniffed, dabbing at his eyes. "Weren't but a few minutes I was in the shop waitin' when I happened to look out the window for the carriage and she was gone. She plum vanished, carriage, horses, and all."

"You didn't hear anything from inside the store—no shouts or sounds of a scuffle?"

"No, sir, nuthin'."

"Can you tell me what she was wearing?"

Rafe nodded. "A blue dress... fluffy like. The color of the sky with white frilly trimmin'."

"Anything you can tell me about how she seemed to you that day? Anything out of the ordinary about her mannerism?"

"How she seemed to me?" Rafe scratched his head. "Nuthin' I can reckon. She was right pert like usual, chattin' up a storm. Happy, I'd say. But she's always seemed happy to me. She's one of the sunshiniest ladies I've ever met. Sure, hope nuthin' bad's happened to her. You'll find her soon, won't you?"

Eugene put his notebook away and shook the man's hand. "With your help, and Lord willing, I will. Thank you for this information, Rafe. This helps me immensely."

The older man nodded and scooted off. Thomas pulled out an ivory snuff box and gave himself a delicate pinch. "He's a good servant," he said as Rafe disappeared into the stables. "I hope he wakes up to reality soon. Otherwise he'll be crushed at her funeral and useless that day."

Comments like his reminded Eugene why he preferred to stick with men who knew how to work for a living, and not gentlemen pampered until they were no longer gentle, nor men.

*Which is why I stick to middle class, still gentlemen, not swayed by currency, and not so poor off to be desolate and depressed,* Eugene thought.

"Shall we?" Eugene asked, trying to keep the annoyance from his voice.

Thomas led him through the oaken doors of the Coldaire Estate. The man turned to the right, going up a circling tower of stairs.

"We gave my dear cousin a room to herself to do whatever her fancy. She would paint, press flowers, that sort of thing. It is as you see." Thomas stopped at the door and pulled out his pipe. Eugene scowled at the door, seeing the locking mechanism from the outside instead of in. He walked around the other side of the door. No scratch marks or markings. Eugene left the thought alone for the moment, circling about the room. Thomas dumped the sooty tobacco from his pipe out in the porcelain water basin near Audrey's easel. Then he took to packing the pipe with fresh tobacco.

*The Devil's weed, as Ma would say,* Eugene thought, walking over to the painting easel near the window.

A lonely dahlia was in the middle, painted orange in a blue vase. Embroidery sat on the cushioned chair, a needle and thread lying neatly on top. Eugene picked it up, reading the red-stitched words 'Charity Never Faileth' in the crisp white cotton.

"Where is her bedroom?" Eugene asked, setting the embroidery down.

"Over there on the left. Said something about wanting to over-look the gardens out in back." Thomas had his pipe lit and seemed to be trying to make perfect rings of smoke. His face gaped like a gasping fish's as the cloudy rings looped up toward the ceiling.

*Let's get this over with,* Eugene thought. *The sooner I'm out of here, the better.*

Opening the door, Eugene found the room surprisingly small to be the home of an heiress. The door also locked on the outside.

Spying Eugene examine the lock closer, along with the surprise on his face at the size of the room, Thomas shrugged and said, "Old home you know, but Audrey insisted on this room."

On the left was a humble bookcase. Two rows on the bottom, both filled with books. Trinkets and porcelain dolls sat on the top two rows. Underneath the white paned window stood the bed, covered in a pink quilt embroidered with flowers. On the bed was her diary.

Eugene went straight for it. He opened it seeing delicately pressed violets on the first several pages. He flipped through several more, seeing sketches of couples strolling down a sidewalk in brick-lined streets.

*My Dearest Friend,*

*How I long to have an adventure of some kind. I feel like little Jane Eyre in Miss Bronte's book, only before she left her finishing school and met her mysterious Mister Rochester, and then found herself the courage to leave his mansion and go off on her own to see what she could take on in the world. She made her own path. I desire the same and—oh! I find myself rambling. But what else can one do on a bright, golden day with no one to talk to but an empty page?*

There was no signature of her on this particular page. Eugene closed the diary and stuck it in his coat pocket for further reading. Perhaps there would be some clue here about what happened to Miss Whitman. He took another look around, his eyes passing over the fanciful dolls and books with flower stems poking out of them. Nothing there of interest. Opening the desk, he found a few letters from friends back East—finishing school acquaintances, most like. All letters in neat, flourishing penmanship, all addressed to girls at a ladies' school in Massachusetts. So, unless her kidnapper was related to one of these acquaintances, here was another dead end. Still, Eugene made a pile of the papers and addresses, slipping them in his briefcase.

Eugene walked out of the door, closing it softly behind him. Thomas leaned against the hallway wall in a haze of smoke.

"So, you have seen her room and the carriage," Thomas remarked. "Anything else you care to inspect or are we done here?"

Eugene thanked him for his time and assured the gentleman he'd let himself out. His footsteps echoed hollowly as he left the empty Coldaire Estate. He needed to speak with Darrow.

# CHAPTER FIVE

Audrey glanced out the window, smiling, tucking some unruly hairs behind her ear. Her hands lay neatly in her lap. Her eyes roamed the passing landscape. Acres and acres of green land were set before her. Herds of horses and bison stampeding held her attention. Audrey could not help but smile. This was the adventure she always dreamt of.

She closed her eyes. The sun filtered through the small glass window, striking her face. The smile that brushed her lips could not be removed. Audrey inhaled deeply, relishing the smell of the wild instead of the perfumed rooms she was accustomed to. She loved the freedom she felt seep into her bones. She loved the thrill of watching the wild horses gallop close to the train, how independent they were.

*I could positively never tire of such a sight!*

Her entire life was routine, schedules and parties. Her life was education, classes, learning many languages to define her as accomplished. But the life she wanted was not the one she lived. Audrey wanted romance. Audrey wanted someone to love her for all she was, not for the money her father accumulated.

Audrey sighed. She wondered what her mother would have

said to all she was doing. But she shall never know. Her mother died when she was a child. She wondered if her father would scold her for what she was doing now. But again, she was to never hear his voice again.

*I miss them*, she thought. *I miss what could have been.*

Audrey opened her eyes when she heard the car door open. Jack, the conductor, came by, helping a woman move her belongings; suitcases in each hand and under his arms. The woman's son sat next to the window. His small face immediately pressed against the glass. The woman thanked Jack for the new accommodations and took a seat beside her son.

"Mother!" the boy shouted, "look at the size of that buffalo! Do you think the Indians rode them too?"

"William!" the mother scolded. "Hush your voice. And no, I do not believe the Indians rode *bison*. Far too ornery."

Audrey snickered.

The woman turned to her with a smile. Audrey stuck out her hand. "Hello, my dear lady. My name is Audrey. It is a pleasure to meet you."

The woman grinned, shaking her hand. "My name is Pearl. It is a pleasure to meet you as well. This is my son, William."

The little boy spun around. "Hello, ma'am."

"This is such a beautiful day; do you not agree?" Audrey said.

"Yes, I do," Pearl replied. "We have been on a train for a few days now. I cannot wait until we are done."

Audrey's eyes went wide. "You do not like the train? I believe it is rather charming."

Pearl laughed softly. "Not when you are on it for several days non-stop."

"Well, it would be rather discomforting, I suppose."

"Is this your first time on a train?"

Audrey smiled sheepishly. "No, it is not. All the other rides I have taken were a rather quick affair. This is my first trip lasting longer than a few hours."

"We are headed to Oregon!" William blurted.

Audrey smiled. "How wonderful! What kind of adventure are you going to take first, young sir?"

William clambered over his mother. He licked his lips and smiled, revealing several missing teeth. "I wanna get me a big ol' black bear and mount him on my bedroom wall."

Audrey gasped. "Sounds ferocious. However, will you take on such a beast?"

"My Pa is gonna get me a big rifle to take 'em down."

"Where are you headed Audrey?"

Audrey fiddled with her hands. "Denver. I am heading to my new job. I got hired as a teacher."

Audrey was rather surprised with herself. She'd never lied before and grimaced slightly. It came out easier than she expected it to. She glanced out the window momentarily, taking a deep breath.

*I can do this*, she reminded herself.

William groaned. Pearl pinched her son, calling his actions rude. Audrey smiled at the boy. She too, loathed school at some point in her life. It had to be around the time she was learning Greek after finishing French. Audrey shuddered. She will more than likely never use Greek for the rest of her life but now it was crammed into her head, taking up space.

"Are you cold, Audrey?" Pearl asked.

Audrey laughed softly. "No, I am not. I shuddered at the thought of seeing a bear."

Pearl chuckled. "I shudder at the thought myself. My husband Bryan went to Oregon to be a fur trapper. Now that he is settled out west, we sold our home in Ohio to join him."

"That sounds absolutely exciting!" Audrey exclaimed.

The car door opened again. Audrey glanced behind her, seeing Jack return with a cart. He strolled up with a smile.

"Good afternoon, fine ladies and little gentleman, care for some refreshments?" Jack asked.

William whined for some licorice. Pearl scolded him and told Jack no. Audrey took several coins out of her purse and purchased some licorice and other candies. Jack left with a smile. William stared at her with wide eyes.

"Oh goodness," Audrey exclaimed. "I am sorely afraid I have purchased too many sweets. William, could you be a dear and help me eat these?"

Pearl smirked, giving her a nod. William looked to his mother who nodded.

"You have to be a sweet, well-behaved boy for your mother."

William raised his right hand. "I do so swear."

Audrey hid a smile, handing him all the black licorice as it was her least favorite. Just thinking about the awful taste made her shudder.

"Thank you, Miss Audrey. Say, if you are my teacher, instead of letter grades, how about pieces of candy?"

Audrey laughed. "I will consider the request, William."

"Oh good. I am sure you would get a lot more kids to pay attention that way."

Audrey made a face and nodded. "Oh yes," she stated in a firmer voice. "Very astute reasoning there, my dear boy."

"Where did ya get that necklace?"

Audrey smiled as she touched it. "It was my mothers. Inside is a picture of her and my father on their wedding day. It is all I have left of her."

Pearl put a hand to her heart. "I am so sorry for you, Dear."

Audrey smiled wanly, "It is all right. It was a long time ago."

Pearl spoke of her husband and their family. Most of hers were back in Ohio while his were in Michigan. Pearl spoke of them for quite some time. Audrey had no idea how much family she had. The only people she knew of were Georgiana and Thomas Coldaire, her father's sister and nephew. After hours of listening to Pearl talk about her family, Audrey wanted a family like Pearl's someday.

The train whistle blew loudly, garnering their attention. Audrey beamed as Jack announced they were now in Kansas City. Audrey felt her insides tingle with excitement.

"Audrey, you must dine with us tonight," Pearl insisted.

Audrey reached out and shook Pearl's hand. "I would be absolutely delighted. Thank you for the invitation."

"We are headed to the Silver Spoon, a dining hotel."

"Sounds wonderful. I shall seek accommodations there myself."

Jack ushered them off the train, standing on the wooden platform to help them down. Audrey's smile covered her jittery insides.

*I made it*, she thought. *I am Jane Eyre. I can "blaze my own trail" as I have heard some others say.* Audrey took a deep breath, taking in the bustling town. *First thing, I need a room and to get refreshed. Second, I need to purchase a ticket for Denver.* Audrey beamed at a woman and her husband in a wagon. *I can do this.*

People smiled. Men tipped their hat to her. Audrey followed Pearl as she seemed to know the way.

Today was the beginning of a grand adventure, made more perfect with new friends.

---

Audrey settled into her room. It was small and quaint, with a metal framed bed under the window. A small dresser was to her left. A wash basin sat on top with a cracked standing mirror. The floor hadn't been swept in a while; dust bunnies accumulated in the corner.

Audrey inhaled deeply. The room she had was cheap enough, leaving her with a substantial sum left in her coin purse. Audrey glanced at the small wall clock, announcing the time as fifteen to five. Her stomach rumbled. She checked her mouse brown hair in the mirror. Pulling at her skin, she checked her green eyes for bags and pinched her cheeks for some color. After quickly washing her face with cold water, she felt refreshed. The dust and grime from riding the train came off on the towel.

With a smile in the mirror, she turned on her heel and exited. She strode down the long hallway and the stairs, turning to the left where she entered a different world, abruptly departing the rugged pioneer entering into the fanciful taste of the east coast. It stunned her for a moment. She wasn't expecting such a change. If she were honest with herself, she was a bit disappointed. She was leaving all this opulence behind simply to find it at the hotel she chose to stay at.

She stood back for a moment, pushing aside her disappointment and looking about the room for her newly acquainted friends to dine with. Audrey spied them over to the right. She walked over with a pep in her step. Audrey sat on the outside chair next to the walkway. The little boy sat across from her, drinking his water with a spoon.

"William," Pearl scolded, "do not slurp."

"Sorry Mama."

A waitress came over, bringing Audrey some water. The waitress leaned over Audrey with a quick "excuse me," handing Pearl a newspaper.

Audrey took a sip of water, slurping it like William, winking at him from above her spoon. The boy laughed.

Audrey whispered, "It is amusing," she chuckled.

William leaned over, whispering back, "I know."

The waitress came back taking their order. After she left, Pearl began reading the paper aloud softly, but only the little tidbits Pearl found interesting like scandals - especially the Soapy Smith ones. Audrey added her amusement as she giggled and asked Pearl to have the paper when she was finished. William sat, listening enraptured to his mother. Pearl told him about what the sheriff had been doing according to the stories in the paper. The boy's eyes lit up, going wide as the sheriff single handedly took out three wanted criminals with a gun firing shoot-out.

"Mama, I want to be a sheriff," William stated.

Pearl smiled lovingly down at her son. "I thought you wanted to be a trapper like your Pa?"

William shook his head. "Naw, well... sorta. I wanna catch bad guys too. Maybe I can be both."

"Listen to his speech," Pearl said with a wink. "You are in the presence of a teacher and you talk like you are uneducated."

"Oh Mama," William gave a lopsided grin. "That's what school is for."

Audrey laced her fingers, putting them in her lap. She straightened her back, gazing at young William, "Well, in my classroom, you will speak and write correctly. It is not 'wanna' it is 'I would like to' and it is not 'sorta' it is 'sort of'."

"Well, my Pa doesn't care," William retorted.

"Your father may not care, but being a respectable sheriff will make a difference. Sheriff's duties include writing papers, talking publicly, attending courts and meetings. There is a lot of etiquette to being a sheriff."

William looked at her dejectedly, then turned to his mother. "I will speak proper from now on, Mother."

Pearl winked at her.

Their food was served in a flourish of people. At least four different people came out bringing all the food they'd ordered. Pearl picked up the paper again, reading the front of the paper this time. Pearl gasped. Audrey took a sip of wine.

"Oh Audrey!" Pearl exclaimed. "There is a kidnapped heiress out of St. Louis."

Audrey spit out her wine barely catching it in her cloth napkin. "Come again?" Audrey asked, coughing and dabbing her lips. William laughed.

"William!" Pearl scolded again. "Eighteen-year-old Audrey Whitman has been kidnapped. A reward offered for any information about her whereabouts. Oh, how awfully tragic. Her poor family. And how incredible, you share the name."

Audrey peered out the window, sipping her wine. "Indeed," she commented. "However, my last name is Lucas and not Whitman." *And how fortunate for me they didn't put a description in the paper.*

Pearl folded the paper exasperatedly, "Well, enough of that dreary news. Let's eat."

Audrey picked at her food, *I am going to have to be more cautious.*

# CHAPTER SIX

Audrey bid Pearl and William a good sleep, promising to be on the next train with them. Little did they know, she had no intentions of being there. Audrey felt horrible for lying.

She stopped by the front desk to inquire about assistance with finding a dress shop. However, the line was long, so Audrey left. Pearl and William passed in front of her, nodding and waving to her as they went to their own chamber. Audrey gave a smile although, she felt it forced.

*I cannot even imagine Jane Eyre lying, she is much too forthright for such a devious thing,* Audrey thought. *And yet... Mine is unfortunately necessary.* Audrey tucked her brown hair behind her ear. *I do not want to go back to St. Louis. It may be a bit dramatic, but I truly think I may die if I have to marry Thomas.*

She stumbled up the stairs to her bedroom. She walked past three closed doors with interesting sounds coming out of the third one. She made a face. *Goodness,* Audrey thought, *I wonder what Ms. Eyre would have to say.* Audrey pondered a moment. *I suppose something along the lines of 'I would always rather be happy than dignified'.* Audrey pressed the back of her hand to her smiling lips.

She opened her chamber room, shutting it gently behind her.

The noises from next door thankfully muffled. She let out a deep breath. A lantern lit the top of the wardrobe. Audrey stopped in front of the mirror, wondering how she could change her look. Carefully, she took the pins out of her hair, letting it fall past her shoulders in ringlets. She looked down at her blue taffeta dress, comparing it to the simple yellow one Pearl wore.

"I need new clothing," she said to herself.

Audrey braided her hair back off her face, wondering if other people wore their hair like she was. She turned toward the bed, sitting on the edge. Audrey sighed deeply, hanging her head.

*I miss the ease of home, my bedroom and the like,* Audrey thought. *But I do not miss being told what to do, whom I ought to speak with or write letters to. I do not miss my aunt or my cousin who have never uttered a kind word to me and who made me feel like a prisoner. In the Bible – When you go through deep waters, I will be with you.* Audrey raised her head, staring defiantly at the door. *I love my freedom, my ability to choose. I love this adventure.*

Horses whinnied. Audrey glanced outside, seeing a massive herd of cattle being driven through town. Audrey gasped, clambering on the bed to gaze out the window. A smile split her face. She watched men drive the animals through the town. They whistled and yelled, moving swiftly and calculated. The horses jolted from left to right, keeping the cattle in a line. The men rugged, their tattered clothing dusty from travel. Some appeared to have not shaved in weeks. And as quickly as they came through town, they left.

Audrey laid her head in her arms and sighed eyes still on the cloud of dust in the distance. How much freedom these men must have from living a grand life. They could marry whomever they chose. They could live wherever their hearts desired. No galas, gowns and boorish propriety.

Audrey spun away from the window, going back to the mirror. She gawked at herself for a long time, gauging how much she truly changed over the past few days. Her pale skin seemed to have a sun-kissed glow. She learned how to book a train ticket, find accommodations, and pay for meals. Audrey was proud of herself. She learned a lot but there was still so much she did not know.

Audrey tilted her head and scowled, catching her green eyes sparkling from the reflection in the window. "I can learn and have my freedom too like those men do." She glanced out the window. "I want a life like that."

Audrey startled at a knock coming from her door along with a muffled, "Good evenin' ma'am. My name's Mary, last name Celeste. Do you need anything? I saw you in the line earlier."

Audrey called out, climbing off the bed, "One moment." She walked over to the door, opening it a wide crack and peeking through. A blond-haired young woman stared at her with a smile and a small gap between her front teeth. The hems of her dress were worn and slightly tattered, but didn't take away from the brightness of her smile or the sparkle in her blue eyes.

After a moment of uncomfortable silence, Mary dipped into a curtsy. "Mary ma'am. Can I get you anything?" She held out her hand and looked expectantly at Audrey.

Audrey clasped Mary's hand and shook it gently. "Audrey. I would like to find a dress shop to purchase a more suitable traveling garment."

"Well ma'am I can take tomorrow off and take you there myself."

Audrey smiled. "How wonderfully generous of you. I do not wish to put you out."

Mary held up her hands. "No problem at all miss. They were overstaffed for tomorrow anyways. I'd be happy to oblige ya."

"You are too much. Thank you."

Mary nodded, offering a friendly smile. "See you in the mornin' Audrey. Good sleep." She waved, walking off down the hallway.

Audrey smiled back. "Thank you, Mary. Good sleep."

Audrey locked the door for the night. With a contented sigh, she twirled in her room. Happily, she undressed into her underclothes, hanging up her blue dress on a peg on the back of the door. Taking her coin purse with her, she tucked it under her pillow.

*I have made a friend of my own, and not someone from a school,* Audrey thought. *Today has been a wonderful day.*

Audrey glanced outside, the streets slowly emptying of people as the sky darkened. She laid on the bed, hands behind her head with a smile that refused to fade.

"Lord, today was an adventure. Keep Pearl and William safe on their travels to Oregon. And tomorrow, I get to explore with a new friend," she prayed. "Tomorrow will be even grander. Thank you, Lord, for all my blessings."

# CHAPTER SEVEN

E ugene sat with Wilfred Darrow in the private dining room at a local St. Louis gentlemen's club. He glanced at the older man, contemplating his past with him. He liked Darrow. Not only was the man his employer in this, and other cases, but Darrow was a colleague, one Eugene admired greatly since he too, rose up from nothing, becoming the most elite lawyer on the east coast. And here he handed Eugene a case that could very well launch his career, getting him noticed by the aristocratic society.

The old lawyer twirled his glass of brandy in one hand before not so gently slamming it down. The noise grabbed Eugene's attention. Looking up from his meal and his thoughts, Eugene noticed the perturbed lines crease the lawyer's countenance.

Darrow had been silent since they left the Coldaire Estate, aside from ordering his brandy and steak. Eugene chewed his food and went over every scenario imaginable that might have taken place for the young woman Audrey. Nothing jumped out at him to point him in a definite direction in regards to what happened to her. Everything seemed suspicious regarding her disappearance, from the carriage to her family.

Eugene rolled his eyes, *Georgiana is about as inviting as small pox and Thomas is a pompous, reeking pig. If Audrey did not runaway, I would be very surprised.* Eugene raked his fingers through his hair. *Hopefully Darrow has some ideas*, he thought perking a brow at Darrow, waiting for him to speak.

Darrow's face scrunched. "I am not sure what happened to Audrey and this frustrates me to no end," he said with a slight English accent. "I do not believe she was murdered. She is worth far more alive. Unless one of her idiot relatives did way with her. But they aren't smart enough to plan her murder," Darrow scoffed.

Eugene agreed with a nod of his head. "There was no ransom note though."

This time Darrow nodded.

Eugene pulled out the notes he took on the carriage and speaking with Rafe. With a breath, he scanned the documents while also wracking his memory of what he saw. There was no blood anywhere on the carriage. The rips and tears were made in a rapid hurry while the window was carelessly smashed and nowhere near the handle.

He pursed his lips. This was a peculiar case. Audrey Whitman's room was immaculately clean. Every doll, trinket, and luxury set just right. She appeared to live the life of a coddled toddler. Everything Audrey could ever desire was at her fingertips for the taking. And nothing was taken in her disappearance. Yet something nagged at him.

*However,* Eugene thought, *the more I think on this, the more I find her disappearance disturbing. This might be the toughest case I ever took.*

"Could she have kidnapped herself to escape her family?" Eugene asked, strumming his fingers on the table.

Darrow shrugged. "Possibly, but not likely. I've watched Audrey grow up from afar. Her father and I were colleagues, and even with her ... interesting relatives, Audrey was always much too obedient for nonsense."

The old lawyer ran his hands through what was left of his hair. The top of his hair lined receded into his head. Gray and silver hairs peppered themselves around the hair that was left. A woman came in removing their finished plates of supper.

"The meal was delightful. Thank you," Eugene complimented the fare.

The woman flashed him a bright smile. "I'm pleased you enjoyed it, sir."

Her light brown hair was tightly coiffed at the nape of her neck, and sparkling blue eyes held his for a moment. Eugene smiled. She was a pretty woman; one he would have liked to come to know. However, with this new case, he would be leaving shortly to investigate. She tucked hair behind her ear, offering a smile in return, while collecting the plates on a tray.

"Fine meal," Darrow added. "More brandy and another glass when you get a moment." He said holding his almost empty glass up.

Eugene withheld a groan. He disliked brandy. But knowing Wilfred did love the drink, being polite demanded he take a few sips.

"Yes, of course sir," she replied, taking the full tray with her.

Eugene moved from the dining table to a cushioned chair by the fire. Darrow joined him, sitting across from him with his glass of brandy in hand.

"What did you find?" Darrow asked.

"The carriage torn to pieces. Too much energy went into making the slash markings for it to be murder. There was no blood either which is unusual if it is being considered a murder. I believe Audrey has been kidnapped."

"Agreed," Darrow said, smacking his lips after taking a swig.

The serving woman came back with a silver tray. Another small glass with a decanter of brandy resting on top. She smiled shyly at him, dipping out of the room before he could thank her. Eugene inwardly cringed. Wilfred reached over, filling Eugene's glass halfway then filling his own to the brim.

"Audrey is a sunny girl, bright, and full of love," Darrow said after a swig. "This greatly angers, and saddens me. I fear greatly for her safety."

"I would like a list of all her friends, acquaintances and

contacts. And a portrait if you have it please," Eugene replied, taking out a piece of paper and a pencil.

Darrow leaned forward, handing him a miniature of Audrey. The lawyer began listing names the girls from the finishing schools Audrey attended. Eugene wrote down every new contact that wasn't on the papers from earlier, annoyed at all the inquiries he would have to make from all the friends this woman accumulated. After the meeting, Eugene decided to head straight to the telegrams office to begin sending queries.

*I have eighteen to send to her friends alone, not to mention all the telegrams to the sheriffs from St Louis to San Francisco,* Eugene thought.

Eugene scowled. "I will find her."

Darrow got out of the chair, groaning. "These old bones. I know you will find Audrey. It is why I hired you for this case especially. I admire your tenacity. Those thieving Coldaire's want what Audrey has. I would rather not give it to them if I can help it."

Eugene stood, shaking the lawyer's hand. "I have some work to do, then."

Darrow shook his head. "Here are some monies to get you on your way," Darrow said, handing him an envelope of bills. "I have kept an eye on her from afar. And I love the girl like she were my own flesh and blood. Find her for me. Bring my goddaughter home. Night, Eugene."

"I'll do my best. Night, Wilfred."

Eugene looked over the list then glanced at the clock on the wall. Even though it was seven in the evening, he was going to telegram each and every one of these people. Eugene contemplated a missing person's poster, but decided against it. A poster would welcome unwanted troubles. It was the last thing he needed in case Audrey was not abducted.

He went out into the humid evening air. The clack of his footsteps drowned out the whickering of horses. It was soothing to his racing mind. Voices were buzzing as shopkeepers closing down for the night. A few people milled outside begging the shop-keeps to open up for a few more moments while others closed their doors with a bang. Men walked alongside their women, taking them home after a day of shopping. The train whistle blew for the last time that evening. Its sharp tone rang through the air. Eugene made a mental note to head there next.

Eugene paused by a newspaper stand, flipping the boy a nickel for the paper. The headline read "Missing Billionaire Audrey Whitman". Eugene folded the paper angrily under his arm, storming off toward the telegram office. He paused in the middle of the walkway, yanking the paper from beneath his arm, his dread not allowing him to wait to read the story.

*Thomas Coldaire reported his beloved cousin missing after her carriage was found shredded to pieces behind an abandoned warehouse. The eighteen-year-old billionaire heiress of the late Philip Whitman went missing two days ago after stopping to order an arrangement of flowers for her aunt.*

Eugene rolled his eyes. "Of course, the brainless dandy did."

He stormed into the sheriff's office.

"Sheriff, I am Pinkerton Eugene Turner, and I am investigating Audrey Whitman,"

The sheriff held up a hand, interrupting, "No need. She's dead."

He paused a moment, taking in the pungent aroma of alcohol and vomit. The sheriff's shirt was unbuttoned at the top, and stained. His face unshaved. The man swayed on his feet, plopping down in the chair behind him that screeched across the wooden floor from the sudden force.

Eugene rolled his shoulders back. "I beg to differ. No body was found and no blood at the scene."

The man scowled. "I investigated, *Pinkerton* Eugene. The woman is dead. Please get back on the train to the town in which you came. Case is closed."

Eugene nodded. "Perfect. I shall be sure to do so and have your job by the end of next week when I find her alive... Sheriff John-son. Have a great evening."

He stormed out the office, slamming the door behind him.

"Now just you wait," Sheriff Johnson called. The high-pitched clatter of the chair bouncing reverberated from the office. Eugene paused outside the door. Sheriff Johnson stumbled, opening the door forcefully. It slammed against the wall on the other side.

"What is it you need, Mr. Turner." He asked gruffly.

Eugene scowled. The tone and manner of this man repulsed him. "Shut down the missing persons ad Thomas Coldaire has done. I do not need unwanted attention."

Sheriff Johnson ran a hand over his face. "Will do. Anything else?"

"Find another job," Eugene stated.

He strolled down the wooden walkway and into the dirt streets. A lantern lit the inside of the telegraph office a few doors away.

*Excellent, still open*, he thought.

"Good evening," Eugene called to the man inside.

The wiry looking man glanced up from his stack of papers. "Evening, sir. How can I help you?"

"Evening. I am Pinkerton Eugene Turner. I'm investigating a missing persons case and need some telegrams sent with some confidentiality, if you please. Send this message post haste to Kansas City, Denver, Amarillo, San Francisco, San Antonio and Philly." Eugene ticked each city off on his fingers as he said them.

The man eyes widened. "Yes, sir. What will the message state? Same for all the major cities, sir?"

"Yes, same for all the major cities. Message is – contact Wilfred Darrow in St. Louis if missing heiress Audrey Whitman arrives, stop. Pinkerton Turner, stop."

"Excellent. It will be done."

Eugene nodded. "Thank you." Eugene pulled out his notes on Audrey's friends and their locations, sliding it over to the postmas-ter. "Send a message to these ladies. The message will state – contact Wilfred Darrow in St. Louis with any information regarding Audrey Whitman and her location, stop. Pinkerton Eugene Turner, stop."

The man squinted his beady eyes, focusing on his handwriting. "Anything else, sir?"

"No thank you. That's all for the moment," Eugene stated, shuffling through the bills Darrow left him. He slipped fifteen dollars over to the postmaster. "I don't need change. Thank you."

The man nodded his head eagerly, his eyes wide, barely suppressing a grin. "Right away, sir."

Eugene dipped his head, striding away from the telegraph office heading toward the train station two streets over. The train engineers and conductors were outside the train talking and laughing. Eugene made for them, hoping they would have seen Audrey. He needed some leads. According to the carriage driver Rafe, she was in a blue frilly dress, more than likely taffeta.

"Evening," Eugene called from a ways away.

The three men by the train scowled.

"Next train leaves tomorrow mornin'," one hollered back.

"Eugene Turner, Pinkerton," he announced, drawing near. "I'm looking for Audrey Whitman. Last seen in St. Louis wearing a sky-blue taffeta dress, with brown hair and green eyes. Have you seen her?"

All three men shook their heads.

He walked away. "Thanks," he called over his shoulder.

Eugene grumbled to himself. Still, it didn't hurt him to look and ask around. Someone must have seen her. Eugene had yet to encounter someone who simply vanished. If so, Audrey Whitman would be the absolute first.

# CHAPTER EIGHT

Audrey woke refreshed. The sun warmed her through the sheer white curtains. The raucous din of the streets below wafted up. The shrill train whistle blew. Horses whinnied, startled at the sudden noise; their owners cursing their frustration as they struggled to control the animals. Audrey rolled over and grabbed her pocket watch from the little table next to the bed.

She sighed with regret. "It cannot be helped. I do not desire to be exposed this short into my journey and I need better traveling garments. No matter how warm the bed is, the day has started."

With a yawn and a stretch, she threw the sheets off, her bare feet hitting the cold wooden floor. Audrey wriggled her toes and relished the cold. She always fancied the sharp coldness of the floors in the morning. It was better than coffee when waking her up. Turning around, facing the bed, she wondered how she should leave it. She tried to remember what it looked like before she got in, but her memory was foggy. She pulled the blankets over the pillow and tried to smooth out the wrinkles. With a shrug, she went to the wash basin and washed her face.

A knock sounded at the door.

"Just a moment!" Audrey yelled, scrambling to get ready.

"Mornin'," Mary yelled through the door. "I'll wait, but you'd better hurry. It's goin' to be a mite busy in a bit."

Audrey looked at her watch, brows furrowed. "It is not even eight o'clock."

Mary giggled. "The day is startin', so's people from outta Kansas City are getting' here and their shoppin' done early. Then after the next train, those peoples will be leaving. The shop-keeps have the best deals first thing in the mornin'. If we're gunna beat the locals, we need to get goin'."

Audrey left a water splattered mess on the table, drying her face with her slip skirt. Raking her fingers quickly through her thick, long brown hair, she braided and pinned it at the nape of her neck. With a skip in her step, she dressed, realizing now the fool-ishness of not taking at least one change of clothing. She laced her dress and pulled on her small shoes.

With a bright smile, she threw open the door. Without a single care to aristocratic propriety, she gave the waiting girl a hug.

"Thank you for being such a dear, and taking me shopping. I hope I did not put you out," Audrey said to a stiff Mary.

Mary pulled back with a tight-lipped smile, patting Audrey's shoulder while stepping away. "Naw. I took the day off to help you. I traded workin' days, here at the hotel, with another gal, so it ain't much trouble at all."

Audrey stepped forward to hug Mary again, not seeming to notice her back away. "Good Lord, you are such a wonderful dear!"

Mary climbed out of Audrey's embrace, patting her hand. "Think nothin' of it. Let's get goin' to Doreen's Dresses. She is about to open up."

Audrey double checked she had everything. Her rings were on, and her bracelet. She ran back in to grab her coin purse, fastening it to her secret pocket while Mary waited outside the door. Walking back out after one final check, Mary led her down the stairs, out the hotel doors and into the bustling city and bright sunshine.

Immediately, Audrey was struck with the busy-ness of the world around her. Mothers dragged their children down the wooden walkways ignoring the protests of their whining offspring. Men spat tobacco on the ground, avoiding the ladies, while gossiping about the early morning happenings. A man stood outside the barber shop, white shirt neatly pressed with black bands on his arms, waving at all the pretty ladies as they passed.

*Oh my*, Audrey thought, *this is grander than I ever expected. It's so unlike the novels and penny reads. Those stories do not accurately describe the industriousness and vivaciousness.* A smile crept its way across her face. Her green eyes soaked in all the fanciful lives she imagined these people lived. *This is wondrous. All the stores, all the people! All the freedom!*

Mary held onto her hand, taking her left out of the dining hotel and into the stream of folks. Men trotted their horses through town, tipping their hat to her. Audrey smiled back. She watched Mary, her blue eyes scanning intently the flow of the street.

"How long have you been on your own?" Audrey asked.

"For seven years now. Since I was thirteen." Mary answered.

Audrey dipped her head toward a group of children. They stood a few yards down the walkway, staring at her. She waved at them with her free hand. A boy in front, no older than twelve, pulled his bowler down over his eyes and quirked a smile.

"Have you always worked at the hotel?" Audrey asked pulling her attention away from the boy.

"Nope. I worked at a mercantile before."

The children Audrey noticed approached, surrounding them on one side. Audrey's eyes widened. The kids grabbed at her clothes. Mary swatted away some of the unruly, dirty children that were bouncing around them. "Get, you thievin' little rats!" Mary yelled.

Audrey put a hand to her chest. *Just like Dickens*, she thought. She scowled, following Mary. "Why on earth would you call them that?"

Mary spun around to look at her briefly. "Because," she stated, watching the children scamper away, "they are tryin' to steal yer things. Yer new. You walk around all wide eyed and gawkin' they know yer not from around here."

"Oh," Audrey said. "So, what should I do?"

Mary smiled. "Act like you know where yer goin'. Come along now. Those little urchins won't bother us none."

Audrey walked along with Mary, still holding her hand. She tried to look around out her peripheral but couldn't see much.

"Watch where yer spittin' that cud!" Mary yelled at a man sitting a few feet away.

"Cud?"

"Tobacco," Mary said matter-of-fact. "Have you never been out much?"

Audrey shrugged. "Not until recently."

Mary snorted.

"Mary," Audrey began, "what is it like being on your own?"

Mary paused outside the dressmaker's shop. "What d'ya mean?"

"Like earning money and sleeping all by yourself, putting your own roof over your head. Is it hard?"

Mary scowled, tapping a finger to her chin. "Naw. Long as you work and work hard, give no lip, you have food and a roof. It gets lonely but it ain't difficult. Now, in you get. We're here."

Audrey walked in, immediately loving the plainness of some of the dresses. They were beautiful but not overly so like hers. All sorts of colors attracted her eye. She needed something plain like everyone had, like green. Lots of women wore green including Mary. A larger woman came out from the back, smiling as she came to her.

"Good morning, Miss, I am Ms. Doreen, owner, proprietor, and seamstress of this shop. What can I do for you?"

Audrey grinned broadly. "An absolute pleasure to meet you Ms. Doreen. My name is Audrey. I am here to sell this blue taffeta while also making a purchase of some better suited traveling dresses."

"Of course, my dear!" Doreen replied. "I was about to say, traveling in silk would be mighty uncomfortable."

Doreen looked Audrey up and down, then swiftly turned, striding to the wall, grabbing a peach colored cotton dress off the peg making sure to grab a light key lime green next to it at the same time. Doreen handed them to Audrey while spinning her in the direction of the screen to change.

Audrey nodded. "It is indeed. I am meeting my father in Denver and would love to appear like everyone else."

"Well, you go try these on."

Audrey went back behind the screen, carefully taking off her blue dress. It was dirty at the bottom hems, nothing a light cleaning wouldn't fix. In fact, she hoped it would sell well so she could get both beautiful colors.

Audrey poked her head around the screen, spying Mary sitting on a chair, waiting for her. Mary was such a great friend to have. She was honest, confident and completely self-reliant, reminding her of Jane Eyre. Mary was what Audrey wished herself to be.

*I can be like that,* Audrey thought.

Audrey stepped into the peach dress, lacing it up the front. She strode out from behind the screen.

"My, my," Mary stated. "That color does fit you quite well."

Audrey went in front of the mirror, twirling and staring at her reflection. "You think so?"

"Absolutely," Mary encouraged with a thoughtful expression. "If yer wantin' to look plain, you'll need to ditch the jewelry you have."

Audrey looked at her friend shocked. "Oh, I could never."

"No one around here wears jewelry like you have. Everyone else has weddin' bands on their left hands. Somethin' to consider. Now, go try on the other one."

Audrey left, going back behind the screen. She looked at the adornments on her hands and the bracelet on her left wrist. Mary was right. She may be able to dress herself down but she would never be able to explain her niceties.

"Here are a few more Audrey," Mary said, handing her three more dresses.

"Thank you, Mary."

"Try on the purple one. I think it will bring out yer eyes and a plain bonnet matches everythin'."

Audrey smiled, hanging the dresses on the pegs attached to the screen. She tried on the key lime dress, liking the way it fit but not much admiring the color. Luckily for her, Mary agreed when she modeled it.

Next, she tried on the dark blue one Mary found. It had the right look and style Audrey was going for. It was a tad long but not overly so. Audrey put the dress in her yes pile which consisted of the peach gown so far, Audrey chuckled to herself. Mary brought her a few more dresses including a calico.

Audrey liked trying on dresses, especially with her new friend. This was something new as she and all her finishing school friends had private seamstresses, and Audrey was loving it. Mary was a wonderful friend to stick by her the entire time.

The last dress Audrey tried on was the purple one. It was a beautiful dress that differed from the others since it had black lace fringe instead of white. Audrey loved it. As did Mary.

"Gee willikers Audrey!" Mary gushed. "You sure are a sight!"

"A good one I hope."

Mary laughed. "That's what I just said. Now, take off those fancy things and let's get a feel for what you really look like."

Audrey looked at her locket in the mirror, fingering it. Reluctantly she took it off and putting it in the tray in front of the mirror. She took off her three rings and her bracelet. Her coin purse was tucked safely inside her blue taffeta. She mentally reminded herself to grab it before leaving. Audrey took a step back from the mirror, looking at herself for the first time in years without any jewelry on. She felt naked without the locket.

But Mary was right. No other women had adornments like she did. Even a wedding band was a lot. Very few women had even one beautiful piece, let alone many. And she so wanted to be like everyone else for a while. Especially now, being alone and on her own. Denver was calling. There was no way she would fit in wearing all her jewelry.

"Wowwee Audrey," Mary said with a smile. "Just like everyone else."

Audrey whirled around with a smile. "You think so Mary?"

Mary nodded, her blond hair bouncing. "I surely do.

Audrey danced on her toes, leaping over and wrapping her arms around Mary, "You are such a dear friend to me. Thank you so much!"

Mary held Audrey back at arm's length with a tight smile. "Go try on the calico again. I rather liked it with yer brown hair, but I want to make sure once more."

Audrey skipped back behind the screen, taking off the purple and adding it into her yes pile. Soundlessly, she peeked into her coin purse. Audrey breathed out. *This should take me far enough,* she thought. Fifty dollars and change snuggled itself back into her coin purse. Audrey removed the purse, holding it tightly in her left hand until she could secure it safely elsewhere. *This should last me quite a while, I hope.*

With a grin, she put on the yellow dress she wanted to purchase. Her fingers tingled from excitement. Now, she was like everyone else in the city. She would be able to travel comfortably and blend in.

She finished dressing and gathered all her items in her arms. Coming out of the screen, she called for Ms. Doreen. The portly woman came over, taking the blue taffeta in her wide fingers, going over the seams and hand-stitching.

"How much for these dresses?" Audrey asked, holding out her laden arm.

Without looking up, Doreen replied, "A dollar fifty a piece and I will give you five dollars for the taffeta."

Audrey bounced on her heels, "Most excellent," she said chipperly. "I shall also like a traveling bag, some camisoles, stockings and a bonnet or two, if you would please."

Ms. Doreen perked a brow, going behind the counter with the blue taffeta. Audrey spun around, "Mary?" she called.

Only silence answered her.

"Excuse me," Audrey said. Doreen rang up her purchases, glancing over the top of her ill-sitting spectacles. "Where is my friend?" Audrey asked.

"She left a few moments ago dear."

Audrey dashed over to the small container where her jewelry

CHAPTER EIGHT | 53

waited. All of it was gone. Audrey shrieked, putting a hand to her mouth. Her heart raced. Her mother's locket was gone! Tears tracked without conscious thought down her cheeks.

Ms. Doreen came over, clucking her tongue. "You poor thing. You've been had. You'll need to speak with the sheriff."

"What?" Audrey asked. She sniffled, drying her tears with the back of her hand. Ms. Doreen handed her a kerchief. A rush of new tears came over Audrey and she cried into the rose-colored cloth.

"She conned you. So, you will need to speak with the sheriff, the lawman here in Kansas City. Now, do you at least have money to buy these items?"

Audrey nodded pitifully, her lip quivering. "Yes, ma'am I do."

Audrey paid the woman and immediately left. She had to find Mary. She didn't care if Mary kept the other pieces, they all meant nothing to her. All she wanted was her mother's locket back.

She walked quickly, clutching her items tightly to her person. Her stomach rumbled in the now, afternoon sun, but Audrey did not care.

*I have to find her,* she thought, *but where to start?* Everything was so large and there were people everywhere. Clutching her traveling bag with her money inside, she went next door to a mercantile.

The shop bells tingled at her arrival.

"How can I help you Miss? The man asked.

Clearing her throat and holding back her tears, "I am looking for someone who stole my locket. Her name is Mary, she is about my height, blond straight hair with blue eyes. Was wearing a dark green dress with tattered hems."

As she spoke, the man shook his head. "No one fitting her description came by here. You ought to report it to the sheriff."

Audrey nodded, biting her lower lip. "Thank you, sir. Have a good day."

The shop door clanked on her exit. *I have to find her, even if it means going to every store.* Determinedly, she walked down the wooden platform.

"Wait miss," the man called.

Audrey plastered a wan smile to her face. "Yes?"

"Sheriff's office is that way, past the Silver Spoon dining hotel, on the next street. You'll see a large sign."

"Thank you," she replied, wiping away the moisture from her eyes with the back of her hand.

Determinedly, she went across the street, bustling to where the man said the sheriff would be. She dodged past wagons full of families and goods and the people getting off the incoming train. Her green eyes scanned frantically for Mary, praying the woman would appear out of the shadows. Mary never did. The foot traffic from the people disembarking the train was incredible. So many people came west and finding one particular person was proving impossible. Audrey stepped down off the wooden walkway to run across the street.

"Watch where yer goin', Lady!" a man hollered.

Audrey clutched her traveling bag tighter, ignoring the man. Pressing on, she hiked up the hems of her dress to walk quicker. Deciding she wasn't going fast enough; Audrey took off at an unladylike sprint. She crossed the final road to where the sheriff was supposed to be.

Huffing for breath, she raised her head and strode down the short platform toward the Sheriff's door. Audrey fixed her hair, calming herself for a moment. *I can do this.*

Audrey yanked open the door. "Excuse me, Sheriff?"

A man rocked back on two legs of a chair; hat pulled down low over his face. A hard snore ripped past his flapping lips.

She cleared her throat. "Excuse me, Sheriff!"

The man snapped forward, tipping his hat back. The chair struck the wooden floor with a thud that shook the floorboards.

"Ma'am," he replied curtly. "To what do I owe the pleasure, since the sign outside clearly stated I was busy."

Her nostrils flared. His indignation was something she expected from the socialites back home. Clearly it existed out here also.

"To whom, if you may, benevolent sir," Audrey's green eyes

bore into his red rimmed ones. "I am here to report someone stealing my locket."

The sheriff smirked. "It's gone, lady. Check the stores that sell and pawn, but it's gone and it ain't worth my salt and time to fetch. Have a nice day ma'am."

The sheriff rocked back on his chair, wriggling down into his seat. Without looking at her, he pulled the hat down low over his eyes.

"Will you not even take a report?" Audrey asked exasperated.

The man chuckled. "Again, not worth my time. Good day ma'am."

Audrey stormed out of the sheriff's office, slamming the door behind her. Tears welled along the edges of her lashes. Sniffling and taking a deep breath, she spent the entire day getting lost in Kansas City, looking for the person whom she thought was a friend.

# CHAPTER NINE

Eugene wandered the streets of St. Louis. Holding a makeshift map out in front of him, he ticked off yet another area where Audrey Whitman wasn't. The hot afternoon sun peppered his neck. Sweat trickled down the sides of his head. Eugene's cinnamon brown eyes narrowed in on a place he hadn't checked.

*She seems to have completely vanished,* he thought. *Not at any of the ladies' clubs, flower stores, and boutiques seen her. The carriage was thrashed, horses not stolen, nothing really stolen...* Eugene crinkled the map in his fists in a fit of temper. It all seemed to elude him. *Was she truly kidnapped?* His face twisted in a grimace. He stepped off the raised wooden walkway, shoving the map into his pocket.

The clues did not seem to add up. He wanted to believe she was kidnapped, but there was no ransom note even days later. If someone wanted her and her money, knowing her worth, there would be a note. Or at least something of a lead to follow. Plus, the shape of the carriage; something nagged at Eugene but he couldn't put a finger on it. Again, there was nothing. In his mind, the clues told him a different story. He did not think she was kidnapped.

*She ran away,* he surmised. *Hastily slashed carriage, no blood, nothing stolen and all possessions left behind.*

Sighing deeply, Eugene looked at the heavens. *When you find yourself in a bind, look at the heavens. God will warm your back while leading you to the answer you seek*, his father used to say. He wasn't so much in a bind, more of a mental block, but he figured his father's advice still applied. It was a clear, sunny day, mildly hot but mainly humid. Most people were inside, trying to escape the humidity. Women fanned themselves in the shade the buildings provided while the saloons were packed with men going for drinks. Eugene glanced at his watch. It was fifteen past noon. He checked the poorer west side of St. Louis. No one had seen her. A low growl passed his lips. Eugene was becoming more and more frustrated with this case. He was beginning to think the money and possible prestige wasn't worth the headache.

A rugged man strolled into the saloon called The Drunken Nag. Eugene stood watching other men walk in behind the first one. Eugene glanced around. He pulled his homburg hat low over his eyes.

*Why did I not think of this before*, he thought. *She might go someplace no well-bred woman would go. If she did runaway, she would want to hide. If she was kidnapped or keeping unsavory company, someone in there might be speaking.*

He walked into a different hotel across the street, making it appear like he wasn't at all interested in the ruffians across the street. He kept his eyes focused on the hotel ahead while he felt the eyes of others prickle the back of his neck. He strode in with all the arrogance and bravado the aristocrats he'd met use. It seemed to work in his favor, he was being ignored. Once inside, he peeked out the paned glass window. The remaining saloon goers went back inside.

"Can I help you?" the hotel clerk questioned, his voice laced with superiority and annoyance.

Eugene glanced around. Wallpaper adorned the walls with gold gilded lanterns spaced intermittently. A dark stained wooden desk separated Eugene and the clerk. The place was lucrative, something Audrey would know and enjoy.

He brought out the miniature of Audrey, flashing it in front of the man's face. "Eugene Turner, Pinkerton, have you seen this woman?"

The clerk shook his oiled head. "I have not, sir. No one that young, has stayed at this hotel all week."

He nodded, sliding the picture back into his coat pocket. "Thank you. Is this the latest paper?"

"Yes. Five cents if you wish to purchase."

Eugene flipped the man a nickel, taking the paper off the tray. He strode back outside, sitting on the bench to the left side of the hotel door. He sat down with a huff. He opened the paper, making himself appear disinterested. He skimmed through all the headlines of people supposedly striking it rich out west or disappearing. Audrey's article was on the front page.

After waiting a particularly long while, he folded his paper, tucking it under his arm. Eugene sauntered across the street to The Drunken Nag. He could smell the pungency of the people before he ever reached the saloon doors. He strode straight in, ignoring the stares of the regulars as he went to the counter. Eugene sat next to a particularly large fellow.

"What'll be?" the barkeep asked.

Eugene peered at the bottles on the back of the counter. "Whiskey neat."

The barkeep slid a glass across the counter. Eugene caught it. The barkeep sauntered over, pouring him a shot of the amber colored, fiery drink.

The barkeep didn't look up. Instead, he cleaned a few glasses, setting them back on the shelf. "Tab?"

*Time to blend in*, he thought.

"Yeah." Eugene answered. Eugene took a sip and smacked his lips. "Good stuff."

"That's shit," said the man next to him. "Apparently, you don't drink much d'ya lawman?"

Eugene twirled his cup. "No lawman here."

The man chortled. "Fooled me just fine. You dress like one."

"In disguise." Eugene replied meeting the man's fierce gaze.

The man rocked back and turned toward him slow, revealing

the .45 caliber on his hip and the two knives in front of it. "Runnin'?"

Eugene shook his head. "No... Lookin' for my woman. Tryin' to find the wench and bring her home."

The man laughed uproariously. "Got burned by a witch, did ya?" he continued to laugh. "Women are good for one thing, friend. Better forget about her."

Eugene drank his whiskey, tapping the bar for another. The barkeep poured him one quickly, then went to the other end of the bar to speak with another man.

He peeked around casually. The men he saw walk into the bar were to his right, one watching his every move. He spun around, leaning back against the bar top as he'd seen other men do before, watching for the type of women who would come in here. He hadn't seen one yet.

The man beside him laughed, slapping his shoulder. Eugene grunted at the shocking weight, spilling some of his whiskey. "Maybe she is upstairs, giving a good ol' rompin' to someone," the man next to him suggested.

Eugene shook his head. "She ain't like that."

The man snickered, patting him on the shoulder, a touch softer this time. "Women will fool ya left and right. They be right smart, more than we give'em credit for. They use us, take our money and leave. I tell ya friend, they be only good fer needs and maybe a meal."

Eugene made a face, shaking his head glumly and hanging it low. "Not sure mine is. She seems to have gotten herself kidnapped. Was in the paper."

The man grumbled. "I heard o' that one. Haven't seen her nor heard of her whereabouts."

The bartender leaned over. "Run-away from you, did she?"

Eugene laughed, twirling his cup. He tapped it on the counter. The barkeep poured him another. Sighing despondently, Eugene answered, "I can't imagine why."

The barkeep poured him another. "You'll never know. Women are strange as the day is long."

Eugene spun back around, raising his glass to the fellow. "I'll drink to that."

He slammed his glass down on the counter, along with the money for the drinks. "Thanks, fer the conversation friend," Eugene said, getting off the barstool.

He walked out into the bright light. If the gangs here didn't know of her whereabouts then most likely she was not in Missouri. But The Drunken Nag was one saloon. He needed to verify at a few more before he started jumping to other conclusions.

*Food first then more investigating,* he decided.

Eugene strolled down two blocks to a restaurant. While getting a meal, he listened and inquired about Audrey. No one had seen her. Nowhere turned up any leads, only confirming in his mind she wasn't in St. Louis.

After the meal, Eugene went to the east side of the city. The heat of the day backed off a little, making the walking easier. He disliked paying for a carriage when his legs worked fine. He continued to check hotels and other saloons for her. For some reason it was easier to discuss her if he claimed he was her intended and she'd left him. He lied through his teeth, telling people she broke his heart. People spoke more freely even if it was the farthest thing from the truth.

Eugene walked along the wooden walkway, his boots clicking against the rough-cut pieces. Another saloon caught his attention. A man stumbled out of the swinging doors. A larger one followed. The drunk man turned, ready to throw a punch. As he did so, the larger fellow, got the other in the stomach. The drunk one doubled over gulping in a breath. The other, grabbed him by the cuff of his shirt and tossed him in the dirt road.

"Stay out of 'ere!" The man spat.

Eugene watched the younger man on the ground scramble to his feet. He ran to the dappled mare tied to the post and swung up in the saddle, swaying a bit on his horse. He spurred his mare, bouncing in the saddle as the mare's galloping hooves pounded the dirt. Some men stood at the doorway chuckling before going back inside.

*Last bar for the night. This may not turn up answers but I can leave no stone unturned,* Eugene thought. He glanced down at his makeshift map, writing down the names of places then crossing them off. Eugene squinted at the saloon sign across the way — Sneaky Leak. Eugene wrote it down.

He walked across the dirt street. People were already heading inside after the commotion. He spied a man on the opposite street corner, walking a lady into a hotel. The man shook his head at him. The warning the man gave was understood, but he needed answers. This supposed kidnapping was looking more like a runaway case.

The music played sonorously, and slightly off key. Eugene ambled through the swinging saloon doors. Everyone stared at him. Eugene went to the bar, sitting down on a rickety stool. One of the men he saw from outside sat next to him.

Eugene dipped his head, glancing around for the barkeep. The man beside him nodded back, returning to his drink. Taking in his surroundings, Eugene dipped his head at the people who made eye contact with him.

The barkeep threw the top back on the bar and entered with a tray of glasses and a sigh. He pulled out amber bottles of liquor, putting it on the shelf behind him. The barkeep's white hair was slicked back on his head, greasy and wet looking; his cheeks rosy and mottled. He slammed a glass down in front of Eugene.

The barkeep's rheumy eyes glanced over at him. "What would you like, young sir?" he asked.

"Eugene, and can I get some rum in the far-right bottle?"

"I'm Barney," the barkeep replied. "And rum it is." Barney fetched the bottle, popping it open.

"From out of town, eh?" the man next to him grunted.

Eugene watched Barney pour him a glass. Eugene dipped his head to the barkeep. Swirling the drink in his glass, Eugene took a small sip. "What makes you say that?" Eugene asked, turning to stare at the man who asked.

"Out of towners always want rum."

"I'm from Philly," Eugene replied with a shrug.

The man on the other side of the fellow who first spoke yelled, "You owe me ten cents, Lowry! He's from Philly!"

"Damn it all!" Lowry cursed from somewhere across the room.

The other man leaned over the counter, looking Eugene in the face, "You look like you've been drug through mud, friend." He chuckled.

Playing it off, Eugene shrugged. "Looking for my woman is all."

"The one in the papers?" Lowry asked approaching Eugene from behind.

Eugene shook his head. This time he wanted no connection to her. "No, her name is Lillian."

The other man leaned back and muttered, "Sorry."

Eugene nodded, taking a long swig of brandy. "Yeah. Me too. Have you seen the woman in the papers? Heard tell she is beautiful."

"And rich," the man added.

"That too."

"But naw, haven't seen her yet. Waitin' to see if a reward is offered first 'fore I go lookin'."

Eugene nodded. "I'm sure there would have been by now if the family really cared."

Lowry snorted. "No kiddin'. If she's as loaded as the papers say, I want a piece of that action."

"As would anyone, I suppose." Eugene said, taking a drink.

Eugene finished his drink and bought one more. He needed to head back to his hotel for the night and plan a different strategy. Audrey obviously was nowhere in St. Louis. And it was easy to deduce from the multiple bars he was in today along with all the hotels, no one had seen her.

Lowry clapped him on the back. Eugene rose from his seat. "Hope you find your woman."

Eugene put his money down on the table when he caught Barney's attention. "Same." he said and went off into the night.

# CHAPTER TEN

Audrey walked back to her hotel, dirty, hot and fresh out of tears. Mary was gone. Audrey spent all day looking for her, calling her name, speaking to anyone who might have seen her. It was as if Mary had completely disappeared. Now it was dark. Street lamps came on, and she was bone tired.

*And the sheriff was so mean,* Audrey thought dragging her feet. *What an awful, insufferable man!*

She walked up to the hotel check-in, seeking an accommodation for another night. Fortunately, there was a room available. Audrey paid the fifty cents and signed her name in the registry. The delicious aroma of food from the dining hotel room tickled her nose. Her stomach rumbled.

"You all right miss?" a woman walking through the dining room doors asked when she spotted Audrey's red eyes, nose, and tear stained face.

Audrey shook her head. "A woman by the name of Mary Celeste stole my mother's engraved locket, watch, and other jewelry. I have been looking for her all day. She wore a green dress, blond hair with blue eyes. She said she works here."

The pretty woman tilted her head to the side, her light brown hair falling over her eyes at the movement. "Mussy blond hair and green eyes, about six inches taller than yourself? Was working here yesterday evening?"

Audrey perked up, "Yes, exactly so!"

"She didn't show for work today, although her name wasn't Mary. It was Beth. And you are not the first person to mention items have gone missing."

Audrey felt the tears fall down her face.

"OH sweetie! I'm so sorry! Don't you worry. John over there behind the desk will alert the sheriff and deputy tomorrow mornin'. His night deputy isn't the most reliable. The sheriff can be ornery at moments, but John has a way with him."

Audrey flashed a relieved smile. "Thank you ever so much. Your kindness is a breath of fresh air. I saw you just walk in from there; would you happen to know if the dining side is still open?"

"It is! In fact, join me. My name is Kayla Langmoore. Today is my last day working here. I've been studying baking with my friend Amelie and she's headed back to France next week. As a farewell she baked me a little care package and I'd like to share it with you. You look like you could use a friend. Especially after a day like today." The girl barely stopped to take some air, much to Audrey's amusement.

Audrey smiled at the girl and couldn't help but giggle a little. "Thank you! I can't ask you to share your care package with me. It's yours! But I'd love the company."

Kayla smirked, "Nonsense, Miss. I want to share. Besides, you've not lived until you've tried one of Amelie's cinnamon rolls!"

Audrey gave in and looped her arm with Kayla, leaving her dresses and other purchases with John at the front desk. "I will eat a cinnamon roll only if you call me Audrey."

"Absolutely, Audrey. Now come. Make my last day special and share a roll with me."

Already she felt immensely better. She spent an hour in Kayla's bright presence, laughing a few times at the stories she told of growing up with two brothers, something Audrey envied. By the end of the evening, Audrey found a kindred soul and was loath to leave, but knew she needed time to process everything that happened over the course of the day; and Kayla needed to leave to begin the new chapter in her life. Audrey embraced the beautiful girl whose green eyes sparkled with life and bid her goodnight, making her way up to her room. Once she entered it, she was relieved to see her packages on her bed. She quickly undressed and crawled under the blankets after placing the package on the little table next to her bed.

*Let's see*, she thought, *after today's expenses, I have forty dollars and ten cents remaining to get me to Denver. It should be plenty.* Audrey cleared her throat, sitting up in bed and taking a sip of water from the glass next to the package on the bedside table. *A report will be filed with the deplorable sheriff about my locket but that is rather dull. I cannot stay. I would be caught and sent back to St. Louis. And my adventure is far from over. Best of all, I met a truly kind soul. Kayla has restored my faith in people. Such kindness. So different from those I've lived with for so many years.*

The thought of being back in St. Louis with Georgiana and Thomas sent a chill down her spine. By now, they assumed her dead and inherited her father's fortune, which was fine with her. Either way, through family, marriage, or marriage to Thomas, everyone but her would inherit her father's fortune. Audrey never cared for the money, or the estates. What she wanted was her father's time and it came far and few between. Philip Whitman was an industrial business man, loving but distant.

She laid back down, pulling the covers up to her chin. She was certain her father would comprehend her reasons for leaving everything behind. Even Philip did not care much for Georgiana and Thomas. Every holiday he spent mayhap an hour total in their presence then retired to his study. Philip called them 'a family obligation' which was said through his teeth and tight lips. She smirked at the memory. *God rest his soul.*

*I will leave tomorrow morning and find my father's hotel in Denver. No more tarrying here.* "I shall change my name and become a waitress," she mumbled as an afterthought remembering the waitress who served Kayla and herself.

A waitress would be perfect. Much like a governess in her favorite book, Jane Eyre, she got to interact with people and children, but she wasn't stuck with one child or a lying rich man.

*It is perfect*, Audrey decided, sitting up in her bed excitedly. *The people come and go, and no one will know who I am. And our waitress was extremely kind and professional. If I recall, her name was Priscilla.*

"Priscilla," she said testing the name. "I like the sound of it."

# CHAPTER ELEVEN

Eugene was growing more frustrated by the moment. He searched all the hotels, both high class and low. He searched saloons, spoken casually with gangs and merchant owners. Seems like no person had seen the missing heiress.

He scoffed, kicking a rock with his shoe. This woman had it all, yet she abandoned all the luxury she could ever desire. She confused him to no end. Thankfully he snagged her diary, hoping inside contained clues to why she ran away. Or about her life so he could piece it together, and understand it.

He strolled back to the train station. Previously, he came when it was dark and there was a shift change. The night operator did not see her. Mayhap the day one had. At least he hoped so. This was his last option before searching all the main roads out of St. Louis.

*Someone ought to have seen her. No one disappears,* Eugene reasoned, approaching the platform.

The afternoon train blew out steam. It was like the engine itself was taking a deep breath. Three men stepped down, two of which were covered in coal. Another man stepped down out of the back, breathing heavily, and stretching his back.

Eugene went to the ticket window, holding up Audrey's picture. "Have you seen this missing woman? She was also in the papers recently."

The man at the ticket office glanced up, adjusting his spectacles, and wrinkling his nose. His eyes narrowed on the miniature. "Looks awfully familiar."

Eugene resisted the urge to clench his hands and retort. It had been a long few days with no leads looking for this spoiled woman.

"Do you believe you have seen her?" Eugene asked through tight lips.

"No need to get all huffy," the ticket man said. "When did she go missing?"

"Apologies. It's been a long few days. I'm Eugene Turner, a Pinkerton, hired to investigate. Audrey went missing three days ago, midafternoon."

The man nodded, fumbling through some sheets. Wrinkling his nose and pushing his glasses back on his face with a poke of his finger. "Hold on, Eugene," the ticket man said. "I'm looking to see what trains departed here and to where."

"Much appreciated."

After three days of investigating, he was finally getting somewhere in this case, and it thrilled him. He left no stone unturned. While he was confident, she wasn't in St. Louis, now the task of truly finding her was at hand. There was no doubt in his mind now that she ran away.

No ransom note arrived at the Coldaire Estate in those days either. He went back to check every morning, staying briefly. The fake whimpering from Georgiana along with the aloofness from Thomas grated on his nerves.

*They solely want her inheritance,* he surmised.

"Mornin' Luke," a man shouted.

Eugene snapped his head around to the voice.

"Morning Jack," the ticket man replied still rifling through train schedules.

Eugene peeked over his shoulder. The train conductor he

observed stretching earlier, entered the building's office. He sat down in a wooden chair along the far wall with a thud and sighed, loosening the collar around his neck.

"Hey Jack," Eugene called, holding up a picture of Audrey against the ticket window. "Have you seen this woman? Her name is Audrey Whitman and she is missing."

Jack scowled at the picture, getting out of his chair with a groan.

"Here it is," Luke said. "We had two trains coming in that day within forty-five minutes of the other. One left to Kansas City, the other to Philly."

Jack leaned in toward the glass, nodding at the picture. "Yeah I have seen her," he replied. "She was on the train I was working. Headed to Kansas City."

Eugene smacked the ticket counter. "Thank you!"

She wasn't kidnapped, but a spoiled little brat who ran away. Eugene ran a hand over his face, trying to keep the anger inside. However, he was boiling mad. All of this time, wasted, hunting down a little girl who got too big for her perfectly stitched dresses.

It was the same arrogance he ran into time and time again with the aristocrats. Something is ruined or flawed, it is thrown away. Something is not good enough, it is discarded. The same arrogance the Coldaire's had.

Eugene let out a breath slowly, *if she worked hard for everything, she might appreciate it more.*

"When does the next train leave for Kansas City?" Eugene asked through gritted teeth.

"In two hours," Luke replied.

Eugene whipped out his coin purse. "I need a ticket," he demanded, slapping two one-dollar coins on the counter.

"I need fifty cents more for the ticket. A dollar if you want first class," Luke replied.

Eugene slapped another dollar on the counter.

"Train leaves at eleven thirty and not a moment later."

Eugene nodded, storming off back to his hotel. He seethed the entire way, hoping when he caught up to Miss Audrey Whitman, she would have realized the errors of her cosseted ways.

*I want to spank the spoiled woman, and make her pay extra for all my wasted time,* Eugene breathed out heavily attempting on calming his temper. *Working for the high class may pay well. Not worth the headache at all. Not at all.*

Eugene wrenched open the hotel doors. He clambered up the creaking stairs to his room. Gathering his small traveling bag, he checked inside for Audrey's diary. It lay on top of his clothes.

*I hope it contains something useful,* he thought.

Whipping it out, he began reading until it was time to catch the train.

# CHAPTER TWELVE

Audrey could not stop fidgeting in her seat. The landscape changed dramatically from when she left Kansas City. The conductor said another couple of hours, and they would be in Denver. That was a while ago, and she was still waiting.

*I'm so excited I am beside myself,* she thought, tucking stray brown hairs behind her ear. *I wonder if Jane Eyre felt this way going to Thornfield. No, she would be poised.* Audrey grinned. *However, that was my life before this. I have the freedoms as an unmarried, regular woman, to be who I choose.*

A smile broke across her face. The gloomy clouds parted ways, giving her a glimpse of the Rockies. Audrey caught her breath. The snowy peaked mountains stared at her. Her grin widened; nose pressed against the glass. Wild horses galloped alongside the train.

Audrey turned her head, her face still smushed against the glass.

"Oh, my stars!" she exclaimed.

A sleepy town came out of the low-lying fog. Wooden houses and smoke billowing from the peaks, brought life to the place. People milled about, covered in thicker coats. The train whistle blew, and the train itself came to a satisfying stop. The engine let out a large sigh of relief as everything settled.

Shivers ran down her spine. Audrey waited for the conductor's call to off board, and her legs bounced excitedly. She grabbed hold of her small bag with her new clothing. She double checked her coin purse to make certain all of her money was still there, safely tucked inside her bag, sighing in relief when she heard the familiar clink of coins.

The conductor called. Audrey jumped up, desiring to run for the exit like a small child, but instead walked with propriety.

"Safe travels, Miss," the conductor said.

Audrey smiled. "Thank you, Curtis. Safe travels to you as well."

Audrey breathed in the crisp air. It burned her lungs. Audrey grinned, inhaling another lungful of nippy freedom. The change from the stale air of the train to the freshness of Denver was exhilarating. She walked down the wooden sidewalk past the vendors selling items to tourists. She smiled at the ladies with their hair in braids. Some wore it up, elegantly, but even the fancy ladies didn't look stiff and formal like they did back in St. Louis.

She loved it. Mist clung to the low plains, hiding the slight rolling hills from view. The train whistle blew again. Audrey smiled. She made it to Denver. She walked along the sidewalk, passing people hustling to get out of the morning chill weather. Audrey watched gruff looking men swagger out of the saloon. She hastily made her way past them even though they were on the other side of the street, slogging slightly uphill.

She was huffing when she came to the top. Across the street was Whitman Hotel. She was so excited to get a glimpse at what her father set up. Philip Whitman never spoke of what he did for business or any people he employed. The sole mention of his dealings were cities where he stayed at his own hotel. Audrey smiled, taking in the magnificence of what her father built. A pine carving of a bear graced the threshold of the hotel.

Tilting her head to the side, she stared at it. *Father mentioned previous to his passing he imported something for mother. I wonder if the bear is it,* she pondered.

Audrey made her way straight for the hotel, dodging the traffic of rolling wagons and swift moving horses with their riders. She climbed the stone steps, reaching the tall bear on its haunches, mouth open. She touched it delicately, grinning at the likeness of such a ferocious creature.

She peeked around the carving, finding a plaque on the side. *For my darling wife. Like this bear, I will always protect you, Philip Whitman.* Audrey put a hand to her chest. *Oh, father,* she thought.

Father never spoke about her mother and when he did there was a distant look in his green eyes and the moment of reminiscing was brief. His eyes barely misted over. If she looked away, she would have missed it.

Audrey kept her hand on the carving, staring up at the magnificent creature trying to feel closer to her parents.

The door opened and a woman emerged carrying a note in her hand. "Why, good morning!" she exclaimed. "Are you coming inside? It is a little chilly out."

Audrey grinned. "Yes I am. My name is," Audrey paused, looking at the foot of the carving. A pot of small roses limply sat by the door, dying with the change of weather. "My name is Rose. I came here to seek employment if you please."

The woman brightened. "Why sure! Our last girl gone off and got married. My name is Lena Jenkins. What's your last name Rose?"

Audrey stepped inside the door, looking around at the hotel. She glanced behind her and across the street before Lena shut the door. There was a smithy on the other side, hammering away. A horse stood waiting in a stall, its breath frosting in the air.

Turning back to Lena, her mouth became dry. She opened it to reply but nothing came.

"It's all right," Lena encouraged. "I won't bite."

Audrey smiled. "Smith. My last name is Smith."

Lena grinned, looping her arm around Audrey. The woman was more than a head taller than she was with long dark brown hair that almost appeared black. Her gray dress hid her voluptuous figure and enhanced the beauty of her dazzling hazel eyes.

Lena smiled. "Well, Rose Smith, let me take you to the head of this hotel, Ms. Jane McCarthy."

Audrey followed Lena around the hotel to the back, almost jogging to keep up. Lena's long legs strode too fast and the hotel was rather large. Lena rounded another corner, calling for Jane.

"In the office," Jane responded.

Lena pushed open a door. A small office with a desk much too large for it, was before Audrey. Papers in neat stacks lined one side of the desk. Jane continued writing something on one of those papers. Her dark blond hair neatly done at the nape of her neck spoke to her professionalism as did the dusky purple dress with a high collar that hugged her frame.

"Did you put the help wanted flyer out Lena?" Jane asked without looking.

"Didn't need to ma'am. Found a girl right here. Meet Rose Smith."

Audrey stepped out from behind Lena. "Pleasure to meet you, Ms. McCarthy."

Jane clasped her hands together, resting her chin on them. Her blue eyes narrowed as she gazed at her. Audrey resisted the urge to swallow. Jane perked a brow, her eyes scrutinizing her appearance.

"Do you have any experience in the kitchens?" Jane asked.

Audrey smiled meekly. "No ma'am. This would be my first ever job. Father never let me out of the house much."

"And he let you out now?"

"Needs the money to purchase new seeds. We had a poor harvest this year," she lied.

Jane nodded. "I am willing to give anyone a chance. Just one, mind you. If you don't pan out, you're gone. Lena, she bunks with you."

Lena turned around and embraced her. "I know we are going to be great friends, Rose."

"Best friends," Audrey replied with a grin matching Lena's.

Jane coughed, getting their attention. "Lena, show Rose to her room then to the kitchens. You need to get to the dining room to help Cassie."

"Yes ma'am," Lena replied.

"Rose, your wages are a dollar a day which is fair since you are given breakfast and supper along with room and board. Wages are given every week on Friday at six in the morning. Ask me, and I will hand you your pay. Because this is Tuesday, you will get paid for today, Wednesday and Thursday, then your week will start regularly if you pan out."

"Thank you, Ms. McCarthy," Audrey said, dipping into a curtsey.

Jane raised a brow, a hint of a smile on her lips. "Indeed. Hurry along. I am not paying you to look pretty."

Audrey smiled, following Lena out the door. She shut it softly behind her, grateful for this opportunity that fell in her lap. Here, she would be a little bit closer to her father, off on her own and away from her vile aunt Georgiana and her disturbing cousin.

"Follow me, Rose!" Lena exclaimed. "I am so excited we are sharing a room together. This will be grand!"

Audrey grinned, linking arms with her new friend. "I am rather excited myself. This will be such a wondrous adventure!"

# CHAPTER THIRTEEN

Eugene leaned back against the seat. The train swayed sideways, zooming across the plains. There was still a good chunk of time until he arrived in Kansas City. He shuffled through his notes, making a checklist of places to search for Audrey starting with hotels. She couldn't have gone too far.

He whipped out a separate sheet of paper with a list of her fathers' dining hotels across America. The man was wealthier than the Queen of England, owning several large estates on the east coast and in the south. Without a shadow of a doubt, Audrey would not have gone to those estates, which left the dining hotels.

After speaking with Wilfred Darrow, Eugene discovered Philip Whitman died when Audrey was twelve. To him, it made sense Audrey would go to a hotel where she could be close to her father as opposed to one of the estates he'd bought through business deals and hadn't ever personally been to. The only issue he found was there were numerous hotels in several states owned by Mr. Whitman.

*Answers have to be in Kansas City,* Eugene surmised. *She had to have stayed somewhere and purchased a ticket.*

He groaned thinking about it. He was tired and ready to find this young lady. It would have been easy to stay irritated and angry with her for running away so foolishly, but after meeting her family and reading her diary, he could sympathize with her loneliness if not her choice to run away. He was tired and wished to be home so he could begin his own search for a family, and this search for a Whitman, delayed his own search and prolonged his loneliness. He sighed and rubbed his eyes. Eugene stuffed all the papers on his lap back into his briefcase, pulling out Audrey's diary and began rereading the story of a lonely girl.

*Dear Friend,*

*I am lonely. I find myself reading more and more being kept up in this finishing school. I hardly have time to visit with friends due to mundane, time consuming and boring tasks and classes like Greek, table settings, voice lessons and embroidery. And the rules about socializing past curfew are strictly enforced. Books, and writing to you, despite being a diary, are my only solace. I long for a pet. However, they are not allowed so once again I turn to you. I'm talking to you so often, I feel I need to name you. What do you think of Brittany? I rather like the name. Anyways, back to real life.*

*Currently, I am reading Jane Eyre by Emily Bronte. I find it absolutely enthralling how forthright she is. Jane is whom I wish to be like, a free woman, not tied down to people through means and money. She chose her occupation and met an aloof yet handsome man. Mayhap someday I shall remit to be so fortunate. Everyone deserves love and companionship. If I do not receive love, I pray to hope for a companion instead.*

*Enough with the dreary news. Bethany Shapiro is hosting a gala in two weeks. I have already seen the seamstress about a dress. While others are boasting of pearls and lace, mine is simple. I want to be seen for myself, and all the lace and pearls speak to my money, and I loathe people only seeing my money.*

*Bye for now, my friend. I am off to finish this enchanting novel and may pick up another by Charlotte Bronte.*

The train jolted to a stop. Eugene tucked the diary back into his traveling bag. Eugene pinched the bridge of his nose, crinkling his eyes. Running a hand over his face, he took a deep breath. He'd read multiple entries, much the same.

*Yes, I can definitely relate to her loneliness. Still this doesn't explain her need to vanish, so abruptly. Surely a story book would not elicit such an instantaneous decision.*

Eugene off boarded the cramped, muggy train, trading it for the cramped and muggy outdoors of Kansas City. The end of the platform faced a large dining hotel – The Silver Spoon. Eugene slogged past the crowded area. The sheriff sat on horseback, sleepily watching the area.

*At least look alive to the town you protect*, Eugene thought.

People milled about outside the hotel and inside the foyer, standing in lines for food or a room to rest. Moving into the foyer, Eugene got in line for a room behind a portly gentleman, huffing and dabbing his head continuously with a kerchief. The line moved rather swiftly to which he was grateful for.

Eugene checked his pocket watch after moving three people. Impatience was getting the better of him. He felt positively certain he was on the right track for Audrey. God only knew what she was doing right now or where she truly happened to be. He hoped she was all right and hadn't found herself in any trouble.

As he waited, he spied the register. Eugene quirked a brow. *Surely, she did not sign her name to the register?*

"How can I help you, sir?" The attendant asked.

Approaching the desk, Eugene slid the register over to himself. "I would like to book for a single night please." Eugene thumbed through the register, going back a few pages. Audrey and her neat hand were here not two days prior. Eugene grinned. *Foolish girl,* he thought to himself, *running away but still using your full name.*

"Sir," the man said gaining his attention. "That will be fifty cents for the room."

Eugene took out the coin purse to pay, but also the miniature of Audrey. Holding up the photo, he said, "I am a Pinkerton who is looking for this woman. Have you seen her?"

The man nodded. "Yes sir, I have; two days ago."

"Do you know what she was wearing?"

The attendant shook his head. "I don't remember. But I do remember her locket getting stolen. Filed a report with the sheriff myself."

Eugene smirked, happy to be on her trail. Audrey losing a locket was small compared to what she could have lost – her life, virtue or other monies. Eugene decided to check with the sheriff anyways to best tie any loose ends. "Perfect I shall head there next. Do you remember her mentioning where she was headed?"

"Denver."

"She left for Denver two days ago?"

"Correct."

"Excellent," Eugene exclaimed, handing the man four, dollar coins. "Book me a ticket for the morning train to Denver. The extra is your tip."

"Yes sir," the attendant smiled and hurried to do Eugene's bidding. Another man took over the booking of rooms with a tight-lipped smile directed to him.

Audrey was indeed a naive young woman, out gallivanting on her own. How she'd managed to not get into deeper trouble, killed or otherwise, he did not know. It was extreme luck or divine intervention by God. Eugene figured it was a touch of both. God did work in mysterious ways. He spun on his heel, going back outside into the bustling streets of Kansas City.

Eugene politely maneuvered past people, tipping his hat to groups of gossiping women. He strolled down the street to the giant white sign hanging on the corner building that read SHERIFF. A large dark-haired man with a stained cotton shirt underneath a cowhide vest came out of the building, heading toward a tethered appaloosa stallion. A golden badge hung off his vest pocket glinting in the setting sun. Eugene was still a few yards away.

"Sheriff," Eugene hollered, "a moment please!" Eugene rushed to the man before he could mount his horse.

The sheriff turned slow on his heel. His dark brown eyes narrowing at him.

"Sheriff," Eugene called, "I am Eugene Turner, Pinkerton on a case of a missing woman."

"Audrey Whitman, by any chance?" the Sheriff replied in a rough voice, bunching the reins of his steed in his hands.

Eugene nodded. "Yes, her. So, you have received my telegram about her?"

Sheriff grumbled. "Yeah, I did. I still haven't found her, the missing locket, or the woman she claims took it," the man finished with a yawn. "Now if you'll excuse me, I am missing out on supper with my wife."

"One more thing sheriff."

"Yes."

Eugene crossed his arms, "Why weren't you at the train station to catch her before she left for Denver?"

Sheriff cracked his neck. He dropped the reins, leaving the horse ground tied. His countenance changing from weary to irritated as he approached Eugene slowly. "Do you by any chance happen to know how many people get off a train in a day? Lots. Going out west with big dreams that won't come true. I have more problems on my hands than one missing woman who shouldn't be in Denver on her own to begin with, but is too stubborn with her head, high in the clouds to listen to anyone tellin' her different. Good day, Pinkerton."

The sheriff mounted and headed off. Eugene stood there a

moment seething from the lack of concern for Audrey but also at the sheriff's apathy delayed his return home.

Eugene sighed. *I want to be back in Philadelphia by now. Use the money I get from this case to buy a house and settle down and start a family.* Eugene kicked the dust. He watched enviously as happy couples strolled side by side chatting happily.

He strolled back the way he came. A large white sign with dresses in the window caught his eye – Doreen's Dresses. Eugene made his way to the store. *I have a feeling she most assuredly came here,* he thought. *If she was wearing an expensive taffeta, she would want a change of attire.*

He opened the door, striding inside. The woman behind the counter looked stunned to see him inside.

"The gentlemen's store is down the street on the right, Percy's Tailored Suits," the woman said.

Eugene removed his hat. "I am Eugene Turner, Pinkerton. I am investigating the disappearance of the lost heiress." Eugene said, unfolding the picture in his pocket, showing it to the woman. "Have you seen her?"

"Why," the woman said sucking in a surprised breath, "she was in here not three days ago, buying dresses." The lady paused, tapping a finger to the side of her jawline. "Yes," the woman began again, "sold me the blue taffeta one hanging in the window. She exchanged it for plainlike clothing more suitable for traveling."

"Thank you for the information. Did she happen to say anything about any future plans?"

She shook her head. "No, I'm afraid we did not discuss anything like that. The woman was so bright and sunny. A very kind, pleasant young woman. Had her jewelry stolen, poor dear. I do hope she is safe."

Eugene dipped his head. "Thank you, ma'am, for your time. Have a lovely day."

Eugene stepped outside into the bright afternoon. He turned on his heel, heading for the hotel. Tomorrow morning, he was headed for Denver. With all this new information, he would have her back home in Philly by the end of the week. Then his life could return to some normalcy.

*Then I can start the life I've always wanted. With the prestige this case will bring me, I'll be free to find a wife and settle down. I will finally be able to support her and whatever family we have,* Eugene decided.

# CHAPTER FOURTEEN

*This is wonderful*, she thought. *New clothes, my hair done up all pretty like them ladies, and no one knows my real name*, Mary smirked. *How grand. I can be like the aceto-cats like back east. Maybe I can use my name now – Florence Miriam Lockburn and keep goin' by Mary tils I get out of here.*

Mary walked down the street with a smirk on her face. Men stared at her, often doing double takes. Rightfully so. The dress she wore was magnificent. A daring neckline, lacy frills, and golden silk. It hugged her figure in all the right places, bringing out her ample bosom. It billowed around her like a fluffy perfect cloud.

Mary twirled her parasol, smiling and waving at a man who had a heifer of a woman on his arm. The man scowled, shaking his head at her. The woman harrumphed. Mary smiled all the more, strolling to her extravagant hotel room.

She rounded the corner, spotting her hotel ahead, The Ice La Vie. The tall white pillared building was the most beautiful site on the entire street. Black and white twisted marble columns stood on either side of the entryway. She passed between the columns, looking up each time at the impressive architecture. Mary went through the double French doors of glass opened by the butlers. She smiled, nodding to each of them. She turned the corner to the right, heading up the curved staircase to her room on the immediate right. Upon opening the door, she let out a contented sigh, closing it with an audible thud.

*Who knew stealing could get me a life like this?* She thought. *No more being hungry at night, cold and scared. I can get hot meals three times a day! No more smelling like a manure pile. I can smell like lemon verbena.*

Mary twirled around the room. "It might be wrong, but I'm not hungry!"

She stopped. Guilt clawed its way inside of her. She took from many people over the years but more so yesterday than she ever had in a week. Usually it was something small to get a meal. This time, it was more.

*No one will understand,* Mary grimaced. *Ma walkin' out on us. Pa goin' to the ale house instead of being with us. Being left at ten years old to care for three youngers. Aunt Winnifred taking in everyone else but me on account of, "I was too much work."*

Mary shook her head. A determined scowl creasing her face. "Not anymore," she said, stamping her foot. "I ain't going hungry or cold again!"

Reaching into her coin purse, she looked at the money she had left. The smile vanished. Twenty dollars would not take her far with what she was doing. Mary went over to the vanity on the far side of the room, looking at the coins there. She closed her eyes and sighed. Thirty-seven dollars and fifty cents. Not much to buy a house or land. She could get a horse or two but animals would require shelter and feed.

"This is the first time I am not out on the streets beggin' fer food," she said, holding the locket and opening it. "I gotta be smart." Mary opened the locket, staring at the couple inside. "Her mother, sure was a beaut."

She grimaced, staring at it. Slamming the locket down on the bed, she stomped over to the closet where two dresses hung. She wiggled out of the gold one and into a plain, green one with no lace or frills. Pulling out her traveling bag, she crammed in her gold dress and stuffed the other on top of it.

*Darn guilt,* she thought. *Don't matter. My luck was turnin' sour here anyways.*

Mary went over to the bed to where the locket rested. Gathering it in her hands, she opened it again, growling at her internal indecisiveness. She stuffed it inside her dress. Taking her belongings and money, Mary stormed out the door.

She passed the butlers who opened the doors for her again, letting her out into the fading afternoon light. Immediately she went to the train station. She waited in line impatiently for everyone else to buy their tickets for tonight's final train.

"Where to miss?" the ticket master asked.

"Denver."

"Two dollars."

Mary pulled out coins, handing it to the man.

"Train leaves in twenty minutes ma'am." The ticket master said.

Mary dipped her head. With her ticket, she stormed down the street. She carefully picked her way to a jewelry dealer on the outskirts of town. She already visited the other two dealers yesterday, selling Audrey's other jewelry. They most likely wouldn't want to deal with her again. This was the last one.

Mary carefully checked her surroundings for the sheriff and deputy who liked to loiter in the area. With no sight of their hides, Mary went in the shop.

"We're closing," a grumpy man yelled.

"Not yet you ain't." Mary retorted.

"What's yer name, gal?" the man said.

The man reminded her of her grandpa, big belly, grizzly gray large beard and two beady blue eyes. Mary's eyes narrowed, *looks like'em, smells like'em, and I don't like'em, this man or my grandpa.* His shirt had tobacco, food and pit stains. Mary wrinkled her nose in disgust. In all, he could pass for her grandpa if he wasn't dead and, in the ground, already.

"Lucille."

"What can I do fer ya Lucille?"

Mary brought out the watch. "What can I get for this?"

"Solid gold, engraved, diamond in the middle of a ticking watch," the man said, rubbing his beard. "Ten dollars."

"No way," Mary grouched. "Thirty."

"Fifteen."

"Forty."

The man laughed, leaning over the counter. "Yer supposed to be coming down, gal," the man said.

Mary put her hands on her hips. "Yer supposed to be comin' up."

The man chuckled, turning the watch over. "Whitman, huh? You the missin' Whitman gal?"

Mary shook her head. "Nope. The Whitman gal gave this to me. I wanna sell it. Thirty dollars."

"Fine, fine," he said getting into the cash drawer.

The man handed her the money. Mary grabbed it and took off at a run, not caring who saw her. She needed to catch that train.

*My new life is about to begin*, she thought grinning with her money in hand. *I cain't miss that.*

She dashed her way down the wooden platform. With relief, she spotted the train. People were already boarding. Smiling, she made headlong for it.

# CHAPTER FIFTEEN

"Sweet Mother Mary and Joseph," Audrey exclaimed, watching horrified as smoke rose from the hot griddle.

The breakfast order she was working on almost burst into flames. Fortunately, she was quick enough this time to swipe it all into a metal pail. Audrey felt the sting of defeat rise up in her eyes. She hadn't gotten anything right all morning. Try though she did, still, she failed.

Jane and Lena threw her into the kitchen, sticking her on the griddle to make eggs. It looked simple enough. However, it was a skill she could not seem to master. Immediately upon pouring the eggs on to the griddle, they began to bubble and snap from the heat. She burned it faster than she was able to turn it over and cook.

Audrey dabbed her eyes with the back of her hand.

"Rose!" the head cook Claudia yelled. "That's the third breakfast in a row you've ruined. What on earth were you doing?"

Audrey fiddled with her apron. "It... It didn't look done enough."

"The eggs didn't look done enough," Claudia paused. "They are scrambled eggs. Light, fluffy and yellow NOT black, crumbly and almost on fire, girl."

"I'm sorry Claudia," Audrey said hanging her head.

*Everything's all right, chin up,* Audrey told herself.

"Wash some dishes. Don't go near the griddle anymore."

"Yes ma'am."

Audrey strode to the giant sink. Hot soapy water filled the tub. A stack of crusty white plates sat on the right, beside the sink. Audrey let out a long breath.

"I can't screw this up," she whispered under her breath. "I will NOT mess this up."

Audrey washed all the plates and silverware. Next, she grabbed a giant black flat pan-looking thing and began scrubbing it. The pan was heavy and all metal. It clanked in her sink as she scrubbed it. The black metal began to turn red in spots. Audrey scrubbed harder to get it all off, but more kept appearing.

"Rose, have you seen my cast iron skillet? I need to make a ham steak," the other kitchen cook Ada said.

"No, Ada I haven't," Audrey replied, pulling the one she just washed out of the sink.

Ada screeched.

"Ada," Rose began, "what is the matter?"

"THAT!" she seethed pointing to her hand, "is a cast iron skillet you do NOT wash," she said hanging her head and shaking it back and forth. "Goodness Rose, you wipe it out. You don't wash it. It's seasoned."

"Seasoned with what? Rosemary?" Audrey asked.

Ada chuckled while holding her head in exasperation. "No darlin', it means the pan is good and used. Oh biscuits."

"Can you not use it now?"

"No, I can use it," Ada sighed. "It's goin' to take it a while to get back to proper. For future though, because you didn't know, if you see a pan like this, don't wash it," she finished, squeezing Audrey's shoulder. "It's all right."

Audrey nodded but inside she felt like a failure. She put the skillet down and grabbed a large stack of dishes she'd just washed.

They were heavy. However, their resting place was on the other side of the kitchen. Audrey hefted the lot in her hands. The door inside swung open.

"Claudia, I need three biscuits and a plate of eggs," Lena hollered, bursting through the door just as Audrey walked by.

Audrey tried to hold onto the plates the best she could. A few slipped from her hands, smashing around her feet. Audrey took a step back, slipping on one of the fallen plates. Her body was thrust backwards, the rest of the plates falling from her hands. Audrey closed her eyes, hands out as her body collapsed to the floor with the rest of the plates falling around her. Her hands slipped along the ground. She felt a plate strike the back of her hand.

Audrey screamed.

"Rose!" Lena yelled.

Opening her eyes, she looked around. Lena stood over her, hands covering her mouth. Audrey checked her hands, seeing a cut on the back of her left one. The blood oozing to the surface made her gag. She looked her body over, only seeing the one scratch. Audrey let out a deep sigh of relief. Carefully, she got off the floor.

"What is going on?" Claudia asked. "Rose are you, all right?"

"Yes," Audrey replied.

Claudia shook her head and sighed. "All those broken dishes... Well, I'm glad you are all right."

Jane came in through the other door, standing to the side of Claudia. Audrey felt flames strike her cheeks. She was in trouble now. Between burning breakfasts, washing a not-washable pan, and now all these dishes, she was certain she was fired. Ada looked at her despondently before turning back to the head chef and hotel manager.

"Everyone all right?" Jane asked.

Audrey nodded.

"I opened the door and didn't see Rose," Lena explained. "It was an accident."

Jane sighed, looking at the floor. "Let's be more cautious please. No one's pay is getting docked, let me make that clear first. Second, Rose, are you all right?"

"Yes ma'am," Audrey replied.

Claudia gasped, going over to the sink. "Is that truly the skillet next to the wash sink?" Claudia asked.

"I washed it," Audrey replied, her voice barely above a whisper. "I didn't know."

Claudia put a hand to her head. "Oh, bright stars... Jane, stick her somewhere else."

Jane came over, her heels clicking on the wood floor. "Rose, what *skills* do you have?"

Audrey tilted her head to the side. *What skills do I have*, she thought. Everyone waited expectantly for her to answer. Butterflies danced inside of her.

Audrey took a deep breath, "I can sew, cross-stitch, embroider, lace, needle point, paint, play piano, harp, and flute. Oh, and I can sing a little."

Jane blinked at her. "Interestingly impressive list Rose Smith."

Audrey curtsied. "Thank you, Ms. McCarthy."

Jane shook her head, eyebrows raised. Audrey flashed her a nervous smile, hoping her list of skills would redeem her after the kitchen fiasco. Audrey glanced around at the other faces. They all wore the same bewildered expression as Jane. Audrey felt more nervous now than she did when taking a test on proper table etiquette.

*Surely, one of my skills can be helpful*, Audrey thought.

"Come with me, Rose," Jane said. "I'm going to put you in laundry," she finished walking away to the back door.

"How exciting!" Audrey exclaimed, following.

Jane flashed her a look Audrey didn't know how to interpret. She took a few deep breaths, calming herself from the chaos of moments prior. All morning long, she tried her best, but it did not seem like she was getting anywhere. Lena told her to sweep the dining room before guests arrived, however she simply made a huge cloud of debris. Then she was told to make coffee, but accidentally included the grounds in the liquid. Even the task of dishes became overwhelming when she washed the wrong pan.

*I can do this*, Audrey told herself.

Jane held the door open for her to go outside. The immediate change in temperature made Audrey thankful to be out of the hot kitchen and away from so many rules. Sewing could not be so hard. She could sew in a straight line, add embellishments, and make people feel handsome with her stitching; like the story of the lady spinning straw to gold. Audrey tilted her head to the side, wondering about the ending of that particular story. She waved it off with an outward flick of her wrist.

Back in finishing school, she won a competition on stitching. This would be a walk in the park for her. She was excited to get her hands on some garments and turn them into something magnificent. People were going to love it.

Jane pointed to a large wash bin. "We are in the back of the hotel. Outside here, is where you will be, washing. Drying is inside next to a woodstove. Mending takes place in the back room after the clothes have dried. You will be doing the mending."

Audrey clasped her hands in front of herself. "Wonderful!"

"Surely," Jane paused with a lifted brow. Opening the door to a small room, Jane announced, "Meet Kelly and Eliza. They clean the rooms and wash the sheets. Upon request, they wash people's clothes. Guests do pay for the service. Your task will be to hang the garments to dry and mend them."

"Yes ma'am," Audrey replied with a bright smile.

*Finally,* Audrey thought, *something I can do exceptionally well at.*

The manager spun on her heel and left. Audrey refrained from letting out an audible sigh. She returned her attention back to her two new work friends. Kelly was an older woman with short curly blond hair, cropped above her shoulders. Eliza's soft brown hair hung in two braids down her back; with a cheery cherub like smile adorning her face.

"Hello everyone," Audrey said enthusiastically. "My name is Rose. Is there anything I can help with?"

Kelly turned her back on her, heading out the door to the vat of washings. "I need you to bring the lye."

"Lie?" Audrey blinked. "I will not bring that. It is bad form."

Kelly rounded with the door halfway open. "What?"

"You said lie. I do not like to lie."

Eliza snorted into her hand. She rotated around, hiding her face in her apron. Kelly shook her head with a slight smile on her aging face.

Kelly chortled. "Rose, L.Y.E. is what we use to wash clothes, and sheets with. L.I.E. is what people do. So… I need you to bring the Y.E. not the I.E."

Audrey laughed delicately into the back of her hand. "Oh goodness. How silly of me."

*Goodness,* Audrey thought, *I hope they do not realize I was serious. I wonder if Jane Eyre ran into such particular troubles.*

Eliza put an arm around her neck. "Good joke, Rose."

Audrey hugged her. "Thank you, Eliza."

"Here, I will show you where we keep the Y.E."

Audrey followed her to a cupboard. Inside, everything was marked and set into neat rows. The entire top row was filled with lye while the bottom row was different colored dye.

Below the dye, sheets folded neatly, filled the last three rows. Blankets and quilts lined a blanket ladder to the right of the cupboard. Everything had its place.

"How extraordinary!" Audrey exclaimed.

Eliza paused, her face scrunching slightly. "Sure… So, grab some *lye* and let's go." She said already by the back door. "We are washing sheets today."

Audrey reached in, without looking, and grabbed a bag. She shut the cabinet, skipping off, arm in arm with Eliza.

"We can have fun while we work you know," Audrey remarked. "What do you like to do?"

Eliza stared at her. "What do you mean?"

"Do you like to press flowers, go on picnics, play the piano?"

Eliza laughed heartily. "Oh Rose, you are too much. Come, Kelly is waiting."

"All right."

Audrey did not know how to take that particular remark. *Surely, after the work day is completed, they must do something of trivial enjoyment*, she thought. *Needle point, or something, even knitting is superb.*

Audrey came outside after Eliza. Kelly was stirring a large bathtub full of hot water with a stick. White linens swirled inside the somewhat soapy water. Eliza went on the other side to a ribbed instrument that hung on the side. She began to rub the garments against the instrument. Eliza became engrossed in her task. Audrey observed her for a while, watching, impressed, as dirt lifted off the garments.

"Rose," Kelly called, breaking her out from watching Eliza. "Add a sprinkle of the lye to the sheets," Kelly instructed.

Audrey opened the bag, going to the tub. She sprinkled some in.

"A little more," Kelly said.

Audrey sprinkled more. The water began to turn red. Audrey gasped.

Kelly's horrified face stared at her. "What did you do?"

"I grabbed a bag. Red is such a lovely color and it caught my eye."

"I said grab some *lye* not *dye*," Eliza said, putting a hand to her head. "Goodness, Rose! Sorry Kelly, I should've watched her."

"Eliza," Kelly sighed, pointing to the wash, "get Jane. She will have to decide if the sheets will be acceptable for use."

Audrey hung her head, waiting for the manager to come. She was in trouble now. In fact, she would most likely be let go. She needed this job. She couldn't return to her aunt and cousin.

*What am I good at,* she thought. *I have been so secluded behind fanciful walls, am I even capable of living out here?* Audrey breathed in slowly, feeling the tears sting behind her eyes. Before her tears could fall, she patted her eyes. *Of course, I am. I made it from St. Louis to here without hindrance. This will not stop me.*

"What did she do..." Jane trailed off. "Oh dear, well they can be used as employee bedding." Jane came in front of her. "Rose, this is your last chance. I understand this morning was an accident with the plates. Burning food, and ruining skillets costs money. And now this…" Jane sighed. "The burnt food and the ruined sheets are coming out of your pay. Come with me."

"Pleasure meeting you, Kelly and Eliza," Audrey said despondently, following Jane away from the laundry.

Kelly shook her head, pulling the dyed sheets out of the tub. Audrey swallowed, following Jane McCarthy to the front of the hotel.

# CHAPTER SIXTEEN

E ugene's room overlooked the train station. He sat on the rickety bed, watching the final train for the night pull in with a screeching stop. The people dis-boarded. Eugene watched, in case Audrey happened to return to this city. No one got off looking remotely like her.

The people he encountered today, who knew anything, remarked she was heading to Denver, Colorado. It felt right in his gut; and his gut was hardly wrong. According to Wilfred Darrow, Denver was the hotel Mr. Whitman built for his wife before her untimely passing. Eugene figured she would head there to be close to the last bit of her parents.

*If I was in her shoes, it's where I would go,* Eugene thought. He glanced over at her diary by the nightstand. Grabbing for it, he fiddled around the pages until he found one he hadn't read yet. Leaning against the pillows in the bed, he opened it further to read by the fading light of the day.

Eugene let out a harsh breath. *Probably another party.* He stared at the page. It was marked a month prior to her disappearance.

.  .  .

*Hello Dear Friend, Brittany,*

Eugene rolled his eyes.

*Bethany Shapiro's gala was exquisite. She was such a vision. Bethany even found herself a suitor; a gentleman from New York. However, I did not. I tried to not use my last name so I could find a man who would be interested in only me; like Jane Eyre. However, someone discovered my name. Immediately I was flocked to. It was utterly disheartening.*

*How I long for an adventure like in Ms. Bronte's book. How exquisite it must be to feel love! I wonder how Jane felt to feel love in return. To not be lonely anymore. I wish to feel the same at some point. I wonder if that is what my dear friend Juliet will feel at her ball. Goodness, did I not tell you? I am to attend a ball this Saturday for Ms. Juliet Bordeu, a finishing school girl friend of mine. It is her birthday and her parents wish to find her a suitor.*

*Mayhap there I shall find a happily ever after all my own. Juliet said the man she fancies will be there. Hopefully her parents approve so she too can have love with him. I do hope she has her happily forever after.*

*Aunt Georgiana picked me out a dark purple dress. The color is beautiful; however, I am not overly fond of all the gaudy lace. The French do love lace. I think the lace looks like an overly frosted cake. It's been overused. Cousin Thomas is to attend with me. My stomach churns at the thought of being with him in the same carriage for any length of time. Sigh. I will survive this too. Ciao for now, Brittany. I am off to plan my hairstyle.*

. . .

Eugene slapped the book shut, shaking his head. It was the typical entry almost consistently. *She is lonely,* Eugene thought, staring at the diary in his hands, *this is a side of the aristocrats I did not think existed.*

A knock came from his door. Eugene groaned, getting off the bed.

"Who is it?" he hollered grumpily.

"Telegrams!" a voice bellowed from the other side of the door.

Eugene opened the door. Large yellow pieces of paper collided with his face. He grunted and grabbed the paper, flipping the boy a penny. He shut the door, opening the paper immediately.

Eugene Turner, Pinkerton, stop.

Audrey Whitman is not with my family and I in Maryland, stop.

Signed, Bethany Shapiro, stop.

Eugene ripped open the next one.

Pinkerton Turner, stop.

Audrey Whitman is not with me Delaware, stop.

Please find her, stop.

Juliet Bordeu, stop.

*How ignorant of me,* Eugene cursed himself, *I should have telegrammed the hotels earlier today. Hopefully it is not too late.*

Eugene grabbed his coat, heading out into the night. With his hands in his pockets, he went to the telegraph office.

He passed by young women with parasols, hanging on the arms of men hurrying to get inside out of the chilly night. Eugene peered to the left seeing there was a show going on tonight featuring the local musical talents of Annie May. Eugene shook his head, chuckling, *"Musical talents" code words for screeching every word*.

Eugene made it to the telegraph office, seeing the older man inside getting ready to shut down for the night.

"Excuse me," Eugene called. "I have a few telegrams to send."

The man didn't turn around. "I am closing son, come back tomorrow."

"I am Eugene Turner, Pinkerton, I am on the case of the missing heiress, Audrey Whitman. I will tip well."

The old man turned around, sighing. "Very well. What is the message?"

"Contact Wilfred Darrow in St. Louis if missing Whitman heiress arrives, signed Eugene Turner, Pinkerton. I need telegrams sent to every hotel in Wichita, San Francisco, Omaha, Denver and Oklahoma City."

"Yes sir, will do," the man said writing down the missive. "Anything else?"

"No," Eugene said, putting down a five-dollar bill. "Thank you."

Eugene walked back to his dining hotel room. The place was quieting down with the last train docked sleepily for the night. It's people now settling into their rooms. Eugene strode to the dining side, following his nose and feeling his stomach rumble.

He sat down at a lonely table in the back of the room, ordering the prime rib dinner. He again, pulled out Audrey's diary, reading about the last ball she attended and her disappointment for not finding the love of her ever so pampered life. Audrey pined for a Mr. Rochester and her own Thornfield Hall. Eugene couldn't help but smirk. She may be woman, but her brain was that of a daydreaming child.

Eugene put the book away when his dinner came. *Dinner then Denver*, he mused.

# CHAPTER SEVENTEEN

Audrey swallowed, striding toward the front desk following Jane. The dark polished wood glistened. The counter top was bare, with only a bell in the far-right corner. Jane paused in front of it with a sigh. A handsome man behind the desk stood up. His slender frame not much wider than Jane herself. He raised his hand to her, dipping his head with a tight-lipped smile.

"Audrey, meet, Bartholomew or Bart for short. You will be helping out at the front desk. With your chipper personality, it should not be too… difficult a task, I would hope."

Audrey forced a smile. "No ma'am!"

"This is your last chance Rose," Jane said with a point of her finger. "Greet people, and take them to their rooms. Basic rooms are on the right side of the staircase. Grand rooms on the left."

"Absolutely," Audrey agreed solemnly, then adding with a significantly lighter tone. "Do the grand rooms have paisley wall-papers? I have heard it's in fashion this season."

Jane blinked, shaking her head. "No. It is painted blue with gold accents."

"Oh, how charmingly proper! I am certain people will love how crisp it sets the room."

Jane opened her mouth to say something then closed it. Jane glanced Audrey up and down with raised brows, "Indeed. Bart, show her what to do."

Bart nodded. "Yes, Jane," he said quietly. Bart beckoned Audrey with a hand to come behind the registration desk. "I go by Bart," the man said softly, opening the side door for her.

Behind the counter was a cut out little inlet with a chair to sit in. A small booklet was pushed to the far-left side. Keys hung on pegs with a small piece of paper attached to each key labeled with a number.

Audrey beamed, greeting people and interacting with them was much more suitable to her skills. She was good with people. At parties, she talked and flitted about the room, hardly leaving time for dancing or refreshments. She did not like seeing ladies by themselves off in a chair or corner, so Audrey went to them, taking turns about the room, chatting up a storm.

*I can most assuredly, handle this*, Audrey thought.

"You stand and wait for a customer. Basic room numbers are from two hundred to two hundred twenty. Grand room numbers are from one hundred to one hundred six. We charge fifty cents a night for a basic room and two dollars a night for a grand room because morning refreshments are served in their room. We keep records of people who stay in this booklet right here," Bart instructed looking at her seriously, pushing the book to the far-left corner of the desk. "And it stays right here."

Audrey smiled, clasping her hands together. "How exquisite! I'm sure every person is positively charmed with the service."

Bart paused for a brief moment, a smirk twitching on the right corner of his mouth. "You are going to do well with your personality."

"Thank you."

"Which are basic rooms?" Bart asked.

"Right side of the staircase. Fifty cents a night and are labeled from two hundred to two hundred twenty."

Bart sat down on the stool. "Correct. I suggest you walk around the hotel and become more familiar. All places are open to employees. The doors which are not, remain locked. Jane is the only one with a key," Bart began folding yellow papers and organizing a cupboard. "We have one guest at the moment in Grand Room one hundred six, but they are out at the moment. Check in every few minutes or so to see if other guests have arrived."

"Absolutely," Audrey replied.

She dipped into a curtsey and almost skipped out the door leading to the stairs. She could feel her insides tingling with giddiness. Out here, this far west, no one would know who she happened to be. It was perfect. She'd a fresh start with an identity all her own. Long as she didn't mess this task up though.

*This is wonderful. I'm doing a job I'm more suited for. I'm at my father's hotel,* Audrey stifled a giggle. *I am just like Jane Eyre now! How positively enchanting.*

She skipped up the stairs to the song she remembered at Juliet's ball. A giant picture of her father and mother graced the middle of the wall of the staircase. Audrey paused, her eyes misting over. It was the same picture in her locket Mary had stolen. It was the sole photo of her parents and it was so precious to her.

*They look so happy,* she thought. *I wonder if they married for love or convenience. I bet it was for love. Father looks so happy, and proud. Mother looks radiant in her purple dress.* Audrey sighed contentedly, smiling. She continued her way up the right side of the curving staircase. The rooms at the top of the stairs were labeled with even numbers on the left and odd on the right.

She paused in front of room two hundred two, hand on the knob. *I bet even the basic rooms are beautiful,* she thought. *Father always worked hard in his study, surely this must be a representation of such work ethic. And according to father, people were always at his hotels.* A wide smile, split her face. Butterflies filled her stomach. Audrey opened the door.

Much to her enthusiastic dismay, the rooms were quite plain. Audrey blinked, *how plain, yet charming.* White painted walls gave the room a comfortable feel. An oversized patchwork quilt adorned a full-sized bed that slept in the middle of the room under the window. A dark blue rug spread out from under the bed on either side. A four-door dresser sat to the left of the bed with an armchair to the right. The curtains were a sheer blue, adding a little more color to the already bright room and polished hardwood floors.

It was like that in every room on the basic side of the hotel. Each room was small and plain, could fit around two people on a bed. Audrey walked back the way she came, heading down the stairs then up to the more expensive rooms on the left of the curved staircase.

Audrey opened the first room on the right, room one hundred two, walking into a carpeted room. Dark wooden polished trim ran about a third of the way up the wall separating the deep blue, gray tinted paint of the bottom half of the wall closest to the carpet and the bright white paint on the top of the wall. It was gorgeous. Gold oil lamps hung on the walls, affixed with dark brass hooks shining with a dull glimmer. There was even a formal living space complete with several arm chairs.

Audrey walked further inside, seeing a rolltop desk to the left. Beyond, there was a door, allowing entrance to the sleeping arrangements. Audrey peeked inside, spying a large bed with several expensive wedding ring quilts. The windows were adorned in velvet curtains, a deep gray to add elegance to the already beautiful space.

*How charming,* she praised. *It reminds me of how I would picture The Bennett's residence from Ms. Austen's book.*

She went back down the stairs, realizing, after peaking in another Grand room, that every room would be decorated in the same way.

Bart gave her a nod. "Continue familiarizing," he said quietly, but his voice sounded louder with the stillness of the hotel. He looked back down at this task.

Audrey turned to the right, going past the sitting lounge to a closed French door. Hand on the knob, she quietly twisted it. Audrey stepped into the dark room. Going over to where a small stream of light seeped in, she threw the curtain back. Little specks of dust floated carelessly around the curtains. The walls were painted a rich plum. White marble floors glistened under her feet. Silver lamps were fixed to the walls. A fireplace sat clean and empty to the right of the room. Lounge chairs and divans, with white sheets over them, coldly slept before the fireplace. A large table rested in between one wall and curtained windows.

*A ballroom,* Audrey deduced. *No one's been here for quite some time.*

Audrey went to the piano, her soft hands caressing the dark oak wood. A small silver plate rested on top of the piano lid. Audrey ran her finger over the plate, squinting at the small letters.

"To my bride, with all my love, P. Whitman," Audrey read with a wan smile.

She pulled out the bench, sitting in front of the piano with a sigh. Her hands smoothed along the surface, disturbing the thick layer of dust. Audrey sneezed. Her hands left track marks in the thick dust that'd long since settled on the piano. Audrey slowly lifted the box blanketing the keys. The cold ivory kissed her finger tips.

Audrey looked to the door, half expecting to see Jane. No one happened to be there. She spun around, her fingers hesitantly pressing down on the keys. A soft noise came from the piano. Audrey smiled, closing her eyes. A shiver ran down her spine. Her fingers stroked a couple more keys of her favorite song.

Audrey looked to the door again, to make certain Jane did not happen to be there. She whirled back around, attention to the cold, music-hungry keys. With a deep breath her fingers danced on the keys, in return for the cold sensual greeting, music came pouring out of the piano. Audrey couldn't place the tune. Her lips turned into a moue, trying to remember the internal melody that captured her fingers. Her brows furrowed. She hummed it suddenly realizing where she remembered it from.

Her heart ran with the tune, the soft melody taking her back to when she was a child. The music box in her room playing the same tune as she danced around like a ballerina. *It was your mother's,* her father told her once right before he left for New York. Her fingers stopped. The room became icy. A shiver ran down her spine. Her mother died when she was a toddler from a sickness in her lungs. Audrey only had vague recollections of her.

"I sing to you, this lullaby," Audrey whispered.

With a haunting realization, she put a hand to her mouth. Her father once hummed the melody she was playing. It was one of the few moments where she had a warm memory of her distant father. Audrey fanned herself with her hands, forcing back the tears wanting to come forth.

She gave her attention back to the piano, gazing at the engraving on the wood. Her hands kept playing but her eyes were riveted to the spot that held a long-forgotten memory, one she desperately wanted to grasp for herself. The music swept up the room, making it brighter. She could feel the opulence of the room, how people would gather here for festivities and grandeur. Now, it was a lonely chamber out west; nothing to set it apart. Cold, dark, unwanted. Like her. She was a girl, all alone, with no family and maybe a friend in Lena.

*I am a tragic failure. I'm not like my favorite books nor their excellent characters. I am barely surviving. I cannot even make scrambled eggs or grab the correct bag of lye. A person I thought a friend turned out to be a thief. What am I even doing out here? I should return to St. Louis and accept my nightmarish fate – marry for convenience and not love. Surely love is a work of ultimate fiction. I've seen little of it myself.* Audrey hit the final key to her concerto and sighed.

"Rose," Jane called.

Audrey scrambled out of the seat and closed the lid to the piano. Her fingertips rested momentarily on the silver plaque, feeling a little warmth and comfort her parents were able to give her in life. Jane poked her head inside, her eyes pinching in the corners.

"Rose, was that you playing?"

Audrey grabbed her left arm with her right. "Yes ma'am," she said softly.

Jane blinked. "It was lovely, but we have guests now. Come and see how we provide service."

Letting out the breath she held, Audrey briskly left the room. *I can do this*, she thought.

She followed Jane out into the reception area. A man and his wife waited by the desk to get a room. Bartholomew stood behind the desk, eyes wide and shaking his head.

"Slower please," Bart said. "It's hard to understand."

The man leaned against the counter, his face turning red. "I want a grand room for a month," he said in French.

"Room?" Bart asked.

The man's face contorted, snarling even more at Bart.

"Excuse me," Audrey said in perfect French dipping into a curtsey. "How may I be able to meet your accommodations here at the hotel?"

Brows raised; the man smiled at her. His wife clapped her hands. The man came forward, smiling brightly. "Thank heavens, someone who speaks French. I would like to book a grand room for a month here. Maybe longer as we build our home."

Audrey smiled brightly, "Absolutely. Grand rooms are going to be two dollars a night and will be going up the stairs on your left. Refreshments are served in the mornings in your room. Would you like one with a view?"

The wife came forward linking her arm with her husbands, "Please," she said, "one overlooking the city."

Audrey went behind the counter to grab the keys to room one hundred five. "May I get your names for the books?"

"I am Donovan Tedoro and this is my wife Adeline."

Audrey turned to Bart. His mouth slightly dropped open as was Jane's. Audrey smiled, motioning to their guests, "Jane, Bart, this is Donovan and Adeline Tedoro. They will be staying here a month, maybe longer, while their house gets built." Turning back to the new guests she said, "I shall take you to your room. You're going to love it."

Audrey took their bag and headed up the stairs. *Finally*, she thought, *something I am good at.*

# CHAPTER EIGHTEEN

The train swayed back and forth, racing down the tracks. Victor Del Avilasto could not keep the smile from his face. His minions in Kansas City acquired what he was after. It wasn't a difficult task. He knew it wouldn't be. No woman could make it far on their own. They needed guidance, a firm hand. Ms. Whitman was like all the other women – guileless and dull.

Yesterday, he received a telegram back from his head man in Kansas City that the Whitman woman had been captured. Victor had laughed aloud. Inside, he was still chortling.

*Women,* Victor mused, *good for nothing wenches.*

Victor rubbed his hands together. His head man, Earl, had caught his girl and took her back to his hideout. Earl was going to get a raise. Maybe he would just kill Earl instead, and not waste the money nor breath. Either way, something would happen to Earl.

Victor brushed his black slacks clear of dirt. Grimacing, he picked fuzz off his black suit coat. He loathed dirt and the outdoors. Glancing down at his boots, he frowned at their dust covered tops.

"Ya look nice, boss," Hank commented.

Victor whipped his head around, facing his employee. His eyes narrowed. "I know," he growled.

Victor removed his black broad-brimmed hat, running his fingers through his dark oiled hair.

Sun beams flitted across the travel car, striking his face with warmth. "I have waited long for this day to come, Hank," Victor said, puffing on a cigar. "A day which would make us all infinitely rich."

Hank shook on the opposite bench seat. Victor smiled. He loved how his minions cowered before him, unquestioning his superiority. It made his blood bubble with delight at how simple his men could be. He employed the castaways of society. They were more apt for his lines of work.

"Indeed," Victor began again, tossing his cigar at Hank, "I have waited *too* long."

The conductor came into the car announcing their stop was approaching.

Hank licked his lips. "We're almost there, boss."

"Really? I hadn't the slightest notion you brainless frog!"

Hank shrank against the seat, scooting closer to the window.

Victor sat in the back of the first-class train seat, eagerly awaiting the arrival of Kansas City. It pleased him Hank acted swiftly, getting a telegram to his head men to be on the lookout for the rich woman traveling alone. He would never praise Hank however. It was enough he allowed the incompetent man to breathe.

The train came to a lurching stop. Victor caught himself on the back of the seat in front of him. "Cursed contraption," he complained.

Victor shoved his way past people, landing on the boardwalk. Immediately he went to his awaiting coach, barely allowing time for Hank to board with him. Victor nodded to the driver. Hank's heftiness rocked the carriage to the right as he boarded beside the driver. The driver took off, but this time Victor was prepared for the spontaneous rush forward.

His leg bounced. Victor barely contained the ecstatic shout as he drew nearer by the moment to so much money. Audrey Whitman was going to make him a rich man and it wasn't too long now.

"Eastman Hill up ahead boss!" Hank called out.

Victor clapped and rubbed his hands together, *wonderful!*

The horse pulled up to the log house. His lead man, Earl came down the stairs two at a time, a smile creasing his greasy, tobacco speckled face.

"Second room on the left boss," Earl said, opening the carriage door.

Victor shoved his way past him. Inside the house his twelve other members of his gang rose to their feet. They removed their hats, whispering "howdy boss" as he strode by. He ignored them, going to the room Earl specified. In front of the door, he paused, straightening his black jacket and removing the brimmed hat.

With a sigh, he opened the door. He raised a brow at a blond headed woman by the window. The woman on the chaise lounge glared at him. Her hands tied behind her back with rope, a white handkerchief gag in her mouth.

Victor strode past her, gazing out the window. A man with a rifle stood outside her window. He smiled. His prize would not be escaping.

"Hello, my dear," Victor said taking the gag out of her mouth. "Do your accommodations find you well?"

Her blue eyes locked on his with an eagle-like stare. Her mouth worked itself back and forth. She licked her lips, attempting to moisturize them. "For a common dwelling such as this? I suppose it is tolerable."

"I am very sorry to hear that," Victor said, taking up a chair across from her.

The girl imitated his vile smile. "I'm certain you're not."

Victor grinned wolfishly, already tiring of her lip. "Well, my dear, I will attempt to make your accommodations with me more suitable. Please, come join me in the study for some refreshments."

"How gracious of you," she replied, "however, I must decline. These bonds hinder me."

Victor grabbed her by her left upper arm, forcing her to her feet. He shoved the girl forward. "You shall do what is courteous, my dear," he said untying her bonds. "Try and escape and these men will shoot you."

She shoved him off, glaring at him. Victor pushed her forward toward the doors.

The room his henchmen just occupied was vacant. Victor led her past the open area to another part of his dwelling. He opened the study door, guiding her inside first. Without waiting for him to pull out a seat for her, she sat down. Victor grimaced at her disrespectfulness. He went over to the decanters on the right side of the room, pouring himself whiskey and her some sherry.

She made herself comfortable, wriggling in her chair. She fiddled with the edges of her skirts ever so slightly, lifting the hems to her knees and itched her calf. Leaning forward her breasts practically fell out. The blonde woman adjusted herself, popping back up in her seat. With a smile, she looped an arm over the back of the chair. Victor stared at her.

"That's mine!" the woman exclaimed. "They took it off me as I went to the train! I demand it back, at once!" She pointed at the traveling bag one of his men brought in. Victor nodded to the man, and handed her the glass of sherry. Setting his whiskey down, he opened up her suitcase. He pulled out a gaudy orange dress with frills and lace.

"I think not, my dear," he replied drolly.

Glancing over at the girl, her glass of sherry was empty. Victor smiled at her like a wolf cornering a deer. She grinned back matching his expression.

"Tell me," he began in a patronizing tone, "Why did you ever think it sensible to leave your cushy lifestyle?" he asked, sitting on the arm of a chair.

"I will do what I please," she replied, matching his condescending tone.

Victor chuckled. "Indeed. Why on earth would you ever sell this?"

He pulled out the watch, seeing her face go blank.

"Obviously I needed the money."

Victor grinned. "A precious family heirloom? Why Audrey," he crooned. "Did you have a little too much fun buying ridiculous colored dresses?"

"It was not a ridiculous purchase," she retorted with narrowed eyes.

Victor's gaze narrowed. He hated flashy colors and low-necklines on women. Audrey clearly had no sense of fashion or bodily propriety. No matter, he was going to get her money then kill her.

"So, tell me, Audrey, why escape your fancy lifestyle?"

Audrey crossed her legs, hiking up one leg and crossing it over the other knee. *Legs not crossed at the ankles. Daringly low necklines. Hands not in the lap but slung behind the chair like a man, this is not the refinement I expect of a woman out of finishing school,* Victor concluded. His head tilted to the side, eyes scrutinizing her. Audrey let out a burp. Hands in his lap, he stared shocked at her, *this is not Ms. Whitman.*

"Where did you go to finishing school?" he asked, setting the watch aside.

"Philadelphia," she replied, flicking her hair back. "I would have preferred going to Italy but Father detested the idea."

"I'm sure," he said evenly. "What does your father do?"

Her mouth flapped open, then quickly closed. She wriggled in her seat, tucking her hair behind her ear. "I'm certain," she stuttered. "He struck gold in California and ingested it," she said with a smug smile.

Victor laughed, pulling out his pistol, cocking it and putting it to her head. "Now, I know you are not Audrey Whitman. Its invested not ingested. A lady wouldn't have crossed her knees, but crossed her feet at the ankles. A lady wouldn't have belched, slung her arm behind a chair, wore a scandalously low neckline, or bought something as foolish as that awful orange dress."

She swallowed, leaning back in the chair. She closed her eyes. The tip of his barrel kissed her forehead. "It's gold," she interrupted.

Victor ignored her. "Who are you and how did you come by this?"

"I am Audrey Whitman."

Victor shot the gun in the air, putting a hole in his perfect ceiling. "Last chance."

She screamed, holding up her hands. She spoke, her words stuttered and rambled, "I am Florence Miriam Lockburn. I go by Mary. I was at the Silver Spoon when the real Audrey Whitman walked in. Had no clue who she was, only she was rich. I took her dress shopping and stole her jewelry. She said she was headed to Denver."

Victor released the hammer. "See, that wasn't difficult… Mary."

"Yeah," she said breathy.

"Unfortunately, I'm going to kill you. Don't want you giving me away to the sheriff."

Mary was white as a sheet. She put her hands up, her voice shrieking, "Wait, I can be useful!"

Victor pulled his finger off the trigger. "How so?"

"I can get Audrey. She knows me. I can get her to you."

He tucked a stray hair behind her ear. She flinched at his touch. Victor smiled, grabbing onto her chin. "Prove it," he whispered in her ear.

# CHAPTER NINETEEN

Taking people into the hotel was far easier than Audrey imagined. She was good at it. And people, to her, seemed to enjoy her company and service. Over the course of three days, she learned a lot more about the hotel and seemed to find her own place.

Lena was her dearest friend. The other women in the hotel came around quickly, which was refreshing. Audrey even learned to make scrambled eggs from Ada, although she mostly steered clear of the kitchen, unless she needed to help wash dishes.

Audrey stepped out into the fresh morning air with Lena. Today was payday and even with her previous mistakes, she made out with three dollars in her hand along with Jane declaring her a permanent hire. Audrey was thrilled with the prospect of staying in Colorado and making her own way.

She felt prouder of herself in this moment than ever before.

"Let's shop!" Lena said. "We have a few hours off, let's go see what Mrs. Birch got in off the train!"

Audrey smiled, taking the stairs down to the street. Arm in arm, she strolled with Lena. The bright morning sun and fresh open air were incomparable to Philly, where it was stuffy with factories emitting heat, making areas pungent; and the squalor of so many people packed into an area. Out here, her skin prickled with quiet freedom that enticed her. She loved everything about being in Colorado. Waking up in the morning, to gaze out the window as the sky slowly changed from a light gray to bursts of pinks, oranges, and purples over the Rockies was her favorite part of the day. And the sunsets she got to witness were also breathtaking. The way the light struck the mountains, or how the fog laid like a sleepy blanket over the base left her in awe. *I love being away from my miserable conniving relatives*, Audrey sighed. *Colorado won my heart and I shall never leave.*

All her life, Audrey had searched through school books, or through small travels, for something that felt remotely like home. With her mother dead and her father always away, she strove to find somewhere her heart could call home. Something, that would make her heart peaceful yet invigorated. The money her father accumulated, the empire he built, held her to the ground, restraining her from traveling, being on her own, from finding love. Back in St. Louis, she could not even walk without an escort, now she can walk to the mercantile and back without hindrance.

Now, she had it all; her freedom, her chance to find love on her own, with a new beginning and name. There was no money to tie to her name, no titles, no mansions. *Or some pompous man who disgustingly kisses my hand, leaving a spittle residue*, Audrey shuddered. *Introducing Lady Audrey Whitman heiress to the Whitman empire, all the unattached males would glance up and stride toward me like an ant does to food*, she thought glowering. *Not anymore.*

Since being at the Whitman Hotel, she confirmed what she suspected all along. She truly learned and verified there was so much more than fancy dresses, tea parties and masquerade balls. There was friendship, like the one she found with Lena, a true friendship and not something decided over social status and money where the friendship was purely a veil. She discovered working hard was satisfying and money stretched relatively far.

There was a quality to life money could not touch. And Audrey was loving it.

"You alright Rose?" Lena asked, pulling her out of the way of a passing, hurrying man and out of her own thoughts.

"Yes, I was thinking of how grateful I am."

Lena linked her arm, "Grateful for what?"

Audrey turned to her. "Your friendship, life, waking up each and every day to this gorgeous place. These past few days have been exhilarating!"

Lena grinned. "You caught Colorado fever."

Audrey paused, putting a hand to her head, checking its temperature. "I don't even have a fever!"

Lena laughed. "Just means you love life and bein' out here."

"Yes, I do." Audrey burst out laughing.

"Come on Rose," Lena ushered. "We need to get back."

They clopped the stairs together laughing. Rose tripped over her dress, taking Lena down with her.

"Maybe I do have a fever," Audrey said snorting with laughter.

Lena giggled, helping Rose to her feet, "Oh, Rose."

Audrey brushed off her dress. Linking her arm back with Lena's, they continued up to the hotel, discussing the new dress material that came in from Boston. Audrey opened the door, permitting Lena to enter first. Audrey followed close behind making her way to the counter. Soon as Audrey stepped behind the counter, a woman in an obscene orange dress grabbed her pulling Audrey back into the foyer and to the door.

"Let her go!" Lena cried, beating her fists on the woman's arm.

Audrey screamed, trying to push the woman away. The woman held onto her wrist with a vice like grip.

"It's me, Mary," the woman cajoled loudly over the raucous. "Mary from Kansas City."

Mary still held her wrist. Audrey wrenched it free. She glared at Mary, taking in her appearance. Her dress, cut low, revealed the tops of her very ample bosom. Audrey's eyes widened, her lips trying to curl slightly. The orange coloring did not flatter her face.

Neither did the dress, it was quite large, giving her slender figure the appearance of being obese.

"Hello Mary. where is my locket?" Audrey asked with bitter force. Then raising an eyebrow, she said, "That is… Quite a dress."

Mary shifted from foot to foot. "I'm sorry," she began, head hanging, "I am so thrilled I found you. I came to return your locket."

Audrey scowled. Mary had taken it. No one else had been in the dress shop but them. Audrey looked in her eyes. Mary's eyes glistened. The girl hung her head, holding open her hand, locket draped across her palm.

"I'm sorry," Mary said again.

Audrey snatched it out of Mary's hand, opening it to see if the miniature of her mother and father were still inside. She let out a breath she didn't realize she was holding, tears welling behind her eyes.

"Thank you, Mary. I thought for certain it was lost."

Mary linked her arm with Audrey. Audrey stiffened, politely removing herself from the too familiar embrace. Lena was on the stairs, looking as apprehensive as Audrey felt.

"Thank you, Mary," Audrey growled, putting distance between them, "for returning what you stole. I would like you to leave now."

Mary turned to her, head down, her voice thick with unshed tears. "Listen, I am sorry. Can we take a walk, real fast, so I can explain?"

Audrey stole a glance at Lena. Her friend raised a brow. "I'll be right back," Audrey said to Lena.

Lena's tense face nodded back.

Mary opened the door for Audrey, standing to the side. Audrey strode past, going through the second door and waited for Mary, arms crossed by the carving of the bear. Mary made it out of the door, hiking up the layers and layers of fabric to make it down a single step. Audrey turned a polite head, stifling a laugh.

"This dress makes it hard for stairs," Mary commented.

"Indeed," Audrey replied levelly.

Mary made it down the stairs with a huff. She straightened the horrid fabric. Audrey looked at her, arms crossed.

"Shall we?" Mary suggested.

Audrey walked with her, side by side, arms still crossed. She kept the locket in the hand farthest from Mary. Audrey paused to put it on. They walked back toward the train station, pausing at the first mercantile store.

"I stole it," Mary admitted.

Audrey couldn't keep the anger from her face. "Why?"

"I was in a bad way and needed the money. People were after me. I felt like I'd no other choice. They were goin' to kill me. I sold the bracelet and was about to sell that," Mary pointed to her locket. "But I couldn't, so instead I used the money to find you because you said you were headed to Denver."

Mary launched herself at her grabbing her in a tight hug. Audrey caught her, patting her back. "And buy yourself this garish dress with the leftover dollars?" Audrey let out a hard breath, fixing her tone. "I had no idea you were in so much trouble. I could have helped you."

Mary sniffled. "I am so sorry Audrey. I thought I escaped trouble but," she trailed off.

Audrey patted her hand. "If you ever need anything, ask me first, please."

Mary nodded, wiping tears with her hand. Her face frowning; more tears coursed down her cheeks.

Audrey patted her shoulder. "I have to get back to the hotel." Audrey spun on her heel, going back the way she came.

Mary smiled. "I am staying there, so I will walk with you."

Audrey nodded. She didn't mean to be hard or sound aloof. Audrey couldn't shake the hurt Mary inflicted by taking her most precious possession. She never expected to see Mary again after Kansas City. However, she was grateful she had now, otherwise she would have not gotten back her mother's locket.

*I will never take this off again,* Audrey vowed, her hand closing around the locket.

"Wait for me," Mary said. "This dress is hard to walk in."

Audrey slowed her pace slightly, still keeping ahead of Mary. "You can always work at a hotel to earn your way," Audrey commented, waiting for Mary at the landing of the hotel. "I'm sure Jane can find you a spot."

"That would be nice," Mary replied, catching up beginning to huff a little.

# CHAPTER TWENTY

The train rocked around the corners. Denver was but a few more moments away. He couldn't wait. His fingers thrummed against his pant leg. Finally, this blasted goose chase was almost over and he could get home, back to working hard to buy a house and finding a wife.

Eugene sighed irritated, leaning against the uncomfortable backing of the train bench. *Do I want to go back to Philly*, he pondered. Life was industrial and changing with the growing factories and the population but after being out in the less dense areas, he liked the fewer cramped spaces. *Maybe I could settle in Kansas City. There was a pretty woman at the Silver Spoon. I wonder if she'd mind having a Pinkerton husband.*

The landscape was level with sparse trees. Giant mountains were off in the distance to his right.

"Denver up ahead," the conductor called.

Eugene opened his briefcase, taking his handcuffs from them and sticking them in his coat pocket. He snapped his briefcase closed, grabbed it and his small traveling bag. From the information he gathered from her diary, and the people he'd spoken with, Audrey was a smart woman. Sheltered, though she was about tasks of daily life, like cooking or laundry, she was astute in other areas like language and art.

He glanced to his traveling bag where Audrey's diary lay inside. He smiled slightly to himself, *Audrey is a kind, articulate woman. Never a bad word from her pen nor can I imagine any coming from her mouth, about her relatives.* He stared out the window, *that quality in a woman appeals to me.*

Eugene rose from his seat as the train rounded the last corner. Denver approached. Fog clung to the tops of buildings like a blanket. The people in the town moved slowly. The train screeched and lurched to a stop.

The conductor bellowed for people to depart. Men politely stepped to the side, allowing the women and their broods off first. Eugene waited, strumming his fingers on the hat he clenched in his hands. The seconds ticked by like hours. His eyes were fixed on the Whitman Hotel. The tall building seemed to tower over the rest of the city.

His gut clenched with anticipation, *I hope Audrey is there and not vanished. My instincts tell me it is the former.*

A woman in a gaudy orange dress, stuck out like a beacon in a rainstorm. Eugene's lip quirked. He set the hat on his head, pulling the brim down low. With sure foot strides, he made his way to the hotel.

Another woman in a red calico dress paused at the base of the stairs leading up to the hotel. She waited for the one in orange to clump the ostentatious fabric in her hands. Together, they ambled up the road, heading further into town.

Eugene smiled, pleased he wouldn't make eye contact with the flashy woman. He dodged rolling wagons, jumpy horses, and men hollering to one another about mining supplies or food. On the other side of the road, he grinned. The Whitman Hotel was close at hand. He would be paid, his name plastered across papers with his success, bringing him more business. All he had to do was find her, cuff her and take her back to St. Louis. Although, hopefully he wouldn't have to cuff her. She seemed kind and reasonable in her journal and according to everyone's firsthand experience with her. Maybe she'd come with him willingly.

Eugene breathed in deeply the crispness of the Colorado air with smug satisfaction. The aroma of fir tickled his nose. The choking smog of Philly was hard at times, here the freshness of Colorado appealed to him. Birds soared high overhead, screaming out their hunting call. The whicker of horses sounded from behind him. Eugene moved out of the way. A wagon pulled up near the hotel.

A man emerged from the hotel. Casually he leaned against a bear carving, lighting his pipe, and puffing. The man raised his hand, acknowledging the driver of the wagon that pulled up, as pipe-man jogged down the stairs. Hat pulled down very low over his face, he almost bumped into Eugene.

"Beg pardon," he said.

Eugene moved out of the way. The woman in orange was having a difficult time maneuvering the next step toward the hotel. The hems of the God-awful dress were dirty and ratted. The other woman desperately tried to help the lady in orange walk while maintaining some propriety. There was no helping the homely woman nor the fabric she wore.

Eugene tipped his hat to the women, "Can I possibly be of assistance?" he offered.

The woman in orange smiled at him. The other was bent over, face full of fabric, trying to bunch it up for her. The man with the pipe also approached the ladies. Orange woman lightly patted his chest.

"No thank you, sir," she said, her voice high and chirpy. "My intended is here to accommodate me."

"Ladies," he said, tipping his hat.

Eugene left the scene at the base of the hotel. He jogged lightly up the steps, his hand reaching out to open the door for himself. Taking one last fleeting look at the women, he caught the woman in red calico's eyes. Eugene paused, dropping his bags. He ripped the picture from his pocket of Audrey Whitman. The red dress made the woman appear paler than she was. Heat crept to her cheeks, making her appear flushed. The look on her face, told him she suspected why he was here. Slowly she took several steps back, making a point to move around the couple to go up the hotel steps and avoid him.

Eugene took the stairs down two at a time. Six men emerged from the wagon. Each wore dark colored pants with a sand colored shirt. Two grabbed Audrey. The other four surrounded the wagon with pistols in their hands. One put a hand over her mouth. Shocked, she tried to scream and couldn't. Her legs flailed, striking nothing but air. Audrey was rushed into the back of the wagon before Eugene got to the bottom of the stairs. The lady in the orange smiled, clambering into the wagon up front with help from the pipe smoking man.

Eugene bolted for the wagon. "Stop!" Eugene yelled, garnering the attention of two of the armed men.

The audible click of the hammer pulling back, caused Eugene to pause feet from the wagon. He raised his hands.

"Well, I do declare," the man with the pipe said grinning, standing by the corner of the wagon. "And who do we have here?"

"Thomas Coldaire," Eugene blurted out. "I have been looking for my beloved cousin, Audrey. Thank you for finding her."

The man released a plume of smoke. "Wonderful. Two birds, one stone."

Another man emerged from the back, pistol drawn and pointed at his head. The other men in front of him pointed to the back of the wagon. Eugene clambered in the back, making a point to seem clumsy. It worked. The other men laughed. He took a seat beside Audrey, tears brimming, sticking to her long, dark lashes. Her body shook. His eyes met hers. He reached out, lightly touching her arm. Even through the fabric, her skin was chilled. Her beautiful gaze locked with his.

"Dearest cousin," Eugene began calmly. "I have searched all over for you!"

A man shoved a gag in her mouth. The wagon lurched forward. Audrey fell over, trying to right herself but her hands were tied behind her. Eugene gently grabbed her upper arm. Her delicateness malleable under the clothing. Soothingly, he set her up, running his hands down her arms.

The man in front of him, held a cocked pistol at him, finger near the trigger.

"Arms out to the side," one man said.

Eugene put his arms out in front of him.

"To the side," the same man said. "Daft fool."

Eugene did as he was told. Another man searched him, pulling his pistol from his belt. His investigating journal, on the inside coat pocket, was next. Eugene wanted to cringe. If these kidnappers dared to read what was inside, his ruse as Audrey's intolerable cousin would be up.

*How in God's name are we going to get out of this*, he thought, gazing at Audrey's tear streaked face. He tried to portray a face to her that seemed stoic and brave. If she caught onto it, she didn't indicate it.

One of the kidnappers wrapped a dirty bandana around Audrey's eyes. The little woman quaked in her seat. A gush of tears tracked down her face and Eugene longed to comfort her. He peered around quickly, trying to see if there was anything to help them escape. The view of the front of the wagon was blocked by canvas.

"Night," a burly man bellowed. A butt of a pistol struck the side of his head.

# CHAPTER TWENTY-ONE

Wherever she happened to be, it was frigid. Goosepimples prickled her skin. Her stomach rumbled loudly. Her eyes were covered, hands tied behind her back. Audrey wanted to be back in the homey white walled room with cozy patchwork quilts and small beds she shared with Lena.

Audrey sniffled. Tears coursed down her cheeks unchecked. The stench of leather and sweat filled her nostrils. *I want to be back at the hotel, eating meals like a family with everyone, talking about our day after everything closed for the night. The hotel was the closest I've ever been to a real family. Even at finishing school, there was no familial atmosphere; meals were lessons. And now it's all gone.*

The man who happened to be taken with her, was strikingly handsome. His dark brown hair cut short against his head. His brown eyes attempted to portray assurance while being fierce and stoic. Why he lied about being her cousin Thomas, she wasn't certain. However, here they were together, although he was currently passed out from being struck. She was grateful she wasn't alone. Whatever this man was here for, she suspected he came to take her back to her horrid Aunt Georgiana. She was not going back to St. Louis.

Audrey wriggled against the rope binding her hands. It brought burning pain to her wrists and achiness to her arms, so she stopped. *I will not be locked in my room nor treated like I am daft,* Audrey thought, biting her lower lip. *I will not be told any more by Georgiana that I am the most worthless abhorrent mistake made by God and my father and birthed by a common whore who doesn't deserve my father's money.* Audrey wriggled in her bonds, *and I certainly will not spend an iota of a moment with Thomas.* She wriggled fiercely against the ties.

"Hold still," a man shouted at her.

"I will not!" she tried to bark back but the gag was in her mouth.

A man dragged her out of the wagon, her feet striking dirt. Audrey dug her heels into the ground but they were quickly swept out from under her. She was carried bride style by a man smelling of tobacco and sweat. He strode for a while, pausing momentarily.

"Get the ladder in," the one who held her commanded.

The clash of the ladder struck wood. "Be still," the same man said to her, "I'm carrying you down the ladder."

Audrey whimpered. Fear of falling to an unknown death left her quaking inside, but she held still. The man set her down on a floor, cutting the bonds to her hands. Her hands immediately went to the bandana covering her eyes. The man's hands slapped hers away from her eyes.

"Don't remove the bandana 'til I say or I'll shoot you dead," he growled, removing the gag from her mouth. The click of the hammer of his gun emphasized his point.

Audrey nodded vigorously, not trusting her voice to speak. Something heavy struck the ladder. It tumbled down, landing close to her with a thud and a groan. The groaning person moved, colliding with her legs.

"You bastards," the man pretending to be Thomas muttered.

Men laughing echoed down. "You can remove the bandana," the one man said.

Audrey's shaking hands went to her eyes, pulling the bandana off. She blinked rapidly, scrunching her eyes to adjust to the lantern hanging from the ceiling of the room. The man claiming to be her cousin lay on his back, both hands holding his head. Thick wooden walls surrounded her, creating a space the same size as a horse stall with walls without windows. Thick slabs of stone lined the floor. Not even a mouse could sneak into this room. Audrey stood. Her head thankfully did not strike the ceiling. The ladder was gone. Over in the corner was a large bucket. Her lip curled at the thought of having to do her lady business in front of a man.

She nudged the man with her toe. "Hello?" she whispered.

He moaned. Dried blood caked to the side of his face and hair. Stubble peppered his stern, square jaw. She studied him closely. He was a handsome man with his chocolate brown hair cut short in the back and left a little longer on top. Slowly, he opened his cinnamon brown eyes.

*He has beautiful eyes*, she thought.

"Hello," Audrey whispered again.

"Lower your voice," he grumbled.

"My voice is lowered." Her whisper had a hint of laughter.

The man grumbled, sitting up. A long black duster, covered his body. Nicer black pants hugged his trim, muscular frame snugly around his waist, with a button down, olive green shirt tucked into it. His clothes were made for travelling. His shoes were not the typical boots she saw around Colorado but something her cousin Thomas would wear.

"Who are you?" Audrey asked softly.

The man looked around, his narrowed brown eyes searching for something she couldn't even find herself. Audrey stared at him as he scrutinized every inch of their confinement.

"Are you Audrey Whitman?" he asked.

Audrey blinked. "I am she. And who are you?" she followed his lead and no longer kept her voice quiet.

"Eugene Turner. I'm a Pinkerton."

"I'm not going back," Audrey replied seriously.

Eugene rolled his eyes. "Don't you want your money for parties, dresses, and whatever else?"

Audrey felt the tears stinging behind her eyes. "I don't care for any of it. I'm not going back. I have found a life I want to live."

Eugene groaned, shaking his head. He stood up, wobbling a bit and leaned against the wooden walls. After a few seconds, Eugene pushed himself away from the wall, striding about the room. The walls were thick and wouldn't budge when he pushed on them in several places. Eugene sat down on the other side of the room, staring darkly at her. Audrey met his gaze. She wasn't going to cower like she'd been taught proper ladies did. She'd learned from Lena, Claudia and Jane, women can be assertive and kind.

*This is my life*, Audrey thought. *I shall live it how I please.*

"I don't wish to go back to that frippery," Audrey said, firmly. "My cousin Thomas is overbearing, rude and scandalous. My aunt Georgiana only wants my father's money and has planned for me to marry Thomas to get it. My father gifted her money before but it wasn't good enough. She summoned me from finishing school in Philly to St. Louis for me to marry Thomas the moment I turned eighteen. But I couldn't do it. Making myself appear dead seemed like the fresh start I needed to get away from society, money and my wretched family. I want to live and find a man of my own choosing," Audrey sighed. "Things I wouldn't get if I was back in Philly or St. Louis."

Audrey caught Eugene staring at her, the corner of his mouth twitching. His handsome face split into a large grin then he laughed, softly at first then it became thunderous.

"You did a horrible job with the carriage. The window had me for a moment, but the seats were cleanly ripped. And no blood? The neatly slashed tethers? Nice try though. The lazy sheriff bought it, but anybody worth their salt in law enforcement, would have known something wasn't right," Eugene commented.

Audrey grinned. "It was," she replied, laughing too at the memory of slashing the seats and cushions to make it appear she was dead. Her lock of hair was still noticeably short on the underside.

It seemed like months ago she'd escaped. However, it was a little over a week ago. The life she found, leaving behind the ball-gowns, parties and money was a simple life, full of good folks and genuineness that could not be found amongst the higher class of Boston, New York or Philly. *I wouldn't trade what I have found for all the luxuries money can buy*, Audrey decided.

At those parties, everyone was so familiar. She knew most by name yet she knew very little past the facade each showed, using veiled words and double meanings to communicate. At the hotel, she didn't have to guess what people thought, they said it. Everyone was friendly, and they meant it.

Although, thinking back, there were fake people everywhere. She hadn't expected to find them in the west too. Her naivety had been revealed to her rather quickly.

*Like Mary Celeste*, Audrey cringed. *How foolish of me to decide her a friend so quickly. Stealing my jewelry then partaking in this heist. How dare she!* Audrey seethed, scrutinizing her surroundings again to find a trace of a way out she missed in her previous scan. There was nothing. *I hope she can redeem herself someday. Although to someone else. If I get out of this, I never want to see her again.*

Other people like Rafe, her aunt's driver, Lena, and Jane were good people, the kind she always wanted to be around but wasn't allowed to be because of social status. The binding cuffs of her father's empire tied her to lands, holding, titles and more, all lashed together with a promise of an arranged marriage and very little freedom. She ran from it all and tasted freedom. Now she never wanted to go back.

In that previous life, she survived, put on a good show and a pretty face for all to see but inside she was lonely and crying for companionship. Here it was different. Here in Colorado, or wherever she was at the moment, it was out of choice. She chose to work hard in dealing with unruly customers, helping clean and do dishes, but she had real friends and was free, finding her niche in hard work and honest people.

She glanced over at her companion. He stared at the ceiling, groaning a bit and holding his head. *He is dashing*, she thought *even though he's here to take me back to my gilded prison.*

Audrey flashed her companion a smile. "Where are you from?"

Eugene perked up at the sound of her voice, his eyes hardening at the corners. "Born and raised in Philly, in the working-class slums," he sighed, adjusting his position.

Audrey ignored his last remark. "What made you become a Pinkerton?"

"Money to get out of the slums. I wasn't born with a silver spoon."

She wasn't going to rise to his bait. Oddly enough, she'd dealt with this previously with a few of the girls at finishing school, where their parents would spend all their earnings, to send their daughter to finishing school in hopes of winning over a suitor. It worked. The girls would marry the first man who called on them. Audrey reached deep for her patience and clasped her hands together, putting them in her lap. "There must be another reason to why."

Eugene smirked, scratching the back of his neck. "I wanted to help people find the ones they love."

"What made you decide to be a Pinkerton and what is the difference between your profession and a police officer?"

"An officer obeys laws and enforces the laws. A Pinkerton investigates missing people or things to make a conclusive decision. For instance, the sheriff deemed you killed. I investigated and find you quite well." He rubbed the back of his head grimacing. "I wanted to become a Pinkerton because someone killed my little sister. I was sixteen. My sister was eight. The police nor Pinkertons cared who did it because we were just another poor family. I investigated and brought the man to justice myself. Ever since, I wanted to bring closure to people." Eugene snorted, staring at the ceiling. His face twisted into a grimace. "How clever. It opens from the roof."

Audrey put a hand to her mouth. "I am so sorry," she whispered.

He nodded. "It's all right."

"What happened to your sister?"

"She was walking down the street, when a corner store got robbed. The mercantile owner took a shot at the man, striking him in the shoulder. The robber, returned fire, getting my little sister. The robber left the scene and my sister for dead. I went around asking everyone who the man was. I finally caught up to him, six days later with an infected wound. He hung for killing my sister."

Audrey flinched closing her eyes. "How dreadful. How horrible for you and your parents."

"It was a hard time," Eugene agreed.

She shook her head. *His poor family and sister. How they must have endured*, she thought. *Makes sense to his tone of voice and gruff nature.*

Audrey stood, pacing in the small room. It was five manly strides from wall to wall. And the only way out was through the roof. It was a clever set up. One way in and out, with sheer unclimbable walls.

"I'm going to try something," Audrey mumbled.

Eugene snorted. "Like what?"

"Kindness. Maybe they will be nicer," she replied, looking point blank at Eugene. Audrey cupped her hands around her mouth, the way she'd previously seen Lena do. "Excuse me, sirs!" Audrey hollered.

Nothing answered her.

"Excuse me! Sirs!" she bellowed.

The door to the roof opened. It was like they were in a cellar of sorts. A man with a grizzly beard and mustache answered. The light from outside stinging her eyes.

"Whatcha want woman?" the man growled.

*Hope this works*, she thought.

"If it is not too much trouble, may I please acquire some water and a coverlet?"

The man blinked. "Lady just state whatcha want," he said in an exasperated, confused tone.

Audrey offered him a warm smile. "Water and a blanket please. I hope the weather is treating you nicely."

His face softened. The hard lines around his eyes and face turning the weather-beaten hardness to gentleness. "Yes, lady, it is. I will see what I can do fer ya."

"Thank you very much. My name is Audrey. What is your name?"

The man was about to close the lid to their confinement when he opened it a crack. "Name's Richard."

"I appreciate it, Richard."

He tipped his hat to her and shut the door. Eugene scoffed at her, sitting up against the wall. Audrey took a seat on the other wall, their feet keeping a respectable space of maybe seven feet apart. Audrey fidgeted with her hair. To say she was nervous was an understatement. The men here would not kill her. She was worth far more alive. Even she was not too naïve to understand that. She needed to get out of this predicament then escape again from the Pinkerton. She was determined not to be bound to the monies and obligations of her father's empire.

Hands in her lap, she fidgeted with the lines of her red calico dress while her mind wandered to why Mary Celeste betrayed her. Surely, she was not a bad person, mayhap surrounded by constant bad tidings, like a death in the family or taking care of many younger siblings by herself.

About fifteen minutes later, fifteen long, silent minutes, the door in the roof opened again, revealing Richard. He tossed down a blanket for her. In a basket he lowered refreshments. Audrey beamed.

"Thank you very kindly, Richard."

Richard tipped his hat, taking a step back from the open hole. Another person came into view. His thin moustache and goatee did not distract Audrey from the malevolence in his dark eyes. He wore an expensive pressed black suit with a red kerchief peeking out of the pocket. Audrey withheld a cringe. He smiled, revealing tobacco stained teeth, ruining his put-together debonair style.

"Ms. Whitman, how kindly of you to visit my estate," the man began.

Audrey dipped into a courtesy. "Pleasure is all mine."

The man laughed wickedly. "I am pleased you feel that way, my dear. Is it safe to assume you know why you are here?"

Audrey did indeed. Many a man came vying for her hand,

many men such as Brom Gaffney, more preferable suitors to Thomas Coldaire, but her cold as ice aunt Georgiana always stepped in to announce her engagement to Thomas, shooting down any would be suitor.

"It is."

"Splendid. You have a few options, my dear. The first is transferring over your fortune. You will be allowed to live but in destitution with no tongue. I don't want it wagging to the sheriff. The second is marrying me and you live, and keep your tongue. You can show me the mansions and pick one to live in and raise our heir."

Audrey felt her insides quake. She forced a visibly fake smile, hands clasped before her. "And the third option, if you please."

The man's eyes darkened. "There is no third option."

"Oh," she began with fake shock, "please correct me if I am mistaken but you did mention I'd a few options. I assumed at least three."

"I beg your pardon, my fair woman, I simply meant two options. I shall leave you to your refreshments and to ponder your choices."

"I appreciate the momentary reprieve to dine. If I may inquire, how is Mary Celeste?"

"Needn't you worry none. She's been let go from her position."

Audrey couldn't hide the shock from her face. *I hope she isn't dead*, she thought. *And what does it mean for me? And what of Mr. Turner? I'm at least useful alive. I need to get us out of here.*

The latch closed overhead. Audrey sat back down against the wall with her head in her hands. Silent tears poured down her face. She leaned back, taking deep breaths. *What am I to do?* Either option was not preferable. Living with her tongue was, but marrying that man and giving him an heir, forced bile into her mouth. *I can't do either of those!*

Eugene's handsome brown eyes locked on hers, a twinkle shining in them she wanted to assume was due to the lantern. Surely, this man could not find her exchange with her captor, or even this predicament amusing.

"What is amusing?" she asked softly.

Eugene grinned. "Reprieve to dine."

Audrey laughed with Eugene's deep tone joining hers. "If you plan on keeping up the pretense as my cousin Thomas, please try to be more flamboyant and egotistical in your behavior. And a touch more demanding. Like 'Mother, my tie doesn't match my suit. Buy me another,'" she said, mocking Thomas's tone and waving her hands about like Thomas did.

Audrey giggled at herself.

Eugene chuckled. "He is quite the dandy."

Audrey nodded, going to the basket, pulling out dented metal cups, bread, cheese, meat, and a skin of water. She split the meal evenly between her and Eugene, fixing his plate and handing it to him.

"Were you born in St. Louis?" Eugene asked.

Audrey shook her head, "No, I was born in New York. Then when I was older, I lived in Philly."

The small talk kept going for what felt like hours, as it more than likely was. Audrey enjoyed chatting with Eugene. It was nice to have someone to genuinely speak with instead of guarding her answers so they could not be used against her.

*He is quite charming*, she thought. *Now, how to get out of this situation...*

# CHAPTER TWENTY-TWO

Eugene studied Audrey from across their small space. The lantern afforded them enough visibility to make out each other's features. Other than that, it was rather dreary. Audrey separated the food in the basket evenly. She munched on her fare with no care to dabbing her mouth, keeping her posture straight or any etiquette rules he'd seen some women do.

Her quick humor in the exchange with their captor, not moments before still startled him. Eugene hadn't expected it to come from her, yet it charmed him to see some wit come from someone so refined.

*She impresses me,* Eugene thought. *She managed to keep ahead of me for quite a while. Paused to help the despicable woman in the orange dress and exchanged her money for simplicity. She is beautiful and charming.* Eugene rubbed the back of his neck. *She was not what I was expecting. I was wrong about her.*

When he'd done investigations for Darrow, for the other upper-class socialites, they were bland as flour. Audrey, as Rafe and Darrow once put it, was sunshine – happy, charming and drew people to her with her kindness and love for life. Audrey had a spirit like a candle in a winter's storm, bright and warm, it drew people... and him to her.

Her emerald eyes sparkled with a yearning for life that begged to be taken on adventures. Her neat chocolate brown hair took on a life of its own as wisps pulled free from the braid resting on her left shoulder. What he thought he would find was a blithering mess of a woman, searching for a place to belong and direction. What he found was the opposite; a lonesome girl searching for genuine connections. The only friend she happened to have was a blank page in her diary and naught else. Much like himself.

"Tell me," Eugene began, garnering her attention away from the meat she was nibbling on, "how must I be more like Thomas."

Audrey laughed melodically, her voice like a harp. "Have you met Thomas?" she asked, pulling her knees to her chest.

"Unfortunately," he replied, taking a swig of water.

"Take what you have seen and add in some tantrums for not getting your way."

Eugene choked, sputtering his water a little. "You're jesting. A grown man throws a tantrum?" He wiped his mouth with the back of his hand.

"It is quite the spectacle. For instance, one Christmas, I left school in New York and went to my father's estate in Philly. Aunt Georgiana was there along with Thomas. I attempted to hide the entire time to not be in their presence," Audrey cleared her throat and began to wag her hands in grand gestures. "I demand a better gift. This shall not do. It is insufficient. How dare you!" she said mocking Thomas, rolling her eyes. "His gift from my father was an envelope of twenty-dollar notes. Thomas threw a fit so gargantuan, that he broke several pieces of furniture on his way out of the parlor," Audrey changed her demeanor, pitching her voice a bit higher, "Oh Philip, we have been utterly destitute, could you not help out your family? We are all you have dearest brother," Audrey rolled her eyes again. "Georgiana pleaded with my father for more money to which he replied, 'paying off your estate in St. Louis as a Christmas present was more than sufficient, Sister."

"Unbelievable."

Audrey made a noise as she swallowed some water. "Indeed. They have always been after my father. When he passed on, they thought to inherit being Thomas is the sole male heir. Except it was bequeathed to me and I do not want it."

Eugene blinked several times. He thought he'd heard wrongly. "You don't want it?"

Audrey shook her head, fidgeting with her hands. "Not at all! Money breeds negativity and greed. To be around boorish men, gossiping ladies, trollops for daughters and dandy's for sons, I believe I am rather content where I am. I want true love with someone, a man who loves me for who and all I am; not someone wanting what I happened to inherit or something arranged as a financial contract."

He nearly choked on his food while Audrey resumed her meal, washing it all down with a final unlady-like gulp of water. Of all things he expected from her, a reasonable conversation and a blunt perceptiveness of society was not. She was intelligently observant of people in the aristocratic world, seeing them plainly as being motivated by money. Out here in normal society where middle and lower class people mixed, there was a duplicity she hadn't expected and the oversight landed them both in hot water.

Her attractive smile made the edges of his own mouth perk. She was a gorgeous woman. Her small mouth with full pink lips could swoon any man. He admired her bravery and how put together she'd been through this whole predicament. If he was honest with himself, he liked her a lot.

Eugene ran a hand over his face. The floor was stone, solid with no cracks to give way to loosened pieces. Every stone was unyielding. The thick rough-cut timber planks were a few inches thick at least, butting up perfectly together to form an almost invisible line. And the only means to escape being in the roof.

"How to get out of here?" he mumbled to himself.

Audrey tilted her head to the side. "I have an idea."

"That is?"

"I can do all the exchanges. You can hide from view. Maybe

they will forget you are with me and then you can escape to get help."

Eugene pursed his lips. "Not a bad idea but I don't like the idea of leaving you here alone with these men."

Audrey smiled. "I don't either. However, I have value to them. Having me leave their sight will be rather difficult."

He sighed, leaning back against the wood. Audrey was correct. He could start a fight, but it would be insane. The men had guns while he only had his fists. He would be dead before he ever poked his head out from the roof top.

Eugene glanced in Audrey's direction. She swept little hairs off her face; shoulders hunched in concentration. She tilted her head, thoughtfully, her green eyes lighting and a smile forming on her lips.

He rested his head against the wood. *There has to be other ways. I cannot put Audrey at risk either*, he pondered. *I gotta find a way to throw a spanner in the works.*

"Money never appealed to me," she stated, breaking him from his thoughts. "Mainly because as a wealthy unattached woman, I was to be married to any gentleman with as much or equal wealth. Makes you feel like livestock. Paraded around for little more than your monetary worth and possible baby making ability. It brings out the greed and hate in men. I cannot stand it. Nor the deplorable idea of being married to Thomas," Audrey shuddered.

"Of that, I do not disagree," Eugene laughed. "He is exceedingly unpleasant. Mr. Darrow does not like your aunt or cousin at all. And I do not blame him."

Audrey smiled fondly at the mention of Wilfred Darrow. "He is a good man. Darrow and my father were great companions." Audrey perked, a gleam in her eye. "I believe I have come to a decision."

---

Audrey stood, cupping her hands over her mouth. "Excuse me," she hollered. "Richard?"

The roof was yanked hastily open.

"Yes miss?" Richard said.

The light from outside had waned. A lantern lit his face enough she could see up. Two other men peered down the rooftop at her.

"I have come to a verdict to your employer's proposal."

Richard ran a hand over his face, down to his beard. Audrey stared at his eyes, hands in her lap.

Richard blinked. "Miss, plain-like if you will," he finally said disheartened.

Audrey smiled brilliantly at him. "My apologies Richard. I did not mean to hurt your feelings. I would like to speak with your boss man please."

"Fetch Victor," Richard mumbled to the man next to him.

That man scurried off the rooftop. The other two sat with the hatch open.

"Thank you for the blanket and food from earlier Richard. Have you eaten yet?"

He shook his head. "Yer welcome, and not yet, miss."

"How dreadful. You have been up there all afternoon."

"I'll be all right, miss."

Audrey fumbled with her hands. Her heart pounded in her chest she swore she could see her dress move with every erratic beat. She certainly felt it pulsate up to her throat. She glanced at Eugene. His countenance softened to her considerably. He was a handsome man, observant and straightforward, which she liked immensely. His gruff and hostile nature was a façade for a lonely and hardworking man. Eugene cracked a smile at her, one she returned fondly, hoping her smile would hide her shaking insides.

*I hope my plan to get these men to focus on me and forget Eugene works. I can't think of anything else. Sheer walls that are unclimbable, one way in and out and it opens from the roof,* she put her hands on her hips, staring down at the floor a moment. *If I can't get them to forget Eugene, then maybe I can make one my friend. Maybe both.* Audrey prayed her plan would work. Otherwise, she hadn't the slightest inclination of what to do next.

Voices echoed down to her, causing a chill to creep down her spine. She closed her eyes a moment, willing her body to stop shaking and took a deep fortifying breath. Eugene inched closer, being careful to stay out of sight from the men above. Audrey dried her sweating hands off on her dress, straightening out the fabric. The man who captured them came before her. She clasped her hands in front of her, squeezing her fingers to keep from shaking.

"Audrey, made a decision, have you?" the boss man called.

The man exchanged his black suit for a plain black button-down shirt, with the top button left open, revealing hair poking out of the top. His own dark mop of hair was slicked back. Brown eyes coldly greeted her own.

"I am quite astonished you called upon me so early in your visit," he said. "I expected to hear from you on the morrow."

Audrey moved the little hairs from her face, then put her hands back to their previous position. "It is rather impolite to keep a man waiting in regards to such an important proposal."

The man laughed. "Do tell me, what verdict have you reached?"

"Please tell me your name?"

"Victor Del Avilasto," he bit out impatiently.

Without missing a beat, for fear of breaking down, Audrey replied, "I accede to your second proposal. However, I find it necessary to apprise you that my lawyer Darrow will have to be present. Darrow is the binding witness to my father's holdings."

The man fiddled with the ends of his moustache. "You are an exceedingly clever woman, Ms. Whitman. I regret to inform you none but the minister shall be present at our nuptials."

Audrey smiled delicately. "Then, however are you to attain my father's wealth? Without Darrow for either suggested proposal, I'm afraid you shall not inherit."

The man's countenance darkened. "Truly?" he growled.

"My father bequeathed it all to me. In the articles, I can only inherit if I marry with Darrow being a present witness. And tell him to bring Rosalinda."

He straightened. His dark eyes peering down at her as if he could see right through her. Audrey ignored the chills creeping like icy fingers down her spine, keeping her gaze open and pleasant.

"Very well. I shall telegram him immediately. And who is Rosalinda?"

"My cat. It is all I ask to have."

"Very well," he nodded.

Audrey curtsied. "When is our intended date of marriage?"

The rooftop door slammed on her without an answer. Audrey deflated, sinking to the cold stone floor, exhausted from faking the pleasantries and silently praying he did not see through her sham of a lie. Her body trembled with relief and fear. The darkness about the man was almost too much to bear.

Eugene came to her, taking off his duster. He wrapped it around her shoulders. She thanked him with a smile, putting her arms through the duster.

"That was brilliant," Eugene commented. "And you don't have a cat"

Audrey smiled. "Rosalinda is a horrible picture of a cat I drew when I was seven that Darrow kept," she chortled at the memory. "After my father passed, Darrow checked in on me. Since we had some similar social circles, he said if I run into any trouble, or find myself in a situation telegram him, or call on him to bring Rosalinda and he will get me help."

Eugene grinned. "Very clever."

Audrey sighed. "Thank you. I hope it works."

# CHAPTER TWENTY-THREE

Days passed with the only glimpses of sunshine being the brief stretches the guards allowed for her to stretch her legs. Four men were always posted around the perimeter, at every corner. One man constantly on the roof, of the somewhat large home, rifle in hand. Audrey took a turn about the property again, three men followed her. This time, however, they carelessly left a ladder in her cage.

Her captor had yet to tell her the fate of Mary and if he telegrammed Darrow. Audrey assumed he hadn't. He was a cunning man who made her skin crawl with fright. And according to her captor, they were going to be married soon.

*I hope we can escape from here before that happens*, Audrey prayed.

Audrey continued her stroll, certain to keep her back to her timbered cell. Her mind prayed relentlessly that Eugene would be able to escape. They decided she would interact with the gang members in hopes of their abductors becoming careless and forgetful of Eugene. And she would continue on for as long as it took. Finally, the day came.

Head down toward the ground Audrey smiled wanly. Thoughts

of Eugene crossed her mind again. He was a nice man, even if his job required him to take her back to St. Louis if they ever made it out of this. If she dared admit it to herself, she fancied him.

*I really like him*, she thought, resisting the urge to peek over her shoulder. While in confinement together, they'd spoken in whispers to keep up the pretense it was merely her locked down in their hovel. Eugene opened up, speaking of his family, and hobbies, and his goal of having a house in the Pennsylvania country with a wife.

Audrey swallowed, walking with her allotted parasol over her left shoulder. She paused, greeting Richard with a kind smile.

"Thank you, Richard," she said.

"Ma'am," he replied with a dip of his head.

The kindly man brought her a shawl and a chair to sit in the sun for a moment. Audrey sat with Richard standing to her left.

"What brought you to Colorado, Richard?" she asked.

Richard looped his thumbs through his belt loop, "Well ma'am, I was makin' a livin' trappin' for furs. Sold a fur to Victor," he paused, shaking his head.

"And then he decided to own you," she finished.

"Yes ma'am."

She swirled her parasol, allowing the sun to strike her face. She dared a glance over her shoulder, seeing Eugene slip out of the wooden container unnoticed. Carefully, she turned back around slowly to not garner attention toward him.

Wanting to continue to distract Richard and seeing a few clouds in the distance and feeling the chill in the breeze, she remarked, "The weather turns quickly here, more so than back home."

"Where ya from, ma'am?"

"Philadelphia."

Richard whistled. "Sure, a long way from home ma'am."

Audrey nodded. "Please, call me Audrey, if you all could for me... please," she said with a smile.

"Yes ma', Audrey," Richard replied.

Audrey wriggled in her seat. "When I was around seven, there was such a terrible storm that blew in to New York, where Father sent me for school. The skies darkened so, it appeared like night during the day. Snapping flashes of lightning stretched like claws across the heavens," Audrey had their undivided attention, as she detailed a particularly bad storm. Her heart pounded, praying to the good Lord that Eugene escaped unharmed.

---

Eugene lay in the corner for the last four days, staying hidden from view of their abductors. They seemed to have forgotten about him. Audrey stayed in the middle when the hatch opened in the bright light, chatting amicably with the kidnappers. She was sweet to them. At first, he assumed it was because she was trying to convince them to let her go. After about the ninth interaction, he'd determined the kindness was who she was. Audrey talked the most, hours at a given time, about books, animals and places she wanted to see someday, with the next place on her list being California. At first, he assumed it was rattled nerves from being captured and forced into an enclosed space. Then after about an hour, her talkative nature just fit her.

Eugene didn't have the slightest about the inner-workings and conniving nature of high society until Audrey. He was employed by the rich or Darrow to find certain people or items. Their snobbish, boorish behavior was what he was used to. Through Audrey's stories, what he discovered was their ruthless cunning, bitterness and aloofness to the rest of the world that did not pertain to them.

Audrey's father, being protective, secluded her from family and other people inside her mansion home and instructed with a tutor. Or she was sent to finishing school, instructed by the finest teachers, and only around three other ladies due to her father's money affording her private accommodations. Audrey was confined and alone, trapped by money and lashed to societal standards of appearance, and decorum. And Audrey, like him, craved compan ionship of someone who was themselves, and wanted the simple life of happiness and a home.

*She is a genuine lady, kind, compassionate and loving*, he thought, *more so than I ever gave her credit for. She is the epitome of a woman I want to find and marry, if I ever make it out of this.*

He shook his head, waiting until Audrey's voice faded.

Audrey convinced the kidnappers she needed to stretch her legs for a few moments. She surprised him with her charming smile, kindness and good nature to make even the toughest man, quirk a smile. She was like a ray of sunshine, sweet and happy, no matter her predicament. People like Rafe and Darrow or even Doreen from Kansas City, were right in their assessment – Audrey was a sparkling, joyous person.

Eugene smiled, picturing her warm smile and the twinkle in her eye. Eugene decided Audrey's plan of getting the gang members to forget about him was working. As Audrey described before, she was under heavy watch, she would not be able to escape. The plan was to get him to escape, and he would ride the road out of there, hoping it would take him to Denver, get help and hopefully be back in time before anything drastic ever took place.

Carefully, he climbed the ladder. Three men surrounded her. Audrey chatted like nothing was ever amiss. He caught her eye and winked. Swinging one leg over, then the other, he made himself seem small as he slid down the roof.

To the left, was the ranch home, and a few tethered horses out front. Men walked around, rifles loaded and ready. The gang members scouted the area for any sign of an intruder. Audrey took the men to the back of the property as planned, away from the main road. Eugene turned right, around the side of the shack and to a larger shack with neatly stacked wood for winter.

Eugene entered the wood building, hiding behind the open door. The vantage point afforded him the visibility of what happened to be around him without getting caught. Eugene slunk back to the shadows. He paused for a while, allowing his eyes to adjust to the light.

*Where is the barn*, he thought, scanning for the building.

Carefully peeking his head out of the door, the barn was to his left with whinnying horses inside. It was unguarded inside the wooden walls. One man stood on the roof, sitting, feet splayed out in front of him, leaning against the weathervane. Hat pulled down low over his face, faint snores rumbling from the man. Eugene smirked.

He crept out of the shadows, staying low. Audrey had yet to return to the darkened box. It clenched his heart she would have to be sent to the awful confinement at all and without him. Eugene glanced to the right, seeking a quick opportune moment, he dashed for the barn.

Along the right wall were organized lines of tack, with bridles, pads and saddles. Along the left was a solitary rifle. Looking all around him warily, Eugene rushed for the rifle, popping open the barrel to see if it was loaded.

"Blast it all," he cursed under his breath. The rifle was empty.

"I was wondering how long it would take you to attempt an escape," Victor stated, leaning against the entrance to the barn door and pulling a cigar out of his breast pocket.

Two men smirked with drawn pistols pointed at him with the hammers cocked. Eugene raised his hands, moving toward the horses. Keeping his eye on the three men in front, he backed up. A barrel of a gun shoved into his back. Eugene stopped.

"I have a wearisome time believing you are, in fact, Thomas Coldaire." Victor stated.

Eugene cleared his throat. "How unfortunate for you. My apologies if I decline in speaking with anyone," he said in a snobbish tone.

Victor smirked. "Indeed," he jeered, clapping his hands together. "No matter. Care to join Audrey and myself for a meaningless stroll about the property? Of course, you would. Why, what else could you possibly be doing. Furthermore, as a concerned cousin, I'm certain you would like to check on her well-being."

Victor wrapped an arm around his shoulder, with the barrel of a pistol shoved in his side, leading him out of the barn. Eugene's stomach roiled. Coming out of the barn, the sun struck his face. Victor led him to Audrey; her back turned to them.

The three men surrounded him, one on either side and the other behind, pistols drawn and cocked. Victor's pistol still in his ribcage. Eugene and Audrey waited four days for a telegram from Darrow. The lawyer hadn't responded. How they were going to escape now was beyond him.

# CHAPTER TWENTY-FOUR

Audrey felt her heart sink to her feet. Eugene gotten himself recaptured. Her hopes of escaping this miserable place were dashed. For four days, she plastered a fake smile to her face while around Victor Del Avilasto. The arrogant, coward of a man used henchmen to carry out duties, using fear and promises of death to his henchmen or their loved ones.

She sat in the chair, Richard on the right of her. The sun warmed her face, yet chills still crept down her spine. Wallace, another gang member, to her left. His dour face, turned the other way, rifle clenched in his hands and jaw set. Audrey squirmed in her seat, heart pounding in her throat.

Eugene and she needed to escape. Victor would surely kill her after their supposed nuptials. Wilfred Darrow hadn't responded to the telegram Victor mentioned he sent to St. Louis. Audrey doubted he did. Darrow would have responded with the comment – Rosalinda is in the box. Her father's friend wasn't coming. She was trapped. The only other man she trusted was now recaptured.

Audrey glanced at Wallace once more, his face hardening, lips pressed together. Out of the corner of her eye, Victor walked slowly with Eugene in her direction.

"You do not like him," she whispered to Wallace, noticing how quickly his demeanor changed.

Wallace spun to her, tipping his hat down low, attempting to cover their whispered conversation. "No, ma'am."

"Why be here?"

"He has my baby sister locked up in Kansas City. Says she ruined his silk shirt," Wallace snorted. "She didn't. Took her anyway because she's a beauty of a woman. I want to get her back."

Audrey gasped, putting a hand to her mouth. "Is there any person here actually loyal to Victor without the threat to a loved one?"

Wallace turned toward the sun while Richard whirled to face Victor. "Over half here are loyal to Del Avilasto. Richard and myself are two of the seven that don't like him. Sorry for bein' curt with you earlier, ma'am."

Audrey smiled wanly, "I understand Wallace. It's quite all right."

Her hands sweated profusely. Her heart clenched together. There was no escaping this madman who held her and Eugene captive. There was no reasonable way to get away from here without getting discovered or shot or risking innocent lives. Victor's henchmen watched her every move. She could not even walk a step out of place without a gun being pointed in her direction.

Tears sprung in the corners of her eyes. She and Eugene were in deep trouble, and it felt as though not even God could not save them now.

*Lord, I am not angry with Mary*, Audrey prayed, *I hope she's safe. Please*, she paused, feeling tears sting her eyes, *help me and Eugene get out of here.*

Sweat trailed down her spine. Victor's ominous presence made her skin prickle. His opulent aroma made her gut churn. It was the same spiciness she equated to Thomas and the devil himself.

"Why my dear," Victor cooed to her.

Audrey patted her eyes with the back of her hand discreetly trying to pass it off as dust in her eyes. She pinched her cheeks to give herself some color. Her mind willed her to plaster a smile to her face.

"Whatever do you cry about?" Victor asked taking his place to her right.

Audrey offered a wan smile. "I had dust in my eye. My apologies for leading you to believe otherwise."

Victor snorted, smiling down at her. "Oh, you are a horrid liar, Ms. Whitman. Did your escape plan fail? Do not fret yourself. A minister shall arrive today along with your lawyer, Darrow, was it?"

Audrey's tongue felt thick against the roof of her mouth. "Indeed, that is correct."

Eugene stood several paces in front of her, men surrounding him. Victor smiled wickedly at her. He took a cigar from his breast pocket and the snippers, cutting off one end. A man to his right struck a match off his boot, lighting the cigar for Victor. Her captor took one large puff, blowing smoke right in her face. Audrey closed her eyes. The smoke stung her face. She coughed once, forcing a small smile. She dared a glance at Eugene. He rounded his shoulders, his countenance darkening on Victor. She set her hands delicately in her lap. Rising from her chair, she moved her parasol in front of her face briefly to make a face at Victor. It made her feel better for the small rebellion. Rotating it behind her back, she tilted her head at Victor.

"Shall we partake in a stroll?" She asked.

"Thomas," Victor called without turning around, "please sit while I take my bride inside. I shall be with you momentarily. Tie his hands behind his back."

Victor held out his arm. Audrey took it, placing her hand delicately on top. Touching the fabric of his attire, being so close in proximity, sent a wave of nausea through her. The aroma of his clothing and cigar made her want to retch.

Audrey caught the eye of Eugene, his gaze held hers firmly, lips stretched in a tight line. She removed the uncertainty and fear from her face before Victor could see. There had to be a way out of her predicament. She could not ever go through with this scheme.

*There is many a slip betwixt a cup and a lip*, her Aunt Georgiana used to say when speaking to her about marrying Thomas. Audrey shuddered. *I found my slip for that situation. I need to discover the slip for this one too.*

"This way, my dear," Victor boomed.

Audrey almost jumped from her skin.

"I have a wedding gift for you, I believe, you shall appear ravishing in. I kept Mary alive for you, seeing how you will need her assistance."

Audrey offered a polite smile. "How generous of you."

"Indeed, it is," he said, letting out a plume and twirled his abhorrent moustache with the fingers not holding the cigar.

Victor led her inside his wood home, built out of rough-hewn logs pieced together. The solid polished door opened. She hesitated to enter. Unlike her previous jail, this had windows but she was still surrounded with no means of escaping her horrid captors. She may not be able to run but she could see the men and the surrounding areas now and plot a means to get away.

Audrey swallowed, taking trembling steps inside the new hellish pit. Victor was a man of opulence. Italian rugs graced the floors, French décor furnished the hallways with walnut demilune tables. His style did not match anything in particular. Victor clearly, needed to have whatever money could purchase.

Victor led her down the hallway to a room on the left with dark wood polished doors and brass handles. The small French doors, carved to resemble cherubs floating on clouds with a Greek Parthenon below. Audrey closed her eyes briefly, groaning on the inside. She despised the Greeks for their infidelity, polygamy and death. Outwardly, she gave an appreciative smile.

A henchman opened the door, revealing a snow-white dress with a long French train. Lace covered the skirting while the bodice was embroidered with purple flowers and cream and pink pearls. Audrey put a hand delicately to her mouth, swallowing to disguise her shock. It was a beautiful dress and one she would never be wearing, nor would she have picked it out herself.

"I do hope you like your new arrangements. Oh, and do not fret yourself, my men will be stationed around the perimeter continuing your safety," Victor stated, standing to the right with a hand on the knob.

"Much obliged," Audrey replied. "Your style is certainly unique."

An evilness crossed over Victor's face. "Well, my dear, I am *certain* your dowry will supply enough to alter any grievances you have."

"Agreed. I anticipate there is enough to permit such an undertaking."

Victor placed a hand on his lapel and spoke to the guard on the other side of the door, "Paul, no one comes in or out but myself," he finished, slamming the door. The click of the lock sunk her heart to her feet.

Audrey sighed, taking a seat on the ottoman. She was finding it difficult to keep a civil tongue, to keep the terseness from her voice and a chipper smile on her face.

Now that she was inside his dwelling, how was she ever going to escape?

# CHAPTER TWENTY-FIVE

Eugene watched helplessly as Audrey was taken inside the homestead. With the three men still holding guns at him, he had no choice but to remain behind. The horrible woman in the same unflattering orange dress, emerged from the side of the house swearing worse than an old drunkard. Hands behind her back, she was forced from the house. A man grabbed her roughly by the upper arm, shoving her forward.

"Move," one man growled at him.

*Serves her right*, he thought.

Eugene was forced to follow the men taking the girl. They walked past the shack he was held in and down the road. Boulders and scraggly planted trees lined either side of the dusty roadway for a while. Eugene glanced behind him, five men with loaded rifles followed. Two men in front also with rifles. Eugene ran a hand over his face, wondering how he was going to get him and Audrey out of this predicament. He looked at the woman struggling between the two men ahead of him and sighed. *She may be despicable but no one deserves to be held here against their will.* Now escaping from here with the woman who got them kidnapped was going to be more difficult.

They moved off the road, to the right, heading off onto a trail. About a half mile in, their little group came to an abandoned small shack with a smoke stack coming from the top. One of the men opened the door, revealing hanging racks for meat. Another man in a red bandana cut the bonds of the woman, shoving her in first. Eugene made his way inside the cramped space. He took a breath before the binds behind his back were cut. The shack smelled of dried meat and wood smoke. The door slammed shut, cutting off most of the light.

The rustling shuffle of numerous boots created a dust cloud under the door. Eugene got down, peeking between the door and the floor. A set of boots stood on either side. Random streams of light filtered through the holes in the wood siding and the few in the ceiling.

*I can handle two men,* he thought. *Shouldn't be too difficult then I can get back to Audrey.* He pictured her sweet smile, his lip quirking upward.

Eugene straightened up, dusting off his pants. The woman with blond hair eyed him suspiciously. Hands on her hips she glared at him, breasts pressed firmly together almost under her chin. Eugene snorted, shaking his head at her.

"Somethin' funny, Mister?" She grouched.

Eugene smirked. "That dress does not become you in the slightest."

The woman huffed, eyes narrowing at him. "Well, I happen to love it."

"Thanks for getting us kidnapped. You must be the belle of all the balls."

Arms crossed over her ample chest, she breathed out sharply. "In case you haven't noticed mister, I'm locked up with you."

"Serves you right."

"I never wanted this!" she exclaimed

"Neither did I, yet here I am," he seethed. "Now," he said quietly, "if we are to get out of this, we need to work together. What's your name?"

"Mary Lockburn," she said, busying herself, adjusting all her skirting.

"That dress has to go if we are going to get out of here."

Mary scowled. "Like hell! I love this dress."

Eugene rolled his eyes, approaching her. He leaned down, whispering, "There are two men guarding us. If we want to escape, we cannot be a shining hideous beacon."

Mary harrumphed, murmuring under her breath, "It's not hideous." Sighing, she conceded the point by turning around. "A little help," grumbled Mary.

Eugene grimaced, his fingers lightly touching the stays on the back of her dress. "There." He said, turning around.

The rustling of the fabric swished as Mary came out of it. She stood, arms crossed trying to cover herself modestly in her underwear and bone corset. Her blue eyes glared harshly at him. Eugene smirked, shaking his head, keeping his eyes at face level.

"Now what?" Mary hissed.

"We wait until they bring us a meal, then we attack."

Mary crossed her arms, taking a seat on the crate. Eugene got down on the floor again, peeking under the door. They needed to get out of here and quick. He also needed to figure out a way to save Audrey before Del Avilasto got his way and married her.

Two sets of booted feet were still outside the door. A light snore came from the lips of the man on the left. Eugene grinned. Getting up, he strained his eyes at the hinges on the door. The wooden pieces were on the inside. Eugene stifled a snort. Deftly his hands fiddled with the wooden clasps holding the door together.

"What are you doin'? It's not meal time!" hissed Mary.

Eugene whispered, "Escaping. One's snoring. Stay in here until I take them out. And stay low in case they start shooting."

"Then what?"

"Hide until I can get back here for you."

Mary got off the crate, going into the corner. Eugene went back to the last hinge on the door, carefully, pausing intermittently to listen to the breathing of the guards. His foot held the door up. With a deep breath, the door broke free. Light came streaming in. And so did bullets.

---

Audrey paced her room in the wedding dress. Mary came in and left quickly, being forced out by Victor to keep them from conversing. A man stood on the inside of the door, pistol in his hand as she got dressed behind a screen. Audrey tried to ask why Mary done what she did but Mary didn't answer. Mary's blue eyes vaguely glanced in her direction at times but mostly kept her eyes focused on her feet. Audrey tried to ask about Eugene and how many people were guarding the property. Mary shushed her, cinching the corset tight and inclining her head toward the guard. Once Audrey was dressed, Mary and the guard left.

*What am I to do*, Audrey thought frustrated, pacing the room once again. *What would a character in Ms. Brontë novels do... trap door? Maybe there is such a wonderful thing in this room.*

She stopped in front of the wardrobe. Thrusting open the doors, she moved all the ladies' garments to the side. Nothing luxurious as a hidden door revealed itself. Slamming it shut, she got behind it. Grunting with the weight, her slippered feet slid on the wood floor. Audrey moved the wardrobe to the side, her dress snagged on the right shoulder. Again, there was nothing.

Stamping her foot, she lifted the rug, peeking under the bed. She walked the room, stomping around, listening for differences in footstep sounds.

*This is dreadful*, she seethed, *there has to be something.*

Her skirts dirtied with her frantic rapid movements, moving about the room shoving things around, desperately looking for an escape. Audrey moved the bed off the wall, revealing more wall. There was naught to utilize to save herself. Audrey moved the curtains, moved furniture and moved it all back carefully just in case. She scoured every inch of her jail cell, and found nothing resourceful to save herself with.

Sweating, she dabbed her forehead with a kerchief.

"My dear," Victor called, his knuckles rapping on the door. "Have you readied yourself."

Eyes wide and breathing quickly, she glanced about the room. Everything appeared as it had before her frantic search. Audrey took a seat on the bed, adjusting her skirts to hide the dirt she made. The click of the latch sounded. The double door to her freedom opened with armed men on either side, hammers mechanically pulled back. Audrey fanned herself with her hand.

"I am readied. However, I find myself rather bilious."

Victor stood in front of her, his pitch-black brows creased. His black hair slicked back, shining in the afternoon light like a beacon of death. His suit a soft gray linen with a white muslin under shirt freshly pressed and crisp on his caramel colored body. Audrey resisted the urge to crease her own brows, opting for an open, innocent gaze.

"You look rather unwell, dearest."

Audrey nodded woefully. "If I dare say, I suspect I feel indisposed. May I inquire if I could perchance repose myself for naught but a few hours? I do not hope to inconvenience you in the slightest."

An older man with a bible approached the door, standing on the entryway to her room. His shirt was nicely pressed blue tucked into a pair of dark trousers. A black tie situated itself around his collar, bringing out the darker colors in his salt and pepper hair. He appeared every inch the colonial minister she read about in newspapers. Audrey swallowed.

"No troubles at all, young lady," the man spoke. Victor tightened his jaw. "Victor, let us retire to your study for an hour and see how the bride feels then?"

"Quite," Victor replied. "Fancy idea, Mr. Emsley."

Audrey fanned herself with her hand, "Any word from Darrow about bringing my cat?"

"Afraid not, dearest." Victor replied.

Victor nodded to her, exiting the room with the minister in front of him. The guards shut the door. The lock sliding in place sounding like thunder in her ears. Audrey flopped back on the bed.

"One hour… I have one hour to figure this out."

---

Soon as Eugene opened the door to the smoke shack, bullets came flying at him. If Eugene hadn't used the door for cover, a couple of them would have been lodged in his brain. Eugene threw the door toward one of the men, startling them. Eugene charged like a ram at the first man he came to. He knocked the vagrant down, landing on the rocky ground with a groaning thud. The man he took down with him moaned, fists raised to defend himself. Eugene rolled over and landed on top of the moaning man, sinking a right hook on the side of the man's face. Eugene scrambled to his feet. As he did so, Eugene yanked the pistol from the man's holster, pulling the hammer back with the other hand. Eyes wide, the man stared in shock for a brief second before Eugene pulled the trigger. The bullet embedded into the man's chest.

Whipping around, Eugene shot as another man came into view. The man hissed, the bullet entrenching in his shoulder. The man gritted his teeth, raising his hands feebly.

"I concede," he stated, licking his lips. His one good hand in the air, he got on his knees. "I didn't want any of this. Don't kill me."

Eugene scowled. "Appears otherwise to me."

Mary came striding out, ripping the pistol from the gang member's person. She rolled the barrel out, checking it and slammed it back in place. Pulling the hammer back, she pressed the barrel to the man's head. "Strip!" she yelled to the man with his hand up. Turning an eye in Eugene's direction she grouched, "I am not escapin' lookin' like a sight."

"Long as it's not the orange dress, I think anything shall suffice," he chuckled.

Mary's eyes shot daggers at him. Eugene cocked his pistol pointing it at the man.

"Strip," Eugene commanded.

The man hesitated. "You ain't gon' shoot me?"

"I am not going to kill a surrendered man in cold blood. But if you try anything funny, I won't mind."

"Mister," Mary harrumphed, "your pants."

The man pointed to the dead one in the dirt. "Take his clothes. At least leave me those," he begged.

"Take the dead man's clothing, Mary," Eugene said.

Mary scowled, taking the black pants off the dead man. She huffed, rolling the man over to get his blood-stained red shirt off. Mary made a face, putting on the clothing. Eugene took a tentative glance over his shoulder to where Mary was. She cursed under her breath as she dressed.

"Done," she grouched, tucking her hair up under the dead man's hat. Grabbing the dead man's jacket off the ground, she shrugged it on.

Eugene wagged his pistol for the man to move. Rising off the ground, the man held his good hand in the air. Sweat poured like rain down his head.

"Grab your jacket to hide your shoulder," Eugene commanded. "I don't want to give anything away."

The man snagged his jacked off the ground, slapping it against his pant leg to remove the dust. Hissing, he put his bad shoulder in the jacket first. The blood stained dark red at the right shoulder of his fir-green shirt. With the jacket on, the blood simply looked like sweat. Eugene made the man walk in front. They strode down the trail to the open road they'd come up naught a few hours previously.

The man hissed as he walked, lowering his injured arm to the side while his other one remained in the air.

"I can help you with your woman, Audrey," the man said.

Eugene scoffed. "How?"

"They are keepin' her in a room on the backside of the house. Guarded, no less, but I can create a distraction."

Mary's quick booted strides sounded from behind him. She

kicked up dirt and dust, trampling along, making more noise than necessary. The woman grumbled under her breath, tucking her blond hair under her hat. Dirt covered her face masking her feminine features. She fiddled with the gun belt at her sides, moving it around to her back.

"What's yer name?" Mary yelled.

"Shhh," Eugene admonished, sending a glare her way.

Mary glared back, but lowered her voice, asking again, "What's yer name?"

"Ross."

"You're Richard's brother, right?"

Ross nodded, shrugging his good shoulder. "Half."

"He's good." Mary stated glancing at Eugene. "Richard told me, there are like seven of them who hate Del Avilasto. And no one hates him more than his half-brother."

The shack was little more than a speck behind them. Eugene focused on the dirt road leading out. Going down the path, Mary and Ross lagged behind Eugene a few paces speaking of all the horrid things Del Avilasto did to them and to others. His mind wandered to Audrey. In a few moments they would turn the bend leading to the property, and he was without a plan to rescue her or anyone else. Eugene scratched the thin beard forming along his jaw.

Eugene paused turning to Ross and Mary, "Take me prisoner. You both need to make it past the men loyal to Del Avilasto. Gather the men who are not loyal. We cannot waltz in without something appearing amiss. Once grouped, we will formulate a plan of action to get Audrey out."

"I can pretend to be the dead man back there. If it doesn't work, I can change loyalties all a sudden and say I got tired of the dress hinderin' how I walk. Figured I knew who would keep me alive. And keepin' you from escapin' will cement my loyalty. I'll just say I aimed wrong and shot at you but hit him instead after you went off and killed the other guy. I took his duds after securin' you," Mary stated, glancing between Eugene and Ross hands on her hips.

Eugene sighed and handed over the gun to Ross, "Betray me, and I will haunt you from the grave. You and all you love."

Ross moved toe to toe with him, his head tilted to the side as his brown eyes met Eugene's with determination. "You have my word. You can trust me," Ross promised, hand out.

Eugene took it, praying their plan would work.

# CHAPTER TWENTY-SIX

E ugene held his breath as they walked through the homestead unhindered. Mary kept the hat low over her eyes, gun pointed at his back. From a distance with the other man's clothes on, she looked like any other gang member. Ross kept the gun pointed up at shoulder level on his right side, alert, ready for anything, while his injured arm hung limply, wound hidden by the jacket. Eugene followed, keeping his gaze fixed ahead, and on the ground to not attract those loyal to Del Avilasto. Out of the corner of his eye, he saw men wandering the perimeter, a few toward the front of the house, and several to the back, facing the house.

*Audrey must be back there*, he thought, returning his attention to the men at the front of the house.

The man on the roof whistled. Ross raised his good hand with the gun, hollering back all was good. Ross walked ahead, going straight for the barn and to the left. Eugene followed Ross's quick booted strides to the end of the very large barn. Eugene entered an empty outside stall, peering cautiously out to the homestead.

Three men were on the house rooftop, each facing different directions. The man on the barn paced, his strides echoing down like a hammer on a coffin nail. Two men stood on either side of the window in the back of the house. Eugene saw Audrey peek outside through a white lace curtain, her face flushed and drawn. Four men stood not two hundred feet away from the back of the house, each facing a different direction.

An older man rode in on horseback, followed by two other men. They reined in at the hitching post in front of the house. The older man removed a book from his saddle pack. Eugene ran a hand over his face.

"That's the minister man," Mary commented. "Came all the way from Black Hawk 'cause Victor paid him handsome to turn an eye."

Eugene stared at her for a moment. "Where are we?"

"In Denver but way in the hills, about a full day's ride from town."

Eugene wasn't one to curse although he felt like it in that moment. He would have to break Audrey free then ride like hell was chasing them to Denver. Eugene paced the small stall, pondering all thoughts of shooting and breaking through the windows.

He stopped. "Fire."

"What about the horses?" Mary countered. "We need those."

"There are saddled horses everywhere," Ross pointed out. "Fire it is."

Eugene exited the stall going toward the other end of the barn, where he had a better view of the back of the house. Two stalls to the back were occupied by a roan and pinto horse. Quiet as a mouse, Eugene let them out, pushing them out the back to the pasture. The horses trotted, ears twitching like they knew what he was about to do.

He backtracked, peering in a door on his left. Inside, a pistol and a rifle lay on a table beside some tack being repaired. Eugene took the rifle, taking the strap on it and slinging it over his shoulder. Revolver in hand, Eugene pushed the barrel over, grimacing at the four bullets inside. Ross came up beside him, handing him a box of matches.

"Horses are out on the other side," he whispered.

Eugene nodded. "Horses here too. I am gonna light this side."

Ross nodded, heading back to Mary. The woman raised her hat, peering at him guardedly. Eugene wiped his forehead with his duster sleeve.

Eugene struck a match against the side of the box, tossing it in the first horse stall. The hay caught fire, whooshing into the air like a gust of wind. He lit another match, flicking it in the second stall. Eugene scurried back to the other side of the barn, lighting another match and lobbing it into another stall as he ran by.

The giant barn was consumed behind him by hungry flames. Ross tapped him on the shoulder and motioned Eugene to follow him. Shouts of "Fire!" filtered through the sounds of crackling flames. Eugene followed Ross, exiting the side door while the outlaws went through the front barn doors with buckets of water. Ross and Mary dashed toward the wagon not far from the barn. They rounded the side, hunkering down as not to be seen. Ross drew his pistol, rotating the chamber to reload the ammo. Mary passed her pistol to Eugene, getting flat on her belly. Eugene rushed for the wagon, hiding himself behind one of the wooden wheels, peeking around it occasionally.

Victor Del Avilasto exited his home. His dark-as-hell hair slicked back on his head. A gray, pressed suit adorned his body making him appear slender and weak. Victor's face was drawn tight and flushed with anger matching the flames pouring out of the barn and climbing high into the sky.

Eugene, crept forward around the wagon wheel, keeping hidden from Del Avilasto. With everyone's attention turned to the barn, Eugene left Ross and Mary at the wagon. He crept on his haunches across the open yard. The men on the roof descended to help put out the rapidly spreading flames. Horses whinnied in terror, adding to the chaos. Eugene brought the rifle he'd found in the barn out in front of him, loading it as he crept forward.

Eugene rounded the house, glanced up and saw Audrey come to the window. Audrey yanked the curtain back, her eyes widened at the sight of the engulfed barn. Her frightened green orbs blinked several times before she disappeared. Eugene got close to the window, tapping on the glass. Audrey was at the door, slamming her hands against it, yelling at the top of her lungs, trying to get out. The door would not budge.

The window came to his chin. Eugene tapped on the glass window urgently, garnering her attention. Audrey spun around. A yelp escaped her lips. She put a hand to her chest, sighing with relief, and a small smile graced her lips. In her white dress she dashed to the window, scanning along the seams for it to open. Tears lined the edges of her lashes. She mouthed his name, panicking as her nails dug into the wood. Eugene whipped the rifle off his person, smashing the window open with the butt of the firearm.

"Eugene!" Audrey cried.

He set the rifle against the side of the house. "Come quickly," he said, taking off his duster and placing it over the glass shards.

He held out his hands for her, taking her in his arms as she leaned through. With her hands on his shoulders, he hoisted her out of the window. Audrey wrapped her arms around him, breathing deeply. She pressed her face into the side of his neck. Her wet, hot tears tickled his skin. He set Audrey down beside him, impulsively kissing her cheek.

"Are you all right?" he asked.

She nodded, wiping her eyes with the back of her hand. "I am now. The minister was about to marry me to that man," she sniffled. "I have missed you so. What now?"

Eugene couldn't help himself and pressed his lips to her forehead. "I've missed you too. Follow my lead."

Eugene glanced over his shoulder. The door handle to her room jiggled. Eugene let go of her hand, jumped slightly half inside the window, pulling the curtains somewhat closed. Ducking down, he grabbed his duster off the sill. He shook it out quietly, wrapping it around Audrey, concealing her bright white dress and stilling the slight shivers. *Most likely from shock,* he reasoned. Snagging the rifle, Eugene grabbed Audrey's hand, pulling her along the side of the house.

"Did you save Mary?" Audrey yipped a little too loudly.

Eugene shushed her sharply. "Yes. She is fine. And Ross is with us."

Audrey nodded.

Glancing behind him, he witnessed Mary and Ross dash out from behind the wagon, running toward the house. They crept alongside the homestead, keeping low and from sight. Black smoke billowed into the heavens; the barn completely consumed by the havoc they wrought. Horses screamed in the distance; their corrals too close to the flames for their comfort.

Eugene rounded the house corner. Creeping along the side to the front. Three horses were tethered to the post still. Victor was on his porch, screaming at the men to stop trying to save the building and look for Thomas and Mary. The minister stood beside Victor, bible open and praying; ignoring the chaos around him and the vileness beside him.

He glanced over his shoulder. Ross's grim, soot covered face shook side to side. Victor was too close. They wouldn't be able to escape without getting shot. Unfortunately, Eugene saw no other options. There was no other place to run nor hide. They needed the horses. They all had to get away from Victor and this place.

"I want him found!" Victor yelled. "I want him dead! Mr. Emsley, marry us at once."

The pastor shook his head. "No mister. I shall not, this was not a part of the bargain."

Victor whipped a pistol from the holster on his hip, pulling the hammer back and aimed it at Mr. Emsley's head. "Now," the tyrant ordered.

Victor stood toe to toe with the minister. The older man raised his hands in the air, turning on his heel back to the house. Eugene reached behind him, squeezing Audrey's hand. The door to the homestead slammed shut. Eugene bolted from behind the house, running to the nearby horses.

He dragged Audrey behind him, hoisting her up on the wide-eyed animal closest to them. The horse tossed his head, whinnying shrilly. Eugene unfettered the reins, taking them in both hands.

Eugene guided the leather straps over the head, before he mounted behind Audrey.

"Audrey!" Victor bellowed from inside the house. The door to the homestead wrenched opened. "You idiots!" Victor screamed, "There they are! Get them!" Hellfire blazing in his eyes. "Get them!" he bellowed.

Victor whipped out his pistol again, aiming for him. Eugene leaned over Audrey to protect her; urging the horse forward with his heels pressed into the horses' belly. Mary and Ross, each on their own terrified, whinnying mounts were not far behind him. Victor fired a shot, missing him, instead hitting the small tree to his left. Eugene glanced to the barn, most everyone still occupied with the flames and terrified horses, giving them a slight advantage. Victor released several more shots. Ross crumpled forward over his own mount, staying seated as the horse continued to run.

"GET THEM!" Victor yelled again.

Eugene didn't turn around, but in his mind's eye, he saw the bodies of many men scramble around like water over an ant hill as they took off toward freedom and safety.

# CHAPTER TWENTY-SEVEN

Audrey's eyes filled with tears as Eugene and her left the horrible place behind them. Her body shook with relief and shock. They were on their way back to Denver, back to where it was safe. Already they had ridden for hours.

She hadn't thought anyone would come for her, believing she would be stuck married to the atrocious Del Avilasto forever, or until he had her fortune and killed her. Seeing Eugene through the square wooden paned window brought her immense relief. Her heart fluttered, even now, remembering his handsome face as he helped her through the window. Eugene was like her very own Sir Lancelot – her knight in shining armor, saving her from certain destruction.

The getaway almost seemed too easy. It was too quiet. Everyone had their ears straining for the whinnying of other horses or the shouts of men. So far, nothing. *We got lucky, thank God.*

Audrey leaned back into Eugene. He let out a harsh breath. The heat from his body radiated through Eugene's duster she still wore, warming her. The trees around them stood tall and bushy. The trail narrowed to where a wagon was almost too large to fit.

Audrey loved the scent of the wild and the long needles of the pines. Their horse frothed at the mouth and breathed heavily, yet Eugene continued to push the horse onward.

Glancing to her left, Mary rode in tandem with them while Ross rode slightly behind. His bleeding finally stopped.

"We need to get him help," Audrey said.

"Where out here would ya expect that? It's at least a days' ride from Del Avilasto's to Denver," Mary answered.

Audrey stared at her. She wanted to glare. She was grateful Mary wasn't dead. No one deserved death. However, Mary's callous attitude only brought Audrey's previous anger about Mary getting her kidnapped to the surface. She wanted to yell at the girl. However, right now, it would accomplish nothing.

"I am glad you are safe, Mary," Audrey said forcefully, keeping her eyes forward.

"Thank you," she replied despondently, a sniffle in her nose.

Audrey took a glance behind her. The billowing smoke from the barn fire could no longer be seen. She let out a breath of relief. No house. No Victor Del Horrible. She chuckled to herself, then sighed. They were free and safe. She snuggled into Eugene again. He groaned behind her. She quickly sat back up.

"Are you all right?" Audrey asked.

Eugene sucked in a breath and gritted out a "Yes."

"We need to stop," Mary said, peering over, her eyes narrowed concerned.

"No," Eugene said tersely. "We need to keep going. We have to reach a safe point."

Mary harrumphed. "Can't find our way in the dark. Damnation! Yer right. We do need to get far away and quick, but night is catchin' on us."

"You kiss your mother with that mouth?" Ross laughed and groaned.

"No," she smirked. "I kissed yer brother."

Ross snorted, shaking his head. "You sure didn't."

Mary shrugged, clicking her tongue, pressing her horse forward. Audrey admired her confidence, the ease in which she maneuvered. She wished she could be like that out in this rugged world; however, she wasn't.

Audrey glanced over her shoulder to Eugene. His face drawn tight and slightly pale. The lines on his forehead crinkling slightly. He was a handsome man with his short beard complimenting his brown hair. His strong cinnamon brown eyes gazed for a moment into hers and she swore she swooned. It never happened to her before. If the flutters in her stomach were like those of the penny novels, she swooned. Eugene was a kind person despite his gruff exterior. His aloof, observant personality charmed her.

"What are your plans when we get to Denver?" Audrey asked.

Eugene grimaced. "See a doctor about this gun-shot wound then telegram Darrow you've been found."

Audrey frowned. If Darrow knew where she was, she would certainly be made to go back to St. Louis, unless of course she were married. Audrey put a hand to her heart. She'd no desire to go back to St. Louis to see her wretched aunt and Thomas.

Tears tracked their way down her face. Mary suddenly went off the road to the right, blazing her own trail. The horse leaving barely visible dents in the grass with most of the green vegetation springing back to life. Eugene leaned forward, his head bending around to meet her gaze. He dried her tears with his gentle fingers.

"It will be all right," he soothed.

Audrey nodded softly, giving him a wan smile. He straightened back up, following Mary's slightly discernable trail. The pine trees thickened, forcing them from their saddles. Audrey dismounted gracelessly, tripping over her horrible dress.

Eugene dismounted with a groan, taking a peek at his right shoulder. "Clean through," he commented.

Ross taking up the rear, "That is mighty lucky," he hissed, leaning on a tree. Ross stayed against the tree for a while, breathing hard.

Mary forged on head, coming out into a clearing. She gathered brush and larger pieces of wood. In the clearing that would be their camp, Mary made the fire into a triangle.

"Do you still have the matches?" Mary asked Eugene.

Eugene reached over his body with his good left hand, getting the matches from his pocket and handing them to Mary.

"Why are you making a fire that way?" Audrey asked.

"In case Del Avilasto comes, the logs can be pulled apart. It makes it harder to see the flames. Then when the danger passes, they can be brought back together to light again."

Audrey smiled brightly. "That's brilliant!"

Mary shrugged, getting the fire going in moments. After the fire caught, she led the horses to a nearby stream for water. Ross dragged his saddle over, tossing it near the flames. The man was pallid, sweat pouring from his forehead with his eyes dark and sunken in. Audrey took a seat across from him, watching his labored breathing. She'd not seen death before, how someone slowly withered away. Her father passed on while she was at school, the news delivered by one of her well-meaning instructors. When she made it home to Philadelphia for her final goodbyes, her father was readied for the funeral with makeup to hide the decay, reminding her of a life-sized doll of her father. Now, one of the men who rescued her was losing a fight to live and it was far worse than she'd ever imagined. Her heart clenched. The weight of guilt pressed down on her. He'd not be in this dire situation if it hadn't been for her need to escape.

Eugene scuffed past the fireside, dust covering him from his shins to his boots. Eugene held his right shoulder, grimacing in pain. The horses stood tied to trees, ears back and heads down; exhaustion lingered in their brown eyes.

Eugene walked the perimeter, scanning the trees and listening for anything that might be out there. After a few moments, he came back to the fire and sat across from Ross.

"Take off your shirt," Mary commanded coming around with a clean, wet rag.

Eugene shook his head. "It went clean through."

Ross chortled. "I wish mine did," he chimed, his voice fluctuating between a gasp and a groan.

"You're going to be fine, my friend," Audrey consoled hopefully. "Thank you for saving me and my friends. You are quite the hero."

Ross smiled. "I wouldn't call it that ma'am, but thank you. And you're welcome."

"Are you all right, Eugene?" Audrey asked softly, sitting beside him.

Eugene's lip quirked at the corner. "Yes. Thank you."

Audrey moved closer to him, shoulders brushing. It was enough to make her heart pound yet for propriety's sake far enough to be polite.

"I don't want my old life," she whispered so only Eugene could hear.

Eugene groaned. "You need to take the mantle so your horrible relatives do not."

Audrey smiled wanly. "I do not disagree. However, I do not want to go back to St. Louis, Philadelphia or New York. I have a fondness for Colorado, the people, the air. There is adventure here I do not want to miss out on. And I really, really do not wish to marry for money or convenience's sake."

Eugene turned to her. The fire light playing across his handsome face. Out of all the people she'd met, Eugene made her feel safe and... and maybe loved. Unlike those at balls who made her feel like she was a prize horse to be sold to the highest bidder. Eugene had her heart.

Her mother once said in the journal she left for Audrey – *love was a whisper on the wind that tousles the hair and kissed the face – lovingly and soft, it endears itself to the heart.* That was Eugene and she wanted it forever.

She took her hair out of her coiffed style, sighing deeply, letting it fall about her. She massaged her scalp for a moment. Moving it to the side, she braided it loosely. She threw the rest of the pretty pins, Victor forced her to put in her hair, into the fire.

Eugene watched silently, seeming to admire her hair. "What do you want?" he asked quietly.

Audrey stared at her clasped hands in her lap. "To stay."

Eugene's dashing brown eyes caught hers in the smoldering firelight. "Then I shall make it so."

Audrey could hardly believe what she heard. She swallowed

and allowed a small smile on her lips, afraid to hope too much, "Thank you."

Eugene's serious eyes lighted a little. He smiled and nodded. He spun toward the fire, losing himself to his thoughts.

Audrey turned her attention to the other side of the campsite where Mary lay alone, far enough away to barely feel the fire. The woman appeared desolate and small in men's attire. *Although,* Audrey considered, *at the moment, she'd probably look small and desolate in whatever she wore.* She felt pity for this woman. She was also trapped by the cruelness of Del Avilasto and whatever her past pushed upon her. Certainly, there was more to Mary than a jewelry thief.

"Mary," Audrey called. "Care to have employment at the Whitman Hotel?"

Mary perked up her head, "You're not mad?"

Audrey smiled. "No. I was before about the jewelry. More so about my mother's locket than the rings or bracelets. The kidnapping didn't please me either. But back there with that horrid man, I realized you were trapped by his cruelty too. I want to offer you a job so you may have a place to call home, food and clothes. And perhaps, in time, we can be friends."

Mary's eyes shone bright. Tears tracked their way down her dirtied cheeks. "Aw shucks. I would be more than happy to. Thank you. And I promise, Audrey, no more thieven.'"

"It's settled. Tomorrow we make for Denver and leave this horrendous event behind us."

# CHAPTER TWENTY-EIGHT

They all woke with the dawn. Ignoring grumbly stomachs and thirst, they all desired to get farther away from Del Avilasto. Audrey sat behind Eugene this time. She pressed into him, holding onto his waist. Audrey relished being close to him, galloping down the dirt road. She took a deep breath, silently enjoying his scent of leather, horse and pine. She prayed Denver would be around the next turn but each turn, came up building-less. Her heart quickened with every bend in the road while her gut sank when she saw more hills, grass and brush.

She glanced over to Ross who slumped forward in the saddle, his face whiter than a muslin sheet. Mary rode beside him, her other hand holding the reins to his horse. Audrey wondered if, when coming out of the woods, they'd taken a wrong turn somewhere. Nothing seemed familiar as the day wore on and the heat from the sun bore down on their backs. For Ross's sake, she prayed they were close.

"We gotta be there soon," Mary commented worry coloring her tone. "I don't think he's got much longer."

"Is this the right road, Mary?" Audrey asked glancing back at her, catching another glimpse at Ross. It didn't seem possible, but he looked another shade paler than a few minutes previous.

"It looks right to me."

Their horses dogged along; ears back and tired, they trudged forward faithfully. The hairs on the back of her neck prickled. She glanced behind her. Nothing was there. Audrey let out the breath she was holding, resting her cheek on Eugene's back.

Eugene patted her hand, leaving it rest on hers for a moment. "We will be there shortly, I am sure." He squeezed her hand briefly before retaking the reins with both hands.

Her heart fluttered at his touch, brief though it was, burned into her skin, sending chills down her spine. Eugene was the man her heart called for, the man her daydreams swept her off her feet. And once they got back to Denver, they would part ways. Audrey closed her eyes; her heart clenched at this thought, already breaking even though they'd not parted ways. Eugene was her whisper on the wind. She prayed she was also his.

With a sigh, she peeked around Eugene's shoulder, seeing the town come into view. Mary cheered, urging her and Ross's horse onward a little but not enough to jostle Ross. Audrey grinned, praying glory to God for delivering them safely to Denver.

Eugene clucked his tongue, begging the horse to go despite his fatigue. Their animal perked his ears, sensing the rising mood, and took off down the road at a lively trot. Despite feeling relief at the sight of home, Audrey's face donned an expression of grimness. This final stretch would determine her fate, and she wasn't sure she wanted to arrive. She didn't wish to leave Denver. Even if Eugene promised he would find a way for her to stay, she feared he would not, and leaving the life she'd come to love terrified her more than Victor.

Glancing behind her again brought her relief. Victor and his henchmen were not there. Denver crept closer into view and her stomach roiled with tension. Her hands sweated profusely. The road dropped to go downhill. Lower down the road it curved; Audrey imagined she could see the Whitman Hotel. She closed her eyes, moving her head to the right. The first building met her gaze.

"Pleasant afternoon, my dear," Victor said, leaning up against the porch of the house.

Audrey paled. "Eugene!" she whispered, her voice cracking.

The horse bolted down the road. Closing her eyes tight, the thunderous booming of the gun echoed in her ears. Their horse screamed, falling to the side. Her eyes bolted open. Audrey clung to Eugene as they both fell. She broke free of the horse while Eugene was trapped underneath the dying animal.

Moving her skirts out of the way, Audrey went around front, pulling on Eugene to get him free.

"You all right?" Mary asked, doubling back.

Beyond her, Ross barely rose in the saddle. His eyes sunk into his pale head. Audrey glanced frantically behind her. Del Avilasto approached with at least ten henchmen.

"Ride Mary! Get help!" Eugene commanded.

Mary didn't hesitate. She spun their horses and galloped down the road, her arm back, pulling Ross and his horse with her. Eugene broke free from the dying horse, getting in front of Audrey cocking his loaded rifle. Eugene aimed at the suffering horse. At the last moment, he turned it on Del Avilasto, pulling the trigger. Audrey closed her eyes and covered her ears. The shot boomed through the still trees. Eugene missed. Del Avilasto ducked at the last moment.

Their horse screamed in pain, finally lying motionless; its eyes glossed over. Blood poured from its side. Tears tracked down her face. Audrey closed her eyes tightly, praying when she opened them, it would be a different scene. Slowly she opened her eyes to Del Avilasto and his men surrounding her and Eugene. The Colorado skies darkened.

"My dear," Victor began mockingly, "how discourteous of you to take off on our wedding day."

"My apologies," Audrey stammered. "My feet were incredibly cold."

Victor leaned forward in the saddle. "Not to fret. I am pleased to find you at such an opportune time."

"Why I agree. I always preferred a chapel wedding."

Victor's smug smile left. The ominous gleam in his eye twisted his face into a grotesque scowl, making her gulp. She'd never been more frightened in her life. Scanning around her, a few of the fellows who despised Del Avilasto were also around her. She pleaded with them silently, hoping their few interactions were enough to make a lasting impression of kindness.

"I am afraid, *my dear*, a chapel wedding is out of the question," Victor seethed, pulling his pistol from the holster. "Also, no *guests* allowed at our nuptials."

Audrey covered her mouth. Victor pulled the hammer back. Eugene fiddled desperately in his pockets for another bullet. Crushing her eyes shut, a trigger was squeezed. A man cried out. His body thumping to the dirt road. The man's last breath gurgled out. Audrey's body quaked. Thunder roiled overhead. Audrey opened her eyes, terrified to glance beside her and not see Eugene standing.

She watched the henchmen on her right, guns trained at Victor. Turning slightly, Eugene stood in front of her.

"Eugene," she called quietly.

Tears brimmed along her lashes thankful he was alive. She expected him to be dead or not to answer. His body heaved a sigh. Audrey looked beyond him. Victor Del Avilasto was dead on the ground. His gray suit stained with blood. His cold, calculating eyes stared glassily at the heavens. Dust covered his oily, slicked back hair. Audrey shook, her body a jumble between relieved Victor was no more, sorrow a man lost his life, and horror that she'd been witness to death. Eugene spun on his heel, throwing his arms around her, holding her close. Audrey fell into him, breathing deeply the scent of him and relishing the warmth he brought. She sighed further into his embrace, locking this moment inside her heart and mind for when they parted ways.

Some of the men took off down the road, going back toward Victor's homestead. Three stayed in front of her. She watched them apprehensively; grim faces taut. One wore relief, closing his eyes as he looked to the heavens. The three of them tipped their hats to her and took off for Denver.

Eugene pulled apart from her, taking both her hands in his, "Shall we?" he asked with a tight smile.

"What?"

"Go to the hotel? I have a telegram to send Darrow."

Audrey's face warped into the mask she was used to wearing around the sham of high-class society. "Yes."

# CHAPTER TWENTY-NINE

Her utter relief at his safety made his heart lurch. The relieved sparkle shining in her eyes, had him wanting to smile, but he couldn't bring his lips to do it. Audrey was a task, a payment. The fiscal gains he would get from finding her would not only launch his career, but get him a nice home with property to raise the family he'd been dreaming of. Problem was, that family didn't seem to exist in his dreams without Audrey.

Eugene held out his hand to her. Delicate like a summer breeze, Audrey linked her arm with his, keeping a large distance between them. Her face twisted into a poised, elegant sophisticated mask soon as he'd mentioned the telegram. Eugene's heart sank when he saw the veil drop, hiding the woman he'd come to admire, and wouldn't yet admit to himself, he loved.

*I don't want to let her go, but I have to*, Eugene thought. *I cannot provide for her the way she deserves. I need to get back to Philly anyways.* He glanced out the corner of his eye. She looked to him; a stiff, fake smile gracing her pink lips.

They trudged down the road, heading to the left where the shadows of the Whitman Hotel loomed over the booming city.

Horses barreled up the hill. Their shrill whinnies prickled the hairs on his arm.

"Audrey," Mary exclaimed from around the corner, "Eugene, damnation! That took plum too long. Got the sheriff dawdlin' behind me." Mary finished with a roll of her eyes.

"Victor is dead," Eugene informed with more gruffness to his voice than he intended.

Mary nodded. "Ross is at the Doc's. Hope he pulls through. It's lookin' a might grim."

The sheriff reined in his mount. The black beast of a horse matched his owners countenance to a fault. The man on the back of the animal glowered, eyebrows pinched so far together one could not discern the color of his eyes. The six deputies reined in at least twenty feet behind the sheriff. Their observant eyes keenly taking in Eugene's and Audrey's appearance.

"I'm goin' back to the Doc's. Keep an eye on Ross," Mary commented. She took off on horseback down the road, her hand waving in the air. She reined in her mount not too far off from where they were and stormed inside a building.

"I think she is rather smitten with Ross," Audrey remarked to Eugene with a smile not quite reaching her eyes, although, Eugene observed, it came close.

The sheriff cleared his throat. Audrey offered him a polite smile.

"Ma'am," the sheriff began, tipping his hat. "Mister, mind tellin' me what happened?"

"Pinkerton Eugene Turner from Philadelphia," Eugene said, sticking out his injured hand. Eugene held back the grimace of pain while the sheriff shook it firmly. "I was following a lead on the missing heiress out of St. Louis."

The sheriff's eyes narrowed further. "You should see Doc Collins down the road about your shoulder," the sheriff paused, "the Whitman woman, right?"

"Yes, that is me," Audrey piped up.

The sheriff's eyes widened.

"Audrey got abducted by Victor Del Avilasto and was being

forced to marry him. I impeded his efforts, forcing Del Avilasto to retaliate and come after us. Up the hill, you will find him deceased at the hand of one of his own henchmen."

The sheriff scratched his stubbled face, "Well," he began, "we have been lookin' for the fiend for years. He is wanted in several states on account of murders and thievin'. Since the others split, you will get the reward for Del Avilasto's death. Seeing as Ms. Whitman is safe, I will leave you to your business Pinkerton. See the Doc. Six houses down on the right."

Eugene nodded. "Have a good day, Sheriff."

The sheriff reined his mount to the right, taking off up the hill with others following. Eugene put a hand over Audrey's, relishing the feel of her hand, leading her further down the dirt side of the road. The Whitman Hotel came into view like a white beacon announcing home, food, and safety. Audrey exhaled, a genuine smile adorning her gorgeous face.

The large carving of a brown bear out front shone in the bright sun. The bear, roaring on its hind legs was so heavily lacquered, the brightness of it was almost blinding. Audrey picked up the hems of her soiled white dress, beginning the assent to the hotel. His hand delicately set on her back, he followed her. Audrey turned to him and beamed. Marigolds and wild roses in potted planters lined the entryway. The dark walnut French doors, inlaid with glass and wrought iron handles displayed prominently the wealth of the Whitman heiress.

Eugene opened the door for her, entering the small foyer. Demilune tables were on either side. On the tabletops were pamphlets holding details regarding the Whitman hotel and the dining area meals, prices, and hours of operation. Eugene grabbed one before getting the final door for Audrey.

"Hello!" Audrey called striding to the front desk and ringing the bell. "Jane? Lena?"

A middle-aged blond-haired woman came from the back. "Rose!" she exclaimed. "Wherever have you been? You left for days without notice and we hired a replacement!"

"I was kidnapped by Victor Del Avilasto and have only just

returned," Audrey explained slightly crestfallen at the news her position had been filled already.

"Rose?" Eugene asked.

Audrey turned crimson, shining brighter than her white ensemble. "I'm afraid I lied to you all. My name is Audrey Grace Whitman. I was trying to start anew, live a life without being encumbered by propriety, status, and money. I'm sorry."

"I knew it!" Jane exclaimed, slapping a hand down on the countertop. Her eyes fluctuating between relief and anger. "The day you must have gotten captured, I telegrammed Wilfred Darrow. He arrived this morning."

"Where is he?" Eugene inquired.

"At the Whitman Diner," Jane replied, giving him directions.

Eugene patted Audrey's hand for a moment, then let it fall abandoned to her side. He strode off in the direction Jane pointed to go find the man who could release him from his mission.

---

Audrey watched Eugene leave, practically sprinting past the sitting area and through the small hallway to the diner. Eugene would get paid handsomely for his services, heading back to Philadelphia with a higher standing amongst the Pinkerton's and law enforcement. His mission, his task of finding her, concluded.

*And so we conclude as well,* Audrey thought with an ache in her heart.

Taking a deep breath, goosebumps prickled her skin. Her body relaxed where she stood, her pristine posture slacking, her shoulders rolled forward. She felt pleased to be back inside the walls of her father's domain. The safety it provided along with being surrounded by her friends was what she needed. She also felt depressed Eugene had left so quickly, so eager to be rid of her presence and finish his duty.

The sure heeled strides of Jane approached. The counter top lifted open with the comforting squeak of hinges. Audrey closed her eyes briefly, before facing the potential, and oddly welcomed, wrath of the hotel manager.

Audrey donned a smile on her face, hoping to soften the tirade that might come. "I take it I shall remain unemployed?"

Jane quirked a lopsided grin. "I believe you may do whatever you wish, Madame."

"I shall remain here in Colorado at the hotel, helping in areas where I cannot catch food on fire nor ruin the laundry. I believe I am rather good at washing dishes now," Audrey giggled. "You shall remain manager." Audrey reached over the counter, wrapping her arms around Jane, giving her a squeeze. "I was terrible," she laughed.

"If I may be frank, yes, you were not very adept at most things," Jane grinned.

Audrey laughed heartily, breaking away from Jane. "I do not disagree."

Strident boot steps sounded from down the hallway. Audrey looked to where Eugene previously disappeared. He came back toward the sitting area with a beaming and relieved Wilfred Darrow in tow. Audrey smiled so wide, her face hurt. Darrow, her father's greatest friend and business partner, was her godfather and the only true family she felt she had. No matter he was here to take her back to St. Louis or Philadelphia, she was glad to see him.

Putting propriety aside, Audrey ran to Wilfred, wrapping her arms around him. She inhaled his spicy aroma of the tobacco he smoked mingling with the overly pungent scent of the men's cologne. Wilfred embraced her back in what she assumed was a grandfatherly hug that pinched her arms to her sides as his scraggly whiskers of a beard tickled her cheek. Since her earliest childhood memory, there was no other way to describe Darrow in her mind. The older man held her close, heaving with relief. The scratchiness of his brown wool coat poked her skin. As always, Wilfred was dressed in a simple suit – gray trousers with a cream shirt and black suspenders.

"I am all right, Wilfred," Audrey consoled.

Wilfred held her back. "I promised your father to always look over you. And I have tried. But you, young lady, have made it rather difficult for me."

Audrey pulled back, wringing her hands. "Yes, my escapade did have some minor inconveniencies."

"I would not use the term *minor* in the slightest."

"Yes, well. I suppose you are right. But, while that was grisly, and I did fear for my life and the lives of my companions, I do not regret coming out here. I refuse to go back to St. Louis. Horrid Aunt Coldaire desires me to marry Thomas and I shall never! And being unmarried myself and not in my majority, I have little choice but to bow to her wishes. And I tell you, I will not do it."

Darrow nodded his salt and pepper head. "So that is why you ran-away, and I cannot agree more," he paused scratching the white stubble on his jaw. "Come, we have details to discuss in private."

Audrey turned to Eugene who stood mutely to the side during their conversation simply watching with wide eyes. "Come with me, Eugene. Please," saying the last part softly.

With a slight nod of his head, he stepped in tandem with her. Audrey took the men to the room with the piano inside. As she shut the door, she wondered if she was locking in her demise.

# CHAPTER THIRTY

Audrey sat down on the piano bench with Darrow standing in front of her. Eugene was across the room, bringing back chairs in either hand although the right chair dragged across the carpet and he grimaced with each step. Each man sat, staring at her like a cow at auction. Audrey straightened her back, taking on the poise and class she was born into.

Darrow sighed, rubbing a hand over his face. "In order for your inheritance to not be squandered by your relatives, you, unfortunately, have to marry. I cannot change the directive put in place by your father. I have tried, and spoken with many colleagues." Darrow sighed, leaning forward in his seat. "I am sorry Audrey."

Audrey hung her head, shoulders dropping. "What should I do? I refuse to return to St. Louis and my previous life. I love it out here in Colorado."

"Truly?" Wilfred asked leaning back, his eyes scrunching together.

"Yes," Eugene added. "She has told me so numerous times during our entrapment and subsequent acquaintance."

Her heart raced erratically. Her lungs felt full yet empty. There was no plausible way she would return willingly to her holdings unless it was to obtain some of her belongings. In that instance, she would get them and promptly return to Denver. And if they clapped her in iron to return her to St. Louis, she'd simply find another way to escape, this time making sure to leave blood behind.

Putting a hand to her head, she felt dizzy. The room was crowding her, caving in and forcing her to make the toughest decision of her life – relinquish her fortune, or marry someone. She could not decline it. Aunt Coldaire would disgrace the family name her father worked desperately hard to achieve. She also could marry someone... Anyone for that matter.

Her eager gaze fell on Eugene, then to the floor. *No*, she chided, *I cannot do it to him. He's worked hard to have this moment. People might believe he married me to achieve his status. But I can't imagine my life with anyone else. Would he be willing to risk the opinions of others and marry me?*

Damning propriety, she leaned forward, holding her head in her hands. Audrey sighed deeply. No matter where she went in this world, society and money followed her. However, she also could not turn her back on her father's legacy. That would disgrace his name and hers.

And the person she desired to marry sat in front of her.

"Audrey?" Wilfred queried.

Correcting her posture, Audrey faced the two men who meant the most to her. "I will marry. I do not wish the money to go to my wicked aunt. I also do not wish to dishonor my father's legacy. I ran hundreds of miles to escape this burden. Trying to avoid it does not work."

Darrow nodded. "You have to come back with me to Philadelphia. The paperwork is there, along with your items."

Audrey rose. Tears edging along the corner of her eyes into her lashes. "I will return to Colorado," she stated, looking at each man pointedly. "With or without my future husband."

The train jolted to a stop in the noisy city of Philadelphia. Horses and buggies jogged down the wide street, stopping every few moments for another buggy to pass in front. Audrey sighed, gathering her small traveling bag. Her coral taffeta dress swished with her movements. Even though the color was lovely and in season, she loathed it on her person.

Newspaper reporters and photographers waited impatiently on the landing. Pushing past one another to get a better view of her.

The story decided on between Wilfred Darrow and Eugene Turner was she had been on holiday, traveling to her father's establishments and everyone was sorely misinformed. The outright lie bothered her. However, it was the cost of society, saving her fortune from greedy family and protecting her father's good name.

She stole a quick glance to Eugene. During their entire trip home, they had spoken amicably in short bursts, although she'd tried for more. Their different social standings, created a barrier between them now since she'd returned home. She hated it. She missed their long talks while being entrapped and the way he held her hand. She'd even take the long ride on the back of a horse with him. Anything but this formal distance. It ached her heart. His brown eyes seemed hollower. His smile not often given so freely as before. His black hat dipped low on his handsome face.

Audrey passed the train conductor, flashing him a bright smile and thanking him by name. Her gesture brought out the heat in his youthful cheeks. Her feet struck the wooden platform. Unconsciously, she opened her white parasol.

Darrow set his hand on her back, guiding her. Eugene went in front, breaking up the columnists and photographers. Audrey hid underneath her parasol, navigating her way to the waiting carriage where Rafe waited for her. Hat in his hand, he wrung it. A bright smile formed across his face.

"Miz Audrey!" he greeted.

Audrey flashed him a brilliant smile, embracing him. "Rafe, my dear friend. It is so good to see you!"

"Thank you, Miz Audrey. I be pleased as plum puddin' ta see you. How was your trip?"

"Very well, Rafe," she replied.

She stepped inside the carriage, sitting on the other side and backwards. Darrow and Eugene stepped inside, taking their place across from her. A reporter clung to the side of the carriage, a beaming triumphant smile on his face. Audrey scooted away.

"One statement!" he shouted.

"I was on holiday out west visiting my father's establishments. My dear cousin was sorely misinformed."

"Thank you," he said, hopping off the side and back into the massive throng of people.

"Miz Audrey?" Rafe called.

"Please continue, Rafe, to Whitman Mansion."

"Yes, Miz Audrey."

Audrey stared out the window to the hustle of the streets. Women with arms full of parcels and children, wrangled their brood down the street and to different shops. The carriage rolled along, taking the well-known turns to her father's mansion.

She closed her eyes, letting her memory fade back to where her and Eugene were trapped in the wooden box for days. Much as she loathed the situation she'd been in, she loved spending time with Eugene. How he raked his fingers through his hair when he was about to disclose something personal. She secretly wanted to run her fingers through his hair, but would never admit it. She could only imagine the scandalized look on his face if she tried. Then again, she remembered the hug he gave her and the few chaste kisses on her cheek or forehead. Maybe, just maybe, he'd let her.

The Whitman Mansion came into view. Black cast iron fence and gates surrounded the home. Rafe dismounted, opening the gates wide for the horse and buggy to pass through. Rafe drove up underneath the covered area, opening the door for her. A man jogged down the drive, shutting the gate and confining her in from the outside world.

Audrey strode to the doors. Rafe beat her to them, opening the gargantuan doors to an elegant entry room. Demilune tables graced the walls every so often with lamps and décor. What her mother decorated, never changed. Her shoes clicked on the marble floors. She strode past the large staircase in front of her.

"Gentlemen," Audrey began, "if you could please follow me, I would like for us to retire to the parlor."

The men's heavy booted footfalls fell in tandem with hers. Audrey asked a passing maid to put together a quick spread of finger sandwiches and tea. With a quick bob, the maid was off. Continuing on her path, Audrey went to a door underneath the staircase, opening it with a jiggle of the handle.

She lit the oil lamps on the tables, igniting the room with rich reds and earth tones. Her father's parlor smelled as she always remembered –tobacco, oak, and cinnamon. Her father's leather cushioned chair sat behind a mahogany desk. To the right of the desk, on the corner, sat a silver tray laden with all different liquors.

"Please," Audrey motioned to the sitting area, "take a seat. Can I pour you a drink?"

"Brandy," Wilfred said softly. "These old bones are not meant to travel so far."

Audrey poured the requested beverage, handing it to Darrow. Eugene waved her off. Taking a seat on the same side as Darrow. Going back to the over laden tray, she poured herself a quick respite of whiskey courage.

Since being on the train, she'd grown distant and glum. She did not smile often like she did while in Denver. And none were genuine. It did not go unnoticed by her companions. With a sigh, she turned around, grabbing hold of the edge of the desk. Her legs quaked, wanting to give out. The possibility, the outcome, was too much. Yet she had to. There was no other way.

"Eugene," Audrey squeaked out.

Taking several improper strides, she was to him. She wrung the coral taffeta skirt in her hands, bringing the fabric up past her ankles. Her throat was on fire from the whiskey. She wanted to cough from the lingering burn.

"Eugene," she said again.

"Something the matter, Miss Whitman?"

Audrey caught her breath. *Miss Whitman.* He'd never called her that. Even while riding home. Her heartbeat quickened. Her palms sweated.

*This is it,* she encouraged herself. *You can do it. You have to. Ignore the name, the formality and just say it.*

She fell to both knees in front of Eugene. He reached down, catching her by her elbows. With both hands in front of her, eyes pleading, searching his own, "Will you marry me? Please?"

"Audrey!" Darrow choked.

Stricken, Audrey rose to her feet. "I cannot marry an aristocrat and remain stuffily confined behind stone and money; I would be miserable. And there is no one I fancy here," she confessed. Turning back to Eugene, she took his hand in hers. The tension in his face did not soften nor did it relieve her. Audrey swallowed, almost losing courage but her racing heart and the words she needed to say poured from her mouth, "Eugene, since our time together, my fondness for you has grown. I admire you and I would greatly wish to call you husband, if you will agree."

She closed her eyes, waiting for the rejection. *I said it,* she thought. *Please don't say no.*

What in the world was she thinking? Eugene would politely decline, going back to the inner rankings of law enforcement, returning a champion hero for restoring the lost heiress. She would then be forced to marry a nobleman or gentleman of some kind who would drag her to every ball and gala on the face of America, Europe and beyond. Her life would go back to propriety and fake relationships.

Audrey took a seat across from Darrow, refusing to meet Eugene's gaze and the silent rejection; or Darrow's astonished and scandalized expression. The burning in her eyes and nose begged for her retreat so she could weep in private. She found, she could not. She had to find some solution now.

She hunched forward, sighing deeply, "Wilfred," Audrey's cracked voice broke the silence. "What exactly does the directive state?"

If she was going to be forced to marry, she wanted to be aware of how it was written. Her father married for love. She wanted the same. Although she feared any marriage would do. Her hands gripped the edges of the polished wooden chair, her legs crossed at the ankles.

"Yes," Eugene replied, getting to his feet.

Audrey's head jerked upwards. Silent tears falling down her cheeks. Her heart thundered with hope.

He removed his hat setting it on the coffee table before him. Approaching her, he got down on a knee. "Yes," he stated again, taking her hands. The charming twinkle of cinnamon brown returning to his observant eyes. "Please allow me to ask you in return. Audrey Whitman, will you do me the honor of becoming Mrs. Turner?"

Audrey beamed, wrapping her arms around his neck.

"The directive states," Wilfred Darrow cleared his throat, grinning. His old bones creaked as he rose. "You must marry for love, like your father did with your mother."

# EPILOGUE

The Colorado sunset was more than Audrey ever imagined it
could be. The sky ignited with pinks and purples, swirling
together in the clouds overhead while the sun beamed orange,
descending toward the hills. It was what the newspaper columns
wrote about; only one had to see it in person to truly behold the
magnificence. Below her, chairs and benches lined in neat rows
outside, lonesome waiting for guests to occupy. People milled
about, chatting amicably with one another.

To the right, behind the hotel, Ross took horses and buggies
from people, parking them in neat lines. Ross survived the ordeal
from Del Avilasto and Audrey employed him as the stable master.
The kind and gentle man had a way with horses.

To the left, people wandered from inside to the outside of the
hotel. The hotel's oil lamps and candles shone like a signal in the
oncoming night, exploding their small Denver town in a revelry
glow.

Audrey grinned broadly, closing the curtain. She adjusted her
skirts for the hundredth time. She strode to the door, opening it
slightly for what felt like the fifteenth time.

"Is he readied?" she asked Wilfred.

The old man smiled, hands on the lapels. "I believe he just exited the hotel."

Audrey grinned, squealing softly in her throat. She ran back over to the mirror, checking her hair and positioning her veil again. She paused at her reflection, admiring the changes the past year brought. Her skin was tanned, beautifully kissed by the sun. Her arms stronger, defined and toned from helping the other hotel ladies with chores of dishes, and cleaning. Audrey now took care of payroll and gave everyone a quarter raise. She'd grown into quite the business woman with the help of hotel manager, Jane McCarthy. The woman was more than an employee to Audrey, but now a very dear friend.

She smiled, looking down at her short nails. Turning her hands over, she rubbed her fingers over the callouses. A lot had changed and everything for the better. Eugene transferred his Pinkerton business to Denver. Although most of his investigations sadly ended up with someone six feet under. People from all walks of life, traveled to Denver to find their claim at gold and fur, and most who went missing met with an untimely end. But Eugene was strong and after each solved case, would come for a hug and simply hold her while allowing himself to let go of the sadness.

Laughter wafted up to her. Audrey opened the window, peering down to the scene below. All her friends gathered, ones from back home in Philadelphia, and ones she made here, meandered to their seats, facing the little wooden and flower woven archway. Audrey squealed in her throat, bouncing on her heels.

Thank the Good Lord her aunt and cousin were not to be seen and politely declined the invitation. To be kind, Audrey sent them a stipend each month to live off of. It was more than generous of her and something Eugene advised her against doing since Thomas was most likely to squander it gambling. However, Audrey felt obligated to her remaining family to take care of them. Even though Georgiana Coldaire was like ice, the woman did take care of her physical needs for a few years anyways.

"Oh, good graces," Audrey said, taking another turn about the room.

Audrey fiddled with her hands, waiting for Wilfred to open the door and take her outside to meet Eugene at the altar. After the wedding, the large entertaining room would be opened with food and drink. Although she cannot cook to save her life, she did help put sandwiches together. Under Lena's close supervision, of course.

*A few more moments*, she thought. *Come on clock, tick faster!*

Audrey gasped, grinning broadly as the door opened.

Jane returned her enthusiastic look. "You need something blue," she said. Jane fastened a blue pin to her gown. The stone swirled with all different kinds of blue tones. Jane took a step back, smiling with tears in her eyes. "It's like my sister is getting married," Jane commented, choking on her last word.

Audrey wrapped her arms around her friend. "And you're next. Tonight, my goal is to find you a match."

Jane scoffed, patting her eyes. "Audrey, I appreciate your optimism but I am well past my suitability."

"Nonsense, it is complete swill and you know it well."

Jane smiled wanly, heading to the door. Upon her opening it, Wilfred poked his head in and grinned. He stepped forward and bowed, holding out his hand. Audrey ran over, readily taking it.

"It's time," he said. "If only your parents could see you now."

"Having you here is more than enough. Thank you, Wilfred."

Wilfred patted her hand, leading her out the door. The staircase and hotel were silent. The creaking of the stairs that normally could not be heard during the day, boomed in the silence. Audrey headed around the corner to the back of the hotel. The skirts on her dress drug behind her a tad.

Jane forged ahead, getting the door for them both. Audrey's heart pounded in her throat. Tears immediately sprang into her eyes. The door opened, however, it felt like it was the slowest opening door in her life. The sunset deepened to eggplant purple and a bright ruby. There was just enough light left from the sun to exchange vows.

Audrey took a deep breath. Wilfred led her around the side of the building to where the guests and Eugene waited. Wilfred cleared his throat at the end of the walk way. Audrey's eyes focused on Eugene. His piercing brown gaze caught hers and he stilled. His face morphed, eyes widening, he swallowed. Turning around fully his gaze took her in completely. A smile he reserved for only her, split his handsome stubbled face.

Wilfred led her down the aisle. Her own look remaining fixed on the man she was about to call husband. If it weren't for Wilfred holding her hand, she would have bolted to him. The reverend began speaking, his baritone voice sounding like an underwater blaring blur of words. Wilfred embraced her, catching her off guard. Audrey returned his affection, taking Eugene's hand.

Audrey stepped up, taking Eugene's hand in her own. "I do," she said immediately.

"I do, too," Eugene said, giving her hands a squeeze.

The reverend chuckled. "All right then. I will make this to the point."

The guests chuckled. The reverend flipped through the pages in his black bible before closing it.

"God's love is eternal and unconditional. By Audrey's quick response, her love for Eugene is clearly like God's," he chuckled. "From flesh to ashes, from prosperous to poverty, one thing I can be most certain of is their love will endure. With the blessing of the Good Lord, the state of Colorado, and myself, you are now husband and wife. For the first time, I introduce Mr. and Mrs. Eugene Turner."

Audrey leapt at Eugene, wrapping her arms around him and kissed his lips. Her husband caught her, holding her back slightly, he helped her to right herself. Audrey laughed, holding Eugene's hand. She led him back inside the Whitman Hotel to the grand room. The wedding guests followed, excited for the refreshments, and the entertainment to follow.

The raucous cheers from outside followed them in. Smiles abounded upon all faces. Children flitted inside the grand room first to scope out the tasty treats. Eugene and Audrey stood together, waiting for everyone to make their way inside.

"Blast propriety," Audrey whispered, planting a kiss on his lips.

"Mrs. Turner," Eugene said in a hushed firm tone, smiling. "Don't swear. I have good authority to spank you," he finished with a wink.

"Mr. Turner," Audrey teased. "I shall runaway at your mischievous threat."

Eugene leaned in close, his lips nearly on her ear. "It was not a threat."

Audrey sucked in her bottom lip. Chills crept down her spine, her cheeks turning bright red. "Since you found a Whitman, you shall be excellent at finding a Turner."

Eugene laughed, placing a kiss on the side of her cheek. "That I am."

# II

## TO LOVE A THIEF

# CHAPTER ONE

Kayla raised her tweezers again. "If you'd hold still, this might be easier on you," she snapped, and yanked another porcupine quill from his arm. "How did this even happen, Loren?"

Kayla's stepbrother Loren grumbled, running a hand over his face as she pulled the second to last quill. "I reached behind a bush."

Kayla snickered, pulling out the last quill. "Did ya like whatcha found?"

Loren scowled. "Quiet, woman—and get to work."

"I'm done," Kayla replied.

"Oh, come on Loren," one of his men hollered. "Why did you reach behind that bush?"

Loren rounded on her. The slap across her face caught her by surprise, and she yelped. She found herself on the ground, her hand to her cheek.

*I think I hate him*, she thought. *I can't wait for this new job. I want to earn my own way, and be rid of him. This is not what family does.*

The men returned from seeing to the horses, and gathered nearby. Kayla got off the ground, nursing her face, and sucking on the split in her lip. She brushed the dirt off her tattered dress, sitting back down on the log. With a stick, Loren drew his plan in the sandy dirt.

They were going to rustle two hundred head of cattle off the Circle 8 ranch. In fact, they were on the Circle 8's land now. Kayla didn't like the idea of thieving because she didn't want to be swinging. At nineteen, she had much to live for. Besides, this wasn't the plan Loren told her.

"Wait! This wasn't what I signed up for. You said no thievin'!" Kayla's panicked voice boomed. "I don't want to swing."

No one listened. She begged her stepbrother not to steal, that there was always honest work. Loren would not be swayed.

"You want a ranch, Kay," he snapped, "this is the only way."

"You're a far-gone idiot!" Kayla snapped.

That earned her another smack. Holding her smarting cheek, she glared at him. She didn't say anything else. Loren and his four men saddled up their tired mounts.

"Let's go," Loren said.

Kayla bit the inside of her lip. She got off the ground, facing off with her stepbrother. "Loren you can't be serious. Thievin' is illegal. You'll swing."

"No, I won't," he said.

Looming menacingly over her, he said, "Sister, step aside." Kayla went to kick him where it hurts, but someone swept her feet out from under her. Loren stood over her, lashing her hands together while another man pulled at her hair so she wouldn't move. Loren dragged her by her tied hands to a tree. With another rope, he lashed her back to it, tying the rope tight around her stomach.

"Loren!" Kayla shrieked, feeling a stub of a tree branch smash her shoulder, "let me go!"

Loren tossed another man a smaller rope, tying her feet. Loren came up behind her, stuffing a gag down her throat. He patted the side of her face. "Can't have you ruinin' the plans. I would rather just kill ya," he sneered, spittin on her dress. "Seein' how yer family, I'll be nice this once."

Kayla thrashed around like a trout she snagged from the water only hours before. Loren kicked her in the gut. Mouth agape, she sucked in a breath. She hadn't a clue they would do this to her, that this was Loren's plan for her. The other men treated her well, or close to it. Most ignored her if it wasn't meal time. Still, the pain her blood would do this, cut deep. Loren was all the family she had left in this world.

Kayla opened her mouth to say something, but was met with a slap.

"Hush yer ugly face!" he hollered. "Give us away, and I *will* kill ya!"

Kayla inhaled sharply through her nose, breathing in the sage-brush and dirt. This was not how she expected the night to turn. This was not the brother whom she grew up with. How did life get so out of hand? Why did her once, nice, successful brother turn to liquor, gambling, and stealing?

Kayla yelled through her gag to stop. Her head swished back, and forth, trying to work the cloth out of her mouth.

"To the Circle 8," Loren shouted, mounting his gelding.

"To jail," a man came stepping out of the shadows. "Raise 'em high," the man commanded.

Kayla thought if her eyes could go any wider, they would pop out of her face. Six men came out of the shadows, surrounding her stepbrother's posse. Loren's face twisted, his eyes darkening with the evil now consuming him.

"You bitch!" he sneered at Kayla, drawing his pistol.

Kayla scrunched her face, turning her head away. She couldn't make herself seem smaller if she tried. The raucous of the bullet passing through the chamber of his .45 resounded in her mind over and over. The gag muffled her scream as the bullet hit her leg. Tears streamed from her eyes. The hot metal burned. She dared not look, focusing her bleary eyes on the people who'd come to inadvertently save her.

The man who hollered the warning to raise their hands, shot Loren off his horse. Kayla heard him exhale; his body hit the dirt. Without having to look, she knew her stepbrother was dead. Kayla prayed for his soul, asking God to forgive Loren of his wayward ways, and his soul, for he wasn't always this way. Loren taught her to ride, and would give her wildflowers when he found them. As she thought about it, she prayed for herself too. Certainly, she would be swinging soon enough.

Blood soaked through her dress all the way to the hems. Her eyes made tears all on their own. Her mind twinkled like the stars in the Texas sky, soon fading to black.

CHAPTER TWO

During the morning Ben rode fence, checking along the west section of the property to move the herd to, when he spotted rustlers on the edge of the Circle 8. He watched the party come in, and make camp. How they hadn't spotted him, Ben didn't know. Looking around, there wasn't much to hide a saddled horse, and grown man.

The Circle 8 had its fair share of thieves since they were the biggest cattle ranch on the east side of San Antonio, and the San Antonio River. For some darn reason, thieves thought entering from the most brushy, rocky, and snake invested area, was the most concealing.

*Maybe if they were rattlers*, he chuckled.

Ben, and his hired hands spent the better part of the evening, cleaning guns, and preparing to take on the rustlers. Ben sent George to town to tip off the sheriff about the planned rustling. Sheriff Taylor, was set to be here an hour ago. The sheriff did not yet show.

*No matter*, Ben shrugged, facing the posse of thieves, *the rustlers would be taken in, charged, and hung.*

The night's brand of quiet seemed deafening after two consec utive gunshots with one rustler dead in the dirt. Ben held his breath, observing the remaining outlaws. The rustlers stared back at him, wide eyed. One reached for the shotgun in the saddle holster.

"Throw down your guns," Ben commanded, pointing his gun at the man reaching for the shotgun. "No funny ideas or I will shoot you dead like your friend there. Roy," Ben hollered. "Gather the guns. George, tie their hands."

Now, he had one dead thief, four on horses, and a woman to worry about. Ben ran a hand over his face. He overheard the woman arguing, wanting nothing to do with the rustling. She wasn't going to hang for a crime she didn't, and seemingly wasn't going to, commit. Although she could get in trouble for being a part of the group. However, it wasn't for him to decide her punishment, it was his father's since the sheriff still didn't show.

One by one, the men tossed their guns to the ground. Roy gathered them out of their reach, stacking them in a neat pile to be retrieved later. George took each man off his mount, tying their hands behind their backs, and lashing their feet together, leaving enough room for shuffling back to the bunkhouse. Ben's four other cow hands trained their guns on the outlaws. The sheriff should be here soon.

"The woman," one of the rustlers choked on his words. "Her name is Kayla."

Ben didn't move from his spot. "She will get help," Ben assured.

"She didn't deserve that," he stated, shaking his head. "Nor her getting struck with a bullet. I'm a coward of a man."

Ben scoffed. "Feelin' poorly for a woman won't save your hide now."

The man shrugged, not appearing any more rattled than before he started to speak, "I know that."

"What's your name?" Ben asked.

"Joshua Jackson from Omaha."

Ben nodded. "Kayla will get help then her punishment decided."

Joshua tipped his head back, looking at the stars. "Lord help her," he said, "It's too late for me though."

Curious against his better judgement, Ben approached the man. "Why did you do it?"

"My sister, Leah, she's blind. I was gunna send her money for blind school."

Ben didn't say a word. Thieving was thieving. And the punishment for it was hanging. Ben couldn't do much for the man now. He was caught red handed.

"All tied boss," Roy said. "What about her?"

Ben sighed, rubbing the back of his neck. "Guess we ought to fetch Doc Collins."

Roy clapped him on the back. "I'll go."

Ben nodded. "Bring him to the Circle 8."

Ben holstered his pistol. He got all the men to their feet, taking a long rope and tying them all together. It was clear as dawn the sheriff wasn't coming out tonight, so he should take them to the sheriff himself. He told Garrett to leave the dead man where he was. The facially-pocked-puke of a man didn't deserve a burial. He'd come out later to remove the body. Didn't need it ruining good grazing land. Ben got on his horse, leading the way to San Antonio.

"George, collect the guns and take her back to the Circle 8," Ben yelled over his shoulder.

The young man, little more than a boy, nodded, carefully gathering the dark-haired Kayla in his arms. Her pallid color reflecting in the firelight. The dark wetness of blood seeped through her ruined dress and trickled down her leg.

Ben peeked at the sky. The moon waned over to the west. "Stupid girl," Ben mumbled, tugging the gang of rustler's along.

# CHAPTER THREE

The smell of flapjacks tickled her nose. Kayla's stomach rumbled. Light struck her behind her closed eyes. Kayla groaned at the pounding in her head. She used the heels of her hands to rub the sleep out of her eyes. It felt like she'd been struck by a raging bull.

Her vision bleared. The smells of food and cleanliness assuaged her senses, feeling different and out of place. Was she dead? Was she already hung, dead and in heaven?

Kayla slowly sat up, her surroundings becoming clearer with each blink. "What in the world?"

The lower half of her dress from thigh to hems, was caked in dried blood. It was a stain she was certain would never come out. And the hole from the bullet would be hard to repair. She pulled up her dress, looking at her left thigh where she was shot. Glancing about the room, there were no bars to lock her inside like she thought there'd be. Come to think of it, while plain, this was a far nicer room than any jail cell she could imagine.

*Where are the others*, Kayla thought.

Kayla gulped, wondering why she wasn't joining them on the tree. A few tears trickled down her cheeks. She, by all counts, should be dead too. It didn't matter if she assumed they'd all been hired to work on a ranch. She was with the thieves. She was connected to the rustlers.

*Rustlers.*

Somehow, Loren kept that part from her. And she was stupidly blind enough to follow along, thinking, more like hoping, her brother changed from being an alcoholic and back into the sweet, intelligent person she remembered as a child.

By lordy, was she wrong! She snorted in disgust, crossing her arms over her chest. She turned a blind eye to who Loren really was, who he turned out to be, hoping her kindness would bring back the brother she remembered.

Kayla dried her eyes. She inhaled deeply. "Hello," she hollered out the open door, boldly gathering her courage. "Are you here to string me up too?"

A tall man entered the doorway, leaning his muscled body against the rough-cut frame. He stared at her with piercing bright blue eyes. If she dared to compare, they were brighter than the Texas sky. A long scar trailed the side of his face from right cheekbone to lip. Kayla glanced at it a brief moment before studying the rest of him. The man who faced her was clearly a cowhand. Rough, cracked hands, crossed over his arms. His dirt stained green shirt, brought out more of his beautiful eyes, and his suntanned skin. Lips pressed together tightly, his hawk like gaze narrowed.

Her heart pounded in her throat. She pushed her hair off to the side. "So," Kayla began with a level tone and false bravado, "what do you plan on doin' with me?"

His heavy booted strides echoed in the room. He pulled up a chair by the door, flipping it around. His broad arms resting on the back of the chair. "What were you doin' with them?" he asked, matching her tone.

Kayla licked her cracked lips, the bravado leaving her. "I thought we got hired at a ranch."

"Hired on as what exactly?"

Kayla shrugged. "A cook, maid, another cowhand."

The man laughed. "A woman as a cowhand?" he shook his head. "And rattlesnakes fly."

Kayla scowled. "I am not afraid of hard work. I can do it."

"You can steal it, you mean," he growled.

Kayla shook her head refusing to lower her eyes. "No sir, work. I hadn't the slightest what they were plannin'. I might be poorer than dirt, but I work for myself. Stealin' is a sin."

"Damn right it is," the man said. "You should be swinging with the rest of them. Fact is, I overheard you try to talk them out of it. That alone saved your hide."

Kayla nodded. Her gut clenched for those who swung, like Joshua. He was a nice man, dull as a knife though, but he treated her kindly when Loren wasn't paying her heed. It saddened her Loren was with the good Lord. While the others made their beds and were now, more than likely, lying six feet under - God rest their souls - she got lucky. Relief coursed through her. She closed her eyes to hide her selfish relief at being alive. If she would've known what Loren was planning all along, she wouldn't have come with him. She wouldn't have left Oklahoma. Now, she was going to be stuck here, or joining her stepbrother shortly.

"I owe you a debt," Kayla said, understanding her predicament. "What do I need to do?"

The man's chair screeched back. "If you can oblige it, stand, and walk with me to the dining room."

Kayla moved her feet to the wooden floor, her shoes still on. She sucked in a breath, readying herself to stand. Kayla stood straight, feeling the ache in her leg. She took a step, and hissed, her wound throbbing as she walked. Her left thigh burned, but she didn't feel her stitches tear. Kayla gritted her teeth, pushing back the tears threatening to fall.

"My name is Kayla Langmoore," she stated.

The man stared at her. The boldness from earlier did not work in her favor, so she quit that. Being herself might earn her some kindness in return.

The man reached out, putting a steadying hand under her arm. "My name is Benjamin Coleman."

Kayla smiled tentatively. "Wish I met you under better circumstances, but here we are."

Inside, she cursed herself for being rather forward. Then again, a duck can't change itself to a hawk. She was blunt like the winters were cold. She stumbled over her own feet.

Ben raised his brows, giving a lopsided grin. "You all right?" Ben asked.

Kayla nodded. "Right as rain."

Ben chuckled sarcastically, "Your face tells a different story."

Kayla looked at him. "Then don't look at my face." she said, making it to the doorway. She paused, leaning up against it, taking a fortifying breath, she steeled herself to walk farther.

"Where are you from?"

"Was from Oklahoma," Kayla began, "Ma moved us to Omaha. She married and died there, so I went back to Oklahoma to be with my grandparents. They died too. I was in the orphanage there for a bit. Got out, and worked at the Hitchin' Post Dining Hotel as a cook. My stepbrother Loren found me, and said he got us a job. Now, here I am."

"I didn't ask for your life story," Ben said with an exasperated chuckle.

Kayla shrugged, grinning slightly, "Sooner or later you would have. Better to spill it now."

"You sure are a blunt woman."

Kayla shrugged again moving off the door frame and into the larger room. "Better than a lyin' one."

Ben gestured for her to take a seat at the dining room table. Kayla sat in the nearby wooden chair. Her thigh throbbed. Kayla rubbed it, hoping to not feel fresh blood on her bandages.

Staring at her leg, got her to pondering on Loren. She missed her brother, well, who he used to be. She didn't care for who he turned out to be. Part of her felt relieved he was gone. He couldn't strike her, nor the other willing women he took to his bed. The other part of her was saddened this was where his life led him. Selfishly, she was grateful to still have hers.

With a sigh of relief, Kayla glanced to the left. Ben squatted in front of a small fire, pouring coffee into a tin cup. He set it down in front of her. Ben sat across the table. Kayla took it, sipping the bitter blackness she'd seen so many men love. Kayla choked on it, sucking in a breath after she swallowed.

"Tastes like death," she complained, "why do you men like this?"

The corner of his mouth twitched, "Same as you women like fancy ribbon."

Kayla laughed, relieved he made a joke. She sipped the coffee again, grimacing, "So what do you want me to do?"

"Work off the cost to get your leg fixed. Since you were vouched for, that you weren't in on the rustlin', you will get pay once you work off this debt."

Kayla nodded. "Fair enough."

Ben strummed his fingers against the wood. "Carl Coleman is the owner. He agreed to let you stay on and be our new cook since Larry retired from the position a couple months ago and no one's enjoyed my cooking."

"Nephew or son?"

Ben tilted his head to the side. "What?"

Kayla sipped the sharp coffee, being it was all she had to keep her hands occupied and to fill the void in her belly. "Are you Carl's nephew or son?"

"Why does that even matter?"

Kayla shrugged. "Guess it doesn't. So, what would you like for dinner and supper?"

"Can you even cook?"

"Does a rattlesnake bite?"

Ben's mouth twitched again. She wanted him to smile genuinely, not this sarcastic half smile she was getting used to him doing. He was a handsome man, rugged, and strong like how her mother used to say all cowboys were.

Her Pa wasn't a cowhand, but a thief. Kayla wasn't like that. Her mother wasn't like that. So, Ma left after Pa got caught and strung up, and eventually married a cowboy when she was a small girl. Kayla gained a stepbrother and shortly after another half-brother. Loren was a sweet child, adventurous and smart, going off to do accounting. The woman he married turned him into a thieving drunk when her demands for comfort exceeded Loren's honest wage. Her death, and the death of the unborn child she carried, twisted him cruel. Her half-brother, Donald was long gone and dead in the ground from fever.

Kayla stared despondently into the tin cup, trying to shake her dismal thoughts. The remaining coffee offered her an ebony reflection. She wasn't thirsty in the slightest. However, to be polite to the man who was allowing her to live, she would drink it. Kayla saw him observing her, assessing her like she was him.

He probably thought she was a despicable woman for getting messed in with them. She didn't blame him. She was mad at herself for believing different.

*Some people can't change no matter how much you hope and love them,* she decided.

"What kind of meals do you hate?" she asked.

"What?"

"What kind of meals do you hate, so I won't cook it."

"I don't like peas and sprouts," he paused, shifting in his chair. "How is your leg?"

Kayla rubbed it mechanically. "Just fine."

"If you can manage, I will take you to the cookhouse."

"I can manage."

# CHAPTER FOUR

K ayla Langmoore was not what he expected her to be. He expected a crying, sniveling mess of a lady, begging for her life. She didn't do any of that. She faced the outcome with steel reserve.

Ben watched how her dirty hair was pulled messily off her face in a braid to the side. A black eye formed on her right eye where the man stuck her from the night before. Thieving and striking a woman, Ben would never tolerate. May the Lord forgive the man who hurt a woman. Kayla didn't deserve that. Kayla was a beautiful woman. Too bad she was a thief and her family too. He didn't believe a word she said about not thieving. It was in her blood. Some people can't change their ways and no one can change their blood.

Her small oval face was dirty. Her green eyes scanned the area with cautiousness. Any movement, she spun in the direction, eyes wide, viewing the area intently like she was waiting to be struck once more. He hated watching her get hit, but he also couldn't have his position given away until the opportune moment. There was much more at stake than a thief of a woman, no matter how pretty she was. When the man shot her, his heart leapt into his throat. In all his thirty years, he'd never seen someone shoot at a woman.

Ben shook his head, leading her to the cookhouse. She walked with her head high, slightly limping. Her emerald eyes shone bright. Other than that, she kept her face passive.

Ben snorted. *A thief with pride*, he thought.

He opened the door for her, offering her a hand to step inside. Kayla didn't take his hand, instead hoisting herself into the lifted house.

"Your room is around the corner. Breakfast at six. Dinner at noon. Supper at six. Think you can manage that?" Ben said gruffly.

Kayla's brows furrowed. "Sure can. Grouse sound good?"

"Yeah."

"Shoot me a few, please?"

Ben nodded. "Take a bath before you start cooking. We don't want dirt in our food."

Kayla flushed. She looked uncertainly out the window. She wrung her hands on the cleanest part of her dress. This was the most distressed he'd seen her so far.

"What?" he asked, slightly concerned.

"I don't have clothes. The horse I rode is gone with the spare I had."

"I will get you somethin'." Ben assured feeling a tad guilty at not thinking about it before. "Bathhouse is the building to the left," he said pointing.

Kayla nodded, heading to the place he directed. By all counts he shouldn't be getting her anything. She owed his father a debt for saving her sorry hide, pulling the bullet out of her leg and not stringing her up. He'd have to add clothes to the tally she owed before she could go free.

Ben walked to the stables. His mount, Ridge already saddled and tied out front waiting for him. This morning he was supposed to ride fences with Roy.

He shook his head in disbelief, *I'm getting a thief a dress.*

Ben strode to the back of the barn where his mother's trunks were kept. She put her slimmer dresses inside, hoping to someday, eventually, get down to a smaller size, but hadn't and gave up hope she ever would. Instead, she saved them all for his future wife. Ben rolled his eyes. His mother, Sarah, been so excited to learn another woman was on the ranch. Her happiness quickly turned to anger when she heard the reason why. Sarah didn't care the circumstances of Kayla's plight. His mother and he agreed, Kayla was a thief.

"Ben," his mother hollered from the doorway of the barn, "is the thief awake?"

He nodded. "Making her take a bath. I don't want dirt in my food."

"What are you doing with my trunk?"

Ben popped the lid. "She needs a dress."

Sarah huffed. "Fine. Give *that* wretched girl my green calico. Keep her *out* of the house."

"Yes ma'am," Ben replied closing the lid.

His mother stormed off to the house. Sarah hated thieves more so than his father. Carl believed there was good in everyone, no matter how wrongly they'd done him or anyone else. Sarah, on the other hand, believed once a sin was committed, the person was forever a sinner, especially when it came to killing or stealing.

Ben gripped the dress tight, going to the bath house. Kayla's teeth chattered from inside. He opened the door, stepping inside with his back to her. Ben passed the dress backwards, feeling the gentle womanly touch take it out of his hands.

"Thank you," she said, her teeth clacking.

"Wash up then straight to cooking."

"Yes sir."

"Sir?" he asked, snorting derisively.

"Yes, sir. You are my boss."

"That would be Mr. and Mrs. Coleman you address," he said, walking out and slamming the door behind him.

Last night, he was ready to take her to jail. His father, Carl, stayed his motion. Upon listening to his and the cowhands' story, Carl believed Kayla was a simple woman who was in the wrong place at the wrong time. She, by Ben's reckoning, should be six feet under. Like his mother taught him since he was little – killing, lying and stealing are the worst sins a person can commit. Kayla, he was certain, was both a liar and a thief.

Ben headed back to his mount who tossed his head at his approach. He mounted deftly, leading the way out to the green pasture where the cattle were lazily grazing. Roy and George sat on horseback a mile up. Ben could see their tiny dots sitting, watching the herd.

Ben allowed his horse some lead to trot, burn off the energy his stallion never seemed to be rid of. It was noon now, his night and routine shot for the day.

"Afternoon," he grouched, coming up in between his cowhands.

Roy smirked. "She is a purty thing."

Ignoring Roy's comment, "How is the line?" Ben asked.

"South pasture holds true. There was a break in the west one. Hank is out fixing it now," Roy replied.

"And the cattle, George?" Ben prompted.

The man to the right shrugged. "Fine. Three heifers will be ready to calve soon. The calves that need branding are in the holding pen."

Ben spun his horse around. "Let's get started."

# CHAPTER FIVE

Kayla moved about the kitchen lithely, popping an apple crisp in the oven. It was almost one and there was still no grouse. Kayla resorted to killing two of the many chickens for their dinner. They were frying on the stove.

The feathers she used to plump up the sad looking pillow for her bed. She hung up a screen too. She assumed the last person to use the bed was a man for it smelled like leather and horse. She didn't mind the smell. In fact, she would have gladly slept in the barn if they'd offered.

Her leg was beginning to pain her a little more. Certain movements made her stitches feel like they were tearing. Without a doubt, she would have a scar there. It was the price she paid for being so naive.

Kayla smiled wanly. Her mind took her back to when she was about eight. Ma just married her stepfather. Her brother Loren smiled at her, giving her a bouquet of small wild roses, thorns plucked clean. *I'm happy yer my sister, Kayla. I will protect you,* he told her. And he did. He grew up into a fine man. However, the woman he married was the devil and took him down a path, she didn't think Loren could walk.

Kayla bent down, pulling the crisp out of the oven. She hissed at the pain in her side from being kicked. She never had much of a pain tolerance, but thought she did quite well at putting on a brave show for Ben.

Her mind wandered to when Mrs. Coleman came into the kitchen not one hour ago, fiercely mad, telling her to stay away from Ben. Kayla had no intentions of a relationship with a man who thought her a liar and a thief. She may be indebted to him for fixing her up and not hanging her, but she didn't want him and had no problem telling the crotchety woman this. Aside from saving her, she owed him nothing. She didn't even like him. He'd judged her before getting to know who she really was. She'd kept bad company. She made a mistake. It didn't make her a bad person. However, Ben's mind was made up. As his mothers.

Kayla sniffed, feeling tears sting the back of her eyes. She'd no one in this world to help her through this. No one, but God, although she was certain the man was on holiday, for he didn't answer her prayers anymore.

"Keep your head above water," she told herself.

She walked outside into the warm afternoon sun to a shaded area where a picnic table sat. Earlier, while rummaging for pots and pans, she came across some white linen. A little more snooping found some nice dishes, ones she'd seen on a mercantile shelf. Opting for the cooler option, instead of inside a cookhouse or on the sunlit porch, she set the picnic table with the wares, dessert, and rolls.

Kayla went back into the kitchen, bringing out the heaping tray of fried chicken pieces, along with green beans, soft boiled herb potatoes and butter. Carl and his wife were the first to sit at the table, piling food on their plates. The other five chairs were reserved for Ben and the other hands who followed on their heels.

Kayla went back into the kitchen before anyone could utter a word to her. She began cleaning up, watching out the small side window while everyone ate with smiles on their faces. How she longed to have something like that in her life; it was one of the reasons she leapt at the chance to start anew with Loren. She wanted to be around family, maybe eventually have her own. God obviously didn't want her to have that right now, if ever.

With a sigh, Kayla finished rinsing out the bowl of flour she used to make the batter for the chicken. She saw Ben help himself to more chicken. Another man to his right, heaped his plate full of green beans.

Kayla smiled. "At least they like my cooking."

Dishes done, she inhaled deeply, gathering her courage. "Gotta clear plates. Then I will eat what's left."

She opened the door outside, the people shushing down at her approach. Kayla did her best to hide the limp caused by the bullet wound. Mrs. Coleman glared daggers at her. Heat crept to her cheeks. If looks could kill, she'd have a bullet in her heart.

Kayla smiled politely. "If anyone is done, I'd be happy to take your plate."

Carl leaned back and stretched, groaning as he did so. "Mighty fine meal Ms. Langmoore."

Kayla dipped into a curtsey. A hard breath escaped her lips at the sharp pain from her thigh and side from the movement. "Thank you, sir."

"Is that an apple crisp?" another man pointed and asked.

"Yes, sir it is," Kayla replied.

"At least the horrible thief has manners," Mrs. Coleman quipped.

"Yes ma'am," Kayla said, losing her smile.

The same man got her attention again, clearing his throat. "Can we eat it now?"

"Yes sir. I will be making molasses cookies later. Small ones you can carry in your shirt pocket while riding fence so leave room for those too."

The man struck the table, grinning. "I'll be dogged. Someone who cooks better than Larry!"

Carl Coleman laughed. "Ben, how did you find your meal?"

"Good, Pa. We gotta get back to work. Roy, George come back with me. Garrett and Joseph, keep an eye on the northern herd."

The men split from the table, leaving her to clear it. Taking a cloth napkin, Roy stuck a piece of apple crisp in his hand, holding it up to her in thanks. Kayla dipped her head, smiling shyly. Roy brought his hand to his mouth, pulling on the napkin to eat the crumbly dessert mid-walk.

Carl let out a long sigh. "Moment of truth," he said while putting a piece of crisp on his plate.

Kayla watched him fork a crumbly apple piece, putting it to his mouth. The man made sounds as he chewed, clearly pleased with her cooking. "You are not allowed to leave, young lady," he said with a wink, and a teasing tone.

"Thank you, sir, glad you liked it," Kayla responded, piling more plates into her arms with a small grin.

"Steal or lie to us and we will hang you where you stand," Mrs. Coleman said, rising from her seat. "Is that understood?"

"Yes ma'am."

Mrs. Coleman stormed off to the large house. Kayla looked down, feeling the sting of regret and defeat hang on her shoulders heavier than a beam from a cabin. With a deep breath, she turned back toward the cook house.

"Young lady," Mr. Coleman called.

Kayla paused, spinning around, feeling the stinging sensation in her eyes and nose wanting to spill tears. "Yes sir?"

"Put those down on the table and come chat with me."

Kayla did as she was bid, a bit hesitantly. Her feet faltered, the cumbersome plates shifting with her awkward step, and her thigh and side aching, threatening to succumb at any moment. Kayla's hands fumbled over themselves, setting what she had back on the table. She settled herself a chair away from Carl, her face fixed in what she hoped was an unemotional mask. He gazed at her with hard blue eyes, mouth set in a firm line. Kayla swallowed. This man held her life in his calloused hands.

"Guilty by association," he began, "am I wrong?"

Kayla shook her head. "No, sir."

"Now I heard you thought you were coming here to work. Consider that your interview. You got yourself a job. In one week, you will earn wages if you choose to stay."

"Thank you, sir," Kayla said, not meeting his intense gaze.

He softened, offering her compassion she'd not seen in a long while. Kayla studied him, noticing the eagle-like observance of his eyes while remembering the fairness in his words. He offered her a second chance. She wouldn't squander it. This man, gave her a home, a job and a second chance. To say she was grateful was an understatement.

"You're young and naive. The Lord and I forgive you for that. Stay away from my son and house. Fly the straight and narrow."

"Yes sir," Kayla nodded, getting up from her seat. "Thank you for allowing me another chance, and for fixing me up. I promise to not be a burden and to stay clear of Ben."

"Good girl. You are excused," he said rising after her. His gaze lingered on her a moment, the laughter lines in his face reaching his eyes. "Mighty fine meal," he complimented again.

Kayla dipped into a curtsey. Going past the table, she grabbed the dishes. Her face burned with shame at the way Mrs. Coleman looked at her and Mr. Coleman expressed the need to remind her to stay away from Ben. Her eyes longed to shed tears. She had a good life prior to this mess; friends, a nice job at The Hitchin' Post, and a man who, she thought, was about to call on her. She had a life back in Oklahoma. Why on God's green earth did she ever listen to Loren?

# CHAPTER SIX

Her beef stew was almost ready. She hadn't eaten since yesterday and her stomach was growling in protest. Kayla rushed from inside the cookhouse to the outside table. The dining table was laden with herbed rolls for supper and two plates full of molasses cookies.

The men were gathering around the table. Eager faces greeted her own.

"Roy, can you please carry the stew pot. I don't trust my leg," she shouted over her shoulder, setting the plate of cookies down.

"Sure thing. I'm gonna be a fat hog off your cooking."

Kayla laughed boisterously. "You sure won't be employed long."

Roy's thunderous laugh boomed from inside the kitchen, fading as he walked out of the kitchen with the large stew pot in his hands sniffing audibly. "Smells mighty fine!"

This time, there was an extra chair, situated between Roy and Garrett. Kayla stared at it for a moment, looking to Carl for affirmation. The man nodded, a twinkle in his vigilant blue eyes, gesturing she should sit. Kayla sat down, folding her hands in her lap. Her fingers fiddled with her dress folds, feeling uncertainty prickle at her skin.

Carl blessed the food before they all dug in. Each man, made moaning sounds deep in their throat. Kayla chortled at them all.

"Something funny?" Carl asked with a smile and raised eyebrow.

Kayla fixed her face back into her formal mask. "No sir," she said, shaking her head.

"Ben tells me you're from Oklahoma."

Kayla patted her mouth with a cloth napkin. "Yes, sir."

"Sir is getting mighty old. Call me Carl. Now, which part?"

Kayla made a moue. "I can't remember. I was little when Ma and I left Oklahoma for Omaha."

"Sorry to hear that. What brought you to Texas?"

Kayla shrugged, staring down at her lap. "Hope, I guess."

"Hope for what?" Carl pried.

Kayla fidgeted with her fingers more, beginning to pick at her fingernails. Frowning down at her lap she sighed. "A better life..." she trailed off a moment, taking a hard, deep breath, "You might as well know. When my Pa died, Ma decided to move to Omaha and there she remarried. Life was happy. I gained an older stepbrother Loren and later, a half-brother Donald. Ma and my step-pa died one winter. They went to town for supplies and never came back. I was taken back to Oklahoma to be with my grandparents, only to find they passed on. Loren and Donald went to theirs in St. Louis. I was taken to an orphanage for five years. Once I turned seventeen, I began working at The Hitchin' Post Dining Hotel as a cook. Loren found me at my job and he is the reason I am here right now. He said he found out about me in a paper because of my baking. Loren came to me, promising me a better life, better pay and a chance to be a family again. I made a good life where I was, but I was thrilled to be around family," Kayla trailed off, shaking her head.

Mr. Coleman nodded. "And here you are."

Kayla nodded. "Yes sir... Here I am."

"Glad you are here then. No harm done. I don't know you well enough, but I can say I am pretty keen on reading people. You are not a liar nor a thief. You did keep bad company."

Kayla smiled wanly. "I won't deny that. I surely did."

Carl raised his brows with a warm smile. "Look Sarah, she is blunt like you."

Mrs. Coleman narrowed her eyes a bit. The sharpness of her gaze sent chills down Kayla's arms. There would be no pleasing the woman in this life or the next.

"Great meal, Kayla," Garrett praised, breaking the tension Kayla felt directed toward her by Mrs. Coleman.

Kayla thanked him with a smile and a slight bow of her head. Life might have handed her hard knocks, this being one of her more difficult ones, but she always came through. It was nice of the Coleman's to treat her well. Now, she needed to fly the straight and narrow like she promised Carl by staying away from Ben. Truth was, that could be a bit hard.

Kayla peeked casually to the right attempting to make it appear like she was searching for the rolls. Ben passed her the basket. Kayla sucked in a breath when their hands briefly touched. She glanced away quickly, passing it off by putting two on her plate then passing the basket to Roy.

When people begun to leave for bed, she started cleaning up. Roy lit the oil lamps for her so she wouldn't have to wash dishes by moonlight. One by one, she stacked the clean plates onto the drying rack for morning. Wringing her hands dry on her dish towel, she stepped outside into the cooler night air. Crickets hummed a soothing tune. The horses in the barn whickered softly.

With a smile, she ambled to the barn. Inhaling deeply the aroma of hay and dirt. She closed her eyes, remembering the scent of home, how her step-pa always smelled of hay and leather. How Ma would call his name at night for supper, the sound of his name starting low then rising high with her voice, and the smile Pa made when he took Ma in his arms for a nightly kiss.

Kayla leaned against a stall, watching a large palomino munch on oats. She longed for her family back. How she prayed her parents were just sleeping and not truly dead. It was months before she realized the prayer was never going to be answered the way she wanted. Kayla wiped her eyes, stamping her foot. They were long gone now, more than likely a pile of bones. How much would her life have been different had they lived?

"Tarnation," she cursed, sniffling.

The palomino leaned over to her, nuzzling her with his soft nose. Kayla rubbed her cheek against the side of his sweet face. She patted him, loving on him. The horse stuck his head out of the stall, putting his head over her shoulder.

"You're a sweet boy," Kayla praised.

She spoke to the horse for a while. His ears twitched forwards and backwards, listening to her. Kayla found herself blabbering to the animal about the life she longed to have, but did not think she would ever receive. The horse listened contentedly seeming to understand. Her happy memories got whickers and her troubles received nudge-like hugs. With another hug she patted him, ready to leave when a voice startled her.

"He is green too, so be careful."

Kayla smiled, spinning around to Ben behind her. "I think you need your eyes checked."

Ben frowned, raising an eyebrow, "Excuse me?"

"He isn't green. He is peach colored," she said with a chuckle.

Ben smirked. "Aren't you funny."

Kayla's heart skipped a beat, watching Ben walk near and stroke the horse on the head. A polite smile gracing his stubbled face.

"Good night," Kayla said, rushing off before she said or did something she would regret later.

She had a promise to keep.

# CHAPTER SEVEN

Ben observed her for a while, loving on a beast that would not let many people near it. This woman lied to a horse about some nonsense about not being her given name. Truth was, she was like her given name - a thief. Even if his father cleared her of the name, she was still a thief. His father was too soft and she practically confessed her guilt by making the horse her confidant. No innocent would choose a horse over a person and no amount of righteousness would fix that. God may forgive easily; people were not so simple. A thief could not be trusted.

However, his attention was grabbed by how calm the horse stood there, letting her pet and hug it. He wasn't spooked or agitated, just still. His ears pointed forward on high alert. The horse whickered softly, responding to her quiet talkative manner. In fact, it was the most he ever heard a woman speak to a horse.

Now that she was thankfully gone, he could shut down the barn for the night, lock everyone inside safely. Ben looked out the barn, observing Kayla make her way back to the cookhouse.

"Kayla," he hollered.

Her slender frame turned around. A pensive smile graced her face. Her eyes bright under the awakening stars.

"Can you make sausages for breakfast?" he asked.

She nodded. "Sure can."

She grabbed the handle on the door.

"Kayla," Garrett hollered from the bunkhouse a few buildings down. "Can you make those flakey, sweet, blueberry triangle thingies?"

Kayla laughed. Her honied voice ringing out over the prairie. "Scones. And yes, I can."

Garrett grinned turning into the bunkhouse. Roy came out next, standing in the door frame.

"Can you make more cookies?" he hollered across the way.

Kayla laughed shaking her head. "I will get in trouble."

"For what?" Roy asked confused.

"For making you all plump and unable to work. Good night."

Ben chortled, finally shutting the barn doors. He loathed to admit it, but he liked her sense of humor. His former fiancé, Clara, never laughed and hardly smiled. Everything with her was serious as the scar on his face. His mother chose Clara, the wealthy daughter of a merchant, for him. Clara was lively as a napkin with curls on her head, taut and lifeless like her personality. He loved her, and pined for her to love him back. He sighed heavily. It was not meant to be. Clara tolerated his affections and his presence, and barely. No matter what he did, it was never good enough, but he tried and loved her.

He rubbed the scar on his face, heading to the bunk house. The sun was about set. Creatures of the night would be lurking around. He needed to get up early in the morning to take a few head of cattle to auction in San Antonio.

Ben turned around, at the bunkhouse door. The light went out inside the kitchen. Without another glance, he went inside. A pretty thief should not capture his attentions.

# CHAPTER EIGHT

Kayla woke before anyone else, grabbing the shotgun above the kitchen door. With a handful of bird shot, she set off east, going toward the rising sun. The gray of the sky slowly turning pink.

She picked up a rock, tossing it into the thicker brush. Grouse stirred from their slumber, shrieking, flapping madly into the sky. The gunshot rang like thunder, echoing off a nearby canyon. The grouse she hit, fell to the ground. She grinned at her excellent, clean shot.

Carefully, she made her way to it. Grouse were not the only creatures awake this morning. She needed to be alert for rattlers. Kayla picked up the dead bird, accidentally scaring some more. She took aim and shot another. The grouse fell to the ground.

She grinned at her kills. "Grouse pie," she mused.

"Land sakes Kayla!"

Kayla turned around. The blood draining from her face. Ben, pistol drawn, came barreling toward her, his face contorted in anger. She offered a chipper smile she didn't feel, holding up her kills. Ben neared, and the smile fell from her face. She took a step back.

"Mornin' Ben," she said, tentatively, grateful her voice didn't shake.

"We all thought you were in trouble!" Ben growled.

Kayla swallowed, plastering a smile back on her face. "No trouble. Just getting a meal."

"Where did you get the gun?" he said striding toward her. "Steal it did you?"

His face twisted in disgust. She hoped to never see that look again. His eyes darkened from beautiful turquoise blue to a dark stormy gray. His jawline ticked, ripping the shotgun from her hands. Kayla jumped, taking a few more paces back. She dropped the grouse to toss the remaining shells at his feet before he could rip them from her. Kayla raised her hands, ready to defend herself.

Kayla gulped. "It was above the kitchen door."

"And the shells?"

"On the shelf to the right."

Kayla looked over Ben's muscled frame. Roy, Garrett and Carl were all waiting near the house, rifles and shotguns out in front of them. She wanted to hang her head in shame, but she'd done nothing wrong. Their eyes felt like daggers. Holding her head high, she picked up her kills, taking them with her to the cookhouse. Ben yelling at her back and to the others about what she'd done. With groans, the men went back to their tasks, glaring at both of them.

Kayla fumed. Mornings were a good time to hunt. Yesterday, she asked Ben to shoot her some grouse, but he hadn't. And if she went to him, she would be breaking her promise to both Mr. and Mrs. Coleman to keep away. And everyone else would be busy today.

At supper last night, it was mentioned the cattle were to go to auction today; some to different ranches, others to the butcher shop. Today was a big day for them all, so she needed to feed them a large enough meal to tide them over. More than likely, they would all miss dinner, so a nosebag of food would need to be made. Luckily, she had some left overs that would work perfectly for their meals. But it wouldn't hurt to make extra, hence the grouse.

Kayla set the birds down outside on a back table, stripping the feathers, then gutting them. She got a large bowl of water to soak the birds in. The grainy birdshot came out better.

Glancing up, Kayla caught her breath. The sun rose fully over the hills. The gold of the sun combined with the pink-purple of the clouds was like heaven on earth exploding over the valley. "Better than any painting."

A scruffy brown cat came twirling in between her legs. Kayla smiled at her new friend. "Good mornin' pretty kitty," she said, bending down and scratched the cat under the chin. "Hungry?"

The cat made a large mewl. Kayla reached into the bowl of gizzards, handing the cat a piece. The cat took the gut piece, quickly making an exit with its tail high. Bootsteps stomped through the kitchen. Kayla rose, not paying attention to who tromped through the kitchen and out the back door toward her spot, instead, watching the cat's tail disappear.

"I cannot believe that mangy thing let you touch it," Ben remarked, his deep voice a bit gruff.

Kayla picked up her bowl of grouse. Moving around Ben she brought it inside. "Everything needs a little love."

Ben took his hat off. "I'm sorry,"

"No need," she interrupted. "I get it. Now, if you will excuse me, I have breakfast to make," her tone terse and unfeeling.

Kayla marched into the kitchen, pausing at the shelves to grab the flour and sugar to make some scones. She hadn't meant to be so gruff. Between his words and actions, a bit ago, and her promise to the Coleman's she didn't know how else to be. She had to keep away.

Kayla let out a long sigh. All she would amount to here at the Circle 8 was a thief. But she wasn't. And her dream of wanting a family was far gone. With everyone here knowing about her, none would want her. While she wasn't old, she had to make enough to leave and start anew elsewhere. That could be a long time from now, so once again, her dream of family would have to wait.

She dried her eyes with the back of her hand. "Tarnation," she cursed, letting out another long breath. "Chin up girl."

# CHAPTER NINE

Ben reined in his horse. He spied Kayla coming out of the cookhouse carrying three packs all knotted at the top. She appeared bound to fall over with her arms loaded. With a grin she came up to each of their horses, offering a sack full of dinner. When she handed him the last one, the smile didn't reach her eyes. She looked relieved, walking away from him.

Her breakfast was a quick and filling affair. He wanted to be on the road to auction and she complied. Everyone was fed and readied in about an hour. How she made all of the food happen, he did not know and couldn't help, but admire.

Without a backwards glance, she turned on her heel.

"What did ya pack Kayla?" Garrett shouted.

She stopped, spinning back around with a beaming smile that followed her no matter what she was doing, unless she was near him. This morning's interactions no longer seeming to disturb her. She did not let on otherwise.

Kayla shielded her hand over her face. "Sandwiches with lettuce, tomato and bacon, three molasses cookies, beef jerky, a blueberry scone and two apples."

"Why two apples?" Roy asked.

"One is for the horse," she laughed, spinning back around. Picking up the hems of her skirts, the same skirts she wore yesterday, she jogged back to the kitchen. Ben spun his mount around to face the men staring in the direction Kayla walked off in.

Garrett grinned wider than the Rio Grande. His eyes not leaving the cookhouse. "She be a mighty fine cook."

Roy readily agreed. "Sure is. Best I ate in a long time. I don't think I would mind being fat off her cookin'."

Ben chortled. "I would. Then I would have to hire a new hand."

"She sure is pretty too," Garrett remarked. "I wanna call on her."

Ben spun in his saddle, disgust plain on his face, and in his voice. "Callin' on a thief?"

Garrett blew his lips and frowned. "She ain't no thief. We all know it. She happened to be in the wrong place at the wrong time."

"She *is* a thief, Garrett. She was caught on Circle 8 property with a group whose intentions were to rustle cattle. Best you remember it," Ben said. "Joseph, release the herd, we're goin' to town."

The man on the gate waved his hat, flinging the latch to the corral wide open. The cattle came barreling out, all branded with a large 8 wrapped in a circle on their left flanks. Ben caught a glimpse of Kayla standing by the cookhouse, smiling. She shaded her eyes with her arm. He shook his head.

*How on God's green earth can she smile so darn much? Surely, there can't be much to smile over, or for.* Ben turned his horse, trotting along the fence line, pushing the cattle toward the open road. Taking a fleeting glance in Kayla's direction. She stood on the front steps of the kitchen, a grin from ear to ear.

*Land sakes, either she is part daft, or she loves cows... There has to be something for that woman to smile so much... Sure is pretty though... Damnit!* He shook his head, forcing her from his minds and refocused on the herd.

It was going to be at least a two-hour trip to town with the cattle; more if something happened to go wrong.

San Antonio was a busy place, but more so on auction day. The train whistle blew loudly, calling the other cowboys to rustle their cattle onto the train cars to be hauled back to the busier towns.

"At least we aren't late," Garrett remarked.

"Let's go. Floyd is waiting at the butcher shop. Garrett, take four with you and head there. Roy and I will take the rest to auction."

"Yes boss," Garrett said, cutting out four head and going in the opposite direction.

"I think he is mad at you," Roy said, leaning in the saddle. "Kayla is a good woman."

"She is a *thief*," Ben bit back.

Roy snorted. "She ain't no thief."

Ben turned sharply to him. "She was with them. Only thing saving her hide is her tellin' them not to do it."

"Exactly," Roy exclaimed trotting ahead. "Remember a couple years ago? I killed a man in self-defense, the night we got attacked on the road to Fort Worth. By the definition you're applying to Kayla, I'm a killer and deserve to be hung. Yet you have told me repeatedly, I am not. I did what I had to survive. Wrong place, wrong time. I am no more a murderer than Kayla is a thief."

Ben grumbled, turning away. He let out a shrill whistle, letting the auction master know he was coming. Roy got the cattle charging, running toward the large pen on the outskirts of town. Young boys stopped to watch, awe struck by Ben's herd and men. Roy dismounted when one of the auction hands closed the pen.

Roy smiled tying his mount to the post. "Time for dinner," he announced.

"You go eat. I gotta dicker prices," Ben said, striding off to the man with the board.

He scuffed his boots in the dirt, making his way to the auctioneer. His mind wandering to the woman with dark brown hair and spring grass eyes. Admittedly, Kayla was a beautiful young woman, and so different than Clara. Kayla was funny, optimistic, and appreciated what was around her. Three qualities Clara would never possess, yet he loved her anyways, hoped it was enough to keep her at the Circle 8. It wasn't. Nothing he bought Clara or did for her, was ever adequate. From the wedding invitations to the dress he paid for, nothing was sufficient to gain a modicum of affection.

He looked at the train, remembering vividly the day Clara left for Philadelphia.

*My heart can never be yours Benjamin,* she began with a vehemence in her eyes he'd not seen before. *My brother found me a match more suitable to my lifestyle and needs, in Philadelphia. I have been corresponding with him for a while and I have accepted his engagement instead. I will be leaving on the evening train. Thank you for taking care of me while my family has been away.* She stormed with her suitcases out of his house, not looking back. Roy took her in the buggy to the station. Ben followed, pining after her, knowing it would do no good, unable to help himself. He did not love the woman now, but missed what he could have had – a family of his own.

Now, he couldn't stop thinking about a woman caught red handed, about to steal cattle. What was he even thinking? His parents told him not to get close to her. His mother even told *her* to stay away. True to her word, Kayla did. For some blasted reason he couldn't. There was something about the woman that appealed to him. She wasn't timid in the slightest. Even when the smile didn't reach her eyes, tears pooling slightly at the corners, her smile was mortared to her face, bringing forth her optimism to the situation instead of crumbling. Kayla was kind to everything she came across, even him, who seldom uttered a civil word to her.

*I've been an ass,* he thought, rubbing the back of his neck. *She's been courteous to me while I have disparaged her. Kayla didn't deserve it.*

"Afternoon, Ben," the auction master called. "Come to make me a broke man again, I see."

Ben grinned. "Not quite, Daniel. I aim to try"

"Goin' rate is six dollars a head."

"Make it eight."

Daniel sighed, lowering his board with paper on top. "Now see, that kinda talk is going to make me broke," he finished with a smile.

"No, it won't. We both know that."

"Seven twenty-five."

Ben stared at him.

"It's more than fair," Daniel said.

"You know darn well our beef is best and will fetch no less than ten dollars a head. You may even get twelve if you use your silver tongue," Ben replied crossing his arms.

"I ain't arguing that."

Ben's grin widened, "Seven fifty."

Daniel scowled, but his eyes twinkled. "Fine, fine. You get your way. How many head you bring in?"

"Fifty."

Daniel scribbled on a piece of paper, handing it to him. "Have Earl pay you out."

Ben grinned, shaking his hand. "Thank you, Daniel, much obliged."

Daniel went off in the other direction, shaking his head. He threw over his shoulder, shouting, "I'm sure you are."

With the envelope of money in hand from Earl, Ben exited the small building next to the auctioning corral. Gazing around the bustling town, he remembered why he didn't like coming. The solitude and scenery of the Texas plains appealed to him over the hollering of city folk. Ben strode back to their meeting place at the large oak that marked the way out of San Antonio. His horse's reins fumbling in his calloused hands in a fit of nerves. Roy and Garrett were already there, tucking into the sandwiches Kayla made. His stomach rumbled, eager to dive into the meal under the cool shade. He was also eager to get back home.

Garrett wore a wide smile, Ben was surprised he could chew. "That is a good sandwich," Garrett said. "Have you eaten yet Ben?"

He shook his head. There was another two-hour ride back to the homestead. He could always eat on the way.

"Naw... Wanna get back home," Ben said fidgeting with the saddle on Ridge.

"I wonder what Kayla is going to make with the grouse she shot."

"All you think about is food," Roy teased.

"Don't you, after all those horrible burnt or dry meals Larry made?"

"All right, let's go," Ben said stifling a chuckle and mounting, riding off down the road with them.

Ben dug into his sandwich. The bustling city fading behind him. Garrett and Roy caught up, pulling up on either side of him. Garrett was correct, Kayla's sandwich was scrumptious. He devoured it in several bites, not realizing how hungry he'd been until the sandwich was gone. He tucked into the other items she packed.

"She gave you an extra cookie!" Garrett complained.

Ben rolled his eyes, breaking it in half, "Here you both go, *children.*"

Garrett and Roy took their halves eagerly, shoving them into their faces with smiles.

"So good," Roy mumbled.

Ben nibbled on the remaining food in the sack she packed him. A grin twitched at the corner of his mouth at the food and the woman who made it. The twitch faded and his shoulders fell. Even if he could get past what Kayla had done, there was no way she would love him. Not with the scar on his face and the darkness in his heart.

# CHAPTER TEN

She cooked and baked to keep her mind off of Benjamin Coleman. Truth was, it was mighty hard. Ben was the type of man where the room stilled when he entered it. People held him in high regard and respected him. At least, that's how she saw him.

He was handsome, albeit standoffish which was to be blamed on the circumstances they had met under. Ben deemed her a thief, a cattle rustler and a liar. Even though she hadn't done any of those things, she had kept bad company, and it was sin enough to damn her. Ben would never like her.

Carl cleared her of her crimes. Her only requirement was to pay back Carl who fixed her up. Then she was cleared to go. She had a few days left until her debt was paid. Part of her didn't want to leave. Having a job and being near Ben was enough for her at the moment.

*At least until the next misunderstanding,* she ruefully grinned at herself.

Kayla tilted her head to the side, kneading bread dough.

Ben was tall, much more than her. Kayla was sure she barely came up to his armpit. His blue eyes were prettier than the grandest of bluebonnet flowers or even the Texas sky. When their hands touched briefly the other night, she felt her arms crackle with ice. He sent shivers racing through her body. Her heart felt like it was going to catch fire. She wanted to be the woman he wanted. But she wasn't. His family would make certain they steered clear from each other.

Kayla hung her head, focusing her eyes on the bread dough. She scowled, and punched the dough down over and over again, becoming angry at ever following Loren. Her stepbrother not only put her in harms way, but harmed her too. She raised her right hand and slapped the mixture, irritated at the circumstances. Kayla sighed, going back to kneading. She could be angry all she wanted, but her name was cleared.

"I'm glad I'm not the dough."

Kayla looked up; her brows raised high. Heat crept to her cheeks. "How was town?" she ventured to ask, her voice cracking.

Ben shrugged, coming in the doorway. "All right. Got the price I wanted for the cattle."

Kayla nodded, feeling a lump form in her throat. *Don't make eye contact, you'll swoon*, she chided. *Good Lord, he's already making my legs weak. Don't meet his eyes.*

"I came to ask you, what you made with the grouse you shot? The boys are mighty hungry."

"I made pies in a gravy and rolls to sop it all up," she replied, her eyes focused intently on the bread. "Sweet tea and lemonade are on the table."

She peeped out the corner of her eyes. His dusty boots and pants all she could see. His voice sent an icy shiver up her arms. She wanted him to embrace her. It would go against her promise if she initiated it, and he never would, being he loathed her so much. Kayla swallowed. It was becoming more difficult to keep that promise. Perhaps after she repaid Mr. Coleman for fixing her up, it would be best to leave.

Ben shifted his hat in his rough hands. "Thank you," he replied, leaving immediately.

Kayla let out the breath she was holding. "What on earth am I thinkin'!" she scolded herself.

"The dough won't answer you," Ben yelled back.

Her eyes went wide. "Blast it all," she mumbled.

She set the dough aside to rise to bring out the evening meal. It was a good thing she made four grouse pies. The leftover meat would make an excellent stew for supper tomorrow. She grinned to herself feeling a little lighter. These men ate her food like it was the last meal they would ever have.

Much to her surprise, after everyone ate, Mrs. Coleman praised her for a lovely meal. Mrs. Coleman, or as Kayla was now allowed to call her, Sarah, seemed mostly content Kayla was staying away from her son. Sarah's shrewd gaze glanced over her with a hint of malevolence that bore ill for Kayla.

"Benjamin," Sarah began, "I believe it is time for you to settle down."

The table went eerily silent. Instead of the lively banter taking place, it changed drastically to clanking of silverware on plates. Kayla swallowed. Her heart clenched. She stared down at her hands in her lap.

Ben cleared his throat. "Another time, mother."

"Benjamin, I only want what is best for you. I have made arrangements," Sarah said smugly, pleased with herself.

"Mother," Ben interrupted, his tone a mix of desperate and firm. "Another time, please."

Sarah Coleman went silent, shrugging and sipping on her coffee.

Kayla wanted Ben. She wanted to wake up in the morning beside him, husband and wife, and the like. She wanted to be the one he came home to. She held her breath, struggling not to lose her composure. There would never be any hope between her and Ben. She'd better get used to it. Trouble was, she didn't think she could. Every vision of the future she had, put Ben right beside her.

"Another fine meal Kayla," Carl Coleman praised breaking the awkward tension.

"Thank you, Mr. Coleman," she replied, thankful for the break in her thoughts.

"Settled for Mr. instead of sir?"

Kayla smiled. "Absolutely."

Carl grinned. "All right. I'll allow it."

Kayla got up, clearing dishes away.

"Any dessert?" Joseph asked giving Kayla puppy eyes.

Kayla shook her head, piling plates in her hands. "Not tonight. I am making something in the morning that is quite tasty."

"What is it?" Garrett asked and Kayla wondered if he'd start drooling in a minute. The thought made her stifle a giggle.

"It's called a cinnamon roll," Kayla said with a smile. "Picked up the recipe from a French friend of mine."

"You mean stole it," Mrs. Coleman corrected.

"No ma'am. Learned it." Kayla did her best not to snap back.

Mrs. Coleman glared. "A leopard cannot change its spots, *Ms. Langmoore.*"

"Sarah," Mr. Coleman warned.

"Ma'am, I ain't tryin' to change my spots. I was in bad company. I'd no desire to thieve either. All I wanted was family. I am no thief, rustler, or liar. While you seem bound to stick those titles on me, Mr. Coleman cleared me of them."

"For once, my husband has made a grievous mistake."

Mr. Coleman rose to his feet. "Sarah," he hissed. "Let's take this conversation inside."

Carl helped his wife from her seat, taking off inside like a storm was on their tails. Ben followed without looking back. Kayla let out the breath she held, taking the dishes to the kitchen. Her cheeks flaming with anger and her eyes pooling with indignant tears. Any hope she held, no matter how small, that she'd a chance with Benjamin, fled with his mother. She knew her chances were slim, and the hope faint, but they all crashed with Mrs. Coleman's cruel words.

# CHAPTER ELEVEN

While the oven in the kitchen was getting hot, Kayla took a stroll to the barn, cracking the double doors a bit. The morning orange sky poked its way through the timber of the barn, illuminating it slightly. The sleepy smell of horses tickled her nose.

Kayla smiled. She loved horses. She was even able to purchase herself one when Loren came promising her a future. She bought a mare to follow him out here. Her shoulders sagged at the thought of her mare. The horse was long gone by now. She would not get her back. Even if she could, people here would automatically assume she stole her.

The palomino stallion stuck his groggy head out of the stall door. Kayla beamed, going over to the horse, feeding him a carrot she brought in her pocket. A curry comb hung on a peg beside his stall. Kayla grabbed it, going back to her big friend.

Carefully she opened the stall door. The horse startled, raising his head high, pawing and snorting.

"Calm down, friend," Kayla cooed, pulling out another carrot. The horse lowered his head. His nostrils blowing hot air against her hand. "See, I am not bad," she told the horse.

Kayla took the comb to the horse, using long calming strokes.

She spoke to the animal about her family, "Ma and my step-pa went out for supplies on a bad winter day. They were trying to beat the winter storm, hoping to stock up more before the snows cut off all travel. The snow came early." Kayla paused and grinned at the memory of past trips to town. "They always brought me a penny candy whenever they went to town and left me home." The palomino stood patiently while her brush strokes stayed steady. "They never came back. I knew they were dead before the sheriff showed up months later, after the snow melted. I had already done a lot of grieving for them, but hearing they would never come home made the grief resurface with a vengeance and I'd been inconsolable. Loren held me, rocking back and forth, crying his own tears. I held Donald. He was too young to understand what happened; our tears were enough to scare him." Kayla sniffed, wiping her nose on her sleeve, having no handkerchief.

The horse twitched his ears listening to her. She took this as a good sign. "When the sheriff came, he took all three of us to his house for a little while. He wired Loren and Donald's grandparents in St. Louis. They wired back for the boys, but not me." She choked again at the thought. Taking a deep breath, she continued on, "The sheriff didn't want me either so he simply loaded me on a train and sent me to Oklahoma, where last I knew Grammy and Pappy lived. I got there, but there was no one there for me. Just a couple of graves in the town cemetery. I've practically been on my own since then. Loren's finding me with the promise of honest work and family was so enticing. I couldn't turn him down."

Her friend whickered. Kayla smiled and boldly hugged the horse, drawing comfort from his solid presence.

"I don't think I heard your proper name," Kayla said. "I am going to call you, Amigo."

"He certainly looks like your friend," Ben said from behind her.

Kayla jumped and gasped, snugging up closer to the horse. Small hairs on the nape of her neck rose. Her heart thundered. Letting out a long breath, she kept on brushing Amigo, being trapped in the stall with Ben. She slowly walked around Amigo, making sure to touch him the whole way, keeping her voice low to not startle him.

"Good mornin' Ben," she said cheerfully, praying her voice didn't falter.

"Mornin'," he responded coming inside the stall.

Benjamin picked up one of Amigo's feet, checking it, "He will need shoes soon. It's another expense I don't care for at the moment." he complained.

Kayla kept brushing Amigo, watching Ben walk around the horse. She shouldn't be in here with him, but she didn't want to leave either. She'd not a clue to the expense of horse shoes. Kayla assumed he didn't know what else to talk about. She grinned at the thought, patting Amigo on the wither. The horse whickered at her touch.

"You should *not* be in here with this mustang. He isn't safe," Ben scolded.

Kayla swallowed, unsure of how to respond, if at all. Ben stood on the other side of the horse, petting it. Ben's hands worked their way down the horse's body, checking for something. Kayla watched him intently. His hawk-like gaze focused on the horse. Stubble lined his chin, covering the scar on his cheek.

"If horse shoes," Kayla began, clearing her throat. Ben perked up, waiting for her to continue. "If horse shoes are supposed to be lucky, you better get Amigo shod quickly."

Ben snorted. "Why?"

"You might get lucky and ride him."

Ben grinned. Reaching down he checked the last hoof. Kayla fed Amigo another carrot, basking for a final moment in Ben's presence. He was the forbidden fruit she promised she would not have. But that didn't mean she couldn't revel in his presence for a few moments. She inhaled deeply, enjoying the scent of horse, laying her head on Amigo's back for a moment then turned away.

Quietly, she strode out of the stall, and the barn. She made it outside into the daylight, letting out a long breath on her way back to the kitchen. The oven would be more than ready for her now.

# CHAPTER TWELVE

B en heard her melodic voice before he ever saw her. Without a shadow of a doubt he knew she was with the green mustang. Women always seemed to pick the most dangerous creatures to befriend.

Knowing Kayla, little as he did, he realized she was friendly and determined enough to make that mangy cat and this horse part of her little social circle. He stood outside the door, listening to her talk as she curry-combed the horse. To his surprise, the beast endured, stone still; alert and listening.

That horse listened to Kayla. Ben observed her jaw move while she spoke, not really hearing what she said. He loved how she blew a puff of air to shift the stray hairs off her face. It was amusing to him; it was unlady-like, unlike Clara who would have been horrified if one hair was out of place. Kayla transferred her long, dark brown braid to the other side, chatting away.

When he entered the stall after she named the horse, the startled look on her face was beautiful. She jumped, catching her breath. Heat rushed to her cheeks, giving her some other color besides her sun-kissed glow. Kayla's green eyes lit up for a brief moment. She focused again on her work, hiding those stunning eyes from him.

He checked the last hoof and noticed she was gone. He grimaced. He didn't want her to leave. Though he didn't know what to say to her either. Afraid of saying something wrong, like every other time he'd opened his mouth around her, he spoke about the horse needing shoes.

*That made her stay, great line,* he chided himself.

Ben patted the horse, locking Amigo in the stall. Walking out of the barn, he saw Kayla step inside the kitchen.

He shook his head, opening the other doors wide. Kayla was probably irritated he told her to stay away from Amigo. However, he was concerned for her safety. He did not want to see her hurt or bleeding. Ben sat on a nearby bale of hay. For some reason, he couldn't get the woman out of his head. She was kind, thoughtful, and based on the last few days of careful observations, most certainly not a thief. He'd been wrong about her.

Grumbling at his own stubbornness, he got off the bale, passing chunks of hay around to the other stalled horses. He studied Amigo, lazily munching on the feed. He would break him in today, so Kayla could ride him. Ben shook his head. This was his father's horse. He would break him in so Carl could ride Amigo. Ben kicked a nearby bucket.

"Oh good, you're chipper this morning," Roy said coming inside the barn.

Ben rolled his eyes at his best friend. He'd known Roy since they were toddlers. Roy was more than a friend, closer to brothers; Roy being the very witty, sarcastic one.

"Mornin'," Ben replied dryly.

"Kayla says breakfast is ready," Roy said. "You should see this plate of rolls," he finished holding out his hands to show the size of what Kayla made.

Ben followed Roy outside to where everyone was gathered for breakfast on the porch. Garrett let out a whistle, sitting down with a large grin on his face.

"That boy is smitten," Roy whispered so only Ben could hear.

Ben grunted his agreement. *He isn't the only one,* he thought.

Kayla went around the table, filling cups with black coffee. Carl was already tucking into breakfast. Sarah ate the cinnamon roll delicately. The way her eyes lit up though spoke volumes to Kayla's cooking. Kayla took her seat respectively between Garrett and Roy. She gave herself a spoonful of eggs and a smaller roll.

"Kayla," Sarah Coleman began genuinely, "you are an excellent cook."

"Thank you, ma'am," she replied appreciatively.

"Thank you, Kayla," everyone else said.

The smile splitting her face, and twinkling in her emerald eyes, made his heart skip a beat. Ben watched her sip her coffee and cringe as the liquid slid down her throat. She shuddered, taking another sip. Ben laughed small at first then it roared. Everyone stopped eating, but he didn't care.

Kayla met his gaze with a smirk, coffee cup in hand. Ben's laughter quieted, going back to his meal. Head down, he watched Kayla out of the corner of his eye.

Kayla licked her lips, shuddering again at the taste. She set down the coffee cup. "I don't like coffee," she giggled, pushing the cup away.

"Ben," Carl frowned, "are you laughing at Kayla?"

Ben grinned. "No sir."

Kayla snorted, eating her roll with a smirk. Ben caught her eye and smiled, winking at her. She beamed back. His heart felt like it skipped a beat... or several. After that, the meal was quick work, leaving nothing to be given to the hogs.

His parents went inside. His mother couldn't make up her mind on a few items for their market run and needed Carl's help. Ben did not pay attention to his parents. And clearly, they did not care, or notice, he was distracted by the woman in the kitchen. Benjamin remained on the porch, sipping coffee, lounging in one of the big chairs near the door. He watched Kayla enter the large garden. Picking up her skirts, she got on her knees, cultivating vegetables.

Roy shoved his arm when he came out with his own cup of coffee. "You like her," he stated with a smirk.

"Nope," Ben said getting up. "Time to go break in Amigo," he winced.

He scratched the back of his neck, gawping at his boots with a wan smile. How she thought of the horse as a friend, he didn't know. The mustang was a jerk. But based on the way her face lit up at the horse, she loved the beast. And if Carl ended up not wanting the horse, Ben would gift it to Kayla.

"Amigo?"

"That is uh," Ben paused, "what Kayla named the palomino."

Roy grinned like a fool. "Oh," he said, dragging out the words. "She named the horse... *Amigo.*"

"Shut it," he grumbled.

# CHAPTER THIRTEEN

Kayla caught her breath whenever he looked at her. His laughter reached his bluebonnet eyes. A wide white smile split his handsomely stubbled face. She had to finish her meal quickly to get away. She promised Mrs. Coleman she would stay away from Ben. She kept her word so far. Being labeled thief was bad enough, innocent or not. She didn't want liar tagged to her name as well for breaking the only promise bound to her.

Kayla washed the dishes then made it out to the large garden. Ripping weeds out of the ground was soothing. It was something that kept her mind off the man she could never have. Garrett was smitten with her. With his boisterous high praise and his eyes always on her, it was difficult not to notice.

She made a face. "Sweet and cute, but that's a big nope," she mused to herself.

A soft mewling caught her attention. The brown cat came swirling its way toward her. He or she was purring softly.

"Hello my other friend," Kayla said, scooping up the cat in her arms.

She felt along the cat's stomach to her swollen tits. Kayla smiled. "Hello my mama friend. What shall I name you?"

The cat mewed a response.

"Come with me," Kayla said getting out of the dirt.

The cat followed her into the kitchen. Kayla poured her some goats milk, setting the small dish down. She gazed at the soon to be mother lap up the milk hungrily. Kayla bent down scratching its bottom. The cat purred noisily.

"I will name you," she paused, tapping a finger to her chin, continued conversationally, "Belle, that is French for beauty you know."

The cat didn't respond.

"I will be outside Belle. Come right out when you're done."

Kayla bent down and scratched Belle behind the ear, smiling. She got up to head back outside. Ben stood in the doorway.

"Makin' more friends I see," he said.

Kayla smiled wanly, and shrugged. "Animal ones are easier than people."

Ben nodded. "I came to ask if you could make those sandwiches again for dinner unless you had other meal plans."

Kayla smiled wider, crossing her arms. "I can. I have grouse stew in the pot, but I can do sandwiches too."

"And cookies?"

She laughed, rubbing one of her arms. "Yes."

Ben smiled. "Thank you," he paused replacing his hat on his head. "I am gonna break in Amigo if you care to watch."

Kayla shook her head. "No thank you. I've seen it before. I don't like how mean it is."

Ben tilted his head to the side. "It ain't about bein' mean. It's what needs to be done."

She shrugged. "Agree to disagree."

Ben nodded, leaving her and Belle in silence. Her friend mewed, licking her satisfied lips.

"Should we watch?" Kayla asked.

Belle scampered outside to the garden.

Kayla smiled. "Good idea my little friend."

Amigo's frantic whinnying assaulted Kayla's ears. The animal cried in distress. Wooden fence posts rattled thunderously as Amigo's body struck the fence to knock whomever was riding him to the ground. The noise was getting to her. She closed her eyes tight. Her fingers gathered dirt in the ground. Her heart broke. No, it shattered. Amigo heaved loudly, whinnying in protest. The frightened animal couldn't take much more.

Determined, she got off the ground. She marched to the corral where everyone was sitting on the fence watching. Ben was on Amigo. The horse bucked and kicked, trying to get him off. Ben fell with a thud.

Roy hopped off the fence, going to the horse and cracking a whip in the air. The sound pushed Amigo to the other side of the fence, trapping him in the corner. Amigo's nostrils flares, panic filled his eyes.

Her heart lurched. Amigo was spooked beyond reason. Scaring the horse would not help in breaking it.

"No!" Kayla called out.

"Get back Kayla," Roy warned. "We don't need you hurt."

Awkwardly, she climbed over the fence. Joseph made a grab for her dress, but missed.

"Kayla get out of there," Mr. Coleman said in a commanding tone.

She peeked over her shoulder, seeing five angry, manly faces gaze at her. "With all due respect, *no*, Mr. Coleman," she replied, reaching for Amigo.

Kayla held out her hand to the horse. Amigo came to her, nuzzling her. Kayla smiled. Amigo shuddered at her touch, whickering softly. She pet him, talking softly, not above a whisper. Amigo's head dropped.

"It will be all right now," she spoke to him. "I am going to put my foot in the stirrup."

"No, you're not," Roy said, making a grab at her.

Amigo got in front of him, knocking him flat.

"Trust me," Kayla said calmly.

Kayla put her foot in the stirrup. Carl yelled at her to get down.

She wouldn't though. No one was going to hurt her friend. Amigo was the first animal here to love her, to be kind. Animals didn't care for a person's past. People did. Sure, the folks at Circle 8 were kind. To her it felt rather forced at times. Amigo let her get her other foot in the stirrup. She sat there, unmoving. Amigo shuddered again. Kayla leaned forward, patting his neck. Amigo tossed his head. Kayla soothed him, talking to him, petting every part of him she could reach.

"Catch more flies with honey," she said keeping her voice low.

"It's a horse," Ben growled.

Kayla turned her head on him. "A horse is your friend, your partner, a being you trust and rely on. You put your life on Amigo's back every time you mount. I think Amigo deserves a little more respect than that."

She clucked her tongue, and squeezed her legs. Amigo moved, going around the corral at a walk. She got him to trot, his gait smooth like butter. He bucked once with Kayla fortunately staying on. She made Amigo stop trotting. Leaning forward, she put her hands on his neck. Amigo tossed his head, stamping his hooves. Kayla stayed in the saddle, talking in low tones. Amigo stilled. She got him to trot the other direction. After a few laps, she dismounted, handing the reins over to Roy.

She spun around, kissing the horse on the nose. "You're a good boy."

Kayla strode away. Her heart lighter than before. Her friend was safe. He was no longer hurting or about to be hurt. If she lost her job for this, then so be it. She was sure another ranch or nearby dining hotel would hire her. She doubted if she did leave, her heart would forget Ben Coleman.

# CHAPTER FOURTEEN

Loren woke groggily, the sun shining in his face. He groaned, feeling the side where he was shot and obviously left to die. He raised his head slightly, feeling the muscles strain in his neck. He pulled his legs up, feeling them protest beneath his jeans.

"Shit," he groaned.

A horse whickered softly nearby. Loren sat up, inhaling sharply at the pain in his ribs. He touched his left side seeing the dried blood on his shirt. Dirt festered in the open wound. He hissed, looking down where he'd been shot.

"Not so bad."

Breathing out, he got to his feet. The other men with him were more than likely strung up now. No one wanted to string up a woman. However, it'd been done before. Knowing how sweet and soft his baby stepsister was, she was alive and likely at the Circle 8.

"Damn woman," he cursed. "I'll get her for this. I will get her good."

Loren swayed on his feet, staggering over to the horse. Surprised, the animal jerked its head. Loren smiled when he realized it was Kayla's dumb mare. He had to get out of here, and the dumb animal was his ticket. San Antonio would not recognize him. The place was too large and bustling for the sheriff to care two wits about him. He had a fresh start. He could get away or something else. And that something else called to him like a thirsty man to water. He would take the ranch, the cattle, the money, and head to Colorado or Nevada. He would pull off the biggest, greatest, cattle heist in history. Everyone would remember the name Loren Pattsen.

With a smile, he rummaged through her pack, pulling out an undershirt of his that she hemmed. Women were not good for much else. Especially his stepsister. She was too cheerful, always smiling. It made him angry. Life wasn't about smiling; it was about revenge. He learned the hard way from the woman he loved, who took everything from him. The bitch took his money, his home, everything he held dear, and lit it on fire, cackling like a witch burned at the stake. Then she had the gall to up and die on him, taking the one thing he looked forward to: his unborn child. Life was about taking, survival of the fittest, the strongest. And he *will* survive.

Grunting, he changed out of the spoiled shirt, leaving it in the sandy dirt. Loren glanced down at the wound. He'd been clipped on the left ribcage. Whoever shot him thought he was dead. Suited him fine. He pulled the clean shirt over his head, tucking it in his jeans. The vest went over that, pulling his somewhat clean appearance together.

Exhaling sharply, he mounted the mare, fitting his feet in the stirrups. It was past midday at best. He needed to leave the Circle 8 property and regroup. He needed more men to do what his other men didn't. The ranch would pay for shooting him. This ranch was going to make his dreams come true. The ranch he envisioned would come to life.

His father thieved his own ranch the wrong way, only to die in a snowstorm. Marriage was no way to get a ranch, and Loren refused to make his father's last mistake. Loren was determined to make his father's dream happen, but Loren's way. Better yet, Kayla would pay dearly too. He always hated her and it pained him to have pretended otherwise when they were kids. His hatred growing with age and distance. His father only married Kayla's mother to help clear his soiled name. Loren didn't believe the "fresh start" angle his father tried selling him.

Loren grinned, taking off toward the road. Glancing back over his shoulder, the ranch stood tall on the rising hill. He would take his time instead of rushing in. He would lay in wait, plot, get the exact details for when to make his move.

It would be flawless, effortless, and something no one would trace back to him. He would wait weeks, but not longer than a month. Loren knew he couldn't keep up a pretense longer than a few weeks.

Loren glanced over his shoulder again. The Circle 8 disappearing from view.

"Not long now," he said to the horse, patting her neck. "Not long at all."

# CHAPTER FIFTEEN

Ben called to her like flowers to rain. Kayla could not even get to sleep without thinking or dreaming of Ben Coleman. It was a curse that plagued her the last two weeks, since she first came here.

Ben would come talk to her about dinner, every day before starting his day. She often made his favorite meal-for supper when he got back from riding fences. And she did it to receive one of his smiles aimed at her. It made her heart melt faster than honey butter. And it was all she wanted right now.

Kayla was more than tired of fried chicken, but all the men loved it so she made it at least every other day. She loathed the mess and the clean up after, but Ben's genuine smile kept her making it. Today's supper would be different though. Herbed beef roast sounded like a welcomed change.

Sometimes, after dinner, Ben would come chat with her in the barn as she brushed Amigo and fed him carrots before she started supper preparations. If she was lucky, he would stay and chat for almost an hour. More often than not, he left after a few minutes.

Kayla smiled, remembering when he helped brush Amigo's right side the other day. It was like they were friends. He told her about Clara, how she left him and it broke his heart. Benjamin was a gentle soul. A side of him she would get to see in a few quick, quiet moments when it was only them. The trust he put in her, made her heart swell. Kayla sopped up every moment she could get knowing, with her luck, it would never last.

She shook her head, putting the large pitcher of tea in front of her so she wouldn't forget to put it on the table. Trouble was, she'd a hard time remembering things when all her mind could seem to focus on was Ben. It was like she was drowning and he was the water.

Ben walked past the window and waved to her. Kayla smiled, raising her hand. She breathed out, her heart bursting with fullness and longing for him at the same time. She peered out the window noticing the sky, the change in light announcing the evening. There was maybe one, two at most, hours of daylight left. She opened the oven, pulling out the roast and vegetables. She made her way outside to the long table on the covered porch. The men and Mrs. Coleman were seated, waiting for the meal.

Ben came jogging up to her arms open for the roast. "I got this," he said.

"Thank you," Kayla replied with a smile. "I will fetch the rolls and dessert."

Ben smiled at her. "Smells great!"

Kayla beamed. Her heart danced like a butterfly at the same time it exploded like Fourth of July fireworks. Kayla went back, balancing the rolls and cherry pie on one arm. In the other hand, she held a pitcher of sweet tea.

"I'm gettin' fat and I don't even care," Roy announced.

Kayla smiled. "I think Ben and Mr. Coleman do."

Everyone's laughter rang out.

"True that missy," Mr. Coleman said. "I care very much."

"Then Kayla, stop making delicious things."

Kayla shook her head. "No, you just need to eat less."

Roy laughed. "You win."

Kayla smiled and winked, taking a roll from the basket. "I know."

She glanced to the right where Ben was sitting at the end. He smiled again at her, making her heart stop. If she were allowed, she would stare at him all day. He was a kind, respectable, honest man. And finally, she felt like she was belonging to this ranch. Maybe she'd found a home. No one, not even Mrs. Coleman had called her a thief in days. She began allowing herself to hope that maybe, she could find the life she wanted out here. However, readily as she permitted the thought of hope to enter, Mrs. Coleman shattered it. Sarah complimented her on the fine spread and announced guests would be coming for tomorrow night's supper.

"These are *special* guests, so we need a fine table and an apple pie," Sarah commanded. "Also make some cookies. And sweep the inside of the house for me."

"Yes ma'am," Kayla replied.

A knot formed in her stomach, and tightened. If she didn't know any better, Sarah Coleman was matchmaking Benjamin to whomever was coming to call. She thought she was about to be sick. Kayla stared at her hands, not brave enough to meet Ben's eyes. If she did, she was certain she would cry. Instead, she forced herself to meet the harsh gaze of Mrs. Coleman.

"And *you* are to eat somewhere else. This is an intimate supper setting," Sarah glanced to Carl. "I invited the Fletcher's."

Carl nodded, sipping his coffee.

"Yes ma'am," Kayla whispered.

Roy cleared his throat. "Sandwiches for the rest of us tomorrow night sound mighty fine," he added trying to soften the blow.

Kayla smiled wryly. "I will make some."

Inside, her heart was falling apart, like the unraveling of seams on a dress. If it showed on her face, no one made a comment about it. She tried to make a real smile return; however, it was hiding. She felt like she'd been struck in the chest. This news hurt more than getting shot by Loren.

She cleared the plates and silverware, washing them all promptly in the warm water. Kayla set them in the rack to dry. All the people left, their meals and conversations completed. Looking past the open door, beyond was flat land, no fences for a quarter mile.

Kayla took off running. She hiked up her dress, bounding off. Her legs pumping furiously. Tears streamed down her face. She leapt over smaller brush, dodged her way past Belle who was hunting. The cat mewed her annoyance. Kayla hit the wooden fence post, crashing into it, hugging it like it was a lifeline. Her sobs the only sound besides the rising song of the crickets. She crumpled to the ground, feeling the ache in her heart crack farther open like the Rio Grande.

She wiped the tears with the back of her hand. "Pull yourself together," she told herself, eyes to the heavens. "God, keep my head above water. Help me to see what I'm lacking, what makes people turn from me."

The crunch of dirt under foot, sent a chill up her arms. "Kayla," Ben's voice said softly.

Kayla sniffed, wiping her eyes and cheeks hurriedly. It was too late to hide her breakdown, but she hoped to salvage some dignity. "Yeah?"

He got down in the dirt beside her meeting her green eyes with his brilliant blue ones. "You're not lacking."

She smiled wryly. "Must be lackin' something."

"Why do you say that?"

She couldn't stop more tears falling down her face. Her heart was crying out like a lone wolf at night, full of sorrow and aching for something it could never have. She wanted to tell him, she loved him, but it wouldn't be helpful to him.

"It's nothing," she said quickly. "I'm fine," Kayla added cheerfully, despite the tear tracks on her cheeks.

Ben reached over, wiping her tears with his calloused thumb. "You look more than fine."

Kayla laughed and sobbed simultaneously. "You should go. Please."

Her heart screamed. She didn't want him to go. She wanted to be nearer to him, put her head on his shoulder. She wanted his arms around her and promises of forever. Kayla bit her lip, staring into his wild blue eyes. Ben drove her crazy. If this is what love felt like, giddy and hopeless at the same time then when would the feeling end?

"I am going to town tomorrow. It's another cattle sale," Ben said looking at the setting sun.

"See if you can get eight fifty, a head," she suggested.

Ben snorted. "Yeah? Why?"

Kayla shrugged and bit back a grin. "We are going into winter months. Supply will be in high demand."

Ben nodded. "Want anything?"

Kayla laughed. She didn't mean to, but she did. Of course, she wanted something. She wanted a new dress and a hairbrush, a blanket without holes. But she had no money. She hadn't gotten paid. She wasn't expecting to be for some time despite Mr. Coleman's promise of earning wages after a week. Kayla was in no position to ask for those wages.

"No, thank you."

Ben nudged her. "Come on, tell me."

Kayla stood, shaking the dirt from her dress. "Good night, Ben. Pleasant dreams."

She ambled back to the cookhouse. Eyes closed, she felt herself become colder than the evening chill. "I love him. I'm about to lose him," she said to herself. "God..." she whispered mournfully, "please take this hurt away."

# CHAPTER SIXTEEN

"I told you to stay away from her!" Sarah seethed. "At least the *wretch* listens."

Ben strummed his fingers on the kitchen table. Thinking in retrospect he was pretty sure it was his mother, that drove Clara away. Sarah Coleman was, if nothing else, controlling. And she did so with an iron fist. His mother tried to control his courtship with Clara, from telling him how he should dress and hold her hand. Then from the planning of their wedding, to what food would be served, to the lace on Clara's dress. He obeyed like he thought a good son was supposed to do, like the Good Book said to do. This time, Sarah Coleman was wrong.

Kayla Langmoore was far from a wretch or even a wretched person. Everything the woman did, was in pure kindness. Her job was to cook, but she also did everyone's laundry, mended clothes and helped with chores when she could. How she wasn't dead on her feet each day was beyond him. Goodness, the woman rose each morning with a vibrant as sunshine smile on her full lips and a sparkle in her emerald eyes.

"She is *not* a wretch mother," Ben growled.

Sarah smacked the table.

Carl cleared his throat. "Now Sarah, Kayla is a good woman. She just made a mistake. She didn't steal anything from us or do us harm."

"She is a Langmoore. Everyone knows that name is no good!"

"And you are a Waltz," Carl said leaning back in his chair. "If memory serves me, your brother swung for being a thief."

Sarah huffed. Ben smiled. His father was a good man. How he chose such a judgmental person to be his wife was beyond him. He loved his mother, however, moments like this, the difference between his parents was glaringly obvious. Carl Coleman told him he didn't care who he and his brothers married, long as they were happy. Ben was happy around Kayla. Ben felt like a nicer, better man around her.

The way she sobbed earlier was something he cared not to see again. Her heart was breaking because of his mother's announcement, even if she didn't admit it. Her beautiful sun kissed face never seemed so desolate. It struck her, harder than a slap across the face. Although she played it off well, the sunshine left her eyes and her smile. And damn if he didn't want to put it back.

He'd followed her out slowly so she wouldn't notice him, she even tried to make it seem like she was all right, for his sake. How any man passed her up, he didn't know. How any man did not see the beauty inside of her, he didn't know. He almost didn't see it. He'd been too busy with his own hypocrisy, thinking her a thief and a liar. She wasn't either. He'd never been more wrong in his life. However, he was grateful she was here, that God somehow brought them together. Kayla Langmoore, God willing, would be his wife.

Ben glanced out the window; one of the lights in the cookhouse extinguished. Carl peered over his shoulder then back to him; a knowing smile spread across his face and twinkled in his eyes. Sarah, grumbling, made her way up the stairs to her bedroom. She slammed the door loud enough to echo down to them.

Carl went outside, sitting on the porch. Ben followed, standing beside him, and facing the kitchen.

"Pa, you passed me this ranch," Ben began.

"Yes, I did." Carl interrupted, the rocking of his chair creaking in the nighttime stillness. "You're my youngest boy, something ought to be left to you too."

Ben smiled. "Thank you, Pa."

"Circle 8 is a ranch left to me. My legacy will live on in you and your children. Your brothers left wanting more, wanting better. You wanted this," he said, gesturing to the land and cattle grazing. "This ranch and what you do is on you from here on out."

"Yes Pa."

"Call on her son," Carl said with a smile. "After Clara, all I wanted was to see a smile return to your face. Kayla brought that."

"I love her."

Carl smiled, getting out of the chair. "I know." Carl patted his back and strode inside. The door softly shutting behind him.

A lone light in the cookhouse shone, offering shadowed silhouettes through the window. Ben sat in the chair, watching Kayla's slender figure move about the room. She pulled the screen, taking off her dress. Ben rocked on the front porch swing unashamed, viewing her shadow, the nighttime descend, and the stars coming alive.

The backdoor to the kitchen slammed. Kayla's soft voice called to the cat she loved so much. Between the cat and horse, if there were any more animals around to become friends, they would be at her door.

Ben got off the porch, heading in the direction of her small bunk. She sat on the step in her nightgown, looking at the stars. Her eyes were closed, but her lips moved.

"Wishing on stars?"

Kayla's eyes burst open. "Ben," she hissed quietly, putting her arms over herself. "you're not supposed to be here."

"I'm callin' on you Kayla."

Kayla's eyes got wider than barrels and her mouth dropped open. "You can't," she said shaking her head. "Your parents won't have it. And I will lose my job."

"I can and I will," he replied, hat in his hands. "I'm in love with you. Kayla Langmoore, you bring out the best in me, you make me smile, you make me happy. You're the woman I want. Please," he paused, hands out to his sides, "may I call on you?"

Kayla flew off the steps and into his arms. She pressed her full lips against his. Her hands flew to the back of his head, holding him there. Her fingers wove themselves into his hair. Her sweet lips remained on his as she inhaled sharply. The world seemed to stop ticking. Ben held her slender frame against him, feeling her heat through the nightgown. The smell of her hair tickled his nose. Ben adjusted his arms, so one of his hands could weave itself in her loosely braided hair as he set her down.

Kayla pulled back; her green eyes hazy and sparkling. "I love you, Ben Coleman."

Ben smiled, kissing the top of her head. "I love you too, Kayla. Now off to bed with you."

She smiled so bright he swore the moon trembled from her brilliance. He watched her go inside, shutting the door quietly behind her. Ben bent down, picking up his hat. His heart never felt fuller.

# CHAPTER SEVENTEEN

Kayla's heart swelled. She'd a hard time sleeping. She tossed and turned, reliving the kiss she shared with the man she loved. Kayla reached over, petting Belle who slept at her side. The cat purred as she scratched her behind the ear.

Belle got up, jumping off the bed, mewling to be let outside. Kayla groaned getting up and opening the door. Fire raged. Kayla shielded her eyes. With a gasp, she turned on her heel, running out the door barefoot in her nightgown.

She went to the bell on the ranch house porch, ringing it loudly.

"Fire!" she screamed. "Fire!"

The men woke groggily coming outside. The hazy orange lit up the entire Texas night. Ben came out of the house, boots on. Mr. and Mrs. Coleman followed shortly behind him.

"Get the wagon," Carl said. "Sarah, get your belongings."

Sarah dashed inside. Kayla stood, momentarily fixated on the fire. She took off toward the barn, drawn by the horses whinnying with fright. The men roared at her not to go, to stay back. She ignored them. Kayla went straight to Amigo, letting him loose. She helped Joseph get the other horses out, taking bridles off the walls with her. Somehow, they all needed to get away.

Kayla spun around, frantically calling for Belle. Her cat could not be found.

"Kayla," Joseph coughed, nearing the cookhouse, "get your belongings."

Kayla shook her head, coughing. "I don't have any."

The fire reached the barn, tearing it apart faster than a child with a wrapped Christmas present. Kayla put a hand to her face, observing the flames eat everything. Amigo came over, tossing his head at her. Kayla worked the bit into his mouth which the horse seemed eager to receive. She mounted bareback and barefooted. Kayla led Amigo over to Ben.

Briefly, she watched Garrett and Roy hook horses up to a wagon. Frantically they went to the ranch house, loading possessions in the back. Mrs. Coleman sat in the front, tears spilling down her eyes. Carl climbed in the front, urging the horses down the road with Sarah glaring at her.

Kayla turned to Ben. "What do you want me to do?"

"I need you to help me with the cattle. We are going to drive the herd off to the south pasture. It's going to take all of us."

Kayla nodded, but Ben already turned away. The crash of the barn toppling in on itself made her jump and Amigo spook. She'd never seen fire like this, nor drove cattle before. Most she'd done was feed the herd or help fix a fence. Ben brought his horse close to hers. He reached over, cupping her face as he kissed her forehead.

"It will be alright," he assured. "Come with me. Joseph, open the gates!"

Kayla nodded, not trusting herself to speak.

Joseph opened the gates to the rushing cattle. Their frantic cries to get away sent chills down her spine. All the cattle piled through the opening to stampede to the non-burning pasture.

Kayla nudged Amigo forward, keeping the cattle going in a straight line.

"Like that, Kayla," Ben hollered. "Keep them going!"

The long-horned cattle moved quickly. Amigo trotted beside them. She reined in Amigo and spun herself on his back to search for Ben. He galloped off into the night, the other way from her.

"Ben!" she yelled.

He was out of ear shot.

"Kayla!" Roy shouted. "Come on!"

"What about Ben?" she hollered over the din of cattle.

"Went to go let the other's free. It's all right. He'll be back!"

Kayla kept the cattle going down the road. Her heart was in her throat, waiting for Ben to come back over the hill. She didn't want to lose him like she lost her parents.

She looked west, to the moon headed down to sleep. They kept moving, catching up to the Colemans in their wagon. The cattle passed around them, parting like the Red Sea. Kayla peered again over her shoulder, praying this time, she would see Ben.

He came galloping down the hill. Relief flooded her and she smiled. Roy came up beside her, grinning. Ben reined in Ridge beside her. Ben reached for her hand. Kayla let him take it, entwining their fingers. She relaxed, with Ben safely back to her.

"Cattle are gone," he said somberly. "Someone clipped the fence."

"Do you think the same people who clipped the fence started the fire?" Roy asked.

Ben nodded. "I bet my life on it."

"How many head are gone?" Kayla asked.

"About a hundred."

"Good lord," Roy said. "That's over half the damn herd."

Ben nodded to Roy, dropping Kayla's hand to gesture with his own. "Let's get these cattle to Floyd's to the holding pen. In the morning we will ride out to find the rustlers."

Roy agreed, taking off to tell the others. Ben departed, walking his horse, tailing the cattle. Kayla followed beside him.

"I'm so sorry," she said.

Ben took off his coat, wrapping it around her shoulders. "Not your fault, love. Besides, if you hadn't warned us, we would all be dead," he said, holding out his hand.

Kayla took it, weaving her fingers between his. "I couldn't sleep. I kept thinking about our kiss. Belle jumped off the bed, wanting to go out and that's how I found out the place was burning."

"You let that mangy critter in your bed?" Ben asked in mock horror.

Kayla smiled at his jesting. "She isn't a *mangy* critter. She is my sweet little friend."

Ben snorted, shaking his head. "we're gonna keep animals outside our home."

"Just dogs."

"And cats."

"Belle is the only animal allowed inside."

Ben sighed, amusement lingering on his lips. "Only *that* cat. Nothing else, *ever*."

Kayla laughed. "Deal."

She peered over her shoulder to where the fire was dying down. It was still too dark to tell if the house stood or not. Kayla prayed it did. There was already enough damage done between broken fences, stolen cattle and the fire destroying buildings already.

"Hey," Ben said getting her attention back. "It will be alright. We are both alive and I love you. The rest are just things."

Kayla grinned. "I love you too."

# CHAPTER EIGHTEEN

"I want her arrested Sheriff!" Sarah Coleman screamed.

The Circle 8 cowhands were occupied with cattle, putting out the fire and assessing the damage. While the resident thief was out buying a new dress and shoes, Sarah seized an important opportunity. She knew Kayla started the fire. It was the sort of thing a love-struck fool would do for attention. And the wretch certainly had eyes for Ben.

Sarah noticed the way Kayla looked at her son. She needed to interrupt their affections before they developed further. Getting the Fletcher's to agree for Ben to begin courting their daughter took some coaxing. The Fletcher's believed Ben was too gruff for their youngest. As always, Sarah came to the rescue and smoothed things over.

Ruby Fletcher would be a suitable, and agreeable wife for her Benjamin. Much better than a thief and a liar. Kayla had been a thorn in her side for long enough. And the thorn needed to be dealt with, promptly.

The sheriff sighed, running his hands through his graying hair. "I can't arrest her. You don't even know who really done it. Least-wise you can't prove it."

Seething, Sarah crossed her arms, "I *know* she did it. She is in love with my son. She was upset over supper when I announced Mr. Fletcher and his family were coming over tonight."

The sheriff shook his head. "Still doesn't mean she did it."

"She was with those band of rustlers Ben brought in a while back."

"Well did she rustle cattle?"

"No. Ben said she tried to get them to stop and got shot for it." Mrs. Coleman shook her head adamantly at the sheriff's statement, but didn't say anything more.

The sheriff ran a hand over his face. Sarah stood her ground. Come hell or high water, Kayla Langmoore would be gone from Texas and her son's heart.

Sarah placed her hands on the desk, leaning over. "You owe me... remember?" Sarah whispered.

---

Ben came to the sheriff's office to inquire about some help in going after the rustlers that left a distinct trail leaving the Circle 8. What he found was his mother trying to get the woman he loved strung up. Rage boiled over him from head to toe. He did not think his mother would be so callous.

His mother leaned over the sheriff's rickety desk; a finger pointed in his face. His mother's expression twisted in disgust. Her tightly coiffed hair pulling back the wrinkles on her face, adding to her age and anger.

"Ben said she tried to get them to stop and got shot for it," the sheriff's voice replied evenly, almost like he was repeating himself.

"She did get shot," Ben testified. "And she didn't rustle."

He'd been to the ranch to see if it still stood. By a miraculous act of God, it did. The barn and surrounding buildings were ashes. He came back to tell his parents it was safe to return home. He also wanted to go after the rustlers. Only to come here, and catch his mother try to get Kayla arrested for something she'd never done.

"Ask her for yourself, Sheriff," Ben growled. "Put my mother's ignorant heart to rest."

Sarah Coleman scoffed. "How dare you! I only want the best for you and that *wretch is not it!*"

"Do not call her a wretch *ever* again!" Ben said pointing a finger.

The sheriff stood, getting in between them. "Now hold up. I will speak to the woman. In the meantime, since cattle have also been rustled, I will send my deputies and your cowboys out in search for the cattle."

Ben shook his hand, somewhat mollified. "Thank you, sheriff."

---

"Do you know why you're here?" the sheriff asked her.

Kayla shook her head. She hadn't the slightest inclination to why she was sitting in cuffs before the sheriff of San Antonio. Kayla bit her lip to keep herself from crying.

Goodness, what would Ben think? He would probably not want her now. Everyone in town witnessed her being escorted away from the dress shop in cuffs. It was a shameful public humiliation she suffered. Ben wouldn't want her, now or ever after this. He wouldn't want to be seen anywhere near. The cuffs made a proper criminal.

Kayla bit her lip harder, feeling the blood trickle between her teeth.

"You're here," the sheriff began, his back turned to her, "because you rustled cattle and started a fire to the Circle 8."

"No sir, I did not," Kayla protested.

"But you did when we tell everyone," Sarah Coleman said from the doorway.

Startled, Kayla jumped and squeaked out, "Why?"

It was all she could seem to ask. This woman always loathed her. Now there was downright hatred in her eyes. This was all to keep her and Ben away from each other.

Kayla hung her head, tears bursting forth faster than a thawing spring river. She'd known deep down she was never meant to have Ben. Sarah Coleman would have made it her life pursuit to see to it and now she had. Ben would believe his mother. He would believe the townspeople who saw her getting arrested and dragged away. Whether she'd done this or not, she was guilty, a criminal, in the eyes of the public.

Sarah sat in a chair smugly in front of her. "I believe you know."

Kayla nodded. She knew now. She would wipe her eyes if her hands weren't behind her. Kayla sniffed, wondering what she should do next.

The sheriff came behind her, uncuffing her hands. Kayla rubbed her wrists, happy to be free of the chafing metal. Her hands automatically went to her face, attempting to dry her cheeks. The sheriff's spurs hitting the floor and the creak of the door opening told her the man left her alone with this wicked woman. The sheriff turned a blind eye.

"I want you far, far away," Sarah Coleman began, "here is ten dollars and a train ticket to Denver, Colorado. *Never* return." Sarah Coleman rose to her feet. "Oh and now that the town's seen you in handcuffs, they will believe whatever I tell them. You are a thief. A no good, rotten to the soul, thief. You will *never* be good enough for Benjamin."

"And if I refuse?" Kayla asked defiantly.

"You'll hang," Sarah said softly, "I will make sure of that. And don't you dare think of writing to Ben. I will make sure you hang in Denver too. Don't worry, after a few months, you will be long forgotten."

The train whistle blew in the distance. Kayla glanced in the direction, wood paneling greeting her lonesome eyes. Her heart shattered more by the second. Sarah grabbed her face, spinning Kayla toward her, making Kayla meet her maliciously gleeful eyes.

"I believe your train is calling," she said.

Kayla got up, taking the small satchel Sarah packed for her. With her head held high, she walked to the train.

# CHAPTER NINETEEN

It was magnificent how the fire took off without much help. The sagebrush by the barn took the flame greedily. With a snicker, Loren loped around to the other side of the ranch where the cattle were separated.

With these new henchmen, he took the cattle and headed east. The dopey sheriff would take them all west, thinking because the area was wide open, they would be hiding or getting away.

Loren peered over his shoulder, seeing the flames lashing out greedily toward the cookhouse where he knew his stepsister would be staying. With a grin he tipped his hat to the building. He was free of the attachment of a sister. He hated Kayla as a kid, how his father doted on her. He hated her mother and how, his father and her, gave him the unwanted burden of his half-brother Donald. Women ruin life. Kayla's mother took his father from him and Kayla took his father's affections from him. Then his wife killed any hope he had of women being different. At least now, the last problem would be dead.

Looking ahead, Loren spurring his horse on. The other men got the cattle charging east. This was easier than he expected.

He looked behind him with a grin. "Burn bitch!"

It wasn't hard to track an entire herd of cattle going east. Ben left Roy and Joseph back at the ranch to help his parents unload their belongings and help put out any remaining hot spots from the fire.

Right now, Kayla was probably making something delicious. That woman of his could make the finest meal from nothing at all. Ben smiled. Kayla was the bright sunshine in his heart.

He looked to the left at the five deputies that came with him. Each had two pistols on their person and a rifle in the saddle bags. Hopefully it didn't come to a shoot-out, but with rustlers, one never knew.

Ben crossed the ridge, seeing his herd in the valley below. A fire was going in the middle. One by one, the rustlers were rebranding the cattle.

"Damn it all!" Ben cursed.

"We caught them all red-handed Ben. They will hang for this if they don't die by a bullet first," one of the deputies said.

Ben nodded, leaning forward in the saddle. "Funny thing is, they didn't make it far."

Garrett chuckled. "For how badly they wanted these cattle, they sure didn't."

"Me and Deputy Virgil will head in," Ben announced. "The rest of you fan out in case shooting starts."

Virgil nodded, spurring his horse onward. Ben kept his eyes forward. If he glanced behind and the rustlers saw, he would lose all surprise. Calmly, they entered their way through the throng of cattle, to the middle of the herd where a cow screamed from getting rebranded. Five men looked up, each ragged and dirty. One of them with facial pock marks was oddly familiar to him.

The man he stared at dipped his head. "We meet again," he said.

"Glad to see you're still kickin' so I can hang you," Ben quipped.

The man spat at his horses' feet. "God seems to favor me."

"Not for long."

The man grinned. "We'll take these cattle and be on our way."

Ben charged forward on his horse, getting in between the man and his own mount. "Like hell."

The man looked up at him, eyes squinted from the sun. "Listen... *friend*... There are six of us and two of you."

"Listen, *friend*," Deputy Virgil mocked. "You're going to hang by the law of San Antonio and Texas."

The man laughed uproariously. The others behind him laughed. Ben's blood boiled. The small click of the hammer went back on Virgil's pistol. Ben reached for his.

"How's your house?" the man asked.

"You started that?"

The man shook his head. "My stepsister did. I believe you kissed her last night."

Ben's heart clenched. His gut tied itself in knots. Kayla wouldn't do such a thing. She was the kindest, sweetest woman he'd ever come across. There was no way she would have ignited the fire.

"She's a Langmoore you know," the man said making a disgusted face. "Tainted blood, she has. She's of the same Langmoore's that belonged to the Jacks Gang from Oklahoma City."

The other rustlers drew their weapons. The hammers drawing back echoed in his ears; all barrels pointed to his chest.

"Now," the leader said. "We *are* taking these cattle."

# CHAPTER TWENTY

W alking out of the sheriff's office, Kayla's heart tightened. People stopped dead in their tracks to stare at her. Women pulled their children closer to their bodies. If men were near, they stood protectively in front of their wives. Kayla never felt more shame in all her days. How could she be so stupid to think she could out run her given name.

*Langmoore,* her Pa once said, taking a swig of firewater, *is a name that will go down in history.*

He could not have been more right. According to her Ma, Pa belonged to a gang in Oklahoma City, stealing and wreaking havoc. Her dear mother tried to outrun her married name by moving to Omaha to start over. Once in Omaha, Ma remarried, forgetting to change Kayla's last name.

Dust clung to the hems of her skirts, giving her a final San Antonio farewell. She inhaled deeply, crossing the street, keeping her stare focused ahead. Tears threatened behind her eyes.

"Goodbye, Kayla," Sarah cooed from behind her.

Kayla bit the inside of her lip. The long black train in front of her stared her dead in the eye. She couldn't meet the gaze of a judgmental train, opting for the creak of the wooden platform.

"Next," the conductor called.

Kayla handed the conductor the train ticket. Kansas City would be her new home until the next train came to take her to Denver, Colorado two days from now. With a shaking breath, she boarded the train, not daring to glance behind her.

"Miss, you're in the last car," the conductor informed.

"Thank you," she whispered. "May I stand outside on the landing?"

The man nodded sympathetically, reading her face like one of his train tickets. "Yes Miss."

She remained still as stone. People piled their way past her. She was riveted to the spot, beholding all she was leaving behind; all that could have been.

"Last call!" the conductor yelled.

When no more came forward, he whistled loudly for the train to move. He hopped up beside her.

"I will leave the door unlocked for you," he told her squeezing her shoulder gently. "So you can stay out here long as you like."

Kayla barely whispered back her thanks. The man nodded, leaving her alone. Kayla lurched forward then backwards. Picking up speed, the train left San Antonio and Ben. The town faded from her eyes; Kayla sunk to the ground, leaning her head against the metal rail and cried.

---

Kansas City was busier than she ever thought a town could get. Kayla didn't like it. The tumbleweeds weren't the same. The dirt wasn't the same. Neither was the landscape or her heart. She felt emptier than a grain barrel in winter; like she'd been swallowed, drowning, but spit out on dry land, simply a part of the plague of bad luck that followed her. The much desired happily ever after, like in fairy tales was unattainable for a Langmoore. The last Langmoore. The thought made her sad, but relieved. At least she couldn't pass on this luck to anyone. She would have to live with the heartache.

Kayla went straight to the Silver Spoon Dining Hotel and booked herself a room. The delicious smells from below wafted their way to her nose. But it wasn't appetizing. She gazed outside to the beautiful sunset, how the sky went from pink to purple, fading slowly to darkness. Kayla sighed.

Ben would be back by now. He would be covered in dirt and cow hair. Right now, he would be passing by her little cookhouse window, if it stood, smiling as he raised a hand to her before going to wash up. She would have made his favorite, fried chicken and taters to help ease the anger and the ache of losing everything. Kayla couldn't imagine how he must be feeling, losing his ranch in one night. At least he was able to get the money from the auction somewhere safe, along with the cattle. Knowing the tenacity of Benjamin Coleman, starting again wouldn't take much effort at all.

Kayla leaned her head against the window sill, looking in the direction of San Antonio.

"I miss you," she whispered.

Tears did not plague her journey like they did yesterday or the day before. It was like her heart was frozen cold. Or ripped out. Either way, she couldn't feel it. Kayla stared blankly out the window, watching her new town come into view.

A long, lonely sigh escaped her lips. This was the town she was supposed to call home. Kayla inhaled sharply, holding her breath a few seconds before releasing it. Denver would never be home, not without Ben.

The conductor called everyone off the train. Kayla ignored him, long as she could. This was the final step in her journey. Getting off meant saying good-bye to Ben Coleman would be all too real. It would be like viewing the caretaker drive the final nail into a coffin; like what she'd seen the last one do to Ma; goodbye for good.

Kayla sighed, feeling the sting behind her eyes.

"Miss," the conductor finally came to make her leave, "it's time to get off."

Kayla nodded, slowly moving toward the exit with her small bag clutched in her hands. Stepping out onto the desolate platform, she caught her breath. Fog cloaked the town like a fluffy blanket, and disappeared quickly.

Denver was colder than she expected. She crossed her arms over her chest, walking up the boardwalk. She peeked in every window, looking for a sign or a place where she could work. Nothing was hiring at the moment. She looked up the hill, spying a large hotel.

With a wan smile, she crossed the road, making her way to the place. A giant carved bear growling ferociously stared at her. Kayla admired it for a moment. Opening the door, she stepped inside.

"We need another cook," a woman behind the counter said.

"No, we do not! Claudia is enough," the other woman argued.

Kayla licked her lips. "Excuse me," she called. "My name is Kayla Langmoore. I am a cook. I will gladly try out in the kitchen for room and board."

The woman with dark brown hair smiled at her. The other one with sandy-blond did not. Kayla scowled a moment. The dark brown hair woman looked familiar to her. She tilted her head to the side, approaching the women.

"Do you have any credentials?" the blond-haired woman asked.

Kayla nodded. "I worked at The Silver Spoon Dining Hotel in Kansas City, The Hitchin' Post in Oklahoma, and at the Circle 8 ranch in San Antonio."

The dark-haired woman brows furrowed as she tapped a finger to her chin. "Kayla? The same one who shared cinnamon rolls with me in Kansas City?"

Kayla nodded, "Audrey?"

Audrey squealed in delight, prancing forward and wrapping her in an embrace. "It's been too long! How have you been? Oh goodness, I'm so delighted you are here!"

Kayla wrapped her arms around her friend. "Thank you," she replied, swallowing down the lump in her throat.

Audrey held her back at arm's length beaming.

"Can you bake?" the blond asked.

"Yes ma'am," Kayla replied, ending the embrace with Audrey. "Scones, cakes, cinnamon rolls, cookies, whatever you please."

"This is excellent, Jane!" Audrey exclaimed. "Claudia wanted someone else to take up the baking. And here our little baker is."

The blond-haired woman sighed deeply while Audrey seemed to almost bounce off the walls. Kayla waited awkwardly while Audrey persuaded, or more like stared, the blond into submission. Finally, the blond conceded.

The blond sighed. "You have a week to see if you pan out. Wages are given every week on Friday at six in the morning. Pay is a dollar fifty a day. Room and meals are included. My name is Jane McCarthy. I am the manager and Audrey is the owner."

Kayla dipped into a polite curtsey.

"Enough of that," Audrey said. "Come with me. You're going to love it here and I can tell you are a fabulous cook."

Kayla smiled at this woman's assertion. "Thank you, ma'am."

Audrey laughed. "Please call me Audrey. Here is where you will be staying…"

Kayla grinned wanly. Audrey showed her around the place she was now supposed to call home.

# CHAPTER TWENTY-ONE

Benjamin stared down the barrel of a .45. Sitting taller in the saddle, Ben glared at the man who pointed the gun at his chest. The man made the sound of the gun going off like he a five-year-old child. Ben didn't blink, but continued to stare at him.

The man laughed and shooed Ben away with his free hand. "Better get back home."

"I will," Ben said, "with my cattle."

"With your life."

"You're stalling. If we are gonna do this, I suggest we get started."

The man made a fashionable bow. "I suggest we do."

Ben dismounted, grabbing the rifle out of the sheath. He studied the men standing in front of him. Their demeanors changed. The once hardened looking criminals appeared almost yellow now.

Ben smirked. They didn't want to get caught or hung, and facing a real challenge wasn't something they anticipated. Trouble was, that was the law. No one was ever going to be above it. He gripped his rifle closer. The others took a moment to load their guns as they faced off. Ben grimaced, hoping his cattle weren't going to be hit. He silently cursed, truth of it all was some were.

He slapped his horse Ridge on the bottom, hoping it would take off to get somewhere safe. The blasted animal didn't go twenty paces. Ben shook his head. He would need Ridge to get home to Kayla.

Ben stared hard at his loaded rifle. The smile that accompanied his lips so many times when he thought of her wasn't there now. If she knew what he was about to do, she wouldn't approve. He gripped the gun tighter, praying to God for the first time since Clara he would make it home to the woman who captured his broken, scarred heart.

"You can surrender," the deputy said when everyone was finishing loading their guns, "and not die from bleedin' out."

"Yeah," another man said, "because chokin' to death by hangman's rope is better."

"If you're lucky the rope will snap your neck, and it will be quick," Virgil countered.

A shot came out from behind him. A man dropped, face down in the dirt. Ben ran, hiding behind a heifer who hadn't the good sense to run. From over the back of the ridiculous cow, he began shooting. Virgil and two other rustlers were dead in the dirt.

Ben scanned the rock, and sagebrush for the leader. He spotted him, tucked up behind a rock, his head the only visible part. Ben took careful aim and fired.

"Jesus!" the man cursed.

"You're goin' to meet him today!"

Ben caught another man trying to sneak around and shoot. Ben dropped down flat on his belly. He watched the man pop his head up like a weasel. Ben shot at him.

"Ben!" George's baritone voice rang out.

Ben moved, sitting on his bottom with his back against a rock. "Yeah?"

"Got him."

Ben smirked. "Thanks pal."

Ben carefully poked his head above the rock. Two of the

rustlers remained. Everyone else laid out in the open, dead. The cattle scattered. For some confounded reason the same heifer didn't move, and Ben was glad for it. One of the rustlers decided to make a break for it to a nearby horse. He didn't make it far. Garrett shot him in the back. The man yelled, falling to the ground. The rustler struggled to make it to a nearby horse when Garrett stood and shot him again.

The pock-marked leader rose and shot Garrett in the shoulder.

"Ben," Garrett cried out, his voice shaking. "I've been hit."

"Where?" Ben hollered back

"Shoulder," the gasped in pain. "Lucky for me he has no aim."

Ben laughed. The man was like Kayla, looking on the bright side of everything. Ben squatted on his heels, moving around the rock and the brush. He needed to get to the other side and take out the man who caused all his problems before he could finish Garrett off.

He spied George dash up the hill, charging like a roaring bear. The rustler's leader scrambled back down the small hill. George fired, hitting him in the leg. Garrett came around the side to gather horses, his shoulder bleeding profusely.

Ben strode up to the outlaw, putting a foot on his hand before he could retrieve his fallen gun. The coward cried out.

"Take your medicine, boy," Ben said.

Deputy Everett, nursing a foot, tossed him handcuffs. Ben lashed it to the man's hands. He motioned for the deputy to toss him some rope off the horse tied near the fire. Ben tied his feet together, flipped the man over and tied it to his hands.

Ben and George gathered the horses together, loading the two dead deputies onto a horse. It took them all of a half an hour. When finished, Ben passed the reins off to Garrett and Everett, letting them leave ahead the rest of them to go back to San Antonio.

The rest rode out, gathering the scattered cattle. It was already late in the day. Ben grimaced, taking a peek at the sky. They would have to make camp for the night. Garrett and Everett would make it back to San Antonio as the moon rose.

Ben rode the dusty plains, rounding up the cattle. He peered down at his holstered rifle, silently sending up a prayer of thanks for making it out alive. To have found love with Kayla, it would have been a crying shame to be buried six feet under. Ben smiled, grateful to be breathing and to have the love of a good woman waiting for him back at the Circle 8.

He rode for an hour or so, in a large semi-circle, managing to find twenty head. Ben pushed them back to the meeting place, seeing the others ready and dismounted. The cattle merged in with the remaining herd.

He dismounted, quickly uncinching the saddle to give Ridge a break. The horse whickered and shook with pleasure. Ben patted his neck, guiding him back to camp.

George made small beds on the ground. The other two deputies stayed with the herd for the time being, understanding they would be compensated for their work and time.

"Tomorrow morning, we go home," Ben announced.

"Kayla's cookin' is callin' my name," George replied.

"Mine too," Ben said with a grin. "I don't think I will ever tire of her fried chicken."

George laughed, his baritone voice startling the horses, "I don't think any of us will, but especially you."

Ben's head shot up. "What?"

George winked, "You're smitten."

Ben shook his head. "More... I love her."

"Imagine that, Ben Coleman admitting he loves someone," George said.

Ben smirked. "I can't wait to be home."

# CHAPTER TWENTY-TWO

The kitchen was amply large like The Hitchin' Post's, but not homey like the Circle 8. In fact, nothing felt right to Kayla and it made her shudder despite the kitchen being stifling hot. Kayla shivered, pouring gravy over top of biscuits.

"Kayla," Lena called, "are you all right?"

Kayla smiled wanly. "I'm all right. Rough night."

"All right," Lena replied. "Go take a break. This is the last meal at the moment."

Kayla promptly removed her apron. She went out the back of the hotel. Opening the door into the bright sunlight, her hands went to her eyes, shielding from the brightness. Kayla leaned up against the door, feeling the familiar stinging behind her eyes. Her nose twitched and burned. Kayla bowed her head, taking a deep breath. She moved toward the bench on the other side of the door. She crumpled on the bench, feeling her body tremble and quake. Tears burst forth from her eyes. Her heart broke for the tenth time this morning.

"Dear Lord, I miss him," Kayla said out loud, resting her head against the exterior wall.

She took in a couple deep breaths, feeling herself regain

composure enough to go back inside and finish the morning services. Dinner would be coming within a few hours. She needed to clean up and prepare a daily special.

Kayla wiped her eyes. Ben brought her so much happiness, especially toward the end of her stay at Circle 8. She figured that kind of happiness been long dead; something she hadn't seen since Ma and step-pa died. Ben was her heart. And now her heart might as well be dead. There was no hope in going back or him coming for her.

"Here you are," Audrey came outside, chipper, "I came to say you are a permanent hire here at the Whitman Hotel."

Kayla bowed her head. She didn't want to let on that she was crying. "Thank you, ma'am. I very much appreciate it."

"Oh, my dear," Audrey said, sitting down beside her and embracing her. "No need for tears. Wages are room and board along with a dollar fifty a day. Sound fair?"

Kayla nodded. "More than fair ma'am."

"Wonderful," Audrey said. "Can you bake some cookies? Claudia is a dear but she cannot bake cookies well."

Kayla laughed a little, wiping her eyes. "Yes, I can bake some cookies."

Audrey clapped her hands together. "Excellent! My husband Eugene will be glad to hear! Can you make some applesauce muffins too please?"

"Yes ma'am."

Audrey embraced her again. Standing, she said, "I understand life out here can seem hard maybe even terrifying. Leaving behind all you know for something unknown is the most courageous and quite the scariest moments. I understand, and I am here if you need to talk."

"Thank you," Kayla whispered.

Kayla got up, leaving Audrey on the bench, walking back inside the hotel. Baking would take her mind off of Ben Coleman. For a brief little moment, she forgot about her troubles. Kayla looked south. Even inside she knew which way San Antonio happened to be; Ben would be out with the cattle, more than likely forgetting about her, finding another cook, another woman to love.

Kayla shook her head, numbness seeping in. "Life goes on, I suppose," she mumbled, her back against the outside door.

She wiped at her eyes again. If she even went back, she would be dead.

# CHAPTER TWENTY-THREE

In the morning daylight, Ben sighed with relief at seeing his home rise up over the charred ground. The herd of cows came stomping over the burned remains of the barbed wire fence. Roy and Joseph were busy making a temporary holding pen for the cattle.

His mother rocked on the porch outside the main house, watching her knitting grow as her fingers moved the needles. Miraculously the house stood. It was incredible to him nothing else besides a few hundred acres, a barn and a few out buildings burned. Thankfully Kayla acted when she did. Everyone owed their life to her.

Ben trotted toward the makeshift cattle fence smiling. George whistled, driving the cattle into the hold.

"Fencing comes in five days from Kansas City," Roy yelled.

Ben nodded, observing the cattle swarm tightly into the hold. Joseph tossed over hay purchased from the neighboring farms. He glanced over his shoulder wondering where Kayla might be. He didn't see her. Ben scowled, worry creasing his face. He assured himself more than likely she was inside using the ranch kitchen to make something delicious for them all to eat. The metal clank of the gate shut on the last cow.

"Who helped with the fence?" Ben asked.

Roy removed his hat. "The Wilsons' and Jarvis'. Your Pa is in town, ordering some other supplies," Roy paused. "And, there is something you need to know."

Ben smiled, dismounting his horse and tying it to a nearby post. "Tell me later, I want to find Kayla."

"About her," Roy murmured.

Ben scowled, turning back around. "What about her?"

"She's gone."

Ben leaned slightly against Ridge. The horse turned his neck, staring at him. Ben looked at his horse, his confusion plain on his face.

"What do you mean gone?" Ben asked.

Roy bowed his head, fidgeting with his hat, "According to the sheriff and your Ma, Kayla admitted to startin' the fire. She admitted to helping the rustlers steal the cattle. Your parents showed her mercy by letting her leave San Antonio; to not come back. They knew how much you love her and tried to not let her hang."

Ben's jaw dropped. All the air in his body left. "She would never do such a thing."

Roy shook his head, exhaling sharply. "I wouldn't believe it either, but she admitted it, Ben… Can't beat evidence like that."

Ben ran a hand over his face. His heart felt like someone ripped it out and stuck it in somewhere else. Roy's face paled and tightened. The man's brown eyes held nothing, but truth. Ben let out a breath he was holding. He gazed at his best friend, watching him wring his hat in his hands.

"Let's get to work," Ben said, patting Roy on the shoulder and giving it a squeeze. "Cattle need a better fence."

Ben felt like he'd been kicked in the gut. Kayla was gone. Each day since, rising in the morning been more difficult knowing her bright smile wasn't there; realizing he would never see how the sun shone off her head, making her appear angelic and how her emerald eyes twinkled with happiness. His body felt more tired and old. His heart, heavier than iron. Facing the day didn't seem to matter much to him.

The betrayal turned his heart to ice. He hadn't the need to cry. He wasn't even angry. Numbed, would be an excellent word to describe the odd ache he felt.

The new cook his mother hired to replace Kayla wasn't good, nor as pretty. In fact, most of the men didn't help themselves to big portions much less seconds. Meals were tense and silent. If someone spoke, it was a quick sentence with no need to comment further about the subject. More often than not, the new cook, Jillian, burned food in the oven. Ben told her to take her time, that it wasn't a big deal if the food was an hour late so long it wasn't burned. Jillian cried, blathering that she was trying. Ben was about out of patience with her.

He looked out the window, seeing Jillian lean against the new cookhouse smiling and staring at Garrett. Ben drew his gaze to his cowhand, watching him. The young man smiled rolling up his sleeves. Ben snorted, a wan smile creasing his lips.

"Good for them," he said a loud.

His words echoed through the still house, making the house lonelier. His parents left two weeks after the fire to stay with his sister Alice and her husband in Virginia, giving him complete control of the ranch and its workings along with peace from his mother's matchmaking schemes. He moved into the ranch house, although it felt even emptier. Sitting at the kitchen table, Ben overlooked his men as they began building the frame to the new barn he should be out helping with.

He sighed. In his heart, Kayla didn't start the fire, but no one was admitting otherwise. The sheriff stuck to the story that Kayla did it and admitted it. So did his mother. His father had no comment on the matter, although Ben thought his father was deeply disappointed and secretly hoped something else was going on, but unwilling to dispute his wife. Even his best friend Roy, said his hands were tied, wanting to believe the best of the woman yet found it hard not to believe the sheriff. Ben saw his point. He too, struggled with it. With the previous situation he found Kayla in, the cards were stacked against her. Yet his heart told him Kayla wasn't responsible for the fire or the rustlers. Her leaving was damning though and a betrayal deeper than most realize.

Ben slammed his fist on the table. If he knew where she was, he would seek her out, ask her for himself. Trouble was, no one knew where she was, but his mother and Sarah Coleman said she was taking the information to the grave. He asked the sheriff, who said he didn't know.

Ben asked The Hitchin' Post in Oklahoma to see if she was there. She wasn't. Curiosity getting the better of him, he asked how she was to work with. The owner said she was a delight, lit up the room with her warm smile and good cooking. Ben paid for telegrams to go back east to the major cities he assumed she would go to, asking the sheriffs to find Kayla Langmoore. No one saw her and he was at a loss for what else to do.

Ben laid his head in his hand, drinking his coffee. He looked out again at the barn. He missed her. He missed that whenever he seemed to have an off day, she made his favorite foods and always a kind word for him. He loved her kindness, her brilliance, optimism, and affection. And he still loved her. He loved a thief.

He sighed, putting his coffee down. He closed his eyes and inhaled. Ben swore he could hear her sweet laughter ringing out. Behind his eyes, he could make out her slender silhouette, her vivid green eyes, beautiful smile and her long dark brown braided hair. He threw his coffee mug against the wall. His chair screeched across the hardwood floor as he pushed it out to stand.

A soft mewling caught his attention. He glanced at the open door, seeing Kayla's beloved brown cat Belle. The cat survived the fire and even had her kittens under the porch. Kayla would have loved those babies. Ben pinched the bridge of his nose. The cat tilted her head to the side.

"Come in I guess," he grumbled.

He closed the door behind the cat as she came inside. He went to go sit back down then decided against it. Slamming the door behind him, he went outside, leaving his coffee cup on the floor where he threw it. He got halfway down the steps before spinning around and opening the door for Belle.

"In case you decide to leave me too," he grumped at the cat.

With a groan, he went to help with the barn raising.

# CHAPTER TWENTY-FOUR

Kayla strolled out into the brisk Colorado fall morning. Fog lingered like a sleepy hound dog over the tops of buildings. She ambled down the sidewalk, one arm crossed over the other. The mail came on yesterday's train as it did every Tuesday since being here. A lot of Tuesdays come and gone. Each time, she prayed a letter would find her. Each time, she was disappointed to find Ben never written. No one had. She was naught, but a ghost, a memory. Kayla inhaled sharply, letting out the breath she held slowly.

She stopped herself from going to the post office. There would be no letter for her, welcoming her back to the only place she felt like she belonged in years. A place where waking up each morning was a joyous gift, whereas here, it was simply survival. She missed San Antonio and nothing here could seem to lift her spirits.

Kayla shook her head, deliberately moving her attention from the post office. Turning around, she headed back to the hotel.

"Miss Langmoore," the postmaster, Dane called. "A letter for you today!"

She spun around, the scowl of confusion present on her tired face. "Truly?"

Dane nodded. "All the way from Virginia."

Kayla's stomach tightened in knots and sunk to her feet. She knew of no one from there. Kayla strolled down to meet Dane halfway, gently taking the letter from his hands.

She read the returned address seeing it was from Sarah Coleman, the very source of her misery, and apparently the only one who knew where she was. Anger boiled her blood. She held the letter, wanting nothing more than to tear it to pieces and use it for fire starter. This woman destroyed her life. This nasty woman ruined every piece of her heart. What could Sarah possibly want now? She'd nothing left to give.

Kayla felt the familiar tears burning behind her eyes. She rushed back to the hotel, going around back so she would not be noticed by her kind employer or her straight-nosed manager. She yanked open the door, dashing inside past Lena to her room. Kayla refrained herself from slamming the door, instead slumping against it, tears falling.

Gently, her not yet mended heart, began to unravel more opening the letter.

*Kayla,*

*Here is money for your services at the Circle 8. You have kept your end of the bargain, so I should keep mine. You more than earned your monies worth in being the temporary cook. That is the only thing anyone there misses - your cooking.*

*If you are thinking of coming back to San Antonio to Benjamin, I advise against it. He's moved on and is marrying Ruby Fletcher next month. You are long forgotten. You are nothing, but a thief, and a wretch. Nothing will be able to change the fact.*

. . .

*- Sarah Coleman*

Kayla stared at the twenty dollars falling to the floor. Wracking sobs overcame her. She must have never meant much to Ben at all. Just like when her parents died, she meant nothing to her brothers, her stepfather's side of the family or anyone for that matter. She meant nothing to anyone at all.

"Kayla," Lena knocked on her door, "you all right, dear?"

Kayla scooted out of the way. Lena slowly opened the door. Her shocked, concerned face regarded her. Gently, Lena came to the floor, wrapping her slender arms around her. Lena held her close, stroking her hair. Kayla leaned into her and cried.

"Oh dear," Lena said in a motherly tone, "what happened?"

Without words, Kayla handed her friend the letter. Lena took it from her, reading the words and gasping when she finished. Lena crumpled the letter, tossing it to the other side of the room, holding Kayla tightly.

"Lena?" Audrey called. "Kayla?"

Lena released her for a moment, leaning out the door. The owner came in. Without a word from either woman, Audrey embraced Kayla's other side. Kayla felt like the frosting smooshed between two layers of cake. Lena filled Audrey in on what the letter said. Audrey embraced her tighter, much tighter than Kayla thought such a small woman capable of. And for the longest moment, both women held her.

Kayla wiped her tears, quieting down. She allowed her heart to open, to feel the love and compassion these women were giving her.

"You are worthy. You are loved. You are a wonderful, sweet human being and not a thief at all," Audrey said.

"You are so loved here," Lena chimed.

Kayla smiled, feeling the tears fall anew. Her heart did somersaults and her gut clenched.

"Take today off," Audrey said. "Sleep, take a bath, go do something."

Kayla shook her head. "No thank you ma'am. I would like to bake," Kayla said, getting off the floor.

She turned around offering her hands to the ladies, yet to get off the floor, which they took. Kayla embraced them individually thanking them for their kindness to her. She walked out of the room, leaving her money behind her on the floor. No amount of paper could heal a shattered heart or the way she loved Ben Coleman.

# CHAPTER TWENTY-FIVE

Ben got the barn raised in a day. Tomorrow the roof and walls would start going on. The cattle he sold over a month ago, more than paid for everything. Now, the last of the winter herd would be sold again to help get the ranch through the winter, people paid and money sent to his parents' new residence in Virginia.

He sat in the kitchen, viewing the cold Texas wind whip tumbleweeds across the prairie, getting them stuck in the fences. Winter was coming and it would be a hard one. The hay he carefully stockpiled burned in the fire Kayla started. Only, he still didn't believe it. His mind constantly battled with his heart over whether or not she did it.

Ben glanced over his shoulder, watching the kittens play near the fire. Belle observing from a chair, one eye on her brood. Ben grinned then scowled. The blasted cat reminded him of a traitorous woman. Yet he'd come to rely on the cat to keep the mice away. He rather liked the lack of skittering and mouse droppings.

Whinnying from the temporary corral sounded. Amigo shook his head, alert and facing the road. A rider was coming. The horse was more of a vigilant dog than George's mutt. The rider rounded the corner, coming up to the ranch house.

Ben's chair screeched back, causing the cats to scatter. He opened the door, meeting his visitor outside. The sheriff dismounted, coming up to him slowly, reluctantly. His head was down, his face unshaved for a few days. The sheriff's winkled clothes smelled of whisky and sweat.

"Evenin', Sheriff Taylor," Ben greeted.

"Evenin', Ben," he replied with a tight smile. "Here," he said handing him an envelope.

"What is this, Sheriff?"

"Money for the rustlers. Turns out they were wanted men. You and your men deserve the reward for it."

Ben nodded, sticking out his hand and thanking the man for the personal errand. "Any word regarding Kayla Langmoore?"

Sheriff Taylor shook his head. "No," he breathed out, pausing. He scratched the back of his head, "but she didn't start the fire."

Ben crossed his arms and raised an eyebrow. "You said she did."

The man removed his hat. "I know… it's been eatin' at me since I said it and every time after… I lied. Not one of my proudest moments, especially saying it against a woman."

"Do you know where she is? Why she left?" Ben asked demandingly.

Sheriff Taylor shook his head. He sat on the rocking chair on the porch with a sonorous thud, let out a groan while wringing his hat in his hands. Sheriff Taylor pinched the bridge of his nose and shook his head.

"I have a story for you," he began, "Sarah told me Kayla started the fire and rustled the cattle. Taking your mother's word, I hunted Kayla down and arrested her. In front of the town too, a fairly calculated move, at the request of Sarah. Brought her back for questioning. Your mother said to release her, that she forgave the young woman and wished to not press charges; said she knew Kayla didn't do it, but asked I told you I did. Sarah said I owed her one, and I did because your mother gave me a loan for a house when the bank wouldn't. Sarah told me there would be a day I could repay her on top of the money, of course. The day Kayla left was that day. So, I released Kayla and left. Your mother was there when I released her, but I don't know where she is," the man sighed, staring at the floor. "I am leaving San Antonio. I'm heading to Omaha, settling down, starting over with a clean plate. Deputy Johnston is taking over. Goodbye Ben. And... I'm sorry."

The sheriff got up. His heavy footfalls jogged down the steps to his horse. Ben felt his jaw tighten and clench. "And this money," Ben said getting up, "Is it even real?"

The sheriff nodded. He mounted, spinning his horse to face Ben. "Yes. It's yours Ben."

The man rode off like wolves were chasing him. Ben sat back down in the other chair, glowering at the yellow envelope in his hands. He heard the sheriff, but had trouble believing him. He didn't know what to believe at this point. Would his mother truly go through all the trouble of getting rid of a woman he loved?

Ben opened the envelope, seeing the money inside, and naught else. He stepped inside the house, going to the kitchen. Opening up the silverware drawer, he slipped the money behind it with the rest of the cash he had. It wouldn't be found. Ben left the door open, rushing down the steps.

"What was that about?" Roy asked.

Ben shook his head. "The sheriff said Kayla started the fire and rustled cattle. Now he says she didn't. The only person who knows the truth is my mother."

Roy grinned at him. "Heading off to go find Kayla?"

Ben shook his head. "No. Chores need doin' first. Winter is setting in and if we are going to live here comfortably, things need done. Pa said they would be visiting soon. I'll ask her then."

Roy patted him on the back, leaving to go get more nails from town. Ben looked northwest, wondering if Kayla decided to go that way. He shook his head. Wherever she was, she probably long forgot about him by now.

# CHAPTER TWENTY-SIX

K ayla gawked at the money in her hands, wondering what she should do with it. She didn't want to keep it. She didn't want any part of it. To her, it was blood money. She wouldn't do that to Ben and she definitely wasn't going to spend what wasn't hers.

She sighed, staring at the open envelope on her bed. Kayla put the money inside, licking the envelope closed. She stared at the front, touching the name she wrote on there. As promised, there was no note. On the back was only the place where she was, Denver, Colorado.

*I miss him and I can't tell him where I am*, Kayla thought, her heart clenching.

Letting out a hard breath, Kayla strode out of her room, going to the front of the hotel. Dane the postmaster was there, handing Audrey a plethora of letters and other news. Kayla approached, handing Dane the envelope with a wan smile.

"Please send this," Kayla asked.

Dane took it with a smile, his wrinkled eyes twinkling. "Sure thing Miss Kayla. Do you have money for postage?"

Kayla handed him two bits. Dane closed his old hand over hers. "How about a trade for an applesauce muffin?"

Kayla looked to Audrey who nodded.

"I will whip some up and bring you one Dane," Kayla said. "Thank you for mailing this."

She turned around, heading back to her room to fix her hair before she started work. She walked past a large bright window, seeing snow fall from the heavens.

Usually the cold, beautiful mixture brought a smile to her lips. Instead it brought heaviness to her heart. Ben wouldn't get the letter for weeks due to delays. Kayla sighed, heading to her chamber, then decided against it. She had muffins to make.

Ben sat on the front porch, a scarf wrapped around his neck. The cold fall winds picked up this time of year in San Antonio. The cattle and horses grew their winter coats early. Meals were now taken inside the ranch house with a fire going.

The devastation from a few months ago could not be seen now. Between the wind and the cattle, all reminders of the fire were beaten down. New structures stood larger, bigger than before.

*The good part, I got a barn twice the size,* Ben mused.

He looked northwest, shaking his head. The woman, the thief, who stole his heart, was somewhere out there and he tried to force her from his mind. Some days were better than others. He tried to forget her, but found he couldn't. There were too many damn reminders. He touched the side of his face, where the scar happened to be.

He smiled, thinking of her again. Not once did Kayla ask how he got it, nor was she repulsed by it. He got it from a fight. Rustlers came in, as they always seemed to do. One had a knife and sliced him open good. In return, Ben took his life. Ruby Fletcher, the woman his mother wanted him to court, lips twitched in revulsion. Even Clara's had. Kayla only smiled, lacing her fingers into his. Ben stared at his fingers; a warmth nestled in between reminding him of when she held his hand.

*I miss her*, Ben thought.

Ben clenched his hands, watching the grazing cattle holler out. Joseph and Roy were out with the cattle. Garrett and George went to town to get more supplies for the house Garrett was building on the outskirts of his property. The man loved Jillian, so along with supplies, Ben asked him to find another cook. Jillian was a sweet girl, but a man could only handle eating burned supper for so long.

Ben went down to the horses, each of them having a small holding behind the barn attached to it. He needed to check their feet and shoes. It was about time they all had a trim.

He entered the barn, the quietness calming him. Amigo whinnied, announcing a person coming up the road. Ben smiled at the horse who was more dog than the dog they had. Ben poked his head outside the barn, seeing his cowhands come up the way and another wagon behind bearing his parents.

Ben went back inside the barn. His parents didn't spot him, giving him a couple minutes to finish this task. He opened Amigo's stall door. The horse's ears and lips were back in warning. The ornery horse hadn't been the same since Kayla left. Amigo lunged at him, tossing his head.

"Blasted horse," Ben cursed.

The spurred boot falls of his father clanked behind him.

"Seems like he misses someone," Carl Coleman said.

Ben shut the stall door. "Seems that way."

Carl handed him a letter. "Addressed to you. All the way from Denver. Know anyone there?"

Ben shook his head, his curiosity piqued, a feeling of mixed dread and excitement stirring in his stomach. He held the letter in his hands, turning it over. No return address was there. His finger slid along the edge to open it. He paused, hearing the high-pitched call of his mother.

"Oh Ben!" his mother called. "How are you?"

Ben straightened his back. Holding the letter up, he flashed it in front of her face. "Fine mother. Know anyone from Denver?"

His mother paled. "Why no," she said recovering. "Why on earth would anyone be sending you a letter from there?"

Ben opened the letter, seeing twenty dollars in paper money tucked inside. "Ma," Ben began, "this is the money I sent you last month."

"Sarah Coleman," Carl growled. "You sent that to Kayla, didn't you?"

Carl pinched the bridge of his nose, shaking his head. His father seemed to age another ten years with more gray peppering his head and beard than he'd noticed before. He looked at his mother, her lips pursed, drawing age lines on her face. Carl's eyes narrowed on his wife.

"I don't have to answer either of you," Sarah seethed. "The wretch is gone, and everyone is better off."

"Yes, you do," Carl said, his eyes darkening and his voice raised. Carl took a step towards Sarah. "Our son has been miserable since Kayla left. I knew she hadn't started the fire and yet heard tell she did, tell coming from *you*. I wanted to believe you'd nothing to do with it, that I'd been wrong about her. I see I was wrong; wrong about *you*. Have anything to say for yourself?" Carl seethed.

Sarah Coleman crossed her arms. "I did nothing wrong," she said haughtily with her head raised.

Carl turned to his son. "Bring her home. I'll take care of your mother."

Ben opened the stable door to Amigo. He grabbed a bridle off the outside peg, fighting to put the bit inside the animal's face. Ben mounted bareback, stuffing the money inside his shirt pocket as Amigo took off down the road.

## CHAPTER TWENTY-SEVEN

Kayla laughed, tossing flour at Claudia. The older woman tossed some back, getting her across the face. Kayla laughed uproariously. She flung some more at Claudia. Lena came inside and Kayla threw a small pinch at her, getting Lena on the apron.

"Oh, it's on!" Lena said, taking a handful from Claudia.

Laughter rang out as they got each other. Their hair turned white from the flour. The white substance covered almost every inch of themselves and the kitchen. Claudia smeared flour on Lena's face while the girl licked her lips. Kayla laughed, choking on the flour causing everyone to laugh more.

"What is the meaning of this!" Jane McCarthy demanded.

Kayla spun around, blowing some flour on Jane with a smile. "Baking," Kayla said.

Jane picked up a handful of flour, dumping it on Kayla's head with a mischievous grin. "Clean up when you're done. Keep your laughter down. I can hear you from my office."

The other women paused watching the manager leave. "You made Jane smile," Lena said.

Kayla shrugged, going back to her cookies. "Yeah."

Claudia got the broom, sweeping the floor. "Jane doesn't smile often."

The laughter quieted with an occasional chuckle escaping someone's lips. Kayla nodded, popping her cookies in the oven. She helped clean up the kitchen. Lena checked the ovens every few minutes, her face longing for a tasty treat.

"Kayla," Claudia began, "you haven't been the same since the letter. What happened if you don't mind me asking?"

Kayla stopped cleaning with her rag. She took a deep breath, letting it out slowly. "I love a man named Ben. His mother didn't like me. She said I rustled cattle and started a fire when I didn't. Had the sheriff on her side too. Told me to leave or hang. So, I left. The letter said Ben was marrying someone else, and has forgotten about me."

Claudia gave her a consoling smile. "Sorry dear."

Kayla shrugged. "Time for me to move on too. My heart is having trouble knowin' it, though."

Kayla pulled her cookies out of the oven. Lena had her nose close to the tray. Kayla smiled. The silly woman was pretty close to burning her face.

"Ouch!" Lena yelped.

Claudia laughed. "Don't stick your nose so close," she admonished, "Now you look like one of those dogs, the mis-colored ones with the pink noses."

Kayla set the tray down, erupting with laughter. Lena rubbed her burned nose.

"Better put somethin' on it," Claudia said handing her some ointment.

Lena grabbed it scowling. "I am no dog!"

Kayla cackled, trying to keep her face straight. "But it's all wet and shiny! Woof!"

Claudia stared at her a moment. They both began howling. Kayla fell to the floor, holding her gut as she laughed. Lena stood over her, sticking out her tongue. Kayla got up slowly holding her stomach. She inhaled deep, handing her a cookie. Lena chomped it angrily. Kayla went outside to get the cold milk and some snow wrapped in a cloth for her friend's face. Kayla came back inside, handing her friend the cloth.

"I'm sorry," Kayla said sitting beside her friend.

Lena rested her head on her shoulder. "It was funny."

Kayla smiled, "It's only funny when the person we are teasing is also laughing."

Claudia handed Lena another cookie. "Sorry Lena."

Lena smiled cheekily, biting with a silly grin into the cookie. "I love cookies."

Kayla smiled, giving her friend a hug. She grabbed her warm wool shawl off the peg, going to sit outside in the fading afternoon light. She sat outside on the bench with a sigh.

---

Ben looked out the train window, seeing the snow fall steadily. The train moved slowly, not wanting to derail and crash. It was the end of October and already snow fell heavily here. According to the man sitting next to him, it was unusual, but has happened. It took the train three days to finally make it to Denver. The conductor came by saying they would reach Denver within minutes. Once there, the train would wait until the snow cleared up a bit.

Ben fidgeted with the brim of his hat. He never felt more nervous in all his days. He wondered if Kayla happened to be here, waiting for him. He wondered if she still loved him; if she was unmarried. A great woman like her, he was certain she wouldn't be. His heart broke a bit at the thought.

He wiped the sweat off his brow. His leg began to shake.

"Please remain seated," the train conductor yelled causing Ben to jump in his seat. "We are going to try to make a slow and steady stop as we come into Denver."

Ben glanced out the window, seeing nothing, but houses and snow on one side. He crossed the walkway to the empty seat on the other side, seeing the bustling town. His eyes scanned the area for Kayla. She wasn't there. Ben dashed to the back of the train, opening the door to the frozen air. The train didn't stop when he jumped off startling a group of people. He tipped his hat to the people, pushing his way through the throng of many waiting to board or for people they knew.

He strode along the boardwalk hurriedly, turning a small corner. Peering up, a giant hotel with a large carved grizzly bear, stood out like a beacon. Ben made for it. He jogged across the roadway, his frozen breath coming out in white puffs. He went inside, glancing around at the opulent establishment. A dark brown-haired woman with a welcoming smile greeted him.

"Welcome to the Whitman Hotel," she said. "We have rooms to meet every need along with a dining area. Would you like a tour?"

Ben stared at her a moment, the smile didn't leave her overly friendly face. "Ma'am," Ben began, removing his hat, "does a Kayla Langmoore work here?"

The woman nodded; her head tilted to the side. "Ben Coleman, I presume?"

His scowl deepened. "Yes."

She came around grabbing his hand. Without warning or a care for propriety, she dragged him through the hotel. Ben followed the petite, fast-walking woman through doors into a kitchen. The kitchen women scowled at him as this woman took him through a final door. The woman who held him let go, troubled lines creased her porcelain face.

"She is out there," the woman said standing in front of the door. "Before I allow you passage, do you love her?"

"With all my heart," he replied, grabbing around her onto the door handle.

The door opened with a groan. Kayla sat on the bench, her head bent next to the door, staring at her feet. Her hair was dusted in white, but not from snow. He closed the door softly behind him, sitting down on the bench next to her. His heart pounded in his chest, feeling like it was going to burst. Sweat covered his palms. Ben removed his hat. Kayla didn't look up.

Her hands went to her face. "I am alright Lena," she said. "I need to breathe. A man came in today, his voice deep like Ben's.

With the same dark hair and beaten leather hat," Kayla sniffed, choking back tears. "And…" she paused her voice breaking, "I thought it was him… I thought it was him," she said turning and leaning against the person she thought was Lena without looking up. "And my heart stopped because I prayed it was him. I thought he found me. But it wasn't Ben," she cried. "I love him so, but I'm long forgotten like the letter said."

Ben moved, putting an arm around her. He felt tears track themselves down his face. After all this time, she still loved him. Ben sniffed, smiling. He kissed the top of her head, leaving his lips to linger. He inhaled the vanilla scent he'd come to love on her. Her warm body crashed into his, her grief so palpable it made his skin crawl.

Kayla breathed in deep. Ben embraced her fiercely. He watched her face wrinkled, her nose wriggle. Her brows furrowed deep over her beautiful face. Kayla leaned up slowly, looking down at his worn pants and dirty leather boots. Slowly, her eyes trailed up to meet his.

With a scream, she pounced into his arms, wrapping them around his neck. She cried as he held her close to his body.

"I thought I was going crazy when I smelled leather and horses," she said.

Ben laughed. "If it has to be by smell, that is surely how I wish to be recognized, but I prefer to be seen by the woman I wish to call wife."

Kayla leaned back the smile dropping in disbelief. "What? I thought you married Ruby Fletcher."

Ben dropped to a knee, damning the snow and the coldness of the flakes soaking through to his skin. Her face lit up and frowned simultaneously, her brows questioningly, furrowing tighter.

"Kayla Langmoore, I love you. These past few months have been torture without you. I sent out letters and telegrams looking for you, thinking you went east, but stupidly I didn't think to look west even though I wondered deep down. I found out the truth, found out where you were and came right here. Kayla," he breathed, feeling relieved to get it all off his chest, "I've missed you every second of every day. I have loved you with every beat of my heart and I will be damned to spend the rest of my life alone without you. Be my wife... please."

Kayla smiled, tears tracking down her face. "I love you Ben Coleman," she said dropping to her knees, she kissed him. "But how could you want me? I have been labeled a thief by San Antonio. They'd seen me arrested and my last name... it's tainted."

"I don't care. Your last name will never be Langmoore again, but Coleman. You are all I need, Kayla."

"Truly?" she sniffed, tears sneaking down her cheeks.

Ben wiped them away with his thumb. "Truly. I love you. Please be my wife."

Kayla nodded. Ben slipped a ring on her finger. Kayla smiled, wrapping her arms around his neck. Never had he been happier to love a thief who'd certainly stolen his heart.

A sniffle came from behind him. The same brown-haired woman stood with the hotel door slightly ajar. She dabbed her eyes with a kerchief.

"This is better than any novel I've ever read," she said.

# EPILOGUE

Fall came on slowly this year compared to last. The cattle sounded in the distance. Amigo whinnied from the corral. Dust clouds came puffing into view. Kayla smiled, a hand resting on her large belly.

The land hadn't changed much from last year's fire. If anything, it helped the garden grow better crops. The rain from spring brought grass for the cattle and a good haying season for this winter. Much to her pleasure, Sarah Coleman resided in Virginia, close to Ben's sister Alice.

When Ben brought her back from Denver, Sarah hopped the next train out. Kayla was torn in her emotions. Sarah missed their wedding and Kayla knew it pained Ben deeply. However, she was grateful the nasty woman left. Carl Coleman was too happy to give her away to his son. She adored her father-in-law and was excited to be seeing him soon, per his letter.

Roy and Garrett came leading the large herd of cattle through the barn and out the back into the north pasture. Ben sat on Ridge in between the house and barn, blocking the cattle from scattering. He waved his hat to her, a large grin on his face. Kayla raised her hand, happy and relieved he was home.

She sat in the rocking chair on the porch, wrapping the blanket that hung off the back around her shoulders. She spied Ben's commanding form pass orders to the new members who joined their ranch. Hector was a great addition and also a great cook. Since she became pregnant, Ben insisted on her not cooking for everyone; not wanting her on her feet all day. She agreed, so long as she could bake.

The smell from the ranch house oven wafted to her nose. The babe inside her swirled, hungry for some peach cobbler. Kayla rubbed her stomach, hoping the pressure on the sides would get the babe calmed.

"Kayla," Ben said, jogging to her. "You all right?"

She removed the pained look from her face, replacing it with a smile. "Yes. Just a hard kick."

His boots thundered up the stairs to her, planting a kiss on her lips. His hands caressed the side of her belly, the babe inside calming to his touch. Kayla let out a breath of relief.

Ben grinned. "Busy today?" he asked.

Kayla nodded, rubbing the back of her neck. "You have no idea. This child moves at all hours of the day."

"Pa should be here today."

"Wonderful," Kayla replied with a smile. "I'm excited to see him."

Ben's hands worked their way around to her back, massaging the sides. Kayla moaned, leaning into him. She rested her face against his chest, inhaling the scent of dust and hay. She would be thrilled when this child came out and she could sleep comfortably for a few hours. Already, sleeping in a chair was getting old.

"Come inside and I will rub your feet."

"Talkin' sweet will get you everywhere," Kayla replied hands on the back of her hips, following him inside.

Ben pulled the peach cobbler out of the oven while she sat in a chair. Ben took a seat across from her, taking her sock covered foot in his hands since her shoes no longer fit. He massaged the instep of her foot, putting her to sleep almost immediately. The screen door sounded rousing her slightly. She hardly paid attention, figuring it was Roy or George.

"Ben," a feminine voice called.

Kayla rolled her head to the side. Her sleepily lidded eyes barely opening far enough to see Carl and Sarah Coleman at the front door. Ben rose, getting in front of her protectively. Kayla groaned, sitting forward, putting her skirts on the floor. Standing, she stretched her back slowly.

Ben walked to the door and opened it cautiously, permitting his mother entry first, but did not greet her. Carl came straight to Kayla with a beaming smile, kissing her on the cheek.

"Kayla, Ben! I'm glad to have made it. Traveling this time of year is a bit treacherous in some places. Kayla, you look beautiful! Absolutely stunning. I can't wait to meet my newest grandbaby!"

Sarah stood by the doorway, wringing the clutch purse in her hands looking around awkwardly. She'd yet to remove her hat or hang her parasol.

"Mrs. Coleman," Kayla beckoned, taking a seat on the divan. "Please come in, and sit with us."

Sarah came, smiling tersely at her. Sarah stiffly took a seat beside her. "Thank you. You have done nicely with this old house."

Kayla dipped her head in a silent thank you. "How does Virginia find you?"

"Quite well, quite well. Humid." Sarah offered a wan smile. She took a deep breath. "I'm sorry... I was wrong."

Kayla wrapped her arms around her mother-in-law. Ben took his mother's hand, patting it with the other. The older woman sniffled, wiping the tears from her eyes.

"I'm so sorry," Sarah said again with a hitch in her throat.

Ben got the reunion he always hoped to have. Even though he never mentioned it to her, it pained him greatly to not have the approval of his mother. Now he had it. Kayla, however, gained more. She gained a completed family, full of loving people who loved her back.

"Any names picked out?" Sarah asked.

"Benjamin Carl for a boy," Kayla replied.

Ben smiled at her, kissing the side of her head. "Lillie Sarah, for a girl."

Sarah dabbed the sides of her eyes with a kerchief.

"I told you, you did not want to miss this," Carl said.

Sarah nodded. "I wrongly labeled Kayla a thief," she put both their hands-on Kayla's belly, "But she is one. A thief who not only stole your heart, she stole mine too."

# III

## TO SAVE A LIFE

# CHAPTER ONE

Clenching the reins in her hands, Mary's horse thundered down the road, taking a wounded Ross with her. Her heart pounded in her chest, feeling like it was about to come out her throat. Victor Del Avilasto, a horrible, abusive man, hell bent on murdering her and her companions, was behind them. She dared not look over her shoulder, fearing Victor and a bullet would be there. Scrunching her eyes, Mary strained for any sign of a building.

Peeking over her shoulder, seeing a house on the outskirts and tucked back a way off the road. The road went downward and curved to the right.

"Pleasant afternoon, my dear," Victor said, leaning against the front porch of the house.

Eugene's worried eyes met hers briefly. Digging her heels into the horses' side, Mary urged her tired beast on. Out of her peripheral, Victor pulled a pistol from his side. The bullet leaving the chamber made her skin crawl. Her heart leapt in her throat. A shriek of a horse split the morning air. Mary caught her breath. Eyes wide, she glanced behind her.

Eugene and Audrey were caught under their fallen horse. The

animal whined, in pain. The light in its eyes slowly waning as the whining slowly faded.

"You all right?!" Mary asked, doubling back.

"Ride Mary! Get help!" Eugene commanded.

Holding her breath, Mary spurred her horse. Her mount nickered, tossing its agitated head. Her heart pounded quicker than her horse's hooves. Ross, slumping over in his saddle, barely hung on. Mary bunched his horse's reins tighter in her hands, arm out behind her, dragging his reluctant mare along.

She swallowed hard. *Gotta get help for Audrey and Eugene. First though, Ross ain't goin' to make it much longer. Gotta get him safe first. God, give me time!*

Sweat poured down her forehead; its salty beads falling on her lashes and stinging her blue eyes. She whipped her blond head around, gazing frantically for those who chased her. Mary let out a breath. Squeezing her legs tighter, she pleaded the horse to go quicker than he already was. The swinging sign of the local doctor, greeted her eager eyes.

"Hang on, Ross," she called behind her.

Taking a peep over her left shoulder, she reigned her horse in, noticing Ross slouched over the front of the animal, with his brown hair hanging in his face. Mary's horse barely came to a stop before she dismounted. Her men's clothes sagged on her body. Her light blue shirt had holes every so many inches, not to include the large, blood stained one in the shirt's shoulder put there by the bullet stopping the previous owner from hurting her or Eugene. And her black pants had a belt that would not tighten enough. Grabbing the waist with one hand, she dismounted.

Sprinting behind her to Ross's horse, she put her hands over her head. Grabbing hold of Ross's pants, she yanked him to her, stumbling a bit as Ross's weight hit her.

"Help!" she shouted, gasping at Ross's bulk. "DOC! DOC!"

Mary struggled to keep him upright in her arms. Ross was a head taller, if not a bit more, than she was. Mary grabbed around his good side, careful of his gunshot wound on his left side.

"DOC!" she yelled again.

A middle-aged man ripped open the dark wood door. His face staring down at the floor, eyes scrunched, he pinched the bridge of his nose. "What in the world," he grumbled, lifting his head.

Mary scowled. "He's bleedin' bad. Been shot by a gang of riders."

Doc came taking Ross from her completely. Ross's feet stumbled alongside, almost dragging behind him. Mary held the closing door open for the man to take Ross inside. Once her companion was safe, Mary turned on her heel, leaving the shocked doctor and Ross behind.

"I'll be back! Gotta get the sheriff!" She yelled over her shoulder.

Mary only ran a few steps when a man stepped outside of a building, arching his back and stretching his arms out to the side. The glinting golden shimmer of a badge caught her attention. She changed her footing, heading headlong for the man.

"Sheriff!" Mary hollered.

The man groused, taking a slow, deliberate spin on his heel. "Ma'am. It's not yet dawn."

Mary stopped, grimacing at his lack of interest. "Victor Del Avilasto shot my friend and is about to kill two more. You need to come!"

The man fully faced her now, brows raised with a sarcastic disbelief on his face. "Ma'am, the man you speak of is a wanted criminal, a very dangerous man."

Mary crossed her arms. "I speak true," she growled. "One of 'em is at Doc's now."

Without uttering another word, the sheriff strode past her and up the road from where she came. Mary walked quickly behind the long-legged man. The sheriff strode into Doc's building, going to the back.

Ross lay on the table, the white sheet under him made him appear paler than he was. Another sheet covered his lower half. Doc's hands were covered in blood. An instrument settled itself in his right hand, hovering above Ross's shoulder.

Doc glanced up, blinking multiple times. "Sheriff," Doc began, "this man came to me a few moments ago."

Mary perked a brow. "Believe me now, Sheriff?" she bit out.

*This dawdling sheriff wasted enough time like all men,* Mary grumped. *Ya go off tellin' the truth yet they believe otherwise or have ta see for themselves,* she rolled her eyes. *Think we're right dumb, they do. Women are smarter.*

The sheriff glowered at her. Mary matched his ill gaze.

"Del Avilasto, you say?" he questioned.

"Yeah," she replied, matching his condescending tone. "I'll take you right to him."

Doc stared at them both for a moment. Ross groaned on the table.

"Miss," Doc began, "are you not staying with your husband?"

Mary chortled. "He ain't my husband. He's my friend though. I will be back for him in a moment. C'mon Sheriff."

Jogging out the door, she headed to her mount. The sheriff walked briskly back to the door she first saw him come out of, yell inside, and mount his horse. Mary mounted hers with ease, waiting impatiently for the rest of the men and the languid sheriff to hurry.

*Take another hour why don't you,* she seethed. *Check to make sure I'm riding a horse and not a turkey.* Mary's upper lip twitched.

Six deputies came one by one out the door behind the sheriff with rifles and revolvers on their hips. It took forever as each man went back inside to grab either another gun or more ammunition. Mary's fingers strummed on her leg. Even her own horse was irritated if the constant twitching of his ears was anything to go by.

Finally, posse assembled, and with the dark countenance of the sheriff leading the way, Mary spun her anxious horse around, taking off at full speed up the hill. The sheriff and his deputies trotted their horses behind her.

Mary exhaled sharply, *let's take ten years.*

Her horse, tired already from their journey, frothed at the mouth. She silently promised him lots of carrots and oats soon as her friends were safe. Glancing behind her again, the sheriff was galloping now, but still some ways behind.

Focusing on the road ahead, she rounded the corner, nearing the final stretch of the road toward her companions. Mary breathed out; eyes wide. She reined in her horse.

"Audrey," Mary exclaimed from around the corner, "Eugene, damnation! That took plum too long. Got the sheriff dawdlin' behind me." She finished with a roll of her eyes.

"Victor is dead," Eugene informed gruffly.

Mary nodded. "Ross's at Doc's. Hope he pulls through. It's lookin' a might grim."

The sheriff reined in his mount a bit behind her. The firm look on his face annoyed her. His lack of concern and need to affirm accusations of a woman furthered her desire to steer clear of men. The sheriff glowered; eyebrows pinched so far together one could not discern the color of his eyes. The six deputies reined in at least twenty feet behind the sheriff. Their observant eyes keenly taking in her companion's appearance.

"I'm goin' back to Doc's. Keep an eye on Ross," Mary commented. She took off on horseback down the road, her hand waving in the air.

She breathed out relieved. Her task was done and Audrey was safe. Guilt clawed at her for what she'd done. She never intended for things to get too far out of hand and when they did, it was too late to stop it. And by then, she too was controlled by Victor Del Avilasto.

She reined in at Doc's door, dismounting and leaving the beast ground tied where he stopped. She burst through the door. The curtain fluttered where Doc just pulled it closed on the room Ross happened to be. He turned toward her, drying his hands on a clean towel.

Mary's heart embedded itself in her throat. "Is he dead?" she ventured blaming her weak voice on fatigue.

Doc shook his head. "No," he stated firmly, setting the cloth down on a table. "God seems to favor him. The bullet lodged in his lower left quadrant," he paused.

Mary made a face. *It's his gut not his quade-runt.*

"The side of his stomach," the doc clarified, "missed everything vital and was quite easy to remove. The other bullet in his shoulder was close to exiting. I was able to remove it." He sat down in his black chair, heaving an exhausted sigh. "I have no idea what trouble found you, and I don't want to know. Whatever it was, put it behind you, but go forward with God in your heart. You may go back and see him."

"Thank you," Mary replied.

She didn't know what else to say to the man. God left her when she was a child when her mother left the family. God left her again when she was forced to care for her younger siblings by herself while her dad drank himself stupid and her aunt couldn't be bothered. Mary knew God was around, that he was as real as a tree, but when it came to her, God turned his back.

Mary pulled the curtain gently. Ross lay still on the table. Bandages covered his shoulder and his stomach. He breathed lightly; his color still pale as the sheet he lay upon.

Approaching him from the left, she plopped in a chair by his bed. Tears stung behind her eyes but she sucked it all in, making it stop. She wiped her nose on the dirty, light blue shirt.

Gently she stroked his hair, pushing it to the side. Dark stubble lined his jaw. Mary smiled wanly.

*Sure, is a handsome man*, she thought. *Kind too. He makes my heart beat all crazy*, she sighed, letting her fingers linger on the back of his head. *This is all my fault. None of us would be here if it weren't for me. I damned us all.* She ran a hand over her face. *By Lordy I damned us all. I'm a fool of a woman. If I don't hang for this, I swear I'll do good.*

She reached for Ross's hand, taking a deep breath, "I'm so sorry, Ross," she said, giving it a squeeze. "I almost got you killed; Audrey and Eugene... I'm so sorry. I hope ya'll can forgive me at some point," she breathed out, tears falling down her cheeks unchecked. "Please... pull through."

Ross didn't move. Mary laid her head down on the small space on the table Ross lay on, never letting go of his hand. Her nose sniffled. One last, lone tear rolled off her cheek.

*I'm going to do better from here on out*, she vowed.

# CHAPTER TWO

M ary woke with a start. Someone put a hand on her head, moving their fingers about her blond hair gently like one would do to a child. She raised her head, turning toward the feeling of the person touching her.

Ross's hand removed itself from her head flopping itself on the table with a thud. Mary raised up, stretching her back and shoulders. Her body aching from the awkward position of sleeping. The blanket resting softly on her shoulders rolled off.

With the heels of her hands, she rubbed at her eyes. Her mouth opened; a soft yawn escaping. Rolling her neck to the side, she heard it pop. Mary leaned forward in her chair, her dirty clothes feeling stiff on her body. Ross's eyes crinkled at the faint sunlight streaming through a crack in the curtain.

"How d'ya feel?" she asked softly.

Ross moved his head to the sound of her voice, his eyes barely opening. "Like shit," he replied hoarsely. He licked his chapped lips. "Have you been here the whole time?"

"Yeah... I couldn't leave ya," she breathed, putting a hand on his arm then promptly removing it. "Doc said yer gonna pull through, but shouldn't move for a bit."

"Got any water?" he asked, his voice cracking and becoming breathy.

Mary scanned the room for a pitcher and a cup. Her eyes landing on the small table to the right of Ross. Getting up, her tight muscles throbbed with each boot step. Her lower back and calves ached. She poured a small cup of water, holding it in one hand. With her other, she lifted Ross's head, putting the cup to his cracked lips.

Ross coughed after taking in a large gulp of the liquid. He sputtered, shooting some of it down his body.

"Easy," Mary said.

Ross pulled his head away. "Thank you."

"What?"

"For saving me. If it weren't for you, I'd be dead."

Mary shrugged, feeling the guilt she thought she repressed surface. She wasn't a good woman, or kind. She was a fighter. She had to be to survive on her own. How Mary wasn't at the end of a hangman's rope, she could only guess God had plans for her or she got really lucky. By all accounts, she should be swinging for her crimes. She was so desperate for money and a decent life, she helped Victor Del Avilasto and his gang kidnap Audrey. Only to find herself soon facing death from Victor.

And that was just the tip of all the things she'd done. Stealing from anyone she could was a bad enough sin. God stated it in his commandments and she was certain she broke every one of them too, except adultery.

Mary put a hand to her throat. "Think nothin' on it," she dismissed.

Ross rolled his head to the side, his gray eyes more open and gazing at her. "Now stop that guilt right there. Don't deny it. I see it cuz I feel it some too. Like me, you got messed in with bad people." His brown hair stuck out all over the place, dirty and greasy.

She didn't reply. It was more than something so simple. Growing up, she was left by her Mato be raised by her father. He was a good man, in of it all, he tried the best he could for her and her three younger siblings after their mother split one night. Father moved them to Kansas City to be close to his sister, Winnifred, taking up odd jobs before landing one as a barkeep. After that, swill became preferable to family.

Mary sighed, shuffling her feet. *I surely did and now I will pay for those crimes in some way.*

Ross's cracked lips tried to grin. "It's all right," he said, reaching for her hand.

Mary let him take it. The warmth and reassurance coursing through her. She closed her eyes, allowing herself to bask in the kindness and tenderness of something so simple as holding her hand. No one held her hand before.

He gave her hand a squeeze. Mary relished in the protective power. She closed her eyes, savoring the moment. Ross slipped his hand away, resting it on the table. The coldness of his departed hand sent a chill down her spine.

*I ain't so sure things will be all right,* she thought, brows furrowing. *I had to make them so growing up and it didn't pan out much.*

No one in Kansas City would hire a kid, let alone a girl. It didn't help she couldn't read and write. Boys were the preference in stores to lift hefty objects. Her solution was to steal to put food on the table for them all. And soon stealing became a way of life from Kansas City to St. Louis, all the way down to San Antonio. It was all she knew, until someone finally hired her. She never told her siblings how she got the money. The shame was enough being on her, still plaguing her now at twenty years old.

*I cain't change what I'd done. I can change the now,* Mary decided. *No more thievin', rustlin, lyin', nor cheatin'. From here on out, I'll be good. I don't want that life no more.*

"Hungry?" she asked, breaking the silence and changing the subject.

Ross's eyes narrowed on her. "Yeah... Thank you," he said again. "I owe you, Mary."

Mary felt herself begin to sweat. Ross made her feel twitter-pated, like she lost her damn mind somewhere and couldn't find it. Not once had he judged her; even while they were with Victor together and now since being free, there was no judgement, only reassurance. Not once did an unkind word pass his lips. He regarded her in a neutral expression and spoke in a gentle, warm tone.

Her heart pounded so hard, it felt like it could slap her across the face. She fancied Ross, even back with Victor, she would ogle him from a distance. There was something about his easiness, his calmness she liked. He was a quiet man, not speaking unless he felt it important and he was fair in his words.

She shook her head, forcing herself out of the day dream. "You owe me nothin'. I'm pleased we got outta there alive."

"Same," Ross groaned, shifting on his bed.

Doc came in, throwing the curtain back. Dark bags hung under his eyes like suitcases – heavy and clunky. Grumbling under his breath, he rubbed the back of his neck. He threw back the curtains hanging over the window.

"Glad to see you both are awake," the Doc yawned. "It's morning. You have all been asleep for a while. Slept all through yesterday," he said in a droll tone.

The Doc leaned over, pulling back the bandages on Ross's shoulder. Mary scrunched her eyes, peeking in toward the bandages. The wound on his shoulder was not red and festering like she thought it would be.

She made a face at the black, neat stitches. She wanted to gag. She was not one for blood and guts. In all, Mary could deal with it, but it made her nauseous. Animals she could handle, the gutting and skinning of them. After all, she had to eat and that part was necessary. People though, not so much. Mary covered her mouth to keep herself from dry heaving.

Ross met her eye, giving her a wan smile. Mary returned it, feeling heat creep to her cheeks.

"Looking good," Doc commented

Doc pulled down the sheet covering Ross, peeking down the top of the bandage on his stomach. He made a face, poking at Ross's wound with his finger. "Take it easy. No heavy lifting for a few weeks. Come see me in about four days or so to change the dressing."

Ross groaned, sitting up. Mary grabbed his hand, gently helping him to a sitting position. She went to the end of the table, getting his boots, and Ross helped wriggle his feet inside. Ross thanked her with a genuine smile reaching his gray eyes. Mary gulped, taking a step back from him.

"What do I owe ya Doc?" Ross said.

Doc shook his head. "Nothing. The Whitman owner paid for everything. Her message is to come see her when you're through here."

Ross nodded. "I'll head there now. Thank you, Doc."

The Doc headed toward the curtain, pulling it completely back. "This way when you're ready."

Mary swallowed, *I'm swinging now.*

# CHAPTER THREE

Mary helped Ross up the stairs to the Whitman Hotel. Inside, she was shaking like a leaf. She felt sick. If Ross felt her shiver, or the cold, clamminess of her skin, he didn't comment. He tucked her arm inside his, holding it in place protectively. The warmth from his body did little to settle her nerves.

Her mind raced with what would happen once inside. Would the sheriff be there to escort her to jail? Would she be banished and told not to return to Denver? Mary bit her bottom lip until it indented and almost bled. Part of her was terrified to find out what lay in store for her behind those doors. The other part desired to face her demons, her mistakes, and own up to what she'd done to Audrey, Eugene, and Ross.

Ross groaned, taking another step.

"You alright?" she asked.

They were almost to the top of the landing where the large wooden carved bear greeted their entrance. Ross hissed, nodded, and took another step. Mary's foot hit the top of the landing. All breath and nerves escaped her, only a definite resolution to walk inside was left.

"I'm so sorry Ross," she said, tears burning behind her eyes. "This is all my fault. If we…"

Ross gently, pulled her to him by her chin. He wiped her tear with a stroke of his thumb, "No," he replied, sucking in a breath, letting it out slowly. "You were trapped like the rest of us."

Mary sucked in her lips, daring not to speak. It *was* her fault. Audrey and Eugene getting held captive, Ross getting shot, and they all barely escaped with their lives; all of it was her fault. How things panned out the way they did, Mary surmised God must want her to keep her skin for now. She knew He existed, but now He must want something from her. There was no other way to explain why she was breathing.

*God*, she thought, *iffn' yer really there, thanks for savin' me, and keepin' me alive. I appreciate it.*

Feeling better after thanking the Good Lord, she reached for the door, opening it and allowing Ross in first. He stood there, blinking.

"No, ma'am," he said firmly.

Mary put her hands on her hips, "Yer injured."

"Don't care. A woman, in a man's presence, *never* gets the door," Ross stated, holding the door open with his good shoulder and leg.

Mary walked in, getting the other door. An iron brick weight lay on the other side of the door. Using her foot to grab it, she propped it open. "I didn't get this one," she said with a smirk.

Ross gave her a pointed look, but said nothing as he awkwardly strode inside. Catching up to him, she glanced up, spotting the remnants of a small grin on his lips.

Going to the front desk, her heart pounded in her chest. Her palms sweating profusely as she rang the bell on the desk corner. Audrey came out of the back with Eugene behind her. Audrey appeared every bit fancy, like how she, herself, tried, and failed, to be once. Mary swallowed.

Audrey came to the front of the counter, a beaming smile on her face. Eugene's dower expression held Mary's a moment. His eyes blazing into hers like fire and she gulped again.

"I'm happy to see you both are doing well," Audrey said.

Ross dipped his head, removing his hat. "Ma'am, I'm indebted to you."

Audrey smiled. "I would like to hire you both. Mary, we need an extra hand in laundry, and general help. Ross, you will run the barn out back. Two meals and board are included. Pay's a dollar fifty a day."

Ross lowered his head, wringing his hat in his hands. "Mighty generous of you, Ma'am. I accept yer offer. However, Doc said I cain't do much for a few days."

Audrey leaned over, putting a hand on his good arm. "I understand. Doctor Collins told me everything. And do not tax yourself, you helped saved my life and so your debt is paid. Just start with what you can. An hour here or there, and no lifting. Maybe familiarizing yourself with the equipment and horses at first then, as you feel better, you can do more."

All the air in Mary's lungs left her. She gaped like a dying fish. She didn't know what to say or how to feel. She almost got Audrey and Eugene killed. She almost got them *all* killed and now she was getting offered a job? A place to stay? It made no sense to her. Yet she felt immense relief to not be on a tree, swinging in the wind. And she felt confused at how this woman could offer her, the one who wronged her so much, a lifesaving job and place to stay.

For the first time in her life, she was being offered money for hard work and a home. A place to lay her head and not fret about where her next meal was supposed to come from; and if she could get enough food for three other mouths along with a decent enough roof to cover their heads. She sent money back when she could, and as much as she could, even if her siblings didn't need it now. When Winnifred married, her siblings went with her, finally cared for with hot meals and a roof, more than she could ever do. Mary spun on her heel, facing the door. Exhaling slowly, she urged the tears back into her eyes.

*A home*, she thought. *A bed all my own with a real blanket. A good meal and not something dumped in the dirt. Good Lord above, I don't deserve it.*

"Mary?" Audrey beckoned. "Is that not satisfactory?"

Mary spun around quickly, facing Audrey, "By Jove," she breathed out. "You serious about hirin' me on?"

Audrey nodded. "Quite."

"Is that a yes?" Mary asked.

Audrey smiled. "I am serious, Mary. If you would like employment, you are hired here, or you can go elsewhere."

Mary let out the breath she didn't know she'd been holding, "I will work for you."

Audrey clapped her hands together. "Splendid. Let's put this entire event behind us and move forward," she stated, embracing them both. "Here are a few dollars to get yourselves new clothes," Audrey said, handing them each an envelope. "Now, let me show you to your rooms."

Ross followed in step behind Audrey. However, Mary found she couldn't. Her mind reeling from all the events, and trying to process it all. She stood by the front desk, eyes fixated on the lower hems of her dress and the floor, worrying the envelope between her fingers.

Mary pinched her side and jumped when she did it a little too hard. *I'm still breathin',* she thought. *It all feels unlikely, like a great dream that's too silly to be real like.*

Ross paused, holding out a hand to her. "Mary," he said softly, "come on."

Mary tentatively took his proffered hand. Ross put her hand on the outside of his arm, falling in step beside Audrey once more. The owner of the Whitman Hotel took them past the staircase and around the side. Eugene brought up the rear.

Mary closed her eyes and sighed. *I've got a second chance and a new beginnin'... I won't squander it,* she thought, giving a wan smile to Ross who reciprocated her grin and patted her hand.

"You all right?" Ross asked.

"Peachy keen." Mary replied through tight lips.

Her insides quaking like at any moment, all of this would be a farse and she would be on the street once more, trying to fend for herself. She didn't want this to be a dream, but she also didn't feel like she deserved it all. Her mind jumbling with reasons she should be dead.

She put a hand to her forehead, taking a deep breath in.

"Mary," Audrey said, stopping in front of a door. "you're staying in this room with Lena. And Ross, you're the last door on the right. I will see you both in a while. If you need anything, speak to Jane McCarthy. She knows about your employment."

Mary stood in front of her room, staring at the door and the shiny brass knob. Peeking over her shoulder, Ross had a hand on the knob with the door already open. He smiled, nodding at her, and stepped inside. Mary turned her head, focusing on the door. Closing her eyes, and turning the knob, she stepped inside.

# CHAPTER FOUR

The sun beat down on Mary's back as she scrubbed the laundry. A cool wind softly blew past her, bringing some relief to the hot sun on her shoulders and the warm waters of the laundry. After three days of being in laundry, she got a good grasp of what was to be done. She also got a good grasp of how others felt about her.

The first day everyone was indifferent to her. They weren't mean, but not kind either. She deserved it. She deserved all of it for what she'd done. Now, the others were coming around to her a little, although most left her be, and often refused to talk more than a word or two while in her presence. Her roommate Lena was the happiest and most talkative of all of them, treating her no differently than anyone else. The manager, a straight nosed, sharp eyed woman, hadn't spoken to her at all.

Mary swept her small blond strands of hair off her face. She braided her hair down the back of her head, but even then, her hair managed to escape. Mary rolled up the sleeves again on her navy-blue dress, not wanting her new garment all sopping wet.

Eliza came out, getting more of the clean clothes. Mary flashed her a smile; Eliza returned a terse one.

Mary sighed. *Everythin' will work out*, she thought, scrubbing the last of the linen. *Lena is nice. And so is Ada.*

Eliza came out again for a few of the other garments and items she washed, taking them inside, and hanging them to dry by the wood stove. Kelly was in an opposite room, mending anything that might have frayed or been damaged.

Mary scrubbed the last women's dress, wringing it out and putting it through a machine to get out more water. Taking the garment inside, she handed it to Eliza, who hung it on a wooden drying rack.

Kelly glanced up, her keen old eyes taking her in. "All finished?"

"Yeah," Mary replied. "The last of room 205 brought in."

Kelly nodded. "Go tend the garden out behind the barn. Bring anything ripe to Claudia in the kitchens."

Mary went out into the bright sunlight. The moment she was out of the door, she could hear Kelly and Eliza speaking in hushed tones. Mary swallowed the lump in her throat.

*I don't have to stay*, she thought. *Just work to get a bit of money and go somewhere else.*

Strolling down the pathway behind the Whitman Hotel, around the back of the building, a few horses whinnied from their stalls. Ross was out with a horse, taking a bridle off.

Mary went inside the barn, looking around. Like the prettiness inside the hotel, it was the same in the barn. Everything was in neat, tidy rows. Neatly labeled barrels lined the outside of the tack room. Mary lifted the top of a barrel peeking inside. *Oats.* Mary shut the lid and walked farther into the barn.

Ross came in from a side door, flashing her a smile. Mary tucked some stray hairs behind her ear, returning his smile.

"Hey Mary," Ross said, shutting the door behind him.

"Aren't you supposed to be takin' it easy?" she chided.

Ross shrugged, hanging up a lead rope. "I am. I'm not lifting. Already saw Doc Collins this mornin'," he pointed to his side. "Healin' good."

Mary nodded, rubbing her left hand on her right arm. His

handsome gray eyes stared into hers. Stubble lined his jaw, adding to his ruggedness. Mary swallowed.

"I'm glad to see yer healin' fine," she offered.

"Thank you."

Mary bit her lip. Last time she had feelings for another person, it screwed her over. Her intended left her for another woman, stranding her in Kansas City, penniless and without care. Right then, she swore off men. Swore off the name of Charlie too; vowing to never name her kid that either.

She reminded herself Ross was only being nice because they were once stuck in the same predicament. *He don't like me*, she cautioned. *He's a nice man, bein' nice like nice men do.*

"I'd best be off to tend the garden," Mary announced.

"I'll help you," Ross said, coming up beside her.

Even in the barn, away from the heat of the sun, she felt her cheeks flame and warmth creep down her spine. *I've plum lost my mind*, she thought.

"Thank you," she replied. "I appreciate it kindly."

Ross dipped his head, going in front of her and opening the side door to the back garden. Stepping back out into the Colorado sun, the aroma of freshly turned soil mixed in with the hay and horses, brought back memories of her Ma and how they would garden together. Mary pushed the memories aside. Her Ma was probably long dead by now.

Mary went to the far side of the garden by the carrots. Checking the long stems, she pulled some out of the ground. Ross knelt beside her, picking zucchinis.

"Where you from?" Ross asked casually.

Mary licked her chapped lips, feeling her mouth turn to cotton. Peeking over, she caught his tanned face focusing on pulling vegetables.

"I was born in Cincinnati, Ohio. Then when Ma left us, my Pa moved me and my three younger siblings to Kansas City. There I met my former fiancé," she rambled, feeling the words tumble from her mouth without wanting them to, but not seeming to make it stop, "his name was Charlie Hilbert... he left me for another woman." Inside she cringed, not wanting to tell him that part of her life and not knowing how he would receive it. "I was young, about seventeen."

Ross remained silent. Her blood turned to ice. Silently, she cursed herself for being forward with him, more than she planned on being.

*He asked where I was from not my life story. Good Lord, Mary!*

Setting her pile of carrots beside the zucchinis, she moved along to the cucumbers farther down the neat row; leaving the tiny ones while grabbing the prickly big ones. The corn was about ready to be pulled off and eaten though it would be a few more days since the little hairs sticking out the end weren't quite long enough.

"Where you from?" she asked, breaking the small silence between them.

Ross paused, leaning back on his heels. "All over. My Ma left us too, so Pa moved me and my sister around where he could get different jobs. My sister died of scarlet fever. Pa remarried and I got a half-brother, Richard," he removed his hat, scratching his head. "I was once engaged. She left me too, sayin' she needed more stability than what I could provide."

"That's the most I heard you speak to anyone," she replied in a teasing tone.

Ross shrugged; his lip quirking in a half grin. He moved, working beside her on the cucumbers, checking them and turning them over. Mary plucked a few, setting them beside the growing vegetable pile.

"What's yer full name?" she asked.

Mary swallowed, feeling more heat creep to her cheeks. Being in close proximity with a handsome, kind man was new to her. She enjoyed it. She enjoyed him.

Ross paused in pulling up a weed. "Ross Evan Montgomery. And you?"

"Florence Miriam Lockburn."

"Pretty name," he said, smiling. "Thank you again, for savin' my hide."

Mary paused her work, staring into his stormy gray eyes; twinkling at her under the shade of his brown hat, gazing into hers with a knowing like he could see the real her, deep down inside.

"I couldn't leave you to die," she answered truthfully.

Picking up her hand, he kissed the back of it. "Thank you."

Mary felt her cheeks flame hotter than the kitchen oven. Hotter than that too, more like the sun. If she could swoon over someone, she felt it would be him. Charlie never made her feel valued or appreciated. She was his tool, a means to get rich and then let her take the fall. She hesitated with Ross too. How their relationship began, casual and kind, was the same way hers and Charlie's began.

She closed her eyes. *I cain't let myself get too close,* she reasoned. *I won't make the same mistakes.*

Turning back to the vegetables, Mary moved along to the bush beans. Her mind wandering to when Charlie took her to St. Louis, almost getting her strung up for what he'd done, and blamed on her. He stole jewelry right off a woman, planting the items on Mary, while he went back, taking the woman's purse full of money. Mary barely made it out alive as the sheriff's deputies saw her wearing jewels too good for the likes of her and chasing her half way out of town. Right after the trip back to Kansas City, Charlie left her, but not before taking her to bed and then taking her money.

Tears tracked down her face. Shame for the time period creeping into her heart, and filling her with immense guilt; not for what she'd done but what she'd let be done to her. She was a fool of a woman. Believing and hoping someone could love her for being different than who she really was – a miscreant.

Wiping her tears with the back of her hand, she picked beans off the bush. She wouldn't be able to right the wrongs she'd done if she spent the rest of her life trying. She'd stolen from so many people, hurt so many. She'd never be able to repay the hurt she'd done to Audrey. But she would try, damn it, because she was tired of hurting people.

Mary sniffed, piling the bush beans in the apron part of her dress. It was awkward for her being here, working. She wasn't used to eating meals together like a family, talking about the day or laughing about rowdy customers who came through the doors. She wasn't used to belonging anywhere. She wasn't sure if she belonged here yet, or if she would ever belong anywhere. She was used to being alone, always alone. And she deserved it after all the hurt she'd dealt.

Wiping her nose on her sleeve, she sniffled, blowing out her breath.

"Mary," Ross called softly.

"Yeah?"

"We'd all done bad things."

"Yeah," she sniffed, hiccupping, trying to keep herself from blubbering.

"Doesn't make us truly bad hearted people."

Mary shrugged. "I've done terrible," she trailed off.

Coming beside her, he set down his tomatoes. "As have I."

Mary dried her eyes, gazing into his. Tears tracked down her face. Ross swept her tears away with a dirty thumb leaving behind slight smears on her light skin. His stormy gray eyes held hers firmly. Pushing his hat back off his face a bit, his messy brown hair matted with sweat to his forehead. His tanned and dirty face brought out the brightness of his eyes and white of his teeth.

*Mighty handsome man*, she thought. She closed her eyes at his gentle, sincere touch, wiping away the last of her tears.

"I've killed a few men," he whispered. "I ain't proud of it."

"I won't tell," she whispered back.

"I know."

Mary bit her lower lip. "I've stolen lots from people. I got sucked in by promises Charlie made me. He used me, in lots of ways, and left me in Kansas City without anything," she admitted, tears coming anew. "I didn't want that life, with Charlie... or the stealin' on my own... I've done terrible."

"I'm sorry for it," Ross offered, giving her hand a squeeze.

Mary shrugged, head down, staring at the dirt. "Lesson learned...again and again."

Ross lifted her chin. She met his steady, kind gaze. His eyes left hers as he nodded toward the hotel, "We got a new start here. Past is past now and it don't matter."

"Is past truly past?"

Ross shrugged, rising off the ground. He offered her his hand which she took. "It is with me," he stated. "Always with me."

Mary smiled. "Thank you."

Ross gave her a lop-sided grin. She liked seeing him smile, how his gray eyes, so focused and eagle like bore into hers with kindness and wisdom. He made her feel like a person. He made her feel wanted. She'd pondered leaving several times in the last few days. Ross made her want to stay.

"I'll help you carry these to Claudia," he said, piling the bigger vegetables in his shirt.

Mary smiled, putting the last veggies in her apron. "Thank you, Ross."

He nodded, going ahead of her and opening the door.

*If I ever get fortunate, I would like a man like him on my arm*, she thought. *Maybe here, past* can *be past.*

# CHAPTER FIVE

Mary took the vegetables to the kitchen, putting them all beside the sink. Ross dumped his load beside hers, tipping his hat at her and leaving promptly to go back outside. With the other kitchen hands busy, Mary washed the vegetables, being sure to keep her head down and any opinion to herself. In the days since being here, Mary found it best to keep to herself since most of the time her attempts at conversation were met with silence or terse one or two worded answers. Some, like Jane and Claudia didn't care for her enough to even glance in her direction. On the other side, her roommate, Lena was more talkative than a child. Mary smiled a little at the thought of Lena. How the woman had words to say every few minutes was beyond her.

Uneasiness filled her again. Mary swore she could feel daggers of eyes on her, driving their invisible knives into her back. She tried to put on a brave face, surviving by acting like she knew what she was doing, or nothing bothered her and displaying confidence. Truth was, she felt like she was drowning, floundering around, gasping for air but getting sucked deeper.

Peeking over her shoulder, Claudia's hovering gaze, like a carrion above a carcass, bore down on her. Reaching for a carrot,

Mary turned her attention back to her washing, acting like she never saw the older woman's death stare.

Being at the Whitman Hotel was almost harder than being on the streets. Here, people knew what she'd done since Eugene told Jane to keep the money locked up, and Jane must have told everyone else; they judged her hard and went to church on Sunday like nothing was ever amiss. They disliked her, treating her indifferently, not really having a true interest in getting to know her. She was better off than on the streets since she'd a roof over her head and food in her belly. On the street, she was cold and hungry; stealing was a necessity. People looked down their nose, spitting in her direction. But it was expected. She hadn't counted on the same intolerance here.

Peering over her shoulder again, she caught a glimpse of Claudia's death stare again. *Just keep scrubbin' for land's sake*, Mary thought. *Cain't get ornery with me over dishes.*

Drying her hands on a towel, Mary went out to where customers sat and ate. Clearing the tables of empty plates, silverware and glasses, bringing them back to the kitchen. Washing all of those, she set them to dry and went back for more.

"What are you doin'?" Claudia barked when she came through the doors again, arms laden with plates and cups.

"Clearin' tables," Mary replied, placing her second load in the sink.

Claudia scowled. "You're in laundry, I suggest you get to it."

"Laundry is done. Same with tendin' the garden and washin' vegetables," she replied levelly. "Would you like me to wash dishes for ya or would ya rather hop down my throat about workin'?"

Claudia threw a drying towel at her. Mary caught it, returning the older woman's level gaze, hopefully without the heat.

"Wash then," Claudia hissed, turning back to the hot stove.

Taking a deep breath, Mary spun on her heel, filling the sink with more hot water. *Maybe Ross is wrong*, she thought. *Maybe here, past cain't be past at all.* Glancing over her shoulder, Lena gave her a wan smile and a shrug. Lena's long dark brown braided hair fell off to the side while her hazel eyes lit up bright when she looked at Mary.

Closing her eyes, she took a deep breath. She washed the dishes, putting each one above her on the rack to dry. One clattered in the sink, the sharp sound of it breaking to pieces echoed in their silent kitchen. Mary pulled the broken pieces out of the sink, tossing it in the garbage.

"Are you all right?" Lena asked, coming up behind her.

"Yeah," Mary replied. "I'm not cut."

"Come. Take a break with me," Lena said, looping her arm in with Mary's. "We've been going at it all morning and some down time with fresh air is just what we need."

Mary allowed herself to be pulled out of the kitchen by Lena. She stumbled to keep up with the fast paced and long-legged Lena, leading her to the back of the hotel. Lena opened the door into a tranquil space with nicely trimmed trees and potted plants. A bench was on the other side of the door to the left. Another bench sat underneath a tall fir.

Plopping herself on the bench by the door, Mary leaned forward with her head in her hands. Some of her small blond strands crept out of her braid. With a sigh, she leaned back, undoing the white apron covering her navy-blue dress.

Lena sat beside her, taking the stays out of Mary's hands and completing the process. Taking the apron off, Mary folded it messily in her hands.

"You all right," Lena asked.

Mary shrugged. "Kinda. Not really."

"Wanna talk about it?"

Again, she shrugged. Would this get back to the others? If she shared what was bothering her, would she even feel better or more guilty? Mary ran a hand over her face. She didn't like being here, made to feel like she didn't belong but there was no other place to go. She had no money. She'd nothing but a few new dresses to her name. What honestly could she do if she wanted to stay truthful?

Leaning against the back of the bench, eyes closed, Mary sighed deeply as the sun struck her face. "I don't fit in here"

Lena put a hand on her arm. "Of course, you do," she assured. "They just don't know you. No one else has been through what you and Ross have. If you tell everyone tonight at dinner, help them understand, then you will gain more respect and feel like you belong."

Mary opened her eyes, taking in Lena.

The woman smiled, nodding at her. "Trust me," Lena urged. "I have my past I don't talk about, same with everyone else. But to make it easier for you, to talk about what you've done," she fidgeted in her seat, biting her lower lip. "I haven't told anyone in a long time except Jane and Audrey. I was once a woman of the night. I was a starving girl; came from the slums of New York. I slept with men to make my way out here to start a better life. Jane believed in me and gave me a job here. I've been at the Whitman Hotel for almost eight years."

"How old are ya?" Mary asked.

"Twenty-three."

Mary squeezed Lena's hand. Life dealt them both hard blows in different ways, forcing each to choose a path. And each path got them judged horribly by the same people who claimed to be righteous.

Tucking the hairs behind her ear, Mary wondered if Ma would've stayed around if her life would have played out differently. Mary scowled, racking her brain for any memories of how her Ma was. She didn't have many recollections of her. Mary sighed, *I did what I had to. Doesn't make it right. Now all I can do is make it right from here.*

"I've been stealin' since I was a kid. At ten years old, I had to feed my three younger siblings. I stole from Audrey; took all her fancy things. Then Victor found me thinkin' I was her. Wanted to kill me right then but I told him I could be useful on account of I didn't want to die. Then… Well… Here I am."

Lena squeezed her hand, a wan understanding smile on her lips. "Don't leave. Stay here and be a better person than you were yesterday. God forgives. You may not think it, feel it, or know it, but He does. He forgives you. It's time to forgive yourself."

Lena got up, going to the door and back inside. Mary stared at the fir tree in front of her, how the roots came above the dirt and back underneath. Lena's words echoed in her mind.

*I cain't forgive myself for what I've done... Not yet leastways,* Mary decided, wadding the apron tighter in her hands. *I got apologizin' to do, startin' with Audrey, and Ross.*

# CHAPTER SIX

Ross wrinkled the brim of his hat in his hands, watching Mary speak to Lena. Since she saved his life, he felt connected to her. She was more than what she painted herself to be – a hard, stone-faced woman. Mary was gentle, authentic, a kinder person than she gave herself credit for.

Spinning on his heel, he headed back to the barn, losing the urge to go speak to her. It startled him that he wanted to talk to her. He wasn't the talking type, much too shy and disliking the sound of his deep, grumbling tone. But talking with her was easy. He enjoyed it; being in her presence and seeing the light shine in her sky-blue eyes. He enjoyed her smile, how there was a small gap in between her front teeth adding to her sultry genuineness.

Peeking over his shoulder, Mary was by herself, staring at the fir tree in front of her. She wrung her white apron in her hands, tucking her constant small, wispy blond hairs behind her ears.

*Prettiest thing in Denver,* he thought. *Personality of a small mouse but wears the clothing of a lion,* his lip quirked... *She's a good woman. I don't rightly know when my feelings for her changed. It was somewhere between running from Victor and being here. I'm glad for it... Now...* he swallowed, beating his hat in his hand, *what do I say?*

He smiled, going toward her. He didn't have a clue what to say to her. Each time he spoke, he expressed his gratitude for his life. He was grateful, but he couldn't keep thanking her. Along the same line, he didn't know what to say without sounding dumb.

Ross stood awkwardly to the side, hopping from foot to foot. Her eyes were softly closed, her breathing deep and slow. Finally, he sat beside her.

"Would you apologize to those you wronged iffn' ya got the chance?" she asked.

Ross scratched the stubble on his beard. He hadn't ever thought about it before. Pushing the guilt of what he'd done aside again, for it didn't change the outcome.

"No," he said softly.

Her blue eyes burst open, her body turning toward him. "I thought you were Lena."

"Sorry," he said, quickly rising to his feet.

"Don't go," she called quickly, "please."

Ross plopped back down, his mind reeling for what to say. If he could apologize for what he'd done, it wouldn't bring back the people he killed or heal the families he hurt. It wouldn't end the nightmares or the sounds of their dying screams. He'd never been cold blooded. Every kill had been kill or be killed. Every torture was torture or be killed. Victor ordered him to do it with a gun to his head, and more guns of the gang members at his back. It was either he killed the man and live or they both died. Taking the cowards way out, he lived.

Ross ran a hand over his face, pushing the memories to the far reaches of his mind. He kicked a rock with the toe of his boot. "No, I wouldn't," he finally said again.

Mary's beautiful blue eyes narrowed; the corner of her mouth and nose scrunched. "Why?"

"It wouldn't change what was done."

Mary sniffed. "Then why do I feel so terrible?"

"Because you believe you should be dead, or at least punished, for the crimes, yet you breathe."

Honestly it was how he felt most of the time. He should have died numerous times over. This last time, he swore he did. Then Mary saved him. Right then he decided God must have a purpose for him. Surely once born, every person's marked with an end date, given a purpose, and put on earth to fulfill whatever was needing done; and he hadn't reached his yet. Somehow, God needed him alive. At least, it's what he thought and made sense to him.

Ross stuck his hat back on his head. "I'll see you at dinner."

Mary grabbed his arm. "Wait."

He stilled, relishing her warm touch on his arm. Mary was like sweet spring air, riddled with fruit blossoms he could breathe in forever. Her navy-blue dress brought out the sun-kissed color of her skin and the blond of her hair. It became her in a manner he couldn't describe, making him catch his breath and relish in the angelic like appearance of her. Her bright blue eyes pleaded into his for companionship, an invite he couldn't deny.

Slowly he sat down once more, her hand still on his arm. Like a cold slap of snow, she removed her hand.

"What should I do?" she asked meekly.

"Pray," he stated. It was a simple answer, one his father often said in response to a lot of his questions. And the answer he always got never made sense until recently. "Pray because God will help you find answers."

She nodded, leaning back against the bench. Her defeated, dour expression clenched his heart. Being forced to do things against one's will to survive brought on more heartache than the lucky ones would ever understand.

Removing his hat, he wrung it in his hands. His life was similar to hers. Being alone and left to care for youngers was hard enough but then to care for a weak, pathetic father on top of youngers made the situation worse than herding rattlesnakes.

"I'm thirty-one," Ross blurted.

He hadn't a clue why he announced that. She made him feel twitterpated in the head like nothing else, and everything made sense when he was around her. She made him want a family and to settle down; to be a better, more loving husband and father than what he was given.

"I'm twenty," she replied.

Ross tilted his head to the side, acting like he had an itch. *So young,* he thought. *Her whole life is ahead of her while I got plenty of years on her. I'm halfway dead and in the ground.*

Mary put her hand back on his arm. "Age don't matter to me none." Her blue eyes shining bright into his. "I...," she smiled at him, squirming in her seat.

Her bright eyes bore into his, full and wide. Mary swallowed, biting her lower lip. He put his hand over hers, removing it from his arm gently and firmly as he could. "I'll see you at dinner, Mary," he said, whispering her name.

Striding away from her, and back to the barn. *I can't be a burden on her young life.*

---

Mary sat open mouthed on the bench, watching the muscled backside of Ross leave her. A lump formed in her throat. She bitterly forced it down. Ross's rejection stung worse than being dumped off in a strange place by Charlie or her mother leaving her at a young age.

Biting her lower lip, she rose, heading back inside. She went to the kitchen to where dirty dishes had multiplied around the sink while she'd taken a break. The suds died down and the water cooled considerably.

The back doors to the kitchen swung open with a whoosh of air and then closed with a bang. The whispering of Claudia and the high pitched, nasally snorts of agreement from Ada grated on her ears. She wanted to lash out, reprimanding them to speak plain in front of her but at the same time, she tried not to care.

Tonight at dinner, she would do what Lena said and tell everyone; give people a glimpse into her life and how sorry she was. Mary was truly sorry for all she'd done. It wasn't who she was but who she had to be.

*Past is past*, she thought. *I gotta put it behind me.* She set another plate on the drying rack, moving along to the cups. *Dear... Lord*, she began, *I be mighty sorry for what I've done up until workin' for Audrey. I hope you, of all bein's can forgive me of my trespasses. And maybe... help me forgive myself for it all too. Amen.*

Lena burst through the door pale and staring right at her. Mary tilted her head, sticking the white cup on the rack.

"Somethin' the matter?" Mary asked drying her hands.

Lena came in close, whispering, "Sheriff Mobley is here."

Mary shrugged. "Did he find the rest of the gang?"

"He's here for you."

Mary paled. "Me? I've done nothin' since bein' here."

"Come out and talk to him."

Mary set the towel beside the sink. Her bootsteps out into the dining area felt like thunder hammering in her heart. Cold crept down her back, settling like ice on the small of her back.

The sheriff sat back in his chair, sipping his coffee. Two deputies sat at a smaller table by the front door, glancing in her direction. Mary shuddered, approaching the sheriff. Her forehead felt cool, like beads of sweat drying now being out of the kitchen. She shivered a little, blaming the temperature difference between the two rooms.

"Sheriff Mobley," Mary greeted.

"Florence Lockburn?"

"Yes, that's me," she confirmed. Mary turned to Lena's scowling, questioning face. "My full name's Florence Miriam Lockburn, but I prefer Mary."

The sheriff's countenance tightened. "Mary," he said flatly. "I'm here because someone said you stole a watch and some other items."

Mary shook her head. "No sir, I have not. I've been here working."

Sheriff Mobley glanced past her to Lena. "Is that true?"

Lena nodded. "She's been with me Sheriff. I left her outside a moment but it was brief."

"Then Ross came by, chatting with me," Mary added quickly. "After, I came in and did dishes."

The sheriff's chair screeched back against the wooden floor. He stood, stretching his back and putting his black hat on his head. "Then you won't mind me searching your room."

Mary crossed her arms. "No sir, I would not."

She led the way through the back of the kitchen and out a side door opening into the hallway where all the employee's quarters were. Mary strode to her door, ripping it open, allowing the sheriff to go inside.

"Hands behind your back," he growled, whirling on her.

"What?" Mary inched away. "I didn't steal nothin'!"

"The items on your bedside table just walked there?"

Mary paled, poking her head inside. "I've been set up! I didn't steal!"

The sheriff grabbed her arm. "Tell it before a judge. Come easy. Hands behind your back, Miss."

Sheriff Mobley spun her around, holding her roughly against the wood. A deputy strode in past her, securing the stolen items. Struggling to turn her head to the left, she met Lena's startled face and accusing eyes.

"Mary," Lena whispered, "how could you do this? After all Audrey has done for you!"

Mary stared Lena dead in the eye. "I didn't. I ain't like that no more!"

Sheriff Mobley grabbed her shoulder, spinning her around to face the door. He gave her a little shove to get her moving. Mary stood her ground, planting her heels in, turning her face to glare at the sheriff.

"I did not steal!" she snarled.

"Again," Sheriff Mobley said, shoving her forward. Mary stumbled. Mobley caught her before she hit the ground. "Tell it to the judge tomorrow morning."

Tears sprung into her eyes. *Damnation,* she cursed. *I didn't do this. By Lordy what will happen to me now? I'm surely swinging. I know I am.* Mary blanched. *What will Ross think?*

# CHAPTER SEVEN

R oss brought the horses in for the night, locking them in their stalls; feeding each a hefty chunk of hay and a portion of oats. The gentle whickering and swooshing of their tails from side to side echoed softly in the barn. His mind wandered to Mary. A small smile crept across his lips.

He never felt the way he did about a woman before. Every woman he was remotely interested in never gave any indication they felt the same. He never really pursued them to find out whether they liked him either. He didn't want their stinging rejection. But he also felt undeserving of their love, believing no beautiful woman would want someone like him. Until Mary; and he still knew he was undeserving of her, but she showed interest and his was more than a little piqued. He couldn't help but want to pursue her. She made him feel wanted, seen, worthy.

Mary made it clear she liked him, even with her simple statement of his age not mattering to her. She was forward which he enjoyed because he wasn't. Growing up, he learned about what *not* to do to a woman from his father. A man was meant to protect and provide not strike and disgrace. He wasn't sure what *to* do in all the other aspects of being a husband. Ross had a pretty good idea, but it wasn't enough to make him good or an expert.

He ran a hand over his face. *I should tell her*, he decided. *I liked her since Victor's, with her wit and defiance. Her savin' my life solidified it.* Taking the hat off his head, he brushed his hair back. *She's sweet as cream even if she acts like a burnt biscuit*, he smirked at his analogy.

Hanging up the last bridle, he strode out the double barn doors, locking it shut for the night. With a long breath out, he went up the pathway to the hotel, going slowly to figure out what to say to Mary. He wasn't good with words, often stumbling over them, especially when the words he wanted to say were important.

Head down and hat wringing in his hands, he focused on the pathway. *Mary, I've been reckoning about this for a while and I like you,* he thought scratching his head. *Nah, Mary I like you*, he shook his head. *Mary I've liked you since Victor's and I was wonderin'.* Ross beat the hat in his hand.

Glancing up at the lantern light on the back of the hotel, Lena sat on the bench outside. Her drawn face fixated on the tree in front of her. Her eyes shone in the almost moonlight. In his days since being here, he hadn't seen her with any other emotion than grinning.

Brows furrowed over his eyes. "Everythin' all right?" he asked softly.

Lena shook her head. "Mary got arrested for stealing. Her trial is tomorrow."

His heart beat stilled. There was no way Mary could have stolen since being here. She never left. He paused, *she could have left during the night, but I don't think she would have. No, she wouldn't have,* he confirmed.

From the way Mary spoke, she wanted better and different. She wanted a new life, free from her past like he did. He wanted to walk away from it all and because of Audrey, they both were able to accomplish it.

"She didn't steal," Ross stated.

Lena leaned her head to the side. "I want to believe it. Sheriff Mobley found evidence in our room on her nightstand. The thing is, I don't remember it being there this morning, or this afternoon. And she was here at the hotel the entire time. I'm just not sure what to believe. Evidence is against her but she didn't seem to have time nor did she seem to want to."

In his heart, Mary didn't do it. He'd seen the guilt and how her beautiful smile turned into quick frowns and knew she couldn't have done it. Someone set her up. But who? Victor and some of his men were dead. The other's dispersed to different areas, so he thought. Could it have been one of Victor's cronies? Or with her past, perhaps someone she'd wronged come to haunt her?

Ross scowled, looking at Lena. "She didn't steal," he stated again. "Don't know how I know, but I do."

Lena shook her head. "I don't know... I hope you're right. I just... I'm going to the trial tomorrow," Lena announced, getting off her seat.

"Me too."

He had to find out for himself if Mary did this or not. In his gut he knew, but he had to be sure. If she did steal and was lying, there was no possible way he could love her. He couldn't allow himself. He couldn't trust her. For if she did this, what else is she capable of? Would she lie and hurt him too, only to gain a temporary upper hand? He was on the path to change and better himself. He put all the wrongdoings behind him, put Victor behind him. If Mary couldn't do the same, she would pull him back into where he didn't belong. He prayed his gut was right and this was a huge misunderstanding or a setup.

# CHAPTER EIGHT

Mary sat on her jail cell bed; legs tucked under her on the patchwork quilt. Claudia came in shortly after she'd arrived, bringing her a meal. The old cook's smug expression as she handed Mary her food, irked her. She did not steal the watch or the money. She was making her own way now and was doubly indignant someone was trying to drag her back into a life she'd decided she was leaving.

Sighing, she leaned back against the wall. Cold air blew down on her head from the jail window. The black iron bars mocked her, jeering at her for finally locking her away for all she'd done over the years, and this time for something she didn't even do.

Two other cells were on her right with no one inside. The dark wooden walls and iron bars surrounded her. An iron door locked her in and a thick wooden one was also locked, leading to the main office area.

Mary sighed, pulling her knees to her chest. Jingling of keys sounded from outside the wooden door. She ignored it, feigning sleep so she didn't have to hear the mocking jabs of Sheriff Mobley, the same ones he and his deputies been throwing at her since she arrived.

"Here she is," the sheriff said.

Instead of the sheriff's clunky bootsteps with the high-pitched jingle of spurs, it was a softer, polished step. Mary kept her head down, ignoring whomever it could be.

"Oh Florence, how I've been searching for you my sweet honey bee."

Mary's head jerked up, eyes already scowling at the person she hated most in the world. Charlie Hilbert, her former fiancé stood before her in a pressed gray linen suit with a black top hat sitting delicately on his blond hair. She could not see much in the darkness of her cell save for what the minimal light from oil lamps showed. Mary swore she could see his brown eyes shimmering with merriment at her predicament.

A beautiful red headed woman was hanging on his arm. Her pink bushy dress, almost as horrible as the gold dress she once loved. The woman's brown-black eyes, gleamed at her in the dim light. Mary brushed hair off her face with a swipe of her hand, and stared at the couple.

After a minute, she glanced around them for the sheriff but he was out of sight.

"Are you not going to say hello to me and my wife, Opal?" Charlie asked. "It is obscenely rude if you don't."

Mary remained silent. She hated him more than her mother who walked out and her alcoholic shit for a father. Leaning back, she rounded her shoulders. Her blood boiled.

*Good thing bars separate us,* she thought, *otherwise I would be hangin' for murder instead.*

"Maybe she is too dim to speak, dearest," Opal cooed venomously.

Charlie patted her hand. "Quite right my love."

Striding to the iron bars, he grinned wolfishly at her. Mary remained where she was. Her jaw clenched tight. She could feel the veins in her neck pulsate. Her jaw aching from remaining silent. Her hands balled into fists that she tucked in her dress pockets.

Charlie grinned at her. "You weren't hard to find," he whispered. "You stayed in Kansas City too long, Mary," he admonished clucking his tongue. "You know better."

Mary cracked her neck, not saying a word. Yawning, she leaned back on the timbered wall, feigning disinterest.

"Remember when you stole from me and buried it somewhere in Texas?"

Mary smiled smugly, shrugging.

She did indeed remember where and how much was buried in the dirt. She caught Charlie with another woman and while he was busy making the other woman scream in the bedsheets, she snuck in, stealing his entire loot — one thousand American greenbacks. She boarded a train, going to San Antonio, then changing her mind, boarded one to Omaha, burying her treasure five miles east outside the city. Mary planned to go back for it, after returning the locket to Audrey and establishing herself as a respectable woman. Now, it was too late. But she would never tell him where she buried it.

Mary sighed, leaning comfortably back on the wall. Charlie pressed his face against the iron bars seething. His white face mottled red, lip curling upward as the devil danced in his eyes.

"Tell me, Honey Bee, where my money is. Where in Texas is it?"

Mary curled up on her bed with her back to Charlie. Inside, she was shaking. Charlie had a temper more explosive than gun powder. The stomping of his booted feet clattered out of the room. Mary let out the breath she was holding. If she didn't die by the judge tomorrow, Charlie would surely kill her. Turning her head, she watched from the corner of her narrowed eye.

"My good Sheriff," Charlie's voice drifted toward her as he headed for the back desk where the sheriff sat leaning in a chair, "I believe I've made a terrible mistake."

Mary's insides trembled.

"Sir?" Sheriff Mobley's voice boomed.

Charlie slipped the sheriff something Mary couldn't see. "I've made a terrible mistake in having this woman arrested. She didn't steal anything from me or my wife. It was a dreadful misunderstanding."

Sheriff Mobley perked a brow, nodding and tucking the "something" inside his pocket. "Put it in writing and sign your mark," he stated sliding a piece of paper in front of Charlie.

Her former fiancé happily scribbled something. Sheriff Mobley's chair screeched back as he stood and groaned. Charlie's wife Opal glared at her. Her perfectly coiffed red hair pinned extravagantly at the nape of her neck.

"Well dear," she cooed softly while still managing to glare and twirl her parasol in her hand, "now you will have to show us where it is, won't you?"

Mary swallowed. The sheriff came back, keys rattling in his calloused hands. The grinding of the lock sent chills down her spine. Mary stayed where she was on the cot, much preferring to face the judge in the morning. Her stomach churned icily, fearing if she moved, she would vomit on the floor.

"You're free to go Florence," Sheriff Mobley stated. "I'll let your employer know about the mix-up and get your job back for you."

"Thanks," she whispered.

Sheriff Mobley took her under the arm, guiding her out of the cell. The man wasn't gruff like he was previously; maybe he did have a heart, way down deep. Whatever happened next, she hoped he would be able to save her hide from this man, his wife, and associates. The iron door boomed shut behind her. Mary flinched at the sound, feeling vulnerable in the open with Charlie. Sheriff Mobley let go of her arm, tipping his hat to her.

Striding out of the jail, Mary made a fast-paced line straight for the Whitman Hotel. Two men stepped in front of her, blocking her path. Glancing behind her, Charlie came out of the building, Opal on his arm. He pulled a pistol out of his waistband. Mary tried to shove her way through the men in front of her desperate to get away. They pushed her down to the damp ground.

"Shit," she cursed under her breath. Righting herself, she dusted off the dirt from her favorite dress.

"Honey Bee, I believe you remember Barrie and Danny," he said casually, sauntering up to her and cocking his gun. "See when you stole from me, you stole from all of us."

Mary whirled around. "Part of the loot was mine. I took the rest as emotional comp-ension for walking in on my intended with another woman." she seethed.

She deserved the money. She needed it. She wanted to build a better life for herself, with her own house and a couple head of cattle. Mary wanted to have a value to others, find herself a respectable husband since Charlie betrayed her heart and treated her like a common harlot. Men saw her with her mussed hair and tattered clothes, and looked the other way; viewing her flawed and unworthy. With money, she had value.

*I want to be wanted,* she thought. *And the money would help me have a family. I can start over in a new town I never been in since so many are ruined for me.*

Charlie strode up to her with a condescending smile. He took his finger and bopped her on the nose like one would do to a silly child. "Oh Honey Bee," he purred with a hint of a laugh in his throat, "sweet, stupid Mary," he sighed, grinning wolfishly, "how simply naïve. The money was never meant to be yours. You merely escaped death."

Taking a step back, she blanched as Charlie pointed his cocked gun at her forehead. She glared at him. For years she had been afraid of his booming voice and his vicious fist. He was little more than a wimpy child, taking out his frustrations on her knowing she couldn't fight back. For that very reason, she feared him.

She rolled up her sleeves. Today, she wouldn't take any more abuse. Men were not supposed to do this to women. At least the little she'd seen of Ross, even Eugene, despite her certainty that man despised her. And she was willing to fight for herself.

"Do you like breathing, Mary?" Charlie asked taking a step toward her.

Mary didn't back down, stepping to him, standing toe to toe. Charlie grinned, his upper lip curling. Tilting her head back, taking another step and forcing him back. Charlie put the cold barrel of his pistol to her forehead.

She nodded, breathing shallowly.

"Take us to where you buried it and you can keep breathing. Don't and we will kill you where you stand."

Peeking out her peripheral, Barrie and Danny whipped back their dusters, exposing the guns on their hips. Opal pulled a pistol out from the pocket of her dress. Four guns cocked and ready, waited patiently to discharge.

"What's your choice Mary?"

Mary took another step to Charlie, forcing him back while the pistol dug a little more in her head. "Get tickets to Kansas City then San Antonio. I buried it in Texas."

Charlie wagged a pistol at Danny. The man strode off down the road to the ticket office. Barrie grabbed her upper arm. Forcing him off, she took another step toward Charlie.

*I'm done with this*, she decided.

Charlie stood his ground, grinning; almost on the verge of chuckling.

*I'm gonna wipe the stupid look off his face someday*, she seethed.

She'd enough of being Charlie's pawn. No more neglect, no more abuse, and never again would she ever come willingly to his bed. No one ever treated her worse than he. Charlie struck her whenever he wanted, burned her on her thigh with an iron fire poker and tied her behind a horse once, dragging her halfway through town. And she was stupid enough to stay long as she had because he offered shelter, food and predictability. At least her own mother had the decency not to care and leave; and her father to die of alcohol.

The only people who treated her worth more than the dirt on their shoes were Audrey and Ross. She'd hoped to call Audrey a friend and she fancied Ross a lot, not like she'd ever be brave enough to admit it out loud. He treated her kind; kinder than anyone else. He spoke to her kindly as well, not judging her.

Closing her eyes for a brief second, she pictured Ross's handsome face staring back at her. How his observant gray eyes bore into hers and the stubble of a beard lined his square jaw.

Another gun jammed itself into her ribcage. "Enough, Florence," seethed Opal.

"This ain't over, Opal," Mary hissed.

Charlie chuckled, releasing the hammer of his gun. Flipping it over, the barrel in his hand. "I believe it is," he said, striking her upside the head with the butt of the gun.

Everything went black and Mary crumbled to the ground.

# CHAPTER NINE

R oss woke with the dawn, dressed for the day and was ready to head to the courthouse. He had to find out for himself if Mary was a liar and a thief. Deep down, something burned inside, telling him she didn't do it. The other part of him needed to hear it from the horse's mouth, to see her face before it could be laid to rest.

Running a hand over his face, he sighed. Sipping his coffee Claudia poured him, she gave him a dour look. Ross perked a brow but said nothing. His mind reeled with all the possibilities that might happen in the next few hours. If Mary had stolen, would it mean she would hang? Not many fancied the idea of hanging a woman but if the shoe fit the crimes, it did on occasion.

*She didn't do it*, he reminded himself, *she couldn't have.*

Ross finished his coffee and headed outside. The crisp morning air going deep into his lungs refreshed him. Striding down the path leading to the barn full of sleeping animals, and kicking rocks along the way, his mind wandered to the blond-haired, blue-eyed woman who wouldn't get out of his head.

If this was what smitten felt like, then by Jove, he was so. She didn't judge him for what he'd done, nor for his age, or looks. She was gentle with a rough exterior, all bravado, not even real, but people mistook her protected vulnerability for rudeness and indifference. Ross smirked, *I don't think she even reckons how kind she really is.*

Ross put his hand on the barn door ready to pull it open and start his morning chores.

"Ross!" a female voice shouted.

Spinning on his heel, a livid hotel manager came striding down the pathway. The Colorado wind couldn't, and probably wouldn't dare, move her dark purple high-necked dress and precisely coiffed hair on her person.

"Ma'am," he greeted, tipping his hat and head slightly.

"Have you seen Mary Lockburn?" Jane asked.

"Not since yesterday afternoon, ma'am."

He didn't want to tell the hotel manager where she happened to be, if by some small chance she hadn't known already. She would lose her job and reputability in the town. The closer Jane got, the more he observed the hard lines on the woman's face and the quick, brusque steps were from worry. Ross let go of the barn door, taking a few quick paces toward Jane. His heart pounding in his chest as possible scenarios raced through his mind.

"Sheriff Mobley released her last evening stating the man who accused her made a mistake. She was let go to come back to the hotel but she's not here. I'm not sure she ever made it back."

"I will check the garden," Ross said.

"Thank you. When you find her, direct her to my office," Jane turned on her heel to leave but spun back around. "Almost forgot. Here is your pay for the week," she stated, handing him coins.

Ross thanked her, tucking them inside his shirt pocket. Opening the barn doors wide, he allowed the weak Colorado morning sunlight in as the horses shook off their cozy sleep.

Jogging to the back of the barn, his heart pounded in his chest. He hoped Mary would be out back, gardening like he often found her in the mornings after her wash was done but she wasn't there. He could usually hear her sweet, melodic humming before he saw her. Today all he heard were birds and horses over the beating of his own heart.

Closing the gate to the garden, his gut churned. Something happened to her. Scowling, he gazed about the barn for any clues to items that would be out of place. All four horses were stalled, staring at him intently and whickering. All the bridles hung on pegs by the tack room door.

Ross let out each horse into their appropriate paddock. His mind reeling with what might have happened to Mary. His brain cooked up several different scenarios ranging from serious, like getting kidnapped, to silly like spending the night with a friend, a friend he knew didn't exist yet. Once the last horse was out, Ross hopped the back fence, jogging up the pathway to the hotel.

Lena, Eliza, and Kelly stood outside in the employee break area, gossiping quietly. Ross ignored their hushed conversations, making a straight line for Jane McCarthy's office. He planned on telling the manager he was taking the rest of the day off to search for Mary.

The sheriff's office was three buildings down and diagonal across the street. It should have taken her maybe five minutes to walk back here and yet she wasn't here and hadn't been all night. Taking a swift detour, he checked her room. Her dresses still hung on pegs.

*She should be here*, Ross thought. *Something happened. Something bad.* He paused, feeling his blood run cold. *What if Victor's men got her instead of me? They might be lookin' for me too. I gotta find her fast!*

Crossing the foyer on his way to Jane's office, he glanced up, spotting Ada walking down the stairs with a full tray of morning refreshments.

She peeked at him with a smile. "The guests are not in their room. And I'm getting too old to go up and down those stairs often." Ada explained with a relieved sigh of being on level ground. "Can you be a dear, and see if they checked out?"

Ross went to the register, flipping it open in one smooth motion. The last name in there was Opal Hilbert who checked out this morning around 5:30. Ross's eyes narrowed, *Hilbert. The same name Mary mentioned her former fiancé had.* His mind reeled searching for answers but there were too many pieces to the puzzle. All he knew for sure was he needed to get started looking for her.

"She checked out," Ross replied.

"Thank you, son. I will tell Claudia," she stated rolling her eyes. "Those guests," she complained, "wanted something extra besides the grand room coffee, tea, and scones. They requested a five-course breakfast, and are not even here to receive it. Odd if you ask me. They just up and left so early this morning."

Ross nodded, putting a hand on the hall door continuing on his way to seek Jane, dismissing Ada politely as possible in his hurry to find Mary. Stepping inside the doorway to the hall, he passed Bartholomew and went to the door on his right. Jane's office door was wide open. Papers scrambled on her desk, with monies in neat little stacks.

She didn't glance up, but kept scribbling on paper. "Something the matter, Ross?"

"Mary isn't here. I would like to go search for her today."

Jane put her pen down in the ink well, her brows furrowing together. "She's not?" A brief frown graced her face. "Are all your duties done?"

Ross nodded. "Until tonight when the horses need to be put back inside."

"Very well. And Ross, please make sure she's ok."

Ross bolted out of her room and down the hallway. In his gut, Mary was in danger. He had to find her. Starting with the sheriff and if the sheriff had no answers, he'd head to the train ticket office. He was taking no chances.

# CHAPTER TEN

The faint light, the odd rocking and jarring screech of metal woke her along with a horrid pounding in her head. She moaned, touching the left side of her head near her face. Hissing at the pain when her fingers lightly brushed the dried blood and oozing scab. Her hair matted to the wound. Mary held her breath as she separated the hair from her injury.

"You had such a pretty face," Opal purred rancorously across from her.

Mary didn't rise to the bait, closing her eyes. The high-pitched screeching whine of the train wheels made her cringe and the pounding in her head worsen. Sitting up straight, her back and body aching.

Opening her eyes, the bright light of the afternoon sun streamed in through the dusty glass window causing her to squint as her eyes slowly adjusted. The glare of the light made her head scream even more. She didn't even know that was possible.

Looking away toward the left, Charlie, Barrie, and Danny sat caddy-corner in the other train bench. Barrie, facing her, sat beside the window with his cocked pistol trained on her. Opal sat properly across from her; her red hair coiffed just so and her expensive silk dress fluffed out around her. Opal set her needle point to the side, folding her hands in her lap, giving Mary her full attention.

*Shit*, she thought, *no escaping now.*

"Do you want to tell me where you buried it, Florence?" Opal asked in a firm tone.

"It's Mary," she replied annoyed, facing the pompous, smug, man stealing, woman.

Opal's face hardened. Her brown-black eyes glaring daggers at her. She whipped out a fan, it seemed from nowhere and aggressively fanned herself. Mary kept her appearance casual, leaning back against the uncomfortable seat, ignoring the throbbing in her head, refusing to appear weak. Mary arrogantly propped one arm over the back of the bench and smiled.

"I'll call you Florence if I choose to, *Florence*. It is your God given name and you will adhere to it."

Mary rolled her eyes. *Charlie sure picked a winner*, she mused. *I gotta get out of here*, she wriggled her shoulders, working out the achy stiffness. She stared at her feet a moment, trying to get the headache causing spots in her eyes to clear away. The pounding in her head lessened slightly, gazing at the shaded area by her feet.

"Florence?" Opal cooed like one would to a child.

Mary scowled. "Yes?" she returned in a sarcastic childish tone.

"Do you agree to adhere to your God given name during our journey?"

Mary mockingly folded her hands in her lap. "Oh absolutely, Mother."

Opal glared, angrily picking up her needle point. She forcefully stitched whatever she was doing. Mary grinned, turning her attention to the small window to her right.

The train began to slow, going uphill. Mary felt the difference in pressure being forced back in her seat. *I once heard there's a gapin' hole in the bottom of some trains for people to use as a shitter...*

Keeping her face passive, Mary stared out the window. The

CHAPTER TEN | 363

train slowed a bit more. Mary scratched her hair, wriggling in her seat. Out of the corner of her eye, Opal glanced at her. Mary wriggled again. *If I can get to it, maybe I can escape.* She sighed, wriggling a bit more.

"Something the matter, Florence?" Opal seethed.

"Where's the shitter?"

Opal curled her lip. "The *lavatory*, is at the end of the way," she pointed behind her. "And don't think of doing anything *but* using the lavatory. Danny will be positioned outside your door."

Mary stood, hands on her hips. Opal rankled her more than she cared to admit. Even Audrey who was richer than anyone she knew wasn't arrogant, bullheaded, mean, and crude as the person in front of her.

Mary's lip quirked, picking her words carefully. "I have to take a piss, all right, miss hoity-toity."

Opal put a hand to her mouth. "Use better language!"

"Listen here," Mary seethed, leaning in close, "I won't make it easy."

A gun nestled itself into the middle of her back. "Go use the lavatory," Danny whispered vehemently.

Turning on her heel, Mary ambled to the back of the train car. Yanking open the door and locking it. Inside the small area was a swing door and a washbasin. Mary went to the swing door, smiling at the drop chute below. Someone seemed to have the same idea before her. The chute had been widened enough to fit a small person.

Mary grinned, thinking of the heap of trouble some person found themselves in. *Thank you, whomever you be,* she thought.

The train picked up speed, forcing her off her feet a bit and to the left. Quickly, the train changed speed once more, forcing her to the right. Mary stared down at the chute in front of her, the wheels on the train slowing significantly again, trying their best to turn on the track as the train went up another hill.

Her amusement died. Her skin crawled, hairs standing on end. Below, the train cars' wheels whistling on the metal tracks. Mary swallowed, *I can do this. Just drop down and lay flat on the tracks. Ain't much to it. Then run to Omaha and get the money. Or... go to Ross?* Mary stared at the moving ground through the chute. *Then what? What happens after that?*

"Mary!" a man's voice boomed. "Hurry it up!"

"I'm takin' a shit! Hold yer guns, meat head!"

Her lip quirked at her response. Getting on the floor, she wriggled down the chute feet first, thanking God she wore a simple dress. The rushing of air whipped any loose fabric of her dress up against her. With a deep breath and shaking hands, she moved farther down, letting go of the nasty drop chute wood to grab hold of the metal bars underneath. Mary tried not to think about what she was touching and getting on her clothes.

She held her breath to help hide the pungent aroma of the drop chute. She wrapped a foot around the metal bar under the train to hold her in place. With her head under the drop chute, she moved down the metal railing using her hands and sliding her feet slowly down the bar. Unlinking her left foot, she used it to drag on the tracks to slow her speed. The train chugged slowly, lurching forward like a horse that thrown a shoe. With a deep breath and eyes closed, she let go of everything completely.

Her body bounced on the wood tracks and rocks. Staying low, not covering her hands with her head like instincts told her to do. She didn't want to lose an arm. Her already throbbing head took a strike as she bounced. Eyes closed; she lay there breathing for a moment. Tears coursed down her cheeks from the pain in her body and the sweet relief of freedom she'd found once more. The final train car whooshing over her head. Opening her eyes, Mary scrambled to her feet, getting off the road and into the scrubby bushes near the tracks.

She breathed out, utterly relieved to be away from Charlie and Opal. "You go that way, and I'll go this way," she muttered at the disappearing train.

Limping down the tracks in the opposite direction, her left foot stung from letting it drag earlier, but the pounding in her heart made it feel not too terrible. She didn't have a clue how far she was from Denver or in what direction, but she couldn't be far from Denver. After a few minutes, the pounding in her head ceased, as the aching in her body began. Her right wrist hurt something fierce and was swollen.

Pausing, Mary gazed down at her clothes. Rips and tears pocked her dress. Dark spots of blood formed on her elbows from hitting the tracks. Finding a flat, secluded place, she sat on the ground, taking off her left shoe; observing a gaping hole in the bottom and her heel bleeding. Mary tossed the shoe away. She gasped on a chuckle, tenderly touching the wound and inspected the rest of herself. *Lucky I ain't dead. With a hurt wrist, minor scrapes, and a few bruises, God Almighty must like me today.*

Shielding her eyes, she glimpsed at the sun. It waned toward high noon. If the train left on schedule it would have been around seven in the morning, which was per usual for a Friday according to Lena anyways. She was roughly five train-hours outside of Denver.

Mary racked her brain for any town outside of Denver near the train tracks and came up with either Walsenburg or Pueblo. Running a hand over her face, and sighing, *lots of walkin' now. I better get there quick before they stop and come after me, iffn' they already haven't.*

Getting up, she started limping in the opposite direction the train had gone. Peeking over her shoulder, hoping to not see the gang behind her. She breathed out, stumbling on the tracks.

*I need a plan,* she thought. *I need to get back to Denver.* She paused, *but what about the money? I could head to Omaha and get it, leave Denver behind me and start over again. But I would leave Ross behind... but... he wouldn't want to start a life with stolen money or with me. He would want a fresh beginnin', workin' for it. And he certainly wouldn't want another man's leftovers. He already made it clear I wasn't good enough and I don't blame him none. Even if he don't want me, I feel safe with him and he's one of the only friends I have.*

She sniffed, using her good hand to wipe her nose. Blowing out a breath, torn between going to Ross in hopes she was wrong about him wanting another man's leftovers, or taking the money and never looking back. *I'll walk more and see how I feel when I come to the next town.*

Picking up her dress for easier walking, she limped along the tracks to whatever town she came upon.

# CHAPTER ELEVEN

Ross left the sheriff's office madder than a bull. Sheriff Mobley didn't know what he was talking about when it came to Mary not making it home when she got released, or anything else. Ross had a feeling the sheriff knew more than he was letting on, but if he pushed for more answers, he would find himself in jail and no use to Mary.

*Damnable sheriff*, he thought. *Where are you, Mary?*

Running a hand over his face, he strode down the road. *I need to find her!* His gut clenched at all the possibilities Mary could be hurt. When Victor Del Avilasto's gang disbanded, he didn't think they would come back for her. Or him for that matter. Unless it wasn't Victor's gang but someone from Mary's past.

Hell, he was surprised his own past hadn't come back to haunt him yet. For all the terrible deeds he'd done, he was certain to be lynched good by now. The fact he wasn't, still surprised him and filled him with a brief moment of relief.

*If it isn't Victor, who is after her? Maybe the saloon will provide an answer?*

Ross pondered the thought, ambling into the saloon near the ticket office. If Victor's gang were after Mary, he would find out in a saloon. Some of Victor's men were like fish to whiskey. Ross didn't want to bring around old ties into his newly established life, and he didn't want to be in a saloon, but in order to find Mary, he'd do what he must, including rekindling old ties.

His eyes adjusted to the dimly lit building as the doors swung shut behind him. Older men sat at tables, nodding and chatting with hushed tones. Out of the corner of his eye, Ross spotted one of his old gang members to his left. Ross pretended not to see him, heading straight for the counter.

The barkeep cleaned out a glass with a towel, putting it on the counter. "We got whiskey or brandy."

"Whiskey," Ross replied, putting down a coin on the wooden countertop.

The barkeep took it, then poured him the amber liquid over two fingers deep into the glass. Nodding his thanks, Ross turned around, keeping an eye on the gang member out of his peripheral. His mind thrummed, looking for the name of the man he'd seen when he'd walked in. He'd even interacted with the man a few times and his mind came up blank.

"Ross," the man called. "Come 'ere and chat."

Ross silently cursed at being called out, especially before he could remember his name. Ambling over to him, Ross took a seat in a rickety chair.

"Mornin' Quint," he replied, the rough man's name suddenly coming to him.

"What you up to since?"

Ross shrugged. "Workin' 'round here."

Quint nodded, throwing back the drink in his hand. "Same, friend. I got hired on a ranch west of here. The others went east and south, along with your brother. Ain't no one left from Del Avilasto here, 'cept us."

Sipping his drink, he let out a relieved breath into the glass through his nose. *Gang doesn't have Mary*, he thought. *That's good news. Too bad about my brother*, Ross hung his head, sighing. *Richard was never able to turn away from a bad thing. Like the fur trapping busi-*

*ness, he told everyone about. It was killing the trappers and taking their stock.*

It pained his heart Richard didn't cut ties when he'd gotten the chance. Richard was always one to follow a golden goose even if the consequences of getting caught wound him strung up; he simply wasn't one to say no to what he believed to be a quick way to get rich.

Ross downed the drink. The fiery liquid coursed through his body, spreading warmth to his veins. Slicking his tongue over his teeth to remove the taste, he stood, his chair screeching back. The noise of the saloon diminished for a moment as people glanced over at him.

"Good to see you, Quint," Ross stated. "Take care now."

Quint raised his hand in a sort of salute. "You do the same."

Taking quick strides out the saloon, Ross turned to the right. His feet hurriedly taking him to the ticket office. No train docked itself at the station. No person waited around for anyone to return or to leave. The platform surprisingly quiet like a church mouse.

Ross strode to the ticket window. A man with a nice pressed white shirt, black arm bands and a tie slept in a kicked back chair. A hat pulled down low on his face.

"'Xcuse me," Ross hollered into the ticket window.

The man snorted, coming forward catching himself while his chair clattered to the ground, pinching the bridge of his nose as he stood.

"Next train will be here at eleven," he stated.

"Thank you kindly. But I need to know when the train left this morning."

The man's brows furrowed. "At seven like it always does on a Friday."

"Was there a woman in the group with a navy-blue dress on, blond hair and blue eyes?"

The ticket master nodded. "Yes. She left to Kansas City with three men and a woman. Poor thing fell down hard, striking her head. It was bleedin' pretty bad and she could barely stand on her own. The others seemed to be carryin' her."

Dumbfounded for a moment, he didn't say a word. Ross slammed money down on the wooden ticket window. "I need the next train to Kansas City."

The man took Ross's money, handing him a yellow paper ticket. "If the train arrives on time, its," he paused, looking at his pocket watch, "its eight thirty-six now, it will depart here at eleven headed to Kansas City."

Ross tapped his hand on the countertop. "Thank you."

Tucking the ticket into his shirt pocket he ambled down the street. Brows furrowed low and hands in his pockets. *I wonder who took her,* he thought. *Three men and a woman wouldn't be anyone from the Del Avilasto gang. It has to be someone from Mary's past.* He paced back and forth a moment. *Like that Hilbert name... It has to be one in the same.*

He stopped across from the saloon he was in before, staring at the dark weathered wooden walls and the chipping saloon paint. Men ambled in and out. Horses hitched outside whinnied, ears back and moving from hoof to hoof; annoyed at being tethered with no grass to munch on. Quint sat by the window, sipping another drink.

*Quint knew people,* Ross recalled. *I wonder if he would have heard something, or knows someone who has.*

Looking both ways for barreling horses and wagons, Ross jogged across the street, careful not to jar his tender, healing wounds. He went into the saloon again, the barkeep perking a brow as he cleaned another glass. Ross took a chair opposite Quint. The startled man set down his half empty drink, staring curiously at Ross, tilting his head and raising a brow, inviting Ross to speak. The whites of Quint's eyes turning a light red from drink.

"I need your help," Ross said softly.

Quint shook his head. "Nope... I ain't in that business anymore."

Ross furrowed his brow, quirking his lips, puzzled. "I need help finding a woman."

Quint scratched his forehead, pushing his beaten hat back. "Oh.

Wrong business," he chuckled. "Finding a woman... I can," he leaned forward with a smirk, whispering, "*assist.*"

"You need to sober up first."

Quint pointed a finger at him. "You need to lighten up." A goofy smile crept across his face as he finished his drink.

Ross felt his blood simmering. He hadn't the patience for drunkards or fools. When he drank, he limited himself to no more than three. He didn't care for the man he turned into when drunk.

"The woman I fancy got taken. She is on a train headed south. I would like your help to find her."

Quint beamed. "How can I say no to that?!" he bellowed, rising from his chair. "Let's go!"

The intoxicated man came to him, his chair clattering to the floor. Quint threw an arm around Ross before Ross could get away.

"Where'd she go?" Quint asked.

Ross ignored the drunken question, leading his friend out of the saloon and into the bustling morning. Taking Quint up the walkway, he headed for the Whitman Diner. Getting Quint sobered up with some food and strong coffee would do them both some good.

"I'm hungry," Quint said.

Ross bit his tongue, dragging Quint along the way. In a few hours, they needed to head to Kansas City, where Mary more than likely would be soon or at least stopped somewhere along the way. Quint dragged his feet, head rolling around as he tried to focus his bleary eyes.

"We're going to take a train in a few hours. Can you sober up?" Ross asked, approaching the dining side of the Whitman Hotel, dragging his drunk associate behind him.

Quint clapped him on the back. "Sure thing, pal," he beamed, putting a foot on a step of the stairs going up the dining side of the hotel. "Ya know, I've always liked you... yer," he held onto the 'r' sound for a moment, "a good man. Broody, but good."

Ross didn't reply, helping Quint up the few steps inside the diner. Lena bustled around, filling coffee cups and taking orders for the three occupied tables. Ross picked a table out of the way of everyone else. Quint sat with a hefty thud, his chair screeching on the wooden floors.

Ross removed his hat, hanging it on the ear of the chair. Quint did the same. The man messed with his wiry black hair, mussing then flattening it out on his head.

"Mornin' Ross," Lena said chipperly, putting two coffee mugs on the table, and filling each to the brim.

"Morning," he replied, taking a sip.

"Have you seen Mary? I saw the sheriff and he said she got released, but she's not here."

"We're goin' after her. She got taken."

Lena put a hand to her mouth, setting the coffee pot on the table with a thump. "Taken?"

Ross nodded, taking another sip of coffee. "Train leaves at eleven. Quint and myself are gonna find her."

"I'll tell Jane."

"You're the prettiest woman my eyes ever seen," Quint commented, staring dreamily at Lena while sipping his coffee.

Lena's cheeks heated. "Thank you. Ross, want the specials?"

"Yes please."

She scurried away to the kitchen with bright red cheeks. Quint sighed, gazing at the door while mindlessly drinking the entire cup of coffee. The empty mug clanked on the tabletop.

Quint sighed. "She's mighty beautiful."

Ross didn't comment. The only woman on his mind was Mary. Getting to know her over the last three weeks taught him love was something he could finally consider. Before her, he never gave a thought to settling down, making a home, or raising a family. But with Mary, it was all he wanted. She was more than her past and more than she gave herself credit for. Broken, like him, they both longed for the same things – love, a home and family; they both just went about it the wrong way first.

Ross scratched the back of his head, wondering on what he would say to her once he found her. *If I find her.* He sighed, his heart constricting a bit.

"Here you fellas are," Lena said, setting down two plates of food.

Hearty helpings of sausages, eggs and potatoes dished neatly on a plate, slid before him. Lena refilled their mugs with coffee, hurrying off to tend the other diners; taking a peek at Quint before she focused on her other customers. Quint watched her leave, stuffing his face with a sausage.

"Love at first sight," he swooned.

Ross chuckled. "I never believed in it until I saw Mary."

Quint stopped chewing, staring at him. "The same Mary from Victor?"

Ross nodded.

His friend let out a long whistle, "Damnation! Ross liking someone who isn't his horse!" he finished with a foolish grin.

Ross let out a hard breath. Having feelings for Mary left him awe struck. He never planned on finding someone and settling down. Especially finding someone with similarities, one who understood his past and did not pass judgement upon him, but empathized with his predicament.

Mary was a special kind of woman, and one he desperately needed to find.

# CHAPTER TWELVE

Mary removed both of her shoes at some point in her walk. Her feet bled under the terrain, but eventually they numbed and she preferred it to the lopsided walk of one shoe on, one shoe off, that hurt the already achy bones and muscles. She stayed on the tracks, walking briskly in the hot sun. Her heart pounded. Fear of Charlie catching her kept her mind active with infinite possibilities, each imagined scenario worse than the last.

Glancing over her shoulder once more, she saw nothing behind her. Breathing out, she wiped the dripping sweat from her head. *Keep goin'*, she urged herself.

Her legs aching, she forced herself to keep moving up the small rising hill. Dropping to her hands and knees, she crawled up the hill. The momentary reprieve in her feet made her body relax.

"Up the hill," she breathed. "Gotta move up this damned hill."

Her fingernails dug into the dried, cracking dirt. Snagging whatever she could for purchase, she compelled herself to the peak of the small hill. A city bustled below her. A smile materialized on her weary face.

Groaning, Mary rose to her feet. She jogged down the hill, a beaming smile splitting her face wide open. People stopped in their tracks. Women put hands to their chests or mouths, taken back by her appearance.

Mary paid no heed, continuing straight for the horse trough in front of a mercantile store. With a leap, she splashed into the shallow water, sighing contentedly. Closing her eyes, relishing the cool water, an excited, disbelieving giggle escaped her lips at the thought she was alive and made it back to civilization.

"I made it," she announced to the horses standing at the trough.

The sun became blocked by shadows. Mary ignored the change in light assuming one of those horses was coming back for his drink.

"Ma'am," a baritone voice called softly.

Mary opened one eye. "Yeah?"

"What in God's name are you doin'? Have you lost your mind?"

Mary sighed, rising out of the trough reluctantly, and stepping out of the liquid. The large man before her was a mountain – tall, burly, blond, and the local sheriff. How he found clothes that even fit, she didn't have a clue. He leaned forward, bending slightly at the waist with hands on his hips. An eyebrow raised expectantly for her to answer.

Mary perked a brow. "No sir, I lost the men who kidnapped me and walked here."

"Walked here," he repeated, disbelievingly.

"Yeah," Mary retorted with crossed arms over her chest, and showing a bare foot. "*Walked.* I was kidnapped in Denver, put on a train, and I jumped off. Now what town am I in?"

"Pueblo."

A crowd gathered around her. One elderly lady's gaze softened to her. The other's wore mixed expressions ranging from suspicion to shock to pity. The people of Pueblo stood a way back from her, yet it felt like they were crowding in, eyes peering, narrowing in, and judging her worse than a pawn dealer.

The sheriff poked his hat with his finger, pushing it off his head a bit. "How did you get off the train?"

"Through the drop chute."

He nodded, saying softly, "Come with me."

Mary held firm. *Ain't no way in hell's fiery pit*, she thought, taking a step back. *I don't wanna be locked up or worse.* She crossed her arms, covering herself, now realizing how immodest her dress had become. She wiped the water off her face, slicking back her unruly blond hair. Her feet stung, burning from the open cuts and sores and the dirt getting inside.

He leaned in close, whispering, seeming to try and put her at ease, "So, I can help you."

Mary's blue eyes narrowed. Her heart pounding in her throat, she took another step back.

"Sheriff Parson," an older lady called, stepping out of the dissipating crowd. "I may be able to help."

Sheriff Parson smiled kindly. "Thank you, Mrs. Cottie."

Mrs. Cottie scoffed. "I think by now you would call me, Ida." The old lady, spry on her feet, spun to her. "Come along now, child."

Mary held firm for a moment, her mind reeling with her options, or lack thereof. She'd no money for food, water, board or to catch a train back to Denver. *Or to Omaha*, she thought, hissing at the pain in her feet. *This old woman seems kindly enough*, she reasoned. Mary took a few hesitant steps forward.

Ida came briskly to her, looping her arm in with Mary's, not bothered in the least by the water dripping from Mary's dress. "Come with me, dear."

Mary practically jumped out of her skin. Chills ran down her spine. For the first time in her life, she was without a plan, a means to take care of herself or even an inkling on what to do. She would be an idiot to admit it didn't scare her. Not many people showed her kindness in her short life. Audrey and Lena were two people, Ross made three. This old woman now made four. The sheriff may be five but she wasn't holding her breath. Most men turned into scum after the first couple of conversations.

"I won't bite," Ida said with a teasing smile and a wink. "Missin' too many teeth."

Sheriff Parson tipped his hat with a grin hiding on the edges of his lips. "I'll leave you to it Mrs. Cottie. I'll try to swing by later to get the details on the kidnappin.'"

Mary's eyes followed the sheriff across the street, back into his small building. Mrs. Ida Cottie pulled on her arm. Mary jumped, being forced to follow along since she didn't have the energy to do much else.

"I live here in town at the end, dear," the old woman spoke.

Mary eyed her. Ida was a strong, short old woman, barely coming to her shoulder who walked with a hunch, making her look shorter and weak. A long white braid went to the middle of her back. Mrs. Cottie walked briskly for being small. Mary was hard pressed to keep up the pace. She stepped lightly where she could, unsuccessfully avoiding the dirt scratching her, burrowing into her open wounds, and taking up residence in her bones.

"What can I make you to eat?" Mrs. Cottie asked.

She barely remembered her mother and certainly no maternal caring from her, so Mrs. Cottie's question and demeanor caught her off guard. It was completely foreign to feel cared for. Mary pressed her lips together, forgetting Mrs. Cottie's question, concentrating on keeping herself from groaning. Her body ached every time she breathed, let alone moved.

Her mind wandered to what she was going to do next. She needed a plan, a means to get back to Denver from Pueblo, putting distance between her and Charlie and get back to Ross and Audrey.

*Denver...* she thought for a long hard moment on that solitary word. She'd heard the saying "home is where the heart is," but never understood its meaning until now. Not only had Denver become like a home with her friends and Ross. It put a roof over her head, food in her belly, and wages in her pocket. It became what she needed. *Denver,* she decided, nodding to the idea. *I am headed to Denver.*

*Now that's settled, how to get out of here?* she thought. *I'm hungry. I don't even know when I ate last. I could eat a meal and keep on from here.* Mary snuck a peek at the sun. It waned past high noon. *I could head north to Denver on foot and a bit off the track to not be found. Then*

*I can rest someplace off the tracks. Gotta rest soon though. This poor body of mine needs some time to rest.* Mary moved the clumped drying hair off her face and gave an irritated grunt. She hated how, when her hair dried, it clumped together, and no matter how many times she separated the strands to help dry it quicker, it didn't make a lick of difference. The only thing saving her hair now was a brush.

"Child," Ida called again, "what can I get you?"

Ida opened the door to her lonely wooden home. A mangy black cat with a missing piece of tail and permanently shut right eyed meowed at her, hopping off the chair and twirling around Ida's feet. The cat eyed her for a moment, its solitary green orb assessing her. Mary chuckled a bit, feeling less judgement from a person.

"That is Fester. Pay him no mind. He runs the place and is kind enough to let me live here too." Ida smiled fondly at the cat; amusement thick in her voice.

"I don't wanna put you out ma'am," Mary finally spoke. "I'm all right."

Ida didn't turn from walking toward her pot over the fireplace, waving her left hand out to the side. "That's a bunch of nonsense, child."

Mary cleared her throat. "My name's Mary Lockburn."

"Nice to meet you, child. Through the small door, is a trunk full of my old dresses, from back in my youth," she chuckled, "pick one out to wear while this one dries."

Mary's face scrunched. She didn't know how to take this woman's kindness. It was so unfamiliar. Back in Kansas City, with Charlie, the kindness she knew consisted of one hot meal a day, a warm bed, and clean clothes, but only when she pleased him. If she stepped one toe out of line, she found herself on the floor nursing a fat lip or black eye with no meal. Even the time he "honored" her by allowing her into his bed, for a heist well done, he'd never given her anything from affection to true kindness.

Aunt Winnifred's kindness was, at best, a visage. The hag was nice to her and her siblings in front of other people, but in private, she was nastier than a bear caught in a trap. But during those moments of brief gentleness, Mary soaked it in, hoping the affection would last a little longer than the time before.

Her lips pursed, moving to the right side. *I don't think it was kindness*, she surmised. Mary shook her head. *No, it wasn't kindness at all. It was somethin' else.* Mary shuddered in her dress. Her garment was drying slowly, becoming itchy as it sat on her skin.

Mary moved hesitantly toward the back of the house. Pausing, she stared at the trunk.

"For Heaven's Sake, child, get changed. It will be alright. Stew is almost done," Ida encouraged.

Mary strode to the back, opening the trunk. The contents were neatly folded, organized piles of fabric. A dark green dress on the top caught her eye. Quickly, she shrugged off her navy blue one and got into the green. Taking a ribbon from the chest, she wrapped her hair in it, tying it at the nape of her neck. The dress was a bit large, hanging off her shoulders, although not immodestly, and well past her feet. Mary pulled a pair of stockings out of the chest, quickly covering her aching feet.

*No shoes will make this hard*, Mary thought. *But I ain't takin' none more from this lady. I cain't.*

She felt strange wearing someone else's clothing, even if it was offered to her. Mary came out of the back room to the kitchen. A steaming bowl of stew sat at one of the empty places while a basket of warm biscuits waited in the middle of the table for her.

"Come eat, Mary," Ida encouraged, sitting at the table herself. The old woman folded her hands and bowed her head waiting a brief second before murmuring under her breath. "Thank you, Lord for the meal we are about to eat. Bless Mary and keep her safe. In God's name, Amen."

Mary sat trying not to disturb her, eating her fare quickly. She needed a plan to get back to Denver. Her skin prickled. *They're comin'*, she shivered. *I know it.*

# CHAPTER THIRTEEN

R oss stood outside a ramshackle building not even fit for chickens. He could hear Quint inside, speaking low, his voice still wavering a bit from the whiskey he consumed. In an hour, they would take the train south to Kansas City to find Mary. He hoped in the amount of time it took to get there, nothing happened to her.

Ross fidgeted, moving from foot to foot while Quint spoke with a man whom he remembered visiting on occasion while traveling with Victor. Aside from the dirty dealings this man previously had with Victor, Ross knew his reputation for finding outlaw's wives who often ran with money or treasure. He often subdued them quickly, ensuring they didn't speak of their husbands' thieving and murdering ways. Ross never cared for the man or his reputation, but he was exactly what they needed if they had any hope of finding Mary soon. With Mary being taken by unsavory sorts, who better to find outlaws than someone who tracked them down on the regular?

Casually, he peered around for any sign of a lawman or anyone who could report them to the law. Seeing nothing, Ross spun on his heel, his back to the door and eyes on the small trail leading down to the main road to Denver.

The shoddy, dark wood door slammed shut startling Ross. Spinning on his heel, he got ready to defend himself. Breathing out, Quint strode to him, head shaking.

"Got nothin'," he stated. "We can't come back here again. He knows Victor's dead and the man still owed him money. He was talkin' to us, bein' nice." Quint snorted. "The man's a rat. Ain't nothin' nice about him."

Ross ran a hand over his face. It was like that with every old acquaintance they asked. This man was the fifth on their list. It was either no one saw Mary, or it was a blond man and a red headed woman with an injured blond woman in a brief passing by. And if someone saw the blond man and red headed woman, they were boarding a train. In all his time with Victor Del Avilasto and his gang, he'd yet to meet another gang with a red headed woman in it, which made him suspect this woman was the one to follow to get Mary back especially since red hair stuck out in a crowd.

*These people have to be from Mary's past,* he surmised. *I can't think of anyone from here to Tennessee fitting a redhead description. It makes me wonder to what she's done... And what she's about to do now. Obviously, the redhead and her companions are dangerous. They kidnapped a person. Hopefully that's all they're willing to do.*

Quint scratched his scraggly hair. "We have something in all this," he began, "your woman went south."

"Yeah," Ross nodded. "I don't think she went to Kansas City though."

"What makes you say that?"

Ross grinned. "She is far too lively to go willingly. She's a mouth on her, and balls the size of a bison. There's no way she let them take her to Kansas City."

Quint laughed. "Sounds like a ripe match for you."

Ross breathed out, a cross between a chortle and a sigh. Mary was the best match for him. Her lively personality charmed him. She was blunt, a force of a woman, more powerful than the grandest prairie tornadoes, but an honest one. They were kindred souls, both broken, but both desiring love, acceptance and companionship. And Mary was right beautiful. More so than the Rockies on a foggy fall morning.

"She is…" he affirmed, feeling warmth spread through his body. "I believe she got off in Walsenburg and headed north. Just a gut feeling, but my gut's never been wrong before."

Quint scratched the stubble on the side of his jaw. "So like Pueblo. Wanna stop there first?"

Shaking his head, Ross replied, "No. Best stop in Walsenburg and work our way north." Ross strode down the trail leading back into Denver. "I'll pay you to come with me," he offered.

"No need," Quint shrugged, walking tandem with Ross. "Feels good to do somethin'… *good*… for once. Plus," he paused. "I don't start at the ranch for another few days."

"I know what you mean. I appreciate the help."

Quint stopped, offering his hand. "Thanks for givin' me the chance."

Ross shook it. He continued down the trail leading back toward town. His mind wandering to what kind of trouble Mary found herself in or if she happened to go back to the life she previously knew best. If she did happen to go back, he couldn't stand to be with her. He wanted better for himself since Audrey Whitman employed him. He hoped Mary wanted the same.

They stopped, unhitching their horses from a post outside the last mercantile going out of Denver. Ross borrowed a horse from the Whitman Stables with Jane's permission. He took the same horse he rode escaping Victor Del Avilasto, figuring since the animal helped save him from being dead, it may help to find Mary.

Quint mounted his gray dappled stud, the beast tossing his head with eagerness to bolt. Ross mounted the bay mare, turning her toward the train station. The town bustled with life, people rolling in on wagons from the outliers for supplies fresh off the train. The long black hunk of metal sat waiting on the tracks.

"We best hurry," Quint said.

Ross nodded, hastening his horse to trot.

"Last call," the conductor yelled, resounding over the Denver city.

Spurring their horses into a quicker trot down the middle of the road, Quint was a few paces behind. Ross's horse leapt onto the wooden platform and slid to a stop before running into the train. He and Quint dismounted, handing their reins over to the boy who put the mounts inside the livery box car. The boy shut the door to the box car after patting the rump of Quint's stallion.

Ross let out a relieved breath, thankful he made it. The train whistled. The metal wheels grinding on the track. The conductor waited on the railing of the passenger car, offering a hand inside onto the back platform of the rail car. Ross didn't take it, leaping onto the platform and stepping aside to help Quint.

Leaping, Quint slipped. Ross grabbed him by the collar, the conductor grabbed Quint's hand at the same time, pulling him inside.

"Thanks," Quint huffed.

Ross handed the conductor his ticket and the one he picked up for Quint earlier when he agreed to come along. Striding back, he took a seat on the left-hand side of the window. The train, picking up speed heading out of Denver. Ross's heart raced, hoping when he found Mary, she was alive and well and not going back down the dark path they just escaped from.

# CHAPTER FOURTEEN

Mary wanted nothing more than to take a quick nap. However, her gut churned at the thought of being stuck in someplace too long. Pueblo was a day's walk at most from Walsenburg and for sure, Charlie and his gang got off there once they realized she was gone. Charlie was coming after her; there was no doubt of it. She needed to leave before he found her, or could hurt anyone who helped her.

Mary swallowed.

The thought of Charlie finding her, terrified her. Charlie would lynch her for sure, whether she told him where the money was or not. If he caught her, she was good as dead.

Glancing over to Mrs. Cottie, the old woman slept in her rocking chair in front of a lazy fire. The kindly woman offered her a place to sleep and stay for as long as she needed. Mary wouldn't take the offer. She couldn't. Not if the old lady wanted to keep breathing, and Mary wanted to make sure she kept breathing.

Mary sat in her chair at the table, strumming her fingers hoping the motion would spur her mind into making a plan. Her mind was torn again between heading to Omaha and getting the money and going to Denver to be with Ross. It would make starting over for a final time easier if she went back for the money. She could head west to San Francisco, living it up in a nice home and meet a gentleman. However, her heart begged her to go to Denver, back to Ross Montgomery; back to the man who captured her heart, who saw goodness in her instead of her soiled past. Ross and her were one in the same – kindred, she heard it said once.

*If I go to Omaha, I can bet my sorry self to never see Ross again*, she concluded. *I don't want that...* Mary slammed her hands down on the table, rising from her seat. *Denver it is. Back to Ross*, she decided. A smile crept across her lips.

Mrs. Cottie snorted, her head lolling to the other side of her rocking chair. Mary grinned endearingly. Ida was a kindly old woman, doing more for her in the last hour than most had her entire life. A crocheted blanket slid off her lap. Mary replaced it gently, whispering, "Thank you."

Tip-toeing out the back door of the shack, Mary opened the door. Observing neatly chopped and stacked wood lined to the right of the door, Mary grabbed a few pieces, stepping inside and stacking them near the fireplace so Mrs. Cottie wouldn't have to later.

*To Denver I go*, Mary thought. *Gonna take me a few days, but if I stay close to the train tracks, shouldn't be too difficult.*

Taking one last look at the woman who'd been so kind to her, she shut the back door. Strolling past several other outlying buildings on her way toward the train tracks, her eyes scanned for the sheriff or anyone following her. Her gut churned with each step. Her mind racing at the thought of Charlie and his men being behind any corner or bush.

*Naw*, she thought. *I'd hear him before I see him. Bastard cannot stand the heat of bein' outside for too long and he'd be complainin' to high heaven about everything.*

Mary quickened her pace. Turning north, she walked briskly along the back of the buildings and keeping the train tracks in view. Nothing but rolling hills, sparse trees and scrubby bushes were along her right side. Mary breathed out, relieved no one would be able to spring the draw on her.

Pueblo, much like many of the other towns along the way from Kansas City were boom towns for one reason or another. Why Pueblo was one, she didn't rightly know. There wasn't much to the place in her mind aside from a river which was good for cattle and other livestock.

*Maybe I'll learn of it later,* she thought. *Sure is a pretty place though.*

Mary's eyes scanned her surroundings starting to the right of her and carefully moving left. Stopping dead in her tracks, her heart pounded fearing what she'd see when she looked back. She cautiously glanced behind her.

Nothing.

Years of being on her own taught her to never underestimate what may be behind her; it could be just as dangerous as what lay in front. Nothing could ever be taken at face value. And nothing, like safety, was ever certain. Mary cracked her neck, hustling along, ignoring the rocks digging into her already tender feet. Moving toward a house, the second to last on the way out, she slid along the perimeter, staying below the windows.

*Gotta make this look not-suspicious-like,* she thought.

Peering around the last corner before her, there was nothing else but open prairie and mountains in the distance. Whipping her head around, nothing was behind. Stepping out, using the bustling of the crowd, she melded into the traffic of the city. Walking along, her head slightly down, eyes scanning for any unattended saddles.

*I ain't goin' to steal money,* she decided, *I just wanna grab a skin of water.* Mary bit her bottom lip, hesitating when she came to a saddled horse whose owner was elsewhere. The horse moved its giant white head, staring at her expectantly. *Nope, I cain't,* Mary thought, moving along, *I am turnin' a new leaf. I'll be fine.*

Crossing the street, Mary stayed within a hundred feet or so of the train tracks. *Carryin' somethin' will only slow me down anyways. Time to put some distance between us.* Peeking over her shoulder a final time, Mary was thankful nothing else stirred except the people of the town.

Ross strummed his fingers on the train bench. The rocking sway of the train speeding across the tracks put Quint fast to sleep and thankfully so. The man was a talkative drunk. Not that Ross minded on account of he didn't speak much, however, it was nice to listen to his own thoughts.

The dry, wheat colored grass sped by. A few wild animals bolted away from the screeching whine of the metal kissing the train tracks. Within a few hours, they would be at Walsenburg and off boarding. He was secretly thankful none of his old contacts saw Mary, or asked about what he was up to save for Quint. Both of them were different from the rest of the Avilasto gang; they wanted a righteous life.

Slouching forward, Ross hung his head. Guilt for all he'd done in his life clawed at him worse than a starving wolf at a cabin door. He wasn't the most educated person, not going past the fifth grade. It was one of the reasons, Emerald, his former intended, left him. She wanted more than what his two hands could provide. And she deserved as much. The beautiful woman was smart, sweet and a better woman than he deserved. Working on a cattle ranch wouldn't ever bring him enough income to have his own or give Emerald the house of her dreams.

When she left him, calling off their engagement, and taking a call as a mail-order bride to Ohio to some rich lawyer, he went on a downward spiral. He stole cattle, money and did anything that could bring him money. He wanted to prove himself a worthy man to Emerald before she married the rich Ohio stranger. He wanted to make her dreams come true at whatever the cost. Because of this time period, he had money in the bank of St. Louis, but he didn't want to touch it.

*It's damned blood money*, he seethed at himself. Hanging his head, reliving all he'd done to get it.

*I own you*, were the words he woke up to after a cattle rustle. Little did he understand in the moment, his life as he knew it, was over. Victor and twenty men overtook him and the three others who rustled with him. All of them turned into Victor Del Avilasto's men on pain of death. Thus, began the five years of *employment*, Ross scoffed, under the tyrant. And his brother's involvement as well, though it had nothing to outrightly do with him, merely coincidental. Richard joined after visiting Ross a year into his forced indentureship with Victor.

Raking his fingers through his hair, *I can't right all the wrongs I'd done*, he thought. He removed his hat, setting it on his knee. Folding his hands, he whispered, "God, I haven't been the most righteous person. You know all the terrible things I done with my two hands. I'm sorry. I want to live a better life from here on out. Live right and right wrongs when I can; and in Your name," he paused, opening his eyes to gaze around at anyone watching him. Putting his hat on his head, he whispered a hasty, "Amen."

"Closing in on Walsenburg," the conductor called, causing Quint to stir.

Ross's heart pounded. He hoped she would be somewhere in this town. If not, then he would go north to Pueblo, stopping at Colorado Springs before heading through to Denver. His gut churned with the feeling she was on her way to Denver. He just had to get there before anyone after her did.

*Hang tight, Mary*, he thought.

## CHAPTER FIFTEEN

Every hundred paces, Mary unconsciously checked over her shoulders. Her cracked feet bled through the brown stained stockings. Pausing, Mary folded the fabric over her feet again, hoping the added layer might make her feet feel better. It helped for a few moments.

Mary sucked in a breath, stepping on a particularly painful rock. Stumbling, she caught herself before she hit the ground. She grumbled, rising to her feet. The hot sun waned toward the west. It was going to be dark in a few hours, bringing out a different kind of wildlife Mary didn't care for.

*Damnation*, she cursed. Trees were few and far between. Rolling hills and low valleys went on for miles. The train tracks she followed split the middle, going on into the fading sunlight.

Mary hissed in pain. Her body protesting the continued torture she was putting it through. Her legs ached for her to stop. Her upper body screamed at her for hitting the train tracks earlier; muscles pulled and ached underneath her clothes. Mary swallowed the dryness in her throat, causing her mouth to dry out more. Picking up a rock, she popped it in her mouth. Her Pa used to say it helped. A frown pulled the edges of her lips down. She spat out the dirt on her tongue, her mouth still dry and now gritty.

"Doesn't help worth a lick," she griped, spitting out the rock.

Mary made for a tall, scraggly pine tree a few hundred feet from the train tracks. She wanted to make a fire, keep the chill and the animals at bay. But her head cautioned her. She could sleep a night cold and survive. It would suck worse than a weevil in flour but it was doable. Being caught was not.

Climbing the tree, her arms shook from fatigue and strain. Slowly, she made her way up the knotted pine, going about fifteen feet up. Mary slipped, sliding back down a ways. "Come on," she huffed, "a little more." Roughly twenty or so feet off the ground, she rested, breathing heavily and leaning her head against a branch directly in front of her. Here. She'd settle here for the night.

Resting her head against the trunk of the tree, she breathed heavily. Sticky sap stuck to her hands and dress. Mary frowned, not liking how it clung to her skin.

Night came on quickly. The sun waned, painting the sky in fire of many colors. Closing her eyes, allowing herself to revel in the beauty of the Colorado sunset.

"Next stop Colorado Springs, or somethin' like it," she whispered.

Propping her feet on a branch in front of her, helped her balance as she allowed her body to relax. The relief she felt should have put her fast to sleep; however, the fact she was outside, under the stars, in the wild kept her from relaxing completely. The dark came alive before her eyes and ears. Bats screeched overhead, catching bugs out of the air. Stars peppered the sky, like someone spilled fancy colored sugar on a cutting board and rolled dough in it. They were everywhere and Mary couldn't see where they began or ended.

*Sure is pretty*, she thought with a sigh. Nestling down on the branch, she jostled around, putting the trunk in the middle of her back. She wriggled her toes relishing the freedom and testing her balance. The fresh crusting on the wounds cracked and broke open. Mary hissed at the new pain, biting her lip.

A soft wind blew through the tree branches. *Tomorrow, I gotta put more distance between us. They're after me. I know it and I cain't allow no sore muscles and hurt feet to slow me down.* Sitting up, she peered all around her in the almost absolute darkness. Her eyes strained for any sign of a fire. She closed her eyes and sighed in relief, leaning back down on the branch. *I'm all right for now,* she breathed. Mary crossed her arms over herself to both preserve her body heat and help her stay balanced in the tree, and let exhaustion claim her.

---

Horses whinnying shrilly woke her from a dead sleep. Mary snorted, wiping the drool off the side of her mouth. She moved her head to the side, peering down at the base of the tree. The morning sky barely crackled with the dawn. The gray light faded, bringing on pink tones, hardly enough light to travel by, but just enough to be doable.

Using her knuckles, Mary rubbed the sleep from her eyes. Nothing was below her. Carefully, Mary sat up on the tree branch, her muscles straining, bones cracking with her slow deliberate movement.

A posse of riders barreled toward her. Stealthily, Mary climbed higher into the pine, moving to the more thickly branched backside of the tree. She was at least forty feet up now, holding perfectly still, and praying to God to keep her concealed. She was thankful she chose the dark green dress from Mrs. Cottie. Any other color would have her spotted for sure, even in this light.

Peering down, she spied Opal's flaming locks and Charlie's pristine attire when they stopped only a few feet away from her tree. Opal twitched in her seat, cooling herself with a black, fanciful fan. Charlie leaned forward in his saddle, adjusting himself in his seat.

Mary suppressed a snicker.

"We searched all over Pueblo," Barrie complained.

"Yeah," Danny chimed, "she could be anywhere by nows."

Charlie spun in his seat, the darkness he oozed sending chills down her spine, "And we shall continue to search for the horrible bitch!"

Opal leaned over, putting a white gloved hand on his arm, "Don't fret dear. She is poor and uneducated. She couldn't have gotten terribly far."

Charlie picked up Opal's hand, putting a delicate kiss on the back of it. He smiled at her, straightening himself in the saddle once again. Mary wondered if his pants were too small or if Opal refused to scratch his itch this morning. "Dearest, you are correct. Knowing Mary as I do, she would need to steal supplies in some local town before getting too far. We'll head to the closest town. She is sure to be there. Boys, let's go. She's so close, I can smell the money!"

Mary's muscles ached, begging for her to move, for relief from holding her so rigidly. Mary refused to move. Sweat trickled down her forehead. She licked her cracked lips, praying to God to help keep her still. Charlie took one more look around, spurring his horse onward, the others following suit.

Mary leaned over slightly, watching them follow the train tracks north to Colorado Springs. Leaning her face against the tree trunk, she breathed out slowly. Pulling her face back, sap and bark clung to her cheeks and the wispy hairs not in her braid. Relieved, Mary moved down onto a lower, sturdier branch once the horse hooves dissipated from her hearing.

Sitting on a branch, head in her hands. "Tarnation!" she cursed under her breath. "I cain't go back to Pueblo; people will have their eyes open for me. Cain't go north to Colorado Springs," she breathed out. "Damn it all…"

Swinging her feet and keeping her eyes north she pondered on what to do next. Nothing suitable came to mind. She needed water and food soon. East or west would take her to food and water at some point. Pueblo would bring her to people and to the sheriff. North would be Charlie and sure as a horse shits she wasn't going north. Nothing was worth the possibility of running into Charlie.

Mary ran her sticky sap hands over her face, grumbling when

sap on her face came in contact with the sap on her hands. *Damnation*, she cursed. She sneakily clambered down the scraggly pine, checking all around her for Charlie.

*I'm gonna head east,* she decided. *I know there's a river that way. And then I'll head south. Gonna have to find me some other way to get to Ross and to Denver.*

# CHAPTER SIXTEEN

Ross smacked Quint on the shoulder, waking him as the train screeched to a stop in Walsenburg. The afternoon waned toward evening. Ross dis-boarded the train with Quint stumbling behind him, rubbing the sleep from his eyes. For being a Friday train, there wasn't many people on board or a waiting crowd outside.

Ross's eyes immediately began scanning for blond haired women. The door to the train stable cars opening brought his attention back around. He waited patiently on the platform for his animal. His bay mare poked her head out, ears forward and eyes wide. Ross jogged forward, taking the reins from the boy who hardly held her tossing head. Quint strode past him, getting his mount before the timid boy could attempt grabbing the animal. Quint's stud whinnied loudly creating a raucous with the rest of the animals on the livestock holding car.

Ross walked his mount off the platform and into the bustling street, scanning Walsenburg again for all the blond headed women. There weren't many out in the evening air. Most he saw were small toe-headed children by their parents. He grimaced. His sweaty palms threatened to drop the reins, but his fist gripped tighter. Walking his horse through the middle of town, Quint on the other side of him, their eyes scanning rapidly for any woman who could be Mary.

"D'ya see her?" Quint asked.

Ross shook his head. "Not yet."

Glancing over his shoulder, Ross's heart pounded in his chest. The need to find Mary urged him onward. He wasn't able to save his sister from the fever that took her when they were only kids. He wasn't able to save many calves on the ranches he worked from sicknesses or natural dangers like wolves. But if he could save Mary, to just save her life, it wouldn't right all the wrongs he'd done, but it would make him believe he wasn't chalked up to shit.

*Plus...* he paused, *I wanna call on her.*

"Should we stop for the night?" Quint asked with a yawn.

"No," Ross replied firmly. "I wanna find her."

"All right," Quint readily agreed, stretching his arms.

Chills tingled his skin, creeping up his arms to his shoulders. His gut churned with the sense Mary wasn't in Walsenburg. He had to check, because if she came back this way, and he wasn't there, hadn't at least checked, he'd never forgive himself.

She'd saved him, now it was his turn to save her. Mary made him believe he was redeemable, a good person, that he was worth living and breathing. Her simple words, her way of being there for him when they were both trapped by Del Avilasto, and then again when he seemed to be on death's doorstep, touched him more than he could admit aloud. She was the nail holding his ramshackle self together, only she didn't know it. Or how much he'd come to love her. Fact was, he was now realizing himself, he loved her.

Ross sighed, straining his eyes for her. No blond and no Mary; no shining blue eyes meeting his own. Spinning on his heels, he gazed behind him. Also, no sign of her.

Ross mounted, swinging his feet over. Quint quickly mounted, leaning forward in the saddle.

"So," Quint began, "wanna split up and see where she's not?"

Ross nodded. "Yeah... Might as well. You check saloons and I'll check diner's and mercantiles."

"What was she wearin'?"

Ross scratched the stubble on his chin. "Dark blue dress with sleeves to the elbows. White on the seams. Blond hair and blue eyes."

Quint grinned slightly. "She sounds pretty. Prettier than I remember, for sure."

"She is."

Quint nodded, moving behind him to the left where the liveliness of the evening was beginning. The whooshing of saloon doors banging back and forth startled Ross's mare who hopped a little. Lively, boisterous laughter came from a building a way down the street. Ross spun his horse around going back the way he came. His eyes strained in the fading sunlight to see the names painted on the wooden signs of buildings.

He hitched his horse outside a large dining hotel where he could see people sitting to eat through the large, clear windows. Striding inside, removing his hat, he gazed around at the people, seeing no one looking like Mary.

Walking back out, he stood on the threshold of the dining hotel, turning right he strode into the hotel side. The man behind the counter pushed his spectacles back on his face with a poke of his finger.

"Excuse me," Ross began, approaching the counter, "any blond woman with a dark blue dress by the name of Mary book a room here?"

The man shook his head. "No sir. Might want to ask the sheriff. He watches every train comin' in and out of Walsenburg."

"Where can I find him?"

The man leaned over the counter pointing across the street, "Over yonder, three buildings in from the end here."

"Thanks," he said, putting his hat back on his head.

Ambling out, turning to the left, he went down the way passing a mercantile. He peered in through the paned glass windows to the darkened store. The man inside wearing a white apron and standing next to an oil lamp set on the counter pointed to the "closed" sign hanging in the window.

Ross nodded his head, moving on down the raised wooden platform, stopping at other shop windows and peering inside. Jogging across the street, he made straight for the sheriff's office. The building was dark inside, the door locked and a "closed" sign hung in the window. Ross shook his head, clenching his fists.

*Where else to check?* Ross thought. *Sheriff isn't around. She's not in the hotel. Quint is checkin' saloons. Everything is closed down... Tarnation, I started too late. She could be anywhere... Confound it all, Mary, where are you?*

Ross made toward another dining hotel on the corner of the street he was on. It wasn't as bustling as the first place. He paused on the raised wooden platform a few buildings away, gazing up and down the darkened, lonely street.

He spied Quint's horse farther down the road outside a rowdy saloon. His own mare was tied outside the dining hotel where he began. Adjusting the hat on his head, Ross jogged down the platform toward the other dining hotel, entering through the white washed door. A bell jingled overhead announcing him to the serving women.

"Sit wherever you like," a young brunette said chipperly, setting down plates of food in front of an elderly couple.

Ross didn't move toward any of the empty tables, but stood near the door and wrung his hat in his hands. The same woman came back, smiling at him like one would a shy child.

"Sir?" she said softly. "Can I help you?"

"Ma'am," Ross began, "I'm lookin' for a woman. She's about a head smaller than myself, blond hair, blue eyes wearing a dark navy dress. Have you seen her?"

The woman shook her head. "I haven't. But my sister was watchin' today's train, looking for her intended," she said with a roll of her eyes. Putting a hand to the side of her lips she whispered. "Been lookin' for him nigh on a month," she giggled. "I tease her. It's 'sposed to be mail order bride, not husband," she snorted. "I'll fetch her. Mayhap she noticed your girl."

Ross shuffled from foot to foot, waiting off to the side watching the few diners. He didn't care for busy places. It made his skin crawl with nerves, and while this place wasn't busy as the first hotel, it was busier than he liked. His arms tingled, urging him to bolt out the door.

Instead, he shifted toward the door, standing next to a chair placed against the wall. Leaning against the wall trying to look casual, he continued to observe the room. Since working for Del Avilasto, he learned to always be on his guard. The vile man had connections from San Francisco to France, with more being enemies. Ross never knew what to expect, but opted to remain ever vigilant.

The brunette woman came back with a smaller, meeker honey brown haired woman in tow. Her pink dress made her appear childlike with her twin braids by her ears. She hid behind the serving woman.

"My sister says she didn't see your woman. The only ones she seen get off here were a few brunettes and two red heads."

Ross perked at the information of the red headed women. "Was one of them in the company of a blond-haired man with two other men following them?"

The meek one moved her head around her sister and nodded.

"Which way did they go?"

The meek woman poked her head out, "North on horses."

"Thank you. I appreciate it much."

Ross strode out of the dining hotel pausing on the landing to make sure Quint's horse was where he left it. It wasn't. Ross cursed under his breath. His mind imagined all the trouble Quint could have gotten into. Ross jogged down the street to his own mount. Reaching for his mare, the animal's ears flicked back and forth, whickering irritably.

Ross patted her neck, "I know girl."

*Where's Quint at. I need his help. Sounds like those people after Mary came through here and left,* Ross surmised. *I need to get to Pueblo, but I gotta waste time looking for Quint now.*

"HEY! Ross!"

Ross turned around slowly wincing at the slur in the words.

Quint staggered forward, grinning foolishly. "There you are!" he giggled. "I lost my horse... And my boots."

Ross ran a hand over his face. "What did you do?"

Quint held his hands out to the side. "I've no idea! But... I found somethin'..." he grinned clucking his tongue.

"Yeah?"

"A man name's Charlie purchased horsies today and... suppplies. Headed to Pue-bb-low."

Ross's head jerked up. The sudden movement spooked his skittish horse. *"There I met my former fiancé. His name was Charlie Hilbert. He left me for another woman,"* Mary's voice rang through his head. *It is someone from her past. And she's runnin' from him. Good God, I gotta find her.*

A woman came jogging down the boardwalk, her breasts practically bouncing out of her low-cut dress with every step. Ross looked away.

"You lost these... *cowboy*," she said in a sultry voice, trailing a finger down his arm.

"My boots!" Quint exclaimed gleefully, putting his boots on and ignoring the woman. "Hey!" he shouted with the same enthusiasm. "There's my horse too. He must'a got excited." He pointed with a chuckle as the stud approached a tethered mare.

Quint took a step, wobbled, catching himself against the wooden beam of the building. The woman, tired of being ignored, walked away. Ross let out the breath he was holding, thankful he didn't have to deal with another issue. Tying his mare back to the post, he jogged across the street to Quint's mount. The dark stallion reared at him, ears back. Ross stepped back, avoiding the kicking hooves, talking soft nonsense. Grabbing the reins, Ross led the horse over to where his inebriated master barely held himself up.

"Mount up," Ross said, tossing Quint the reins and mounting in a swift motion. "We're goin' to Pueblo."

Quint put one foot in the stirrup. The drunk fell backward, hands not even out to catch himself. Foot still in the stirrup and back in the dirt, the man put his hands behind his head and grinned.

Grumbling, Ross dismounted. *Gonna be a long night*, he thought.

"All those twinklies," Quint commented with a grin.

Ross removed Quint's foot from the stirrup, accidentally taking Quint's boot with him.

"Buddy," Quint complained. "It won't fit you."

Ross offered him a hand up. Quint took it, standing with a hazy, mottled grin and a rheumy gaze. Without warning the man, Ross lifted him by the waist and tossed him in the saddle.

"Whoa…" Quint said astonished, managing to keep his seat as his horse shifted nervously beneath him. "I didn't know you could do that!"

Ross ignored him, unfettering Quint's reins, putting them in the man's hand. Quint sloppily took them, leaning forward in the saddle looking like sleep would overtake him whether he was ready or not. Perking a brow, Ross took the reins back from the man, holding onto them himself. Ross mounted his mare, the horse grumbling underneath him.

"I hear you. Let's go find her," Ross replied, patting his mare. "Off to Pueblo."

"Yeah!" Quint cheered. "What're we doin' again?"

# CHAPTER SEVENTEEN

The high noon sun beat against her back. Mary's feet pained her with each step. The blisters from yesterday had cracked open, bleeding again and again. The bleeding eventually stopped, but it didn't stop the pain. The lucky part, as she figured it, was her skin was sticking to the stockings, hopefully providing a barrier between all the dirt and her open wounds.

Grumbling, she pressed on through the low brush and moving through scrub oaks. The rushing crash of water caught her attention. Carefully, she maneuvered through the rest of the obstructing plants, going slowly toward the river she'd finally spotted. She banged the ground with a stick she picked up, scaring off any rattlers lurking in the brush. She knew she'd hear the nasty critters before she saw them... if she saw them, but this way she gave advanced warning, hopefully avoiding them altogether.

*Nasty things*, she thought. *Makes for good eatin' though.*

Mary looked all around her before taking another cautious step. Creeping down toward the bank where the river sped by looking for a good place to sit. Off to her right, about 100 feet, she spotted a rocky mudbank and some low, slower flow. Pushing herself to walk the few more steps, she dropped over the edge, landing on the rocks below. Mary knelt down, eyes scanning up and down the bank for those hunting her. Setting down her stick, she maneuvered nearer to the water, more out in the open.

The hems of her dress sopped up the liquid on the rocks, turning the dust covering her hems to mud. Trying to be inconspicuous as possible, she crouched; sneaking to the mudbanks edge. Cupping her hands, she scooped water, splashing it on her face.

Mary sighed. *Now to follow this to Pueblo,* she decided. *Or should I go to Walsenburg?* Slurping up water, her throat instantly cooled. She wanted to stick her entire face in the river. *Gotta avoid Charlie, and he's plannin' on going to Pueblo. So I'll by-pass Pueblo, to Walsenburg and hop a train north.*

Mary laid on the cool rocks, sticking her face in the water, drinking her fill. She pulled back, getting to her knees, crawling back to the bank. Her eyes constantly scanning up and down the river. Grabbing her stick, Mary clambered out of the bank's edge, walking south, and keeping along the river's edge.

She peeked behind her, relieved at not seeing Charlie or Opal. However, it didn't set her nerves to rights. They were still coming for her. Charlie wouldn't stop until she was good and dead, or he had the money. She wasn't going to give him the location of it. He may have claimed it, but in her estimation, she's the one who did all the work for it, then he goes and cheats on her. The money is hers, or it would be if it weren't for the fact the money was dirty.

*Well then, I don't want it neither,* she decided. *I'm gonna give it away to a school for girls. Hopefully it will make their lives better. One thousand dollars would go a long way for them.*

Striding along the brush, she banged her stick every few feet or so. A train whistle blew in the distance. She was still a way off from Pueblo. Luckily, her early start helped her make good time, plus the periodic sprints she forced on herself when the fear of being followed almost swallowed her.

She'd turned east about two hours before and now, the town of Pueblo appeared below her as she crested a hill. Pueblo spread out in even rows of streets with wagons and horses moving all around.

Peeking over her shoulder one last time, she descended the hill, sticking this time to the outskirts deciding to stop there for the night before heading to Walsenburg to catch the train north.

The scraggly brush oaks offered her no concealment doing her little good. Although on the flip side, she could see quite a distance out; and all she saw was more brush, which both relieved and unnerved her. Life taught her to never turn her back on the enemy, to always be in a position to see everything, so open spaces made her nervous and in her current situation, scared her to pieces.

*I don't want to always peek over my shoulder wonderin' when the past will come back alive,* she thought, walking briskly past houses on her right. *I want a home. Someplace sturdy with walls no one can rip from me. And a husband like everyone else got.* She paused a moment, keeping her back to the brush. Her eyes skimming up and down the street. *I want to be educated. Learn to read and write.*

Forcing herself to keep walking, her feet ached with protest. She kept a keen eye on the bustling street to her right.

Her heart lurched as her thoughts strayed to Ross again. In all the time she spent running from Charlie, her thoughts were on staying alive to get back to Ross. Mary smiled at the thought of him. In all their time together, he never once condemned her. He teased her, but never was he mean.

*You kiss your mother with that mouth,* he joked once. She quipped back, *no, I kissed yer brother.* The smirk gracing his lips in that moment had her swooning on her feet. Only she let the feeling go. No one like him would want broken and troubled manure like her. Charlie didn't; although he'd pretended well. Her aunt Winnifred didn't want her and neither did her parents.

Mary ran a hand over her face. *I wonder what happened to my brothers and sister,* she thought. She hadn't heard from them in years and didn't bother to track them down. Aunt Winnifred married up in society, taking her family with her, thankfully. They were years younger than her anyways. *They won't remember me. Milton and Pauly would be thirteen now. And little Maggie would be almost eleven.* Mary breathed out; a wan grin quirked on the side of her lips. She brushed a lone tear off the corner of her left eye.

Pausing, she scanned the area again. Horse hooves thundered nearby. Mary slunk back into the brush, crouching low. She hung her head, wiping more tears threatening to fall into the thirsty dirt.

*Ross won't want me either. Everyone always leaves*, she breathed deeply, trying to still the tears. *Ross said once to pray because God will help you find answers. God doesn't answer prayers*, she frowned. *If He did, then I wouldn't be thievin' to live. I would have a family and be smart.*

Horse hooves paused near her hiding spot. Rough hands grabbed her from behind, dragging her backward. Mary closed her eyes, her back striking the rocks as the hands dropped her in the open.

A man clucked his tongue. Her blood turned colder than an Ohio winter.

"Hiding in the pine was smart," Charlie began, "only we could still see you," he snarled, giving her hair a tug, "Honey Bee."

Righting herself on her feet, Mary took a swing at Charlie. He caught her fist, shoving one of his own into her stomach. Doubling over, Mary inhaled sharply. Catching herself before she hit the ground, she was unable to dodge before Charlie brought a knee to her face. Mary's body jolted back. Another fist struck along the right side of her face.

Tears, unrelated to her previous thoughts, streaked down her face. Someone grabbed her, forcing her to her feet. Mary took another swing at Charlie connecting to the left side of his face. His lip split open. Mary grinned. Opal strode forward, slapping her across the face. Mary balled her right hand into a fist. Taking a step forward, she threw a punch at Opal, missing by a hair. The woman flinched, hiding behind her husband. Dashing forward, Mary took another swing at Opal. Charlie stood in front of his wife, punching Mary on the right side of her face as she focused on Opal.

Mary fell to her backside in the dirt. Clutching her face, she glared at Charlie. Her heart pounding in her chest. Barrie and Danny stood on either side of her.

"Get a rope and tie her up," Charlie hissed.

Barrie stormed off to the horse. Danny forced her to her feet, holding tightly to both her arms. Wriggling, Mary tried to break free. Danny swept her feet out from under her forcing her to her knees.

Charlie grinned, standing over her, "You know what's wonderful, Honey Bee?"

"You dyin'," Mary seethed.

Charlie laughed mockingly, spitting on her face. "No... When *you* die, no one will know. *No one* will miss you or care. You'll be a poor woman buried in an unmarked grave *no one* will miss."

Icy shivers crawled up and down her arms. Her heart thundered in her chest. Barrie came back, tying her arms together behind her back, wrapping the rest of the rope around her body. Charlie slapped her across the face just because he could.

Mary licked her split lip, staring at the darkness in his brown eyes, wondering if he was always this cruel. Closing her eyes, she wracked her brain for memories of her time spent with Charlie. Mary cringed. *He was cruel. Always mean, shoutin' and strikin' me when somethin' went wrong. I was too young and stupid, too blinded by food and shelter and the occasional affection.*

Danny yanked her to her feet. Mary shrugged him off, stepping away from him. Her eyes blazing as she approached Charlie. Grinning fiercely, she stood toe to toe with the man she'd come to loathe. All the months of abuse she took from him came rushing to memory, and with it the hatred and anger came boiling to the surface. The fear once rattling around in her bones, replaced by animosity and fury.

"No one," she growled, "will miss *you*."

Charlie dipped his head to her, bringing his nose close to hers, whispering, "But you, *Honey Bee*, will see God first."

Taking off at a dead run, not hesitating even a second, she headed back the way she came. Her feet thundering in the dirt.

"Help!" she yelled. "Someone, help me!"

Before she'd gotten more than a handful of steps, Mary felt herself being pitched from the earth. Her body thrust to the left, sliding in the sandy dirt. Spitting out the dirt, she scrambled to her feet, hardly getting traction under herself. Sprinting toward town, still unbalanced due to the blows to her head, Mary fell face first back into the dirt. She moaned, rolling to her side, she glanced back. Danny caught her foot before she was able to move it, lashing rope around it. He climbed her legs, pinning her to the ground despite her struggles. Barrie jogged forward, kneeling down on her back. Thrashing around, she tried to get away again. Barrie held her face in the dirt.

Kicking her feet, Mary strained to get out from underneath the henchmen. She couldn't. Her feet were now lashed together. Taking the rope, Danny drug her on her belly back toward Charlie and Opal; both now mounted and facing the way she came. Her dress bunched underneath her; hands lashed behind her. Grumbling, Danny came back with a smaller rope, binding it around her knees with her dress pulled and tucked down for modesty. Taking a blue kerchief out of his pocket, he tied it around her mouth.

Mary thrashed in the dirt, attempting to crawl using her shoulders. Danny gave the rope a pull, dragging her to the horses. She frantically worked her head back and forth. The gag would not release.

"How wonderful you decided to join us, *again*, Florence," Opal snickered behind a fan.

Charlie's lip twitched. Danny mounted his horse, lashing the tied end of her feet bindings to his saddle horn. Using her shoulder's Mary inched away from the posse.

*I need to get to Denver. I need Ross*, her mind cried. *This cain't be the way I die. This man will not be my end.* She grunted with each wriggle of her shoulders inching in the dirt like a worm.

"Drag her," Charlie commanded, urging his horse forward.

*I need Ross. I need to get to him*, she repeated to herself. *I love the man, even iffn' he cain't love me back. I sound mighty stupid lovin' someone who I don't know more than salt, but I do. It's what Audrey called 'instant connotation' or somethin' like.* She laughed silently at her thoughts. Of all the things to think of at a time like this, Audrey's fancy words shouldn't have been one of them.

"Boss," Danny replied, glancing down at Mary.

Charlie sighed irritably, leaning in his saddle. "Drag. Her."

Mary inched away, flopping around worse than a dying fish. She struggled to get her body to move in the sandy dirt, away from the people who wanted to off her. She breathed frantically, the gag in her mouth sopping wet with saliva.

Shaking his head, Danny dismounted. Mary squirmed, trying to wriggle free. Picking her up, Danny threw her over his shoulder like she weighed nothing more than a small bag of carrots. He tossed her on the back of the horse, mounting in front of her.

Mary closed her eyes, tears once again seeping down her cheeks. Whatever came next would have her dead for sure.

# CHAPTER EIGHTEEN

Ross ran a hand over his face. The exhaustion and frustration bore heavily upon him. He swore it was the longest night of his entire life.

Reaching over, he righted Quint in the saddle for what felt like the millionth time. The man, so intoxicated, dismounted every few yards to either take a piss or speak to an object he believed had curves of a woman.

Ross tied Quint's reins around his saddle horn. Spurring his horse into a light trot, Quint bounced in his seat, groaning.

"Ugh, my head," Quint complained.

Ross kept silent, eyes vigilantly scanning for a blond woman in a navy-blue dress. He saw nothing but more scraggly brush oak and tall pines. Sighing, he scratched the back of his neck, pulling his hat down low over his eyes.

A choking garble made him pause, glancing behind him. Quint leaned forward vomiting all over himself and his poor horse. Ross flinched, turning back around. His horse tossed his head, moving around another brush oak as they crested a hill. A train docked at a station, smoke rising from the stack. A town bustled with activity behind the train. Ross urged his mount forward. His nerves tingling with anxiousness to find Mary.

*She has to be here*, he surmised.

Ross made straight for the train. A saddled sheriff sat on horseback in the middle of the throng of people; sharp eyes scanning for any unsavory people.

"Town!" Quint exclaimed. "We can get somethin' to eat."

Ross didn't care to eat. Not with Mary still missing and in trouble. His gut churned, roiling with the fear Mary was in deep trouble. Untying Quint's reins from the saddle horn, he tossed them back to his friend. The hungover man fumbled hand over fist to get a grip on the leads, finally smiling triumphantly, when he gained control.

Ross shook his head, moving carefully through the throng of people. "Sheriff," Ross called approaching the man. "What town is this?"

The blond sheriff cocked his head to the side. Green eyes skimming him up and down. "Colorado Springs."

"Shit."

"What town did you think this was?"

"Pueblo."

The sheriff laughed. "You overshot by quite a way. It's another half day ride, if not more, the way you just rode in on."

Ross dipped his head, turning his mare back around quickly. His blood boiled. Clenching the reins in his hands, his knuckles turned white. His heels dug a bit forcefully into the side of his mount. Thankfully, the animal didn't bolt at his show of temper and the people around him avoided the dancing feet of his mount.

Leaning forward, Ross apologized, stroking the mare's neck.

"We're leavin'!?" Quint complained.

"Yeah," Ross stated, not keeping the terseness from his voice. "Wanna stay?"

Quint, scratched his head, "Well," he began, "yeah... We need food. The horses need to eat and drink and we can all use a few hours' sleep."

Ross ran a hand over his face. *He's not wrong*, he surmised, not liking the fact. Spinning his mount back around, careful of the crowd around him, he went into town. Staying to the right of the road, he meandered through the busy streets.

Quint stopped outside a livery, dismounting and stumbling to the ground. Ross reined in his mare, dismounting as well. Quint fumbled through his pocket, pulling out a few coins and handing them to the waiting man.

"Food and water," Quint said, motioning to the two animals. "We will be back in a few hours."

Ross crossed his arms, watching his bay mare being led away. Quint clapped him on the shoulder.

"I'm sorry," Quint said. "Let me buy you breakfast."

Arms crossed; Ross leaned away from the friendly gesture of the smelly man beside him. His mind wandered to what kind of trouble Mary would be in because of their delay. She could be anywhere by now and his breathing hitched. Somehow though, in his gut he knew, she wasn't out of Colorado.

*She could be dead for all I know*, Ross worried. *Or bit by a snake. Fallen down a cliff. By Jove, I sound like a mother hen... But I love her. I have to find her, bring her back to Denver to call on her proper.*

Swiping a hand over his face, he allowed Quint to lead him somewhere. Quint led him to a diner, automatically ordering two of the specials and coffee. Sitting down in the high-backed chair, Ross sighed with defeat. It felt like the moments ticked by slow, taking years off his life.

"Hey," Quint said softly, gaining his attention and surprisingly sober considering only a little bit ago he'd vomited all over himself and his horse. "We'll find her. We have to take care of our horses and ourselves to do it though."

Ross nodded, sulking in his chair. A woman poured them coffee, hastily moving away to the next table wanting some of the black gold. Ross took off his hat, hanging it over the ear of the chair. Leaning forward, he sulked with his elbows on the table and head in his hands.

"Do you have a gun?"

"No," Ross stated. "I don't wanna kill anyone. Not since Victor."

"I have one," Quint replied softly. "And heck, no one wants to kill no one, but sometimes you can't help the fact. Do you wanna stay alive for Mary, have a life with her, then you may have to shoot someone. Doesn't make you bad."

A woman brought them food, setting the fare down with a smile. She refilled their coffee cups and backed away quickly, her nose scrunched up as she turned away.

"I'm sorry for last night," Quint said between bites of fried eggs.

Ross picked at his meal ignoring his companion, lost in thought. His body in a crossroads of starving and nervously wanting to be back on the road.

*Somethin's not right*, he thought, scowling at the burnt toast. He bit into it, washing the crumbly dust down with a large gulp of coffee. *Somethin' doesn't feel right.*

Ross forked the two fried eggs, stuffing them into his mouth. He quickly washed it all down with coffee and grabbed the sausage off the plate, sticking the greasy rounds in his shirt pocket. Grabbing his hat, he stamped it on his head and bolted out the door.

Quint's chair screeched back and he garbled, "Wait for me," jumping to catch up with his friend. Ross peeked over his shoulder. Quint slammed money on the table, hurrying out the door.

"Just wait, Ross," Quint reasoned. "If Mary's adept as you say she is, then she will be all right."

"You don't know it!" Ross seethed. "I never once doubted her ability to take care of herself. What I fear, is me not bein' there when she is in trouble, of her gettin' hurt or killed because this lowlife former-fiancé may not hold back and she cain't do anything about it."

Quint conceded. "All right," he said, standing in front of him with his hands out. "Where do you wanna look first?"

Ross shook his hand. "Head south to Pueblo. She's gotta be somewhere between Walsenburg and here."

"Do you wanna look around here first?"

Ross nodded. "Yeah... Thank you."

"All right then. You take the left and I'll take the right."

Ross jogged across the road to the livery, getting his mare. Thanking the man and mounting up, he began his desperate search for Mary in Colorado Springs. *If she ain't here, it leaves one last place*, Ross thought. *I sure hope to find her breathin'.*

# CHAPTER NINETEEN

Mary bounced in the saddle. Her head aching from trying to keep it still. Every time she thought the road smoothed out, there was something else causing her body to jolt.

Closing her eyes, she dared not open them. Each time she did, her eyes bleared, and involuntary tears made her head ache worse. Wherever they were headed to scared her more than Victor; at the end of this journey, she knew she wouldn't be breathing.

*How in blazes am I getting out of this one?* she thought.

Mary wriggled on the horse, rocking back and forth. Danny, reaching behind, smacked her on the bottom. Mary seethed, rolling into Danny. Using her head, she drove it into his side. Danny swatted her away with the back of his hand. Desperate to escape, Mary rocked side to side, hoping to jostle herself free.

*Then what*, she thought. *I'm stuck worse than a fox in a trap. Lord Almighty, my hide is tanned for sure.* She fought the bonds holding her hands, rolling her wrists. She grunted, *long as I'm breathin' I won't be sittin' like a stuck pig.*

The horses tail swished, flicking her in the face. Scrubby brush oak and pine trees dotted along their pathway. The sound of rushing water had her mind reeling and her imagination wandering to what could happen once they stopped.

Mary licked her cracked lips. Her mind a mud puddle of ideas for escaping but the physical ability evading her. Sweat coursed down her head, running into her hair. She struggled to make a decision.

Fighting her bonds, Mary rolled her wrists over themselves again. Biting her lip from the pain, she got her left hand partially free. Grinning triumphantly, she worked her other wrist free, tears coursing down her face.

Moving her hands around slowly, she wiped her eyes, removing the gag from her mouth. Her wrists, rubbed raw from the scratchy rope, bled freely. Mary could care less. Bringing her feet up to her, balancing carefully on the horse's rump, she worked the knot binding her feet while keeping a careful eye on the riders in front.

Smiling, she got part of her legs free from the rope. With nimble stealth, acquired over years of pickpocketing, she fingered the knife on Danny's right side; carefully pulling it free of its sheath. Knife in hand, she gripped it tight.

*No, I cain't kill him,* she determined. *Ross wouldn't like it. I don't want blood on my hands. I've never killed. Don't rightly know if I could.* Mary brows furrowed. *But I can do this.* Biting her lip, she sliced the horse's croup enough to make it painful but not deep enough to do damage. Not the animal's fault for doing what it was supposed to.

The horse side stepped, tossing his head. Danny reined in hard, gaining little control of the animal. Knife in hand, Mary sliced the animal again. Finally, the horse reared throwing her off.

Closing her eyes, Mary hit the dirt, landing on her back. All the air, gone from her lungs. Quickly sitting up, she cut the bonds below her knees. Scrambling to her feet, Mary bolted through the scrub oak, weaving her way around the obstacles.

"Damnation!" Charlie cursed. "After her!"

"Shiiiiiiit," Mary breathed.

Horse hooves thundered behind her. Mary weaved her way

past rocks and bushes, heading for the river. *I can't swim worth a lick but I'd take my chances*, she thought.

Peeking to her left, Barrie was hot on her heels. The river still a way from her. Mary's eyes darted back to the man barreling after her. He whipped a pistol from his belt, drawing the hammer back with his thumb. In her racing mind, the clicking sound reverberated.

A loud crack split the silent air. Mary tumbled to the ground. Breathing heavy, she rolled to her side. Her right calf bled profusely.

"Shit!" she shrieked.

Barrie dismounted, glaring at her, jerking the hammer back again, he pointed the pistol at her head. "Drop it," he growled.

Mary let the knife fall from her hands. The rest of the posse reined in their animals around her. Charlie dismounted, glaring daggers at her, fists balled at his sides. Mary closed her eyes, knowing what was coming next; pain radiated from her left jaw to her skull as his fist connected with her face.

"Well Honey Bee, I dare say you found the perfect spot," he hissed.

Charlie raised his boot, kicking her in the chest. Mary flew black, inhaling sharply for breath. Rolling to her side, she tried to stand. Her calf throbbing, refusing to bare her weight.

*Stand*, she urged herself but her throbbing, bleeding body refused to obey.

Charlie loomed over her. Peeking back over her shoulder, the malevolence radiating from Charlie sent chills down her spine. With a gleam in his eye, he kicked her in the back, holding her down with a booted heel.

"Bind her hands and her feet, then drag her to the river."

Barrie tied her hands behind her back, knotting the rope all the way up to her elbows. Tears coursed down her face. With another piece of rope, she felt her legs being tied at the knees, wrapping all the way down to her feet.

*God*, Mary prayed, licking her lips. Snot trickling out of her nose while hot tears coursed down her bowed head. *Knowin' I'll be meetin' you soon, I wanted to let you know how sorry I am for all I've done in my life. I haven't been much good at anything or to anyone. For that, I'm sorry. I don't know where you'll be sending me. I deserve whatever I get. Please keep Ross safe. Iffn' you see it fit, let him know, I loved him. It sounds right dumb not knowin' him well enough, but I cain't help it.*

She paused, an image of Ross forming in her mind. The way his gray eyes shone underneath his hat. How the brown stubble forming along his jawline added to his handsome ruggedness. The way he would smile, giving a half lopsided grin while looking at his boots then back into her eyes. It made her heart swoon and fall in regret. *It's what's called an 'instant connotation' or somethin'. Keep him safe, please. Thank you, God... Amen.*

Eyes closed; Mary felt her body lift off the ground enough to allow for movement. The sharp whistle followed by horse hooves pounding dirt, made her heart lurch as they began to move forward, dragging her beside the horse. She never faced death quite like this. Even in the clutches of Del Avilasto, she not once felt this isolated and trapped. She had people around her, working together to escape, bringing her with them. Now, being alone, she was done for.

The forward momentum of the animal forced her to roll to her back as she was drug through the brush. Mary didn't notice the scratchy brush, rocks and bumps along the way. Her body numbed considerably. Her eyes fixed on the sky. Her mind wandered to a thought, *wonder if God lives in the clouds. What's His heavenly palace look like? Guess I'll be finding out.*

The harsh movement of water drowned out everything else around her. The rushing whoosh of the river crashing over rocks was met with a beautiful view above her. The horse paused on the edge of a small bank. The moist soil below her cushioned her weary body.

"Right here!" Charlie yelled. "This place is perfect!"

Sitting slightly up, Mary skimmed the area around her. Three pine trees and a few others dotted the nearby bank. The steep bank dropped suddenly on the sides. A sloped side made a pathway down to the water, but even it was a sharp walk. The water below rushed by with little white capped spots. A thick pine jutted out to the side, overhanging the water by a few feet.

Laying back down, Mary closed her eyes, feeling her feet being dragged and lifted. The dirt and sweat of the henchman carrying her made her nose twitch against his chest. Booted steps sloshed through the water then stopped. She kept her eyes closed, not wanting to see the final moments of her life. The rope on her feet tugged and she felt herself drag a little. With a *swish*, she heard the rope toss, smacking on a branch, which made her shudder. A second later her body jolted into the air. Swinging back and forth by her feet, her blood rushed to her head. Tears trickled to her forehead.

"Where is the money, Honey Bee?" Charlie asked.

"Go to hell," Mary spat.

Charlie laughed, "Ladies first."

Mary bit her lower lip at his laugh and gasped as she dropped sharply into the river. Cold water rushed over her face. Mary held her breath, closing her eyes trying to ignore the stinging in her nose. Quickly she was pulled out of the water. Mary gasped for breath, snorting the water out of her nose.

"Mary," Charlie began condescendingly, "where is the money?"

She remained silent. She would never tell him where she hid it. Some other fellow can find it and put it to good use. Charlie wouldn't ever get his bloody, killing, backstabbing hands on it. Glaring at her, his face mottled red. Opal sat on her horse, fanning herself, appearing bored as Mary hung there facing her final moments.

Charlie nodded to Barrie, lowering Mary under the ripping current once more. Eyes closed; Mary held her breath for as long as she could.

# CHAPTER TWENTY

R oss checked every mercantile and diner in Colorado Springs. Checking with the sheriff, the train master, and the people working on the train; any person he came across, he asked if they'd seen her. Mary wasn't seen anywhere in the last two days.

Changing directions, Ross and Quint headed on the main road south to Pueblo. Ross's eyes lingered on those he passed. He asked everyone he came across if they'd seen Mary. With shakes of their heads and a quick 'no', the people headed to their own destinations, leaving Ross frustrated and on edge.

The hot, autumn sun bore down on his back. A cool wind whipped through the trees. Off to the east, storm clouds swirled darkly overhead. Ross groaned. Adding horrible weather on top of this already stressful situation was more than he could take. If it started raining, he would have to worry about flash floods on top of losing any possible tracks.

*Where is she?* Ross thought, his heart sinking to his gut. His stomach roiled at the thought of getting to her too late. He panicked she was already in serious trouble and he wasn't there to save her, like she had him.

Pausing along the river, he sat on the back of his horse, head in his hands exhausted beyond reason, but too worried to rest. Mary had to be somewhere. She wouldn't leave Colorado without telling him. Or would she? Mary was flighty, scared of settling down because she feared never belonging. But she did – in his heart and in his home, hopefully, if she'd have him.

"Hey," Quint shouted riding up to him. "We'll find her. Have some faith."

Ross exhaled sharply, running a hand over his face. "Yeah."

"Come on," Quint encouraged.

Picking up the reins, he steered his horse to travel along the bank headed away from Colorado Springs. Quint trotted ahead of him.

"Mary!" Ross hollered.

Nothing answered him.

"What's she like?" Quint asked, slowing his horse.

Ross perked a brow. "What d'ya mean?"

Quint shrugged. "Is she sassy or proper?"

"Sassy," Ross said smirking. "When we were escaping Del Avilasto, she was cursin'. I asked her if she kissed her mother with that mouth. She smiled and said 'No I kissed yer brother,'" Ross smiled. "Her face lighting up how it did, she was beautiful even in the too big man's clothes she was wearin'."

"She sounds nice," Quint said softly.

"She is. You know how people say, when you feel it in your heart, it must be right?"

Quint scowled, nodding politely. "Yeah, I'd heard, what is meant to be will."

Ross nodded. "Mary is right for me."

Quint nodded.

Sighing, he urged the mare to trot. Already it was well past noon, heading into the evening. There was still a way to go to get to Pueblo before nightfall and the impending storm. One thing he disliked about the mountainous state was the changing weather. Almost incredibly, it seemed to turn in a matter of a few breaths.

His fingers strummed on his pant legs. Sighing, he ran his fingers through his hair.

"I found somethin," Quint called. "Look at the bank!"

Ross spurred his horse, his eyes straining for what Quint saw.

Quint pointed. "Looks like someone slipped on this mudbank."

Ross dismounted, going in for a closer look. He sprinted to the spot, jumping down into the dried out mudbank. Footprints depressed in the mud, on the side of the bank, going up into the grass.

Scowling at the tracks, he moved around them, trying to figure them out. *Someone walked weird on their feet, like on the sides,* he thought. *Who would be out in this with no shoes? Could this really be Mary?*

"Tracks look like they head south," Quint remarked.

"Let's go."

Renewed with a furious determination to be after Mary, Ross mounted quickly, startling his exhausted mare. Taking off south, he forced his horse to gallop. He wouldn't stop until he found her, even if it meant a full gallop to Pueblo, and had her in his arms for good.

His eyes strained, scanning up and down the riverbank for her. No blond woman was there to meet his gaze. Heart thundering in his chest, he moved the mare away from the river opting for the open road. Brush oak and dry grass quickly passing him by. The trail toward Pueblo fading in the waning sunlight.

If Mary was anywhere, it had to be Pueblo. His mare's sides heaved, foam frothing at her mouth. Ross urged the tired horse onward. He couldn't let Mary die, not when there was something to be done about it; not if there was still breath in his lungs, he would save her.

Glancing behind him, Quint rode hot on his tail, waving his hat. Ross leaned over the mare's neck; the horses' hooves pounding the sandy dirt.

"Ross!" Quint shouted.

Ross reined in slowly. The horse shuddering under him, relieved to stop. Quint's spirited mount tossed his head, ready to get running once more.

"There's horses and people back there," Quint stated pointing behind his shoulder. "Maybe they've seen Mary."

Ross spun his horse back to the river, trotting slowly. The terrible sky seemed to inch closer. Thunder crackled overhead.

A red headed woman perched on a black roan, adjusted her hair piece. She snapped her fan out, flicking the fan at herself with a hand on her hip. Three other horses tied to various trees surrounded her. Still a way back, Ross dismounted, tying his mare to a scrub oak. Quint dismounted, checking the pistol at his hip while pulling another out of his saddle bag.

"I know you don't want to," Quint began, rolling the barrel over and checking the bullets. Quint rolled the barrel back in place, "but just in case."

Ross took the pistol, taking the bullets out of the gun. Striding off toward the tethered horses, he shoved the bullets down into his pocket, while the gun went into the belt on his left.

*Somethin' doesn't feel right*, he thought. *The lady on the horse hasn't moved. Three other horses are rider-less.*

Peering over at Quint, his steady, even gaze focused on what was ahead. By the brief nod and terseness of his friend's face, Ross surmised Quint must feel the same. Something was wrong.

Quint jogged up beside him, pointing to the left. Ross nodded, crouching down low and creeping forward. Horses whickered softly at his approach. The lady on the black roan didn't glance in his direction, her gaze fixed on whatever was happening in the river.

Ross moved stealthily through the brush and pine trees, past a few new pines beginning to grow. The rush of water and a sharp inhale met his ears. Someone sputtered water. A tree branch creaked.

*What is going on here*, Ross wondered.

Moving in slowly, he pushed a bush out of his way. Leaning against a pine, he peered down the embankment. Three men were on the bank fifty feet away from him. Someone, shoeless in a green dress secured at her knees, swung on a tree. The rope swung the person around. Blond hair covered a face.

Ross's heart sunk to his feet. "Mary," he breathed.

Quint grabbed his shoulder, putting a finger to his lips. "There's only four," Quint whispered.

Ross nodded, moving along the river bank quietly. The water rushing by. Thunder cracked overhead, clouds darkening the area. The horses whinnied, moving closer to the tree line. Creeping forward, Ross closed in the distance, hiding under the tree Mary was strung up to. Quint moved beside him.

"Shit," he whispered. "That's Charlie Hilbert."

"Who?"

"The gang leader in St. Louis," Quint shook his head. "Back before you, Victor and Charlie were at war over territory. Charlie won, forcing Victor out," Quint shook his head. "This is bad."

Ross's stomach flipped. Out of all the things he imagined hearing, Mary being tied in with this man wasn't one of them. She told him before, however, he didn't think much of it, being engaged to someone himself. Never in a million years would he have guessed the Charlie that'd done her wrong was a rival gang leader, one powerful enough to beat Victor Del Avilasto.

*If she got tangled up with this man, what else has she done,* Ross pondered.

"Darling," the woman called from her horse, "can we be done promptly. I do not wish to be caught in this storm."

A man in a gray suit spun around to answer the woman. "Hold on, love." Turning back around the man pointed to one of the men holding the rope.

Mary swung on the tree, spinning in a slow circle. Ross peeked his head above the bushes, eyes locking on Mary. She'd her eyes closed, scrunched up. Her lips sucked in tight. Her long lashes held, what he was certain were tears on the edges.

"Honey Bee," the man purred, "my little... *Mary*," he crooned with a menacing tone. "Tell me where the money is and I will let you go. You will live."

Mary said nothing. Eyes open, she swung in a slow circle. The man sloshed through the water to her, moving her wet blond hair off to the side.

"Mary," he said softly. "This is your last chance. I will not pull you out of the water again."

She kept her mouth shut.

"I will give you a share of the one thousand dollars you stole."

Quint flopped back on his butt. The man's mouth hanging open. "She does have bison sized balls," he whispered.

Ross silenced him with a glare. Mary swung in a slow circle. He peeked over the edge, catching her doleful blue eyes. Ross's heart sank, the wind knocked clear out of his lungs.

*She's given up*, he thought.

"Do you wanna shoot them?" Quint asked.

Ross shook his head. "No killing. Best let them think Mary's dead."

"You're gonna let them drown her!" he seethed in shock.

"You hear that Barrie?" one man hollered.

Ross hunkered down low. Lightening splintered across the heavens, illuminating the sky and water with a creepy jagged hand. The woman on the horse called again, her voice lost in the din of thunder.

Quint pulled out his pistol. The hammer clicking back on the next round of raucous thunder.

"Drop her and let's go," Charlie said, heading up the bank.

The sky darkened further. Barrie lowered Mary into the water tying her off, her head just under the rushing water, and left, joining the rest of the posse up the mudbank. The red headed woman moved her horse, looking south. Removing the pistol from his belt, Ross handed it forcefully to Quint. Ross shrugged off his hat and vest, slipping through the brush and down into the water.

Charlie and his gang had yet to leave. Their horses whinnying behind Ross. The sharp coldness of the river stung him for a moment causing him to suck in his breath. Ross waded to her. Air bubbles floated up from Mary. Taking a deep breath, he submerged himself. Ross found her face, pressing his lips to hers, blowing in air.

Coming to the surface, his ears waited for the sound of

galloping horse hooves. He stole a quick glance in the direction he remembered Quint being in. The man wasn't there.

Diving back down to Mary, he put another puff of air into her lungs. Rising up, the area around him was dead of any noise aside from the river around him and the thunder above him. Ross, pushing himself up, sloshed to the rope where Mary was tied.

*I should have brought a knife*, Ross chided himself. His anxious fingers fumbled with the knot, finally breaking it loose. The rope slackened. Mary fully submerged in the water. Hand over fist, Ross pulled her to him, wading out into the depths to bring her back. Grabbing hold of her body, he swung her over his shoulder.

Ross's heart thundered wildly in his chest. His mind battling with thoughts he was too late to save her from a watery grave no one ever deserved. He forced his ears to strain harder, listening for any faint whisper of life.

*I'm too late.*

Ross gently set her down on the muddied river bank. Her blond hair, wet and clumping to the side of her face. Ross put a finger under her nose, begging to feel a warmth.

"Mary," he whispered, caressing her cheek. He pressed a kiss to her forehead. "Mary!" he called, his voice cracking under the din of thunder.

He pushed her onto her side, smacking her back. "Come on, Mary!" he urged. Striking her a few more times on the back, Mary didn't move. She rolled on her back, listless, lips turning blue. Ross rocked back on his heels, pressing the back of his hand to his mouth.

"Mary," he said softly. "Come on, Mary," he pleaded. Hand balled in a fist, he struck her on the chest. "Come on, Mary!"

She didn't stir.

Ross rolled her to her side, striking her two last times on the back. Her long blond hair sticking to the side of her face. Gently he swept it to the side, pressing a kiss to her cheek. Resting his forehead on the side of hers, tears snuck down his cheeks.

"Mary," he breathed. "Please."

Mary's body convulsed. Ross held her in his arms. Her mouth

sputtering water, she inhaled sharply, coughing. She breathed in deeply. Ross cradled her in his arms, resting his head against hers.

"Thank God," he said. "I thought I lost you."

Mary smiled, breathing out relieved; for a moment contented to breathing in Ross's arms. "Never thought I'd see you again."

Ross helped her to a sitting position, untying the knot binding her hands. Ross unfettered her arms, unwinding the tightly bound rope. When the rope fell off, Mary wrapped her arms around him. Not in his years of breathing, had he ever come to love such a meaningful embrace. Mary clung to him. Her deep inhales on his neck and long exhales while her hands dug into his body made him feel like the man he always wanted to be.

"I love you," she whispered.

He held her snugly in his arms. Her body fitting perfectly against his. Smiling, he relished the ardor of her embrace.

"How did you find me?" Mary pulled back asking.

"When you didn't come back from being let go by the sheriff, I felt something wasn't right, so I began looking for you. Heard you boarded a train to Kansas City only I knew you wouldn't head back there."

Mary grinned. "I jumped off the train."

Ross's eyes widened. "Jumped?"

Mary nodded. "Through the drop chute. I had to get back to you."

Ross held her close to his body, kissing the top of her head. "And I had to get to you," he said, moving around to unbind her feet.

He unwound the rope starting at her knees working to her ankles. Mary sighed, rubbing her wrists and wriggling her toes. He checked over her legs. Blood came off on his hands. Mary's eyes winced at his touch. Lifting her leg, a bullet wound grazed the right side of her calf. Ross exhaled the breath he didn't know he held.

*It's not in her leg*, he thought. *My poor Mary.*

Ross scowled at her bare feet. Muddy stockings covered her toes while blood stains littered across the rest of her feet. Gently,

Ross pulled the stockings off. Raw scabs peppered her feet, while a gaping wound on her left heel bled intermittently. He checked over her wrists, her skin chaffed and red from the rope. Moving her hair to the side, her beautiful tanned face was bruised by her eyes with splits in her lip, and scrapes on her cheeks.

Ross caressed her cheek, "You all right?" he whispered.

Mary leaned into his hand, nodding slightly. "Thank you," she breathed, closing her eyes.

Lifting her chin to meet his gaze, her weary blue eyes bore into his. Her poor face, puffy with scrapes and deep scratches from her ordeal, were slowly scabbing over.

"You sure you're all right?" he whispered softly, his thumb softly stroking her cheek.

Mary leaned into his embrace. "I am now," he breathed. "Here with you."

Scooping her up in his arms, he trudged up the slick mudbank. Horses whinnied, their hooves thundering across the landscape. Ross climbed up the bank, going to the right to take cover in the thick riverside brush. Mary's head rested in the crook of his left shoulder.

"Ross!" Quint yelled. "Time to go!"

Scowling, Ross looked to the south where moments before Charlie Hilbert and his gang left Mary to die. The wind picked up, rain falling from the heavens. Thunder cracked overhead. Mary put hands to her ears.

"It's all right," Ross crooned.

"We gotta go, pal," Quint urged.

Ross gently threw Mary on the mare. Quint came to the side, holding her up while he mounted. Ross adjusted her, putting her on his lap, and spurring his horse north.

# CHAPTER TWENTY-ONE

Mary's heartbeat had yet to slow. She thought for certain she was a goner. Seeing Ross through the bushes gave her hope breathing would be possible for a bit longer. She honestly thought she'd hallucinated, but it was enough for her, until she felt him in the water. Having him come into the rushing river, giving her air was not what she expected him to do. Her heart fluttered with relief and love she did not think possible for someone like her to experience.

She'd spent all her time, planning her next move to stay alive, she didn't give herself time to think on when she decided she loved Ross, only she did. And the relief Ross felt the same to come after her, turned her body to grits. She was more than certain Ross was meant for her, in some weird way.

In the twenty years she's been breathing, Mary only knew about being left. From her mother to her father, aunt, and siblings, everyone eventually went away from her. The only constant to her ill-begotten life was the sun always rose the next day. Now she had someone who proved she mattered.

*Thank you, God, for sendin' him.*

Closing her eyes, she relished in the warmth Ross brought.

Picturing his stormy gray eyes locked on hers, and smiled. Rain pelted her face as they galloped across the hill and brush filled landscape north toward Colorado Springs.

The other man with Ross was in the lead, pistol in his right hand with the hammer back. Glancing over Ross's left shoulder, no one happened to be there. Mary sighed, relieved Charlie and Opal believed her drowned.

"Why were they after you?" Ross's firm tone demanded.

"I caught Charlie with another woman, so I stole all his money and buried it in Omaha."

"One thousand dollars?"

Mary shrugged, "I don't know. I can't count."

The rushing surge of water made her skin prickle. Gazing out to the right, the water from the river rose steadily. Fear had her peeking over Ross's shoulder. Mary's eyes widened.

"Ross," she breathed.

Ross peeked behind him; horses hot on their tail. "It's all right."

The mare foundered over a bush, rearing and falling to the side. Mary shrieked falling off the horse, landing on her stomach away from Ross. The animal screeched in pain, trying to rise but couldn't. Mary crawled away from the horse.

Ross pulled the saddle and pad off the horse. The other man with Ross slowed, turning back but keeping his eyes to the south.

"You all right," the man hollered.

"Yeah, Quint," Ross affirmed. "Go on without us. See you in Colorado Springs."

Quint scowled, his horse eagerly prancing under him. "What about Mary?"

"She'll be fine," he yelled. "Take them away from us and right past the sheriff."

Spinning his mount around, Quint galloped north. Ross knelt beside the horse, keeping it still and quiet. The mare whickered. Mary crawled beside the animal laying on her stomach with her back to the horse, her legs toward its hindquarters.

If Charlie and the gang were after her, she wanted to appear small if not dead. Ross laid by the horse's head, stroking the mare.

His eagle like gaze, skimming north to south for the riders that followed. Whoever they happened to be, neither of them wanted to take any chances.

Rain coursing down her face, her body chilling with the liquid pelting her back. Mary shuddered. Her hands digging into the sandy dirt to keep herself from fidgeting. She willed herself to still, waiting with baited breath for the danger to pass. Mary felt her stomach roiling. Without warning, she turned around and retched, her body quaking on its own accord. The mare whickered softly, it's labored breathing quieting.

The horse's hooves moved in rhythm to the rain and thunder. Ross's stormy gray gaze followed the riders. He let out a breath. Mary closed her eyes, staying still as a tree. She dared not move. Fear of getting back into the clutches of Charlie scared her more than lightning storms or the dark.

"Mary," Ross whispered, "are you all right?"

"Yeah," she whispered back. "Are you?"

"Yeah," he said, eyes alert and watching the north.

"Ross?"

He turned toward her, giving a wan smile. His hand reached out for hers. Mary grabbed it, giving it a squeeze. The power she felt through the small embrace sent her heart fluttering.

"When we get back to Denver, I would like to get some learnin'."

Ross's face scrunched. "Learnin'?"

Mary nodded. "I don't want to be stupid. I don't want," she paused, scrunching her shoulders, "I don't want you to feel embarrassed to know me. I want to read and write."

"All right," Ross smiled. "If it's what you want," he said scooting closer. "Mary?"

She glanced up, peering into his stormy eyes her heart came to love. "Yeah?"

"I'm not embarrassed to know you. I'm grateful... blessed."

Mary shuddered from the rain. Watching the north, her eyes labored to see any people. Overhead the sky darkened. Thunder boomed while lightning crackled across the heavens like angry gnarled fingers.

"Mary?" Ross called.

Peeking up, she met his stoic gaze. His fingers softly caressing the side of her face, moving the hair away from her cheek. Mary closed her eyes at his touch. Their hot breath plumed in the cold rain. She moved, sitting up and resting her back against the horse. Ross did the same. Lacing her fingers in with his, her eyes looking north to south through the dense brush and rain.

"Mary," his deep voice murmured, "can I call on you?"

Grinning, Mary threw her arms around his neck, kissing him on the lips. "I'll do you one better."

"What's that?" he chuckled.

"I'll marry you."

# EPILOGUE

M ary jogged down the steps of the Whitman Hotel, a bundle of laundry cradled in her hands. This morning guests dared to brave the snow-covered ground to head south to Pueblo. Mary thought they were idiots, but kept quiet about their decision.

*Plum stupid*, she thought with a snort.

The hotel was booked full of people, giving her and the other women plenty to keep busy. All the grand rooms full of very respectable people while the others were full of miners and trappers, or other families coming to Colorado to try and find their fortune.

Going around the corner, she opened the back door to the laundry. Kelly stirred the hot vat of liquid. Eliza, bunched over, used a washboard to clean the linen Mary just brought down from the previous guest. Mary set the bundle of laundry beside the washing station.

Eliza glanced up, grinning ear to ear. "It's Christmas tomorrow," she announced.

Mary grinned back. Eliza announced every day how many more days it was until Christmas. To Mary, it was another day.

This year was different for her though with a roof over her head and a husband.

"Are you hopin' for something?" Mary asked.

Eliza shrugged. "It's my favorite holiday is all. I hope Claudia makes cinnamon rolls."

"With extra icing," Kelly added.

"Sounds good to me," Mary replied. "All the laundry's been brought down. I'm gonna head to the kitchens to do dishes."

"Thanks Mary."

Mary waved her hand, already to the door. The bustle of the hotel brought a smile to her face. Audrey flitted from place to place, adding decorations on top of all the decorations she already purchased. The ballroom was open with people scurrying in and out, readying the place for what Audrey called an employee party. Mary paid no heed to the room, not really knowing what the employee party was supposed to be only that it was tonight and she was to attend it. Audrey called it 'mandatory'.

Opening the door to the kitchens, the heat smacked her in the face, taking her breath away from the rest of the hotel. Mary propped open the door with a stool. Standing in the doorway for a moment, Mary took a deep breath of the mingling smells of Christmas fir tree in the foyer and Claudia's baking in the kitchen.

Coming into the kitchen, Claudia glanced up, giving her a terse smile. The cranky old bitty came around to her a little bit but not by much, constantly muttering on about what happened back in her day.

"Dishes need doin'," Claudia stated as always.

Mary rolled her eyes, pushing up the sleeves on her dark red dress. She stared down at her left hand where a gold band sat on her ring finger. Mary smiled, twisting it. A broad smile flourished on her face, remembering when Ross got her the band in Colorado Springs on their way back to Denver. Right in town, that day, they got married, bruised, battered body and all.

*Thank you, God,* Mary thought. *You gave me more than I deserved of ever getting. I appreciate it. Amen.*

Mary glanced over her shoulder, half expecting to see Ross

meandering inside from being out in the Whitman Stables behind the hotel. He wasn't there. With a shrug, she spun around, washing the soiled white plates and cups in the hot soapy liquid. The busyness of the diner could be heard through the swinging doors.

Audrey and Eugene came through the diner, walking briskly out the back of the kitchen.

Claudia whistled, "That woman doesn't ever stop."

"No, she doesn't," Eugene ducked back in the kitchen to add with a chuckle. "Since the dinner rush is finishing, there won't be a supper. You can close down the kitchen."

Mary paused, watching the surprised and curious lines cross Claudia's wrinkled face.

Eugene held up his hands. "Mandatory Employee Party."

Claudia threw a rag on the counter. Chuckling, Ada brought her the rest of the dishes. Mary scrubbed, growing more curious as to all the hype of this party. Her boss made a huge deal of it, reminding everyone a few times a day to be there.

Drying her hands, Mary put the dishes away. Grabbing a broom to sweep, she quickly made a pile and tossed it all in the can. Audrey's quick, clicking heels came tapping in the room.

The woman squealed like a pig being fed. "Come, come!" Audrey urged. "This all can wait. Time to get this soiree started."

"Soiree?" Mary replied.

"Party, event, celebration!" Audrey squealed again. "My dear, it's going to be wonderfully grand! A Christmas Employee Party! Don't you just love it?"

Mary's face scrunched. "Sounds... pleasing," she replied, using a new word from school she picked up.

"Oh, it is most pleasing, I do agree," Audrey said hurriedly. "Come, come! Claudia please put down the rolling pin. It doesn't need to be put away. Come! Let's go."

Mary leaned her broom against the hutch, following the impatient hotel boss out of the kitchen. Curiosity getting the better of her, she entered the ball room. Two trees were on opposite corners of the room, decorated with ribbons, popped corn, and candles. Gifts wrapped in boxes sat beautifully under the trees. Refreshments lined the two back tables with giant bowls full of spiced punch.

"Go get some refreshments," Audrey encouraged.

Mary stood to the side of the room, waiting for Ross. She hadn't seen much of him over the last few days. Mary understood there was lots to be done with the barn and the animals with feeding and breaking the ice in the water buckets. But she felt there was something else going on.

She fiddled with the hems of her dress sleeves, shuffling foot to foot. Mary eagerly watched the door for her husband, wondering where he happened to be and if he was all right.

"Hey, Mary," Lena greeted, bringing her a cup of punch. "Careful, it's strong."

"Did you make it?"

Lena rolled her eyes. "Quint." Taking a sip of her drink. Staring at the door, she asked, "Ross still working?"

"Must be. I haven't seen much of him in days."

Mary gulped her glass, setting it down on a doily covered demilune table. Looking both ways for Audrey, Mary snuck out of the party. Heading around the back to the employee door, she opened it up into the fading evening sunlight. Ross's snow crunching boot steps strode to her. With a peck on her cheek, he came inside.

"Grab your coat," he said, standing off to the side of the door.

Without question, Mary went to the room they shared, grabbing her coat off the inside peg. Ross took it from her, holding it open for her to slip her arms inside. Mary spun around, moving her hair out of the back of the coat. Ross's nimble fingers, buttoned it up for her.

Mary wrapped her arms around his neck, placing a chaste kiss on his cheek. "Where have you been?"

"Working. But now that I'm off, I've got something to show you."

Heading back outside into the cold, Ross took her hand, leading her down the pathway toward the Whitman Stables. Mary's mind wandered to what it might be. Being back in Denver since their ordeal, Ross rescued a plethora of animals he found, nursing them back to health. The animals were either used by the hotel or sold once they got better.

*Please don't be another cat,* Mary sighed, following her husband. She didn't care for cats. For some reason her husband found them the most. Mary kept hoping he would bring home something useful like a dog.

Ross led her past the barn and up the road. He paused at a home, two houses up from where the barn was. A lone light was on inside the house. The yipping of a dog inside. Ross strode up to the door, hand on the knob.

"What are you doin'?" Mary chided. "This isn't ours."

Ross grinned, jogging back to her and sweeping her off her feet. "Yes," he stated, kissing her lips, "it is. Welcome home, Mrs. Mary Montgomery."

Mary choked back tears. "A home."

Ross kissed her lips, pressing his head against hers. "Our home. Where we belong, together; now and forever."

# IV

## TO LIFT A DARKNESS

# CHAPTER ONE

The horse tore through the landscape, its hooves pounding the sandy dirt north to Colorado Springs. Glancing behind him, the riders pursuing him closed in the distance quicker than he anticipated.

A bullet zipped by his head, ricocheting off a boulder. Thunder cracked overhead unleashing a torrent of water and a gnarled hand of lightning snaked across the sky ahead of him.

"I don't wanna be sober for this," Quint groused under his breath.

Whipping out his pistol and leaning back careful not to lose his balance, he took a shot at the man to the left. The man crumpled off the back of his horse, lying flat on the ground while the horse reared in panicked confusion. The posse of riders huddled closer together, barreling for him.

Quint slowed his horse, turning to face the oncoming gang. His left hand reached around, grabbing his right shoulder. Bringing up his pistol, he rested it on the crooked elbow, aiming another shot at the man on the left.

His bullet fired as another gun cracked and, struck the man in the chest. The man on the horse didn't fall, lying flat back and dead in the saddle; the horse charging forward. Quint watched the man's body flop, a bullet caught him in the left thigh.

Quint winced, moving his horse to face the shooter, stopping to shout above the rain, wind and thunder. "I'd stop there, Charlie Hilbert."

Charlie reined in his mount, fifty yards from him. "Quint Morris, we meet again. Sadly, you always seem to choose the wrong side."

The other rider with Charlie reined in a few feet behind him. She leaned over, adjusting her skirting in the stirrups and pulled her hat lower on her face. Quint's horse shook under him. Rain cascaded over his face. Quint wiped the river of water out of his eyes and off his nose. Lightning's yellow tendrils reached out over the blackened sky to his right; the storm moving quickly west.

"Not this time," Quint shot back.

Charlie laughed. "The woman you're allowing to get away hid a great deal of money; money you could have a cut of."

Quint pulled the hammer back on his pistol hoping the storm would hide the click and let the loaded firearm rest on his good thigh. His anxious stallion pranced in the goopy soil. Quint pulled the reins, keeping his heels to the ground. The animal snorted, irritated.

"We don't have to end this way, Quint," Charlie called over the din of thunder. "We can work together."

"I've no intention," Quint replied.

"Too bad," Charlie said, firing his pistol.

The bullet whizzed by his ear. Bringing his pistol up, Quint fired blindly in reaction. The bullet caught Charlie's horse in the neck. The horse foundered, dumping Charlie sideways. The woman screamed, scrambling off her horse to check on Charlie. The sudden movements of the woman and Charlie's horse spooked the woman's horse. The beast side stepped, bolting a few yards.

Charlie wriggled out from under the dying animal, stumbling to his feet. The woman put a supportive hand endearingly on his shoulder. Charlie smacked her hand away, unknowingly shoving her to the side as he brought his gun up to shoot. Firing another round, Quint got Charlie in the head. The man rocked back on his heels, finally falling backwards.

The woman, unphased at her lost lover, grabbed the gun from Charlie's dead hands. The pistol shook, waggling at him.

"Ma'am," Quint hollered sternly, "I wouldn't."

The woman wiped wet hair off her face. "Or what?" she seethed, hellish eyes narrowing on him. "You'll shoot me dead?"

He nodded and shrugged. "Yes… I'm not above it."

The woman blanched at his comment, dropping the gun. Her pistol fired at her feet; the bullet pinging off the rocks. She screamed, bending down for cover, and crawling toward Charlie's body. Quint trotted his horse toward her, bullet fresh in the chamber. She rifled through Charlie's pockets quickly, taking what she could off the dead man.

Quint watched her emotionless figure crawl about her dead husband and his dead horse, taking what she could from them. Finally, hiking up her skirts, she sauntered to her horse, apparently lacking the good sense to run.

"Don't come back to Colorado," Quint shouted.

She spun on him, eyes dark as venom and glared at him. Mounting, she sped off south. Quint let out the breath he was holding, pushing the hat off his head.

"That woman has the devil in her," he commented to his horse.

The beast shuddered under him.

"I wasn't gonna shoot her… well," Quint scratched his head. "Nah, I wouldn't have."

He trotted over to the animal he shot on accident. He winced when he saw it still breathing, eyes wide and nostrils flaring, blood trickling from its lips. Quint dismounted, careful of his angry, bleeding leg. Bending down, he covered the horse's eyes with a bandana from his pocket.

"I'm sorry bud," he said to the horse, patting his neck. "I didn't mean to get ya."

Drawing his pistol, he let out a harsh breath, pulling the

hammer back. His mount whickered softly. He stroked the animals head, ruffling his fingers through its dirty mane.

"I'm sorry," he whispered again.

Pressing the barrel to the suffering horse's head, he closed his eyes and squeezed the trigger. Getting up with a pained groan, his eyes searched for the other rider-less horses. The horses stopped where their mounts fell, heads down with ears back, breathing heavily; the rain pelting their bodies.

"That saves time," he said, gathering his horse's reins.

Quint grabbed the body of the dead Charlie Hilbert, throwing him on behind his saddle. Taking out some rope, he tied Charlie on. Mounting, he trotted off toward the first horse. His mount whickered under him, ears back and agitated. The beast side stepped, tossing his head. Quint leaned over, patting the horse's neck.

"It's all right, Joey," Quint soothed. "We'll be back in Denver soon."

Joey snorted, bolting off to the rider-less horse. Joey slowed to a halt nearing the animal. Quint dismounted carefully, inhaling a hiss when his shot leg hit the ground. The exhausted, soaked horse didn't balk at his hurried appearance. Quint checked over the animal, unleashing the dead man from the saddle, letting him drop unceremoniously. On the horse's croup, two deep cuts oozed blood.

"Shit," Quint breathed. "Gonna need to get you some help."

The weary horse whickered, shuddering in the cold, bone-soaking rain. Quint unsaddled the horse, tossing all the gear on the ground by the dead man. Picking up the person he killed, Quint tossed him on the wounded horse.

Gently, he tied, the person on, careful not to see his face. Quint's heart clenched. In all his years of making poor decisions, he killed three people. Now, he'd ended three more. Sighing, Quint strode to the other person, face down in the muddied soil.

Thunder boomed overhead. Chills from the icy rain crawled up his soaked arms and permeated the rest of his body. Quint adjusted the hat on his head, pulling it low over his eyes. Unsaddling the last horse, he tossed the tack by the dead man. Picking up the fellow, Quint caught a glimpse of the man's face.

Quint sighed, closing his eyes. "Damn it, Danny," he breathed. "Stupid kid."

Quint flung Danny over the back of the horse, tying him down beside the other one on the uninjured horse. Running a hand over his face, he sucked in a breath. Gathering the reins to all three mounts, he led the horses across the plain to where he last remembered seeing Ross and Mary.

"Ross!" he hollered; his voice drowned out by the passing tempest.

Shuddering from the rain, he backtracked toward the river. "Mary!" he called, being met with no sign of his companions.

The surging river roared with the driving rain. Lightning crackled, spindling out like a spider's web across the sky to the east. A booming roll of thunder followed, making all three horses whinny shrilly. Quint frowned. *I can't wait to be back in Denver*, he thought.

"Ross!" Quint hollered again.

"Quint? That you?" Ross answered to Quint's left.

"Yeah. Charlie's dead," his voice faltered slightly. He hoped the storm covered it up.

Ross stood with a drawn and pale Mary in his arms. Quint changed direction, heading toward him. Approaching his friend, his eyes toward the ground at Ross's questioning gaze.

"What happened?"

Quint shuffled from foot to foot. "They were closing in and shot at me. I shot back. I killed them. Charlie, Little Danny and another."

"Danny Roister? And the woman?"

Quint met his gaze. "Yeah. That kid we saved from hanging when Del Avilasto was looking for a scapegoat a few years back," Quint shook his head. "I let the woman go. She headed south."

Ross nodded. "I owe you much."

Quint shook his head. "No... I got to right some wrongs. Call this straight."

Ross offered his hand. "Deal."

Shaking Ross's hand, Quint brought Joey around, offering up the saddle to Mary. Ross hoisted his woman on the horse's back, taking the reins from him. Quint let them drop, holding the horses with the dead people on their backs. Ross helped him switch out horses, alleviating the wounded horse of his horrible burden.

The rain abated, bringing instead a light drizzle with a stiff wind. Quint didn't mind. The stinging of his skin helped to remind him he was breathing. Walking, he headed to the open road. He let out a breath. In a few hours he would be in Colorado Springs, inside a saloon, drinking away the memory of what he'd done.

# CHAPTER TWO

Quint sat at the Whitman Diner, in the back corner, counting the money he got from the Colorado Springs sheriff for killing and bringing in the body of Charlie Hilbert and his gang. Quint shoved it all in his pant pocket. His heart swelled shut at the killing of three people. Even though in self-defense, the killing shamed him, just as the previous three killings he'd done.

Drinking the rest of his cup of coffee, he leaned back on his chair. Fork in hand, he played with his fried eggs and biscuits. Closing his eyes, his mind flashed the images of the boys he killed.

*Not even a moustache between them,* he shook his head. *And I killed them because I was so blinded by greed and what Del Avilasto promised to see straight. Running for a bit with Charlie Hilbert didn't better my odds either. Lord, I am unforgivable.*

Quint ran a hand over his face again, trying to swipe away the memories and the pain they brought forth. Six lives taken. Taking the life of the horrid Charlie Hilbert wouldn't ever correct the pain he'd inflicted but at least he was able to bring the man's reign of terror to an end.

"Where did it all start going wrong?" he questioned himself quietly.

Screeching of chairs echoed in the stillness of the diner as people paid their tab and left, leaving only him. Glancing over his shoulder Lena's beautiful hazel eyes caught his.

"You all right?" her melodic voice asked him.

Quint tilted his head to the left. Lena smiled at him, a coffee pot in one hand and a stack of dirty plates in the other.

"Fine," he responded with a smile and a shrug.

Lena leaned over, filling his mug to the brim with the black gold. "Mary says you saved her."

Quint snorted, shaking his head. "No... I surely didn't."

Lena smiled softly at him. "Still, mighty brave of you to go with Ross and face those men."

Quint took a sip of coffee. Lena walked away, going back to the kitchen, leaving him alone, the only patron in the entire dining room. He sighed, running a hand over his face and scratching the back of his neck.

*I am a damned man. Ain't no woman like her would want me*, he sighed. Getting off his rickety chair, he put his worn hat back on his head. Lena came out the kitchen with a magnificent smile on her honeyed face, holding something behind her back.

"Here," she said abruptly.

Quint took the offering of a molasses cookie, smiling at the morsel wrapped in a cloth napkin.

"Don't tell Claudia," Lena whisper-chuckled. "She counts them now with Eugene and Ross stealing them throughout the day. And if she notices and says anythin', tell her you saw Eugene sneak out with one." Lena winked and giggled.

"Thank you," he said quietly. "Lena," he began, choking on his words, "can I... if you want," Quint choked some more.

Lena stood patiently in front of him. Her hazel eyes frightened and shocked at his attempted proposal. Lena grabbed her right wrist with her left hand, biting her lower lip.

"I'm," she choked out.

Seeing her stricken face, Quint held up a hand, giving her a lopsided grin. "Have a good day, Lena. I'll see you at supper."

Lena cleared her throat. "Yes, see you then Quint."

Quint strode out of the Whitman Diner to his tethered stallion. The horse whickered gently at his approach. Quint patted Joey's back, gathering the reins in his calloused hands. Peering over his shoulder, Lena waved at him from the window. Quint raised a hand to her.

He tucked the cookie Lena gave him in his pocket. Mounting up, he spun his horse south toward the train station. Getting his horse into a smooth trot, he headed out of town to the Rocky Pine Ranch, silently berating himself for embarrassing Lena.

The train whistle blew loudly; the engine roared, coming alive to take people south on their travels. Quint crossed the tracks heading east, following the main road to Black Hawk.

Joey whinnied underneath him, ready to stretch his legs. Letting his horse have lead, Joey opened up, barreling down the road. Quint allowed himself to enjoy the freedom he felt on Joey's back. The wind whipping his body brought a smile to his face. Taking the second road to the left, Quint followed it down a small hill, curving down until it flattened out.

Down below, a small house plumed smoke from a chimney. A barn settled itself to the right of the house. Cattle lowed out behind the buildings, across a small creek in an open pasture.

"It's peaceful way out here," he said to Joey, pulling him to a walk.

The horse tossed his mane, irritated he didn't get to run more.

Quint reined in at the top of the last hill, gazing down at the beauty below. *I want something like this – a house, a wife, my own small slice of Colorado heaven.* Sighing, Quint rubbed the back of his neck. *It's not going to happen for me. Not when a woman learns of what I did, she'll leave me quicker than meat spoils.*

"Shall we?" he asked Joey.

Spurring his horse, the animal galloped the last half mile or so to the ranch house. Quint dismounted out front before his horse ever came to a stop. Taking the cash out of his front pocket, he shoved it all in his saddle bag. Looking down at his gun belt, he contemplated taking it off.

Spurred bootsteps and the slam of the door, caused him to peek over his shoulder. Quint smiled, at the older man coming out onto the porch.

"Quint Morris," his boss hollered. "Good to see you again and just in time."

Looking up, Quint smiled. "How goes, Mr. Kirby?"

"Frank," he said with a twinkle in his eye.

The ranch owner rocked back on his heels, leaning against a beam of the house. Taking off his hat, Frank ran his fingers through the salt and pepper hair covering his ears and flopping over his forehead. "Not too bad. Branding calves and making a larger holding pen for them."

"Where's the party?"

Frank chuckled. "Out in the east field, across the bridge. Albert quit this morning, hopped the train, and headed south to Kansas City. So, it's only you and Brandon from here on out. Or at least till I can find a replacement for him."

Quint nodded. "I'm certain we can handle it, Frank."

The older man scratched his beard. "Thank you. See you later then."

"Are you staying for supper?" Frank's wife asked, coming around the side of the house. A dead chicken, plucked clean, dangled in her left hand. The woman's bright eyes held warmth and kindness. Streaks of gray weaved through the braid holding her hair tight.

Quint shook his head. "No ma'am. Thanks though."

"Heidi," the woman corrected, coming up and lacing her right hand in with her husband's, holding the chicken away from their bodies.

"I'm going to dine at the Whitman Diner," he smiled, thinking of Lena.

"A woman," Heidi commented to Frank, winking at Quint before going inside the cozy home.

"Remember, the bunk's out back, the small building attached to the barn," Frank said in a teasing tone, hand on the door knob. "Heidi already put blankets out there for you."

"Much obliged."

"Pay is once a month. Twenty-five dollars. See you later, Quint."

Before Quint could respond, Frank turned and went inside his home. Taking off Joey's saddle and pad, he carried it and the saddle bags to the bunk house. Opening the door, Quint set his items just inside, heading back to Joey. Leading his horse around the back, and crossing the bridge, he let him loose with the cattle in the west field. Joey took off bolting out of sight.

Spinning on his heel, he went toward the east field where Brandon stoked a growing fire. Glancing at the sky. Not even noon. He pulled the molasses cookie from his pocket, stuffing it in his mouth. He moaned, smiling at the thought of Lena and the secrecy she held him to.

*I'll tell Lena,* he decided. *See where it goes… Tonight.*

# CHAPTER THREE

Lena watched Quint ride away from the diner, heading south toward the train station. Her heart tumbled in her chest. She didn't know whether or not to be fond of him or write him off. The man was illusive, harboring more than what he let on.

*Everyone has their secrets,* she thought. *I know I surely do.*

There was something about Quint which drew her to him. She thought him rugged and handsome with his deep brown eyes and coal black hair. His clean-shaven face with the upward quirk of his lip sent her heart fluttering. At the same time, her head cautioned her to remember her past and avoid the male gender all together.

Lena brought the soiled plates back into the kitchen, depositing them by the sink where Mary washed and dried. She offered a genuine smile to her friend thankful she was back and alive. Mary glanced up, her right eye swollen and discolored from the kidnappers who took her.

"You doin all right, Mary?" Lena asked.

Mary nodded. "Yeah. I'm not as sore today."

"Lena," Claudia called.

Lena spun on her heel facing the elderly and gossip-loving cook. She offered the woman a polite smile. "Yes, Claudia?"

"Could you run to the mercantile to see if they have any eggs, milk and flour in?" Claudia asked, strumming her fingers on the counter. "Leonard said more would be in today."

Lena nodded, heading toward the back door leading into the hotel. "Sure thing, Claudia. Anything else you, or Ada need?"

Ada poked her head above the oven, pulling out another sheet of cookies. "Molasses and sugar please."

Lena waved her hand behind her head. "I'm on it," she said, heading out of the stuffy kitchen.

Taking a deep breath, thankful to be out of the hot kitchen, she strode toward the manager's office. The cool air felt refreshing on her face. Lena breathed in deep, relishing the wafting scent of cookies mingling with the aroma that was all Colorado.

Her mind wandered back to Quint, wondering if someone like him would love her, if he truly knew her past. Lena shook her head; *I could never tell him. He wouldn't want me when he learned of what I had to do...* Lena shook off the uneasy nerves crawling on her skin, forcing the handsome cowboy from her mind. *No more,* she decided. *No man would want me and I don't want the rejection. I have friends here, food, a roof over my head, and it's good enough for me.*

Striding past Bartholomew at the front desk, she went to the door, leading to the back office.

Without glancing up at her Bartholomew called, "Jane left you money for the shopping in the envelope in front of me."

"Oh," Lena said. "Do you know where she went?"

Bart shrugged, reading the *Denver Times.* "Checking in on Ross and the new girl, Natali."

Lena nodded, grabbing the envelope. "Thank you, Bart."

Striding out of the Whitman Hotel, the autumn sun warmed her face. A cool, gentle breeze blew the wispy chocolate brown hairs off her face. With a smile on her lips she headed down the stairs of the Whitman Hotel. Pausing at the bottom, she looked both ways, waiting for the wagons and horses to pass. Men tipped their hats to her, smiling as they passed. Lena nodded, keeping her face pleasant but impersonal.

Her skin crawled. She didn't mind going to the mercantile. She minded the looks she got from men she passed along the way; they made her anxious. Taking a cleansing, calming breath, she jogged across the street, turning to pass a couple stores.

Seeing all the cowboys in town made her think of Quint Morris. She admired his easy laugh, how his brown eyes twinkled whenever she neared. He made a point to come see her almost every day since he and Ross had returned with Mary.

*Good Lord*, she thought. *What am I even thinking? I have to get him out of my head before he ever gets into my heart. He mustn't know. I could never tell him or anyone else. No one would like me then.* Lena sighed and shook her head as she stopped in front of Handover's Goods. *No more thoughts of Quint Morris. No, no Lena Jenkins.*

Opening the door to the mercantile, the bell tingled above her head.

"Good morning, Lena!" Leonard exclaimed. "Claudia send you for more eggs and milk?"

Lena grinned, at the old shop-keep. Leonard moved behind the counter slowly, bent at the knees and hand on his back. His snow-white hair combed over the bald patch on his head endeared her more to him. Small black spectacles sat on the tip of his nose.

"Yes. I also need molasses, sugar and flour."

Leonard shuffled behind the counter, going to a barrel. "How much flour?"

Lena opened the packet of money, pulling out coins. "I will take two bags each of flour and sugar."

Leonard nodded, taking a seat on the stool. "I'll let my help take over. It's why I hired the young kid," Leonard chuckled. "I'm thinking of retiring," he winked at Lena then raised his voice, yelling over his shoulder, "Clyde, I need you out front."

"Yes, Grandpap?" the blond-haired boy around thirteen said.

"Help, Ms. Jenkins. She needs two bags each of flour and sugar, eggs, milk and molasses. And help her carry it to the hotel."

Clyde nodded, getting busy. Approaching Leonard, Lena set the money on the counter. Leonard took it, counting it and put it in the cash register. The old shop-keep handed her back some change.

"How are you doing, Lena?" Leonard asked. "Any man around here catch your fancy yet?"

Lena blushed and shrugged. "One has, although I'm not sure."

Lena felt herself burn hotter than Claudia's oven. *No more, Quint. No more,* she chided herself. *I can't let myself get close. I can't let him know.*

Leonard smiled kindly; one of those smiles she figured a wise grandpa would show. "God sends people to us when we least expect it," he said, taking a seat on his stool once more. "God sent me my Ethel when I'd just gotten my advances rejected by Ethel's cousin," he chuckled, shaking his head and smiling fondly. Leonard glanced heavenward, his gaze seeming to pass through the beams in the mercantile shop. "God knows what you need and sends it exactly when you need it most."

"Amen," she said softly.

His comment made her skin crawl. She didn't want Quint; not right now anyways. She wasn't ready to confess to another man what she did back in New York or all the way here. It was sinful. It was against everything she knew and the bible.

"Shit," she cursed under her breath.

"You say somethin', Lena?" Leonard asked. "Or did you sneeze?"

Lena blanched, rubbing her nose. "I sneezed. Sorry, Leonard."

"Bless you. Clyde, after you help Ms. Jenkins, I want you to sweep the shop."

"Yes, Grandpap," the boy answered, putting all her items in a crate.

Lena got the door for Clyde, heading up the small incline of a hill back to the hotel. Clyde spoke a few sentences to her about helping his Grandpap at the store and how he liked it. Lena responded absentmindedly; her thoughts elsewhere. Lena bit her bottom lip, glancing to where she remembered Quint ride off to. If God sent Quint to her, how long could she keep from telling him about her past and if she did tell, would she be forced out of town like after the last man she told?

# CHAPTER FOUR

Hours after speaking with Leonard, her nerves remained rattled. If any of her friends could tell, they were polite enough not to say anything. To remain busy, she cleaned all the windows, inside and out, all the tables and chairs as well; swept the dining area until she was certain she could eat off the floor, and cleaned the kitchen from top to bottom. Even after all the labor, her nerves had yet to calm.

She swallowed, stepping into the dining room and glancing again toward the door. Any moment, Quint would walk through for supper, taking a seat in the very back, far right corner as per his usual; his back to the crowd of diners.

"Lena," Natali said, tucking blond hair behind her ear. "Anything I can help with?"

The soft-spoken new hire, more skittish than a fawn, poked her head out of the kitchen door to ask.

"I'm all right. Take a break and go relax. I will need your help during the supper rush," Lena replied.

Natali nodded, sticking her head back inside the safety of the kitchen. Lena let out a breath. She wanted to be alone for a bit more. Taking the broom inside the kitchen, putting it back against the right side of the wall by the hutch, she made her way outside.

Taking in a lungful of air, she moved to sit on the bench on the right side of the door. Closing her eyes, she ran her hands over her face and let them linger on her cheeks.

"There's no way," she said softly to no one, "no way, I could tell him."

Sighing, she leaned back against the bench and groaned. She was making a mountain out a prairie dog hill. But to her, this secret was everything. It was her reputation here in Colorado. It could ruin her if her past got out. Adding her fancy for Quint on top of it all, made it feel like her small, contained world was crumbling to bits.

*Oh Mama, how I need you now*, she thought through misting eyes. Mama wasn't coming back, dying the day after her fifteenth birthday from lumps all over her body. Lena still remembered hearing the doctors whisper about her mama being a "medical mystery" and "nothing to be done" for her. Those words still struck fear in her.

Lena swallowed hard, wiping a tear from the edges of her lashes. *Mama*, she thought, *I miss you so much. What would you tell me to do? You know I didn't want to do what I did. I had to eat though, and get away from the slums of New York if I ever wanted to be free of the position life had forced me into there.*

The door creaked open. Lena straightened herself. Closing her eyes, she feigned basking in the sunshine.

"Hey Lena," Natali said. "Mind if I join you out here?"

Lena shook her head. "Not at all."

Natali took a seat, blowing air through her lips. She put her head in her hands, leaning her elbows on her knees.

"What's the matter?" Lena asked, thankful to not be focusing on her own issues.

"I miss my mama. I'm worried about her," Natali confessed. "My step-dad is a mean bugger."

Lena put a hand on her back. "It will be all right. Sometimes you have to save yourself as horrible as it sounds. Then you can have hope to save others."

Natali shrugged. "You're right. Doesn't make it any easier," Natali sniffed.

Lena wrapped an arm around the young woman. Natali leaned against her, crying the tears she'd been trying to keep in. Lena held her, rubbing her arm while she cried, understanding all too well what Natali had to leave behind in the shack she called a home. Lena's own tears tracked down her cheeks.

With her mother's passing, she couldn't afford to have her buried and too weak from no food and age to dig a grave herself. She remembered kissing her mother's head in a final goodbye and covering her mother with a blanket then burning their shack. It was all she could do; disappearing deeper into New York before she could get arrested for arson or a murder that wasn't a murder.

With nothing to her name and not even grown into her body no one would hire her for respectable employment. She did the only thing she could think of at the time out of complete desperation – become a lady of the night to sailors docking in the harbor and cowboys coming into town for their liquor. After-having their way with her, then passing out drunk, she stole their money, hopping from train to train, escaping New York whoring her way here to Denver, hoping to leave those decisions and her painful past in the past.

Lena's gut churned at the recollection of what she'd done, of the pain and anger she caused the men she'd stolen from and the way she'd prostituted herself. *God, I am a despicable person*, she thought. *How could You ever forgive someone like me?*

"Thank you, Lena," Natali said, rising and wiping her eyes. "You're a good person."

Lena held back a snort, opting for a warm smile she didn't quite feel. "Thank you. Let's go see if the supper rush is here yet."

The door cracked open with Mary stepping outside. "Quint is inside. The only diner for now."

Lena replied. "Thank you, Mary."

"I got the left side for orders if you go for the right."

"Good plan, Mary."

Lena walked inside the hotel, past Mary, heading for the diner. Taking a deep breath, plastering a smile on her face, she put a hand on the door into the kitchen, pausing for one more moment.

"What do you want me to do?" Natali asked behind her.

Lena looked at her to reply. "Do the dishes." Leaning toward the girl she added in a whisper, "and stay out of Claudia's way. The woman is a bear during a rush. If it sounds like she's asking you to do something, don't do it. She already has it but is thinking out loud."

Pushing the door open, she glanced to her left. Claudia was already red faced and flustered, ordering Ada about the kitchen, and there was only one diner so far, and he hadn't ordered yet. The other cook paid no heed to the grumping Claudia, pulling roasted vegetables out of the oven and humming to herself.

Lena pointed Natali toward the sink. "Stay perfectly still and Claudia won't see you," she giggled softly.

Natali smiled, a slight twinkle returning to her emerald eyes. *Poor girl*, she thought. Heading out into the dining room, she looked around; Quint remained the only guest for the time being.

Smiling broadly, she approached the seated cowboy. Realizing her face held a widened smile, and the man who caused it, she corrected herself quickly.

"Lena," Quint greeted warmly, a big grin splitting his face. "How was your day?"

"Fine, thank you."

"The diner looks great. Did you tidy it all up yourself?"

Lena nodded. "Yes, I did," she swallowed. "How was your day?"

"Good. Took on a job at the Rocky Pine Ranch out toward Black Hawk."

"Are you liking it?"

Quint shrugged. "It's a job and one that keeps me close to Denver, so I can't complain overmuch."

Lena smiled tersely. Her feelings for Quint rising since being in his presence. Earlier this morning, she was sure as the sun rose, she wouldn't fancy him. She even made sure that giving him a molasses cookie was simply friendly, like she'd do with Eugene, Ross, even Bartholomew. Now, standing in front of him, she wasn't sure the cookie this morning was simply friendly and she could keep her feelings passive.

His handsome brown eyes bore brightly into hers. The scar on his forehead, poorly hidden by the dirt he'd attempted to wipe off. His coal black hair, flecked with brown dust, brought a smile to her face. Quint, a cowboy, was about to ride away with her heart.

*I need to be careful*, she cautioned herself.

"I hope the new job is treating you well," she offered after a moment of silence.

Quint nodded. "Sure is. I just had to come back to town for a bit, get myself a meal."

Lena blushed, clearing her throat. "What can I get started for you?"

"Tea and the special," he replied, strumming his fingers on the table.

Lena bobbed her head. "Coming right up."

Letting out the breath she was holding, Lena strode into the kitchen. Mary smirked, raising her brow at Lena's entrance, peeking above the small container of powder Audrey bought her to conceal the bruising on her face. Ignoring the look, Lena poured Quint his iced tea.

The door from the diner swung open. "Lena," Quint said, standing in the entrance.

Shocked, Lena took a step back. "Yes?"

"Can I ask you to supper?" he wrung his hat in his hands, shuffling on his feet, as he met her alert gaze. "I mean, obviously not tonight... Like tomorrow... or whenever you have a day off and want to have supper with me," he held up a hand, mouth hanging open a moment. "You don't have to, I..."

"Sunday," Lena blurted, wondering why she'd say it.

Quint nodded. "Sunday," a smile twitched at the corner of his lips. "Sunday... I'll pick you up then."

Hastily, he backed out of the kitchen. Lena let out another long breath, putting a hand to her head. *Oh biscuits,* she thought although she couldn't quite wipe the smile from her lips.

# CHAPTER FIVE

Quint spun on his heel, but not walking away still blocking the doorway to the kitchen and let out a long, harsh breath. He ran a hand over his face, wiping the sweat away, relieved it was over. Asking Lena to supper was harder than confronting Charlie Hilbert or Del Avilasto. In fact, he thought he might prefer speaking to them over talking to a stunning woman who took his breath away each moment he was in her presence.

*Good Lord*, he thought. *I gotta get myself together.*

Behind the door, Lena cleared her throat. "Someone there?"

"Sorry," he choked out, stepping to the side.

Her head and hand poked out of the door, handing him his tea, a grin on her face.

"Thank you," he said, taking the drink.

"Be right out."

*Because of me, I ruined her evening, and now she has to gather herself for work... I shouldn't have asked her right then*, he thought, wiping the last of the sweat off his brow.

He took a seat back at his spot. The door to the diner jingled, announcing more people coming in to eat. Lena came out with a heaping plate of food and a small plate of rolls. Setting it down in front of him, she flitted off to get to the other diners.

Mary came out of the back, her face covered with a powder making creases on her skin and dusted the top of her dress. Quint waved her over.

Brows furrowed; she came over. "Not likin' the meal?"

Quint shook his head. "Not that."

Her mouth twitched, hands on her hips. "Lena?"

Again, Quint shook his head. "Lean down. You got powder all over you."

Mary shot back up, heat creeping to her cheeks. "Where?"

"Go to the wash room real quick."

Hearing his voice, Lena glanced in his direction, a soft brown eyebrow perked. Quint made the motions of dabbing feminine powder of his face, lips pursed and brows raised, eyelashes fluttering. Lena pressed the back of her hand to her mouth, apologizing to the guests for the distraction.

Quint grinned, turning back around to his meal. Chicken, roasted potatoes covered in a thick brown gravy, carrots and corn, greeted his hungry eyes. A side dish of peach cobbler and two biscuits added to the deliciousness of the meal.

More people meandered in, taking a seat in the empty spaces. Mary came out from the kitchen, face and powder set, taking over the left side of the dining room. He tucked into his meal promptly, leaving nothing to the hogs.

Setting money and a fair tip down on the table, he left without saying good-bye. The fear of Lena changing her mind about their date made his gut twist.

*True,* he thought, *no female has ever turned me down. But Lena's not like all the other women. And she means more to me.*

Lena made him forget where his mind was supposed to be. Her beautiful, round, tanned face, and cute dimples made his heart beat fast and skip.

Lena was an enigma to him. Her laugh and brightness outshone the sun and the brightest of stars, and instead of counting his day in hours until his next drink, he'd begun counting hours until he got to see Lena again. With him, she checked herself, hiding behind a demure and passively polite nature, but he'd seen glimpses of the lively, kind woman and couldn't wait to break her out of her shell.

Remembering his hat he'd left on the chair, he spun on his heel to go back inside. Lena met him at the door.

"Here," she said, thrusting out his hat.

Gently, he took it from her. "Thank you," he replied quietly.

"Six o'clock, please. If that's all right."

Quint tilted his head to the side. "What?"

Lena squirmed, wringing her hands. "For supper... Sunday."

Quint grinned broader than the Rio Grande. "It's perfect," he leaned down, giving her a peck on the cheek.

Stunned, and red, Lena backed herself inside the diner. "See you," she choked out.

Quint cursed himself for being so forward and open with his affections, but couldn't really bring himself to regret the peck either. Sighing, he jogged down the steps to his horse. Taking the reins, he led Joey across the street to the saloon.

*I need a drink*, he thought. *I am plum losing my mind.*

Tethering Joey outside the saloon, Quint ambled inside. Lena's reaction to his peck on the cheek brought his demons out in full swing. The mocking torment inside his head made visions of people appear, pointing fingers at him and yelling. Squeezing his eyes, he blocked it out, only it didn't make the people go away.

Quint strode inside, up to the bar. "Bottle," he ordered.

The barkeep nodded at Quint and grabbed a fresh bottle of whiskey from the mirrored shelf behind him, setting it gently on the counter. "Your usual, Quint. Two dollars."

Laying his money on the table, Quint popped the bottle open, guzzling a third of it in one go.

"You all right?" the barkeep asked, taking a step back.

"Never better," Quint bit out, going to sit by the window.

Leaning back in his chair, he watched all the people pass by on the other side of the street. Women hanging on the arms of their men, smiling and laughing; something he was certain now would never happen for him. Lena was much too kind a woman, sincere and gentle for a ruined man like him. His memories and flashbacks brought out the angst and regret, swallowing him whole until he eventually cried and passed out from drink.

Running a hand over his face, he leaned back, taking another long draught of the fiery liquid. *I gotta tell her,* he decided. *She has to know what I've done. I don't want her to regret being with me. I'll tell her tonight after she's off work.*

Quint hung his head, right hand on the bottle, spinning it on the tabletop. *I can't,* he decided. *I'll tell her Sunday. When I'm sober.* Quint nodded to himself. *Sunday, after supper, Lena will know. And if she rejects me, as I'm sure she will, I'll head somewhere else... Probably Oregon or something far away. 'Sides, that'll give me time to finish up this job.* Quint sighed, laying his head on the table.

"I won't be able to stay away from her if I stay," he said to himself.

The barkeep grunted from the next table where he was wiping the table and gathering empty glasses. "It's always a woman, isn't it?"

Rising from his chair, Quint guzzled the last of the whiskey, the burn barely bothering his alcohol desensitized throat. Leaving the empty brown bottle on the table, he strode outside to his horse. Joey tossed his head at Quint's approach. Quint ignored the agitated stallion, mounting in a single leap.

"Quint," Ross's gravelly booming voice called from across the street at the Whitman Hotel. "Come here a sec."

Quint turned slow, feeling his vision blur and refocus. Ross stood in front of him, much closer than Quint had expected with eyes narrowed and lips set firm. Quint scowled, tilting his head to the side to get a better look.

"Hey bud," Quint greeted a bit growly, his voice matching his mood.

"Come with me. I need your help in the barn," he said too loudly for Quint, taking the reins to his horse.

Joey tossed his head. Quint leaned over, snagging the reins out of Ross's hand. "I can follow," Quint bit out.

Ross looked around cautiously. Quint followed his gaze, eyes narrowed trying to spy what Ross happened to see. A fist connected with the side of his face, turning his world dark.

# CHAPTER SIX

Lena's face burned from the peck Quint gave her on her cheek. The diner was practically full of folks, some who saw and thankfully those who didn't. Not too friendly, Lena shut the door on him, breathing out harshly with her back to the door.

Slapping a smile on her face, she went back to doing what she did best. Mary bustled around her, sweat glistening on her forehead as the heat from the diner and the kitchen rose.

Claudia and Ada could be heard through the door, hollering out complete orders ready to be delivered to the tables. Lena waited for the bell to ding just outside the kitchen door, knowing if she came in a moment quicker, Claudia would jump down her throat for being pushy.

The bell to the kitchen dinged rapidly. Lena strode inside. The hard, rosy face of Claudia narrowed in on her.

"Where's Mary?" the cook boomed.

"Taking orders, why?"

"She needs to write it down. She shouts the order and leaves."

Lena sucked in her lip, turning to Natali. "Can you write?"

Natali nodded. "Yes, I can."

"Go get Mary, please."

Claudia huffed. "Breakfast is one thing. Men are typically too drunk and hungry to care if we get something mixed up. Dinner and supper though they've not hit the bottle yet."

Mary came inside, her smiling face instantly drawn. "Somethin' wrong?"

Claudia went to speak but Lena shot her down with a hard glare. Lena wasn't going to let the ornery cook ruin Mary's newfound confidence or use the fact Mary was learning to read and write as an adult be used against her.

"Mary," Lena began, "for supper service, we like to write down the orders when the diner gets packed as it is, since there are many plates going out at once. Natali is goin' to take over for a bit. You'll still get your tips and some of mine."

Mary's face fell. Her eyes bright blue and shining with unshed tears. The woman nodded. Lena wrapped her arms around her.

"I didn't think it would get this busy. I am so sorry Mary," Lena whispered.

Mary pulled back. "Not your fault," she said with a drawn smile. "You're always helpin' me and I... appreciate it kindly," she finished, grabbing an apron off the hook.

Lena smiled. "Thank you, Mary. And don't let it get you down. You're doing so much better. It won't be long before you'll be writing down orders."

Standing by the wash sink, Mary gave her the orders she took and where the people were sitting. Luckily for Lena, the orders were mostly the specials. Grabbing the four plates of waiting food, she strode out, handing out Mary's orders and her own and giving Natali all the new guests who walked in.

Lena let out a breath when she saw Natali taking care of her tables quickly and efficiently. The new hire was a natural in the environment; she flittered swiftly with a smile on her face, serving people and taking extra care to the elderly and those with children.

Letting out a breath, she went back into the kitchen. Grabbing a mug off the shelf, she poured herself some cold coffee, guzzling it in one go.

"Busy out there?" Ada asked.

Lena shook her head. "Dying down."

Claudia scowled. "How?"

"Everyone is eating, but there will be another rush. I give it fifteen minutes or so. Train just came in."

"Another one?"

Lena nodded, pouring herself another mug full. "Didn't you hear the whistle?"

Claudia spun around, muttering under her breath. Ada rolled her eyes, grabbing vegetables out of a basket to cut. Leaving the kitchen, Lena went back out into the dining room, clearing plates from empty tables. Money was left on the table. Lena swept it all into her pocket, heading back into the kitchen.

Dropping off the plates with Mary, she put the cost of the meals into a tray by Claudia, and made change for herself out of the extra. The old cook's eyes narrowed, watching her count the money like a hawk. Lena forced a smile to her face. *She is extra ornery today,* she thought. *The woman needs to retire.*

"Lena," Mary called from the sink.

Striding the short distance over, Lena leaned in close. Mary shuffled from foot to foot, eyes darting from her to the sink. Mary washed a dish, putting it up to dry on the wooden rack.

"I have to tell ya somethin'."

Lena got closer, leaning in.

"Quint is at the saloon, makin' a mess and drunk talkin' about ya. He's really gone to the wind. Ross went down to make it straight. Just thought you should know."

Lena felt herself turn crimson.

Mary set a hand on her bare arm, smiling sympathetically. "I saw him put a peck on your cheek. The man be right smitten."

"Thank you, Mary," Lena choked out, turning abruptly on her heel.

Going out into the dining area, Lena plastered a smile to her face, keeping the looming tears at bay. She greeted the remaining customers, and some of the new with a kind smile, exchanging small talk, swallowing down all that she wanted to release making sure her usual happy, and chipper self was on display.

She cleared tables while humming a tune to mask the slight falter of her voice when she spoke. Going back and forth from the kitchen to the diner, wiping down tables and chairs, and resetting them all with fresh silverware and cloth napkins in the vacant spots.

People came in and left, going around the side of the diner to the hotel to book a room. The supper service was steady for a while, keeping her occupied but not overly busy. Peering out the window, the sun set in perfect Colorado fashion with a burst of vibrant colors over the mountains, leaving the new arrivals and old citizens in splendid awe.

Glancing over to Natali, the woman had two tables left close to the front. Lena walked over, flipping the 'open' sign over. The last inside two families would be it for the night.

Lena grinned at Natali; thankful and happy the young lady did exceptional despite being thrown in under the pressure of a full diner. Luckily the menu had five options, including the special at Claudia's insistence. Audrey had tried to change the menu offering a wider range of meals. The old cook wouldn't have it though so Audrey did what she could without ruffling too many feathers.

*Thank goodness for that. Especially having to throw Natali in last minute. Less confusion to deal with,* Lena thought, taking the last of the dishes to the back.

Lena exchanged the meal money, making change for herself with the leftovers. Tipping out the cooks, and Mary, Lena hastily went outside to sit on the bench. Keeping it all together for so long was beginning to wear down her defenses and make her smile crumble.

In the privacy of outside, she allowed tears to slither down her cheeks. Sighing, she leaned her head against the back rail of the bench. In the almost eight years of being here, she never experienced something quite unfathomable as this – having someone interested in her. It made her heart cry out joyously yet caution her.

Her feelings for Quint were quite strong despite her trying to harness them. The peck he set on her cheek made her skin itch with fire and ice at the same time. However, him going off to the saloon, dug in her heart with a pitchfork. She didn't care he'd went there but the drinking brought back awful memories of what she allowed to be done to her. And Quint talking about her at the saloon, made her cheeks flame. She knew most everyone in town and now their tongues would be wagging.

*I don't want the whole town believing I'm easy, because I'm not. Even with my less than savory past, it doesn't make me an easy person,* she thought, wiping away the tears. Her body shook, *I am a better person now. I am a good person and I did what I had to do – it was never something I wanted to do,* she wiped away streaming tears. *Lord, what do I do?*

Closing her eyes, she willed herself to calm. The anger inside of her waning like the moon morphing into a numbed hurt. *I'm going to talk to him after everything is cleaned and shut down for the night,* she decided.

With a tired groan, she rose; shuffling the several steps to the back door of the hotel. Lena strode down the small hallway, past her bedroom, to the kitchen. Claudia and Ada cleared their pots and pans, setting them beside the sink for Mary to wash. Natali took a large gulp of tea, her white face rosy with a sheen of sweat.

Natali met her with a smile, fanning her face. "Last diner left," she breathed, relieved. "Tables are cleared and set."

Lena nodded, walking up to grab the broom. Claudia moved, staying her hand.

"Have a good night. We're done. Mary let those pans alone for the night."

The clink of a plate clattering on another boomed in the small kitchen area, Lena and Mary exchanging incredulous looks, hoping Claudia didn't catch their surprise.

"All right," Mary replied.

"Night," Lena called, exiting the kitchen.

*Off to find Quint and tell him the date is off,* she thought, her stomach sinking.

Lena meandered down the pathway to the Whitman stables. If Ross got involved like Mary said, then Ross would have taken the drunk man to the barn to sleep it off, saving him dignity with the town and his boss.

A lone lamp hung outside the sleepy building. Opening the side door, Lena walked inside through the low-lit area. A single lantern hung in the middle of the barn. Horses whickered at her approach. Quint's gray dappled horse poked its head above the stall door, thrusting its head out to her.

"Hi Joey," she greeted, petting his nose.

Lena moved toward the stall, peering inside for Quint. Scowling when he wasn't there. Joey nuzzled her, grabbing the ends of her hair with his floppy lips. Laughing, Lena pulled her hair free of the horse, giving him loving pats on his neck.

A snore erupted from the end of the barn. Joey blew his lips, ears back clearly unimpressed.

"Mad at him too?" she asked the horse with a smile, walking to the back of the barn.

Quint lay in a pile of hay, a dark mark forming on his jaw line. Lena frowned, kicking his boot with her shoe. He snorted, stirring a moment but didn't wake. His hat lay on the top of his thigh.

"Quint," she said, kicking his boot again.

His eyes squinted open. "Angel Jesus!" he exclaimed, his face white and stricken. Sitting up, he hung his head, swishing it back and forth. "I'm sorry for all I've done in my life. I repent my sins. I didn't want to kill the first three..."

Lena scowled. "Quint, it's me, Lena," she interrupted, bending down to his level. "It's Lena."

Quint leaned forward, wrapping his arms around her. "Lena!" he said, breathing in sharply. "I thought Jesus came for me."

Lena pulled away, standing back from him. "I came to cancel our date."

Quint's face fell. He stood, brushing off the hay and putting his hat back on his head. "Why?"

"You're a mess, talking about me at the saloon."

Quint hung his head. "I'm sorry," he mumbled. "You're so beautiful... Can I make it up to you?"

"Stop drinking."

Quint nodded rapidly. "No more."

Lena strode out of the barn, leaving Quint inside. She heard him flop back in the pile of hay, breathing out harshly. Feeling slightly better yet shaken, she made her way back to the hotel. She let out the breath she was holding, nearing the back door. *I can't. I can't deal with that. I don't want to be a part of the horrible gossip and everybody knows a saloon is an easy place to start it up. I don't want any part of it, yet I like him. Lord help me and my foolishness.*

# CHAPTER SEVEN

Quint rose when the sky was lit with a light gray; the dawn barely crackling awake. He rode back to the Rocky Pine Ranch before anyone stirred. Running a hand over his face, he allowed Joey to trot down the slight slope to the ranch house. Smoke plumed from the chimney.

He groaned, *I hope no one is up yet.* Trotting toward the house, he crept around to the back of the barn, dismounting swiftly and undoing Joey's tack. He left it all by the bunkhouse door, not wanting to go in and disturb Brandon. Leading his horse out to the west pasture, he let him loose. He was relieved no one came out as he took care of Joey.

Letting out he breath he held, Quint went around the side of the barn and bunkhouse to the back by the chicken coop. Seeing a basket hanging off a peg, he went inside the sleeping hen house to collect the eggs for Heidi.

*I feel like shit,* he thought. *Not only from drink but for hurting Lena. I have to make this right. A perfect woman like her doesn't want a drunk, on top of a killer such as myself.*

Quint put the last egg in the basket, carrying it out of the coop. Setting the delicate parcel down on top of a small outdoor table, he grabbed a cup of feed, tossing it in to the brooding hens.

"Morning," Frank said, coming around the side. "Wife will be mighty happy you collected the eggs. She hates the dang birds," he chuckled.

Quint grinned. "They can be ornery."

Frank took a step closer, lifting his head and inhaling. Immediately his eyes narrowed on him, his chipper face turning sour. "How you squander your money is none of my business but don't show up on my ranch again reeking of it."

Quint hung his head. "Yes, sir."

Frank clapped him on the shoulder. "Every man has his demons. I get that. Whatever your reasons are your own. Go wash in the crick. I'll bring you one of my shirts."

"I got one," Quint replied. "I'm sorry."

Frank held up his hand. "No harm done, boy."

Quint strode to his saddle bag outside of the bunkhouse, grabbing his soap from one of the pockets. Taking out his only clean shirt, he scowled at it. He would have to purchase another, nicer shirt. He wanted to take Lena out for a nice supper, somewhere proper and candle lit.

Shaking his head, he strode down to the water. Shucking off his boots, socks and gun belt at the water's edge, without care, Quint leapt in. The water surprised him. For being close to winter time, it was surprisingly tepid.

Peeking up at the sky, smiling at the Colorado sunrise he'd come to love. It was part of what drew him to Colorado to begin with. On the crowded streets of St Louis, he never once looked at the sky. He was too busy watching his back from folks he got mixed in with.

Quint bent over, sticking his entire head in the water. He wanted the memories behind his eyes to quit haunting him with every mistake he made, every accident he'd been involved in, whether his fault or not.

His mind went back to his youth. Being a stupid teen, who wanted riches and adventure, he got mixed in with Del Avilasto and believed what the crook promised. Little did he realize it was a dark path. By the time he figured it out, he was in too deep. He got the money he thought he wanted, but it lacked meaning, so he sent it back to his grandpa and lied about where he got it from.

Quint shook his head underneath the water, scrunching his eyes. He could never tell the old man how he'd gained the money – especially when pick pocket and sleight of hand turned into something much more. *And then I killed people*, he thought, bringing his head above water. Birds chirped, the world coming alive with the breaking of the dawn. He shook his head like a dog, then ran his hand through his hair. Quickly washing his hair, upper body, and shirt, he hurried out.

*Lena is up by now, serving breakfast*, he thought. *I am going to head over there later, and apologize, proper.*

"Quint," Frank hollered.

"Yeah!"

"A woman is here to see you."

Quint scowled. Throwing on his shirt and gun belt, he made his way toward the house. His mind reeled with who it could be. He didn't have any other women in his life. His ma and pa both passing on to the good Lord when he was about twelve. His grandpa the only remaining relative he had lived in St Louis.

A roan mare, tethered to the front of the house, whickered, shaking its head. Coming toward the house, a woman in a dark green dress with chocolate hair stood with her back to him, holding a basket on her left side.

"Lena?" Quint asked, approaching from the side.

Lena blinked rapidly, holding out the basket to Quint. Taking the offered basket from her, Quint held in in his left hand. Lena went to the horse without saying a word.

"What's the matter?" Quint asked, setting the basket down on the porch.

Frank back peddled, heading inside with a knowing quirk on his lips. The door to the ranch home opened and slammed shut quickly.

"Lena?"

She paused, foot in the stirrup. "My feelings are hurt. I don't like being talked about."

Quint hung his head. "I'm sorry. Please... let me make it right."

Lena nodded. "All right. I know you didn't mean anything by it," Lena sighed, moving a dirt pebble with her boot. She stopped, gazing back at him with rich hazel eyes. "Supper, this Sunday, six o'clock."

He couldn't have grinned wider if his face allowed. "Thank you."

"I've got to get back. Friday breakfasts can be a touch crazy. In the basket is a sandwich and some cookies. Don't tell Claudia...again," she said smiling.

Quint grabbed her waist, hoisting her up on her mare. Lena's cheeks burned; she brushed her braid over her right shoulder. Quint couldn't help but grin, guiding her foot into the stirrup.

"Thanks. See you Sunday," she reminded quietly.

Quint untethered her mare, handing her the reins. "See you Sunday."

Turning her horse, she galloped up the road leading back to town. Quint watched her until she completely faded from view. He ran a hand through his hair, sighing with a smile twitching on the corner of his lips. Picking up the basket, he strode out to the barn, opening the doors wide.

*Two more days*, he thought. *Then, I'm gonna call on her.*

---

Lena felt her cheeks flame when he put his hands on her waist. She could feel the heat of his skin through her dress. Desiring to close her eyes, she forced herself to keep them open as he hoisted her up on the mare. Reaching to hide her crimson cheeks with her hair, she forgot she braided her long dark tresses.

*Oh biscuits*, she thought.

The pain and regret in Quint's voice startled her, making her reconsider rejecting his date proposal. He was genuine in his apology. Seeing how much it meant to him, she accepted his apology.

She not only came to give him some food to sop up the liquor from last night but also so he wouldn't come see her today. He distracted her while she worked. Handsome to look at, charming to speak with, she couldn't keep her eyes off of him. He made her feel like the only woman in the entire world and that every word she had to say was important.

Also, Mary insisted she come to see him, to talk things out and make it right. Her friend wasn't wrong. Only, she couldn't find the words she wanted to say. Maybe during their supper, she would be able to find the words. She hoped so. Quint deserved to know he was getting a broken and flawed woman – a former harlot, lady of the night.

She shoved the thought aside and thought back to the promised date. She smiled bashfully, feeling her insides crumble like an overly done cake. "See you Sunday," she whispered.

Quint handed her the reins, whispering also, "See you Sunday."

His fingers gently and briefly touched hers, sending a wave of chills down her spine despite the warmth of the sun of her back. *Good Lord, I am like a schoolgirl,* she thought. *Get a hold of yourself, Lena Jenkins.* Without saying another word, she spun her horse and took off up the road.

*I have to tell him after supper. He deserves to know. He is much too fine a man to be with me,* she thought. Her horse whinnied shrilly, making it to the top of the hill in moments.

With the road flattening out, she rode back the way she came to Denver.

# CHAPTER EIGHT

Nervously, Quint combed his hair. He went to town twice already, buying three of the same shirts in the same color, a pair of pants, men's cologne, and a bouquet of flowers for his date. Already, he changed a shirt, sweating through the first one.

Pulling at the collar, he swallowed. He hadn't been this anxious since Del Avilasto told him to rob a stagecoach three years ago. Quint cleared his throat, looking at himself through the shoddy mirror in the bunkhouse. He dabbed more cologne on his neck, running the rest through his coal black hair.

"You look fine," Brandon encouraged. "And you smell... strong. I think you are sufficiently purty."

Quint's lips pressed in a thin line and gave him the stink eye.

Brandon chortled at him and winked, "Go pick her up early."

"Do you think she would mind?"

Brandon sighed, leaning forward on the bed. His sandy brown hair long over his eyes. "I reckon not. She likes you. Take her for a stroll or show her your favorite place."

Quint nodded. "I best get going then."

"See you later, Romeo. Except court her, don't kill her with your cologne," he chuckled.

Flowers in hand, Quint strode out into the late afternoon light, Joey stood tethered and saddled to the hitching post out front. He gently tucked the flowers into his saddle bag, hoping the flowers stayed beautiful.

Frank and Heidi sat under the shaded porch in rocking chairs, peeling peas and plunking them into a bowl. Heidi glanced up at him, her smile stretching from ear to ear. Her long-braided hair made a crown on her head. Speckles of white and silver glowed like a halo, framing her face.

"You look pretty, Mrs. Kirby."

"Thank you, Quint. Off to get your lady?"

"Yes, ma'am."

Frank peeked over the bowl, his smile matching his wife's. "Be good. Mind your manners."

Quint gave a breathy laugh, moving a rock with his boot. "Yes, sir."

"Everything will be fine," Heidi encouraged. "Go get her and have a wonderful time."

"Be sure *not* to dine at the Whitman Hotel," Frank mused.

Gathering Joey's reins, Quint mounted in an easy step. "I'm taking her to that French place."

Heidi smacked Frank's arm. "We've been here years and have yet to dine there," she teased.

Frank's mouth dropped open, glancing over at Quint with a roll of his eyes. "Boy, you plum got me in trouble now," he chuckled. "See you later. Have a good time."

With a smiling shake of his head, Quint spurred Joey. The horse trotted up the hill with easy steps, more than eager and happy to run. Quint allowed the animal to run, giving him lead to stretch his anxious legs. The wind whipped his face, cooling the sweat on his head and under his arms, and calming the anxiety he'd been feeling.

*I've never felt more nervous in my life, he thought. I bet she is gonna look beautiful, all dolled up. I hope she wears her hair down.* Quint ran a hand over his face, wiping away the lingering sweat. *I need a drink. Just one.*

The city of Denver came into view. Seeing the bustling town, made his gut churn quicker. Being alone with Lena made him excited and scared. She was so perfect, genuine and kind. Something he didn't think he deserved and certainly didn't think he would ever get a chance to possibly call wife. He wanted to call Lena his wife.

There was something about her, pulling him to her more than bees to flowers; more than any comparison he could think of. Lena was the woman he had dreamed about before getting messed in with bad people. In his dreams, a woman with rich dark chocolate brown hair, greeted him at the door to their cabin with a smile. Her hazel eyes would sparkle lovingly at him as the two children tucked behind her maroon colored skirts peeked out until they saw him; then they'd run to him as she laughed. Her voluptuous figure would meld into his perfectly, putting a joyful kiss on his cheek. In his dreams, it was always a beautiful brunette. Now, he was certain that in his dreams from years past, it was Lena.

Joey whinnied shrilly, bringing his thoughts back to the town coming into view. Quint crossed the railroad tracks, going up the small inclined street on his way to get Lena. He was early; roughly an hour from leaving the Rocky Pine Ranch. He stopped on the other side of the street from the saloon. His mind and body craving one drink of whiskey.

*No*, he decided. *No whiskey tonight.* Moving past the saloon and up the road, he tethered Joey outside the Whitman Diner. Pulling out the flowers from his saddle bag, he frowned. The bouquet wilted, some flowers losing their petals.

*I can't give these to her*, he thought. Picking out the bad flowers, it left him with a less than full arrangement but better than the one he was going to give her.

Taking a deep breath and flowers in hand, he strode up the steps to the Whitman Hotel. Going through the sets of double doors, he went to the counter. Bartholomew stood behind the desk, checking people in for the evening. Quint stood to the side by the sitting area, waiting to catch a glimpse of the woman he fancied.

Lena paced her bedroom, her stomach in tight knots. A new dress, at Audrey's insistence, hugged her curvy frame. Mary told Jane and Audrey about her upcoming evening with Quint Morris. Lena wished no one knew. It made her nervous feeling everyone's eyes on her.

Her palms sweated profusely; she was certain they would drip with moisture. Lena paused in front of the mirror, checking her hair and her face for yet another time. Lena braided her hair off her face in a halo around her head. She pulled out some small strands of hair to frame her face.

Gazing in the mirror, she pinched her cheeks. Rosy color came on her face. She smiled at her reflection, letting out a deep breath.

*Ohhh, I can do this,* she thought. *A nice supper with a nice man.* She shook her body, trying to free herself from the tingles and nerves running through her. *After, I have to tell him. He has to know before we progress to something more. But first, I want to enjoy the evening.*

With a deep breath, she opened the door, going out into the sitting area in the hotel check in. Sitting in a chair, Quint had his head down, a small bouquet of flowers in his hand. A smile crept across her lips.

Quint rose at her approach, eyes wide and bright. Heat flaming his cheeks, he gazed at her up and down with adoration.

"Beautiful," he whispered, holding out the flowers.

Lena smiled, taking them gently from him, "Thank you."

Peeking over Quint, Audrey and Mary stood in the back by the door going into Jane's office. They smiled at her, nodding and waving their hands at her to shoo.

Lena chuckled softly. Quint turned around, catching them mid-shoo and waved to them. Lena covered her face with the bouquet of flowers.

"Shall we get going," Quint asked, offering her his arm.

Lena took it, feeling the icy rush of touching him and being near him crawl over her skin and make her heart flutter, skipping several beats. Lena held her breath.

*You can do this. It's your first date ever and everything will be alright,* she reminded herself. *You can do a dinner with this man.* Lena let him lead her toward the double doors and the foyer.

"I'll take those for you," Audrey said, at the corner of the check in desk.

Lena felt her cheeks flame at the perky and grinning hotel owner. "Thank you, Audrey."

"Certainly! I will put these in your room. Have a great time! Now shoo!" she said over her shoulder.

Quint chuckled. "They sure want you out."

"I haven't been out with a man since coming here."

Quint eyes sparkled. "Waiting for the right man to ask?"

Passing through the door Quint held open, Lena tilted her head to the side blushing. "You can say that."

"When did you make your way out here?"

"I arrived here in Denver on my sixteenth birthday from New York," she said fiddling with her hands. Closing her eyes, she walked down the steps she knew by heart. Her mind screamed at her to keep details of what she was to herself.

Taking a deep breath, she stopped in her tracks. *I have to tell him,* she decided. Quint stopped, holding on her arm still. Lena glanced at it, wanting to remove herself from his respectful embrace but also desiring it to linger a touch longer.

"Something wrong? I planned on us dining at the French place. Don't rightly know how to pronounce it."

Lena shook her head. "Everything is fine," she lied.

"You sure?" Quint pressed. "You got pale real quick."

"Yeah, just really nervous is all," she said, biting her lower lip.

"I am too," Quint admitted. "I really like you, Lena Jenkins."

Lena grinned, feeling the giddiness of a school girl tingle all over her. "I really like you too, Quint."

Quint's smiled went so wide, it crinkled his eyes. He took off his hat, pressing it against his heart. Lena giggled, keeping her hand in his, lacing her fingers in between his. The warmth of his strong calloused hand coursed through her, making her believe all was right with the world with his gentle and protective embrace.

"I be damned, a woman so beautiful as you likes the hide of me," he said, shaking his head and putting his hat back on. "I must be dead."

Lena laughed, leaning her head against his arm, breathing out deeply. "I feel the same."

Hand in hand, they strolled across the street and down a little side road toward the French diner. Lena never ate there before, but according to Audrey, it was like being in France.

The smile covering her face could not be removed. Lena relished the touch of Quint's hand, resting her head on his arm. It was too good to be true, especially for a soiled dove like herself. The darkness in her past seemed to lift, her life becoming brighter with Quint around.

Lena squeezed his hand, lacing her fingers tighter in with his.

Quint stopped in the middle of the sidewalk. With his free hand, he pushed the hat back on his head. "Lena," he said, licking his lips and shuffling his boots. "Lena," he said firmly, meeting her gaze. "May I call on you?"

Tears burned behind her eyes, making a trail down to her nose. Sniffling, Lena nodded, wrapping her arms around his waist. She came up to his chest, eye level with his bicep. Quint gently embraced her back.

"Yes," Lena said exhaling, her body relaxing with his shielding arms around her.

"May I kiss you then?"

Lena nodded, not trusting her voice to make coherent words. Putting his hand around her neck, her insides turned to jam. Her mind went fuzzy as his warm, soft lips landed on hers. Lena pressed her lips against his, her hands resting on his large, strong forearms.

He breathed, pulling back, "A kiss of an angel."

She blushed, lacing her fingers back in with his. "Yeah," she whispered, "I could say the same."

Quint beamed, kissing the back of her hand. "I'm happy I met you and am able to enjoy this evening with you. Thank you for agreein'."

"You're welcome."

Walking past the last several buildings, Quint opened the door to the French diner. Lena was surprised she made it inside without floating away. As she heard once, she felt over the moon, being with Quint. And surely, this was a night, she would remember forever.

# CHAPTER NINE

Quint left her inside the Whitman Hotel a little past ten in the evening. She kissed him on the cheek, setting his entire face to blooming on fire. He couldn't help but to smile being around her. Lena was stronger than whiskey to him and he was getting drunk off her fast.

With a final goodnight and goodbye, he strode out of the hotel feeling like he could walk on clouds. During their supper, they talked about what they each wanted in life – a family, kids, and a cabin home, somewhere they both felt safe and secure. The conversation only confirmed for him he wanted a home with her.

He remembered his grandfather once saying a man may build a house but a good woman's love makes it a home. Quint wanted that with Lena. He wanted to take her, ride into the sunset on Joey, and see what part of Colorado felt like home in their hearts. All he knew for sure was life began and ended with Lena Jenkins.

*She is all I ever wanted in a woman and a partner in life,* he thought. *She's smart, funny, and gentle. A real genuine woman. And maybe, if I'm a lucky man, she might allow me to call her wife.*

Joey whickered at his approach. Quint grinned at his horse, patting the animal on the neck. Gathering the tethered reins, he walked his horse down the small slope toward the road leading back to Rocky Pine Ranch.

The bellowing raucous of the saloon caught his attention. Quint paused on the other side of the street, debating about going inside. Biting his bottom lip, he walked across the street. Joey tossed his head, pulling at the reins wanting to go home.

"Two drinks max, Joe," Quint said. "I didn't tell Lena about what I've done," he told the irritated horse, tethering his reins to a new hitching post. "I have to tell her. I'm gonna tell her tonight. I just need a drink."

Taking a deep breath, Quint went inside. *Telling Lena drunk and not remembering the shame in her eyes might be easier on my heart*, he decided, feeling the heart-wrenching shattering of the joy he'd had just hours before, strip away from him. *She has to know*, he confirmed. *One way or another, it's going to be tonight.*

Striding up to the barkeep, he slapped his money down on the counter.

"Regular bottle?" the barkeep asked.

Quint shook his head. "Half glass."

The man nodded, pouring him his money's worth and then some. "You look like you could use a touch more."

Quint nodded, throwing back the fiery liquid in a few gulps. "One more."

The barkeep poured.

Sitting on the stool, he savored his final drink. The burning liquid torched his throat, making its boiling way down to his stomach. Quint shuddered, closing his eyes.

*I'm gonna lose her*, he thought. *I'm going to tell her then I'm going to lose her for good. She would want this. And I don't blame her.*

Sipping his drink, he put more money on the counter. The barkeep scooped it up, topping off his drink. Quint slammed it back, vowing to stick to his two-drink rule, although he smudged it a bit when the barkeep topped him off. Slamming back the last of his allotted amount of whiskey, he strode out the saloon.

Leaving Joey tethered, he promised the horse he would be back once he spoke to Lena and got his rejection.

Quint dropped her off at the Whitman Hotel a little past ten in the evening. Lena gave him a peck on the cheek, still beaming after such a wondrous evening spent with him. Quint left her inside the sitting area of the hotel, striding out to his horse to go back to the Rocky Pine Ranch.

Lena breathed out, plopping in a chair. *Oh, my stars,* she thought. *How lucky am I to have a man like him. Never in all my days have I given a thought to being truly happy. But here I am. The darkness I swore followed me from New York out here to Denver, all the horrible things I subjected myself to, don't seem to matter around him. I can finally forgive myself as God has forgiven me and move on.*

She smiled, closing her eyes and remembering how it felt when he touched her hand. Quint came into her life unexpectedly, right when she was certain to swear off men for good for fear of never finding happiness once her truth came out. Now, she was certain, when she told him, there would be no judgment from him.

Quint was the kind of man her mama spoke highly of, the way she said her papa was. From what she remembered of her papa, he was a kindly man, unfortunately passing on in a mining accident when she was seven or so. She couldn't recall exactly. But mama made sure to remind her what a gentleman does, a man's man is supposed to be. Lena had forgotten all of it before Quint.

"Date went well?" Audrey asked, coming down the stairs from the grand rooms side.

Lena nodded. "Yeah... He asked to call on me."

Audrey squealed with delight, racing down the steps. "Tell me everything!" the woman demanded excitedly.

Leaning forward, she filled Audrey in on every word. Audrey listened intently, happily agreeing, squealing and stamping her feet. The woman jumped out of her skin with euphoric joy.

"Finally, my greatest friend is finding a suitable match!" she sighed dramatically. "I'm so delighted for you Lena! You deserve it."

"Thank you, Audrey," Lena grinned. "I'm so happy I can hardly stand it."

"All right, well, I am off to bed. I only stayed awake to hear from you so I could tell Eugene."

Lena's brows furrowed. "Is he awake at this hour?"

Audrey was already at the stairs, going up and to the right where the basic rooms were. "He is going to be," she giggled.

Lena rose out of her chair, going to her bedroom. Her mind muddled and euphoric with her time spent with Quint, she couldn't think of anything at all. Her mind was blissfully blank. Walking down the hall, turning to the left, she came to the first door on the left. Opening the door quietly, she walked in, immediately unbuttoning the front of her dress in the dull lamplight someone already lit for her.

Her roommates were long gone and married. It seemed every roommate she ever had went off and got married, except her, but now, her luck was changing. With the recent changes in the past few weeks with Cassie and Mary both getting married, it left her alone in the quaint little room.

Lena hung her dress on a peg mounted on the wall by her bedside. She kept it alone and to the side away from the other dresses she had and wore for work. With a happy sigh, she clambered into bed, rolling down the bedsheet.

"Lena Jenkins," a hushed voice called through the door.

Perking her head to the side, she cautiously crawled out. Going to the door, she put a hand on the knob, balling her free hand into a fist.

"Lena?" Quint called.

Brows furrowed; she opened the door. Quint's rosy cheeks and bloodshot eyes stared back at her. A wide grin, reeking of whiskey tingled her nose, churning her gut and urging her to hurl.

"What are you doing here?" she hissed.

Quint gazed down at his feet, removing his hat. "I have to tell you something... some," he hiccupped, "thing bad, I've done."

Lena stepped to the side, allowing him to enter before he woke anyone up. No matter how improper it happened to be, she was soiled anyways. Quint sat on the bed heavily, sighing with his fingers wringing in his hands.

Walking across the room, she took a seat on her bed, waiting for him to look up and speak what was on his mind. She crossed her arms over herself, moving her long chocolate hair to the side. Her stomach fluttered, wondering on all the reasons Quint would be here, drunk at this hour in her room.

"Quint," she whispered, "are you all right?"

Quint shook his head. "I killed people," he sniffed, wiping his eyes with the back of his hand. "Six people. I didn't want to. But I did it. It was either them or me. The first three, I was made to by Victor Del Avilasto. The last three I killed was Charlie Hilbert and his gang going after Mary and Ross."

Lena's jaw hung open. She didn't know what rightly to say. She didn't like killing. As God commanded, it was a right bad sin. However, she was a sinner too, no better than Rahab herself.

*I like a killer,* she thought. *A murderer...* she snorted, shaking her head. *But I understand, out here in this lawless country and with the no-good likes of Sheriff Mobley a person has to make difficult decisions, Lord knows I've had to. But... Can I be all right with a mass murderer?* Staring into his warm brown eyes, she decided she could. Quint did what he did to survive, to protect not only her friends but his life as well, bringing a horrible gang to its knees most recently. *I am all right with this,* she concluded.

Quint woefully stared at her, then back at his feet. His knee bounced, shaking rapidly then stopping. Lena's brows pinched together concerningly. Her heart thundering in her chest, wanting to find the words to speak but none coming out of her mouth.

Quint rose, putting his hat on his head. "I understand if you can't bear the sight of me. I just had to tell you."

Lena rose, holding out her hand. She bit her bottom lip, her hand wavering between holding its position and letting it drop so he could leave. Taking a step forward, she reached for his arm.

Her body, working and thinking on its own accord. All the things she had done in her life came to the forefront. Now was her time to tell him what she's done, what her past, like his, left her with little choice to survive.

"Quint," she said softly. "I'm not mad."

He perked at her words. His eyes narrowing, zooming in on hers. The redness in his eyes dissipating. The dim lamplight playing shadows on his face, making the stubble more prominent and his masculinity alluring.

"You're not?"

Lena shook her head. "No... I understand."

Quint smirked, letting out a soft snort. "I'll be damned."

She smiled, wringing her hands together. With his confession over, it was time for hers. Vomit sat in the back of her throat. Besides Mary, Jane and Audrey knowing of what she'd done, this would be the first person, let alone a man, she'd ever told in years. Her mind spun with doom. Lena sat down, putting a hand to her head, her previous confidence gone.

"It really does bother you," Quint sighed, slapping his hat in his hand.

Lena shook her head. "No... It's not that. I have something of my own to tell you."

Quint sat back down. The rosiness in his cheeks fading more with each moment. Lena silently wished he was still drunk but it wouldn't make the telling any easier. Drunk or sober, Quint would know and she was certain he would remember.

Sitting back on the bed, her hands shook as she put them to her face. Hanging her head, elbows on her knees, her hands held her head. Her knees bounced. She painfully swallowed the bile in her throat, choking it down with a hard gulp. The squeak of the bed depressing echoed in the small room. Feet moved in her field of vision.

*You can do this Lena,* she encouraged herself. *Quint has to know.*

Lena sighed, sitting up. Her body quaked. She felt sweat pepper her forehead. Quint patiently waited; brows slightly furrowed. Hands on his knees, hat in his left hand, his brown eyes focused on her intently.

"I-I," she stammered. "I have to tell you something because I like you. And the longer I keep it in, the more it eats at me to tell you."

Quint took her left hand, rubbing his thumb over her knuckles.

"My mother died, leaving me poor, hurting for money for food. Living in the slums of New York, it leaves a person with few options. And when no store really wants to hire a young girl..."

Quint perked a brow, his eyes then darkening to a scowl. "Yeah?"

"I slept with men for money, to get food and to make it far away so I could start over. I stole too. I'm not proud of it, knowing I'm tainted and meant for hell. I thought you should know before we go any farther because I really like you."

The room stilled, nothing making a sound. Lena held her breath and it seemed Quint did as well. Lena's heart stopped, lodging in her throat.

The bed squeaked with Quint rising to his feet. He put his hat back on his head, moving toward the door. Tears tracked down her cheeks. Hand on the door, Quint yanked it open. Lena's heart shattered in her chest. Wracking sobs overcoming her, she crumpled to the wooden floors.

*I knew it*, she cursed herself. *My past is so dark it can never be lifted*. Lena picked herself up, moving to the bed. *Who was I trying to kid*, she cried, *no one can ever love me*.

# CHAPTER TEN

Lena couldn't sleep. She faced the wall, warmly tucked inside her bed. She was supposed to rise hours ago to help in the kitchen to get breakfast going. She couldn't bring herself to do it. Her heart throbbed and broke further with each beat.

She wiped the last of the tears from her eyes. Her stomach roiled painfully. Her body chilled despite being tucked under a pile of warm quilts. Lena scrunched farther down in the bed.

A knock thumped on her door. "Lena," Mary called. "Claudia needs you."

Lena didn't care, nor did she move. She hurt too much to do anything. Every fiber in her body ached, bringing more pain and sadness. She resigned herself to being alone for the rest of her life. While all her friends got married and got their happily forever after, she wouldn't. Here, at the Whitman Hotel, she would remain until she died, like Claudia, cranky and old.

Mary knocked again. "Lena, you all right?"

The creak of the door opened. Lena peeked over her shoulder, seeing the blond head of Mary. She turned back toward the wall, not caring.

"Lena," Mary exclaimed, coming to her in quick strides. "What happened?" she asked, kneeling down by her bedside.

Lena shook her head, fresh tears escaping out of her eyes. Mary got up, embracing her tightly. Lena sniffed, reining back her tears.

"I told Quint," Lena squeaked.

Mary pulled back, her face scrunched and eyes narrowed. "About your past?"

Lena nodded weakly.

"He didn't take it too kindly?"

Lena shook her head, tears tracking down her cheeks.

Mary's lips pursed. "What a hippo-crate."

"What?" Lena blinked. "What's a hippo-crate?"

Mary shrugged, her lips pressed together and pulled down. "I heard a fancy word Audrey used once. She called Eugene a hippo-crate. I don't know what a hippo is, but apparently, you put it in a crate," she moved her lips to the side, head slightly tilted and brows furrowed. "She said it when she was lookin' a might cross, so it must be a word to say when mad."

Lena smiled, sitting up. "Thank you, Mary."

Mary got off the bed, standing off to the side. "Get yourself cleaned up, and I'll tell old cranky, you're coming."

Mary strode out the door, gently shutting it behind her. Lena rose, pulling her green dress off the peg by the wall. She stepped into it, buttoning down the front while stepping into her worn shoes.

Going out, she snuck to the back of the hotel to the washroom. Staring at herself in the mirror, she grimaced at her reflection. Her eyes had red lines running through them. The bottom of her lashes crusted. Streaks where her tears ran stained her cheeks. Lena gathered a handful of water, splashing the tepid water on her face.

Lena sighed, blotting her face with a towel. *Time to put on a good face. I have to let everyone see I am fine... That nothing gets to me*, she decided.

She gripped the edge of the wash basin, staring blankly into the mirror. She pulled her hair out of the fancy hair style she had it in, opting for a simple braid, resting on her left shoulder. She wetted the fly away hairs with water, hoping by the time it dried, it would be better.

"Lena?" Audrey called from the door. "May I come in?"

Lena picked up her toothbrush, quickly brushing her teeth. "Yes," she called, spitting in the sink.

"Mary told me," Audrey said, wrapping her arms around her. "Oh, Lena," she crooned. "Everything will work out for the best. I know it."

Lena fell into the embrace, not knowing how badly she needed it. Tears wanted to start fresh but she refused to let them fall. Taking a deep shaky breath, she pulled back.

"Time for work," Lena said, heading to the door.

Audrey cupped her face. "My dearest friend," she began, "you are a wonderful person."

Lena smiled. "Thank you."

She didn't feel like a wonderful person. She felt more like a pile of manure that Ross throws out behind the Whitman Stables. Striding out of the washroom, she went into the kitchen. Claudia's voice raised at her, asking her a slew of questions Lena didn't bother to listen to or care to answer.

Putting on an apron, she went out into the diner with a smile on her face. Natali glanced over her shoulder, relieved at her presence, and pointing to the right side of the diner.

Lena went to a table where a cowboy sat alone. "Can I take your order?"

"Coffee and the special," he said with a smile.

Lena returned his grin, "Coming right up."

Going back to the kitchen, Claudia glared at her, mumbling under her breath. Lena set her paper order on the counter, taking a hot pitcher of coffee out.

*I can do this*, Lena thought. *Smile, fill coffee cups, smile and the day will be over before I know it.*

Quint woke with the dawn, going out to ride fence to see if any lines were broke. He missed breakfast and was going to miss dinner. He didn't care. His gut churned anyways, unable to settle after discovering what Lena had done.

It disgusted him. He didn't want that kind of woman for a wife. It was distasteful. Killing men, as he had, was necessary. He did it to survive, selfish as it was. Killing was the last option he was given. Lena had options for herself. What Lena did went beyond reason.

*I can't have a wife like that*, he thought.

Joey flicked his ears back. He trotted along the fence line in the south pasture. Every head of cattle accounted for and the lines in the fence stable. Finishing checking the line, he trotted back the ranch. Dismounting, he took the saddle, pad, and bridle off his horse, lugging the tack back to the bunkhouse.

Heidi was on the porch, setting out a dinner fare. Frank sat in a rocking chair, whittling a piece of scrap wood. Ignoring them both, Quint strode back behind the barn, picking up the ax left on a splitting log.

He frowned, lifting a piece of wood that hadn't been split yet. Bringing the ax down on the wood, the timber burst apart, a chunk zooming in a different direction. It felt like his heart. Lena broke it. Lena, this beautiful, kind woman, was a no-good whore.

Quint snorted in disgust, his upper lip curling.

"I get splitting wood is a horrible job but it doesn't smell bad," Frank mused.

Quint grinned. "It's not what my face is for."

Frank nodded. "Care to talk?"

Quint shook his head. "Nope."

"All right, boy. Dinner is on the table, come eat something quick. You can get back to this later."

Quint grunted, splitting another piece of wood. He couldn't eat. His stomach was in knots picturing Lena under another man. Quint shook his head.

*There's no way I could ever get over this*, he thought. Quint chopped a few more pieces, picking them up to take to the main house. Frank, Brandon and Heidi waited patiently for him to come and sit. Quint smiled tersely, setting down his bulky load by the door.

Taking up a seat, he bowed his head.

"Lord, bless this meal and those sitting at this table, amen," Frank said, lifting his head to pass the rolls.

Quint heaped potatoes on his plate, smothering it in brown gravy. Brandon passed him pork and another meat on a large platter. Taking his fill, he passed the plate on to Frank.

He tucked into the fare, not realizing how hungry he was. He pushed Lena out of his head for a bit to enjoy his meal. Quint had no intention of thinking on her while he ate, especially not how her bright hazel eyes lit up at him yesterday or the tears and despair in her eyes as he walked away.

Quint threw his cloth napkin down on the table, screeching his chair back.

"Is it not good, Quint?" Heidi asked, visibly hurt by his abrupt actions.

Quint blinked. "No ma'am, it's delicious. I just find myself too troubled to eat."

"Is it that French food?" Frank asked. "I heard they eat them little snails."

He shook his head. "They called it es-car-got and no, I didn't eat any of it. The food was mighty tasty."

Heidi perked up at the news. "We should go sometime, shouldn't we, Frank?"

Frank smirked. "Gettin' me in trouble again, boy," he chuckled.

Quint grinned, staring down at his feet. "Thank you for the fine meal, Mrs. Kirby."

Quint strode back to the woodshed behind the barn. His mind and heart too occupied to eat, battling over Lena. Part of him wanted to understand why she did what she did, to forgive her as she did him, and so quickly, and look past it all. He couldn't imagine being hungry or being so poor. It seemed unreal. He grew up well thanks to his parents and grandfather. He never went without, always a roof over his head and food to fill him.

The other part, was utterly disgusted. How could a lovely, kind woman as Lena be hopeless enough to sell herself and soil her good name. A name is all a person has in this world. A person was judged on their character and their name. Hers was soiled like the devil's as Quint reckoned it. No matter what the circumstances, he couldn't imagine anything worse.

He kicked a rock. Being torn between forgiveness and moving on. His heart wanted Lena Jenkins. She was the air filling his lungs. Now, he wanted to forget everything about her and for some reason, he couldn't; and it bothered him.

Grimacing, he picked up the ax, striking the sharp blade at the rough-cut piece yet to be broken down smaller. He dove into the pile of wood, working out all his anger and frustrations until sweat soaked through his shirt and more.

"Quint," Frank called from behind him. "You've been at this for a bit. I'm sure we have enough wood to last a good part of winter now."

"Yeah," he replied a touch harsher than he intended.

"Date not go well?" Frank pressed.

Quint shrugged. "Went well enough."

Frank sat on a nearby round, grunting as he sat. He stayed silent; hands clasped together. The hat on his head and the shade on the back of the wood shed, put a shadow over his face. Quint ignored his boss, going back to the rest of the stack of wood needing to be split and splitting the smaller, drier pieces down for kindling. Quint took off his shirt, blotting his face free of sweat. He threw his soiled shirt to the side, picking up the ax.

"All right," Frank said, getting up, "I'll leave you to it," he paused, looking back at him. "Maybe you should talk to her."

Quint's lips compressed into a tight line. *I have no idea how to feel, and if I should talk to her*, he thought. *The date with her was absolutely perfect. We had a great supper, an evening stroll, everything was wonderful with her.* Bringing the ax over his head, he split another piece.

Quint stuck his hat back on his head, shuffling his feet. Holding the ax aloft in his hands he drove the blade into a chunk of wood. The crack of the wood splintering apart brought him some relief.

He ran a hand over his face, trying to push Lena from his thoughts. The beautiful hazel eyed woman lingered. Instead of his gut churning, his heart grew heavy.

Quint whacked his ax into the splitting stump. He shucked his gun belt by his soiled shirt, going to the crick. *I'm gonna talk to her,* he decided. *Tell her I won't be calling on her.*

# CHAPTER ELEVEN

Lena sighed, sitting on the bench outside the hotel. Leaning her head against the wall of the hotel, she closed her eyes, willing her heart to stop its breaking.

Their date had been perfect. A delicious supper, an evening stroll and great conversation. It was the highlight of her year. Possibly the highlight of the last several years. It was everything to her, to be treated so kindly by a gentleman. Now, it was dashed to shreds. The happy memory ruined... like her.

A tear tracked down her face. She didn't bother to flick it off; no one was here to see it. The breakfast service went quick enough. Claudia tried to berate her for being out too late and having it affect her work. Lena snapped at the old bitty. She didn't mean to. Eight years of taking the woman's verbal rebuke got to her.

Lena told Natali to handle dinner. It should be a light affair anyways. And if it got too wild, to come and get her. She didn't care anymore. She needed a moment to herself.

Rising to her feet, she gloomily strolled down the pathway toward the Whitman stables. Lena smirked, it was an oversized barn with fancy writing labeling it a stable at the insistence of Audrey.

A horse from an outside paddock whinnied shrilly at another horse Ross was in the paddock with. Lena smiled, *jealousy at its finest*. Without Ross noticing, she went into the barn, searching for where Mary told her Ross settled a batch of rescued kittens.

Opening a side door, where the nicer tack was stored, soft mewling reached her ears. A small orange cat waddled out of the room. Lena picked it up, softly closing the door so the others wouldn't escape.

The kitten purred in her hands.

"Sweet little thing," she cooed to it.

"Lena," Eugene's voice boomed in the barn. "Ross in here?"

Lena spun around. "I saw him in the paddock with a horse."

Eugene nodded. "Thank you," his eyebrows scrunched when he spotted the kitten. "Ross rescue that?" he asked pointing.

"Yes," she cooed to the kitten. "Isn't it the sweetest?"

Eugene came over, petting its little head. He smiled at the little kitten, scratching it under the chin. The kitten purred. "It stays outside, and especially out of the diner."

Lena smiled. "Yes, boss."

Eugene rolled his eyes. "I'm not your boss."

"You will be when you marry Audrey in a few months."

Eugene scoffed, shaking his head and striding out the door. Lena put the kitten back in the small room with the other meowing critters. Spinning on her heel, she headed out the barn doors.

Her heart felt a touch lighter; comforting and loving on something so soft and sweet had done her good. Lena crossed her arms over herself, striding up the walkway to the hotel. She paused, gazing out at the industriousness of Denver.

*I want someone to share this with*, she thought. *I want someone to want me, but I'm not holding my breath.* Looking over at the Whitman Hotel, she sighed, *I should resign myself to be like Claudia.* Lena grimaced, *goodness I hope not.* Crossing her arms, she kicked a pebble. *God, am I meant to be alone?*

She spotted Quint going toward the stable. His dapple stallion was an iconic horse out here in Denver, where everyone had bays or some other look alike. Lena swallowed the lump in her throat, moving her hair off to the other side of her face. She wanted to hide but it was too late. He was approaching fast.

Lena shuffled her feet, moving toward the hotel. She tried to make it seem like she'd always been walking.

"Lena," Quint called.

She tensed, turning back around. Arms crossed; she shuffled her feet. "Y-yes?" she asked.

Quint reined in his horse in front of her. "I came to," he mumbled, removing his hat.

Lena nodded, feeling her throat close around what felt like a ball too hard for her to breath around. Tears peppered the corner of her eyes. The stinging and burning behind her nose made her take a deep shuddering breath to rein it all in. She turned away so he couldn't see the emotions roll down her cheek. Before she could give him a chance to continue, she strode away. Her heart was broken, she felt slimier than mud and she wouldn't add allowing Quint seeing her so upset to the list. She wanted to keep as much dignity as possible.

*Maybe I should leave Colorado,* she thought. *I've been here eight years and have quite a sum saved up at the bank, even after I donated some to the orphanage and squandered a bit on myself.* Lena dared a glance behind her. Quint turned in the saddle, facing the Whitman Stables and the men below. *I'll live in Black Hawk. It's beautiful there too.*

Lena nodded, confirming her plan to be out of Denver and run from the pain one man caused her heart.

---

Quint didn't have the words to complete his sentence. Lena strode away from him quicker than a rabbit hopped toward a carrot. He couldn't bring himself to tell her, but her keen mind figured his reason.

Part of him wanted to end the courtship, because her being soiled as she was truly bothered him. He didn't want to picture his Lena with another, whether being forced into it or not. It was distasteful and wrong of a woman. It was not how he imagined his Lena being.

The other part of him wanted it to continue. Lena was a golden ray of sunshine in his dark and twisted life. She brought out the better in him. In over a day, he hadn't drunk from the saloon or bought a bottle from the mercantile, which was unusual for him. Lena did that. He suspected she did it for a lot of people. And it made it harder for him. He loved what he saw. He just couldn't get over what she'd been.

Sighing, he put the hat back on his head. Spinning in the saddle, he spotted Ross and Eugene, eyes narrowed and curious at his and Lena's abrupt conversation.

Turning Joey in their direction, he went to the middle paddock where they happened to be. Ross and Eugene clambered over the rough-hewn wooden fence, leaving the docile mare in the arena whickering happily munching her hay.

"You all right?" Ross asked, jumping off the top rail.

Quint dismounted, hitching Joey to a post. "Yeah."

"Appears otherwise to me," Eugene scowled, glancing past them all toward Lena. "I have never seen sadness mar her face since coming here."

Quint's heart clenched. He was the cause of it. He gazed out at the landscape to the right. Behind the Whitman Stables was the garden. Beyond it was more empty land the Whitman woman owned and then in the far distance, more buildings popped up in a neat row.

Focusing back on the two men, Ross's arms were cross and he glared at him. "I already saved your face once with her at the saloon. What happened?"

Eugene's brows pinched together, eyes locking on his with all the qualities of an admirable investigator. Eugene waited expectedly for Quint to say something but Quint didn't have the words.

Quint peeked over his shoulder, up the hill to the Whitman

Hotel. He could make out the silhouette of Lena on the bench against the hotel head in her hands.

"She is soiled in a way women not ought to be," Quint finally admitted after a tense silence.

"So?" Ross asked, shrugging his shoulders and shaking his head. "None of us is perfect."

Eugene nodded. "But it bothers you."

"A touch," Quint confessed. "I didn't expect it from someone sweet as her. Not sure I can look past it either."

Ross scowled. "Mary ain't perfect. She stole and got Eugene here kidnapped by Del Avilasto, along with Audrey. It didn't taint my view of her. I ain't a saint, an angel or God himself. Last I checked, you were just as bad as me."

Quint nodded. Shame marring his face, coloring his cheeks red. Joey whickered, tossing his mane. Ross shook his head in disgust, hopping back over the fence. Grabbing the pitch fork, Ross began shoving the horse manure like he was previously.

Quint felt himself go numb. Lena's past shouldn't bother him as it did. He wasn't perfect either as Ross said. He was tainted. He ruined his good name through killing, stealing and working for a horrible gang leader, and he didn't have a noble excuse like survival.

*I'm surely meant for hell,* he thought. *Lena, even knowing her briefly, makes me feel like a better man. I'm drawn to her, more than all the comparisons I can think of. Mary once said "instant connotation" is what she felt with Ross. I have it with her and I think I ruined it.* And part of him didn't care.

Eugene shuffled his feet, taking a step toward him. The clean-cut man stared him level in the eye. A fire he hadn't yet seen in the man flared and brought a glower to his face. Crossing his arms, Eugene asked, "Have you ever gone without?"

Quint shook his head. "No."

"So hungry you cried yourself to sleep?"

"No."

Eugene's upper lip curled slightly. A disdain for his ignorance and judgment, clear as a lamb in a field on his face. "Good for you,"

Eugene said. "For Lena, it was a different world. And yes, I know of her past. She did what she had to do to survive, like you killing Charlie Hilbert. Yes, I heard about it too. Each of you acted out of necessity in a different way," he sighed, hands on his hips. His gaze finally softened a touch. Looking him blank in the eye, "I grew up in the slums of Philly. My neighbor, Evla was a sweet girl. Her parents got sick and eventually died because they didn't have money to get better. Evla was fourteen and turned to selling herself on the streets to survive. And believe me, she looked other places for money. She tried the shops, warehouses, the bar houses as a bar keep. No one wants a young, uneducated girl. I gave her money when I could. It was a little easier for a boy to get a job, so I helped when I could. Seeing her struggle, made me want to be a Pinkerton all the more, to help people, women like her, and women like my sister, killed in cold blood when she was eight. I don't hate Evla for her choices. I pity her. To be so alone, hungry – starving so badly, I could hear her cry, hurt me, made me want to be better so I could help girls like her. For you to turn your back on Lena, shows a callousness beyond imagination. You just told her she's little more than the dirt under your boots and your turning away shows the kind of man you really are," Eugene raised his hands, going around Quint. "That's all I'm gonna say on the matter but I hope you *can* prove yourself to Lena. She deserves far better than what you've shown her and if you can't get over yourself, run far away because you don't need to be anywhere near her sweet self."

Eugene left him dumbstruck by the fence post. Quint hung his head, ashamed of himself. His body felt heavy. Everything felt heavy. And he was the cause of it all. He was a horse's ass. Untethering Joey from the fence, he mounted swiftly; heading on the main road back to Rocky Pine Ranch. He checked himself before he got too far; he needed to stop at the mercantile, picking up the supplies from Leonard for Heidi.

*I'm a cactus,* he thought. *Eugene is right, I don't deserve her.*

## CHAPTER TWELVE

Eugene's words pounded like a hammer in his mind. He cursed himself for wanting to love her while struggling to get past what she'd done. Eugene was right though – they were both tainted in their own way.

Truth was, he didn't know how to describe how he felt about himself either. He'd done terrible things with no noble motivation, where Lena did it to survive. He went looking for adventure and riches and did bad. Lena did it for food.

*I'm worse,* he thought. *And here I am being terrible to her... Lena has been my heart since her first "hello" and smile. She is kind, gentle, hardworking and forgiving; so why should this even matter?*

Scowling, he bent to the side, riffling through his pack for the sack Frank gave him to carry the goods he needed from the mercantile.

*None of it should matter,* he decided shrugging. *I've been on the fence long enough about this, and I need to make a choice. Do I want Lena Jenkins or not?*

Joey whinnied, ears flat back on his head.

"Easy, buddy," Quint cooed, patting the stallion's neck. "Sorry."

Quint sat a moment in front of the hitching post. *I want Lena.*

*Because of her, I don't want to drink. Because of her, I smile more, desire a respectable future, to do better and good. Because of Lena, I feel like I have a purpose in this life and I've done made a mess. I gotta make it up to her somehow.*

Dismounting and hitching Joey, he went inside the mercantile. Old Leonard sat behind the counter at the register, while his grandson Clyde filled orders. Clyde smiled at him, setting Quint's box on the counter, and turning his attention to the customers in front of him. Two more women entered the store behind him with their baskets and shawls wrapped around their arms.

Leonard frowned in concentration, getting off his stool. A blue scarf wrapped around his neck, bringing out his wrinkly blue eyes that were usually hard to see over the spectacles. Hunching over the pad of paper left at the registers, he picked up an old pencil. "On credit?" Leonard asked.

Quint shook his head. "No. Frank sends this," he replied, bringing out money, and setting the clinking metal on the countertop.

Leonard picked it up, counting it meticulously. "Tell Frank thanks, and tell Heidi her scarf is mighty nice for these old bones." Leonard tugged on the scarf around his neck and smiled.

Quint nodded, taking the crate.

"You look like you've been run through." Leonard observed.

Quint smirked and shrugged, "You can say that."

The old man nodded, smiling like his grandfather did when he was about to pass on some unsolicited wisdom. "God knows what you need and sends it. But the tricky question is, are you open to receiving it; however, it comes?"

Quint tilted his head to the side. "I guess?"

Leonard smiled, tapping his fingers on the counter. "Have a good day, Quint."

Eyes narrowed; he strode out the door. *I have no idea what he's getting on about. God does what he wants when he wants and I'm too blind to get it.* Setting the crate down by his horse, he gently packed the sack with the goods, careful not to smash anything or to complain. It beat trying to lug a crate back to the ranch on horseback.

Throwing the sack across the front of his horse, he dispersed the weight on either side of the saddle horn. Joey's ears twitched back and forth. He would go back to the ranch and figure out a way to make it up to Lena. There had to be a way to get back into her heart after what he'd done.

Glancing up at the Whitman Hotel, Lena stood outside, beside the carving of a large bear looking anywhere but at him, her face a touch pale. The rosiness in her cheeks more than likely from the tears he caused on her heart.

Quint frowned. *I don't ever wanna see her cry. I'm such a donkey.*

"Hey Quint," Mary said with a smile in her voice, one he was sure he didn't deserve.

Quint jumped, rounding on her. Breathing out relieved, he grinned. Another blond woman was with Mary, looking no more than a kid. Quint nodded to her.

"I'm going in," the woman said softly to Mary, barely acknowledging Quint as she passed by him.

"Be right there," Mary called after her, noticing the intensity on Quint's face.

Quint shuffled his feet. "Mary, I gotta ask you something important."

Mary's eyes furrowed. "Sure. But if it's about Lena, handle your own mess."

"Where's the money in Omaha again?"

Mary put her hands on her hips, "Why?"

"I wanna get it, donate it, with your permission, to women in trouble. Help them get better."

Mary perked a brow. She crossed her arms over her chest, changing her stance to lean back on one leg. Her eyes gazed him up and down like he lost his mind. And surely, he did. For all he'd done over the past day. He was a right horses' ass.

"You need to apologize first before I tell you," Mary snapped. "You only get an instant connotation once in your life."

"Connection," Audrey corrected with a smile, walking up from behind him. "Instant connection, and yes you do."

Quint about leapt out of his skin. He'd known women were sneaky. He witnessed Heidi suggest something for Frank to do, then Frank would do it like it was his bright idea. But the sneaking up on him, was worse, in his mind, than running from Charlie Hilbert. It might just give him a heart attack and put him in an early grave.

Mary pursed her lips. "I thought it sounded a might odd but I didn't know which word."

The hotel owner came around the other side of Joey, moving around to stand beside Mary, tucking Mary's arm in hers. "I tried to catch you before you left," Audrey said. "One can never pass a chance to shop, especially with girlfriends."

Quint felt his cheeks flame. *How many people knew about what I did?* he wondered. *Ross, Eugene, Mary and Ms. Whitman... shit, it's quite a bit.* Quint swallowed, taking a step back toward his horse.

"Excuse me," he said, ducking out.

Leaving Joey hitched to the post outside the mercantile, he took off running for the Whitman Hotel. He strode up the steps, two at a time, ripping open the doors and bursting through. A couple checking in at the front desk gasped at his sudden and abrupt appearance.

Going around the back, he opened Lena's bedroom door without knocking. She sat on her bed, not even looking up at him.

"Mary," Lena breathed. "Leave me be."

Quint quietly shut the door. "I'm not Mary."

Lena jumped, quickly spinning on the bed to further hide her face. "Go away, Quint Morris!" she barked. "You've done enough."

Quint ambled over to her, kneeling down and taking both her hands in his, holding them tightly so she couldn't take them back from him. "I'm sorry." Quint inched closer to her, wanting to touch more than her hands, to wrap her in his arms and console her, but not daring to after the total jerk he'd been. "I am very sorry, Lena. I'm a cactus. And I really like you, but I handled everything so wrong."

Lena sniffed, not meeting his eyes.

Quint rubbed the back of her hands with his thumbs, placing a kiss on the inside of her palm. "You might not believe it, but I'll prove it to you," he vowed, rising to his feet. "I hope you'll be able to forgive me and consider taking me back someday."

Lena sighed, letting her kissed palm lay open on her thigh.

"I'll prove it to you every day, for the rest of my life," Quint said, backing toward the door, not taking his eyes off her.

Upon going out the door, he turned and jogged across the hotel, out and down the steps. Sprinting back to Joey, he gathered the reins in his hands, clambering on. The women were still huddled, chatting outside the mercantile where he'd tied Joey.

"Mary, where is it?" Quint asked.

Joey pranced underneath him, ready to run.

"East outside of Omaha toward the Missouri River. There will be a patch of ash trees surrounded by pin oaks and some other flowerin' ones. Go to the ash with the initials F.M.L. and it will be buried underneath there."

Quint took off down the road. After dropping the supplies off with Frank, he rushed to the train station. He'd a train to catch.

# CHAPTER THIRTEEN

Quint stared out the window. The train rocking back and forth on the tracks, speeding east to Omaha. Each mile he got closer; his nerves became more rattled. Last time he traveled on the train was with Ross to get Mary and he was drunker than a skunk at the time. Before, it was with Del Avilasto, going to St. Louis to speak with Charlie Hilbert and he was drunk then too.

To say he hated trains was an understatement. But he had to do this for Lena. He had to prove to her he loved her more than life itself, that her past didn't matter to him. He was gonna prove it until the day he died; Lena Jenkins previously from New York was the only woman for him.

His mind wandered back to a few hours before. After explaining everything to Frank and Heidi, he took off for the morning train. Whether he had a job to come back to, he didn't rightly know or care. Some other cowhand would be welcome to take his place. Doing this for Lena was the only thing making sense right now.

He felt like a fool of a man it took someone else making him come to his senses. He was so blinded by his own twisted sense of morality; he didn't realize how hypocritical he'd been.

*God knows what you need and sends it. But the tricky question is, are you open to receiving it; however, it comes?* Leonard said to him yesterday afternoon. Leonard was right. God sent him Lena. And being the giant horses' ass he was, he didn't recognize her for what it really was.

*I'm a cactus*, he thought. *I'll prove to Lena, a million times over if I have to, I love her and I'm so sorry. The instant connection Audrey, and Mary*, he chuckled to himself, *mentioned is true. I didn't believe it. Pa spoke of it once before he passed and I was too young to understand what he meant by it. Pa*, he thought, *you were right.*

Running a hand over his face, he sighed deeply, willing his stomach to cease its roiling. His palms sweated profusely. *I can't wait for this to be over*, he thought. This train ride was different. He wasn't drunk. After confessing his sins and receiving Lena's forgiveness after their fancy French supper, and subsequently walking out on her because of his own hypocrisy and stupidity, he swore off alcohol, wanting every moment, there on out with her to be memorable, not tainted by drink because he didn't want to man-up to his emotions. He didn't need it anymore to drown the guilt. He still felt sadness for those he'd wronged, but he'd begun to forgive himself; and with this new determination to win Lena back, he'd begun to forgive his own foolishness toward her. He'd the ability and love to overcome his own idiocy; and now he'd the opportunity to right some of his wrongs, especially toward the woman he loved.

The train began to slow, forcefully at first, shoving him forward. He caught himself, using the window as a brace.

"Omaha, ahead," the conductor yelled, the relief evident on his face and the slow closure of his eyes.

Quint felt the same. *The ride back will be the last of my life*, he swore.

The train lurched to a stop. Steam billowing out all over. Quint waited anxiously for the women and children to alight first. Once the conductor called for the men next, Quint was third in line to get off. Breathing in deep, shaking the jitters out of his hands, he went to the livestock car for Joey.

When Quint made it back there, he sighed. His horse had sunk his haunches back, locking his hooves and legs, refusing to follow the boy out of the car. Quint strode over, taking the reins gently from the kid, tossing him a nickel. His horse was worse than a tantrum throwing five-year-old in a candy shop.

Mounting, he headed to the end of town, toward the Missouri River. The sky grew dark overhead; thunder booming ominously. Quint scowled, urging Joey to trot.

*I hate being soaked through,* he bemoaned. *Once I get the money, I can head back, get on the train and head for home, back to my Lena. Then never leave again.*

Passing the last building, he gave Joey rein, letting him open up to run off the pent-up energy since being on a stuffy train. The horse's powerful legs surged forward, galloping down the road to the Missouri River and hopefully a road leading back to Lena's heart.

---

Lena sighed, sitting on the bed. Quint busted in, apologized, promised something, and left. She didn't have the heart to listen to him or meet his gaze. She didn't trust the way he looked at her. As if he finally realized she was a treasure worth losing.

She was more. She wanted to be desired for being her, not brought out like a trinket and treated well, then stored back on a shelf for a later time. Plus, she couldn't get the look of disgust he gave her out of her mind.

*I'm done with Denver,* she decided. *I'm going to Black Hawk or maybe... I've never seen Texas.*

Rising off the bed, she grabbed her traveling bag she bought years ago and dragged it out from under the bed. Lena stuffed her dresses and trinkets inside until her bag nearly burst at the seams. She stripped the linen off the bed, folding it neatly and setting it in the wooden chair in the corner of her room.

Mary, Natali and more than likely, Audrey all went shopping at Leonard's Mercantile or to browse Mrs. Birch's Mercantile, farther down the road. She would be able to escape unnoticed. She didn't want to say goodbye; it was too final a word and part of her wanted to pretend she'd be coming back.

*I need to stop and get my money out of the bank*, she thought. *I will need to get my own house unless I am able to get board included in my pay.* She sighed, wringing her hands, and finally grabbing her traveling bag to occupy her hands. *Everyone needs a fresh start at some point. Lord knows I need it now.*

Striding to the door, she peeked out. The hotel was tranquil. No footsteps echoed down the staircase.

Going to the left, she peeked around the corner. The front desk was vacant. Bartholomew must be grabbing a snack. Letting out a breath, she quietly jogged to the double doors and small foyer beyond. Making it out the Whitman Hotel, she smiled triumphantly, walking up the road to the bank.

She looked around her anxiously, not wanting to be spotted by anyone, especially Audrey. The woman would guilt trip her into staying, puffing out her bottom lip and making it wiggle while giving the best puppy dog eyes Lena had ever seen.

Lena ran a hand over her face, swiping the stray hairs away. Striding up the walkway, she jogged across the street to the bank, dodging a rolling wagon and three cowboys.

Opening the door, she walked in, nodding to the two shotgun wielding men she passed. Going up to the barred window, she felt her insides jumble. The man sitting behind the window smiled at her.

"What can I do for you, Miss?"

Lena set her traveling bag by her feet. "I would like to make a withdrawal, please."

The man nodded. "How much?"

Lena scowled, tilting her head to the side. "I'm not sure. How much do I have in my account?"

"Name?"

"Lena Nyura Jenkins."

The man rifled through a drawer of papers, making a satisfied sound when finding her account. "You have one thousand, one hundred sixteen dollars and fifty cents."

"I would like to take it all and close my account."

The man blinked. "Are you absolutely certain?"

Lena took a deep breath and nodded. "Yes. I am moving."

The man pulled out an envelope from a drawer then turned and walked toward the back of the bank where two more armed men stood on either side of a large door. The teller undid the lock, the creaking hinges sounding relieved at finally opening. The man strode inside. The faint sound of money being stuffed into the envelope sounded like nails on a chalk tablet to Lena.

Lena shuddered. She regretted this move. Denver was the place she felt most at home. She'd family-like friends here, a good job and a routine she thrived in. But she couldn't stay if Quint was here. She couldn't bear seeing him while her heart broke over and over because of his words and low opinion of women like her. She discreetly wiped her eyes, hoping no one saw the tears gathering before she was able to push them back. The teller came back out, locking the vault behind him. He passed her the envelope through the gap in the barred window.

"Safe travels, Ms. Jenkins. I would stick that at the bottom of your bag for safe keeping."

Lena smiled tersely, clutching the money tightly in her hands.

"Would you like an escort to the train or stagecoach?" the banker asked.

"I would appreciate it," Lena replied.

"Hugh there would be happy to escort you. You have nothing to worry from him. I trust him with my family," the banker pointed to a man at the door. The same man opened the door for her and followed her out.

*Here I go,* she thought. *Goodbye Denver. It was nice while it lasted.*

# CHAPTER FOURTEEN

Quint rode up and down the bank of the Missouri and found no pin oaks, flowering ones, or ash trees as Mary said there would be. He scowled, lips pulling down. He stopped by every tree he saw, walking around it to see if her initials were carved somewhere.

Trotting south along the river bank, he sighed, coming to another copse of trees. He grimaced, seeing the pin oaks but no ash. Quint dismounted anyways, walking around the trees for any signs of Mary's name.

Nothing.

Quint kicked the dirt. Grabbing the reins, he mounted Joey again. The sun was well past being overhead, although the clouds were so thick it could have been much later than he originally thought. Thunder boomed long and loud to his left. Quint grumbled at the first rain drop striking his skin. Going farther south, he stopped at another copse of trees.

*Ash, pin oak,* he thought. *I don't see any flowerin' ones.* He grumbled, rain pelting his entire body now. *Tarnation, this is worse than chasing hogs.* Quint scowled. *Maybe chickens, actually.*

Sighing, he approached the trees. Dismounting with a tired

thud, he trudged along the sopping ground to the copse of trees. Thunder cracked loud, lightning striking into the water about a mile up. Quint shivered.

He walked around the first ash he came to, grimacing at the lack of a carving. He wondered if Mary could even carve her initials into the tree. Quint grimaced, *she's illiterate not an idiot.*

He strode around the second tree and the third, nothing. Wiping a hand over his face out of both frustration and to get the water out of his eyes, he went around the fourth tree. Nothing. Growling, he went around the fifth.

Quint kicked the tree. *Tarnation! I am getting mighty sick of this.* He turned around to stride back to his horse. He stopped mid stride, looking to his right. There, on a wild pear tree, were her initials. Quint ran a hand over his face and laughed almost hysterically.

*I'm gonna teach her about trees,* he thought.

Going back to Joey, he pulled out a small hand shovel. Water continued to douse his body and that of his poor horse. Quint grumbled. Being soaked through irritated him more than bad cooking by a drunk blind woman – which was an experience he swore he'd never repeat.

Digging into the pliable dirt, it didn't take him long to pull up the sack of money, dripping in water. Quint shook his head, filling the three-foot hole back in.

Joey tossed his head, ears back and irritated. Quint didn't blame him. Being out in this storm was bad. Quint tucked it all inside the saddle pack. Before clasping the bags, he opened one of Mary's bags, then opened another and another, seeing sopping wet wads of notes mixed together with coins.

*Lots of money, tucked inside three wet sacks... I hope it dries out,* he thought. Closing the saddle pack, he mounted up. *Back home and back to Lena. I can't wait to see her beautiful face and hazel eyes. Hopefully this makes up for my being a bumbling idiot.*

"So happy we meet again," a redheaded female on horseback stated, pointing a revolver in his face. She pulled the hammer back, inching her horse closer to him. She smiled, holding the barrel on his face. "Quint Morris."

Quint's surprise was barely noticeable. Merely a twitch of his lips. He sighed internally when he responded, "Ma'am."

---

Lena hesitated getting on the stagecoach. She stood, one foot on the stool to get it and the other on the dirt ground. She'd been so determined, but now her second thoughts held her back from taking the final step up. Part of her wanted nothing more than to leave it all behind. She shook her head. She couldn't. Denver was her home, where her self-made family happened to be. All her life, she spent running from her past, herself and every foul memory. Even here in Denver she'd been afraid of her past. But while she hid in Denver, it'd become her home.

For eight years she made a life here, a home. To throw it all away because of one man was ridiculous and stupid. God gave her a backbone for a reason.

*As God says, what is judged against someone shall be returned in equal measure,* she thought. *Scary, but true. I don't need to run and hide. God will sustain me. Even when doing what I did, my faith didn't remain shaken for long. Probably should forgive him too.*

Gathering her bag, she took her foot off the stagecoach and started to turn, giving the driver an apologetic smile.

"Ma'am?" the driver called, "Change your mind?"

Lena nodded. "Yes. I'm sorry."

The driver held up a hand. "I understand. Let me get your money back from the ticket."

Lena waited patiently to the side while the other passengers clambered on board. The team of horses, eight in all, snorted, whinnying shrilly eager to start toward their destination.

The driver handed her back the money she spent on a ticket to Black Hawk. She felt immediate relief when the money touched her palm. Black Hawk wasn't far away, but it was far enough and running just didn't feel right. Her mother taught her better.

Lena thanked him with a smile and a nod of her head, tucking the money inside her dress pocket. Her heart felt lighter. Running hadn't felt as right as she thought it would. It felt... dirty. She wasn't a woman to turn cheek and run when there was a bump.

With a contented sigh, she strode down the sidewalk, walking up two side roads, and up a small hill. She huffed, *almost back to the hotel.* She stopped on the other side of the street in front of the French restaurant. She sighed, clutching her bag tighter. A wan smile, creased her lips. Her shoulders drooped for a moment, staring at her feet. Turning away, she continued down the sidewalk gradually lifting her shoulders, determined not to let Quint's rejection get her down anymore.

*It was a good night,* she thought. *I had a nice time. Even with everything that happened between us afterwards. And I still really like him. He is kind, funny. At least until he found out about my past.* She pushed the thought aside. *Each time he looked at me, it's like I was the only one in the world. He made my heart happy. I might be the dumbest woman on earth for still liking him. But nothing with anyone is ever perfect. Maybe we can still have a chance. Maybe he's willing. Especially after the last visit he made.*

Lena pursed her lips to the side of her face, glancing back over her shoulder to stare at the French restaurant. *Mama said once two imperfect people are made perfect together in love and with God in their hearts. I know what I got in mine. I wonder if Quint has it in his too.* Lena sighed, blowing out a deep breath through her nose. *Only time will tell. I like him... I like him a lot minus the recent bump.* Lena sighed again. *If it's meant to be, it will be.*

Turning back around, she headed straight for the Whitman Hotel. The building rose high into the sky in front of her like a protective father, shielding her from the outside world. Lena climbed up the steps to the Whitman Hotel. Peeking over her right shoulder, she spotted Mary, Natali and Audrey heading in her direction with paper-wrapped packages. Lena grimaced, heading in and praying she hadn't been spotted. Striding inside, she kept her eyes on where she was headed, hoping not to have to answer questions.

She breathed out, relieved she got to her room unhindered. Her blankets were where she left them in the chair where she put them every washday. Everything was the same, like she never tried to leave Colorado.

"Lena!" Audrey called outside her room. The knob on her door turned and Audrey stepped inside without waiting for an answer. She looked around like a deer in a trap, wide-eyed with a hand to her mouth. "Were you... leaving here?"

Tears stung behind her eyes. "I wanted to... I tried; but I couldn't."

Audrey embraced her. Not another word came from her mouth. Lena rested her head on Audrey's shoulder, breathing in deeply.

"I understand," Audrey finally said.

Lena pulled back. "Could you, if you don't mind, hold onto my money?"

Audrey nodded; a small un-Audrey-like smirk graced her lips. *She's picking up more and more from Eugene,* Lena thought, suppressing a giggle at the thought, but giving in to the urge when Audrey said. "So, the next time you try to run away, I won't give you a penny?"

Lena responded when her laughter ended. "Exactly."

She pulled the envelope of money out from her traveling bag, handing it over to her best friend.

Audrey took it. "I will put it back in the bank with your name on it."

Lena nodded with tears once again spilling down her cheeks. "I'm sorry."

Audrey's perfectly shaped brows perked. "For what? For feeling?" Audrey embraced her. "I understand why. Sometimes you feel overwhelmed and crowded, like you're choking on air."

Lena nodded, wiping the tears away. "I was trying to run away from Quint *and* my past – again. At first, I thought leaving would make my heart hurt less and I could start over where no one knew and no one ever had to know. I then realized I shouldn't let it bother me because I am more than my past. My past is a lesson, not a life sentence of misery and shame."

Audrey embraced her again. "You, my best friend, are incredible. I am happy you decided to stay," she said, heading for the door. "I'm going to stroll on over to the bank now and I will let you get settled back in."

Lena watched her stride out the door. She sighed, putting her traveling bag on the floor. Sitting on the bed, she hung her head. Lena wiped a lone tear from her eye.

*Mama didn't raise a coward,* she thought. *I will face whatever comes. And I shouldn't be ashamed of my past. It was a lesson. A temporary blemish on one year of my life not the entirety of it.* She rose to her feet. *No more of this... shit.* She grinned, whipping out the blankets and spreading them back on her bed. *My name is Lena Nyura Jenkins and my darkness is gone.*

# CHAPTER FIFTEEN

Quint scowled, glaring at the woman on horseback. His insides went cold as she stared him dead in the eye. He leaned forward in the saddle. He didn't particularly care for this woman, and what he was afraid would happen next didn't sit well with him.

He ran a hand over his face. *Shit.*

The woman smiled, leaning back on her white mare. "Hand it over."

Quint shook his head. "No. It ain't mine."

The woman scoffed. "It's Florence Miriam Lockburn's. Mary as you know her. She stole it from me and my late husband."

The pieces in Quint's mind clicked. If color could drain from the landscape around him, it did at this moment, highlighting only her. He'd told her to leave Colorado. And he assumed she had, but apparently she hadn't; going so far as to watch and follow him all the way out here. He didn't care to kill a woman. It would be worse on his conscience than his previous misdeeds. Quint sighed angrily through his nostrils. He let her go once. He didn't know if he could do it again... alive anyways.

"Go your own way," he said, turning Joey to the right.

The woman fired a shot in the air. "Not without the money. I know who you are Quint Morris. I can end you faster than a hangman's noose and the law could."

Quint smirked. "I wouldn't. How about I give you half considering your fellows are dead in the ground."

The woman glared, tilting her head to the side. "I want more than half. I want it all."

Quint fiddled with the ties to his saddle packs, reaching for the money, acting like he was fishing it out. The woman withdrew the pistol, releasing the hammer and holding the barrel toward the sky by her ear. He studied her, wondering if there was a slip. He didn't want to kill her, shoot her or do anything to harm the woman. However, she'd caught him like a fish in a bucket, leaving him with either dodging a bullet or something else.

"How do you know my name?" he asked to keep her talking.

He needed a plan. Something to help him get away from her. But if he got away, she would come and find him, Ross and Mary at the Whitman Hotel endangering everyone there, including Lena. Or she would go to the sheriff with her sob story, getting him in trouble with the law.

"Papers," she said, pulling the hammer back again. "Are we gonna do this or are you gonna die?"

"I am not dying today, Mrs. Hilbert."

The woman smiled menacingly. "Hand over the money."

"Half."

"All," she moved her horse closer to him. The barrel fixated on his head. Mrs. Hilbert smiled sweetly like one would to an idiot of a person. "Do I have to make it simpler for you?"

Quint smiled smugly, matching her condescending tone. "Sure. Why don't you do that."

The woman's face changed drastically into the devil incarnate. Her finger hesitated on the trigger. Quint moved Joey around, walking the several paces toward her. They sat on horseback, face to face. Her gun crossed over her chest, still pointed at him in a lazy manner.

Quint moved his hand. The woman jolted, licking her lips and then biting her upper lip.

"I wouldn't," she muttered, her voice hitching.

He glowered at her, staring at the barrel of the gun. Quicker than a flash of lightening, he grabbed for it, turning the gun on her. Her face paled more than a snow-capped mountain. Her white mount tossed his head nervous with the sudden movement.

"My," Quint grinned. "How the tables have turned. Wouldn't you agree?" he said, mocking the pretentious tone she used earlier.

The woman glared daggers. The horse under her shifted its tired stance, ears flicking back and forth irritated. Quint released the hammer on the pistol. Opening the revolver, he took out the four bullets she had. Quint wanted to laugh. Four bullets went by quicker than she would ever anticipate, unless she was some sort of expert shot. If it happened to be the latter, he shouldn't have been able to take the pistol from her.

Quint tucked the bullets into his pocket, handing the empty revolver back to her.

The woman glared. "You'll pay," she seethed.

Quint shook his head. "A woman shouldn't talk like that."

She pulled her fist back, ready to strike. Lashing out, she nearly fell off her horse, riding sidesaddle like a proper lady. Quint caught her fist, rolling his eyes. He didn't have time for this nonsense now. It was sad. Her grief from losing her husband and her twisted sense of revenge made it difficult for her to see reason and move on from the horrible deeds Charlie Hilbert committed. Instead, she went right back into the hellish pit she just got out of. At least he hoped it was her grief and desire for revenge. He couldn't wrap his brain around an evil woman.

Holding her fist, he unbelted the rope on the side of his saddle. He lashed the rope around her hand, pulling it tight around her one wrist. Her eyes went wider than plates at a mercantile store.

"You unhand me!" she seethed.

"You wanted to kill me and tried to swing at me," Quint reminded her. "I ain't letting you go for nothing."

The woman sobbed. "I *need* the money."

Quint took her other hand, lashing that one together. He tied it tight but not enough to be overly painful. Taking the free end, he tied it to his saddle horn.

"Off we go," he stated, clicking his tongue.

Joey began trotting back toward Omaha. Quint let out the breath he was holding harshly through tight lips. His journey was almost over, save for dropping this woman off with the sheriff.

Going back to Lena made his gut swirl. He wondered how she would accept him, the new him. He wanted her forgiveness more than he wanted air in his lungs. Her distraught and broken face haunted him each time he briefly closed his eyes. Even if she never liked him again, wanted to see him or be around him, he wanted to make it right. And he'd try every day for the rest of his life if he needed to. Lena meant the world to him and he stupidly, arrogantly mistreated her and the pain she carried, making it seem insignificant compared to his own.

*I was such an idiot. A fool of a man*, he shook his head. *By all counts I don't deserve her love after what I've done. I just hope... pray, I can get her forgiveness. But even then, I don't deserve it. Lord, I'm so sorry. You set her in my path and I overlooked her. Please... don't take her from me.*

Running a hand over his face, he wiped the now misting droplets of rain off of him. He took off his hat, leaning over and sticking it on Mrs. Hilbert's head. She scowled at his gesture, moving her hands to her head to adjust the hat over her eyes.

"Thanks," she muttered.

"Why do you need the money?" Quint finally asked.

Mrs. Hilbert shrugged. "Start over. I didn't know what Charlie was about when I met him. I was a saloon gal, wanting out of that life. I changed my name to Opal when Charlie and I married. It was only after we got married, I saw who he really was."

Quint nodded, hanging his head. He finally understood what Eugene was saying to him yesterday. It all the more solidified what he wanted to do to help women – women like Lena and Opal. He wanted them to have a voice, a chance at beginning fresh, much like he had at the Rocky Pine Ranch.

The ride was silent. The tracks in the mud leading into town became heavier and more condensed. Quint stopped, dismounting before getting closer to Omaha. Untying the rope from the saddle horn, he held the lead tying her hands in his left hand. He opened the saddle bag, rummaging through until he got to the money. He rubbed the loose money coins and paper stacks in between his fingers.

"Do you know how much Mary took?"

The woman nodded. "Over six thousand."

Quint's eyes widened; he thought it would pop out of their sockets. "Holy Sweet Baby Jesus!"

"Mary couldn't count. She didn't learn," Opal explained, she fidgeted in her seat. "Tell her... tell her, I'm sorry."

Quint nodded, staring at his feet, hands on his hips. "*If* I let you go this time, *with half*, will you go in peace?"

Opal nodded. "You have my word."

"I'm not giving you the bullets back."

Opal smiled. "I know. I want to go north to Minnesota. I will send a telegram when I make it for good faith."

Quint rummaged through the money, digging out a few stacks of money and a handful of money coins. Striding over, he opened the saddle bag on her mount, shoving the money inside. She held her hands to him. Quint eyed her warily, undoing the bonds tying her. He wanted to be done with her for good. Put the finality of everything behind him forever and move forward.

Taking a step back. She leaned down, taking the hat off her head and setting it on his head. "Take care," she said.

Spurring her horse, she took off.

"Your promise!" Quint hollered after her.

Opal slowed her horse. The mare's hooves digging into the soil until the horse squatted back on his haunches. The horse spun in a tight circle like a fancy show horse in a rodeo would. "I will."

Quint remounted with a groaning sigh. *It's all over. Every bit and piece*, he thought, squeezing his legs for Joey to get going. The bustling city came into view and earshot, the hollering from one side of the street to the other was music to Quint's ears. Quint maneuvered to the train station. Another train sleepily docked at the station, allowing fresh passengers to board and start adventures somewhere new.

Quint trotted, making a straight line for the ticket office. *Time to go home to my lady*, he thought. *And I will spend forever showing her how much I love her.*

Joey, ears back whinnied loudly.

Quint glowered at the horse, suspecting he'd read his mind. "I will prove it to her."

# CHAPTER SIXTEEN

Lena cleared the dining room tables, setting it for supper. Natali swept the floor. The aroma of Ada's baking wafted through the room, making her stomach rumble for a tasty treat.

The supper rush would begin in about an hour. She needed to get freshened up a bit and sharpen her pencil for orders. Friday nights were the busiest with the last train coming in a touch late.

Glancing out the window, she frowned. She hadn't seen Quint in days. Her palm still sweetly burned, like a phantom tingle, with his lingering kiss. She closed her hand tightly, wondering where he was. He apologized to her days ago, vowing to her to make it right. Yet he seemed to have up and disappeared.

*If it's meant to be, it will be,* she reminded herself. *I just hope wherever he is, he is all right.*

The sun waned heralding in evening. The lighting outside was rapidly changing, becoming darker with each moment. The door to the diner creaked open. The bell tinkling, announcing the person. Peeking over her shoulder, she was disappointed to see Eugene creeping forward almost on tiptoes, inhaling deeply.

"Is Claudia in there?" he whispered.

Lena grinned and giggled, leaning in to whisper conspiratorially. "Are you wanting me to sneak you a treat again?"

Eugene nodded, pouting his lip. "Please, and don't tell Audrey. She'd make me work extra hard so I'll fit into my wedding pants. No one will notice if they're a tad tight." Eugene winked.

Lena set down the silverware, crossing the room to the kitchen, shaking her head grinning. The man could eat anything and not gain an ounce let alone enough to make his pants tight. She glanced over her shoulder to Natali, who still had the look of a deer caught in a trap. Lena smiled ruefully at the woman. For being at the Whitman Hotel for almost two weeks, the girl was not adjusting too well.

Striding inside the kitchen, Lena sighed at the perfect timing as Claudia nodded to her, heading out back to the break area. Ada scooped cookies on a plate to cool.

"Smells delicious," Lena complimented eyeing the cookies and trying to come up with a plan to swipe a couple.

Ada scooped three on a plate. "I know Eugene is out there," she added giving Lena a pointed look.

Lena pursed her lips. "Yeah," she squeaked, "he is."

Ada rolled her eyes, allowing a grin to grace her lips. "Here. One for each of you. And tell the sneaky man, no more."

Lena chortled, bringing the plate of cookies back out into the dining room. Eugene frowned, hands in his pockets. Lena held the plate out for a cookie.

"Ada knew?" Eugene asked, his shoulders dropping, his face looking like a disappointed little boy, although his eyes still held laughter.

Lena nodded. "Yeah," she replied with a grin, taking her own cookie.

Natali strode over taking the last cookie. Lena smiled at her, trying to offer her some comfort. Natali, so timid, sat in a chair with her head down.

Lena sighed. She knew all too well the overwhelming feelings of running from something, starting over in a new city and hoping – praying – the past wouldn't follow. More often than not it did.

Fortunately for her, her past from New York didn't follow her out here, but it didn't mean it wouldn't. She prayed it didn't.

*But that didn't mean the consequences of the past hadn't reached me,* her mind strayed to Quint. *I greatly regret what I've done,* she thought, savoring her last bite of cookie. *But regret won't ever right the wrongs. I can only go forward with good and humble intentions.*

She peered out the window, wondering if Quint was all right. She missed him. The way he smiled at her, making her heart giddy like a child getting a candy from the mercantile. She missed his easiness, his banter and thoughtfulness. She hadn't known him long. But in the short time, he'd come to mean so much to her. Not exactly sure when he'd become more than just a friendly face, but she suspected right before the French supper date was about when her feelings grew and somehow it all felt right to her. He made sense.

*We're so broken and healed up completely different,* she nodded to herself. *Yet we are so similar. We know each other.*

She exhaled through her nose, taking a seat across from Natali. The young woman glanced up, eyes pinching together but not in an aggressive manner. Eugene took a seat in between them both, savoring every bite of his one allotted cookie.

Lena fumbled with her fingers, being the first to polish off her cookie. Her heart raced in her chest. Everything in her begged her to run out of the dining side door to get a horse and go to Quint.

This urge in her drove her wild. She had to tell him she wasn't mad or angry. What he did was hurtful. It was mean. But he was protecting himself like how she turned him away to protect herself; she knew it. He was too kind for it to really be his honest opinion.

It was ridiculous. Each of them strove to hide from the other yet desired to be with each other. It was like the night chasing the day to be caught in the twilight for a mere moment then go hide away.

"I'm leaving," she said, rising to her feet, her chair screeching back. "I am gonna ride out to Rocky Pine Ranch."

Eugene's brows furrowed. "Why?"

"I have to tell Quint I've forgiven him and... I'm not mad," she admitted. "And... Goodness I'm plum crazy but I love him... We are both so incredibly broken yet totally the same. And he has to know."

Eugene grinned. "Go ahead. I will help Natali take orders. "Bout time I pull my weight around here. Just be sure to tell Audrey. She needs to appreciate me more." Eugene winked, grinning to let the ladies see he was joking.

Lena strode out the main diner door chuckling while dashing down the steps and up the sidewalk toward the Whitman Stables. Stray hairs whipped in her face and she hiked up her skirts, willing her shaky, nervous legs to go faster.

Every part of her being had to find Quint. He had to know she wasn't mad, and know she loved him. Stupid though it was loving someone she'd known barely a month. But as Audrey and Mary attested to, when it was the right man there was no denying it.

Lena trudged her way up the sidewalk, going past the main hotel entrance to the Whitman Hotel. She turned right, walking down the cleared path way to the stables.

"Lena!" Quint hollered.

She stopped dead in her tracks, breathless. Quint rode up to her, his face drawn and eyes sullen. Her heart went to her feet. What was he going to do now? Break her mended and forgiving heart again or make her the happiest woman alive? All the sudden her excitement and resolve fled and she was left doubting herself and Quint.

Lena swallowed. "Quint," she breathed.

He dismounted his horse, leaving it ground tied. Taking off his hat, he approached with his head down; his beautiful brown eyes hidden. All the breath escaped her lungs.

"I need to tell you something," Quint said looking up at her. Lena noticed his dirty, disheveled look and the bruises under his eyes.

Lena swallowed. "I have something to tell you too."

"I am so sorry, Lena," Quint said, voice thick; taking another step closer to her. "I have something I need to tell you."

Lena nodded, allowing him to lead her around the side of the hotel.

Quint's face lit up. He pulled her to the side, hiding behind the corner of the enormous building. Quint dropped Joey's reins again, walking back to the horse and opened his saddle bags. He pulled something out that Lena couldn't quite see and fumbled in his pockets

*What is he up to,* she wondered, watching him with a slight scowl on her face.

He held out a bouquet of daisies. "I want you to have this," he said, holding out his hand.

Lena didn't make a move.

Quint dropped to his knees. What astonished her most, making her breath stop in her chest was the beautiful, ring nestled in the middle of the flowers. Lena looked up to Quint, tears flowing down her cheeks with a question in her eyes.

He sucked in a breath. "Lena, please forgive me. I am a damnable fool. I have made so many mistakes but my worst one was hurting you. Your past doesn't matter to me... I understand if you never want to talk to me, but I hope you will."

Lena still didn't make a move to take the bouquet or the ring. Quint delicately took her hand, pressing the flowers into her hand. He took the ring out, taking her other hand and put cold metal into her palm.

"It was my grandma's wedding ring. My grandpa engraved 'forever' on the band. He used to say souls were bound by God forever, parting this life and into the heavens. I never understood what he meant, until I met you," he sighed, scratching the back of his head. "I was hoping to get the chance to give this to you because your past doesn't matter to me at all. I was horrible and wrong. Just being with you, it's all I want. But I understand if you want nothing to do with me."

Lena reached out, wanting to touch his arm. She hesitated, her hand hovering over his arm. Quint saw her hesitance and took her hand, rubbing his thumb over the back of her knuckles.

"I'm not saying no."

Quint smiled. "I went to Omaha, where Mary buried the money. I want to donate it, to help women dig themselves out a hole and get themselves started in a better life... I'd like to donate it in your name, if it's alright with you."

Lena felt stinging behind her eyes that trickled down to the tip of her nose. A few tears crept out of the corners of her eyes. She nodded rapidly.

"Yes... It's more than fine."

Quint wiped her tears away with a sweep of his thumb, leaving his hand resting on her cheek. "I know I've wronged you. And I will spend the rest of my life making it right. Lena Jenkins, you make me strive to be a good man. A better man. And if I overstep, again I'm sorry, but I want to call on you proper. I want to marry you someday."

Lena couldn't think of words. She wrapped her arm around his neck, burying her face into the collar of his shirt, inhaling his scent of dust and horses. Lena closed her eyes, committing to memory this moment. Quint wrapped his arms around her, holding her close to his body. His head resting on her shoulder next to her neck and inhaled deeply. The sensation sent a rushing warmth through her body.

"I love you," she whispered.

Quint squeezed her tight, kissing the side of her face. "And I love you."

# EPILOGUE

Lena stood in front of the large cabin she and Quint purchased. A bright red ribbon hung across the porch from one beam to another. Their ten-bedroom home came completely furnished by Audrey into a home where women could come and get their life back on track. It was a place to get away from the chaos of the life they'd been forced to live and receive employment by either the Whitman Hotel or another in the town of Denver, Colorado.

A crowd gathered out front of her new home. Audrey, giddily bouncing on her toes standing in front, off to the right-hand side of her on the porch. Peeking to her left, the tall, proud building of the Whitman Hotel stood protectively over the new charge.

Audrey bought the land and the home on it, adding to the home with the funds donated by Quint to help women like her get back on their feet. Lena never felt prouder and more anxious.

"Thank you all for coming," Eugene announced, his voice booming over the gathered crowd. "My wife Audrey and I are pleased to announce the grand opening of Lena's Doves. Here, women will be taught skills, and given employment either at the

Whitman Hotel or our other partners around this wonderful city. I couldn't be prouder of the young woman heading up this new program. Let me introduce you to Audrey's and my good friend, Lena Morris."

Lena took a deep breath, coming forward. A newspaper reporter, eagerly jotting down notes as his keen, story hungry eyes bore into hers. Lena swallowed. She glanced around for her husband Quint, seeing him standing in the back of the crowd with his horse and cowhands behind him. Quint held his hand up to her in a show of support.

Taking a relieved breath, Lena gazed at the crowd. "I was once a soiled woman, believing there was too much darkness in me because of what I'd done for any man, let alone God, to love," she stated, pausing to catch the hitch in her throat. "I was wrong. A man I now call husband, loves me and so does God. I want to help women see there's more to their life than the trouble they found themselves in. I want to help them overcome, to not be ashamed of a choice made out of fearful necessity. My mama once told me mistakes do not make for a life sentenced to live misery and shame. I didn't realize for a long time, until I met my husband, how right she was. The message of Lena's Dove's is simple – love yourself enough to be brave. It takes a lot of courage to change the path you're on. For those in the crowd considering a change, please come speak with me. I would love to help you."

Lena bowed her head and shrank away. Eugene and Audrey stepped forward toward the ribbon. Audrey reached out, pulling Lena along with her. Lena felt her cheeks flame. Eugene held up a pair of scissors, cutting the ribbon to the sanctuary for women as both women sidled up beside him.

A photographer came forward, snapping their picture for the weekly paper. Lena felt her cheeks flame. Quint strode forward from the back of the crowd, taking both of her small hands in his.

"I'm so proud of you," he whispered, putting a kiss on the side of her head.

Lena smiled. "I'm so nervous."

"You're doing great. I gotta get back to Rocky Pine Ranch. I will see you tonight. I love you."

Quint gave her another quick kiss before walking back to his mount. The sight of his retreating form made her gut swirl. The crowd began to dissipate a little but the newspaper reporter remained. Two women from the back, dressed in brightly colored skimpy dresses slowly made their way toward her. One wore a black eye, hiding it under poorly done make-up.

Lena came off the porch going toward the women. Without a word, she wrapped her arms around them, holding them close. The one with the black eye sobbed into her shoulder.

"I understand," Lena whispered. "If you want out, if you want a better life, come with me through the doors."

The woman nodded. "Thank you, Mrs. Morris."

"Lena," she replied.

The woman smiled. "I'm Maisey and this here is Kittie. We *were*," Maisey remarked pointedly, "saloon gals at the Red Tree. We want out."

Lena smiled. "Let's go inside and get you some fresh clothes."

"Do we need to pay for anything?" Kittie asked.

Lena shook her head. "It's all taken care of. And if you want a job, we have open positions at the Whitman Hotel."

Both women looked at each other smiling and nodding. "We would like that," Maisey said with a tear in her eye.

"Then let's go."

Lena stared off to the left where she remembered Quint walking away. He stood there, on horseback watching her, pride swelling his chest. He moved Joey through the crowd, coming to her. Leaning down he kissed her on the lips.

"I couldn't resist," Quint smiled. "I love you, Mrs. Morris."

"I love you too," Lena replied smiling from ear to ear.

"I told you I would try to prove it, every day forever," he cupped her cheek, placing a kiss on her forehead. "I'm proud of you and so happy to have you as my wife. Ladies," he said, tipping his hat to them. "See you tonight at supper."

Kittie leaned over, "Is that your husband?"

Lena nodded. "It is."

"I want that," Maisey added.

Lena turned on her heel, taking both Maisey's hands in her own. "That one is taken." She giggled a little and winked at them both eliciting a giggle from them. "Let's go inside, leave your darkness behind you and start your new journey."

# V

## TO VEIL A FONDNESS

# CHAPTER ONE

Natali ambled down the elevated sidewalk of Kansas City, glancing mindlessly at the shop windows. Everything she wanted, was everything she would never be able to afford. Even a simple calico dress was beyond her meager self-given budget. A beautiful blue taffeta dress caught her eye with neat white French lacing and pearls around the collar. Stopping, Natali gazed at it, fingers fidgeting and twining themselves in the apron at her waist; wondering how it would look on her, how it would fit, and if it would happen to catch the eye of the man she fancied.

Perth Jones was someone she'd had her eye on for a while. It panned out for her well enough that they worked at the same place in town. Perth was the barkeep and she was the kitchen help. Every evening, around nine, they took their meals together with a few other co-workers. Perth could have sat by any number of people, but he made it a point to always sit by her.

Closing her eyes, Natali envisioned herself in the blue dress and Perth asking her to dance. Perth spinning her about the dance floor, his keen blue eyes on hers, as he remarked on how beautiful she looked. From there, her mind took her from a dance to a moonlit walk where, on a bench, Perth proposed.

Someone shoved her forward, shoving her into the glass of the shop. *Not today,* her mind reasoned. Sighing, she walked away. She didn't dare take a glance at her own dress; it was a fright. Patched holes lined the bottom hem and sleeves. Natali touched her hair, making certain her sunlight-blond braids held tight the slippery fine strands.

Working in the hot kitchen made her hair fall out of other hair styles. Braids were the only style that held her hair back off her face through her long shifts. Natali crossed her arms and continued walking. Rounding the corner to the left, she maneuvered her way past the throngs of people getting off the train toward her workplace. The Silver Spoon dining hotel had a line to the door.

*It's going to be a crazy night,* Natali thought begrudgingly.

More than likely, she wouldn't get home until midnight and their supper would get pushed back to eleven. Then after a brisk walk home, she had to hem her Ma's dress; and it couldn't be put off, no matter how tired she happened to be.

Natali clenched her fists. Ever since Ma married Joel Benson, life changed for the worse. Joel stole most of *her* earnings stating a young woman should not have so much because money made young women frivolous and no family member of his was going to be so shallow. Joel took her earnings and claimed to put them toward the homestead, but she never actually saw what good they did their home. Natali, not wanting to make trouble for Ma, handed over some but not all of it. She hid what she could in the ratted hems of her dress. Whether Ma and Joel ever figured it out, they never let on. Natali hoped what she saved would be enough to take her to Colorado, and hopefully with Perth as they both had spoken about getting away. In Colorado, she would have a new life, starting with a new dress.

Natali went around the side to the kitchen area. Opening the door, Natali groaned. Already there was a plethora of dishes to be washed and dried. Grabbing an apron off the peg, she tied it around herself. She walked to the washing tub already filled with hot water and lye.

"I'm so glad you're here!" exclaimed the head cook Marta.

Natali smiled, plunging her hands into the soapy liquid to scrub dishes. The salty woman rarely expressed her gratitude for anyone. She dared not add a comment knowing Marta would spread whatever her reply was quicker than melted butter.

Stacking the clean plates on the drying rack, her body relaxed, relieved to be here working and not at home. Her step-father more than likely was already intoxicated and rambling about something gone wrong. Natali grimaced, setting another dish in the rack.

She lifted her voice just barely enough to be heard over the other kitchen sounds when she asked Marta, "Where's Sally?"

Marta sighed loudly. "Never showed up. That girl knows Thursday nights are the busiest."

Natali kept her mouth shut. Marta loved to go on, gossiping about whomever wasn't doing their job to the fullest, if a person was late or did something wrong. It drove Natali crazy that someone could stir trouble and complain like Marta did. Most of the time, Natali managed to block out her prattle, but every once in a while, it got to her. Natali scrubbed the dishes harder then hung them to dry in a wooden rack above her wash bin.

"Natali," Marta called, "Prep three slices of apple crisps and a slice of peach pie to go out."

Drying her hands, she got down four dessert plates. She made the plates pretty with a sprig of mint from the potted plant growing on the window sill. Satisfied with her artistry, she cut into the apple crisp first.

*Big as a deck of cards*, she thought. Marta would go on for an hour if she got the wrong size.

The door to the back burst open. Natali paused where she was, mouth open when she observed her mother standing on the other side of the now open door. Her mother's lip was split wide, the blood dripping down her chin. A bruise covered her left eye with a goose egg forming on her forehead. Her emerald eyes were glassy with tears wanting to be shed. The relief on her face when she saw Natali was palpable.

"Ma?" Natali whispered.

Her mother sunk to her knees with her back blocking the back door, tears streaming down her discolored face.

Natali didn't know what to think. Out of her interactions with Joel, he didn't seem like the type to strike. When he drank, he was a mean drunk, with words though, never with a fist. He was also a pillager of money, but that abuse was never seen on a body. Despite his mean words and overbearing ways, he worked hard on the farm Ma owned after her no-good Pa passed away. And in all, appeared to be a decent enough fellow more so than Pa ever was. But as she watched her Ma's tears, she realized appearances and impressions were often deceiving.

"Mama?" Natali whispered.

"My heavens, Mrs. Benson," Marta paused her cooking, coming over to Evonne with a stool. "What happened?"

Fresh tears continued to line the edges of her mother's emerald eyes only to spill over her mottled cheeks. "Natali," she said softly, looking around Marta, ignoring her question. "We need to leave Kansas City."

Natali blinked a few times. What she had in her pockets wasn't much. It was enough for her train ticket to Colorado, a few days of food and maybe a room if she found one cheap enough. She had serious doubts it would support them both all the way to Colorado.

Despite her doubts, Natali nodded. She would figure it out. She had to. She would sneak back into the house and check all his hiding spots. Surely Joel hadn't spent all he'd taken from her? She breathed out softly, her resolve firming. It didn't matter. Natali would find a way to provide for them both. Her Ma needed to be safe and away from the monster he'd revealed himself to be.

Natali's stomach churned. The last time she'd seen her mother this way was when her Pa was living. The Good Lord took Pa the following day from a snake bite when she was eight. Now, at nineteen, it felt like she was reliving that day all over again.

Wrapping her arms around her mother, Natali simply held her while she cried blocking everything else out for just a few minutes. Natali sniffed, blinking away the tears from her own eyes. It stung her heart someone, a person who promised to love her mother forever, could do this. Were all men this cruel?

Banging came from the door her mother's back leaned against, rattling the dishes on the shelves. "Evonne!" Joel called. "Come out, let's talk."

Natali grabbed her mother's trembling hand and whispered, "To the back where storage is."

Evonne stood shakily and wobbled to the back of the kitchen area. Once out of sight, Marta opened the door.

She narrowed her eyes at him and demanded, "We are in the middle of dinner service. What do you want?"

Joel stepped in, wringing the brim of his hat in his hands, looking worried and concerned to anyone who didn't know Evonne had rushed in here bruised and battered. "I followed Evonne. Is she here?"

Natali shook her head. His voice was gruff, as it always was, although there was a hint of sorrow behind his words. Didn't matter. Her Ma promised her after Pa died no man would hurt them again. Or Ma for that matter. And he did. Natali had prayed that her mother finally found a love she deserved to have; that this time around, she would be happy. At first, they seemed happy. But the wolf Joel was finally ambled out of the sheep's clothing and it was dark and menacing.

Straightening her back, Natali glared at Joel. "No, she is *not,*" she seethed.

Joel's expression turned dark, his brown eyes radiating hatred, "Watch your tone with me, young lady."

Natali harrumphed. "Be gone from here. We are in the middle of dinner service."

Joel stepped toward her. Marta blocked his path, holding up a thick wooden spatula. Her wispy gray hairs produced a halo around her head. Marta's eyes crinkled, emphasizing lines along the creases as she stared down the angry spouse.

"Look for her elsewhere, *Mr. Benson.*"

Joel glared daggers at each of them. His calloused hand grabbed the door roughly and slammed it behind him. Natali nodded a thanks to Marta but the woman didn't notice as she went back to her tasks.

Natali kept quiet. She'd seen the way her mother looked at Joel and loved him. Her mother made the man her world and the love she received in return was a strike to the face. Natali cringed, feeling icy tickles crawl on her skin. After watching her mother go through violence with Pa and now Joel, Natali decided right there she would never marry. All it led to was heartache; if she were so fortunate heartache was all she would receive. There was no such thing as love, only ownership.

"Three apple crisps and a peach pie, dear," Marta called out.

Natali plated the dessert. "Ready to go."

A serving girl came in, grabbing the plates, taking them out on a tray. The choking sobs of Natali's mother filtered in through the back. The kitchen stayed silent as each worked at their own pace, calling out orders in between cooking and washing dishes. Evonne stayed where she was, sobbing intermittently while apologizing through the storage door to her for failing as a mother. Natali's heart tightened when she heard the repeated apologies. Ma hadn't failed her. The man who promised to love her forever did.

Natali's mind wandered on what to do. After tonight, they had to go home. There was nowhere else to go. And Natali needed to see if she could find the money Joel took. A train wouldn't come into Kansas City or leave until morning anyway. The earliest one would be eight and Joel would be asleep. Perhaps she could time it where they came home after he slept and left before he woke. Could they both escape safely to Colorado? Would Joel follow them?

*And what about Perth?* Natali thought.

She glanced over her shoulder to where Perth would be, her mind's eye seeing past the walls and the staircase to the other side of the Silver Spoon dining hotel. She would make a point to speak with him tonight. No matter what, she felt Colorado calling her. Hopefully Perth would agree, but even if not, she had to make a move for both herself and her mother.

# CHAPTER TWO

The train rocked back and forth. Natali stared mindlessly out the window, trying her best not to think of anything at all. Her head and heart ached too much. Natali lifted a kerchief to her eyes, dabbing at the tears threatening to fall.

Her mother stayed behind in Kansas City. Natali didn't understand it. She got her money back when Joel fell asleep drunk as a skunk. It was then her mother told her she was staying, but urged Natali to go. Natali wanted to argue. Truthfully, she protested a little, but her mother simply smiled then grimaced as her bruises and split lip pulled taut and shook her head. Natali handed her mother a handful of coin dollars, hoping Evonne hid it well enough so Joel couldn't find it.

Natali snorted, *he'll find it, the horrid man.* She dabbed her eyes again, sniffling quietly. *I don't even know where to begin to process it all.* She inhaled slowly, *Oh Mama, I wish you were safe with me. And I could use a hug right now.*

Her mind wandered to Perth. Last night she discovered his feelings for her were not genuine or at least not of a type for a gentleman's courtship. Perth's preferences went against the Bible. It shocked her at first when he broke down in tears, confessing and apologizing for leading her on. It stung her heart. She'd loved Perth. Had been willing to break her vow to herself never to marry because she'd loved him so much. She shook her head. More like she loved the idea of being with him. And she thought, hoped really, his feelings for her were as genuine as hers. Her naïve heart was put into place although Perth had tried to do so gently. The first few hours stung her heart more than she cared to admit. Now, she made her peace with it. Thinking more about it, she saw where she'd turned a blind eye. Every interaction she recalled pointed Perth in this direction. She hadn't seen it because she hadn't wanted to. She looked out the window and resolved to let it all go.

She sighed, *I need to give it all to God. Lay it at His feet for He will sustain me. God, please keep my Mama safe and in your loving hands.*

Feeling a bit more peace about her Mama and Perth, she turned her mind to her trip. Staring at her hands and inspecting her dry skin, Natali realized she hadn't a clue what she would do once getting to Colorado. Procuring a place to stay was at the forefront of her thoughts. She needed a safe place, somewhere sensible to last her awhile financially. Then, she would go about seeking a job where she could respectfully support herself.

Scowling, she stared out the window. The train whistle blew loudly. The city of Denver came into view as they passed around a sloping hill. Nervousness scuttled on her skin like ants.

"Denver, Colorado!" the conductor announced. "Stay seated until the train comes to a complete stop."

She leaned forward in her seat, nervousness and excitement coiling in her gut. When the train stopped, she stood, grabbed her bag with her few possessions and began filing behind the people in front of her.

The crisp, almost autumn air was a pleasant relief as she offboarded the stuffy train. She looked up at the darkening sky, and breathed in deep loving the smell of pine and rain. Colorado prickled her skin with adventure and an energy she hadn't imagined. She felt alive, ready to take on the challenges she knew would come.

Whirling on her heel, Natali ambled up the slight hill, staying on the right-hand side of the road. Natali took in all the new store fronts, her eyes scanning rapidly for any kind of "help wanted" sign. Scowling, she passed many mercantiles, and other stores to no avail. Clutching her small suitcase in front of her, Natali stayed to the right, going up a slight corner bending to the left. Looking to her right a large building with a sign reading 'Whitman Hotel' caught her attention. A carving of a roaring bear stood guardian outside the hotel. No sign of needing help was in the window.

*I better start trying someplace and if not, I can at least get a room here*, she thought. *I wish Mama came with me.*

Sighing and gathering her determination, she went up the steps. Taking a deep breath with her hand on the knob, she yanked the door open. Stunned at the small foyer, she walked in five steps and opened the next door, letting out another breath she forgot she was holding.

A tall, lanky man stood behind the counter. He stood at her approach, fixing his shirt collar and straightening his sleeves.

Clearing his throat and speaking softly, he greeted her, "What can I do for you, Miss?"

Natali stepped forward, biting her lower lip. "I'm looking for employment."

"You will need to speak with Jane McCarthy. In the meantime, can I offer you a room? Basic ones are fifty cents a night."

Natali nodded. "Basic room please. When will I be able to speak with Ms. McCarthy?"

The lanky man pulled out his pocket watch and stated while handing her a room key, "After the supper rush. My name's Bartholomew. Your room is up the staircase to the right. Room number two-hundred one. If you want a bath, it will be twenty cents, and will be outside the door, over there," he pointed, "and to the left."

Natali nodded, handing over some coins. "Thank you, I would like one."

"I'll let the staff know you're coming for a bath. It will be ready in about fifteen minutes."

Bobbing her head, Natali spun on her heel, heading up the

stairs. The soft clicking of her shoes followed her, the only sound she heard in the giant hotel. Hand on the smooth mahogany rail, she cautiously ascended the stairs. The first time on her own, in a new and wondrous place, made her skin crawl with nerves and tingles of excitement.

*I can do this*, she told herself. *Then I will have fantastic stories to write Mama.* Taking a deep breath, she rounded the stairs to the right. A giant painting of who she assumed to be the owner and his wife, hung in the middle of the wall. Natali swallowed at the stern looking man. The soft elegance of his wife brought a smile to her lips. *She seems kind*, she thought.

A dark, brown haired woman came down the steps chatting with a blond woman with a high-necked dress.

"Good evening!" the dark-haired woman exclaimed.

Natali smiled. "Good evening," she replied quietly, dipping her head as she continued to her room.

The dark-haired woman stopped, spinning on her heel. "Just arrive in Colorado?"

Natali paused, close to the top of the stairs. "Yes. I came from Kansas City. If you don't mind me asking, are any places hiring around here?"

The blond woman perked. "Yes, this hotel is hiring for a laundress."

"I can start tonight," Natali said hurriedly.

"What's your name, dear?" the dark-haired woman asked.

Natali dipped into a small curtsy. "Natali Hawkins."

The woman clapped her hands. "Isn't this splendid, Jane?" she asked her blond companion. "Whenever we talk about needing someone, God provides."

Jane's mouth twitched in a small smile. "Agreed."

The dark-haired woman came toward Natali, taking both her hands in hers. "I am the owner, Audrey Whitman. It is a pleasure to meet you Natali, come with me. Employee's sleep down here. Pay is a dollar fifty a week."

Natali followed Audrey and Jane down the stairs. Bartholomew rose politely at their approach, a timid smile on his lips.

"Bart, could you be a dear and refund her monies?" Audrey asked. "She is our new hire for laundry."

Bart nodded, bringing out the monies promptly, handing it to Natali.

"Thank you, Bart," Audrey said chipperly. "Follow me to your room." Audrey paused mid-stride. "Bart, could you send a note to Katie at Madame Comtois' telling her I will be by later for dresses?"

Without looking up, the man behind the counter, promptly scribbled the note on a piece of paper and walked out the door to the hotel. Natali followed the owner who practically jumped out of her own skin with happiness. Audrey walked down the hotel, going around to the left.

"Your room is in here with Eliza," Audrey said. "Go freshen up, and meet me by the front desk when you're readied. I'm going to treat you to a new dress. Don't be alarmed," Audrey continued not bothering to look at her as she walked away, "I do this for all Whitman family. See you in a bit."

Natali stood on the entrance to her room. *Good Graces, this is certainly an interesting day,* she thought, putting a hand on the knob, and entering her room.

# CHAPTER THREE

Rolling up the sleeves on her new dress, Natali dunked her hands under the hot, soapy water. The owner of the hotel insisted upon a new dress for her. The kindly woman bought her a simple green one, and her old threadbare and raggedy dress was thrown into the fire, after she got the money out of the sewn pockets, of course.

Everyone here was more than kind to her. Already she met everyone working in the hotel, by Audrey showing her around. It was different from the polite gruffness of Kansas City. She preferred the people here. Her roommate Eliza was quiet in the evening, preferring the solitude of a book and tea to talking. It didn't bother her. She enjoyed a moment of peace and honestly enjoyed she wasn't wanting to talk all the time. Natali didn't think she had much to say herself.

Glancing up above the washing tub, Eliza came, taking the cleaned linen from her and running it through a press. Natali scrubbed the rest of the linen sheets from room 205. The lye tingled her nose, and made her hands feel itchy and slimy.

"When we get done with laundry, we either go out and tend the garden or help in the kitchen," Eliza stated. "Which one do you want to do?"

"I'll help in the kitchen."

Eliza breathed out relieved. "Thank you. I cannot stand the kitchen. It's too hot and Claudia can be a pain."

Natali smiled. "She is probably no worse than Marta at the Silver Spoon in Kansas City."

Eliza chuckled. "Yeah, maybe."

Natali finished the linen she was working on, handing it over to Eliza. Her friend ran it through the press, taking it promptly inside to dry by the woodstove. Natali brought up the hems of her dress to above her ankles, moving back a touch. Tipping the washing barrel over, all the dirty water rushed past her bare feet.

She watched the water trail down in a zig-zagged path to the rock covered pathway leading from the hotel to the stables. Natali frowned, thinking of her mother hoping she was doing all right. Natali wanted to send her money to take care of herself but she didn't want Joel to take it.

*Mama, I hope you're ok,* she thought.

Natali moved the wash tub back inside the laundry room then dried her hands on a towel. Shucking her shoes back on, she quickly tied up the laces. Heading inside the Whitman Hotel, she made for the kitchen. Humid heat struck her face upon entering. Ada and Claudia slaved over the hot stoves and an oven, pumping out supper orders rapidly.

Claudia banged on the bell, a deep scowl creasing her face. Ada took a towel, dabbing her forehead. Lena came into the kitchen from the dining side, a brow perked and meeting Claudia's annoyed gaze evenly.

*Claudia is almost as bad as Marta,* Natali thought.

"Where's Mary?" the cook boomed at Lena.

"Taking orders. Why?"

Claudia crossed her arms, leaning over the counter scowling even fiercer. "She needs to write it down. She shouts the order and leaves."

Lena sucked in her lip, turning to Natali. "Can you write?"

Natali nodded. "Yes, I can."

"Go get Mary, please."

Natali strode out the door into the almost packed diner. Her heart rate pulsed. *Oh goodness,* she thought. *Tonight, is going to be extremely busy. Poor Mary, the woman is doing her best.*

"Mary," Natali said quietly.

The woman left the table she was at with a wide-eyed gaze and a huff. Natali beckoned her with a nod toward the kitchen. Stepping to the side, she allowed Mary first, regretting the decision almost instantly with Claudia's ill-intended glare at Mary. The ornery old woman went to open her mouth but Lena shut her down instantly with a look she didn't know the kindly woman was capable of.

"Mary," Lena began, "for supper service, we like to write down the orders when the diner gets packed as it is, since there are many plates going out at once. Natali is going to take over for a bit. You'll still get your tips and some of mine."

Mary's face fell. Her eyes bright blue and shining, wavering on unshed tears. The woman nodded. Lena wrapped her arms around her and squeezed slightly. Natali put her hand to her mouth.

*Poor Mary,* she thought. Her insides rumpled together like crumpled paper. Natali grabbed an apron off the peg, sticking a pad and a lead pencil in her pouch.

"I didn't think it would get this busy. I am so sorry Mary," Lena muttered, holding her in a tight embrace.

Mary pulled back. "Not your fault," she said with a drawn smile. "You're always helpin' me and I… appreciate it kindly."

Natali gave Mary a wan smile, heading out into the packed diner. Starting on the left-hand side where she first spotted Mary, she began talking with the diners and taking orders on the pad. She apologized for the confusion and misunderstandings, telling those who were too upset to speak to Jane.

Gulping, she rushed back and forth from dining tables of people back to the kitchen. Claudia's face relaxed making her look less ornery. However, whenever the old crone glanced in Mary's direction, she scowled.

Natali kept her head down, taking out orders to people quickly. This was all new to her. She'd always been in the kitchen and never this side of the dining room as wait staff and she prayed she didn't make any big mistakes.

The busyness of Denver surprised her. Denver itself was smaller than Kansas City and the people seemed less hurried, yet the diner was packed and always seemed busy and there were always people on the streets and in the stores. Natali jumped as the windows shook. Peeking out and into the sky, she grew even more confused. The noise sounded like thunder booming, yet no rain or dark clouds hung in the setting Colorado sky. Glancing down to the steps coming into the diner, hundreds of cattle mooed and jostled, moving through town at a trot.

The bell to the kitchen rang loudly, breaking her away from her awe at the sight of so many animals. Taking more plates out to the diners, the people quieted as they began to shovel food into their faces. Natali's own stomach rumbled and she threw up a quick prayer of thanks for having found the Whitman Hotel. She never got much in the way of food at the Silver Spoon. One meal a day for her since she was trying her best to save her money to get away from Joel. Now, she had two meals a day, eating with her co-workers like a family and it didn't cost her extra.

Diners got up, clinking money down on the tables and leaving. Natali swept the money into her apron pocket while clearing the plates to take to Mary.

"You ok?" Lena asked as Natali turned around with the plates, smiling with rosy cheeks.

Natali nodded, heading back into the kitchen. She grabbed their food and a pitcher of coffee. *I did not think a town like this could be so busy*, she thought.

Taking the last plates of food out, she set it down, promptly filling the diner's cups with coffee. Glancing out the window, she was disappointed to see the cattle long gone. A cowboy twirled in his saddle, scanning the area behind him. Natali spied him curiously, watching his horse's feet dance in the dusty road. The cowboy raised his hand to her, taking off after the last of the cattle. Heat crept to her already rosy cheeks.

Picking up the last of the dirty dishes, she went back to the kitchen, her cheeks flaming from the busyness of the supper rush. Setting the plates by Mary, she went over to a hutch where a cup for each of the kitchen workers sat. She grabbed her cup and brought it to her lips taking a large gulp of tea, ignoring as a little dribbled down her chin. She wiped the excess drink and sweat off her face.

Going back out with a soapy rag, and a bucket of soapy water, she wiped all the tables down. Starting on one side of the room, she worked her way front to back. Lena came out, taking care of the last customer while she went around setting cups and saucers, and silverware wrapped in cloth napkins.

Natali went back into the kitchen, finishing the last of her drink.

Lena came in behind her. "Last one just left."

She met Lena with a smile, fanning her face. "Tables are cleared and set."

Lena nodded, walking up to the hutch to grab the broom.

Claudia waved her hands, "Stop," he said decidedly. "Have a good night. We're done. Mary let those pans alone."

Everyone went silent, relishing the stillness for a moment.

The clink of a plate clattering on another echoed in the small kitchen area. "All right," Mary replied.

"Night," Lena called, promptly exiting the kitchen.

Natali took off her apron, setting all the money down on the counter. Claudia counted it, brusquely explaining the cost of meals. The extra money was made into small change and Claudia handed it to her.

"What's this?" Natali asked.

"Your tip," Claudia replied, her eyebrows raised, and in a tone suggesting her question was stupid.

Natali nodded, taking the money. She remembered some of the ladies from the Silver Spoon Dining Hotel handing her some change here and there for being nice. Natali divvied up her money, making it fair between Claudia, Ada, Mary and herself making sure each woman knew which pile was theirs.

"Have a good night," Natali said, going out the kitchen door to her room.

*I could send this to Mama*, she thought. She grimaced, her face pulling down into a moue. *Joel would steal it. I need to figure out a way to take care of Mama without Joel getting a penny.*

# CHAPTER FOUR

W yatt set the hat back on his auburn head, his hands folding into fists over the reins on his horse. His mount danced excitedly on his hooves, ready to go and keep the cattle moving the last few miles to Elk Creek Ranch outside of Denver. Wyatt and the other hands had ridden hundreds of miles, herding cattle from Hartford City, Indiana to Denver, Colorado. And finally, their journey was almost over.

His horse trotted alongside the cattle, moving them through the sleepy town. A woman in a window, with her face pressed against the glass, stared at him awe struck. Wyatt smirked, raising his hand to her. The woman disappeared back inside what Wyatt saw to be the Whitman Diner.

Wyatt turned back in his saddle, focusing on the cattle. *Pretty woman*, he thought.

The last of the cattle moved past his horse. He followed sending up a shrill whistle and a whoop now and again, encouraging the cattle forward. Wyatt sympathized with the stragglers. The fatigue seeped deep into his bones too, making the last leg to the Elk Creek Ranch a weary one, but the sooner they arrived, the sooner they'd all get to rest. He breathed out a sigh of relief. *Almost there,* he thought.

With a renewed sense of determination, Wyatt spurred his horse into a trot, giving a few enthusiastic "whoop whoops" to get the slow plodders to gain some speed.

*Only a couple miles more, cows. Come on. Let's go!* He laughed at his own thoughts. He was more tired than he realized. Or lonely if he was imagining talking to the cattle like that.

Heading out of the small town of Denver was strange. The city felt like it could be a booming, bustling town, but was sleepy at the moment. Like the week had exhausted the people of the town and they were all tucked in early on a Friday evening instead of just emerging for the night and weekend like he was used to seeing.

Wyatt turned his attention to the lead man, Kain, and scrunched his face as he guided his horse over the train tracks and headed north. The lead man, and also his cousin, had been following a winding path north, but now he was turning slightly east, the way they came.

*Is Kain lost?* he thought. *Or a looney?*

Kain's horse barreled toward him. Wyatt's cousin's mean-tempered mare had its ears back, always looking ready to dump Kain in the dirt. Reining in quick, the horse's haunches dipped toward the ground.

"Wyatt," Kain said, "head back into town to the telegram's office and see if they know where Elk Creek Ranch is."

Wyatt nodded. "You lost, cousin? We're supposed to be heading west not east," he replied, spinning his horse around.

Kain grinned, pushing his hat back off his head to scratch his sweaty head. "No… Just happened to slightly forget what way out of town it happens to be."

Wyatt chortled.

Kain playfully glowered. "Thanks. Appreciate it. I'm gonna take the others and herd the cattle west just outta town. We'll get moving in the morning when we know where exactly this place is. Unless it's close by."

Wyatt's brows furrowed in disappointment at the thought of spending another night on the hard ground, but he shrugged and answered, "Sounds good."

He urged his tired horse on. The animal grumbled underneath him, ears flicking back in protest. Leaning forward, Wyatt patted her neck.

"I know Daisy, I'm tired too," he crooned to his horse.

The horse trotted back toward town, loping at an easy gait. The light from the setting sun set the town aglow. He moved along the side of the train tracks, going back over them as he entered the town. Daisy whickered under him, shaking her head and rattling the bit.

Stopping in front of the telegram office, he saw a scrawny old man exiting the building.

"Closing son, come back tomorrow."

Wyatt shifted in the saddle. "I don't need a telegram, sir. I was hopin' you might know where Elk Creek Ranch is."

The man pushed the spectacles back up on his hawkish nose. "Ah yes, Graham Oliver's ranch. Back that way," he said pointing west, "Take the first trail you come to. Head north for about five miles and the ranch will be on your right."

Wyatt was taken back by the specificness of the old man's directions.

The man smiled when he saw Wyatt's surprise. "Graham is my daughter's husband," he explained. "He's been waiting for you fellas for a bit."

Wyatt nodded. "Yeah, I can imagine. Between the weather, Indians and wolves, it's been a hard drive."

"Yeah, yeah," the old man agreed. "If you hurry now, you'll make it before the moon gets beyond the mountains. Speak with Lewis Custer, he's the head cowhand."

Wyatt waved his thanks, taking off back down the road before the sun set too much farther. Daisy galloped with her ears back, not pleased she was still moving since most nights this time her job was done for the day.

Approaching the herd of cattle, he spotted a new rider amongst the crew. Wyatt drew his pistol, throwing the barrel over to see if all six rounds were loaded. Flicking the barrel back over with his wrist, he gently set it back inside the holster, waiting to see if he'd need it.

Wyatt cautiously approached the group, spying Kain talking to the man, his countenance open and friendly. Wyatt loosened up a touch, trotting Daisy the rest of the way over. The men spun in their saddles, raising their hands in greeting.

"Hey Wyatt," Kain called. "This man is from Elk Creek Ranch."

Wyatt eyed them suspiciously. "Who's the owner?"

"Graham Oliver," the man with a shade of dark hair replied. "We gotta travel this way," he said pointing north, "for about five miles, then the ranch will be on the right-hand side."

Wyatt let out the breath he was holding through his nose. He didn't rightly trust this man. Anyone could give directions to somewhere especially a big ranch in the area. Wyatt went to open his mouth.

The same man spoke before Wyatt was able to "My name is Lewis Custer. Can I get yours before we head back to the ranch?"

Still suspicious, Wyatt glanced over to Kain and gave a slight nod of his head. His friend, and leader, shifted in the saddle, shifting up the worn hat back on his head. Wyatt's horse jostled under him, head hanging low. Subtly, he moved his duster off to the side, hand resting near the pistol at his side. He didn't trust anyone, let alone someone miraculously finding them at the same time he was looking for the place to go.

Ever since Hartford City, he wasn't the same man he'd been a year ago. Life had changed him. Now he was reclusive and alert to the people around him – especially the women. He was wary, constantly leery and on guard of anyone. He didn't want to be hurt again. His late wife took all he had, preferring the saloon and gambling to his company. It ended only when she got herself shot in a back alley for conning a man – and the man hung for it. Leaving the ranch he worked on, and heading out with a cattle drive seemed to be a legitimate idea to escape the sorrows of Indiana.

Settling down here in Denver appeared like the new start his heart told him he needed. As for remarrying, he would never. Not ever after Lydia. To open up again and reap nothing but sorrow and heartbreak was more than he could bear upon his thirty-year-old frame.

Daisy whickered underneath him, tossing her head. Wyatt refocused on the situation around him, still eyeing the newcomer suspiciously.

"I'm Kain Garland," Kain began, then pointing to Wyatt he said, "That's Wyatt Pearson. The other three in our group are Tod Limbo, Chad Brooks and Des Parges."

Lewis nodded. "Let's get movin' the herd then."

"Before we do," Wyatt said. "Why are you by yourself? And if you're gonna try to cross us, I don't have a problem digging a hole."

Lewis grinned, leaning back in the saddle. The whites of his teeth glowing in the setting sun. "I came to town to check and see if a telegram came from you fellas. Last we heard from you was in Omaha."

Wyatt nodded. "It's a little late for checking telegrams."

He didn't care for the man's tone. He's lucky he got any kind of telegram. Herding three hundred head of cattle was a task in and of itself with five men.

"Happens when you work all day preparing for cattle that are two weeks late," Lewis snapped. "Let's get going." Lewis turned, spurring his horse on up the road a way.

Wyatt went to the back of the herd of cattle past the other three hands. His body relaxing the further away from the conversation he got. He didn't want to put someone in the ground but with so much money invested in this herd of cattle, he didn't want to lose it to a lying jackal either.

*Journey's not over yet, Wyatt. Be on your guard.*

The men got the herd moving for the final time; their raucous mooing protests and groans echoing in the oncoming stillness of the evening. The sunset glowed a golden yellow, getting ready to tuck itself into bed. He guessed an hour, maybe a touch less, to get the cattle to Elk Creek Ranch.

Wyatt groaned, hating herding cattle by possible moonlight. He kept his hand on his pistol in case this job didn't pan out like he desired. The group had dealt with enough thieves on his way to Denver. He scanned the horizon looking for trouble as the sun descended to sleep and the dark gray of night slowly peeked out; and found himself hoping to be at Elk Creek soon. He was anxious to be done.

Lewis came from the middle of the herd, trotting over to him. "Hey Wyatt," he shouted.

The cattle filed past as their horses walked side by side.

"Yeah?" Wyatt replied tersely.

Lewis grinned. "I like your frankness, Wyatt. Care to have employment at Elk Creek?"

Wyatt perked a brow. "Pay?"

Lewis shrugged. "Pay is at the end of every month. Twenty-five dollars, room and meals included."

"I accept," Wyatt stated.

Lewis held out his hand. Wyatt leaned over in the saddle and shook it.

"Let's get to headin' home then, huh?" Lewis said grinning, spurring his horse to gallop into the lead again. "Almost there," he called over his shoulder.

Wyatt sighed. *Whatever's at Elk Creek is better than what was left in Indiana*, he thought, peeking over his shoulder in the direction of what he left behind. *Goodbye Lydia. I loved you and tried to give you my best, my all, like a good husband ought to. I'm sorry I wasn't enough of a man for you.*

The cattle lagging behind mooed, not wanting to jog any farther. Hollering and whooping, Wyatt got them going again, catching up to the rest of the herd. They crested a hill where sparse trees lined either side. Stars peppered the sky like someone took sugar and tossed it into the sky. The moon, looking like a giant oatmeal cookie came into the sky glowing their way to the ranch.

A little calf straggled behind, limping on its front leg. Wyatt grimaced, stopping Daisy to dismount.

"Hold on little one," Wyatt crooned to the runt-ish calf.

The calf bleated pathetically, laying down in the dirt road. Wyatt picked it up, tossing him on the front of the saddle. He scratched it behind its ear and the calf nuzzled into his gentle embrace.

"Hey there, little Norman," he said, naming the calf.

Wyatt smiled, for the first time in months. Mounting back in the saddle, he got Daisy moving, bringing up the rear. The cows groaned, jogging and stopping intermittently from exhaustion. Even though they stopped often enough on the way here to allow the cattle to free graze, they were still a touch under the weight they wanted to bring the cattle in at. Wyatt whistled sharply to Kain, announcing the last cow moved under the archway of Elk Creek Ranch.

Wyatt let out a breath. "We're home, Norman," he said to the calf.

The cattle were pushed farther onto the property, through the wide-open gates off to the left side of the house. Wyatt drove the last one through and out the back to graze, shutting the gate behind of him. With an accomplished grin, he patted Daisy on the neck.

"Well done," he said, taking Norman off the saddle.

He carried the calf to the barn, setting him gently in an empty stall.

"What happened to that one?" Lewis asked.

Wyatt shrugged. "Hurt front leg. I think he'll be fine."

Lewis nodded in the lantern light. "Leave him in the stall and put your horse in another one."

A man strode into the barn with a blond-haired, pregnant woman on his arm. The man, over six feet tall, loomed in the barn doorway like a guardian.

"Hello," the woman greeted merrily. "Welcome to Elk Creek Ranch. My name is Nellie Oliver. This is my husband Graham." She looked up at her husband fondly.

Wyatt tipped his hat and dipped his chin, going back to his task of removing the tack from Daisy. The calf bleated at the stall door.

"Come into the ranch house when you're done here," Graham said. "I got your pay along with a hot meal."

Kain came over, petting the calf on the head through the wooden slats in the stall door. "We made it," he said happily. "I told you this would pan out, cousin."

Wyatt shrugged. "It ain't over yet."

# CHAPTER FIVE

Natali got her work in laundry done early. Taking off prior to the dinner rush, she ambled down to the post office, sending her weekly letter to her mother. She missed her and felt guilty she wasn't there for the older woman. However, living in that hellish pit with Joel was more than her heart or brain could handle.

She slipped a few dollar coins inside the letter, hoping her mother would be able to use the money for herself and not have Joel get a hold of it. She had begun to set aside more for her mother, hoping to eventually send her a larger sum instead of the paltry coins here and there. But only if she left the man for good. Joel was worse than a leech.

Natali stepped inside the post office, waiting in line to see Dane. The kindly man took a parcel from a woman, stamping it and putting it in a sack to go out on the next train.

"Natali," Dane greeted, "sending another letter to Kansas City?"

She nodded, handing over money for the cost to send it. "I believe by now she expects my letters."

Dane smiled, taking the letter and putting it in the bag. "I believe so too. Here is mail for the hotel, if you don't mind taking it for me, and a letter for you."

"Thank you, Dane. Have a good day," she said softly.

Heading for the door, she maneuvered past those entering and went outside. Going to the right, she sat on a bench out of everyone's way. She set the Hotel's mail next to her and looked at the letter addressed to her. The dirtied envelope sat in her fingers. Part of her hesitated to open, wondering what she would find from her mother.

Taking a deep breath, she broke the seal.

*Dearest Daughter,*

*I hope this letter finds you well in Denver. After you left, so did Joel. He's gone. I have no idea where he went. I checked saloons and other places he frequented, no one has seen him.*

*I took your position at the Silver Spoon Dining Hotel and sold our land and ranch home to a man from Ohio. Soon enough, I will be coming up to Denver to be with you in about two months. I'm hoping to be there at the end of November before the snow hits hard.*

*I love you very much. You're a stronger woman than I could ever be. I'm proud of you and the woman you are. I know this change for you was a difficult one to make but if anyone can do this, I know you can. You've always been a hard worker, driven, smart and kind. I'm proud God gave me you as a daughter. I love you.*

*Love, Mooomy*

She smiled. Since a child, and knowing her mother's love of cows, she always called her "mooomy". It was endearing her mother still used the silly nickname she gave her. Natali let out the breath she was holding. She didn't want to seem a cruel woman, knowing how her mother loved the man, but she was relieved her mother was free of the attachment.

*I still will never marry*, she thought.

Rising from her seat, she tucked the letter into her deep pockets; holding the letters for Audrey in her hands. Looking both ways, she crossed the busy afternoon street. The whistle of the train announced its impending departure to some other American location.

Natali rushed across the street, heading back into the Whitman Hotel. She thought about taking back the letter she was about to send, but if what her mother said was true, then she would need the extra cash for the train ticket here to Denver in two months.

Natali tucked the stray, wispy hairs behind her ear. Arms crossed over herself, she paused in the middle of the road while a wagon barreled past her, swaying out of the way.

"Ma'am," a man called from horseback too close to her for comfort.

Natali glanced up. "I'm sorry," she said meekly.

He tipped his hat to her, "Allow me."

He dismounted, holding the reins to his mellow animal. His auburn hair and stubbly beard, illuminated by the sun, made his handsome features more prominent. His blue eyes were startling clear and bright under his crop of hair. Offering his arm, she took it, gently and barely touching him. He smirked, taking her to the other side of the road.

"Thank you," Natali said with a dip of her head.

The man tipped his hat. "My pleasure, Miss."

Natali scurried up the slight hill to the Whitman Hotel, taking the steps two at a time while the man tied his horse to the hitching post below. She went inside, setting the mail on the inside counter of the front desk.

"For Audrey," Natali said to Bartholomew as she quickly passed.

Going straight into the kitchen, she got her apron off the peg.

Claudia nodded to her, barking orders, "Check the dining

room for customers, and make sure you have a notepad for orders."

Natali ignored the old woman, thinking how similar to Marta Claudia was. Tying her apron about her waist, she went out into the dining area. Everything was set to proper, with cups and silverware, waiting for patrons to come in and get something to eat.

Natali flipped the sign over and propped open the door. The weather was still nice enough to allow such a luxury. The heat from the kitchen would make the small dining area hot soon enough and she welcomed the cool breeze.

Men, dressed in work clothes, covered in dirt, grime, and manure wandered in, taking a seat and ordering the specials before they even sat down. Couples fresh off the afternoon train wandered in, hungry for dinner.

The same man who helped her across the road sat down on the left-hand side of the diner. Natali strode over, offering a kindly dip of her head.

"Coffee and the special," he said.

Natali felt her mouth become cotton. His rich, baritone voice made her tingle all over. She scurried off to the kitchen to place the man's order and made sure not to forget the one's before his as well. She swallowed, letting a deep breath out her nose. She went back out with a pot of coffee and pitcher of tea, filling cups and bustling around trying to keep herself distracted. Lena was nowhere to be found which bothered her.

Filling a cup after her first complete round of the dining room, she peeked over her shoulder, spying Lena's happy face, taking an order on the right side of the diner. Lena's cheeks were rosy and her face was slightly flushed. Natali's eyes narrowed but the woman offered her perkiest smiles.

"Ma'am," the auburn-haired man called, his voice making her shiver. "Can I get a fill?"

Natali strolled over to him, filling his cup for the third time. "Should I leave the pot?" she asked in a teasing tone.

Natali immediately felt her face flush. He smiled at her,

bringing the heat crawling to her cheeks even faster. She cleared her throat, setting the coffee pot down on the edge of the table.

He rose from his seat, taking his hat off and sticking it on the ear of the chair. Holding out his hand to her, Natali stared at it a moment. Timidly, she took his hand and shook it.

"Natali," she said, blushing.

"Wyatt Pearson," he replied.

The bell to the kitchen dinged mercilessly. "I… I better go grab your food," she stammered breathlessly.

Putting a hand to the back of her head to check her hair, scurrying off and letting out puff of air to push her stray hairs off her face. The man was handsome with his dark rust colored hair and dark blue eyes. She shook her head, clearing it from the fuzz Wyatt put in it.

*No men,* she thought. *I don't want to end up like my Mama. I won't allow myself to swoon, or fall in love, or anything that will allow my heart to be broken. I watched my Mama get hurt too many times. Not for me. Not ever.*

Claudia glared at her upon entering the kitchen. "The bell rings, you come," Claudia barked. "First set of meals are ready."

Lena rushed to her side, hands on her hips and glaring at the crotchety old woman. "It's busy out there. It's busy in here. Stop it."

Claudia mumbled under her breath, setting the dished plates down on the serving table with a harrumph. Natali was surprised nothing bounced off the plates.

Natali stacked the dishes in her arms, taking the meals backward out the door. She served the first set of diners, finally stopping in front of Wyatt last. He moved his coffee and his paper. Gently she set the plate down and walked away.

Before she'd gotten two steps, Wyatt called, "Natali?"

Spinning on her heel, she went toward him, hands clasped in front of her. "Yes? What can I get for you?"

"Thank you," he said, turning back to his meal.

Natali blushed, "You're welcome."

She closed her eyes, heading back to the kitchen for more plates. *No, Natali, no,* she thought.

# CHAPTER SIX

Wyatt hardly chewed the food served to him by the beautiful blond haired, emerald eyed young woman. When he thanked her for the meal, the woman swallowed, hoping to be out of there before he asked her if he could come back or worse – out to supper.

When she went back into the kitchen for, he assumed, more plates loaded with food, he paid; leaving money on the table and dipping out before he could say something else.

Another woman was not what he needed, not now, not ever. Lydia had been enough for him. He already gave one woman his heart and he dared not do it again. Lydia ripped it out, shattering every hope he had at a loving marriage and life. Her true nature came roaring out worse than a tornado not long after he said 'I do' – vindictive, abusive and hateful. He'd never seen a woman more spiteful than her and he feared to try again because Lydia had been sweet until she'd signed the paperwork and made the marriage official. What if Natali, or any woman, was the same?

Wyatt spent hours after her death trying to discover the reasons to her behavior. He'd wondered if it was him or her secrets coming to light. He'd been dutiful and doted upon her when he could. She never went without and wanted for naught. Yet, he caught her in bed with someone else.

*And I had to hear of her death from the man she slept with instead of the sheriff,* he groused to himself, recalling the man speaking indifferently of his late wife.

He ran a hand over his face, pushing the past and Lydia from his mind. Wyatt sighed. *I got burned badly by Lydia, opening my heart and loving her. I care not to have it happen again,* he thought, striding down the steps of the Whitman Diner. Peeking over his shoulder, he caught a glimpse of blond hair through the window. He shook his head at himself. *No. Not ever again. I don't want to be tied to another failed marriage to a beautiful woman who never really wanted me.*

He jogged across the street to the bank, going inside. Two guards armed with pistols and a rifle stood on either side of the door while two others stood by the safe in the back. Wyatt nodded, approving the security of the bank. He opened the account he wanted, putting all his money inside the black metal container. He'd already counted the money and knew he'd quite a bit. Totaling the chunk he got from selling his home and ranch in Indiana and his cut of the cattle drive, he'd enough to buy a place here in Denver and settle down again, if he chose.

Striding out of the bank, he jogged back across the street. Daisy remained hitched to the post he'd tied her to. Wyatt caught himself looking up in the window of the dining hotel for Natali. He spied her blond hair and her shy smile. Wyatt immediately looked away, focusing on his feet until he reached Daisy.

Daisy whickered where she stood, shifting from hoof to hoof. He patted her on the neck. Gathering the reins in his hands, he walked down the road to the mercantile for some necessities. After spending months in the same clothes, he needed new shirts, pants, socks and boots.

"Wyatt," Kain called over his shoulder.

Wyatt paused on the side of the street, waiting for his cousin and former cattle drive boss to catch up. Kain approached, his hand out. Wyatt shook it with a tight-lipped smile knowing this was farewell.

"Me and the boys are hopping a train back to Indiana," Kain said. "Are you coming?"

Wyatt shook his head, "No. I'm staying here."

"Did you tell the family?"

"Yeah. Left'em each a letter," he breathed out. "I can't go back. Not yet."

"Lydia?" Kain asked.

Wyatt nodded. "Yeah… Lydia."

Kain regarded him sympathetically, pulling him into an embrace. "She wasn't good for you or to you. Time to put the woman behind you. Nothin' good will come from dwelling on her."

Wyatt shook Kain's hand again. Not replying as there wasn't anything that hadn't been said already and not wanting to restart old arguments. He'd heard it all from Kain and his uncle, both warning him Lydia seemed like an off woman. He hadn't listened, loving her anyways simply because he couldn't help it.

"I'll miss you," Wyatt said, foregoing another handshake and embracing Kain.

Kain wrapped him in a bear hug, lifting him off the ground. "Be sure to write. You get hired on at Elk Creek?"

Wyatt nodded. "Yeah. Getting some new clothes then headed there."

"I kinda like it here," Kain said, gazing around. "I think I'll get everyone to move out here."

Wyatt scoffed at the proclamation. Getting his mother to move would be similar to getting a block of cheese from a radish. His father and baby sister would be easy to convince. He smiled at the thought of them. Leaving his family behind for the new start here in Denver was going to be challenging.

The train whistle blew, sonorous in the background. Black smoke plumed from the stack. Ladies in parasols boarded first being helped by the conductor. Men waited by the livestock cars to board their horses.

"I'd best be off," Kain replied. "Take care, Wyatt. I'll be seein' ya."

Wyatt embraced his cousin a final time. "Take care. Send word when you make it home."

"Sure thing, Granny," he said with a grin.

He snorted, shaking his head. *The man's daft*, he thought.

Wyatt continued down the road to the mercantile. He hitched Daisy outside, ambling in past the other patrons more focused on shopping for their necessities than he happened to be. He picked out a few different colored shirts, opting for the reds and brown colors that hid dirt best. He picked a blue shirt for nicer occasions like church.

Lugging all his selected clothing and pants up to the front counter, he inquired about boots. Surprisingly, the store carried the Wellingtons he liked. Incredibly pleased, he paid for his purchases.

"Evening Leonard," Natali called from the door as she entered. "Claudia is in dire need of sugar, eggs, and flour... again."

Natali's stunning face was all red with a wispy, blond, stray hair sticking to her forehead. Her dark emerald eyes focused on the old clerk as he came around to help her.

"Put it on the Whitman tab, Ms. Hawkins?" the mercantile owner asked. "Clyde will bring it up."

"Please," Natali said, rushing back to the door. "Thank you, Leonard. Audrey said she will be down to pay the tab tomorrow," her face turned more crimson as she spotted him before she pushed through the door, "Hello again, Wyatt," she said softly, promptly heading back through the door and up the slight hill toward the hotel.

Wyatt gathered his items, taking them outside to his waiting horse. Daisy whickered at his approach, ears forward and tail whooshing. He stuffed it all inside his saddle bags, occasionally glancing up the hill to where Natali disappeared.

He grimaced, not liking the fact he was purposefully looking for her. *I don't need or want or desire another attachment, marriage or otherwise*, he decided. *Not another failed marriage for me. I'm good and done.*

Unfettering the reins, he gathered them all in his left hand and mounted in one fell swoop.

"Let's get heading back to Elk Creek," Wyatt told Daisy.

Daisy shook her head, her brown mane whipping back and forth. She turned heading down toward the tracks. The train whistled, pulling out of the station. He watched it lug forward, the grinding metal on the tracks creaking forward to head north toward Omaha. His cousin would have to cross the Mississippi on a ferry.

Wyatt felt his body chill. He hated crossing the Mississippi. It was one of the reasons he cared not to go back. There were passable areas to cross with a herd of cattle but he didn't like doing it nor would he ever again.

Clucking his tongue, he pushed those thoughts from his mind and headed down the road to cross the tracks. He could feel his anticipation mounting. Tomorrow was his first full day at Elk Creek.

# CHAPTER SEVEN

The satisfying pop of wood breaking apart brought a smug twitch to his lips. He got back from town to begin splitting the cut wood for this winter's heat. Two of the other cow hands cut the rounds while he split and stacked them.

Daisy grazed out in the horse pasture with the others, although every time he checked she was near the fence line and him. Wyatt peeked over his shoulder again, keeping an eye on Daisy. His mare rested her head on the fence post, blowing her lips like a sulking dog.

Wyatt shook his head, bringing the ax down on another chunk of wood much too big for the stove.

"I've never seen a horse look bored," a cowhand named Samuel said.

Wyatt smirked. "She does that. I'm not sure why."

Samuel chortled. "It's a woman thing."

Samuel and the other man, Avery laughed. Wyatt smiled, not truly caring for the comment made. Men were just as indecisive and bored-looking as women, human or horse. Wyatt swung the ax back around, making another large chunk pop, exposing the yellow sap inside the wood.

The other horses in the pasture whinnied, facing the long dirt road leading up the ranch house. Daisy looked over, ears back and unamused, staying where she was. Wyatt did too, splitting the other chunks Avery and Samuel cut down to size for him.

A buggy came up the drive, parking in front of the homestead. A brown-haired woman exited first, followed by Natali. Wyatt's eyes widened and he swallowed. He turned his back, hefting another round onto the splitting area.

He heard the overly vivacious, happy, and smiling rancher's wife, Nellie, screech from the doorway, greeting Natali and the brown-haired woman. Wyatt shook his head.

*I could never have a wife that... friendly. Well I could tolerate it a bit, but definitely not every day*, he thought. *But that won't be an issue cuz I'm never marrying again.*

"That's probably why Graham is so quiet," Avery's nasally voice said after the women went inside. "Nellie does all the talking."

"Yup," Graham's amused baritone response added.

Wyatt smirked at Avery stiffening, waiting for the bear of a man to comment further. It didn't come. Wyatt swung the ax, splitting the wood down into more manageable pieces.

"Any pieces good for kindling?" Graham asked, picking up an ax.

Wyatt pointed with a nod of his head, "Those pieces on top have good sap to them."

Behind Graham the saw blade hissed through the wood. The timber cracked as the last round piece fell to the ground. Samuel and Avery sighed with relief.

"Samuel," Graham ordered, "Go help Lewis and Parker in the pasture to make the corral for the calves. Avery, finish splitting the wood then stack it. Wyatt come with me."

Wyatt slammed the ax into the wood, walking away to leave Avery to finish the giant stack. Graham led him through the barn and out the back into the cow pasture.

The new cattle brought in yesterday munched on grass, tails swishing the air and Wyatt heard contented moos breaking the quiet surrounding them.

Graham sighed, a contended grin on his face. "We are going to brand cattle tomorrow. Lewis and Parker have been putting together the holding fence for the calves. We are gonna sell them next week."

Wyatt nodded. "All right."

"I'm going to be honest with you," Graham said turning to face him. "I don't have money to pay you right yet. I spent it all on the herd."

Wyatt held up his hand. "A place to sleep and food for me and Daisy is good enough for me at the moment."

Graham raked his fingers through his bright red hair. "I'll pay you, just might be a bit."

"Not worried about it," Wyatt repeated, proffering his hand to his boss. "Like I said, I'm content with what you're offering me, but I'm keeping the calf in the barn."

Graham smiled. "Deal."

The sun waned more over to the west, casting a sleepy shadow on the land. Wyatt strode away from Graham, heading out into the pasture to help the other men building the corral for the calves off the main fence line.

After a little while, the back door to the ranch house opened. The women exited in a chattering bunch, sitting on the back-porch bench, drinking out of small tea cups. Wyatt's eyes landed on Natali who sat herself on the very edge of the bench, away from Nellie and the brown-haired woman.

Natali fidgeted in her seat, hunching down a bit and sipping her tea to keep from conversing. The women's raucous laughter echoed over the stillness of the valley they were in. Wyatt shook his head, clearing it of the blond woman sitting with the women but by herself. He turned his attention back to the task at hand, mentally shaking Natali from his thoughts.

He held up another board for Lewis to nail in. The small corral was coming together smoothly. After about three quarters of the corral was done, Samuel and Parker rode their horses through the herd figuring which ones to sell next week and which cows to brand to keep, breed and further the Elk Creek line.

Glancing up after putting another board in place, he noticed Natali sat farther away from the other chatting women, looking off into different directions. Getting up, she strode out to the main boarded fence line, putting her hands on the wood and watched him and Lewis.

Wyatt held the board in place while Lewis put a nail into it, ignoring her watching them.

"Who is the brown-haired woman?" Wyatt asked softly.

Lewis glanced up, his eyes narrowing, "That would be Audrey Whitman, owner of the hotel in town. She is gonna marry a detective from Philly this fall"

Wyatt nodded, grabbing another board.

Lewis shook his head. "This should be enough for the calves. There aren't many and most of the heifers look pregnant."

The sun cast a glow over the land, erupting the sky in a light pastel pink and orange. Samuel and Parker were still out with the herd, counting and recounting the cattle. Wyatt picked up the supplies, taking what he could carry back to the barn. Graham came into the pasture, helping to carry the remaining wood.

Wyatt's eyes narrowed slightly. He wasn't sure about his boss. One moment he was aloof and distant. The next he was helpful and passably friendly. He wouldn't complain though, he had a roof over his head, food and a job.

Natali stayed on the fence, watching the herd and the men working, her blond hair shining like a lantern in the fading sunlight. The other two women joined her on the fence – watching, laughing, and pointing.

Wyatt tipped his hat to them. Nellie waved, nudging Audrey who nudged Natali with a smile. Wyatt's cheeks heated with the unwanted attention.

He gathered material in his arms, heading toward the barn. If the women were going to stay for supper, he was going to stay in the barn. He didn't want his eyes forcing his heart to become attached to something he didn't want to have.

"Wyatt," Graham called. "Ready your horse. You're taking the women back to town."

Wyatt nodded, setting the tools in the tack room. "Sure thing, boss."

*This is going to be a long night,* he thought.

# CHAPTER EIGHT

Natali didn't want to join Audrey on an excursion to the homestead of someone she didn't know. But seeing how Audrey was her boss, she felt like she couldn't refuse. Not only that, but Ada handed her a giant basket of cookies to take out to Audrey to give to Nellie Oliver. Apparently, Nellie was in the final stages of pregnancy and loved Ada's molasses cookies.

Audrey practically dragged her down the front steps of the Whitman Hotel where a buggy and horses were waiting outside for them. Natali boarded the buggy holding onto the basket while Audrey slapped the reins on the horses back. The lively woman spoke the entire time. The smile on her face never faltering for even a second.

Natali clutched the cookies, hoping that looking out the side of the buggy was enough to tell Audrey she wasn't interested in listening. It didn't work. Audrey spoke, eyes fixed the entire time on the road and horses, chatting up a storm about how much she was going to just love Nellie Oliver.

*Oh, my goodness,* Natali thought resting her head on the basket's handle, *my ears are going to hurt and be sore tomorrow.*

At a lively pace, the road to Elk Creek Ranch took no time at all. They turned to the right, heading down the drive. The beautiful ranch home was directly in front with the barn off to the left-hand side. A roughhewn fence with barbed wire contained horses on the left-hand side. A few bulls grazed on the right-hand side going up the drive.

Natali glanced over to the left where the thunking of wood being split echoed in the air. Her cheeks flamed, spying Wyatt. Her eyes immediately focused on him and his strong arms, bringing the ax down on the wood being split. She swallowed.

*I didn't know he worked here*, she thought, breathing sharply. *Oh, my goodness. I don't want this. I don't want to be here.*

Audrey slammed the brake on the buggy. The front door opened revealing the blond hair of Nellie Oliver and her growing, round belly. Natali swallowed, clambering down out of the buggy. Promptly she handed the basket of cookies to Audrey.

Her boss ran up the steps to Nellie, wrapping the woman in a tight embrace. It seemed Audrey Whitman had friends all over the place. Natali stood awkwardly by the buggy. She glanced over her shoulder, spying Wyatt peeking over at her. She swallowed looking away for a moment.

She swore she could see the deep blue of his eyes and the dark auburn of his hair in the afternoon sunlight. Two men were by the barn, cutting rounds of wood while Wyatt split it.

*No Natali. You don't need any attachments. You don't want to end up like your mother – abused and alone, fighting to provide for yourself.* She took a deep breath, staring at her booted feet. *I don't want my life to end up like that.*

Peeking up, Audrey and Nellie paused, smiling at her.

"Come, come inside," Nellie beckoned. "I will put some tea on and we can munch on some cookies. Thank you so much for bringing them."

"Our pleasure," Audrey replied happily, following Nellie inside the home.

Natali swallowed, following the women inside. *At least it blocks my view of Wyatt*, she thought. *I have never met a man who'd affected me so much in one day, that I wouldn't mind avoiding for years.*

Natali sat on a wooden chair at the dining table at the end while Audrey and Nellie sat across from each other engrossed in conversation from the get go. Both women spoke at almost the same time. It made her head spin. How they each understood what the other was saying was beyond her. It sounded like the constant droning hum of crickets.

She sat in her seat, staring at her hands. The lazy movement of cattle caught her eye and she found herself staring out the window at them. The entire herd from the day before, she was certain, was in the pasture. Nellie mentioned cattle arriving late yesterday evening. Natali was certain these were them.

She spied Wyatt and a few other men moving on to the pasture. Boards of wood were lain out in the grass waiting to be nailed together. Brows furrowed; her head tilted to the side.

"Corral for the calves," Nellie said, groaning as she got out of her chair. "I'm ready for this baby to come. I'm getting huge and awkward." Nellie went to the stove, pouring water from a bucket into a kettle. "I forgot to put the tea on," she sighed, shaking her head. "I've been so forgetful lately."

"A baby is tiring on the body," Natali commented.

"Indeed," Nellie agreed, going off on a tangent regarding babies and being tired to Audrey.

Natali let out a breath, thankful to be out of the conversation loop for a bit longer. The tea kettle whistled, this time and Audrey stood up to handle the affair. Nellie expressed her gratitude, hiking her dress up to show off her swollen ankles. Natali opted to stare out the window at the men.

"Let's watch from outside," Nellie said, winking at her. "Lots cooler out there."

Natali's cheeks flamed. "Sounds delightful," she replied softly.

Audrey handed her a teacup and saucer with cookies on the side. Audrey carried a cup for Nellie as the pregnant woman waddled her way outside. Natali took a seat on the very end of the bench, watching the men put a corral together.

Wyatt's auburn hair glowed in the fading sunlight. Natali loved evenings such as these where the sunset lingered until the very last moment. Where the sky faded gradually leaving behind soft oranges and pinks.

Natali finished her tea and cookies, thanking Nellie for her graciousness and hospitality. She excused herself to get a closer look to what the men were doing. Off the main fence line by fifty feet, she watched Wyatt holding up boards for another man while the board was nailed and set. The corral was small, perfectly so for the calves.

*I wonder how they are going to separate the calves from their mothers,* she thought.

Natali rested her arms on the wood boarded fence, careful of the barbed wire running along the top, and laid her head on her arms. It was interesting watching the men put together something so quickly and efficiently. Two men on horseback rode into the herd, parting cattle as they went, fingers dabbing in the air as they ticked off how many were there.

Audrey and Nellie joined her on the fence. Nellie talking about the man they hired along with Wyatt, her thoughts about the herd and just endless chatter.

*I hope Audrey is quiet on the way home,* she thought. *I couldn't handle a man who spoke incessantly about anything. I can't handle a man at all.* She shuddered. *I don't want to be like my Mama.*

Natali felt her heart stop with the thought, getting swallowed up by her body. It felt like her heart wasn't there anymore, she was only existing, taking up air and space.

*I don't want to be alone forever though,* she rationalized. *But I'm also scared of having a failed marriage like my mother. I want mine to work, to last into old age where we both sit on the porch and watch the day go by.* She took a deep breath, letting it out through her nose.

Wyatt raised a hand to her. A blush snuck across her cheeks. She felt her arm be nudged by Audrey. Immediately her cheeks flamed hotter. She watched Wyatt pick up materials and take them back to the barn for the evening. The sun went lower still, casting its final glows on the land before the gray of night rose into the heavens to take over.

A tall, burly man, strode over, greeting Nellie with a kiss on her cheek.

"Ladies," he said, nodding to them. "Wyatt is going to escort you home when you're ready."

"Thank you kindly, Graham," Audrey said exuberantly. "We should be getting back. I'm sure Eugene will have a posse sent after me if I stay a moment longer."

Nellie chortled. "Thank you for coming and for the cookies my dear friend. I hope to see you soon."

"You must come over for tea after church this Sunday," Audrey encouraged excitedly.

Graham gave a tight-lipped smile to Audrey. Natali looked away, pressing the back of her hand to her mouth hiding a grin. *Dreading the talking already*, Natali mused.

Audrey quickly added, "Eugene will be there. He has been wanting to purchase a cow but needs expert advice."

Graham almost seemed relieved. "I'd be happy to speak with Eugene."

"Splendid," Audrey replied, clapping her hands together. "See you soon enough. Take care my dear," Audrey embraced Nellie, squealing like a toddler receiving a treat of licorice.

"Thank you for your graciousness," Natali added softly.

"Anytime," Nellie said, turning toward the house. "Thanks again."

"Bye my dear," Audrey called over her shoulder.

Natali was already ahead of Audrey walking to the buggy where the horses stayed hitched. Their visit wasn't but a couple hours at most but it was long enough for her. Natali breathed out relieved to be heading back. She hoped Lena was able to manage without her since the supper rush started a while ago. Hopefully it was nothing much. Otherwise poor Mary would have to take over her spot for a while.

She clambered into the buggy sitting in her same spot.

"You drive," Audrey said.

Natali swallowed, taking the reins to the horses. She'd not done this more than a couple times at home. Joel always drove the wagon.

Wyatt strode over, his horse's reins in his hands. "Ladies," he said. "I'm here to escort you back."

"Splendid," Audrey replied.

Natali swallowed.

# CHAPTER NINE

The silence lasted all but a few minutes, at least while Natali got the horses turned around and heading back toward the road. Then Audrey started talking. Wyatt rode on her side of the buggy. Natali felt her skin crawl, catching herself peeking over the side to his dark blue eyes occasionally meeting hers; and strong, stubbled jaw. Natali swallowed. Wyatt was a handsome man – tall, muscles built by hard work, and kissed by the sun.

Natali blinked, focusing on the road and not the person, either one, beside her. Audrey peppered Wyatt with basic questions – where he's from and family – which he politely answered or changed the subject to something trivial.

She fidgeted in her seat, wondering how long it would take to get back to the Whitman Hotel. His presence made her skin crawl, tingling like a bug on her skin. Combined, his presence and Audrey's incessant talking, and she was right uncomfortable. Natali scowled, her eyes adjusting to the low lighting as the moon came out to slightly light their way home.

She hated the dark. It scared her; not because of the creatures or creepy crawlies, but because both her dad and step dad would bellow in the night, throw things or strike her mother. Both her father and Joel would come into where she slept, waking her with a kick, shove or crashing items and holler for her to leave the house for the night. Her father had also been known for striking her when she'd come to her mother's aid. Nighttime brought out the human monsters and it scared her.

Natali swallowed; slapping the reins on the animals backs lightly in hopes of making their journey go a tad quicker. Audrey was silent a moment, sighing contentedly. It was a brief moment the vivacious woman was splendidly quiet.

"So where are you from?" Wyatt asked, scooting his animal closer to the buggy.

Natali shook her head free of her previous thoughts. "Oh... Kansas City. I've lived there all my life."

Wyatt nodded. "Got any family?

Natali swallowed. "My mother. I miss her."

Her brows furrowed. She wriggled in her seat again. She turned the horses around a corner to avoid a copse of trees.

"What made you come to Denver?"

Natali bit her bottom lip. "A fresh start. I needed out of there," she paused, looking at him.

The moonlight illuminated his stubbled face, bringing out his rugged jawline and the outline of his muscles though his dark blue shirt. His eyes shone under the light and his dusty hat.

Wyatt leaned forward in the saddle. "Bad memories?" he finally asked.

"Yes," she whispered.

She glanced to her right, spying Audrey with her eyes closed. Natali eyes widened, shocked someone would be able to sleep so peacefully on the way home on such an uneven road.

"And you?" she asked. "What made you come here?"

Wyatt breathed out heavily, his head hanging. "The same reason you're here."

The light of town poked into view. Natali inhaled sharply, hoping her relieved expression went unnoticed by Wyatt. The buggy descended the hill and rolled into town. The buggy jostled over the train tracks, forcing Audrey from slumber. She began talking like the silence never happened.

Natali glanced over, seeing Audrey's face turn to hide the crimson embarrassment. Natali guided the horses up the slight incline, going around the back to the Whitman Stables.

Ross stood outside; arms crossed beside Audrey's intended Eugene. Both men looked slightly cross and for a moment, Natali was jealous. She too wanted someone to be concerned at her safety, to want her to be home at a reasonable time and be there through all of life's big and small moments.

She gave a slight shake of her head. *No more foolishness,* she chided herself. *You don't want to be like Mama.*

Wyatt trotted all the way toward the men, dismounting so fluidly it was almost a blurring motion. Natali exhaled in relief when she got the buggy to stop in front of Ross.

The buggy came to a complete stop and Natali put the brake on. Audrey hopped out of the buggy first, immediately going to Eugene with long, drawn out explanations as to why she was so late in getting home. The woman spoke to quickly, Natali wasn't sure Eugene got all the words. She certainly hadn't.

Awkwardly, Natali stood to the side, wringing her hands. She watched Ross going around, unhitching the horses from the buggy. Gently, he grabbed the horse's bridle, leading the two tired horses inside for some much-needed rest.

Wyatt came up standing roughly five feet from her. "I hope you have a pleasant night, Natali," he said softly.

"Thank you," she whispered back. "Thank you for escorting us home safely. I appreciate it."

"My pleasure," he replied, remounting his horse.

Natali felt her mouth thicken, becoming gloppy and pasty like flour with little water in the mixture. "Tomorrow night's fried chicken at the diner," she blurted.

Wyatt spun his mare toward her, sliding up beside her. "Sounds delicious. I might have to come."

She smiled, fidgeting with her fingers. "I look forward to seeing you."

"Likewise."

Natali was grateful for the darkness. Heat flamed her cheeks worse than a prairie fire. Wyatt smiled at her, tilting the hat off his eyes just a touch; the moon light bringing some color to his deep river blue eyes. The sun-kissed glow of his stubbled jaw and the glow of his skin sent a shiver down her spine.

*I've never swooned over a man. Not even Perth Jones*, she swallowed. *But I'm sure... absolutely certain... I could faint over him.*

Natali brushed stray hairs behind her ears. "Have a good night Wyatt," she said rushing off in front of his horse and into the hotel before he'd a chance to respond again.

*I have to get out of here*, she thought. Natali stormed up the pathway to the hotel, promptly going inside.

---

Wyatt loved how the moonlight put a glowing halo on her beautiful head. He watched her face light up then rapidly fall.

"Have a good night Wyatt," she called rushing off.

His own face soured, wondering what he did or said wrong to make her suffer. Daisy jostled underneath him, ready to head home.

He didn't know what he said wrong to make her so fearful. It made his own heart lurch and the sinking feeling he got from Lydia came rushing back.

*I can't get myself involved*, he decided. *I can't open myself only to have my effort, my love, thrown back in my face again.*

Audrey and Eugene stood slightly in front of him. Audrey had her hand on Eugene's arm, smiling brightly. Eugene regarded him casually, like any man would do to another bringing home their intended wife. Wyatt understood Eugene's caution. Wyatt nodded to the man, turning Daisy toward the road. He felt himself become a touch desolate. He too wanted the happiness they were experiencing, yet he was scared to pursue it.

"Thank you," Eugene said coming forward, hand proffered. "For bringing home my intended safely. I appreciate it."

Wyatt stopped, leaning over in the saddle to shake his hand.

"Wyatt," Audrey called. "It's late. Stay at the hotel, my treat."

"There's an empty stall," Ross added, coming up beside him.

Wyatt dismounted, keeping his eyes on the direction Natali went. "Much obliged," he said.

"Least we can do for you escorting us home safely," Audrey replied.

Eugene led Audrey toward the looming and protective Whitman Hotel. Wyatt watched them go for a second, keeping his eyes on where Natali disappeared.

"Come on," Ross said beside him. "I'll show you where you can put your mare."

"Thank you."

Ross led him inside the Whitman Stables. The large white sign, illuminated by the moonlight, made him snort with amusement. It was a nice-looking barn although he didn't think any barn warranted a sign. Inside, two lanterns lit the building, showing all the animals ready for slumber. Wyatt put Daisy in the stall, removing her tack and leaving it over the stable door. His horse whickered, happy to be inside and munching on hay.

A woman's grumpy sigh came from the barn doorway. Wyatt glanced over and noticed a blond woman walking straight to Ross. The grumpy sigh made him nervous until she wrapped her arms around his neck.

"Wyatt," Ross said, giving Mary a quick peck on the head. Ross pulled Mary around to face Wyatt with a beaming smile on his face, "this is my wife, Mary."

Wyatt dipped his head. "Pleasure to meet you."

"You as well," she replied politely, sighing deeply and leaning her head on Ross's shoulder.

Wyatt took a comb off a peg, giving Daisy a brush down. His horse shook at the touch, tossing her happy head. Daisy turned her head, nuzzling his arm with her nose. Wyatt grinned, patting her head with a free hand.

"Somethin' wrong, Mary?" Ross asked.

Mary groaned. "The new hire. She's all glum and in tears most the day," she said rolling her eyes. "I got no clue to what's wrong with her."

"Natali?" Ross asked in clarification.

Mary opened her mouth to say something, but Wyatt beat her to it.

"She's nervous and shy," Wyatt answered.

Mary scowled. "Shy... Like scared to talk?"

Wyatt nodded. "Yeah. Like that."

"Well... That's gotta change," Mary decided, hands on her hips. "I'm gonna go talk to her."

Mary's husband raised a hand to call after her, but she tromped off. Ross grinned, shaking his head. "See you inside," he hollered after her.

Wyatt felt his stomach tense. Last thing Natali needed was a talking to about how she shouldn't be some way. It irked him. Natali had the freedom to be how she wanted. If the woman had something to say, she should say it. He patted Daisy on the rump, letting go of the slight irritation. People would do or say what they will.

He hung the comb back on the peg, giving his head a small shake to clear his thoughts. Daisy whickered, swishing her tail happily. He strode out of the barn with Ross behind him, shutting the door for the night.

Ross led the way up to the hotel and inside the back door. Wyatt followed, locking the door behind him for the night. Ross took him to the main part of the hotel, pointing up to the right side of the staircase.

"Room 219 is open and clear of people," Ross said, clapping him on the shoulder. "Have a good night."

Wyatt stared at his boots and soiled front of this clothes. Not wanting to soil anything for the employee's to clean, he immediately sat in the little sitting area out in front of the check-in with a sigh. It was late to ride home and would take him a bit by moonlight. A night in a chair was better than the ground. Picking up a small pamphlet, his eyes glossed over the material. Scowling as it was about dresses, he set it down. He didn't feel like going to bed yet, but didn't want to read about women's garments.

His sunk further down in the cushioned seat, wriggling in his spot. He pulled the hat down low over his eyes determined to sleep in the chair. He was happier out in the open to see what was going on around him.

Wyatt ran a hand over his face. Memories of him and Lydia flooded his tired mind. It irked him, right when he was coming to find himself and make peace with everything, Lydia showed back up. It was how she was, even after she rested in her grave.

He adjusted himself in his seat, pushing the hat down lower on his head. *I thought Lydia was happy with me. She smiled at me endearingly for a bit before and after our marriage, then after being married for a month or so, it was like she changed overnight. Her smile was gone. The sparkle in her eye turned sour. She gave barbed phrases; regarding me, and my ways of providing for her to that of a lazy hound. In the moment, I never saw what was coming. I guess I never really knew my wife,* he thought. He remembered her dark brown hair; brown eyes light and rich with life. Her nasally laugher; how cute it was when she snorted after a few chuckles. *Where did it all go wrong. I worked, provided, did all I could to make her a happy woman.*

Wyatt shook his head. He couldn't pinpoint where his marriage began to fail. He honestly didn't have a clue. Some days, he came home and she was happy. Other days, he spent searching for where she happened to be. He heard the townsfolk whispers stop when he came around, catching wisps of half-finished conversations. No matter whom he asked, or where he ventured, none knew where Lydia happened to be. His heart ached, warring between holding the people responsible and understanding their involvement in his affairs. Hearing about her death in a back-alley gambling ordeal shocked him. Of all the places and ways to die, gambling wasn't one he pictured for her.

He grumbled, adjusting himself in his seat.

"You all right?" Natali's soft voice asked.

Startled, Wyatt jumped out of his seat, pushing the hat back off his face. "Yes," he said, clearing his throat. "Are you all right? Anything I can do?"

She held a plate of cookies in her hand and a glass of milk. "I... I wanted to thank you for bringing us home safely," she stammered, setting the fare down on the table. Immediately she backed away, turning to head back down the hall.

"What's the matter?" Wyatt asked. "I ain't going to hurt you," he told her, not keeping the hurt from his voice.

Natali nervously smiled, coming back and sitting in a chair across from him. "I," she swallowed, taking a breath. She rubbed her upper left arm, turning her head with a sigh. "I'm scared. I haven't met too many kindly men."

Wyatt nodded, taking a seat himself. Finally, he caught a glimpse into who this beautiful woman was. "You have nothing to worry about with me."

Natali bashfully turned to face him, not quite meeting his eyes. "Thank you," she replied, her shoulders dropping a little. "My father was a mean and callous man, and my step-father was much the same. If they couldn't beat or yell at Mother, I was next, or shoved outside at night... I... I hate the dark."

Wyatt scowled. "I'm sorry that happened to you. A man who strikes a woman ain't a man at all."

Natali wiped the hairs from her face. "Sorry..." she said, fumbling for her words. "I didn't mean to trouble you. Those are molasses cookies, Ada's specialty. I hope you like them," she finished, rising from her seat. She wrung her hands, finally taking off to the right and down the hallway.

Before she got three steps, Wyatt rose out of his seat. "Natali?"

She stopped. "Yes, Wyatt?"

His mind went blank, like a scrap piece of paper. He couldn't think of anything at all. His thirsty eyes drank in the sight of her blond hair and emerald eyes. He'd never seen a person, animal, or sunrise more beautiful than she.

"I know how you feel," he said, trailing off at the end.

Natali blinked, hands clasped in front of her, waiting for him to continue.

Wyatt licked his lips. "My former wife... she... got killed. Our marriage was," he tilted his head from side to side looking for the right word, "different, but I loved her. She was like your Pa though," he said with a shrug. "I loved her anyways."

Natali put a hand to her mouth and nodded. Her cheeks flamed in the dim lighting, eyes bright and shining from unshed tears. "Have a good night," she said, back pedaling a bit.

"Have a pleasant sleep," he said.

Natali smiled wanly, disappearing around the corner. Wyatt plopped back in his seat, head in his hands.

"Oh, my goodness!" Audrey squeaked softly from the banister. Wyatt sighed but refused to acknowledge Audrey any more than that.

# CHAPTER TEN

Wyatt left before anyone in the hotel woke up. He didn't want to face the hotel owner and her giddy, and her all to perky self. He didn't feel like conversation this morning, and despite only knowing Audrey for the ride home yesterday he was certain she would say something to him this morning. Possibly wanting to know what he and Natali talked about and while he didn't mind a little conversation, he wasn't in the mood for perky nor did he want to divulge even a hint of Natali and his conversation yesterday. It felt private, precious even and he didn't want to betray Natali's trust. And because he didn't know how to avoid questions without fear of being rude, he figured leaving quickly was the best option.

Riding down the road, he debated going to the Whitman Diner for the promised supper of fried chicken. Although even now, hours away, he'd pretty much decided he couldn't do it.

He liked Natali quite a bit. They were similar – familiar in their past and guarded in their hearts, not to mention they both found peace in the quiet. He didn't expect Natali to open up as she did. The woman was closed off tighter than a nail in a coffin, and he wasn't sure if he should be honored by her trust, or afraid she was willing to get a little closer to him.

He made it outside of town when the light gray of the sky was turning a gorgeous pink and orange. Encouraging Daisy into a trot, he headed towards Elk Creek Ranch, hoping to be there before the other hands started to stir. There was a lot of work to be done and he wanted to be sure not to hold up the progress.

Branding cattle was a tiresome affair but it needed doing. The newly acquired herd needed to be separated into groups for keeping, auctioning and eating. The runt-ish calf, Norman, usually would have been an auction or slaughter calf, but he'd bargained with Graham and now Norman would be part of the keeping group. The little fighter made it across the Mississippi and all the way here. Wyatt would be damned if he gave up on the little calf now.

*Maybe if I had fought harder, like little Norman did to survive the trip to Denver, my marriage might have panned out better,* he thought. Daisy whickered, snorting her disapproval at the turn his thoughts had taken, as if she could read his mind. He sighed and nodded his agreement with Daisy then said out loud to the horse, "You're right, Daisy. It wouldn't have changed Lydia. It would have changed and hurt me." Wyatt sighed, running a hand over his face. *Still, I could have tried harder instead of silently accepting what we were and closing off completely.*

Elk Creek Ranch came into view like a beautiful little painting he'd seen once. Pink, orange and purple bloomed better than a springtime flower over the sleepy ranch house silhouetting the buildings in beautiful light. Whinnying from the barn and clucking from the chickens resounded with the chirping of birds, creating a cacophony of delightful morning sounds.

Wyatt smiled, closing his eyes and relishing the morning. This time of day was his absolute favorite. The cozy, sleepy, quiet smell of the barn upon sliding the doors open and listening to the animals become alert and attentive with an affinity for a little loving cuddle; it all just thrilled him and made him appreciate God's creation.

He led Daisy over to the barn, dismounting and opening the door. The animals' heads poked out of the stalls, alert and watching him come inside. Wyatt inhaled deeply, savoring the comfortable smell and security of the animals. He paused outside an empty stall, taking the tack off Daisy and sticking it over the stall railing and leaning into the grooming box for a brush.

"You stayed late," Lewis commented with a smirk from Norman's stall.

Wyatt jumped at the comment, feeling his cheeks turn a rose color. "Nellie's friend *insisted* I stay."

Lewis chortled. "Yeah... Audrey does that. The woman is keen but you wouldn't guess from her overly friendly personality," Lewis clambered over the stall instead of opening the gate. "She got kidnapped by the Del Avilasto gang last year toward the end of summer, survived and now runs the hotel."

Wyatt's eyes widened. Even out in Indiana, the news of the infamous gang reached their town. "That's impressive. I am just not sure I can handle more than short periods of time with her in the same room," he finished with a smirk.

Lewis chortled, clapping him on the shoulder.

Wyatt shrugged his shoulders, glancing over. "Is Norman all right?"

How the calf survived is a miracle. His own mother rejected the calf and eventually passed away after crossing the Mississippi. With frequent stops to fill a pail with milk, then a bottle so Norman could eat, the calf thrived. And the way Wyatt figured it, God played a role in the calf's survival.

"Yeah," Lewis replied. "Woke up in the night bleating from hunger and I ended up falling asleep with him, holding the bottle of course," Lewis laughed. "I'm gonna see if one of the heifers will allow him to suckle."

Wyatt put Daisy in her stall. Hoisting the tack over his shoulder, he put it on a saddle rack and bridle hook beside the other cowhands'. After he settled the pieces into a position he liked, he ran a hand over his face.

His mind wandered back to Natali's invitation. The idea of

fried chicken being served to him by a beautiful woman niggled at him. *Maybe I shouldn't go to town tonight. It might look bad being gone two nights in a row,* Wyatt thought. *I need to have a meal with everyone here, since this is my new home.*

He peered over his shoulder to where the road and town would lay beyond the rolling hills and sparse trees. *I'll see her tomorrow. Surely the woman goes to church on Sunday.*

---

Natali fidgeted in her seat inside the Denver church. She hadn't been inside one of these buildings in a long time, often working Sundays and forgetting what day it happened to be.

Wyatt Pearson and the rest of the cowhands from Elk Creek Ranch sat on a bench seat two rows in front of her. She couldn't help but stare at the back of his head, seeing the long hair curl slightly at the collar, not paying a lick of attention to whatever Reverend Kester was preaching. She had a hard time shaking their last conversation from her head. Not only what Wyatt disclosed about his marriage, but the high-pitched giddiness of Audrey calling out "Oh, my goodness," and the fact she was so nosey, made her a touch furious. What Wyatt said to her was in confidence.

To make it a little more awkward for her, and honestly maddening her further, Audrey embraced her the next day, going on a tangent about love finding a way in front of Mary and Lena. She didn't care for the attention. Seeing her so uncomfortable, Lena pulled Audrey away to speak of her upcoming nuptials this fall. Thankfully for her, it worked and she was able to escape to help in laundry where Eliza was blessedly quiet.

*She meant nothing by it,* Natali reminded herself. *Everyone at the hotel is really kind... Well, except for maybe Claudia. But everyone is kindly enough. I couldn't have found a better place of employment. I just wish they'd mind their own business a touch more.*

Natali perked her head up as Reverend Kester's bible snapped shut and he announced the closing prayers. She let out a relieved breath. It had been a long time since she sat in on a church service.

She forgot how long they went sometimes, and didn't care for all the crowds gathering at the only entrance to talk about the sermon.

She observed Reverend Kester's stillness on the pulpit and animated tone stating the goings-on of the community. Curious to her new home, she paid attention.

"An auction for cattle will be held here in four days. No squabbling over beef, it all tastes the same once it's well done," he joked.

Natali chortled.

"The fall harvest party will be held at the Whitman Hotel in mid-October with a pie bake off for the women. I am certainly looking forward to being a judge. However, I don't think my wife looks forward to adjusting my pants," he laughed.

Natali felt a twinge of loneliness creep inside her. She wasn't going to compete in anything. In fact, she wasn't sure she would be here when the time came. She was ready to run away, farther this time, possibly east to Ohio; once her mother came to Denver of course, they could leave together. Being so close to Wyatt and seeing him made her anxious. Part of her dared to get to know him, the other vowed to swear him off for good.

*We are so familiar and similar,* she thought, scowling at the Good Book. *Yet I cannot bring myself to allow my affections to grow. What if Wyatt is like Joel or Pa? I would be married and there would be nothing; not even Reverend Kester could save me from.*

Shivers crawled on her skin. Mary took her shawl off her shoulders and wrapped it around Natali.

"It is a bit chilly," Mary said. "You all right?"

Natali nodded, leaning in when Reverend Kester's back was turned. "I am fine... Just deep in thought."

"Don't think on it too much. You'll jump to concussions."

"Conclusions, dear," Ross whispered, putting an arm around his wife and pulling her close.

Natali smiled with fondness and amusement. "Thank you, Mary."

"Have a Blessed day," Reverend Kester's voice boomed in the cozy church.

The pews screeched back as people rose to their feet to head out of the stuffy church building. All at once, chatter filled the church as everyone began to greet each other. Natali turned, following Mary and Ross in front of her out to the right.

She kept her head down, daring to not make eye contact with Wyatt. Her emotions battled worse than the Civil War. A part of her wanted to take a chance and get to know Wyatt, but she'd tried that with Perth and his rejection of her silent affections had stung her to the core, yet she was certain Wyatt would not reject her at all. However, taking the risk was something she refused to do. What if Wyatt turned into a monster after marriage? The other piece of her, fueled by that very question, wanted to run and hide, to not give into her feelings at all; she refused to be like her Mama in love. She wanted better. Even if that meant she never married.

Natali sighed, exiting the church into the bright sunlight. She shielded her eyes for a moment, letting her body soak up the sun's warming rays. She took off the shawl, handing it back to Mary with a "thank you."

Mary opened her mouth to say something, but Natali strode off with a smile and a nod, wanting some peaceful solitude. She ambled down the road at a leisurely pace, taking in the sights of Denver. She hadn't adventured out much since getting to the hotel. Spotting a few stores, she made a mental note to go see at some point.

Natali went up the stairs to the Whitman Hotel, stopping on the landing at the carving of the roaring bear. The creature was around eight feet tall, guarding the entrance to the building. Natali took a seat on the chair next to the bear. Glancing to the left, she spotted a polished silver plaque.

*For my darling wife. Like this bear, I will always protect you, Philip Whitman.*

Natali smiled wanly. How it must be nice to have a husband who was kind and affectionate such as this. Audrey's voice lilted from inside the hotel. Natali blanched; Audrey had beaten her home. She barely rose from her seat before Audrey made it outside.

"Natali, dear, how are you this wonderful day?" the hotel owner asked.

"Very well, thank you," she replied with a small sigh. "And yourself?"

"Simply divine!" Audrey breathed. "Eugene and I are about to go for a stroll. Do you care to join us? We will be back before dinner service. Lena loves having you in the diner with her and I'm sure she will be remised if we cause you to miss it."

"Sure," Natali said out of politeness and a sprinkle of curiosity about Denver, she went beside Audrey.

She descended back down the steps. Together, they crossed the street, Audrey's arm in Eugene's. Audrey lovingly laid her head down on Eugene's shoulder, surprisingly in complete silence. *Why can't she be quiet when it's just me or the ladies? She'd be so much more likeable if she'd talk less.* Natali scolded herself for such thoughts and decided just to enjoy the stroll. They rounded a corner on the right, going down a street she hadn't been before. New shops and people greeted her eyes.

*I will have to come explore this part later.*

Striding in step with Audrey on her side, Natali gazed around like a child, her wonder interrupted by a question directed toward her.

"What brought you to Denver, Natali?" Eugene's voice asked, startling her.

She met his curious gaze, "I needed a change. A fresh start."

Eugene nodded in understanding. "Don't we all?"

"What happened?" Audrey asked. "No one runs from nothing," she glanced over to her and smiled fondly. "I was running from my unscrupulous aunt and horrid cousin." Audrey chuckled a bit and looked at Eugene when she said, "Then a gang of murderous men."

Eugene snorted, a smile on his lips as he shook his head.

Audrey leaned over, linking her free arm into Natali's with a smile. Natali smiled back, keeping her eyes diverted to the places and people around them; not wanting to answer right away, although knowing Audrey as she did, would have to at some point.

Taking a deep breath, she paused her footsteps. Audrey and

Eugene halted, cocooning her on the side of the walkway, creating a protective bubble while people strolled past.

"My step-father Joel is a cruel man and a drunk. He didn't hit anyone I know of until right before I left. Not sure what changed, but my mother came to my workplace battered and bloody. I tried to get her to leave. She wouldn't. She loves the man although I'm not really sure why. Now I am here to start over and begin by myself without my mother. I miss her though."

Eugene perked a brow. "Leave what happened behind. Start fresh here. This place, these people, they're not the same."

Natali nodded and gave him an appreciative, shy smile. "Thank you. I better get back now. Lena is going to need me soon."

Before Audrey's pursed lips had a chance for a rebuttal, Natali took off at a fast-paced walk to the Whitman Diner, relieved to be out of their presence.

# CHAPTER ELEVEN

Natali breathed out heavily when she got inside her room. Quickly changing out of her Sunday best, she strolled into the kitchen. Relief hung on her like a comfortable blanket. She enjoyed, slightly, their company. At least the discomfort was getting better. Eugene's words struck her but she hadn't the time to ponder the meaning just then.

Tying her apron behind her back, she strode out into the Whitman Diner. She stopped in the middle of the room, making eye contact with the only person occupying a table – Wyatt Pearson, sitting where he had the first night she met him. His handsome tanned face and rich blue eyes greeted hers with a twinkling smile despite the resting easiness on the rest of his face.

Clean dark jeans and a nice green shirt tucked in at his waist clung to his broad frame and made his already dazzling blue eyes pop. His gun holster rested peacefully over the ear of the chair with his beaten leather hat over top. Natali had yet to move from her spot by the swinging kitchen door.

"You got that side?" Lena asked, nudging Natali's hip with hers, smiling.

Natali nodded, swallowing the lump in her throat. "Yeah. I sure do."

Striding over to Wyatt, paper and pencil in hand, she offered him a genuine smile. "Evening," she said pleasantly. "What can I get started for you?"

Wyatt rose out of his chair. His face bent down a tick to gaze at her. His lips curled inward. Shuffling of his boots were all she could hear in the deafening echo of the diner. Her heart thumped quietly, almost like she was barely living and breathing.

Natali inhaled, holding her breath.

"I came," he began, clearing his throat, "I came to ask you to supper."

Natali blinked, uncertain of what to say. Her insides fluttered, tingling so much it felt like vomit might rise.

"Supper?" she squeaked out.

"Unless you would rather do dinner... or breakfast... coffee?" he replied slightly high-pitched at the end. He cleared his throat. "I'm sorry," he bent over grabbing his hat. "I will go now. Evening."

"Coffee," she blurted.

Wyatt's brows raised, eyes smiling fondly at her. "Coffee it is."

Natali blushed, letting out a small sigh and the breath she still held out softly through her nose. "What can I get for you now?"

Wyatt smirked. "Coffee."

Natali giggled softly. "Coming right up. Anything to eat?"

"The special."

Natali wrote it down on the note for Claudia, striding back into the kitchen. Lena smiled broadly at her, hands on her round hips. Natali felt heat rush to her cheeks. She set the paper down where Claudia designated for orders and walked out of the kitchen promptly with a coffee pot.

She brushed the stray blond hairs off her face, smiling as she approached Wyatt. It was the first time in a long time that she'd offered someone a genuine smile. Usually she reserved it for her mother or even Perth Jones, but it had remained hidden for the most part. At this moment, she couldn't help but smile. Wyatt stared at her; blue eyes focused on her face.

Her heart pounded in her chest, thumping so hard, it was almost in her throat. His handsome eyes bore into her skin, making her hot all over and leaving beads of sweat trickling down her back. His strong, masculine, face offered her a sweet and simple smile in return. A real smile. Wyatt's white teeth shone in the afternoon sunlight making her legs turn into crumble cake.

Off and on she was undecided about Wyatt. Part of her wanting to take a chance and open up while her other side wanted to shut up tighter than a bear trap and run away. Her fear Wyatt would be a wolf in disguise cautioned her. She knew she didn't want someone like Joel Benson. Men like him were dangerous. However, knowing what she needed to steer clear from didn't make it any easier to know what to pursue. If anything, it made it harder; if only because every man she met had the potential to be her Pa or Joel.

*It's so hard to know what is good, when I know so well what is bad,* she thought, moving the pesky hairs behind her ear.

She poured Wyatt coffee, letting her eyes linger a moment too long on his face. Blushing, she scurried around and poured the other guests who wandered in their fill of the black liquid. She glanced over her shoulder as she poured her last customer's coffee, watching Wyatt take a sip. Turning back around, she lifted the pitcher, thankful she hadn't made a mess.

The bell in the kitchen dinged loudly for her. Natali accidentally tuned out the sound, her thoughts on Wyatt. Claudia started calling her name. Heat flamed her cheeks. She took off down in between the tables, scurrying inside the kitchen.

"Handsome man out there," Lena commented as Natali approached the counter.

Natali blushed. "He is."

Grabbing the plate of food, she strode out of the kitchen and dropped the food off to Wyatt with a smile. Only two tables were filled at the moment. Leaving the guests to eat in peace, Natali backed out of the dining area, retreating once again into the kitchen.

Lena leaned against a hutch, drinking some tea. "Still two tables?"

"Yeah," she paused, fiddling with her fingers. "I want to apologize for being distant."

Lena held up a hand. "No need. We've all been in your shoes at some point in our lives. You're fine."

"What Lena said," Mary added from the washing area.

Natali nodded her head, pouring herself some tea. "Thank you, all."

Lena set her drink down, wrapping her arms around Natali. "You're fine."

She smiled, thankful to be in a good place with good people. *This*, she thought, *is what I needed all along.*

---

Wyatt fidgeted in his seat at the diner, waiting patiently for Natali to show up. After church services she disappeared so quickly, he hadn't the chance to ask her out to supper. He loathed asking her at her job, but there was no other place he got to see her besides the one time at Elk Creek.

*I can't believe she said yes*, he thought, chewing another bite of beef stew.

He peeked over his shoulder, seeing her eyes on him as she poured the other dining couple some more coffee. If she wasn't careful, she would be spilling all over the table and them. Just in time, she turned back around.

Wyatt smirked, finishing off his meal. He left change on the table, scooting out of the chair. He buckled his gun and holster to his waist, making sure it hung low enough for easy access but not low enough to be mistaken as a gun slinger's. He didn't need that kind of trouble. Slapping his old dusty hat on his head, he was ready to leave.

The kitchen door swung open. Natali stood at the threshold of the door, holding a pot of coffee in one hand and a pitcher of tea in the other. He stood riveted to his spot, stunned by her appearance. She was beautiful with blond hair, all prettily braided about her head. Large, keen, emerald eyes taking in everything at once, scrutinizing every detail. And they were focused on him; which were what stunned him when he first met her.

Wyatt sucked in a breath. "It was a fine meal," he commented.

"Glad you liked it," she breathed, setting down the items on a side table.

He strode to her, standing off to the side so he wouldn't be in the way of the kitchen door. "Coffee..." he trailed off softly, gathering his courage. "What day shall I meet you?"

Natali grabbed on to her left elbow with her right hand, clenching and unclenching her left fist. "Whenever you come back my way."

"Thursday," he said quickly before either of them could change their minds. "We should be in town for the cattle auction."

"Sounds nice. I look forward to it."

Wyatt smiled, reaching out to take her hand. Hovering a breath above hers, he stopped himself, putting his hand back down at his side. Instead, he set his hat on his head and tipped it to her, nodding. "Have a good evening," he said, backing to the door.

With a flick of his wrist, he turned the knob, letting out the breath he hadn't realized he held when he got outside. Jogging down the steps, he made his way to Daisy.

"Wyatt!"

He turned around at the high-pitched feminine voice. His heart sank to his ankles. Sprinting up the sidewalk was a woman he wished to never see again.

"Oh Wyatt!" she screamed.

"Charlene," he greeted tersely.

The woman threw her hands around his neck. Gently he pulled her off, taking several steps back. She tried to throw herself at him again, unphased and grinning from ear to ear. Daisy took a step forward, tossing her mane. Wyatt appreciated her interference and smiled to himself at Daisy's protectiveness; even if it was unintentional.

Charlene screamed frightfully. "Oh..." she swallowed. "You still have that."

Wyatt smiled, patting Daisy's neck. "I sure do."

"It took me forever to find you, Wyatt."

He didn't say anything. He didn't even shrug. He just stared at her. Wyatt heard once from his Pa, *marry the woman all you want but you marry her family too.* He didn't think it would be such a terrible thing until he met Lydia's cousin, Charlene Brandt. The woman was worse than ticks in spring.

"I spent all my money to get here to be with you," she said happily.

"Let's spend all my money and get you back," Wyatt replied, tethering Daisy again.

Charlene laughed uproariously, slapping his arm. "How I have greatly missed your humor, Wyatt."

Inwardly, Wyatt cringed. Since day one of meeting Charlene, ironically on his and Lydia's wedding day, Charlene had been a thorn in his side. Lydia had put Charlene in her place a handful of times yet the woman persisted in her pursuit, being so bold as to kiss his cheek. Wyatt went so far as to move across to the other side of Hartford City to be rid of her and find some peace. Yet she found him, not only in a new house, but a whole new town.

Now with Charlene here, avoiding her and getting to know Natali was going to be a huge pain. If he thought it possible, he'd run her out of town, but there was no running, or hiding, from the brown haired, crazy brown eyed monster once she saw him. Wyatt shuddered.

"I went all over Hartford City, hopped a train and checked every city and finally I heard tell you were on a cattle drive going to Denver because some old man in a store remarked about wolves eating cattle and a posse of cowboys headed there and then I spoke to your Ma and she said you were on cattle drive, so I knew you were headed here and now here I am. Ain't that fun!?"

Wyatt blinked, not knowing how a woman got so many words out in a single breath. "You must be tired."

Charlene laughed. "Heavens no! Seeing you has invigorated me.

You see, I spent all this time wondering if I should come and see you and now that I have and seen your face, I am so happy I did. I knew you missed me."

He ran a hand over his face, not saying a word.

"Oh goodness me! I am going to get checked into this hotel. It looks absolutely lovely. Are you staying here? I saw you come out and I thought to myself, surely you must be working or staying here. So, I should too because it looks absolutely divine. How are the meals? Are they good? It must be so because you look handsome and well. Oh gosh," she stopped sucking in a large breath at the base of the Whitman Hotel steps. "Look at that bear! Have you ever seen such a thing? Goodness me! What a sight. I am so thrilled to be here in Denver with you, Wyatt."

Charlene climbed the steps, still speaking and opened the door. Once she disappeared inside, he made haste for Daisy, unfettering her from the hitching post and taking off at a trot down the road.

Wyatt let out the breath he was holding, thankful to be away from the pesky woman and able to hear himself think. He'd believed he escaped his past when he made it to Denver. How wrong he'd been. Wyatt shook his head in disbelief. Not only had it followed him, one of the worst parts of his past was hot on his heels.

*How am I going to avoid Charlene, because that woman is worse than a flower to a bee.*

He was afraid that every time he stepped into town she would be there. Waiting for him. He shuddered, trying to wrap his brain around the problem so he could find a solution. Thursday would be here quicker than he anticipated, and he was looking forward to coffee with Natali. Not only Thursday, but with the cattle auction, he would be needed in town and she would surely be looking for him.

Wyatt ran a hand over his face again, crossing the train tracks and heading north. He grimaced at the next thought but didn't see any other way to save his own hide. *I gotta find someone to stick Charlene with and quick.*

# CHAPTER TWELVE

W yatt entered the barn at Elk Creek, unsaddling Daisy slowly. He thought about how to get Charlene to go after another, unattached, and hopefully willing partner. He hadn't a clue what to do if the man was unwilling. Hog-tying the man and bribery were among the options he was seriously considering. Charlene was in her mid-twenties and never received a suitor, although based on what he knew of her, he was pretty sure she scared most men away. She swore it was God waiting to fit her with the perfect man. Wyatt figured that was only a tiny reason.

He locked Daisy in her stall for the evening, shutting the barn doors behind him. He walked to the house, going around to the back where the bunkhouse was. The other men had come straight back here after the church sermon. Avery sat on the steps playing a fiddle. The others lounged around listening to Avery play. Only Graham and Nellie stayed to shop around a bit.

Nellie said she'd wanted to get some shopping done while they were out and about since it was getting harder to get around with her being heavy with child; although Wyatt wondered if she just liked to shop and it was a Sunday habit for the couple. Not that he could blame them. He remembered how much he'd enjoyed dating Lydia, and he looked forward to the same with Natali.

*Sunday afternoon shopping trips would be an ideal date.*

Wyatt let out a long breath, pausing at the fence of the paddock to scan the herd for Norman. The feisty little calf suckled on the teat of a young heifer. The sight brought a smirk to his face. The happy little calf was a fighter through and through. Between surviving his temporary sore front leg, being a runt and enduring the swift currents of the Mississippi, the calf, he hoped, would grow to be a big ol' bull.

"Hey Wyatt," Lewis called, striding up beside him. "How was Natali?"

Wyatt felt his jaw tense. He didn't like speaking personal with someone he didn't know from Jove. Wyatt turned, facing the senior cowhand head on, studying him. Lewis, with his shaggy light brown, almost blond hair and keen brown eyes might stand a chance to Charlene. He was pretty enough and easy going.

*He just might do the trick,* Wyatt surmised. *Or Avery. One of them ought to catch her eye. Lord knows I've put her in her place too many times to count and the persistent pest of a woman doesn't seem too keen to catch on. Time to pass her onto one of these fellows... I almost feel bad... Nope,* he decided. *I rightly don't. I'm desperate.*

Wyatt widened his stance a touch. "I say we go to town tomorrow and drop off the slaughter-herd and pick up that order of fencing coming in on the train. Some of the calves need selling too to the man you mentioned before."

Lewis scratched his stubbled beard. "Yeah, the Wright's were lookin' for a few head," he agreed. "Would you go with me or stay back? Samuel hates town, but will go if he has to, and Parker, after business is done, always heads straight to the whore house," he said the last part with disdain. "It bugs me," he hissed under his breath.

"I'll go," Wyatt agreed with a casual shrug.

Knowing Charlene as he did, the woman would be awake bright and early, chomping at the bit to go shopping or out to find him. Being at Elk Creek nigh on a week, and no one knowing much of who he was, happened to be his only saving grace at the moment. However, if he could get Charlene hooked on Avery or Lewis, his life would be set. Both men had the rugged, wild look she seemed to want, at least that's what Charlene boasted had driven them together.

*If I can get her claws in one of them,* Wyatt thought, *my troubles are all gone.*

Wyatt rolled his shoulders, tilting his head to the side. "You said the Wrights wanted calves correct?"

Lewis nodded. "They sure did. Preferably six or so from our herd. They wanted Rocky Pine's but Frank wanted too much for his herd," Lewis scratched the back of his neck. "Frank has good beef, so I don't blame the man."

Horses whinnied at the end of the driveway, their noises echoing up to the ranch house. The blond head of Nellie and the tall frame of Graham had him striding toward them to help unload the wagon. Walking around the wagon, Graham went to the side to grab the supplies they purchased while in town. Undoing the chain on the side of the wagon rail, he reached inside to move the tarp.

"Surprise!" Charlene yelled.

Wyatt fell back on his bottom, clutching his chest. "Charlene," he breathed on the ground. "I thought you were at the hotel."

Wyatt rose stiffly, staring at Lewis who had the back of his hand pressed to his mouth in a poor attempt to stifle his laughter.

Charlene clambered out of the wagon herself, smiling brightly and opening her parasol, not bothering to smooth her dress. "Oh, I just couldn't sit still, not with all these new, wonderful places to explore. And all these people to meet. You took off so un-expect-edly, I was rather hurt but I challenged myself to have a divine time shopping with Audrey at Mrs. Birch's store and lo and behold I ran into this lovely woman who knew exactly where you would be. Such a coincidence, do you not agree. I am so pleased to have found you again Wyatt. Are you not going to introduce me? No bother. Hello, friends, my name is Charlene Brandt and I am Wyatt's—"

"Charlene is my late wife's cousin." Wyatt blurted, getting stares from Graham, Lewis and the other hands who came to see the spectacle.

"Yes," Charlene quickly added. "But we love each other."

Wyatt ran a hand over his face, gritting his teeth. His free fist clenched and released on its own.

"Come inside, Charlene," Nellie beckoned coming to Wyatt's rescue. "I would love to hear about your hometown."

Charlene took a deep, audible breath and began spouting off about Indiana. Wyatt stood before his peers; eyes closed. Opening his eyes, his colleagues stood before him, utterly still and silent in their disbelief.

Graham strode over, hands in his pockets. "Put the wagon away," he said, clapping him on the shoulder in an unexpected show of camaraderie.

Wyatt felt his insides rumble between sizzling fury and embarrassment. He refused to hang his head. There was nothing to be ashamed about. He did not bring this upon himself.

"She seems…" Lewis said, swishing his head side to side. "Nice."

Wyatt nodded. "She is… A little too nice," he breathed out. "I am not interested in her at all."

"I can see that."

He clambered in the wagon, steering the team of horses toward the barn. His heart sunk to his feet. If Charlene met Audrey as she said, then his chances and time with Natali just got harder.

*I gotta get Charlene saddled with someone*, he thought. *And quick.*

---

Natali watched Wyatt from the Whitman Diner window get embraced by a lovely woman in a pastel pink dress. Her heart swirled, unbelieving that the kind, handsome man who'd just asked her to coffee would embrace another woman so quickly. Mixed in with the unbelief was sadness. She'd dared to hope. Just a little, and this is what that hope got her. Wyatt held the woman back at arm's length, for propriety's sake of course.

Lena's quiet footsteps approached, almost drowned out by the clinking of dishes shifting in her hands. Dinging from the bell above the door rang in the quiet diner. The last two diners went out into the afternoon, chatting happily, satisfied with their meal.

Lena blew her lips. "He doesn't look too thrilled," she commented.

Natali turned toward her friend. "What makes you say that? The woman looks perfectly pleased."

"His face is tight. See the way his teeth clench and his hands? And the unnatural red of his face. He doesn't look pleased to see this woman," Lena replied, going to the kitchen. "Whomever she is."

Natali nodded; her eyes riveted to the scene below. The woman turned, going up the hill. Wyatt mounted his horse, trotting away from the woman without looking back. Natali perked a brow that quickly furrowed.

*Maybe Lena is right*, she thought, hope rising up in her again. *Maybe he really cannot stand her.*

Natali made her way back inside the kitchen just as Mary finished washing the dishes, leaving everything to dry. Mary turned toward her and made a motion with her head, beckoning her to follow outside to the bench. Lena, who must have anticipated Mary's intentions, held open the kitchen door for the both of them.

They never made beyond the entrance of the kitchen. A raucous woman's voice resounded in the hotel. The woman in the pink dress was inside the hotel, making a fuss over how grand everything happened to be. Her vibrant tone and talkative nature were second only to Audrey. Natali felt her face fall, eyes going wide to take in the scene the woman was making.

*I am not the type of woman he likes*, she surmised.

Lena stood in behind of her, pushing her toward the door to the employee area. "Don't worry yourself. He doesn't like her," she commented.

Natali inhaled the fresh, almost autumn air as soon as the door burst open into the sunlight. Of all the smells she could remember and place specifically in her mind, there was none comparable to

Colorado. She plopped herself on the bench, exhaling through her nose. Mary sat on her right; skirts hiked up past her ankles as she swished her skirts back and forth in an attempt to cool her legs.

Natali breathed out, letting the remnants of the waning sun strike her face. The side door opened. The sweet-smelling perfume of Audrey permeated her nose. The woman took a seat on the other side of Lena, letting out a contented sigh.

"We have a guest staying in the grand room side," Audrey finally commented.

Natali felt her blood turn to ice. Shivers ran up her arm. Mary patted her right arm, letting her hand linger.

"Her name is Charlene Brandt, all the way from Indiana," Audrey continued.

Natali swallowed. She didn't trust her voice to speak. Surely this woman came after Wyatt because they were intended? Why else would a woman make their way across America for a man? There had to be a legitimate reason.

Her face made a moue, staring dead ahead at the tree. A high-pitched droning came from inside the building. All of them turned toward the door, waiting to see who it happened to be.

"Here," Claudia said gruffly stepping aside for something, or someone. "This belongs to you, Audrey."

"Oh goodness me!" the woman exclaimed as she shoved past Claudia. "Thank you so much, Cookie! I have been looking every-where for some decent companionship and here you are." The woman said, turning her attention to the women on the bench.

The door inside the hotel slammed.

Without even noticing the incensed Claudia leaving, the woman continued like she never missed a beat. "And I thought to myself how wonderful it would be to shop with some new companions. See the sights, if you will. Anyone care to join me? I am looking for things to furnish my new home whenever Wyatt and I marry. I'm sure it will be soon."

Natali leaned forward, staring at the woman with mouse brown hair. "Wyatt Pearson?"

"Yes. Exactly so. Were you not listening, dear? My apologies. I do speak rather fast."

Natali leaned back in her seat, staring dead ahead at a tree.

"How do you know Wyatt?" Lena asked.

"He is my former cousins' husband. Lydia, my cousin, was killed in a back-alley accident. The dear had money troubles with gambling, trying to make it rich," Charlene sighed dramatically, sniffing and dabbing her eyes. "Wyatt didn't make enough for my dear Lydia, so she tried to win it and got killed when she bet too much. Wyatt buried her and came out to Denver. Took me a while to track him down. I know he needs me like I need him. We are made for each other. I know it in my heart."

Mary grabbed Natali's hand, leaning forward with a wry smile. "Like a chicken made for a fox," Mary said winking at Natali, pulling her to stand with her. "If you'd please accuse us, we are going to prep for supper."

Mary shoved her toward the door. Mary yanked it open, stepped inside and rapidly pulled it closed behind them. The blond woman stared at her pointedly, before making a face at the door. Natali's lips twitched into a smile. She'd never seen Mary become upset over anything before.

"She's fuller of manure than a horse," Mary commented, shaking her head. "Like I said, don't go hoppin' to con-clues-sons. That woman is mud."

Claudia grumbled coming out of the washroom to the side of them, fixing the kerchief over her graying head. "Cookie," the woman snorted. "The gall of the woman," she hissed moving to the side and going past them.

Mary rolled her eyes and put a hand on Natali's shoulder. "Come on."

Natali strode away from the door. Her mind reeling with questions as to why Wyatt really happened to be here in Denver besides trying to be rid of the painful memories as he mentioned before. Surely this woman wasn't crazy enough to follow him out here for nothing? She had to be his intended. Why else would she be here? Natali took a fleeting glance back at the door, her face twisting in a scowl.

# CHAPTER THIRTEEN

Morning could not come quickly enough. Wyatt paced outside along the fence containing the herd of cattle, waiting for the others to rise. With all the livestock fed, stalls cleaned, and eggs gathered, the morning chores were done. All he'd to do now was saddle Daisy, gather the herd, and ride through town on the way to the Wright's ranch.

Charlene, thank the Good Lord above, was at the hotel, escorted safely by Avery. The man had yet to return to Elk Creek, more than likely staying the night at the Whitman Hotel like Wyatt had done just a few days before. Wyatt felt sorry for Avery. Being saddled with Charlene wouldn't be an easy one. The trip to town wasn't far yet the road stretched on forever when someone jabbered on.

Wyatt ran his fingers through his hair, entirely relieved to have a peaceful morning. The jingle of metal tack sounded behind him in the stillness of the morning. Avery came up the drive, going straight into the open barn without so much as a glance at him. Wyatt spun on his heel, heading toward the barn.

Avery dismounted with a sigh, taking the saddle off his roan gelding speaking without turning around. "Don't get any ideas.

The answer is no. And the other answer is I don't know anyone who would be interested in Charlene."

Wyatt grumbled, pulling the skin on the back of his neck. "I wasn't going to ask that."

Avery stared at him disbelieving. "Just in case you were."

Wyatt sighed. "I hope she finds someone at the auction," he mumbled.

Avery laughed. "I'm sure by the end of the day today, *everyone* will know of Charlene and avoid her."

"I fear that outcome," he grumbled.

Picking up a curry comb, Wyatt helped Avery brush down his horse while Avery checked its feet. His mind ran rampant with thoughts on how to avoid Charlene or more drastically, moving away to be rid of her once more. How on earth she found him, so many miles away, both unnerved and scared him. He didn't like the fact she tracked him down so easily or at all. Wyatt switched sides, making the roan's coat smooth.

"I may know someone who would be a solution to your problem," Graham said from the barn door.

Wyatt looked over his shoulder, hoping his eagerness didn't give him away. "Who?"

"My brother, Zed Oliver. He has three kids. Wife died in childbirth about two years back. He lives beyond this ranch, more north."

Wyatt nodded.

"He's coming down for the auction. Looks just like me but blue eyes."

Avery laughed catching Graham's attention. "That's damn near everyone in Denver, Graham."

Graham turned away from Avery, looking at Wyatt point blank with a smirk playing at his lips. "We're twins. I'm the best looking though."

"Sure are," Nellie replied, waddling inside the barn. "Come; food is ready."

Wyatt followed Avery and Graham out of the barn with the fast-paced waddling Nellie in front. He was surprised how agile she was for how far along she happened to be. Any day, a crying babe would be heard from inside the farm house. Wyatt was excited, nervous and a touch envious of what Graham happened to have – what he thought he'd had with Lydia until she'd left him and gambled herself into an early grave. It still bothered him greatly the woman he gave his heart to didn't want him as much as he'd wanted her.

Striding inside the big house, he took a seat beside Samuel on the end of the long table. The bear of a man heaped food on his plate, passing the dishes with a good quarter of the food to him. Wyatt chuckled silently to himself when he saw the big hole in each dish passed to him.

Nellie came around with a steaming pot of coffee, giving everyone a mug full before sitting down and serving herself from the steaming dishes. The woman sat with a groan; her chair pushed back to allow passage for her belly. Graham peered out the window to his right, scowling at whatever was outside. Rising to his feet, he winked at Nellie and opened the door.

"What do you want?" he bellowed.

Wyatt, Avery and Sam's chairs screeched back on the hard-wood. Pistols on their side, they were ready for any encounter this ranch was in for.

Nellie rolled her eyes. "Eat, this is how he happens to greet someone who comes to make him a *deal*." she instructed, shaking her head.

She rose with another groan and her hands bracing her lower back, she put the napkin on the table; not bothering to fold it, looking longingly at her plate as she turned to follow her husband outside. Not waiting for anyone else, Wyatt eagerly tucked into the fare, shoveling it all in his face. He loved Nellie's cooking and was so pleased it wasn't Kain or him making the meals.

A buggy parked itself in the middle of the driveway about a hundred feet from the ranch house. Wyatt grumbled when he saw who disembarked from the buggy. Someone Graham happened to be doing business with brought Charlene here. The annoying woman wore a gaudy pastel blue dress with yellow trimming, shining worse than a beacon in a snowstorm. The man who brought her here was busy letting his brood of children out the back of the buggy. The children ran for the barn, going for the animals like dogs at a hunt.

Wyatt choked on his coffee, realizing he needed to disappear from Charlene. Sputtering, he moved from his chair and toward the back door trying to stay out of sight of the windows.

"Will she follow you into the privy?" Parker asked chortling.

"Yes," he replied in a harsh whisper as he furtively glanced back to the open window.

Charlene's talkative, grating tone resonated from outside and filtered to his ears. He wanted to chop off his ears to escape her sound. Moving quietly to the backdoor, he could almost feel the coldness of the knob in his hand as he reached for it.

The front door opened and he bemoaned his opportunity to escape. He knelt down, pretending to gather something off the floor.

"Oh Wyatt!" Charlene cried out happily as she bust through the door. "I am so pleased you're here."

Wyatt closed his eyes, getting off the floor with his pretend handful of dirt. Graham raised a brow to him, trying to hide the smirk behind his beard. The man who brought Charlene here, stood by the front door, watching the scene Charlene was about to make. Wyatt tried to keep his face as impassive as possible although he felt himself faltering into a scowl quickly.

"Anyways," Charlene continued without missing a beat. "I was hoping to have found you here. We need to go shopping together since you know we are a couple now and will be purchasing a house very soon—"

"Aren't," Wyatt corrected in the middle of her speech.

Charlene blinked; her cheeks going rosy. "Quite right. You haven't asked me yet. But I'm sure since we are finally here together, you asking me will not take quite so long. Even when you were married to my dearly departed cousin, I knew. I just knew, I tell you! We were meant to be together and it wouldn't take long at all for you to leave her and to marry me. I told myself every day, if you had a chance to know me, you would love me too. So, when I found out you were gone, I sold everything and came out here to be with you. I know you need me too like I need you. We are the same you know. Absolutely the same."

The silence in the room was deafening. He could feel the heat of embarrassment crawl on his skin. He left Indiana to come and make a new life here away from the torment and memories. He also left to escape Charlene. And now, in front of his peers and boss, Charlene had come to stab a knife into his future and plans to start anew.

Charlene droned on, eventually leaving the dining room to scope out the house with Nellie. Graham's good wife led her away from him and the others with wide eyes and a deep breath. He was so grateful to her and regretted ever thinking any ill thoughts toward her chattiness. How the nice woman tolerated someone such as Charlene, he hadn't a clue.

"Wyatt," Lewis beckoned. "Care to get started on the cattle?"

Wyatt let out the breath he held. His insides quaking with anger at Charlene.

"Hold a moment," Graham said, taking a deep breath. The droning of Charlene could be heard across the house. Graham shook his head. "Let's all go to the barn."

Wyatt smirked. Following his boss out the door, he felt relieved at the cool air striking his face. His body shivered, cooling the rage previously consuming him.

Striding into the barn, he and the cowhands circled around in front of Graham as someone who looked remarkably like Graham strode up to Graham's left.

The man lifted his hand in greeting, "I'm Graham's brother, Zed. The better-looking twin." Zed winked as the cowboys chuckled.

Wyatt sighed instead. His chance at springing Charlene on the man was gone. A rock formed in his stomach, sinking to his feet. How he was going to get any man saddled with the woman was beyond him. It would be a drunken chore or cost him all his money – which he would gladly give if it meant to be rid of her.

On his person, he had roughly four hundred dollars, all of it he would give to any man willing enough to marry Charlene Brandt.

*I would give my legs to be rid of the woman,* he thought. Wyatt kicked a rock in the dusty barn, staring at it and wondering why now, of all times and places, God decided to send Charlene back into his life.

*The only reasoning, I can think of is what Ma used to say – the Lord will fight for you; you need only to be still – and I haven't been. I need to let this go and do the best I can. I still want to pursue Natali and that's what I'm gonna do.*

"We are going to herd cattle over to the Wright's. They wanted some of the calves. Wyatt and Lewis, you're going to take them there," Graham instructed.

"I will take Charlene back to town. I'm sorry, Wyatt. I didn't realize..." Zed replied, trailing off. "Think Nellie can watch the kids for me?"

Graham nodded. "Sure," he said, clapping his brother on the back. "Parker and Samuel. You two are going to separate the cows for slaughter. Pick out ten for now. Avery and I are going to tag about thirty head for the auction."

As Graham finished his directions, Charlene's grating voice could be heard on the morning air. Wyatt sucked in a deep breath; reminding himself to be still and not give in to the urge to run or be judgmental. He went straight for Daisy, grabbing his tack along the way to get the calves moving to the Wright's.

# CHAPTER FOURTEEN

Natali strolled down the sidewalk. Cattle and people were already beginning to gather in town, getting ready for the large cattle auction in three days. She'd already seen Wyatt through the window of Leonard's Mercantile ride through town with cattle. A buggy, following behind, dropped Charlene off at the steps of the Whitman Hotel.

After exiting Leonard's Mercantile, she strolled down the walkway and stopped periodically, peering into all the store windows she wanted to see since her short yet enlightening walk from the day prior with Eugene and Audrey. Her mind wandered to the loud woman, Charlene and what Mary and Lena said regarding her. Natali didn't want to believe Wyatt would string her along. Especially since he seemed so genuine. They'd had moments and she was willing to take a step of faith on him. Yet her mind ran in circles, pondering why a woman would travel by herself from Indiana to Colorado if not for a man, or from a man? And the way Charlene went on about Wyatt, Natali was sure it was the former. Nothing else really made any sort of sense.

Natali bit her bottom lip. She decided she would dwell on the good. She was looking forward to Thursday, and was wondering when they would find time to get coffee when the cattle auction chaos from town would start well before the dawn.

*I'm excited and nervous*, she thought with an uncharacteristic giggle.

Her face made a moue at the sound and she looked around to see if anyone had heard her. She pushed the idea of coffee aside for the moment. She wanted to enjoy her mid-morning stroll on the sidewalk mindlessly without her nerves getting in the way.

She stopped at a small dress boutique and looked through the window. She lit up at the expensive dresses inside. The silk and taffeta were beautifully made, detailed with French lace and glass beads; something she wouldn't ever wear but enjoyed secretly dreaming about.

She was jerked out of her dress-dreaming by the distinct laughter of Audrey and the braying of Charlene from a hundred feet away. Natali shrugged the shawl tighter on her shoulders, slipping down a side road to the side of town she hadn't been to yet. She counted the corners she turned, ending her small and victorious escape from Charlene at a small quilt shop.

Natali paused outside the shop. She peered down the road, spying Charlene and Audrey turn toward her. Swallowing, she continued on, thankful she wore darker colors and could blend in with everyone.

A man put a few crates of chickens in his buggy. Wyatt came riding up to the man. Laughter echoed behind her.

Taking a deep breath and swallowing down her unease, she opened the door to the quilt shop and stepped inside. Instead of browsing the cloth swatches and quilting supplies, she walked to the lace curtain covering the window and peeked out, watching the engrossed women pass by. Her attention shifted across the street where Wyatt moved his easy-going animal to the side.

He dismounted, dropping Daisy's reins and offering the man with the chicken crates a hand. Another man rode up beside Wyatt and the chicken man, talking and smiling. Audrey and Charlene stepped out, going across the street toward the men.

"Are you going to shop or take up space?" a woman yelled from behind the counter.

"My apologies," Natali mumbled, stepping to the door once again.

The lady grumbled under her breath about eastern people immigrating west, but Natali ignored her, gently shutting the shop door behind her.

She sidestepped and watched the women speak to the chicken man, and Wyatt. Audrey's animated voice lilting out over the street. Wyatt looked up and seemed to search the area, as if he could feel her eyes on him. His tense gaze found hers. His keen blue eyes locked; his upper lip quirking at her. Audrey immediately turned on her heel. Natali blanched.

"Natali!" Audrey called.

Inwardly, she cringed but her feet mindlessly took her over to the gathered party.

"Hello all," Natali said, dipping her head, "Ms. Whitman. Ms. Brandt."

Charlene laughed uproariously, garnering attention from everyone on the block. Wyatt and the other men turned their heads, trying to mask their cringe, but Natali caught them.

Charlene stroked her arm like a pet and Natali jerked away. "Oh, Natali, you amuse me so. Please call me Charlene. I was just talking to Audrey here about dress shopping with some fine company. You will join us in this endeavor. I am soon to be married and I am looking for a one of a kind dress – white or not, it simply doesn't matter," Charlene made a move toward Audrey and began conversing strictly with her, now ignoring Natali.

She let out a breath she didn't know she held, blinking rapidly at the disbelief at the back of Charlene's brown head. *How can her lips form words that fast?* she thought. Wyatt took a step to his horse looking like he wanted to hide.

Gathering her courage, she took a few more steps toward him. "Hello, Wyatt," Natali said.

Wyatt perked and swung his attention toward her at the sound of her voice. "Good afternoon. How does the day find you?"

"Quite pleasant, thank you," she replied, blushing, and taking a step closer to Wyatt.

"This here is Lewis Custer," Wyatt introduced. "And this is Zed Oliver, Graham's brother."

The men tipped their hats to her and smiling, turned back to their tasks. Natali fumbled the ends of her shawl in her hands, looking down at her feet. Audrey and Charlene glanced over to where she was. Audrey grabbed Charlene's hand, pulling them closer to the party. Natali turned her attention to Wyatt once again.

"Care to go to coffee?" Natali blurted.

Wyatt's eyes pinched together. "I would love to. Is our proposed time getting rescheduled?"

Natali gaped like a fish a few times. She moved stray hairs behind her ear. The cool breeze put a chill on her skin. Biting her lower lip, she pulled the shawl tighter.

"No," she finally stuttered. "I... That is to say... if you happen to have a moment, because I do too... right now, coffee sounds good," she said the last word a touch high pitched.

Wyatt glanced to Lewis and Zed. The bear of a man with a beard nodded while the other clean shaved man grinned.

"Have a good time," Lewis, the clean shaved one, smiled.

"Oh Natali," Charlene beckoned. "you must come shopping with us. Leave the men to their trivial tasks. I'm sure they are rather in a hurry to get back to their little ranch and smelly animals."

Natali watched the vein in Wyatt's neck tick.

"Coffee sounds great," Wyatt replied, offering her his arm.

Charlene gaped like a fish for a moment. She smiled smarmily. Natali swallowed remembering one other person who made that smile and the hell following it.

Audrey stood, fidgeting with the tie on her lace glove but kept her eyes on Charlene. Audrey tried to whisper words to get Charlene to move down the street but the woman couldn't be swayed. Audrey looked at Natali and grimaced, shrugging at her sympathy. Natali tipped her chin at Audrey in understanding.

Wyatt touched her hand lightly with his, bringing her attention forward. "There is a diner down the way here," he said. "Let's get you out of this biting wind."

Natali allowed herself to be led away from the tensest conversation she'd ever had. She felt the warmth of Wyatt's assuring hand through her cotton dress. She let out a breath through her nose, taking in the sights of Denver with much more ease. Wyatt kept his hand over the top of the one that was looped through his arm.

"Have a good time," Lewis called.

Natali smirked to herself and nodded but didn't turn around. *I will have a good time.*

They strolled down two store fronts to a little diner close to the train tracks but two blocks over from the main road. Wyatt got the door for her, taking off his hat as he walked inside. With a hand on the small of her back, he guided her down the aisle. The diner was small and already packed with people. One table, way in the back, was open.

Without waiting, Natali made for it, taking a seat with her back to the door. Wyatt's chair screeched out across the table from her. He took off his gun belt, slinging it over the ear of the chair. His hat rested peacefully over it all. He took a seat opposite her with a smile.

Natali wriggled in her seat. A waitress went around, filling little coffee cups and taking orders. Natali made eye contact with her. The waitress came over, filling her cup and Wyatt's.

"How are you liking Denver so far?" Wyatt asked, soon as the waitress went away.

Natali smiled, meeting his handsome gaze. "It's better now," she replied.

Wyatt let out a breath and chuckled a bit. "I couldn't agree more."

She fiddled with her cup, moving it around in her hands. "Thank you," she stammered. Meeting his eyes fully, she took a fortifying breath and continued, "for agreeing to having coffee."

"My pleasure," he replied, a genuine smile lighting up his lips and reaching his eyes.

Natali smiled, opening her mouth to say something but finding her tongue thick and refusing to move. Pressing the lip of the cup to her lips, her mind took her back to the other day and Eugene's words of leaving Kansas City behind her. At first, she thought it was ridiculous, playing it off and not wanting to read into it. Now, sitting before this handsome man, she realized the depth of his words. She ran away from Kansas City, running from a situation that did not overly affect her. She was her mother's daughter, but she wasn't in her mother's marriage.

*God has not called you to "fit in"*, her mother used to say. She tried so hard for so long to ease the ache Joel caused her mother. She lost herself in trying to help, in trying to make it right or better. And in doing so, she became terrified for no reason. She'd spent so long avoiding feelings of any kind, frightened of a fate like her mother's, she forgot to remind herself that she was nothing of the sort. Her mother's choices were a reflection of her and not of Natali.

She took a deep breath, feeling her body relax. *Leave Kansas City behind you*, she thought. Wyatt sipped his coffee, keeping an eye on the door.

"For so long, I was afraid of ending up like my mother," she began, licking her chapped, trembling lips. "I didn't want to open myself up to be hurt, or abused – closing off from everyone I knew or met; and everything good that came into my life. Then I met you," Natali paused, meeting his gaze. "You came into the diner and there was a kindred connection," Natali waited for some kind of reaction. There wasn't one. Tucking in her lips, she stared at the top of the table. "I'm sorry for being so forward."

Natali swallowed, swirling the coffee in the cup. Her insides swirled, tingling as she waited for any kind of response from Wyatt.

# CHAPTER FIFTEEN

Wyatt rode away from the Whitman Hotel full of coffee and a happy heart. He drank so much with Natali he didn't want to see the black liquid again until tomorrow.

Wyatt chuckled, *may for a couple days.*

The light of the sun began to wane, going from mid-morning to late afternoon. He needed to get back to Elk Creek Ranch but speaking with the beautiful woman had him iron pressed to his chair for a pleasantly long time.

Daisy shook her mane, taking him out of town and north toward home. Wyatt couldn't wipe the smile from his face. Spending the afternoon with Natali was what he needed; making him determined to call on her when he saw her next. He would have asked her officially at the diner they were at but the timing hadn't felt right.

*I'll ask her Thursday,* he decided. *When we meet for coffee again.*

He smiled, reminiscing on Natali. She was gentle and kind – hiding like him from the failures brought into their life by other people. They were kindred souls, brought together, he believed, by God.

He'd studied her mouth, how it moved freely when she spoke

fondly of her mother or of her dog long past. When she was about to disclose her hurt, her lips would tighten like a fish then press down in a hard line.

*Any other person would look ridiculous, but on her, it's cute.*

She constantly tucked hair behind her ear, even if there was nothing to tuck. Her cheeks, often rose colored and glowing during their conversation, brought out more of her alluring green eyes. Wyatt adjusted the hat on his head to block out the shifting sun.

He rounded the final corner as Elk Creek came into view. Lamps lit the inside of the ranch house. The barn door remained open a crack for him to settle Daisy.

Wyatt turned up the road, going straight for the barn. Dismounting, he held the reins in his hands. His eyes scanned the ranch house for any sign of Charlene, knowing she had no boundaries when it came to pursuing him. He spied Nellie and Graham at the table with the other ranch hands. Wyatt let out the breath he held.

Swallowing, he stepped further inside the barn cautiously looking around with each step. Knowing Charlene as he did, she could be anywhere like a silent, stalking cat obsessed with a mouse. Wyatt shoved the hat back off his forehead, forcing his eyes to peer into all the dark places of the barn. Rustling came from the stall to his right.

"Hey!"

Wyatt whirled around, letting out a breath when he spied Lewis. "Damnation man."

"I saw someone come up the drive and wanted to make sure it was you."

Wyatt nodded. "I was making sure Charlene wasn't in here or the ranch house."

Lewis's laugh thundered in the cozy barn. "Naww... She was steaming when you went off with Natali though. Said something again about finding a dress today and making arrangements."

Wyatt pressed his head against the saddle and sighed. Daisy spun her head toward him, nudging him with her muzzle. Mindlessly, he uncinched the tack. Lewis pulled it off and set it on the other side of the barn on a saddle rack.

"Just thought you should hear it from me first before the woman tries anything unpleasant," Lewis finally said.

"I appreciate it," Wyatt grumbled, taking the bridle off Daisy. "I don't know how the woman has the gumption to pull stunts like this."

"Love drives some women mad. She's one of them. She wants to feel appreciated and loved like the rest of us, but Charlene doesn't know how to go about it."

Wyatt let out a hard breath through his nose. "How did you get to be so wise?"

Lewis shrugged, kicking the ground with his booted foot. "I liked Nellie's sister but she didn't like me. In that case, I was the crazy woman. Although I am not sure I was quite at Charlene's level, although I pulled some crazy stunts to get noticed."

Wyatt chuckled at the mental image of a younger love-crazy Lewis as he led Daisy into her stall and shut the door. He scooped some oats into her feed pan then followed Lewis out of the barn, shutting the door behind him.

The bleating call of a calf caught their attention. Norman was at the fence, head tilted to the side, watching the men walk by. Wyatt smiled, going up the calf. He reached through the fence to pet him, but his adoptive mother charged the fence. Norman skittered around her.

Wyatt grinned, kneeling down, "You got yourself a good mama, Norman," he said, petting the calf's head.

He scratched Norman's head behind his ears and under his chin. Norman stuck his head through the fence, pressing his wet nose to Wyatt's cheek. Wyatt patted Norman's little face. Rising off the ground, he continued with Lewis to the ranch house.

"Don't name what we're going to eat," Lewis teasingly admonished Wyatt.

"We aren't eating Norman. I bought him. He's mine and I plan on breeding him. He'll make some great babies."

Lewis rolled his eyes and shook his head. Wyatt opened the

door, heading inside. Graham, Nellie and the others patiently waited for them to come sit down and eat. Wyatt took his seat beside Parker, dishing food on his plate. Nellie smiled knowingly at him, while Graham would meet his eyes then roll them with a smirk.

Wyatt grinned. His afternoon with Natali was worth all the extra chores or tasks he would be asked to accomplish.

"So," Nellie began coyly, breaking the silence. "How was coffee?"

Wyatt smirked. "Wonderful."

Graham snorted. "I'm glad to hear it. You're doing all the dishes for a week."

"Gladly, boss."

Chuckling erupted around the table. Wyatt grinned, tucking into his meal. He would happily do all the dishes for a month if it meant another afternoon with her.

Natali walked up the steps to the Whitman Hotel feeling like she was walking on water. Everything felt soft under her feet. Everything felt magical with little sparkles dancing around her head. If she told anyone, they might dub her insane. But she wasn't. The afternoon with Wyatt restored her faith in herself and in a life unlike any she'd seen much of up close; only hearing about equal and loving partnerships until coming to Denver just a short time before.

Going through the double doors of the hotel, she was careful to look for Charlene. The woman would more than likely be on the lookout for her, to either talk to her about whatever imagined nuptials she had in mind or shame her. Natali felt sympathy for Wyatt. To lose his wife in such a horrid way, and then have this woman after him, would be difficult.

Sure, as the sun rose, Charlene sat in the sitting area off to the side. A paper loftily held in her hands. Charlene glared at the paper. Not a strand of hair out of place on her mouse brown head.

Natali swallowed, trepidation filling her from her feet to her stomach. She made a wide arch around Charlene, heading to her room to freshen up before the supper rush hit with all the people in town for the auction in a few days.

"Natali, dear," Charlene called with a fake smile and seething vehemence in her eyes. "how do you fare this evening?"

"Quite well, Ms. Brandt. And yourself?"

Charlene set her paper in the chair, taking several steps toward her. "Better now, thank you. Tell me, how was your afternoon with my fiancée?"

Natali blinked. "With all due respect, Wyatt isn't engaged to you."

Charlene stamped her foot. "He would have been engaged to me already if a harlot such as yourself would let him alone enough to speak with me! How dare you!"

Natali peered over the top of Charlene to where Bartholomew sat behind the check-in counter; he flipped through the paper, unimpressed and indifferent to the rising situation. Audrey and Jane stood in the doorway leading to their offices staring wide-eyed at the scene unfolding in the middle of the hotel. Natali felt eyes behind her and she hoped it was a friend and not someone who believed her a foe.

"Ms. Brandt," Natali began softly, "Wyatt is free to choose whom he may, be it yourself or I. However, as he stated previously, you and him are unattached."

"Falsehoods seep from your lying mouth," Charlene seethed.

Natali suppressed a smile and a laugh. She'd heard the saying of someone "being off their rocker" although she hadn't understood it until this moment. Charlene's face scrunched; her eyes bore into hers with a vengeance Natali had never seen on a woman before.

"Stay. Away. From. My. Intended," Charlene hissed.

Ms. Brandt stormed off and up the steps to her room on the grand room side. Natali let out the breath she held, pushing the stray hairs off her face. Mary came up behind her, shaking her head.

"Like I said," Mary said, standing beside her, "that woman is mud."

Natali tucked in her lips, ready to burst into laughter. She watched Charlene stomp on the steps and disappear down the hall to her room. Natali shook her head. The entire situation was laughable. She kind of felt bad for Charlene since she was so confused and hurt.

She turned on her heel, heading to the kitchen. Despite wanting to laugh at the whole situation, the lightness she'd felt earlier with Wyatt had dissipated. Her heart still felt wonderous from being with Wyatt, but it also felt heavy for Charlene. She knew what it was like to feel so alone and unworthy.

*I found someone who makes me feel seen*, she thought, picturing Wyatt's handsome sun-tanned face, piercing blue eyes and dark auburn hair. *He makes me feel like a person. I've spent so long being afraid of men and love; and that I am not afraid anymore because of Wyatt is nothing short of miraculous.*

Natali opened the door to the kitchen only to be greeted by fleeing old women. Natali had to fight to keep the laughter down as Claudia and Ada hurried to their spots in the kitchen as if they hadn't just been caught spying. Ada offered her a sympathetic, if perhaps a bit embarrassed, smile while Claudia's normal grumbles increased in volume as her cheeks reddened. Natali shook her head at them, offering Ada a smile of gratitude and grabbed her apron off the peg.

*Come on supper service*, she thought.

# CHAPTER SIXTEEN

Cattle bellowed throughout Denver in the early Thursday morning. Natali set another plate of food in front of a couple cowboys who eagerly tucked into the fare. The bell inside the diner rang announcing more guests. Natali felt her stress levels rise when she looked around, observing how many already occupied tables there were and how many more needed to eat. She'd not a clue how they were all going to get fed. Natali scampered back to the kitchen at the sonorous dinging of the bell. Lena grumbled something about "too early" and "no coffee," and Natali almost nodded her agreement as she strode beside her.

Inside the kitchen was more chaos. Claudia's hair was frazzled; her face dour as she loaded plates of food. Her perpetual grumble lost under the hisses and pops of multiple breakfasts cooking. There was so much food out, for a moment Natali was stunned. She couldn't remember seeing so much food before.

A particularly loud clatter of dishes brought her out of her daze. Mary washed plates and ware quickly, setting them in the drying rack for the next meal that was sure to be only minutes away. Natali stepped up to the counter, grabbing the next order. Swiveling on her heel, she was followed out the door by Lena.

Natali went back out with food, setting it down with a smile and refilling coffee cups. A high-pitched whistle filtered in through the slightly open windows. She peeked outside, spying Wyatt ride in with cattle from Elk Creek Ranch. Seeing the back of his head brought a smile to her face. Her heart fluttered, causing every inch of her skin to tingle.

Mary said that for her, *love was an instant connotation to Ross.* Natali was certain, Mary meant connection and Natali took a brief moment to smirk at what she'd come to affectionately think of as a "Mary-ism." Even still, Natali felt something toward Wyatt that was unexplainable. She couldn't stop thinking about him, wanting to spend more time with the man. Her walls were crumbling around her.

A smile still graced her lips. *I can't wait for our next coffee date.*

Screeching chairs echoed in the small diner. Natali carried soiled plates back into the kitchen. Men full of food, stomped out of the diner, leaving money and more dirty plates in their wake. The diner almost suddenly emptied of people, with only the last few men remaining. Shoveling the last bit of food into their faces and gulping down coffee, within a couple minutes even those men followed the others outside and to the auction down by the train tracks.

Lena sighed. "That was chaos," she breathed. "I need to sit and drink my own cup of coffee."

Natali plopped in an empty seat beside her, leaning back against the chair shaking her head in relief. "What a morning for sure. I didn't think we had enough food to serve all those men."

Claudia came waddling out of the kitchen. Her white-gray hair frazzled and sweat beading on her forehead. She huffed, taking a seat at an empty table two over from Natali and Lena.

"We need more supplies," she said. "Take a breather then Natali, head to Leonard's for eggs, flour, sugar, milk and some vegetables. Pick some, I don't care what, just get a bunch and put it on the tab. Lena, get meat from Randall's, also put it on the tab. I'll tell Audrey so it can be paid."

Natali nodded. "In a moment."

Claudia agreed with a nod of her head. "Turn the sign around. We need a break."

Ada walked into the room and turned the sign to "closed," taking a seat beside Lena. Natali steeped herself, breathed out, got up and headed to the door. With the slight break in people, she might as well get this chore done quickly as dinner rush would be upon them soon. The bell tinkled above her head when she opened the door and stepped out into the flood of people.

People strolled down the sidewalk toward the train station. Cattle herded close together bellowing skittishly. Cowboy's on their mounts kept the cattle from wandering. Natali waited for a clearing in the road so she could cross. She dashed past people, making a zig-zag line for Leonard's.

"Natali!"

Looking over her shoulder, she smiled. Wyatt moved past couples, coming to her with a smile on his face. Natali moved to the side, out of people's way. Seeing Wyatt and having him come toward her, made her heart soar higher than an eagle. She couldn't keep the smile off her face.

His dusty hat was pushed back off his face. A dark blue shirt hugged his muscular frame while dark pants fit him perfectly. He looked every inch a rancher; every inch a respectable owner would look, in her opinion.

Heat crept to her cheeks and the smile on her face didn't wane.

"Natali," he said, coming to her. "You shouldn't be out like this by yourself."

"Then I am glad to have you here."

She shocked herself by flirting. Wyatt smiled, taking her arm and tucking it inside his. He walked on the outside, keeping her near the security of the buildings. His thumb mindlessly rubbed the outside of her wrist as they walked.

She entered Leonard's Mercantile with Wyatt on her arm, feeling like the most special woman in the world. His hand still rested over the top of hers, keeping it there protectively. Leonard glanced up over the top of his spectacles, grinning.

"Ms. Hawkins," Leonard greeted with his usual smile. "What can I do for you, today?"

"Good morning, Leonard," Natali replied. "Claudia needs the usual plus carrots, potatoes, onions and green beans."

Leonard nodded, writing it all down. "Out of food already? Would be a shame if those molasses cookies would be out too," he finished with a wink.

"I will happily save you some. I'll sneak them by after the dinner rush."

Leonard chuckled. "I would appreciate it, Ms. Hawkins. I'll send Clyde up with your order."

"Thank you, Leonard. Please put it on the tab. Audrey will be in to pay it."

Leonard nodded, writing down her supplies for his grandson to bring them as soon as it was gathered. Natali, made a motion toward the door. Wyatt grabbed it before she could, putting his rough, calloused hand on the small of her back.

"Are you headed back to the diner?" he asked.

"Yes. Care to have some coffee?" she replied.

Her insides screamed, hoping he would say yes and chat with her again, if only for a couple of minutes. Even if nothing ever became of this relationship, she was thankful to Wyatt for showing her not to be afraid; to be happy and comfortable with herself. Although she fervently hoped Wyatt wasn't going anywhere.

"I would love to have a cup of coffee with you," he replied. "I can't stay long though. I'm still on dish duty from staying so long last time." Wyatt smirked. "But I also don't want to leave the guys for too long. They're going to need my help soon."

Natali smiled. "Any mere moment with you, is one I would appreciate to have."

Wyatt grinned, showing the white of his teeth. Natali felt her knees tremble. She enjoyed being in his presence, and hoped he felt the same. Wyatt protectively led her back across the street to the diner, opening the door for her. Inside, the entirety of Elk Creek Ranch sat at the largest table.

Wyatt chuckled and grinned down at Natali, winking. "Well,

never mind then. Even the boss is slacking. Guess I got a few minutes then."

The men around the table chuckled. Even Nellie laughed a little despite looking miserable as she sat down, resting her back and neck against the rail of the chair. Audrey sat beside her, talking low and kindly to the woman.

Wyatt let go of Natali's hand, taking a chair from another table and putting it beside the only other empty one. With a tilting nod of his head, Natali moved to the chair and sat while he scooted her to the table. Wyatt removed his hat and gun belt, slinging them over the ear of the chair. He took a seat beside her, his cheeks lightly rising in color.

Lena came out of the kitchen with two pots of coffee. She poured her a cup first, leaning down and whispering, "I got this. Enjoy yourself."

"I owe you one," Natali replied in a whisper.

Lena winked, going around and filling every person's cup to the brim with the black liquid gold. Natali fidgeted in her seat, putting the bitter liquid to her lips. After the other day, she was about done with coffee although she would drink gallons of it if it meant remaining here, by Wyatt's side.

Around her, people ordered their meals. While waiting to replenish their food stores, Claudia would be sending out whatever she could for their breakfast. Luckily for everyone, no one minded.

"What are you doing this Sunday?" Wyatt leaned in and asked.

Natali shrugged. "Church service then I do the dinner and supper service."

"Before church, would you care to go on a walk with me?"

"I would love to," she replied, sipping her coffee with a smile that reached her eyes.

Lena came out, bringing plates of food, setting them in front of a ranch hand then disappeared back inside the kitchen. The door from the kitchen leading out into the diner burst open. Mary stood on the other side, barring the swiveling door from swinging outward into the diner. The blond woman smiled, the gap in her teeth showing as she awkwardly stood there.

"Get her out!" Claudia's voice boomed.

Mary's eyes went wide. She stepped to the side. The door swung open, slamming on the other side of the wall and banging with an echo. Lena came out, two plates of food and a coffee pot in her hands, eyes wide and shaking her head. All eyes waited curiously for someone else to step out into the diner but no one came.

Mary slunk over, creeping along the wall to stand by Lena filling up a cup of coffee for herself. Someone inside the kitchen cleared their throat. Natali's skin prickled, wondering what was going on.

The bell over the door to the diner tingled. Reverend Kester stepped inside, hat in his hands with a wide, toothy smile.

"Care for another to join?" Reverend Kester asked.

"Not at all," Graham Oliver beckoned, scooting his chair over closer to his wife.

Natali sipped her coffee warily. Out from inside the kitchen, stepped out Charlene in a white, overly laced dress. Her mouse brown hair hung in perfect ringlets down her back. Her hands held bouquet of lavender and ivy. She beamed, walking toward Wyatt.

Natali choked on her coffee, scooting out of her seat to stand beside Lena. She wanted to get a good look at this extravagant and unorthodox scene.

"Oh Wyatt," Charlene preened. "This is how I always imagined it would be. An intimate setting full of people we both know, quiet and quaint. Food, merriment and drinks all in one place. This is so delightful. And the kind Reverend already here to join us in matrimony."

The Reverend glanced about him, reading the room warily. He choked on his coffee, setting the cup down and rose to his feet.

Wyatt rose also, keeping the chair he vacated in between him and Charlene. Wyatt appeared perplexed mixed in with anger and annoyance. His eyes scrunched on the corners. He gripped the ears of the chair, his knuckles turning white. His jaw set firmly, and the vein in his neck throbbed.

"I was informed," Reverend Kester directed at Graham, "you wanted to speak with me about a couple head of cattle."

"I knew nothing of this" Graham gestured at the overly fancy Charlene and then back to him "or of you wanting cattle," Graham replied.

Charlene, still beaming, strode up to Wyatt. "Oh darling. I know we cannot bear to be apart from each other which is why I took it upon myself to gather everyone here. I knew you would love this intimate setting. Oh," she said, dashing for him. Charlene ignored the chair between them, putting her hands on his forearms. "Wyatt, my love. This is such a wondrous day. Let us not squander it a moment further. Dear Reverend, we are ready to be wed."

The diner was silent. Not a chair squeaked or coffee cup clanked. Natali glanced about the room; all faces staring at Charlene a mix of wonder and horror at her behavior.

Natali swallowed, waiting to see how Wyatt would respond. So far, the man stood more still than a mountain, eyes darkened and glaring at Charlene. Two of the men continued eating their fare like nothing in the world was amiss.

"Are you not pleased, darling?" Charlene asked. "I did try my best but given the circumstances as they were, I was not left with much to work with in such a minuscule amount of time. I do hope you understand. Now, let's stand over here and the Reverend can begin."

Wyatt took a thundering step toward her. His eyes fixed on Charlene's face like a fox on a chicken. His fisted hands balled at his sides.

"Wyatt," Natali piped up.

He glanced over to Natali, his face softening. She offered him a tight smile, not knowing what else to give.

Turning back to Charlene, he said. "No. I am not marrying you today or any day. I believe I have made it perfectly clear on more than one occasion."

Charlene gaped like a fish. "I thought you were toying with my affections. Playing – hard to get – if you will."

Wyatt laughed. "No, I wasn't. I do not know how else to make it clear to you. But since the Reverend is here at your bidding, perhaps he can help me in telling you, I do not wish to be married to you, this day or any other day. I do not love you."

Charlene seethed. "It's that harlot's fault!" she screamed, pointing at Natali. "She ruined you against me!"

"No, she hasn't. I love Natali. I am going to call on her in hopes that someday soon she will be my wife."

Natali put a hand to her mouth. "Really?" she squeaked.

Wyatt spun on his heel, striding toward her. "Yes," he said, taking both her hands in his own.

Natali's heart fluttered; her skin tingling at his warm, soft touch on her hands. She smiled, meeting his gentle blue eyes. He reached up, tucking stray hairs behind her ear.

"Yes," he repeated. "May I call on you, Natali Hawkins?"

Natali nodded. "I would love that."

Wyatt kissed the back of her hand. "I would love it too."

"What about me?" Charlene screeched, tears trickling down her eyes. "You're supposed to love me!"

"Ms. Brandt, would you care to take a stroll with me," Reverend Kester proclaimed. "Or would you like to change first?"

Charlene stamped her foot, completely ignoring the reverend. "I love you, Wyatt Pearson. I know you love me back. Marry me, so we can be happy together!"

"No Charlene," Wyatt's firm voice boomed.

"You will regret this. Mark my words," Charlene cried, scurrying toward the kitchen door. "I'm going back to Indiana. Don't come for me. I won't be bothered. We are through Wyatt. My love will not go to waste."

Audrey came over to Charlene, wrapping an arm around her. "Charlene would love to take a walk with you, Reverend. Allow her but a moment to ready herself."

Charlene left with Audrey through the kitchen. Everyone in the diner seemed to breathe again, happily relieved of the awkward and interesting situation. Natali held onto Wyatt's hand, smiling as her eyes met his.

Wyatt led her around, back to their chairs. He scooted her in and took a seat beside her.

"Thank you," he whispered.

Natali's brows furrowed. "For what?"

"Making me believe in love again."

Natali leaned forward resting her head against his. "Same." she breathed.

# VI

## TO BIND A HEART

# CHAPTER ONE

J ane strode up the steps inside the Whitman Hotel going left to the grand room side. Hand in her dress pocket, she fiddled with a blue stone pin her mother gave to her on her wedding day. She knocked on room 105 where a patient lawyer sat outside the door on the left-hand side, hands in his lap, waiting to escort Audrey down, and give her away. Entering the room, Audrey's eager face greeted hers.

She returned Audrey's enthusiastic look. The woman practically jumped out of her skin with excitement. Jane smiled. It warmed her heart seeing her friend blossoming so; knowing all too well the tingling, thrilling shivers of marriage.

"You need something blue," Jane said, pulling out the pin from her pocket.

She fastened a blue pin to Audrey's gown. The stone swirled with different blue tones, varying from dark indigo to sky blue. Jane took a step back, smiling with tears in her eyes. "It's like my sister is getting married," Jane commented, choking on her last word.

Audrey wrapped her arms around her. "And you're next. Tonight, my goal is to find you a match."

Jane scoffed, patting her eyes. "Audrey, I appreciate your optimism but I am well past my suitability."

"Nonsense, it is complete swill and you know it well."

Jane smiled wanly, heading to the door. Upon her opening it, Jane took a step back startled. The old lawyer, Wilfred poked his head in and grinned. He stepped forward and bowed, holding out his hand. Audrey ran over, dress hiked up above her ankles, readily taking it.

Jane stepped to the side to avoid being barreled over by an eager Audrey. She smiled brightly, tucking away her own loneliness, waiting to follow Audrey down the stairs. In the months knowing the hotel owner, she'd discovered nothing – objects, people, or problems – stood between the woman and what she wanted.

"It's time," Wilfred choked, tears forming in the corner of his eyes. "If only your parents could see you now."

"I miss them greatly," Audrey agreed, misty eyed. "Having you here with me now and to give me away, is everything to me. I would prefer no one else. Thank you, Wilfred."

Jane smiled, navigating around them both to hold the door open. Wilfred with Audrey's arm looped in his followed her down the stairs. Jane got the door leading to the outside sitting area. The guests rose to their feet, smiling and appreciating the approaching bride on her glorious day. Jane closed the door softly behind her, fiddling with the broach at the base of her throat.

Closing her eyes, she took a deep breath. *Her late husband stood in front of her. Seth's brown hair and light blue eyes sparkling in the Tennessee sunset. A grin from ear to ear split his handsome, tanned face. His white shirt with bluebonnets pinned to his chest brought out more of his stunning eyes. Jane felt the warmth of his hand envelop her skin in an exhilarating protectiveness she swore she would never tire of.*

*"I do," he whispered, pressing his head against hers.*

Jane bowed her head, tears streaming down her face. She took a moment to breathe and allow herself to feel the sorrow hitting her when thoughts of Seth assailed her. Jane opened her eyes, taking in Audrey and Eugene exchanging vows. Her heart was happy for them, but it also ached for herself. Seth had been gone for over a decade, yet she could not get over how much she loved him.

Angrily, she wiped the tears from her cheeks. Glancing around, her eyes pinched together inspecting the crowd, hoping no one saw her slight burst of emotions. Her glance showed her all eyes on the radiant bride and her handsome groom.

Jane let out a breath of relief, patting her hair to make certain no strand was out of place. She spied all of the Whitman Hotel employees in the front two rows on the left-hand side.

"I do!" Audrey exclaimed.

"I do, too," Eugene said, giving Audrey's hands a squeeze that Jane could see from her spot in the back.

Reverend Kester chuckled. "All right then. I can see my job is almost done here. I'll get straight to the point then."

The guests chuckled with the reverend while the bride and groom grinned at each other, almost oblivious to everything around them. Jane smiled, watching the happiest moments unfold. She remembered her own happy moments with Seth, feeling all the love he had for her rush back. Reverend Kester flipped through the pages in his black bible before closing it. He smiled, looking out across the crowd. His tall frame towered over Eugene and Audrey as his arms spread wide, as if to embrace the couple.

"God's love is eternal and unconditional. By their quick responses of - I do - their love for each other is clearly like God's - quick, powerful, and unforgettable," Reverend Kester chuckled. "From fake deaths to kidnappings, and wanted gang members to hardships, one thing I can be most certain of is their love will endure. With the blessing of the Good Lord, the state of Colorado, and myself, you are now husband and wife. For the first time, I am pleased to introduce Mr. and Mrs. Eugene Turner."

Audrey leapt at Eugene, wrapped her arms around him and kissed his lips. Eugene barely caught her, holding her back slightly, he helped her to right herself smiling all the while. Jane smiled, wiping more tears off her face. She was happy for her friend and boss. To be honest with herself, she was also slightly jealous of what Audrey and Eugene had. Granted, she had it once too. Only it was cut short by several decades.

Spinning on her heel, Jane strode inside the Whitman Hotel, going to her office. Besides her room, it was the only place of solitude for herself. She wasn't in the mood, selfish as it was, for merriment.

"Jane."

A lilting voice beckoned her to turn around.

"Jane McCarthy," the woman called again.

Internally she sighed. She didn't want to make nice. Her heart felt too many emotions and she needed to sort through them before she felt she could socialize.

*Smile and nod*, she reminded herself.

Jane plastered a business-like smile to her face. In front of her, with a smile on her face and a man on her arm holding a sleeping baby girl was Kayla Langmoore. The man, Ben, if she remembered right, dipped his head to her. The dark brown-haired woman grinned broadly, embracing her like no time had passed between them.

Ben leaned over, shaking her hand. "Ms. McCarthy, it's a pleasure to see you again," his deep voice rumbled.

Jane felt her lips tense. Ben didn't make her feel uncomfortable. Her emotions were so jarring, she wasn't sure how long she could remain polite. She needed a break from the event. For propriety's sake, she tilted her head and grinned.

Curious to the sleeping child, Jane tucked back the blanket and smiled wanly. "She's beautiful. Congratulations."

Kayla embraced her again. "Thank you. It's so good to see you again. It's been quite some time."

A year had come and gone since seeing Kayla Langmoore. The young woman was a pleasure to have employed, for the few months she was. Three months after Audrey's kidnapping, Kayla Langmoore came to the Whitman Hotel until around January when Ben came to claim his woman.

The entire year since meeting Audrey was quite the wagon ride. And why it took a year for Audrey to plan this wedding, she didn't know but surmised it had to do with society, her money, and estate homes all over America.

"Yes, it has," Jane replied, holding Kayla back at arm's length giving her a quick inspection. "It is very nice to see you again, Kayla. We all sure do miss your baking, even still. Please, head inside and enjoy yourself."

"Very kind of you to say," Kayla grinned. "We will see you inside."

Jane tucked in her lips, heading in behind Kayla and Ben to sneak away since they were ahead of her. She maneuvered off to the side, past people and toward the front desk. Audrey and Eugene stood in front on the left-hand side, of the double French doors leading into the ballroom. Jane stood to the side while people lined up the far left, allowing other traffic to pass by as they all waited a turn to congratulate the bride and groom.

Silently, she side stepped to the door, leading back into the hallway to her office. *I'm being selfish, I know,* she chastised herself. *I should be happy for someone who's my best friend, like a younger, endearing sister. But it reminds me so much of what I lost. And I just... I can't.*

Jane sighed. *It reminds me of all the love and intimate moments I gained with you Seth,* she thought. *I love you. Even still, my heart loves you deeply and cherishes you and the happiness you brought. I remember our wedding day, how the sun set and twinkling little bugs came out. How you adjusted the crown of flowers on my head each time before you kissed me. And now, it's all memories...*

Every part of her desired to run away into her office, her feet moving her that way seemingly on their own, but she stopped them. That wasn't the woman she was. Jane walked toward Audrey and Eugene, smiling genuinely. The party inside was a cacophony of laughter and happiness. Children were at the far end near the food table, giggling and sneaking sweets. Parents were lost in deep conversation with other adults, oblivious to their quiet children and their friends.

Jane grinned, feeling herself loosen up a bit. She strode over the bride and groom, who found themselves alone for a moment.

"Congratulations," Jane said to Eugene and Audrey.

The bride beamed, throwing her arms around her neck. "All of this is possible because of you," Audrey exclaimed. "You are simply incredible."

"Thank you," Eugene added, embracing her next. "You have been the steady rock in this tumultuous adventure."

"You both are very welcome," Jane replied, her voice thick. "I love you both dearly. Congratulations."

"Come," Audrey beckoned. "It is high time to find you a match."

Jane felt her arm whip around her body as Audrey drug her about the room. Jane peeked over her shoulder to find Eugene rolling his eyes.

Jane swallowed. The room was a hive of people buzzing around her louder than a bee's nest. It scared her. Not only the plethora of people but the possibility of finding love after losing Seth. Years ago, though it was, it hurt her heart still.

She'd loved Seth since they were kids, growing up down the road from each other in the hills of Tennessee. Marrying him at seventeen was the highlight of her life. Having his life cut short a mere 8 years later when she turned twenty-six destroyed her inside. And more so with no child of his to have in her arms. Jane took a deep breath. Seth's faded image drifted across her eyes.

Jane bit her bottom lip. "Thank you, Audrey," Jane stammered. "I appreciate your endeavors, but I would rather enjoy the party by mingling with our guests who came from out of town."

Audrey grinned. "Nonsense. You shall be dancing with every available bachelor. It will be thrilling for you."

Audrey grabbed her hand, pulling her deep inside the ballroom. Jane's slight heels skated her along the polished floor. Jane met the amused eyes of Ross and Mary sipping some punch. Mary set her drink in Ross's hand, coming over to Audrey and, hopefully, to Jane's rescue.

"Whatcha got goin' on Audrey?" Mary asked. "I'd figure you'd be with your man."

Audrey threw her arms around Mary's neck releasing what felt like Jane's shackle on her wrist. "My dear friend, we are going to find a match for Jane. And Eugene doesn't mind my temporary absence."

Mary's brows furrowed. "You think that's a bright idea?"

Jane maneuvered her way behind Mary and her rounding belly, using Mary as a form of protection from the enthusiasm of Audrey.

Audrey pouted. "Jane, I thought you wanted companionship?"

Jane licked her lips. "I do. But God provides what He will in His time. If there is ought to be someone, then he will come forth when I need him most. Now forget about me, and go enjoy your brand-new husband. I'll be fine. See, I'm fine." She said, gesturing toward Mary and adorning her face with her best smile.

Jane linked her arm with Mary's, thankful to be out of Audrey's grasp and her sweet intentions. Jane let out a breath she was holding as Mary led over to Ross. She stood by Mary and Ross, relishing in their silent presence as more people meandered inside the ballroom.

Closing her eyes briefly, she let out a long, slow breath. *Everyone here is married. Don't fret yourself so.*

"Can we join your circle?" Lena asked no one in particular. "Jane, you look upset."

Jane shook her head plastering another smile to her face. "I'm fine."

"Here," Quint said, handing her his drink with a wink. "It'll loosen you up a bit."

Jane kept the grimace from her face. She adored Lena, knowing the young woman for nigh on ten years. Her husband, Quint, sweet though he was, had a former penchant for whiskey and if this cup had any of the firewater inside, she was going to be in trouble.

"Thank you, Quint," she replied, taking a small sip.

To her surprise, she hardly tasted any liquor. She took a larger sip. Before Jane knew it, the entire cup was emptied. Jane handed the empty glass back to Quint.

"Glad you liked it," Quint commented.

Jane nodded, her skin tingling with delayed warmth. *Whiskey. I haven't tasted it in years. And now I know why. Downright uncomfortable.* Her entire body tingled with the firewater and the effects it would soon bring forth.

"Jane, I would love for you to meet Mr. Ralph Bordeu," Audrey announced. "He is my dear friend Juliet's father from Philadelphia."

The man bowed, smiling at her with a twinkle in his keen blue eyes. A formal black suit adorned his body; his brown hair slicked back on his head was peppered with silver.

Jane swallowed. Ralph took a step forward, making a grab for her hand. Politely, Jane raised it, allowing Ralph to kiss the back of her hand.

"Pleasure," Ralph said in a baritone voice.

Jane softly cleared her throat, struggling to keep the pleasantry on her face. "Pleased to make your acquaintance."

"Shall we traverse over there a way?" Ralph queried, offering her his elbow.

Jane bowed her head, clearing her throat softly from the cotton feeling from the whiskey. "I would love the company," she replied a bit shakily.

Audrey squealed excitedly, clapping her hands. Mary grabbed her hands, forcing them on her belly.

"Feel that kick!" Mary barked, drowning out the child-like behavior of Audrey.

Jane closed her eyes, wishing Mary's distraction was enough to get her out of this obligatory visit, wishing she hadn't drunk the whiskey as she felt it continue to tingle her body. *Ohhh goodness.*

# CHAPTER TWO

Jane felt her insides roil between nervousness at the handsome older man's presence and anger at the gumption of the now Audrey Turner. Although, she shouldn't be so incensed. After knowing Audrey over a year, she'd come to expect nothing less from the well-meaning nosy, assertive woman.

Ralph led her to a sitting area over by the fireplace at the far end of the ballroom. He helped her into her seat, waiting until she was done and adjusted before sitting himself.

"I thought this a safe place. I saw you getting upset by Audrey's," he waved a hand, trailing off.

"Yes, thank you," Jane replied, offering a polite smile, not quite reaching her eyes.

Ralph smirked, staring at her with bright blue eyes. "Your lip twitched and went straight... Just like my late wife's," he breathed out heavily through his nose and offered her a sympathetic look. "You kept it together very well."

Jane's smile turned genuine. "I appreciate it."

She made sure not to make her lip get tight as her nervousness continued. Instead, she fiddled with her dress collar on her neck.

She swallowed, fidgeting in her seat; not liking a stranger could read her so easily.

The entirety of the situation made her a nervous wreck. She didn't know what to say to him. She was clueless in how to begin a personal conversation outside of business settings. She opened up to others at the hotel and their spouses, trusting them more than a random man off the streets. She didn't rightly know how to make something personal or begin in a personal way when all she did everyday was speak business casual.

Meeting Seth as a kid, and staying sweethearts was all she knew of men. She didn't have to try to get affection and Seth didn't have to woo. There was nothing – no trying. She and Seth were always the same – inseparable.

*One day, after one of the spring gatherings, he looked at me and something shifted. We just knew we were meant to be. Nothing complicated to it,* Jane thought. *I have no idea how to go about doing this – talking and getting to know a stranger... I could make it like an interview,* she decided. *A casual, simple interview...* She cleared her throat, putting her hands in her lap.

Jane took a deep breath, attempting to still her jittering nerves. *Part of me wants to run away and the other is curious about where this conversation could go.* Jane crossed her ankles and uncrossed them, opting for setting her feet flat on the floor. She painted a softness to her face, hoping it came through genuinely and not as uncomfortable as she felt.

"I can tell this is making you uncomfortable," Ralph said, leaning forward in his seat. "I'm sorry. It's been years since I've spoken to a beautiful woman."

"It's been years for me as well. I mean. It's been years since talking to a handsome man for anything other than regarding hotel business," Jane replied, feeling heat rise to her cheeks. "My apologies. This is all so overwhelming."

Ralph nodded. "Then how about we speak... as friends."

Jane smiled; straightening herself in her seat. She cleared her throat and pulled at her dress collar. In her mind, every instinct screamed at her to run; this was not a jar of worms' worth open-ing. But part of her, probably the little amount of alcohol coursing through her, bid her to stay.

"All right," she agreed, taking a slight breath. "My husband died of yellow fever twelve years ago, back in Tennessee."

Ralph nodded. "My wife died of tuberculosis, around ten years ago, leaving me with Juliet as a toddler. It's hard being an only parent to a child as rambunctious as my Juliet. It's been lonely for myself," he paused.

Jane bowed her head. She hadn't ever the time to pause and have meaningful conversation with a man. Anyone for that matter. She buried herself in work, making all the adjustments and even helping when employees married or quit.

She felt like moving on, and getting to know someone, would shame Seth in some way. Not being able to bear a child with his name or anything of him, made the shame worse. She had nothing of him to keep, only his last name and it would change in the next marriage, if she were to have one, further cementing the abandon-ment of her beloved Seth.

Now, she had a handsome older man in front of her; speaking to her like a kindred lost soul. Jane bit her bottom lip. *He isn't asking me for a union*, she reminded herself. *Ease up a touch. It's only talking.* Jane took a deep breath, willing her body to relax.

Her eyes met those of Ralph. He smiled tightly at her, seeming to be just as nervous as she; hands clasped together as he leaned forward in his seat. Jane took a relaxed position, leaning back fully in the chair.

"I haven't taken another wife, fearing I would shame the memory of Penelope," Ralph said, breaking the silence.

Jane's mouth felt like cotton. *I shouldn't be so surprised to discover a man who thinks similarly to me. Yet I am wholeheartedly relieved one does. Both of us are not desiring to move on for fear of shaming the memories of those beloved to us.*

Ralph nodded his head, clasping his hands together.

"I understand. I too, fear forgetting or losing the memory of my late husband," she paused, taking a deep breath. "We were kids growing up down the road from each other. I always knew I loved him and married him at seventeen."

"I met and married my Penelope at eighteen."

Jane met Ralph's kind eyes and offered an understanding grin.

"Astounding... Audrey told me we would be similar, but I did not believe her until this moment," Ralph stated.

She hardened. Either the alcohol or what she saw as Audrey gossiping about her, made her skin feel like it was on fire. *Granted, Audrey loved to talk and would do so to a post if it stood there long enough, but to do this to me? How dare she! Audrey hadn't the right to tell anyone of my past or predicament.*

"Don't be upset," Ralph tried to sooth, backing a bit at Jane's look of indignation. "She didn't tell me anything other than we were similar."

Jane deflated a bit. Still, it rubbed her the wrong way. Jane stood, her chair screeching back a bit.

"Thank you for your friendly conversation," she ground out as politely as she could. "It has been a delightful change."

She wished her words sounded more believable. Her comment was almost backhanded, which she regretted. Ralph was kind to her throughout their surprise encounter. He deserved better than her curtness. She opened her mouth to say something.

"I understand," he said, nodding his head and lifting a hand as if in a gesture of peace. And she was a little relieved because he truly looked like he understood.

With a dip of her head, she strode off toward the ballroom doors. The freedom of the exit almost within her walking reach. Turning her head slightly to the right, she caught a glimpse of Mary and Lena, deep in conversation with Natali.

She made her way past the women. Glancing over her shoulder, she was relieved to see Ralph chatting amicably with someone else, like nothing went amiss with their short conversation. Jane felt her body relax, as the door came within reach.

She strode out into the hallway, going to the left, alongside the ballroom and toward her bedroom. She paused along the wall, peeking over at the sitting area where a couple mingled, talking sweetly and barely touching hands for propriety's sake.

*I'm not ready*, Jane thought. *It's been twelve years and I'm still not ready to let you go.*

## CHAPTER THREE

Jane sat behind her desk, doing her payroll sheet to make certain everyone got their allotment. Since the wedding two days ago and everyone now at church, it gave her the break in the morning she needed after handling the final wedding affairs and the plethora of questions from the people and employees around her. She stacked the money into neat little rows, counting it twice to be certain of the amount.

Audrey decreed everyone got a small bonus on her wedding day of ten extra dollars on payday. The bonus allotment included Jane, which surprised her since she was salary as hotel manager. Jane smiled softly. It would be a nice surprise for everyone and one she was excited to give, even if it was two days late due to everything going on. With Mary expecting in a few months, Bartholomew leaving at the end of the week for Baltimore, and Kelly leaving on tomorrow's train for Omaha, it would be a wonderful gift for them all.

She would have preferred Lena taking over the hotel, but she was busy running her own little corner of the world with Lena's Dove's, working here at the hotel, and a newlywed as well. Adding another item to Lena's already full plate would be a distasteful gesture on her part.

Jane closed her eyes, relishing the stillness. The hotel was simply restful; the kind of quiet one finds alone in a cabin in the woods where the heart can pause and reset itself. Jane took a deep breath, letting it out slowly through her nose.

The ballroom would begin to get cleaned and reset this afternoon and finished by tomorrow. Most of the guests already made for the train, including Ralph Bordeu and Kayla Langmoore and her little family. She'd politely said goodbye this morning, checking out the guests while Bartholomew had the day off, and asking if their stay happened to have been pleasant.

Kayla had thrown her lithe arms around her, hugging her for what would most likely be the last time she ever saw the kind-hearted woman. Kayla would be heading back to San Antonio to her slice of America.

Saying farewell to Ralph made her body cringe at the awkwardness. However, Ralph was polite and steadfastly kind throughout their morning interactions. He gave her a friendly handshake and left with his daughter Juliet in tow.

Jane turned her attention to the mess on her desk. She scoffed at herself. Few would consider a newspaper, 3 stacks of papers and a few bundles of neatly stacked money and envelopes a mess, but for her, it was bordering on unbearable. A sales page in the paper caught her attention. A family was selling their two-bedroom cabin home four miles up the road from Elk Creek Ranch. Jane bit her bottom lip wistfully.

*I haven't had a home since Seth died. Nothing felt like the home we built together and shared. And honestly, I have lived in boarding houses and this hotel since. Not really homes by anyone's estimation,* she thought. *Maybe it's time I did something for me, moved and settled down.*

Her lips pursed, face turning into a moue. Jane shook her head. *No, I need to train Lena or even Eliza to take this aspect over first. Audrey is leaving next week for New York to spend their honeymoon there. We need to make a decision about who takes over before Audrey leaves. I'm anticipating Audrey being gone for some time,* she thought, strumming her fingers on the table top. *And I need to make a decision for myself on either staying here at the hotel or purchasing myself a home.*

Jane rapped her fingers on the desktop. Her eyes narrowed in on a blemish on her polished desk top that had been there since she began. *I thought I wasn't ready to let Seth go... Today I'm ready to make a change for myself, and get a home; to let a piece of Seth go in that way, and live alone in a home which I haven't done in twelve years. I'm not certain what changed exactly. Maybe it's my old age and withering mind,* she thought with a snort. *But I need a change. And now, getting a home is as good as any.*

Sighing, she rose out from behind her desk, going out into the hotel and toward the kitchen for a snack. The smell of Claudia and Ada baking wafted pleasantly to her nose. Her stomach rumbled. Jane's heels clicked on the hardwood floor as she made her way toward the kitchen.

Opening the door, Jane caught sight of Ada pulling a sheet out of the oven. The steam from her cookies rose into the air, filling the kitchen with deliciousness. Ada smiled at her, reaching back into the oven for cinnamon rolls.

*Kayla's rolls,* Jane thought hungrily, *I'm thankful the kind woman mailed the recipe.*

"Here," Ada said, scooping a roll on a plate and giving it a heap of icing. "How are you this morning, Jane?"

Jane took the plate, walking over to the stove top to pour herself a cup of coffee to go with her treat. "I'm well, thank you Ada. I have your pay in my office. How is everyone at home?"

"Thank you," Ada tossed her head back and forth. "And it's been an adjustment."

"Is everyone at church still?" Claudia barked, stirring a large pot of stew. "We open shortly. I need Lena and Natali here."

Jane felt her body internally sigh. The older woman was becoming increasingly agitated in her old age. Claudia was the cook even before Jane had arrived in Denver. Her long-standing position definitely should be a source of pride, even seniority. But this rudeness was too much. Jane poured herself come coffee, scooping a small bit of sugar into the bitter dark liquid.

"Claudia," Jane began evenly. "Exactly how long have you been at the hotel? I believe I'm coming on at least thirteen years myself."

Claudia turned toward her, both hands on her ample hips; her left fist clutched a dripping ladle. "Since Philip Whitman built this place in spring of '59." Her keen old eyes narrowed in on her. "What are you drivin' at Jane McCarthy?"

Jane took a sip, shrugging nonchalantly. "I'm thinking of retiring."

"You're not even forty," Ada remarked in surprise, giving her a wink.

Jane grinned, giving another shrug. "I've made my little fortune; saving and saving because I had no one else to provide for since Seth is no longer with me."

Claudia nodded. "I wish I could say the same. My drunkard of a husband squanders everything. I'm waiting for him to choke on whiskey. I got a few hundred dollars to my name I've hidden. Won't get me far if I left now."

"And as you all know, I got my grandkids to provide for," Ada said. "They made it here a few weeks ago from St Louis and it's been," Ada paused, shaking her head. "an adjustment. I've been saddled with these kids since their mom died and my son, their dad, ran off. Don't get me wrong. I love them dearly, but I'm too old to raise another set of children. I'm in my sixties."

"Oh, be honest, ya old biddy," Claudia teased. "You're almost seventy."

Ada grinned, pointing a finger at Claudia. "Quiet dust cloud. You could be Jesus's mother."

Jane chuckled; hiding her light laugh behind a sip of coffee.

Claudia snorted. "I'm not that old. At least not yet."

Jane bit her lip and hung her head. She felt selfish. Her troubles of a broken, bitter heart were nothing compared to what these other women were adjusting to. She missed Seth, and what they could have had. And she felt guilty. Being a barren woman, she felt like she'd failed Seth. He wanted children in a powerful way, but never blamed her for their lack, stating her barren womb was not a problem; though secretly it was. She knew it, seeing the disappointment and resentment in his eyes even though he never spoke a word of it.

"I say retire if you can," Ada piped up. "If you have the ability and the means, do it. Then do fun things! Life is much too short."

Claudia laughed. "Only short for you because your head is barely past the counter."

Jane hid her grin and the snort of laughter behind the coffee mug and a fake sneeze. "Thank you. I'm unsure... Still contemplating doing so."

Taking her plate with the cooling, gooey roll and half-finished coffee, she went back to her office. Her feet missed a step at the sound of Audrey and the others coming back from church. She caught herself, hurrying along. She didn't want to be caught up in their couple-bliss.

*I believe it's time for me to move on,* she decided. *In all aspects.*

CHAPTER FOUR

Fir trees, tall and proud stood towering in the Utah sky. Clear blue skies stretching far into the horizon promised good weather for the next few days. Derek sighed in relief. The numerous animal pelts weighed heavily on his back and on his mule; the last thing he needed was bad weather.

Derek adjusted the rifle on his shoulder. Pulling the hat down low over his squinting green eyes, he continued through the brush and trees. Soon, as he figured it, he would be following Ogden River west to Ogden, Utah and catching a train east to Denver, Colorado. At least that was his plan.

*Plans always seem to get away from me*, he thought.

He'd spent years traveling and trapping from way north in Montana, west to Idaho and back south to Utah. He was done. Being in his late forties, this life was wearing on his mind and body. His shoulder, currently aching from the weight of the pack.

The loneliness didn't bother him. He saw it as a kind of penance; not desiring to burden anyone else with his issues. The memories he tried to escape from were relentless, tormenting his dreams and waking thoughts with images of his wife's sweet face.

He tried running from the death of Darcy; seeing townspeople reminding him of what he would not have, followed him with the painful reminder she was gone.

Derek ran a hand over his face. Beads of sweat came off on his hands. He groaned from his sore muscles, moving over a large fallen fir to stand in the shade for a moment. "I'm getting too old for this, Harold," he said to his mule.

Harold brayed. His mule effortlessly made it over the fallen tree, shaking his short mane.

"We are retiring," Derek continued, reaching behind the animal's halter, giving him a quick pat.

Derek sighed, moving farther down the animal trail. The rushing whoosh of water sounded to the left. Derek smiled, pausing in the middle of the trail to listen to the soothing cacophony. There was nothing like water to lull his restlessness. Derek hung his head, his heartbeat slowing to match the steady sound.

Harold nudged him.

"Yeah, I'm moving," he grumbled grumpily at the mule for breaking the moment.

Derek continued down the trail, Harold's lead rope in hand. His eyes scanned the trees for grizzlies, black bears, or cougars; even wolves would target him if they were hungry enough. Harold's ears twitched backward, shaking his head.

"We need to settle down," he told Harold. "Take a breather and end this way of life. Maybe find a place with a permanent fireplace, soft clean bed, a regular bath, and newspaper. You're old... I'm old..."

Harold brayed, digging his hooves into the soft soil. Derek stopped, whipping his rifle around. He cocked it, putting the butt of the gun up against his right shoulder ready for whatever threat Harold had sensed to show itself.

A low breathy growl resounded from his right. Holding the rifle tight to his shoulder, he stared down the iron sights. A black bear crossed the trail fifty yards in front of him. It stopped, rising up on his hind legs. The bear lowered back onto four paws, taking a few steps toward him.

Derek held his ground, holding a breath. He didn't want to shoot a bear. He had enough pelts and meat to last him quite a time. He spent a long time living off jerky, and didn't care to spend another month trying to eat it all and then to add bear meat to the mix. That would delay his getting to civilization by at least another two weeks. The bear came toward him. Harold jerked his head against the lead rope Derek held tucked under his arm. Derek took out his pistol from his hip holster, rifle still secure on his shoulder, and fired a shot into the air. The animal paused, sniffing at him and making low growls.

"Move along bear," Derek whispered under his breath, "this isn't your day to die."

The black bear backpedaled, going toward the sound of water. Derek let out a long breath. To him, shooting a bear was bad luck; believing the bear was once in the form of a man and his soul was trapped in the bear. And according to his half-breed late wife, believing the same, killing a bear beyond necessity was enough to damn a soul.

Derek kept the rifle in front of him, walking down the animal trail. Harold's ears twitched and his lips let out a constant bray until his mule was certain the danger passed. Derek patted his old friend on the neck to reassure him.

Since Darcy passed away so suddenly during the night, around three years ago, Harold was all he had left for company. He had a child, but Bryce was a grown man and far away from Derek and his poor choices since Bryce was a young child. Derek sent letters, often with money to Bryce's mother Tara, more or less to appease his own guilt. Derek didn't blame the man, even now, for wanting nothing to do with him.

Last he heard by letter, a year ago - the only letter he got from his son - Bryce was in Denver, and still wanted nothing to do with him; going far as asking him to stop sending money. And since Darcy went to be with her gods, three years hence, he decided he wanted to be around someone of his blood; and to get the chance to know the child he was denied.

Derek ran a hand over his face. *And if Bryce wants nothing to do with me, then I will move along, going back west; maybe to Butte, Montana to settle down. I've got the money and the time.*

Harold brayed, picking up speed to charge in front of him. Derek figured Harold must be sensing the town, eager for a roof over his head. Derek sighed. His stomach swirled with the apprehension of getting there. He would need to find someone to buy his hides for a fair price. He just hoped it wouldn't take long.

Derek loathed towns – the smells, the people, the way people looked at an old trapper like he was unintelligent or couldn't understand their words. He hated how strangers could make him feel inferior, so he tended to avoid towns unless he had business. Harold brayed, nudging him forward. Derek couldn't help the small chuckle that escaped. Obviously, Harold didn't feel the same.

"We get there when we get there, Harold," Derek admonished.

A raven flew across his path, perching on a tree to his right. The bird cawed at him. Derek raised his hand and smiled, his heart clenching. Darcy always said if she were to pass on, she would come back a raven – a sleek, messenger of her gods; often expressing she wanted him to live his life happily and find love again. Derek thought the raven an interesting concept but didn't want to hurt her feelings or demean her beliefs since she grew up with the natives; also expressing he didn't want anyone else but her. He however, believed when you died, that was it – dead. Yet the memories of seeing what the bird brought forth were comforting.

Derek watched the bird as he passed by. The raven tilted its head, flying over his path again, cawing relentlessly. It perched on a tree to the left, moving down toward the end of the branch. Derek paused, glaring at the bird.

"Darcy," he began firmly. "I appreciate your message in coming to find me. But I am not changing my mind in finding someone else. I'm changing locations, not my mind."

The raven cawed, flying off into the sky.

Derek grumbled. "My cow may have died but I don't need your bull," he teased to the retreating bird.

Snorting, his brain brought back memories of teasing Darcy daily about something. How the woman put up with his wit and dry humor, he didn't know. The only reason coming to mind was she loved him too.

After she'd died, he'd thought about taking another wife, but he could never fully get behind the idea. He loved Darcy. And the idea of taking another wife, struck a deep chord of guilt. He didn't want to shame her memory, to forget the only woman he ever loved.

Cautiously, he went down the hill, spying the bustling town of Ogden, Utah and a train already nestled in the station. Even from his distance, the steam of the engine settling in for the afternoon, wafted his direction.

Derek patted his mule's head. "Here we go Harold. I need you to be on your best behavior. I gotta sell all of these pelts. I know. I haven't forgotten Darcy. And the thought of going east again... well, it kind of terrifies me. Never thought I would head east again."

He frowned. Bryce's mother, and him had a thing going for a while a long time ago. Long before he'd met Darcy. After one of his trapping trips, he came to Denver for a spell and met Tara, a saloon dance girl. It still didn't bother him in the slightest what Tara was. He wanted to settle down and marry her, while Tara wanted someone else specifically; so, he went west, forgetting the woman he thought he'd loved.

He came back to Denver once, and discovered he had a son. Spitting image of himself too. He tried to stay for the boy; do right by him. But Tara and her husband ran him off. Trying to be the bigger man, he left peacefully, back into the wilds of the west. Tara supposedly died of tuberculosis a few years back according to his son's letter a year ago. It irked him he wasn't able to pay for her burial or any such arrangements. He felt he owed it to the woman since Tara raised his kid, even if it hadn't been his choice.

Derek moseyed down the hill side, keeping his footing firm. The trees opened up, parting way for the city below. Smoke plumed from cozy chimney's inside of homes. Women strolled about the town with broods of children at their skirts while men purposefully strode from building to building.

He made his way to the end of town, starting there to sell his wares. With winter coming in a few months and this area getting a bunch of snow, having a nice warm pelt would come in handy for many people. In most towns he sold his wares in, he stood on a corner, his pelts hanging over a railing of some sort and people would come. And the strategy never disappointed despite the stigma being a trapper held.

He and Harold paused at the end of a building, out of the way of the raised platform walkway, stairs and the building store front. People had a problem with the nomadic lifestyles such as his and the last thing he wanted for his business was to alienate himself further.

A man, dressed in nicer, casual attire strode up, eyes narrowed in on the pile of pelts on Harold's back. "Got a bear underneath all those?" he asked.

Derek nodded. "One. It's a grizzly."

"How much?"

"Fifteen," Derek said, fishing the hide out.

"Ten," the man countered.

Derek's eyes narrowed, pulling the folded pelt out of the pile. He handed one end to the man and opened it wide, extending it the full ten feet.

The man nodded, running one hand over the fur while keeping the other stretching the pelt. "Very nice," he replied. "Ten."

"Split the difference, thirteen," Derek countered.

The man nodded, swaying his head a bit. "Twelve."

Derek held out his hand, shaking on the price. The man walked away with a slight smile on his face, thrilled he got the 'good deal' he thought he did. Derek shrugged. Pelts and hides were only worth what he decided. With the fur trade diminishing greatly over the years, with beaver pelts on the decline; he didn't care for what he made on the last stock he had. Derek already made his money in fur.

He reached over, patting Harold on the head. "After this, old friend, we are going to Denver."

Overhead, a crow flew, perching on a building across the street. Derek's eyes narrowed on the bird. *New location, but never a new companion,* he thought. *I can't let you go, Darcy. I don't think I'm ready.*

The crow flew off.

# CHAPTER FIVE

The afternoon train rolled to a steady stop in the bustling city of Denver, Colorado. Derek sat with his back against the bench seat, waiting for everyone else to load off before he disembarked. He never thought nerves would prickle at his skin, but they did and it irritated him.

Before he left Ogden, Utah, he paid for a telegram to be sent to his son, asking him to meet at the train station in Denver. To his surprise, Bryce replied, agreeing. Derek tried to prepare for all outcomes. He didn't want to be too disappointed if the kid never showed or too excited and awkward if he did.

With a groaning sigh, Derek lifted himself off his seat. Grabbing his two rucksacks full of his belongings, he headed for the stairs off the train. Harold waited outside for him, tied to a hitching post nearby already taken care of by one of the train's stable boys.

Sure, as the bird flew, he spotted his own reflection waiting with a woman, who he hoped was his wife, and in between them both was an older girl, around six if he guessed. Derek ran a hand over his face, striding to Harold trying to buy himself a few extra seconds. His stomach tightened, tumbling in knots.

Darcy always wanted him to go see his kid and reconnect, stating it's the gods' ways to bind family together, as one does a heart. Derek thought it best to let the grown man be. Since Darcy was no longer by his side, he found he longed for this connection, and just maybe, she was right.

Gathering Harold's lead rope in his hand, he strode over to the parked wagon where Bryce and his family waited.

"Bryce Anderson?" Derek asked.

The tall, sandy blond-haired man perked a brow. "Yeah?"

"Derek Bennett," he said, extending a hand.

Bryce's green eyes narrowed on him, taking his hand but not coming down from the wagon, choosing to stay firmly planted in his seat. Derek wasn't about to say anything. He deserved the lack of courtesy.

"This is my wife, Elena and my daughter Ophelia," Bryce introduced, his face lightening a bit as he looked at his family.

Elena smiled fondly at him. Her welcome reached her blue eyes. Her light blond hair put back in the hairstyle all women seemed to wear once they realized most the other women in high society were too.

*Darcy always had her hair in braids flung over her shoulder*, he couldn't help compare as he took in the kindly woman before him.

The toe-headed girl sat still in her mother's arms, staring at him warily like all children do with the wide green eyes she shared with him and her father. Those beautiful eyes seemed to focus on his scraggly beard. He meant to cut his long, silvering hair and beard. But he wanted to get settled in a new place first. And if this meeting said anything, it said he wouldn't be settled for a while yet. Looked like he was headed back to Butte, Montana.

Derek took off his hat. "Pleasure to meet you, Mrs. Anderson," he said dipping his head. "Hello, Ophelia," he began, offering the child a smile. "How are you?"

Ophelia, tucked herself against her mother.

"Will you be staying with us?" Elena asked.

Derek kept his eyes on his son, watching the man tense at his wife's question. Derek felt his heart pang. *Coming here was a mistake*, he thought sadly.

"No ma'am," Derek replied evenly, briefly glancing her way. "I'm going to stay somewhere else."

"Are you hungry?" Elena asked. "There is a place to eat right up the hill."

"That would be lovely. I am hungry for food other than jerky and coffee."

Elena laughed. "Please come join us then."

Bryce's jaw set tight and Derek worked his back and forth in reaction. Sooner or later they would need to have a discussion. And he was never one to beat around the bush, so sooner seemed better.

"I get it," Derek began to Bryce. "You're angry with me and I know why. I loved Tara. I asked her to marry me twice. Tara refused. She loved someone else – Travis Anderson. I didn't know she was pregnant when I left. I haven't been here for you, so I get the anger and distrust. Soon as I found out about you, you were never far from my thoughts, and never unwanted or unloved."

Bryce's eyes narrowed on his. The whites of his knuckles enclosed around the reins to the team of horses. Derek glanced to Elena, watching him with a softened affectionate gaze.

Derek regretted giving up so easily and walking away from his only son so many years ago. Seeing how happy Bryce was with the man stepping in as his father had turned him bitter and hurt his heart. Plus, the threats of turning him into the sheriff made by Tara made staying less than desirable. However, he couldn't hurt Bryce by telling him. Travis was the only man he knew as his father and Tara was his mother.

Derek shuffled his feet, bringing his eyes back up to meet Bryce's hard stare. "When I came back to Denver to ask Tara to marry me again, Tara married your father, Travis instead. You were just a tot and the cutest thing. I found out on that trip, she'd birthed you and just married this other man, a man she'd apparently loved for a long time, and I was forgotten. I tried to stay and see you, but your new daddy wouldn't have it, claiming you as his own. I understand it though. Travis was a good man and it seemed he loved you and your mother. I can only imagine he was one heck of a father to you."

Bryce's jaw ticked. "As I said in my only letter, I want nothing from you," he said firmly, pulling out an envelope from his pocket and handing it to him. "Here is all the money you sent me over the years. I don't want it."

Derek hung his head. "I deserve that," not making a move to take the money. "Like me or not, that's fine. You came here to get something from me. Closure, revenge, *something*. Keep the money, buy land, cattle, whatever. I don't care what you do with it. I'm old and came here to hang up my hat. But if you want me gone, the train is still here."

"Bryce," Elena whispered, her eyes reflecting sympathy. "Give your father a chance."

Bryce's troubled eyes narrowed on his wife. "Elena," he harshly whispered.

Elena returned his gaze. "Love prospers when a fault is forgiven, but dwelling on it separates close friends."

"It's all right, Mrs. Anderson," Derek said. "I'm going to stay at that big hotel, up the road there and rest these weary bones. Once the week's out, I'll head back to Butte, Montana."

"Is that where you came from?" she asked.

"I came here from Ogden, Utah."

"Why do you wear that hat and strange coat?" Ophelia asked.

Derek smiled at the girl. "The beaver hat keeps my head warm and the rain off. The coat was a gift made by my late wife."

Ophelia pursed her lips together. "Was she a squaw?"

"Ophelia!" Elena admonished embarrassed by her rude manners. "That's not a nice word. Apologize this moment."

"Sorry, Mr. Bennett."

Derek held up a hand. "She was half native, half white," he replied, thinking fondly of Darcy's brown eyes.

"Sorry," Bryce's deep voice cut into his thoughts. "For your loss."

"I'm sorry to you as well Bryce... for everything. Truly sorry,"

Derek said, slapping the side of the wagon. "I'd best be off. Have a good day now."

Derek turned slightly on his heel. Harold nudged him in the back, eager to walk and be as far away from the livestock car as possible. Derek turned once more and stared at his son's face again, hoping to memorize it in case this was the last time he ever got to see it; a mixture of anger and curiosity marred the boy's... man's face. Derek would be lying if he said he wasn't curious about his own son.

The overwhelming emotions of meeting today took a toll on his son's countenance. As it did for him as well. Derek's shoulders dropped, exhaling out his nose.

Bryce sighed. "I will see you around... Derek."

Derek nodded. "Have a good day, Bryce. See you around."

He sighed again, going up the hill with Harold on his left. The mule brayed, ears twitching back and forth. The city bustled around him. More so than any other city he'd been in before. It unnerved him. Not even Butte's wildlife, or Ogden's recent Native attacks got to him like Denver's bustle. The country was vast and people could go anywhere, but the dense, naked population bothered him. There was nothing to hide behind; nowhere to go.

*I wanted to be here,* he thought. *To get to know a son who wants nothing to do with me. Not that I blame the man. I wouldn't want anything to do with me either.*

Glancing up into the bright blue unyielding sky, he shielded his eyes from the glare of the sun. He ambled further up the road, spying to his right the giant carving of the bear mentioned to him previously by a fellow wanderer. The Whitman Hotel stood out like a grand fir tree around a cropping of maples.

Derek hitched Harold to the post outside the hotel. He checked to make certain his money was tucked inside his coat pocket. Harold brayed his annoyance at being left again. With a sigh, Derek strode up the steps and went inside the hotel.

Hand on the iron grip, he yanked the door open. Out came a blond woman, looking over her shoulder and not paying a lick of attention to where she was going. Derek moved quickly out of the way, allowing the oblivious woman to pass through. The blond woman did so, passing by him with her tightly coiffed hair and high neck collared dress.

Derek shook his head, striding inside the hotel. A staircase was in front with a giant portrait of what he assumed would be the hotel owner and his wife, gracing the middle of the wall in between the two staircases curling up each side of the large room.

The aroma of actual, cooked food permeated all his senses. His stomach rumbled.

"Can I help you sir?" a kindly soft toned woman asked.

Derek spun on his heel, meeting her with a smile. The woman stood behind a counter, her brown eyes soft and kind, wearing a dark ruby dress and her hair nicely pulled back off her face.

Derek cleared his throat. "Yes. I would like a room for a week."

The woman nodded. Her petite frame barely visible over the counter. "Grand room or basic?"

"Basic," he stated, approaching the counter. "How much for my mule to board?"

"The room is fifty cents a day and the board for your animal is also fifty cents a day. We feed oats and hay, brush him down daily and put him out in a paddock."

Derek nodded, pulling out seven, dollar coins. He set them on the counter. The woman counted the money, writing something down in her booklet.

"Please sign the register and here is your key," she said with a smile.

Derek scribbled his mark on the paper, taking the key and shoving it deep into an empty pocket.

The woman leaned over the top of the counter, pointing to the right at the door he came in at, as she spoke, "Whitman Stables are around the back. Follow the sidewalk up the way a bit and take the immediate right. There is a large white sign on the front. Ross is our stablemaster. He will take care of your mule."

"Thank you, kindly," he said.

"Pleasure is mine," she replied with a smile. "My name is Eliza. If you are hungry, we do have a diner. Guests get ten cents off their meal for staying and dining here. Dinner service will be over in about an hour. Special today is ham steak, fried potatoes, gravy and beans."

Derek tipped his head, turning for the door. The blond woman who previously left came rushing back in, cheeks flushed and annoyance in her eyes. Derek walked a wide berth around her. Eyes forward, she hadn't even noticed him.

He shook his head, pushing past the outer doors, taking a deep breath of fresh air. Jogging down the steps, the earthy crisp scent of Colorado tingled his nose. It was alluring in a way, much like Montana or the wilds of Utah. There was an adventure here prickling under his skin.

Untethering Harold's lead rope, he went in the direction Eliza mentioned the stables were in. A crow cawed at him from the ledge of the Whitman Hotel and flew off. Derek grumbled at its retreating back.

# CHAPTER SIX

There was so much for Jane to accomplish. Time never seemed long enough to complete what she wanted to do. The ballroom was cleaned and reset for the next person to utilize – most likely Audrey will throw a party before anyone else would think to use it since most in Denver weren't exactly the richest. Although one never knew when the town would need a meeting space or someone else would want a big wedding. Jane sighed, looking at her list as she crossed off the ballroom.

*Now for taking inventory for the kitchen and winter supplies, see if anyone in laundry needs supplies and get each hotel room prepped and recleaned before the winter horde of people arrive.*

Jane bustled past a man who appeared to have just rolled in from being in the hills. His earthy, tree and dirt scent wafted up to her nose. Jane crinkled her face, part of her fascinated by the smell and the other not liking the sharpness of the scent.

The man stepped wide around her; brow raised to her. Jane realized her mistake and fixed her face from looking confused to open. She sighed inwardly. If the man was going to be staying here, she would need to apologize for her rudeness.

Jane held her head high, again hoping her faux pas with the

man could be overlooked or easily mended. She strode over to Eliza, at the front desk, who'd been astonishingly adept at taking over most of the duties in running the hotel. Jane had been pleasantly surprised when Eliza readily agreed to be trained as hotel manager; lifting a weight off her shoulders and Jane looked forward to retirement that much more now.

"Eliza," Jane whispered, approaching her. "See that gentleman there. I may have offended him with some misplaced facial expressions and I want to smooth over any offense. Please let him know his supper tonight is on the hotel."

Eliza nodded, giving Jane a gentle warm smile. "Will surely do."

"Thank you."

Grabbing some papers off the front desk, Jane spun on her heel, going to the door where her office was. Staring at the stack of papers, got her on thinking of retirement again.

The more she thought on retiring and finding her own house, the more it appealed to her. It felt right and like a good time to stop working herself to the ground. She wanted the quiet; the easing of stress off her shoulders wondering if she would be able to keep everyone employed all year round.

*I want my own home. I haven't had a real home since Seth and I were married. Seeing everyone around me marry and their happiness has cemented this decision for me. Part of me is ready; the other is terrified. I haven't known who I am outside of 'hotel manager' in such a long time. Burying myself in this hotel was all I've known for over a decade.*

Jane sighed, heading through the door to her back office. *I'm losing my touch. It's definitely time to move on.* Earlier she passed out everyone's money and bonuses although doing so, while a relief, brought out some guilt since she was 3 days late. Fridays were her usual distribution day but with everything going on, plus her mind on her imminent retirement, it'd slipped her mind. Thankfully no one said anything.

She sighed, picking up a crate left by her desk. She'd set it there to remind her of something. She tapped her foot for a second, trying to remember why she'd brought the crate in. She blew her lips. *My memory's going too. I must be getting old. Oh!* remembering what it happened to be. Biting the inside of her lower lip, she slowly packed up all her belongings in the office. It wasn't much – a few baubles and gifts from years gone.

Taking her crate, she left the office and went toward her bedroom. She mentioned retiring once to Audrey. Although she wasn't as cemented in the idea until now. She needed to inform Audrey once this week was out, she was going to have her own house. Preferably on the outskirts of town, but still near enough as she didn't care to have a horse and a buggy to get to town and an animal to feed; especially in hard seasons like winter. She'd much rather walk.

*I wouldn't mind a cat though,* she thought. *Just to keep the mice away. Dogs scare me.*

Adjusting the crate in her hands, she opened the door leading out into the main hotel lobby. The outdoorsy smelling man from earlier ambled his way up the stairs with two overstuffed sacks on his back. Jane set the crate on the counter, exhaling sharply through her nose.

Hiking up her skirts, she clopped her way up the stairs behind the man.

"Excuse me," she said in a soft tone.

The man turned around. His eagle-like blue eyes locked on hers. His brown hair fell past his shoulders strung with silver at the sides and a touch throughout. His beard, long and curly hung off his face with more silver than in his hair. A beaver hat smooshed itself down on his head. Dark weather-beaten leather from the sun and wind hugged his frame with several knives peeking out from underneath, tucked about his waist. Jane swallowed.

"Yes, ma'am?" he questioned, his voice deep and rumbly.

Jane gawped like a fish. "I wanted to apologize," she said, clasping her hands together in front of her. "I didn't mean to be so impolite earlier."

The man dipped his head. "Alright," he replied. "What did you mean to be?"

Jane blinked. She wasn't sure what caught her off guard, his curious tone or question. Most times she apologized such as this, the person would reply with 'think nothing of it' or some other trivial response. This holding her responsible was startling. She wasn't sure what to think about it.

"I," she began, shifting her feet. "I was in a hurry and did not see you. Once I realized what I'd done, I wanted to make it right."

He nodded. "Accepted. Now, what room is 205?"

"It will be on your left. Third door," she replied, turning to head back down the stairs.

Letting out a breath, she made her way back to ground level and left her crate at the front desk with Eliza to snatch later. She strode into the kitchen, spying Mary doing the dishes and Natali coming in with a heap of dirty plates.

Jane opened the door going into the diner. Only three guests remained at the tables. She gazed around, taking it all in before she forgot to. This place was her solitude, her fortress, her way of life for so long. Now, getting ready to start a new adventure, she wasn't certain about it.

Closing the door, she came back inside the kitchen. Claudia and Ada walked out, turning right toward the break area, chit-chatting as they strolled along. Jane smiled, watching them leave. She stared down at her heeled shoes for a moment, wishing she hadn't always been so proper or frank in all the years she'd been here. She'd always chosen professionalism over personality and being personable with people. Now, she regretted it.

*I could have been nicer,* she thought. *Not so tight lipped or tight faced. More relaxed like I used to be when Seth was alive.* Closing her eyes, she leaned her head back against the wall, nose toward the ceiling, breathing for a moment. *I need to get back to that, back to me.*

She glanced around the kitchen, spying Mary. Instantly her cheeks flamed. Knowing Mary, the woman wouldn't judge her for her thoughts or feelings.

Mary's blond brows raised at her as she scrubbed a pan. "You all right?" She asked, keeping her rounding belly away from the sink as much as she could. Her apron was nearly soaked through with dishwater.

Jane nodded, putting a business smile on her face. "Quite fine, Mary."

Mary tilted her head forward slightly to better glare at Jane, "And ducks have chicken feet."

"You have the most interesting analogies." Jane replied, her lip twitching.

Mary's face fell, frowning. "Thank you, but I don't have allergies."

"Comparisons," Jane explained. "I always like your comparisons."

"OH," Mary exclaimed, her face turning pink. "I appreciate your... candor."

Jane smiled. "Always, Mary. Thank you for all you do. Go take a break. I feel as though we may have a supper rush. And I don't want Ross in here upset about how much work you're doing."

"I'm all right," she replied. "Somethin' seems to be buggin' you. Your face went all blank."

Jane sighed and crossed her arms over herself. "Since Seth passed away, I have busied myself and buried myself in work here at this hotel. I feel like I have lost myself. I want to get back to how I used to be when Seth was alive."

Mary nodded, putting the pan in the drying rack. "Then get back to it. Only you know what you're like. Go for a walk. You hardly leave this place."

"I will," Jane decided. "Thank you, Mary."

Mary picked up a pot, submerging it into the warm, soapy liquid. "Welcome."

Jane strode out of the kitchen, heading for the main front door. Lena was behind the counter, speaking with her husband Quint. Jane nodded to both of them as she passed by, going out the front door of the hotel.

With a deep, cleansing breath, she went for a walk to find some semblance of her former self.

## CHAPTER SEVEN

Derek strode back inside the Whitman Hotel once he got Harold settled into the stables. The bed and room were nice, smelling freshly laundered. It was the nicest place he'd stayed in for the price he was paying.

He unpacked, putting his clothes up on pegs. He needed to go about seeing if he could get it all washed. It had been months since he'd had any clean clothes, at least cleaner than a quick rinse in the river. The other bag he had rested on the ground in the upper right corner by his bed – where Darcy would have slept if she were still around.

Derek grimaced. It had been a few years since Darcy's passing and he couldn't bring himself to be rid of her clothes. Everything else she had, necklaces and baubles, he dressed her in as she desired, before he sent her spirit back to her people via the fires of a funeral pyre. He hadn't even opened the pack since she'd died three years ago, but lugging her things around had always seemed right.

Biting firmly onto his bottom lip, he hauled Darcy's sack onto the bed. Fiddling with the ends, he opened it, spying her favorite red dress she liked to wear going into town. Pressing the material to his nose, he inhaled sharply; the dress smelling faintly of her lemon verbena perfume.

He spun, sitting on the bed with a groaning sigh, holding her dress in his gnarled, calloused hands. His fingers ran over the bead work and the neat stitches. He set it on the bed beside him. Leaning forward with his elbows on his knees, he hung his head with a sigh.

*I didn't want to move on without you. Still don't some days*, he thought. *But life continues to go on. Darcy, I will forever cherish your love and kindness; how you changed this old man for the better.* Derek got up, turning toward the sack. He pulled out all her clothes. Keeping only the red dress she loved so much. Everything else, he repacked, deciding to donate it to a charity.

*May you follow the Great Spirit home to your people*, he thought. *Or however it was you translated it. Just know, I hope you're at peace, I love you and I wish you a safe journey. I got to continue mine.* He sighed, standing in the middle of his room with his head bowed. *I thought back in Montana, where you died, I wouldn't be able to move on and be ready to share my life with someone again. Now, I am not sure what happened. Maybe I'm ready for peace.* Derek ran a hand over his face, pinching the bridge of his nose with his left hand and breathed in deep. *Whatever it is, I'm old and ready to settle down... quietly. I'm ready to move on from this nomadic lifestyle and be still.*

He slung her pack over his shoulder, exiting the room. He locked the door with his belongings inside. Heading down the steps, he spied the front desk lady, Eliza if he remembered correctly, behind the counter.

"Those need a wash?" Eliza asked.

Derek shook his head. "No," he said, his mouth becoming like cotton. "I want to... donate these clothes... Women's clothes."

"Oh," she said, startled, eyes narrowing. "I know women at Lena's Dove's for Women could use these. Dove's is out the main door. Take a right and walk up a bit. It will be on your right. You can't miss it."

Derek nodded, adjusting the stuffed pack on his shoulder. He strode out of the hotel, his mind racing. *I hope I'm doing the right thing,* he thought. *I hope it is what you would want.*

Derek frowned. He assumed it was. Darcy never wanted anything to go to waste. And here her clothes were, gathering dust and specks, being wasted when another woman could have used them.

He strolled up the sidewalk going past the Whitman Hotel and Stables. The next house on his right was Lena's Dove's. Setting his face firm, he ambled up to the dark wood front door. As his boots hit the wooden porch his heart buoyed when he realized he wasn't as troubled at the thought of giving these clothes away as he'd first thought he would be.

Setting his bag down, he knocked on the front door. A tall, brown haired woman answered with a smile on her lips. Her hazel eyes met his, the smile open and warm.

"How can I help you?" she asked politely.

Derek cleared his throat. "I want to donate these women's clothes to you. They were my wife's."

"Thank you," she exclaimed. "May I take a look?"

He gestured toward the sack. She leaned over, pulling out a leather coat. Her head tilted to the side, expression open and thoughtful. Most people he met would scowl at the attire he and Darcy wore. Their clothes were unusual to some – not the typical wool coat most gentlemen wore or dusters of the cowboys; instead tanned deer and elk hides, turned into soft leather clothing and shoes.

"These are beautiful," the woman remarked, taking out another piece. "You sure you want to donate these?"

"Yes," Derek replied firmly. "For you ladies to wear. Not quite sure what Lena's Dove's is, but the lady at the hotel said this would be a good place."

"It is," she smiled. "Lena's Dove's is my work where broken, abused women can come and have a second chance at a fresh start, like I was given at the hotel."

Derek smiled broadly; a weight lifted off his shoulders. *This is exactly what Darcy would have wanted.* He sighed, relieved. "Perfect," he replied, gesturing toward the clothes. "Enjoy. Have a good day ma'am."

He strode away from the building and down the hill. Instead of his heart hurting at giving away pieces of his wife, it felt good; like he set the final stone upon her grave and he was able to walk away from it.

Ambling down the sidewalk, he crossed the street to get his bearings in this giant boom-town turned bustling city. There was an exhilarating thrill to Denver, more than he experienced in Butte or Ogden. He couldn't put his finger on what exactly made him want to say, be it the mountains in the distance or all the rolling hills and areas yet to explore. There was a whispering thrill to Colorado which he previously never felt at all.

*Maybe when you're set in yourself, comfortable with who you are, the land speaks to you,* he thought. *I wasn't set in myself for a long time.*

He turned down the road to his right, going past a French restaurant. He stopped in front, wondering if he wanted to try something different. Shaking his head, he continued on past a butchery, a quilt shop, and another mercantile. Turning right again, he strode up the road, not wanting to stop until he got to the far end of town.

More than wanting to explore, he wanted to clear his head and think. He came here to meet his son, Bryce, and tie up loose ends before God called him home. He believed everyone was marked with a start date when born, a person also had an end date. With getting older and not knowing when his end was, he didn't want to leave it unfulfilled. He wanted to try and get to know his only son, and now, with the chilly reception he received, he didn't know if he'd get that chance.

Head down, he mindlessly wandered. Sighing, he trudged up the road, staying to the right side. Wagons and people passed him, traveling into the heart of the city. He glanced behind him, seeing people wander in and out of buildings.

"OW!" a woman yelled.

He didn't feel his body plow into someone. His only indication he'd done so was the exclamation. Whipping his head around he gazed at the woman he'd accidentally struck down. The tight hair on her head was loose, falling in a braid over her shoulder. Blond strands fell in her face over her earth tone brown eyes. Derek reached down grabbing the proffered hand and pulled the woman to her feet. He thought she looked familiar but with her hair down and a rosy glow to her cheeks, he couldn't be sure.

"You all right?" he asked.

She brushed the escaped hairs out of her face and began dusting herself off. "I'm fine. Were you not paying attention?"

Derek smiled, realizing who the woman was. "No, I wasn't. And clearly neither were you."

The woman straightened and met his gaze. "Oh, I'm sorry."

"Derek Bennett," he said, extending his hand.

She smiled, taking his hand. "Jane McCarthy."

"Care to take a stroll with me? I wouldn't want you to bonk head first into someone else."

Jane blushed. "I'm heading back to the hotel."

Derek nodded. "All right."

"Would you care for a cup of coffee?" she said, gulping and going slightly pale.

Her cheeks immediately heated, with a careful rise to her brows. In a blink, she transformed her own surprise to a shy smile. Glancing down at her feet, the woman fiddled with her hair. Derek couldn't keep the smile from his face.

He perked a brow. "When I get back to the hotel, or with you?"

"Have a good day," Jane replied.

Picking up her skirts, the woman all but ran from him. Derek stood there a moment, shaking his head as he watched her go down the street. He continued up the hill, losing himself in his walk.

# CHAPTER EIGHT

Jane climbed up the steps to the hotel, admonishing herself for asking the man for coffee. What came over her, she couldn't rightly think of. Her head and emotions were all scrambled up worse than one of Claudia's breakfasts. He was a handsome man with his shoulder length hair that curled at the ends. His strong, suntanned face definitely made her look and keen green eyes bore into hers.

Something long dead inside her stirred. She buried it for years, not wanting to acknowledge it, fearing it would cause her more heartache. Adventure and the slight promise of companionship thrummed within her. Jane wasn't sure how to take it or place her feelings on it.

Yanking the main door to the hotel open, she strode determinedly into what was still her office for the rest of the week, deciding to bury herself in what she does best – sitting behind her desk and working. It would do her some good to get her mind off other things she didn't care to focus on. She needed to budget for the oncoming winter months when people were most likely to stay for an extended period and food stores would need to be stocked up more than they already were.

*This task always demands my full concentration.*

The door to her office was open. Jane perked a brow. Inside Audrey and Mary sat in chairs waiting for her.

Mary frowned. "A walk ain't supposed to make you peeved."

Audrey's brows raised. "How exhilarating you went for a walk. I did not believe you ever left the hotel," she teased.

Jane gave a tight-lipped smile, placing her hands on her hips. "What can I do for you, ladies?"

Audrey crossed her feet at the ankles, settling her hands in her lap, a smug smile on her lips. "I came to inform you of two things. Firstly, I got your missive. I have been so busy making arrangements for Eugene and my's honeymoon and handling the affairs of other hotels, I just now read it not two hours ago. Eliza taking over is superb and I readily agree with your selection. Secondly, I further agree you retire and do something for you. Which is why I sent Eugene over to the bank, and we purchased you a home."

"And I came to tell you," Mary's brows furrowed. "Something... Give me a sec. I swear carryin' this child makes me dumb in the head sometimes."

Audrey smiled, setting a hand on Mary's shoulder and squeezed. "We have seen the discontent behind your eyes and feel it is time for you to move on. You have serviced this hotel wonderfully for twelve years."

Jane nodded, choking back tears. The love these two ladies had for her was incredible. Her heart could burst out of her chest from their affection if it wasn't stuck behind blood and skin.

"Thank you... You did not have to purchase me a home. I have enough saved to be able to do it myself."

Audrey waved her off. "For someone who is like my sister, who gave me chance after chance even when I completely failed at most everything, I feel it makes us..." Audrey's face twisted in concentration.

"Square," Mary chimed.

"Exactly so," Audrey continued.

Mary slapped a hand on the arm of the chair. "Biscuits, now I know! Jane," she began rising to her feet and putting her hands on the back of her hips. "You're wise. The smartest woman I know. And it pains me deep to see you sul-lean."

Jane's eyes squinted. "Sullen?"

"Damnit…" Mary frowned. "Sullen face. You need happiness in your life, a new beginning. You gotta find that achin' part of you. Everybody has an achin' part."

Jane nodded, understanding what Mary was getting at. "Thank you, Mary," she replied.

There was an aching part of her as Mary put it. Jane just didn't want to touch it right now. It was frightening. Change of anything was frightening. However, she needed it. Settling herself into a home, making it hers and how she wanted was something she had been desiring for a while but didn't think possible because of her employment here.

Jane smiled at the young blond-haired pregnant woman. Mary was keen in the way of reading people and common sense. Since Mary came here, she'd learned to read and write a bit, at the encouragement of her husband Ross. Jane smiled fondly – Mary and Ross were good for each other.

*Mary is right,* Jane thought. *I'm ready to move on. I'm ready to start something new. Terrified but ready.* Jane took a deep breath. *And this achin' part of me she said, is right. I'm aching for my own life, my own... things... And maybe, companionship?*

"We love you Jane," Audrey said. "We only want to see you happy."

Jane wiped her eyes. "I know, thank you," Jane replied.

"And I want to apologize. At the party, I saw you be so uncomfortable," Audrey continued, "speaking with Ralph, because you both are so similar, I thought it would do you some good to talk to someone who could empathize. I'm sorry. I should not have forced it upon you so."

Jane walked around her desk, embracing Audrey. "It's quite alright. It opened my eyes to what I want."

"Well, what I want is the privy and something to eat," Mary said, rising to her feet. "Find your achin' part, and you find your happiness."

Audrey frowned. "What do you mean, Mary?"

"I was achin' for goodness, to be a good and kind person. I turned myself around and God gave me Ross," Mary said at the door frame. "Excuse me, I'm achin' now for the privy."

Jane chuckled. The waddling woman exited her office with quick booted strides to the main hotel door. Audrey stood in front of her smiling, pulling a piece of paper from her dress pocket. Audrey leaned forward sliding it across her desk. Tentatively, Jane picked it up, unfolding the yellowed parchment.

"The deed to the house and land," Audrey said. "Thank you, for everything… Oh and before I forget, because I know how you are, I've arranged for you to purchase your favorite hutch back from Elena Anderson."

Jane put a hand to her mouth. "Audrey…"

The owner of the hotel rose, heading for the door. "Go see your new home! It's at the end of town, on the left. Your name is on a piece of paper in the window."

Jane stared at the paper, still reveling in shocked awe of what this woman had done for her. She planned on purchasing a home herself, budgeting and planning the rest of the money on what to get for her small cabin home to see her through her first winter and even after. Now, she was set, more so than she ever expected to be. Jane wiped a tear with the tips of her fingers.

*A home,* she thought, *something so trivial to others has been given to me. I haven't had a home in so long. I took this hotel, what could have been a home had I tried, and turned it into only a place of business. I'm an old, bitter, fool of a woman.* She thought, folding the paper down into quarters. *I can't turn back the clock to redo so many things but I can live each new day with a happier heart. The Good Word does say, 'And I will give you a new heart, and a new spirit I will put within you. And I will remove the heart of stone from your flesh and give you a heart of flesh'. Now is a good time to let Him do that.*

She sniffed, sucking in her tears. She breathed out raggedly, the paper shaking in her hands. This gift was more than she could wrap her head around. Jane wanted to thank Audrey, but she'd left before Jane's mini meltdown. Her office, plain and free of the baubles on her desk was void of much else but paper and a tipped pen. It was lifeless, just like she felt her life had become up until this point - drab and boring.

Finishing what she'd set out to do, she stacked her papers and set them aside, ready for Audrey to approve the winter supply list and budget. It took her naught but an hour to complete after going over the previous year's supply list.

Jane rose from her desk, going out the door to the right. She walked past closed doors of storage, holding chairs and extra tables for events. The last door on her right led into the laundry and she breathed in deep the aroma of soap and freshly laundered sheets as she strode past.

Taking a deep breath, Jane stepped out into the afternoon sun, strolling up the road toward her new home.

## CHAPTER NINE

Derek watched Jane leave, trying to wrap his head around the strange and perplexing encounter they'd had earlier. Shaking his head, he continued on down the road away from the hotel, maneuvering past wagons and people on horseback.

His mind wandered to his son and how he could possibly go about making up for all the lost time. He didn't know where to even begin or how. He had done what he could, sending money and coming here now to make it right, or at least, better. Derek didn't know what else to do. They were estranged. Another man raised his son and though Derek wanted to be angry that he'd missed all that time; he was grateful to the man for stepping up to do what he was not allowed to. He wanted to be bitter. He couldn't find an emotion in himself to drive at it though. It wasn't Travis's fault Tara and him could not get along.

*Maybe it's better if I left Colorado,* he thought. *I got nothing holding me down or back.*

Derek walked up the road a touch further, turning right this time to walk back along one of the main roads he'd mindlessly passed. He ambled across the busy street, checking out the town on the left-hand side and beyond. He rounded a corner, spying the large backside of the Whitman Hotel.

Several butcher shops nestled amongst people's homes, lined the street. This side of Denver was busier than he thought it would be. Kind smiles and nods were thrown his way as he walked.

"Hello, Mr. Bennett."

Derek's head shot toward the voice. He smiled tersely, recognizing Bryce's wife coming from the butcher shop on his right.

"Hello to you, Mrs. Anderson," Derek replied.

She came toward him smiling with Ophelia at her skirts. "Care to come to supper tonight?"

Derek shuffled from foot to foot. His son's pretty wife was trying hard to help them both mend ties. It was sweet of her. However, he would not involve a woman in an affair between grown men.

He shook his head. "Appreciate the offer, Mrs. Anderson. However, I have plans. The hotel offered me a meal on the house."

"Oh?" she replied, adjusting the bonnet on her blond head. Her blue eyes waned with desolation. "I'm sorry. I can only imagine how troubling this is for you both to be apart for so long and now desiring to make amends. I know it's hard on Bryce."

"Thank you. There's lots I regret and I certainly missed seeing him grow. It's hard on me too. If he happens to change his mind, I'm staying at the Whitman Hotel," he paused fumbling for the key in his pocket to make certain it was still there.

Ophelia's green eyes peeked around her mother's skirts. "Have you been in the wild?"

Derek crouched down, tipping his hat back a touch. The child went around her mother's back, peeking around the other side. Ophelia, a darling little lady, not much older than six years old, he surmised, was an observant child.

He twirled the ring on his left finger. "Yes. I'm a fur trapper. I kill animals and sell their pelts, bones, meat, and whatever else I can use off the animal," he replied.

"Like bears," she asked, glancing up at her mother.

"I try not to. Killing bears, I believe, is bad, unless you really have to. But yes, I've killed a couple bears."

Ophelia frowned, her sharp little brain chewing on all she heard. Derek rose to his feet, groaning at the sharp movements on his old body. Elena stared at him a moment, her blue eyes trying to discern the kind of man he was. Derek would let her mull it over. He wasn't a bad man, but he wasn't good either. He figured he was just a man.

He tipped his hat to both the women, "Have a good day, Mrs. Anderson, Ophelia."

He strode down the way, turning left and going up the other road. He spied Bryce's backside loading items into a wagon. He walked past. Already this morning was difficult on them both. He didn't want to make it worse with his surprise second appearance.

Derek glanced over his shoulder, spying Elena and Ophelia gaze in his direction. He wanted to duck into a building, but opted against it. He equated hiding to being stuck in a corner, like an animal in one of his traps. It wasn't on his agenda for the day.

Striding up the road, he spied a house for sale with a large black sign in the window. The empty cottage on the outskirts of town, butting up to the sparse trees called his name.

Derek scratched his beard, pulling on it and combing the wiry hairs down. *I could stay here. Own up more for leaving my son and make it a point to stay and be a part of his life. I could also get myself a proper house and not some rigged together teepee or ridge pole house.*

He glanced over across the street to where there were more trees lining the way. Derek nodded to himself, finding the other side of the road more agreeable to his wandering taste.

"Mr. Bennett!"

Derek slowly turned around. His son came up the road with the wagon and team of horses. A content, smiling Elena sat next to his son. The curious face of their daughter between them.

He tried his best to keep his face impassive, to seem nonchalant about their ordeal and meeting earlier although on the inside he was a bundle of nerves and excitement.

"Mr. Anderson," Derek greeted with a nod.

Bryce shifted in his seat. "Would you care to join us for supper, tomorrow?"

Elena beamed with a hint of smugness on her face and a twinkle in her eye.

Derek tried to keep the smirk off his face at the cunning woman. "I do not wish to impose on you and yours," he replied. "A meal is a lot from someone and a great deal of time to honor someone. I will, however, be happy to meet you for coffee."

Bryce seemed to be relieved at his answer. Derek tried not to take it personally. Supper and meals were a great honor to bestow on someone and his son clearly didn't want to invite him into his home yet. Derek tried not to mind. A man's home was a personal refuge. He couldn't intrude on it.

"I will meet you for coffee." Bryce replied, fumbling with the reins in his hands. "I gotta know somethin' first," he began, giving him a hard glare. "Did you ever miss me?"

Derek felt the wind get kicked out of his chest. He didn't expect the question to come from his son. He expected something along the lines of "why didn't you fight for me?" or even, "why are you back now?"

Derek widened his stance and looked at his son fully in the eye. The green in Bryce's eyes shone bright. Bryce fumbled with the reins some more, but refused to look down. Derek strode forward, putting a hand on his son's knee.

"Every day," he replied, his throat constricting. "Every. Damn. Day. Tara named you Bryce after my father. I didn't know she did that for me until later. She loved Travis and I could never fill that love for her...Travis was a good man," Derek paused, taking a deep breath. His voice was cracking, something he never liked about emotions. "You being with them, was your best life. And I could not force myself into that and obstruct it for your sake..." He ran a hand over his face. "I tried to get involved and be in your life. Tara and Travis thought it best not to confuse you. Tara *suggested* I leave and if I didn't, her and Travis would take me to court. I consented, only asking for letters."

Bryce tied the reins on the wagon brake and dismounted from

the wagon, offering his hand. Tears lined the edges of his long dark lashes. His son's green eyes shone even brighter through the tears. Derek looked down at the proffered hand. He stared at it a moment, his heart going between leaping for joy and shattering at all the years lost with his only son.

Derek reached out, taking his son's hand.

"I'm going to take the wife and Ophelia home," Bryce stated. "Tomorrow, do ya think, you'd care to meet for coffee in the afternoon? Let's say two o'clock at Martin's Diner?"

Derek nodded. "I would like that."

Elena wiped at the tears streaming down her cheeks. Little Ophelia rested her tired head on her mother's lap. In a fluid motion, Bryce mounted back into the wagon, throwing the break with the reins now in his hands.

Derek tapped the side of the wagon, holding up a hand as his son sped up the road to wherever his home happened to be. Heart happy, Derek strode back to the Whitman Hotel to bathe and get something to eat. Out of the corner of his eye, a crow flew off a rooftop and Derek smiled to himself.

# CHAPTER TEN

Derek meandered his way back, taking his sweet time, procrastinating taking his much-needed bath; deciding a few more hours of stench won't hurt his body, only the nose of the people he didn't want to get too close anyways. He chuckled and leisurely strolled up the hill going northeast.

Homes lined the edges of the road, making way to larger plots of land toward the end of town. He spied one he found agreeable looking – small, better built cabin, different than the one from earlier, not too large with a decent enough back area for gardening and surrounded by a few trees.

Darcy never had a proper home with four walls and a privy. They were always moving, camping every few months to a different spot where the animals and trapping would be better. Come winter, on the colder days, he would buy them a few nights at a hotel to get clean, hot meals and a place to sleep. Darcy didn't mind much; looking back, he felt poorly for not giving her more.

Derek frowned, pulling at his beard and exhaling out his nose in a contemplative manner. The cabin was well built from what he could tell and something he could easily purchase.

Striding toward it, he found a sign in the window – McCarthy.

He grimaced. His prime location, already taken. The house behind him also occupied and not for sale.

Derek spun on his heel, going back down the road. The hotel manager from the Whitman building strode up the road with a thoughtful gaze. He stood to the side of the pathway. Upon realizing he was here, she stopped.

"Hello," she greeted, her countenance confused.

"Just lookin' at this house for sale only to see it was bought," he explained.

Jane nodded. "Yes… I got it."

"Lucky lady," Derek replied. "And about your offer—"

"No need," Jane interrupted, holding up a hand. "You don't have to. I…"

"I would like to have coffee with you," Derek continued like she didn't interrupt him.

Jane blushed, taking a step back and putting a hand to her throat. "Really… Mr. Bennett, I don't want to trouble you."

"It's been ages since I had coffee with a attractive woman."

Derek felt his heart twitch in his chest. Darcy had been gone just shy of three years. Part of him, while looking at Jane encouraged him to get to know another woman, be it Jane or someone else. The other desired him to remain a bachelor.

He shook his head, pretending a pesky bug landed on him. Living the bachelor lifestyle after Darcy was painful – always alone without a companion besides an old mule and it was not something he cared to repeat. Isolation and thirst for companionship drove him to the brink of madness at times.

*She is a beautiful woman*, he thought gazing at her left hand to make certain it was bare. *She has mighty wide, pretty brown eyes.*

Jane cleared her throat. "Well," she began, slowly making her way past him and toward her new home. "I… I suppose we shall have coffee."

"Tonight, after supper?"

Jane gawped like a trout on a riverbank. "Yes," she agreed. "Tonight, in the sitting lounge."

"See you then," Derek said, allowing her to pass. "Congratulations on your home."

Derek winked at her, enjoying seeing heat rise instantly to her cheeks. He smiled, finding himself smitten with her blush, noticing the extra coloring bringing out the brown of her eyes.

*I better head back and get cleaned up for our after-supper chat,* he thought, finding himself smirking. *A pretty lady and a rough grizzly old man like me... having coffee.*

---

Jane strode to her house. She knew the area like the back of her hand. Audrey's kindness afforded her this quaint cabin home. It happened to be the one she'd been eyeing for a while, but opted against getting since she was on the fence about retiring. Now, it seemed the choice was made for her.

She spent so many years, running from her past, afraid to face it and deal with the harsh emotions it brought – pain, suffering, the loss of everything she could have had with Seth taken from her. To make her loss even more difficult to bear, she had to burn everything as soon as Seth had died to prevent the spread of yellow fever. Not only did she lose everything when her husband died, she literally lost everything with not even a memento to remember him by. Sitting on a tree stump, flames licked the house like children to candy. Her husband's body returning to ashes; God claiming Seth's soul moments after his final breath. Everything, stripped from her in moments.

Jane sucked in a breath, facing the cold dark wooden door. The weathered timber offering her cozy solitude inside, yet she couldn't move.

*I'm ready. I need to allow myself this moment and move on. I cannot bring Seth back, nor my home or belongings. Seth's fish hook box collection is gone. I cannot bring back my mother's quilt or my father's pocket watch.* Jane hung her head, tears rolling down her cheeks. Quietly, she wiped her eyes with her fingertips. *I'm ready to let it go.*

Jane hesitated on the threshold of the cabin. Her hand shakily on the brass knob. Turning the knob, she closed her eyes and took a step inside. The trapped musty scent greeted her nostrils with a familiarity long forgotten. Tears filled her eyes again. She briskly wiped them away.

Her small booted heels clicked on the wooden floor. The fireplace long sat empty. Dried wood piled in the fireplace waited for an occupant. The kitchen, small and tucked in the left corner offered her a window and a few cabinets with a long counter. Walking around to the right, one bedroom sat open and empty of everything. It was a larger bedroom than the one she had at the hotel.

She took a turn about her new home, making a mental note of everything she needed to purchase to situate herself. Her left foot skated on the back of a framed piece of cloth. Her foot left a soiled mark on the back of it.

Bending down, she held the stitched item in her hands with faded blue letters reading – *And after you have suffered a little while, the God of all grace, who has called you to his eternal glory in Christ, will himself restore, confirm, strengthen, and establish you.* Jane put a hand to her mouth, tears silently tracking down her cheeks.

She'd long forgotten about God. Or rather she suspected He'd forgotten her. After Seth died, she'd stopped going to church or praying. It wasn't that she didn't believe; simply, she'd given up like she figured God had. At least she thought He had. Holding this old, soiled embroidery piece in her hands, allowed her to reflect on its meaning to her life. She was ready to move on and begin this new and different chapter.

Jane brushed off the back of it, setting the framed embroidered piece on the mantle. With a wan smile, she moved toward the front door, opening it to go back to the hotel.

"Oh, Mr. Bennett!" Jane exclaimed, putting a hand to her chest. "You gave me a fright."

Derek bowed his head. "I brought you some firewood. In case you wanted to stay here a spell."

Jane moved out of the way, watching his tall, imposing figure stomp across the room with sure footed strides. Brown hair flecked with silver came down to his shoulders. A beard to match lined his entire face, giving him every bit, the rugged mountain man look he happened to be. His scent wafted past her nose, a pleasing mixture of cedar and smoke.

He stacked the wood in his arms off to the left side of the fireplace. Even with no fire, her cheeks flamed, randomly thinking of his calloused, strong hands embracing her. Jane pushed the notions from her head, walking out the door and waiting on the porch to shut the door and head back to the hotel.

"Your roof needs repaired," he said, coming toward her.

"I suppose I might find someone to do it before winter sets," she said, her cinnamon brown eyes scanning the old, rotting wooden boards.

Coming to stand on the threshold of her door, Derek walked backward, looking at the roof. "I can do it. Won't take me but a day."

"I can't impose," Jane began.

Derek held up a hand. "Call it square if you have a meal with me tomorrow evening."

"Mr. Bennett," Jane began placatingly.

"Derek," he said, pushing his worn beaver hat off his head. "Please, call me Derek."

His swirling green eyes, deeper than a pine, bore into hers. In her younger years she would have giggled and shied away. Now, in her late thirties, she smiled demurely at the attention.

*Such a handsome man. And here I am staring like a loony.* Jane stared down at her feet, tucking back imaginary stray hairs behind her ear. *And I find myself fancying him without the clawing of guilt in my heart. Maybe I really am ready for this.*

"Derek," Jane began, eyeing him levelly, "I appreciate your willingness to help, but I really don't feel right obligating you to such a big project. Especially with you being new here and all."

Derek took off his beaver skin hat, holding it loftily in his left hand. She mindlessly checked his hand, looking for any sort of band resting on a finger. Nothing was there. Jane felt the corner of her mouth slightly twitch upward on its own accord.

He grinned at her. "It would be my pleasure to help you. Allow me to put on your roof. All I ask is one meal with you. You won't find cheaper labor," he finished in a teasing tone.

Jane blushed, her eyes darting to her feet. "I agree. Supper tomorrow night."

Derek nodded. "Sounds like a plan, Miss McCarthy."

"How do you know my last name?" she asked, her voice rising suspiciously.

Holding up his hands, Derek replied, "It's on the window."

"Oh," Jane said sheepishly, glancing to the one main window. "So it is."

"Are you headed back to the hotel?"

Jane nodded. "No. I was going to check on something at Leonard's Mercantile."

Derek rolled his shoulders forward then back. Swishing the hair off his head, he stuck the beaver hat back on. "I will see you later then, for coffee this evening," he stated, dipping his head to her. "Miss McCarthy."

She watched the backside of the mountain man stride back into the busy evening Denver street. Jane let out the breath she was holding. A surge of emotions washed over her, sending a bone chilling shiver down her spine colder than a Colorado spring thaw.

*Coffee and supper, all in less than a day?* She thought, clucking her tongue. *Jane McCarthy, you are a smitten woman.*

# CHAPTER ELEVEN

Derek hadn't expected her ready and willing response. Based on her curt, almost abrupt interactions earlier, he thought she would deny him until her lips turned blue and her cinnamon brown eyes rolled in the back of her head. Having her agree reluctantly, and at his insistence, made him feel horrible. He hadn't meant to be so pushy.

*I'm going to tell her so at coffee tonight,* he decided. *If she shows up. I might have just ruined it.* Derek shook his head, letting out a hard breath through his nose. *The first woman you like in years and you chase her away. Good job you old donkey.*

He jogged up the steps to the Whitman Hotel, striding inside to the front counter. The woman he saw before, still standing there and helping another set of guests. Derek patiently waited to the side for the couple to be done.

"Hello Mr. Bennett," the woman greeted.

His brows raised at her remembering his name. "Yes, ma'am. I would like to go about getting a bath."

The woman nodded. "Absolutely. Give us about fifteen minutes and we'll have it ready for you."

Derek nodded, slapping coins down on the counter. He strode

back out the doors and briskly walked down the road to the first mercantile he saw. Now that his mountaineering days were behind him, more presentable clothes were in order. He wouldn't ever get rid of the leather buckskin pants or any of his other garments, but every day wear to blend into society would be nice to have.

*And I wish to look presentable for Miss McCarthy.*

Taking his new clothes, and some other hygiene items, he ambled back up to the hotel. The woman behind the counter announced his readied bath, instructing him on how to get there. The cozy little room was heated by a fireplace. A stool sat to the side of the large tub. Steam rose from the bathtub.

*I haven't had a warm bath in years!*

Derek set his razor, scissors, and soap for his hair and body on the stool and put his fresh clothes on the rack above the towels. Carefully, he lifted a hand mirror laying on a shelf near the drying rack. Derek stared at his grizzly beard.

*I need to shave. I look like a mangled coon,* he decided, setting it beside the other items. A trash bin labeled with big letters – hair – sat under the shelf. Derek chuckled. *Must be for all the men who shaved and clipped their hair themselves.*

Stripping down, he plopped into the warm water, washing his hair and beard first. The water didn't turn as murky as he expected but it wasn't the cleanest either. Derek scrubbed his skin until it was red and the sheen of dirt was floating in the tub.

His lip curled at the grubby sight of the water. Getting out, he wrapped a towel around himself. He grabbed the hand mirror and scissors, setting them on the single shelf. Reaching down for the trash bin, he set it up there as well. He leaned his face over the bin and began trimming the wiry hairs.

He got close to his face, making all the hairs even as possible. Eventually, he might go see the barber, but for now, this would do. Anything was better than before.

His stomach rumbled. With all the events of the day, he forgot to get something to eat. With supper looming shortly, he decided the Whitman Diner would be his place for grub that wasn't jerky or smoked fish.

Completing his beard, he quickly dressed in clean garments and towel dried his hair. Taking a leather strap, he pulled his long hair off his face, tying it at the nape of his neck.

Picking up his soiled clothes, he trucked up to his room. His sack and items sat where he'd left them. Stuffing his soiled clothes in his sack, he took everything down to be laundered.

"Good evening, Mr. Bennett," the woman behind the counter greeted.

"Evening, Miss Eliza. I was hoping to get this sack of items cleaned."

"Certainly," Eliza said, coming around for the sack. "Anything needing special attention?"

Derek nodded. "All the leather."

Eliza glanced from the bag to him. "It's gonna cost you a bit extra."

"That's fine."

Eliza nodded, writing down his name and room number on a slip of paper while telling him the price for the cleaning. He gladly paid, leaving extra dollar notes for the laundress as a tip for all his items and the care they would need.

Striding off to the dining side, he felt like a fresh man. Glancing out the window, he spied Miss McCarthy coming up the steps. He went down the hallway and toward the diner. He didn't want to be a pest any more than he already had been.

Guilt clawed like a bear up his throat and roared, sending melancholy throughout his entire body. Even though Darcy had been gone for several years, he felt terrible for moving on. He loved her in his own way, despite their marriage not starting conventionally. He'd seen a woman in need so he struck a bargain with her. He would marry her, tell people she was Greek to get her out of the cruel clutches of a society who wanted nothing more than to shut her out due to her heritage, in exchange for company on his long and lonely trips, and help with the chores.

Darcy was a good woman – patient, gentle, kind to anyone and everything she came across. Spending time and coming to know her was pleasant. They were companions, sleeping in the same tent but not often under the same buffalo hide. It was an amicable marriage, one he enjoyed.

*Seeing a woman like Jane makes me ready for the next stages in my life, whether the next stage happens to be the pretty blond by my side or not, I'm ready.*

His gut swirled with nerves. In a few hours, he would be sipping coffee with the prettiest woman in all of Denver.

# CHAPTER TWELVE

Jane strode down to Leonard's Mercantile. Out of the corner of her eye, she spied Derek Bennett going inside the Whitman Hotel. She let out the breath she was holding, relieved she would be able to think in peace for a while.

Derek made her brain foggier than a Colorado fall morning; where the fog hovered around the mountain like a bird. She couldn't rightly think straight. Derek's nice smile, silver streaked hair to his shoulders and piercing green eyes made her want to feel his calloused hands on her body.

Jane shook her head and those thoughts from her mind. Mr. Bennet, Derek, was the complete opposite of Seth. Seth was clean cut and shaved. He never had a day where he went without shaving unless he was sick. And he never fixed anything with his own hands, often hiring out for someone else.

She never understood why Seth would do such a thing when he was more than capable and knew how to do it despite his wealthier upbringing. Seth being the son of the judge, and eventually becoming the town mayor, afforded them the money to accommodate such a luxury. Growing up down the road, and being in the same grade throughout school, they weren't much different. However, to her, growing up poorer than Seth, made her feel a man should work on his own house so the money could be saved for unknown circumstances. She overlooked this flaw of self-entitlement in Seth, preferring the amicability of their relationship instead of an unwanted fight.

When Derek offered to fix her roof, she was taken back because while she believed a person should do things for themselves when capable, she hadn't seen the kindness of strangers manifested so incredibly and his kindness left her confused but in awe. It was kind of him to bring her wood for a fire she wouldn't be having until tomorrow. It was nice he wanted to fix her home, in exchange for a meal with her.

Jane was so stricken by Derek's thoughtfulness to save her the money in labor, she overlooked his pushiness. She rubbed a hand up and down her arm, gazing at all the nice dishes and fabric in Leonard's store. Usually she ignored the fabric, going to Madame Comtois for dresses or Mrs. Birch. Now she needed the fabric to make curtains, a quilt, and other necessities.

"Evenin' Jane," Leonard greeted in his grandfatherly tone.

Jane gave him a warm smile. "Evening Leonard. How are you doing today?"

Leonard smiled. "Doing well, considering these old bones. How are you Miss Jane? Anything I can get started for you?"

Jane walked over to a display of dishes. "I am fine, thank you. I came to order a few things like these dishes."

"All right, lemme get the hotel tab—"

"That won't be necessary, Leonard. I'm purchasing these for me."

Leonard smiled. "How nice. Did you buy yourself a house?"

"I own it."

Heat crept up her neck. She didn't know exactly what to say about Audrey getting the house for her. Technically, she did own it.

"I was wondering when you would breathe some fresh air," he replied chortling as he wrote down her order. "Did you want that set or the one from a catalog?" he asked, reaching under the counter.

"This set is perfectly fine for me," she said. "And," she paused, checking over the display of fabric. She pulled out a blue-gray color fabric that caught her eye. "And this fabric please."

Her stomach betrayed how elated she felt. Her first set of proper dishes in nigh on twelve years. It felt wonderful but also a mite scary. She would be on her own. Not that alone bothered her but if someone came to steal or harm her, she would have no one around to truly help her.

*Perhaps overcoming my fear of a dog would be wise.*

Jane set money on the counter. Leonard counted, giving her back money she overpaid with. She was always doing that. Her father used to say, *better to put too much down and get some back than be short.* He wasn't wrong.

The old mercantile owner nodded to himself, motioning to his store helper, Clyde to bring up the dishes for her. "Alright. Anything else for you, Jane?"

Jane's lips pursed slightly to the right side of her face. "I guess I will have to make a list and see what I need. Can the dishes and fabric stay here for a bit?"

Leonard's face crinkled in laughter, bringing out more of his known grandpa appearance. "I will be here when you're ready. And yes, that's no trouble."

"Thank you, Leonard."

Jane hurried out of the mercantile. She walked two streets over to where the lumber mill happened to be. Inside, Jeffrey bellowed orders to some younger men about stacking boards nicely to not damage them. Jeffrey was a nice man. One wouldn't happen to know by his harsh appearance or his constant disapproving scowl, but she knew that was just the way his face fell. His heart was true.

She waited outside for him to see her, not wanting to soil her dress. Jeffrey's large frame angrily spun on a heel. Head down he came outside cursing about the men inside. Jane cleared her throat.

"My apologies, Miss McCarthy, for my cursin'," Jeffrey said, taking off his hat. "I did not see you there."

"It's all right," she said, closing the distance between them. "I came to buy a bit of lumber."

"For the hotel?" Jeffrey asked, confused. "I just checked the roof two weeks ago and the old girl is solid."

Jane shook her head. "I own a house now, and the roof needs a bit of repairs."

Jeffrey nodded. "Where's it at?"

"East end of town," she said pointing.

"The one that backs up to a few firs, up the road from Ross and Mary's and across?"

"That's the one."

Jeffrey nodded. "The old Milner house. I will have Luis bring you up some boards tomorrow. Whatever you don't use, let me know so I don't charge you for it."

"Thank you very kindly, Jeffrey."

The man rolled his shoulders, then dipped his head. "It's gettin' late for a lady to be out. Want me to walk ya back to the hotel?"

Jane glanced at the sky. The sun had waned considerably with around one hour or so left before it set. She hadn't thought about the time or much anything else but getting items for her home and coffee with Derek Bennett shortly.

"Thank you, Jeffrey. I would appreciate it."

Jeffrey held out his elbow. Jane looped her arm in with his. She stared at the gold band on his left hand. It had been a long time since she wore a gold band on her hand. She sold the ring Seth gave her years ago to help pay for her ticket out this way. For years her guilt gnawed like fall at summer. But it was done.

She sucked in her lip, finally coming to the main road up toward the hotel.

"Somethin' wrong, Jane?" Jeffrey asked.

Jane shook her head. "Not at all."

Jeffrey nodded, taking her across the street and up the hill. Something niggled at the back of her brain to ask him. It was childish in a way. But now that she was about to retire and be in town a touch more, she wanted to know what others thought of her.

*I'm wrong in wanting to know*, she chastised herself. *Nothing good would come of it in knowing.*

Jeffery continued talking about his wife and the kids, making her forget about what she wanted to ask. He stopped at the base of the hotel steps.

Jane took one step up toward the hotel doors. "Thank you for helping me and escorting me back to the hotel, Jeffrey. I appreciate it. Tell your family I said hello."

"My pleasure, Jane. Take care now."

His giant frame ambled back down the road toward the lumber mill. Jane climbed the steps to go inside. She forgot to take her small watch with her when she left to see her house and hoped she didn't stand Mr. Bennett up for coffee.

Peeking to her right, she saw no one in the hotel sitting area. Heading back to her office, her own personal small watch sat on the table top. She had forty-five minutes to prepare herself for a bit of conversation-*personal* conversation.

Jane swallowed, shoving her hands in her dress pockets. *It's just coffee. Nothing so serious. He's a kind man, like Ralph*, she breathed out through her nose, heading now to her bedroom. *Coffee with a mountain man*, she mused.

---

Jane sat on the settee, ankles crossed, sipping some black coffee. A scone sat on a plate on her lap. She'd yet to see Mr. Bennett emerge from the staircase or even the dining side. Half-past seven and no sign of the man.

Granted they never set a proper time but to her supper was seven and this was well after. Jane checked herself over, setting her skirts just so and touched her hair. Nothing was out of place.

"Why you sure are a pretty sight," Mary complimented.

Jane peeked up from sipping her coffee. "Thank you, Mary."

Mary waddled over, sitting down with a huff. "What's with the coffee and scones?"

"I'm going to be chatting with someone soon," Jane explained as a blush crept to her cheeks.

Grinning, Mary leaned forward, taking a scone off a plate with four remaining of the delicious treats. "I will make sure you're not bothered."

"Thank you, Mary."

"None of it," she replied through a mouthful of scone. "Least I can do for all you've done puttin' up with me."

Jane sighed, gazing around the hotel for Mr. Bennett and not spying him. She checked her watch again. The time ticked slowly. Only five minutes had gone by.

"I understand what you're thinkin'," Mary began, her scone now gone. Her hand reached for another but hesitated and pulled back. "You've been alone so long it feels normal because you know naught else but bein' alone. You've accepted it as you. A differ'nt part of you is achin' for someone yet terrified to find out," she paused, grabbing another scone. "You're not shamin' you or memories of Seth. You're just too stubborn to accept moving on and part of you is lookin' for excuses not to talk to him or for whatever this is to not work." Mary got up, holding the scone in her teeth while she adjusted her skirting around her belly. Taking the scone in hand. "Have a nice chat. I will tell the others to skedaddle."

Jane blinked. She hadn't thought of it such as that before. Mary put it succinctly. She felt like finding another was shaming the memory of Seth. In a sense, how dare she move on because Seth was her joy? Yet she knew Mary was right. She wasn't shaming Seth. She wasn't shaming the memories or the goodness that was there. She was wallowing in self-pity, terrified to allow herself to get close and love again. And because of that fear looking for reasons to back out.

She closed her eyes, sighing deeply and feeling her body fall into an accepted regret of all the years wasted and determined not to allow herself to waste more. She was done wasting. Twelve years gone, when she could have spent some of those years happily with someone for companionship.

*No more living and feeling this way. This is not how I used to be. Reserved yes, but not so out of touch.* Jane hung her head, the coffee cup tilting and shaking in her hands.

Rising to stand and setting her scone and plate on the table, she glanced around again for Derek Bennett. She heard him before she saw him. Booted steps strode from the dining side. He emerged through the kitchen, getting shoed out by an annoyed Claudia and her flapping apron. Jane hid the smirk on her lips behind her coffee, the liquid now cold.

"Miss McCarthy, sorry I'm late," he said quickly coming to her, "didn't realize how late I happened to be."

He sat down across from her, his beard now neatly trimmed, cut close to his skin with the occasional wiry spot near his ears and under his chin where it looked like the mirror hadn't quite reached. Nice blue pants hugged his frame while a clean brown shirt pressed against his body. His hair, with slight curls at the end, was now pulled back with leather tied at the nape of his neck.

"Quite all right," Jane said, leaning forward and pushing the plate of scones in his direction.

Derek held up a hand. "Just ate. Your diner serves excellent food. I had to finish everything. Why I lost track of time." He gave her a sheepish grin causing her heart to flutter.

Mary waddled out, taking the tray of refreshments with her to the kitchen. The pregnant woman winked at her when her back was turned toward Derek. Jane chose to ignore the woman's teasing and leaned back in her seat; ankles crossed.

"I'm pleased you enjoyed the meal."

Derek copied her relaxed posture, leaning back in his seat with his hands clasped. "Where are you from, Miss McCarthy?"

"Please, call me Jane."

He grinned at her. "Pretty name."

Jane couldn't keep the creeping blush from her cheeks. "I'm from Tennessee. And you?"

"Massachusetts."

Jane turned the tables before he could ask her more questions. "What made you come out this way?"

"Fur trapping," he said. "The money was hot and I got quite a bit of it. Sent the majority to my son Bryce here in Denver."

Mary came back out with a fresh mug of coffee and more scones. She set it down and scurried off. Out of her peripheral, Claudia peeked her head out of the door, smiling. Ada took Claudia's spot and pressed a hand to her smiling face.

Eugene walked from where the employees slept in rooms on the main floor. He paused, mid-stride and spun on his heel. Audrey's lilting voice came in from the back door of the hotel. His quick strides faintly echoed down the hall toward the back door to cut Audrey off. Jane wanted nothing more than to chuckle at the helpful attempt Eugene was bringing her, but it would be rude to Derek; Jane kept her face passive.

Jane ignored her nosy friends, focusing on Derek in front of her. The man relaxed in the chair, slumping his shoulders and clasping his hands in his lap, while casually disclosing a personal item to her. She wondered how he became so natural, oozing quiet confidence she wished she had in her life outside of being a manager.

She wriggled forward pouring him and herself a cup of coffee. "Sugar?"

Derek shook his head. "No thank you, Jane," he said, leaning forward to take the offered cup and winked at her.

Jane plopped a spoonful of sugar in her cup and swirled it all with a spoon. She leaned back in the seat with her cup. "I came out to Denver after my husband passed away from yellow fever. I had to burn everything."

"I'm sorry for your loss," he replied somberly. "I lost my wife in the night. Went to sleep normally but in the morning, she was gone... It was sad, but beautiful. I think... I think when it's my time, I would like to go like that."

Jane nodded her agreement. Surely passing in one's sleep would be the kindest thing. "I'm sorry you lost your wife."

"Thank you. And I'm sorry about your husband," he stated, his swirling green eyes gazing into hers. "Anyway, enough of the somberness. How are you going to decorate your home?"

Jane blinked, a surprised smile sneaking across her lips. "I'm going to purchase a settee tomorrow."

Derek nodded. "And an armchair?"

"Yes," she laughed breathily. "That too. I'm thinking of a light blue color for both pieces of furniture to match the curtains I'm going to make. And I would need a dining table as well."

"I'll make you one," he said, leaning forward and grabbing a scone. "It will be cheaper than purchasing one on order."

Jane waved him off. "Very kind of you but I cannot ask it of you since you're already fixing my roof."

"You're not asking. I'm offering. And all *I* ask is another supper date, after tomorrow's of course."

Jane felt herself heat hotter than a winter wood stove. Any blind and deaf woman would be able to realize this man's attention is obvious. And while Jane could be purposely obtuse, in this case she couldn't deny his intentions. She swallowed, her stomach fluttering and tumbling with emotions she hadn't felt in years.

Spying Mary, who had snuck around the corner, gazing at her and nodding her head in encouragement. Ross, leaning over the top of her took in the scene and scowled, dragging his wife away before she made a scene with her enthusiasm. Movement on the banister caught her attention as Audrey and Eugene grinned down at her like children. The kitchen door opened revealing the three faces of Claudia, Ada and Lena.

Jane breathed out, torn between being annoyed and appreciating their lovingness toward her. She let out a breathy chuckle, tucking her lips in to regain some composure.

"You have nice, concerned friends," Derek leaned in and whispered. "Being out in the wild, you know when you're being watched and how close. There are probably a few behind me and a couple on the stairs."

Jane smirked and laughed at the whole absurd situation. "You're right. We're being watched."

Derek grinned, setting his plate and coffee on the table. "Don't bother me none."

"Me either," Jane decided.

Derek's calm presence made her relax more. Her heart beat steadied, feeling safe in his presence – she felt no need to sprint away from the moment as she had with Ralph. She felt bad about it still, but with Ralph, she was eager to leave, yet with Derek, she was eager to stay. Even being married to Seth and loving him dearly, oftentimes, their moments spent together were forced. Seth carried his work burdens into his home life. Here, with Derek, there was nothing of the sort. No tension or pretense. Just him and his calmness.

*I really like him. He is kind, patient... easy,* she thought. *He's a nice man.* Jane leaned forward, reaching for the coffee. Derek beat her to it, pouring the dark liquid for her. *He makes my heart flutter and still at the same time. He makes me relish the moment, a contentedness I never felt before.* Jane grinned easily leaning back in her chair.

Derek never took his eyes off of her, completely giving her his full attention. She loved it, wishing she would have done the same earlier. Seth almost never gave her his full attention, often talking to her over ledgers and paperwork. It had become so common she forgot about his disconnection to her and had accepted it, not realizing how much it had truly bothered her. With Derek, she relished the feeling of importance he gave her.

Jane sipped her coffee, feeling herself mold in the cushion on the settee. "How old is your son?" Jane asked, breaking their peaceful silence.

Derek shrugged, a frown creasing his handsome face; the first sign he had given that he had anything other than peacefulness in his life at the moment. "Not sure. I wanted to marry his mother, but she refused, marrying someone she loved. I heard about my son when I came back to town, but didn't want to press any more difficult feelings on the kid since all he knew, the other man was his father. Hardest thing I ever did. I think he's in his early twenties though. Fits the timeline plus he has a little family of his own."

"That must have been difficult."

"It was. But now, we are establishing a relationship. At least I hope we are. He's allowing us to meet for coffee tomorrow at Martin's Diner and I'm grateful for the chance he's giving me," he finished, a contented smile skittering across his lips. "Do you have any kids?"

Jane shook her head. "No. But not from lack of trying."

Derek smiled sympathetically at her. "What do you want?"

Jane laughed easily, shaking the slight melancholy that had creeped on her when thinking about the children she never got to have. "What do you mean?"

"In this life. What do you want out of it?"

"Happiness." Jane answered without hesitation.

Derek smiled. "Me too."

# CHAPTER THIRTEEN

Jane woke well past the normal five o'clock time which she usually rose. Checking her watch, it ticked past seven in the morning. Jane grinned. Wiping her eyes groggily, she smiled recounting the previous evening spent in Derek's company.

*It was such a pleasant time,* she thought enjoyably as she stretched her back.

Derek and she had stayed up well into the night talking until they went through their pot of coffee and ate all of Claudia's scones. Jane went into the kitchen to make more coffee, Derek following her, and they stayed in there, sitting at the kitchen table, until they went through two more pots and the rest of Claudia's scones.

The conversation was so easy, flowing from them both like they had always been friends. It was nothing like she'd ever experienced in her life. Even conversations with Seth weren't as memorable as the one from last night, and never so easy either.

Jane rose, going to her dress hanging on the peg. *It was the best conversation of my life,* she decided. *And I'm content for the first time in years. I'm happy. I'm not holding myself back anymore to stay fixed in the past and 'what could have been's' with Seth.* Jane took a deep breath. *I like Derek. And now that I think on it, I believe Seth and I married because we were comfortable with each other and didn't want to accept anything different. I knew him like the back of my hand. And to get to know anyone different in Tennessee was as foreign to me as the stars are bright.*

Jane shook her head, allowing the sweet memories and tid-bits of her and Derek's conversation to filter back through her mind. She relished in his easy company and soft tone.

She dressed in her favorite, well loved, high-necked purple dress, one that complimented her hair and eyes. She grabbed an apron off the peg she bought herself for whenever she needed to help in the kitchen. The dark brown fabric would hide the dirt from cleaning her new home. Neatly, she folded the apron and clutched it in her right hand. Taking her cloth money sack, she put it in her left dress pocket to pay Jeffrey later. Maybe she would stop off at the local carpenters and see if she could order her furniture, minus the dining set Derek offered to build her.

Today, Derek would be fixing her roof for her while she tidied her little home. The hotel duties were completed on her end and Eliza was more than capable of being on her own and running the hotel. She was excited to fully retire, to move out and to have something tangible that would be hers after working all those years.

Heading to the washroom, she took care of her morning routine. Satisfied, she walked out into the main part of the hotel, her folded apron now upon her person so she wouldn't forget it. Bartholomew was already helping two couples check in. Jane smiled, dipping her head as she went past and into her office.

Opening the small office door, Eliza sat in one of the chairs in front of her desk.

"Good morning Eliza," Jane greeted happily, taking a seat for the final time behind her desk. "I hope I haven't kept you long."

Eliza wriggled in her seat. "Morning. And no, you haven't. I've only arrived a moment ago."

"Something the matter?"

Eliza looked at her lap, her hands fumbling over the fabric of her dress. "Do you think I'm ready for this?" she blurted. "I don't want to mess anything up. I don't want to get fired."

Jane smiled fondly, moving to take a seat by Eliza. She rested her hand over the top of the young woman's. "You won't. I already made the list of items for the rest of the year heading into winter. And everything from Audrey's wedding is put away. All you have to do is make certain payroll is done on Fridays, go to Leonard's Mercantile or Randall's Butchery for food for the diner and everyone is happy. At least at first. As time goes on, you'll learn the ropes, put out fires and roll with everything that comes up," Jane assured. "You *can* do this and you're very good at it too. You can always come see me or Audrey for advice."

Eliza smiled demurely, "Thank you for believing in me."

"Absolutely," Jane replied, rising to her feet. "Go get something to eat and start going over ledgers. Even though they are done, you will be able to see *how* they are done. I'm going to my house up the road and will be back later if you have any questions for me."

Eliza tilted her head to the side. "The old Milner house?"

Jane nodded, hand on the frame of the door as she was about to exit. "That one," Jane smiled kindly at Eliza. "You're going to be fine. Audrey and I have lots of faith in you."

Eliza took a deep breath and rose out of her chair. She took small steps around the desk, finally sitting down in the padded chair with a large sigh of trepidation.

Jane left her office. She paused two steps from the door. *No longer my office*, she corrected herself. *And I'm glad to be rid of the burden. Twelve years behind that desk was more than enough for me.*

She strode out of the office area and to the check-in counter. The guests were gone, more than likely settling into their rooms. Bartholomew sat behind the counter, his paper open, as per his usual. She was going to miss him when he left for Baltimore.

Jane took a look around, seeing all the changes the past year had brought; it made her head spin.

Last year, Audrey Whitman came into her life in the tail end of summer, a giddy woman without a useful skill to her name. And right after Audrey's arrival came Mary and Natali at about the same time, both fairly skilled. Jane smirked. Kayla followed roughly a month later. Now Audrey, the proud owner of multiple hotels across America was finally married. Why it took so long for Audrey to marry, Jane could only guess at; but she assumed it had a lot to do with how wealthy Audrey happened to be and appeasing the society she grew up in enough to finally leave it behind as was her original intent when she'd traveled west. All these new women contributed to her life and this hotel and Jane was forever grateful they had, even if change was difficult for her.

Jane walked out of the hotel, and down the front steps. Turning up the road, her heart fluttered in her chest. After spending the entire night talking to Derek, she was excited to see him again; to speak with him, and watch his green eyes, keen and adventurous, gaze at her.

*I feel like I'm in my teens again*, she thought, going past the Whitman Stables. *Like I did right before Seth proposed. But unlike that memory, this new... relationship has me excited, a completely different feeling.*

Quickly, she crossed the street to continue up the slight incline to her new home. The city was coming alive with people. Wagons barreled into town, wanting to get their supplies before their day got too far gone. Men on horses stopped next to stores and throughout the city. Another wagon with a mule clambered her way.

Jane stayed to the far side, away from the road. She sucked in a lungful of the crisp autumn air. She loved this time of year, the smells of the turning weather and changing land and the ever constant of people baking.

Making it to the top of the incline, she paused and looked around the city. A crow flew low over her field of vision, perching on Ross and Mary's house, looking at her. She watched the bird hop along the roof, never taking its beady black eyes off of her.

The bird cawed and flew off. The Whitman Hotel stood like a proud beacon in the heart of the city. It's tall steps and commanding architecture made people pause to look at the feat Philip Whitman built.

She didn't even hear the wagon stop beside her.

"Care for a ride?" Derek asked.

Jane pressed a hand to her heart. "I didn't even hear you approach."

Derek chortled. "The country will do that to you. Make you stop to take pause and gander about; appreciating what God made," Derek breathed in deep, taking a look around. The mule brayed, ears flicking back. "That's enough Harold," Derek admonished.

"Harold?" Jane asked, glancing to Derek and pointing at the mule.

Derek clambered off the buckboard wagon. "Yes," he replied, patting the mule on the side. "This is Harold. When you spend years trapping, you ought to name your companion."

Jane grinned. "The name suits him. Is Harold going to get himself in a relationship?"

Derek kicked back on his heels, tipping his beaver hat back off his face with a poke of a finger. "Should Harold have a relationship?" he asked with a grin.

Jane shrugged. "I believe if Harold wants a relationship, he should be able to have one. And if he gets one, her name should be Darlene."

He chuckled softly. "I agree… I believe Harold is ready for such an endeavor."

Jane felt a rush of heat attack her cheeks faster than fire to tinder. Never in all her days, had she'd been this outspoken, this relaxed, or casual. Even in her marriage with Seth, it was constrained by propriety; simple, quick, and pertinent gusts of conversations to the very heart of the matter. And in those moments, she cherished the conversations; short bursts as they were because she loved him. Never did she stop and believe she needed something more, until she found that something in Derek Bennett: a meaningful and fun relationship.

Walking over to Harold, her hand hesitated, hovering over his back. Her mind took her to the time Seth admonished her for riding a horse, touching one even for his fear of her getting hurt. She felt so free riding the mare bareback across their property those few times she managed it without Seth finding out. Would she feel the same energy from touching Harold?

Derek put his hand over top of hers, forcing her hand the rest of the way to Harold's fur. Harold shook his flank at her touch. The exhilaration she once felt zinged back to her. A smile crept across her lips.

*Goodbye Seth,* she thought, sinking her fingers into Harold's fur and whooshing her hand up and down his back. *I'm at peace with you being gone and where I'm at. You were a part of my past but you're not in my future. It's time for me and my happiness.*

She let out a steady breath through her nose, scratching Harold on his left shoulder. The mule tilted his head, pulling his lips back. Jane could feel Derek's eyes on her. Out of the corner of her eye, she caught a glimpse of him smiling at her.

"I don't think I've ever seen Harold so happy."

Jane grinned, kneading her fingers in Harold's coat. "He's so soft."

Derek patted Harold on the rump twice, moving closer to the steps of the wagon. Standing by the wagon, Derek held out his hand to her to help her onto the bench seat. Jane took his hand, climbing inside. Taking a peek into the back, she spied planks of wood piled and a sack of nails sitting to the back-left corner.

"Jeffrey was going to deliver the wood," Jane remarked

Derek shrugged, climbing in beside her. He threw the break and lightly touched the reins to Harold's back. Harold moved his ears back, lurching forward.

Derek peeked over his shoulder, merging onto the road. "I went down to the lumber mill to get nails and a few other things with Harold and found out the delivery of wood was for you, so I brought it myself on Jeffrey's wagon."

"Thank you very much," Jane offered, sitting down on the bench.

"My pleasure," he replied, giving her a quick smile.

Jane took pleasure sitting beside Derek, relishing in his rugged appearance and the protectiveness he exuded. His hair was tied at the nape of his neck. A re-trimmed beard lined his jaw.

"Somethin' on your mind?" he asked without taking his eyes off the road.

Jane heated. "No. I'm perfectly fine, thank you."

Derek smirked. "That color dress becomes you."

Jane looked out the wagon to the right, staring at the scenery, houses and people passing her by. Derek turned the wagon down the rutted road to her house, stopping as he barely passed the cabin and pulled along the left side. With a quick leap out, he dismounted and turned around to help her down.

She took his proffered hand, carefully climbing down from the buckboard wagon. "Thank you for the ride," she said, when her feet were planted firmly on the ground.

"My pleasure," he replied, holding onto her hand for longer than was proper.

Jane grinned, sneaking her hand back. "Mrs. Anderson is going to be by today," she said carefully, watching Derek's face intently.

He nodded, gazing at her intently to continue.

Last night during their conversation, Derek disclosed more about his son Bryce, what happened with Tara and his relationship and more. It hurt her heart. She knew Tara, employed her once in laundry. Jane hadn't thought she was capable of being so callous as to not allow a man to see his son.

*And poor Derek*, she thought. *All he wanted was to be around his son, get to know the man and was pushed aside. And to not harm his son's feelings, he let him go... And here I am buying a hutch from his son's wife.*

The lines on Derek's face did not change. No flaring of nostrils, clenching fists, some kind of anger she expected was null from this man.

Jane tucked some wispy strands that had escaped her braid behind her ear. She felt guilty the hutch purchase eluded her up until this point. She was so engrossed in last night, she didn't stop to think how seeing Bryce would affect Derek.

Jane licked her lips. "The hutch was once at the hotel in storage. We had a sale of the things in storage and Elena bought it when she and Bryce married. Audrey knew I always loved the hutch and arranged for me to buy it back," Jane explained.

Derek nodded. "I'll help bring it in when it gets here."

She went around the back of the buckboard and headed to the front door of her home. Taking the key out of her pocket, she opened it and stepped inside, letting out a small puff of air.

The caw of a crow outside her window to her right caught her attention. The beady black eye of the bird blinked at her, then it flew off. Jane's brows drew together. *What a strange creature,* she thought.

Picking up a broom that was left behind, she began cleaning her home starting on the dining room side of the house. The dirt lifted off the ground but the floorboards, she decided would need a decent scrubbing.

On the roof, she heard the strident bootsteps of Derek, pulling up rotten wood shingles and grumbling. She wondered how he managed to keep his footing with one side slightly more sloped than the other. She once heard this style called gambrel, but she wasn't entirely certain. She shrugged. Nor did she care very much.

Jane paused in front of the fireplace, imagining a settee in front and both of them on it in the wintertime and smiled. *The settee would need to be a bit larger than I originally planned,* she thought. *Derek is a big man.* To enjoy companionship again was something she wanted. She didn't want to grow old alone and become known as the hermit woman of Denver with an abundance of cats she had heard some old women were known for.

*I'm ready for some companionship... a relationship,* she decided. *Mary was right. I had to find my achin' part,* she mused with a smile thinking of Mary. *I thought I was aching for a house all my own and that may have been part of it. But... I'm aching for a partner. Someone to tie my life to and grow old with. I don't want to die a hermit.*

Boot steps thundered over the roof and she followed where she thought Derek happened to be with her eyes and smiled. *I found my achin' part.*

Looking up through the planked wooden boards, her brows drew together, wondering if their relationship would continue to bloom into something more. *I hope so,* she thought, sweeping the floor.

# CHAPTER FOURTEEN

If Derek had any memorable conversation with a woman worth taking up head space and remembering, it was last night with Jane McCarthy. Even long after their conversation ended and they departed to their respectable rooms, Derek couldn't sleep. He lay on top of the sheets, hands behind his head, thinking of her and all that was said between them. Even now, hammering on Jane's roof to fix her wooden shingles, their conversation was all he could think about.

Jane had buried herself in her work there at the hotel and he had done the same with fur trapping, more so after losing Darcy. They were on common ground, searching for a place to belong and with someone by their side. Even though neither of them thought so, or at least would ever dare to mention it out loud, it was there.

*She's a sweet woman who spent a long time hiding herself... like me after Darcy passed on.* He smirked, thinking of her casual demeanor from last night; the way she leaned forward in her chair, shoulders rolled forward and relaxed. The easy, soft smile that graced her lips and exposed the dimple in her right cheek. *I really like the woman.*

Derek yanked up the rotting shingles, counting how many he needed to replace. On her gambrel style roof, one side was sloped slightly more than the other to help the snow fall off; however even with the sloped sides, eventually the wood would rot. And with more than half the roof rotting, it would take a while to replace.

He grimaced, pulling up another board. *I'm going to replace her entire roof with tin instead of this*, he decided. *It will never hold well. And I don't want her to have to replace it the following year.*

Climbing down, he took several large steps back from the house. Staring at the roof, all the shingles, while made out of better wood than most he'd seen in the towns he'd traveled through, were in the middle of deteriorating. Even though the roof could easily survive the winter, he didn't want Jane to experience any troubles later with a roof completely caving in or leaks.

Going around to the front door, he knocked. The swishing of a broom from inside paused.

"Come in," her voice called.

Derek opened the door, standing on the threshold. Since she was busy making her house proper for herself, he didn't want to track in dirt.

"I would like to replace your roof with tin," he said. "Your wooden shingles would last you the winter but you would be likely replacing them again in spring."

Jane blinked. A frown pulled at the edges of her lips. "All right," she agreed.

Derek hurriedly added, "It won't cost much more than the wood. Tin is fairly inexpensive."

"I trust you," Jane replied, leaning her broom against the wall. She wiped her hands on her apron and pulled money from a small cloth sack from an apron pocket.

Derek didn't know why but her words made him smile. There was something more to them than what she let on. He took a few steps forward and paused. He checked behind him to see if there happened to be a dirt trail.

"It's fine," Jane said with a humorous smile. "I appreciate your caution."

Derek remained in his new location in the middle of the room. He looked around the cabin. She had swept the interior clean and gotten the spider webs out of the corners. In all, the home was becoming quite cozy.

"I'm going to head to the mill then and get your money back. Then I'll hop on over to grab some tin," Derek said, backing carefully toward the door.

"I haven't paid yet," Jane replied, picking up the broom. "Jeffrey was waiting to see what was going to be used before he charged me. And please let me know what I owe you."

Derek nodded, hand on the knob of the door. "All right."

He exited the house, heading for Harold and the wagon. A raven perched itself on the back end of the wagon, spying him and then flying off. Derek grumbled under his breath. He never believed in the afterlife Darcy used to mention. But after constantly seeing the same raven, he was convinced it existed, or it happened to be God looking after his flock of sheep.

*Darcy – even now, you're meddling in my affairs*, he thought. *I'm ready... I'm just taking my sweet time in things. There's no rush. I just met the woman and I'm not set yet on staying in Denver.*

Derek untethered the reins on Harold, and climbed into the buckboard wagon. He got the mule moving back toward the road at a leisurely pace, going down the slight hill and toward the lumber mill.

Off to the right, he spied his son's horse and wagon down a side street. Today, they were supposed to have coffee at two o'clock at Martin's Diner. He looked forward to the coffee arrangement. It was hard to spy his son across the street and not want to go over and say hello. But he knew how hard it's all been on Bryce.

It had been hard on Derek as well; seeing his son after so long and getting to finally hear the sound of his child's adult baritone voice instead of the high-pitched squeak of a child made him want to rant and rave at the injustice of missing out on so much of Bryce's life. It was difficult to be the one looking in on Bryce's life, always sending money, always sending something, but never allowed to interact, do or say anything to save face and not hurt his kid. He wanted to be there for Bryce. He wanted to be the father to his son that his father had been for him. However, he wasn't because he hadn't been allowed to be.

*A father's love never fades... Even if Bryce doesn't want me, I will always love my son.*

Derek sighed, rolling past the side street and down the road farther. He made a right turn, heading straight for the lumber mill. The main man Jeffrey, stood outside, talking to a man with a piece of paper in hand.

He stopped the wagon, going around the back to unload the boards.

The strident bootsteps of Jeffrey reached his ears. Derek didn't have to look up to know the man was there.

"You haven't touched a board," Jeffrey remarked.

Derek nodded. "The roof needs to be completely replaced. I'm goin' to purchase tin. It will last longer."

Jeffrey reached in and grabbed some boards. "Zinc is a bit cheaper if you want it. I got enough to do the roof and then some."

"I would be much obliged," Derek replied.

Jeffrey nodded, carrying the board around back. "Unhitch your mule for me. I will drive it on up there and then make another delivery."

Derek propped the board up against the wagon, going around the front to the wagon. He began unhitching Harold. Taking his animal, he walked forward and out of the way, waiting for Jeffrey to come around with his animal

Jeffrey came around from the back of the mill with a darker and slightly larger mule than Harold, harnessed and ready to go. The molly mule happily backed into place, ears alert and forward.

"She's a pretty animal," Derek complimented.

"Darlene here is a good horse mule," Jeffrey praised, patting her neck.

Derek chuckled and shook his head. A deep belly laugh wanted to rumble out. Derek choked it down, allowing himself to grin broadly as he faced the other direction away from Jeffrey. He didn't want the man he just met to think his random smile insane.

The rustling of leather straps and the stomping of Darlene's hooves reached his ears. Derek wiped the grin off his face, saving it for Jane later. Turning back around, Jeffrey situated himself in the buckboard.

"Darlene and I will drop off the tin roof in about two hours. I have a delivery to make that is a bit out of town."

Derek nodded. "Just fine. I will head up and get the roof cleared and ready."

Jeffrey nodded back, slapping the reins on Darlene's back. Once Jeffrey was a bit away and out of ear shot of his boisterous laughter, Derek chuckled uproariously.

*The cunning woman,* he chortled.

Grabbing Harold's reins, he headed back up to Jane's house to finish taking the shingles off the roof. Wagons of other folks ambled past him to the destinations they wanted to be. Men dipped their heads in greeting while the women smiled.

He headed up the road he remembered seeing Bryce's wagon. He was curious to know his son yet cautious to give the man room. Part of him wanted to overwhelm his boy with love, the other respected the distance Bryce set between them.

*It was courteous of Jane to tell me that my son was going to stop by. It pained me though, watching her face fall and wince, like she expected anger,* Derek thought, watching the wagon. Turning his head, he stared at Harold.

"Jane's a considerate woman," Derek said to the mule. "Should we settle here in Denver?"

Harold tossed his head. Derek switched the reins in his hands while the right hand scratched the mule under the chin. Derek came up to the place where Bryce had his wagon parked. No one was around it. The hutch Jane bought from Elena stood straight up, tied down in the back with many ropes. Shrugging, Derek continued up the road, going down a side one that wound to the left and brought him up to the other side of Jane's home instead of from the main road through Denver.

He dipped his head to Jane, hitching Harold to the post where he'd tied him up before. Three women were outside with Jane, talking animatedly to her. The third woman in a yellow dress with a suitcase stood off to the side. Jane's face, reddened from work. Wispy blond strands poked out of her usually tightly coiffed hair.

Derek paused, gazing at her. She was beautiful, all rosy and bright. Her brown eyes sparkled in the afternoon sunlight. Her sleeves on her dark purple dress that complimented her eyes and skin tone were rolled up to her elbows.

Shaking his head, he went around to the back where the ladder happened to be. Grabbing some tools, he climbed up the ladder and strode across the roof to the front of the house.

Getting down on his knees, he pulled up a shingle. He leaned over the edge of the roof, and hollered, "I'm going to be pulling shingles ladies. You may want to head inside."

"Oh Mr. Bennett! How lovely to see you," Elena Anderson answered.

Derek gave her a polite smile. "Mrs. Anderson, it is a pleasure to see you again. Tell Bryce and Ophelia, I say hello."

"I won't need to. Jane is buying my hutch and Bryce is bringing it over. And Ophelia is right here. Just playing a bit shy," Elena reached behind her, pulling Ophelia forward and to the front door of Jane's home.

Derek nodded, going back to his task. *For this being such a large town, everyone sure knows everyone.*

Laughter and quick talking tones reached his ears even with the door shut. Derek shook his head with a grin, moving along the top of the roof and pulling up shingles. The work was easy enough. The wood was so rotten and water logged, if it didn't crumble in his hands, it pulled right up.

Getting zinc on this roof was definitely the best choice, Derek decided. Moving down to the next row of shingles he noticed they were slightly better but not by much.

A jostling roll of a wagon sounded behind him. Derek didn't peek over his shoulder, trying to get another row yanked out before Jeffrey arrived with the roofing.

"Need a hand, Mr. Bennett?" Bryce called from behind him.

Derek peered over his left shoulder.

Bryce dismounted from their wagon, tying the reins next to Harold. He came over to the base of the ladder, a foot resting on the wrung. Derek pushed himself to standing, walking carefully on the roof to the ladder.

"Let's get the hutch inside first, if you don't mind. Then I'd love some help," Derek replied.

"Not at all," Bryce said, turning on his heel toward the buckboard wagon.

Derek deftly climbed down the ladder, going over to his son. Bryce untied all the knots on the rope holding the hutch in place. The furniture Jane was acquiring was of solid cherry pieces, dove tailed and pieced together. It was a beautiful piece, one that must have cost her something fierce.

"Jane pay you for this yet?" Derek asked.

Bryce shook his head. "Nope. I'm going to let my wife negotiate as it was hers," Bryce bit his bottom lip, chewing on it then looking around cautiously, lowering his voice. "She has too much furniture anyway."

Derek chortled, unsure of how to respond. There was a tenseness between them. Even though their clogged, smokey air was starting to clear, the bitter ash and dust lingered between them. And even though they were kept apart for love and different reasons, coming back together would be harder than freeing a caged bear.

Bryce climbed back into the wagon, carefully scooting the heavy wooden furniture to the end. Taking the top, he gently laid it on its back.

"Why now?" Bryce asked. "Why do you want to be a part of my life now?"

Derek's eyes bore into the curious green of his son's. Anger lingered; along with hurt and sadness. Derek sighed, deflating and defeated. He thought coming back to Denver, at least one more time, would do his old heart some good; to lay it all out on the line to his son before he passed on. Now, he wasn't certain coming here was such a grand idea.

*The hurt on Bryce's face nearly kills me every time I see it,* Derek chastised himself. *No amount of words would ever be able to replace the hurt I've done to my blood.*

Bryce stared at him firmly. The hard, sun-tanned lines on his son's face etched into his memory. There was still anger and curiosity but now Derek saw an openness to his honest answers.

"I've always wanted to be a part of your life. But your mother and father made it clear I was unwelcome and I didn't want to cause you more pain or confusion so I stayed away. Before I left, I watched Travis with you. He treated you well, so I set aside his threats and saw the man behind them. He could care for you, love you. He loved your mother very much and the threats came from fear, not malicious intent. Travis is a good man, a kind man over-all. A man you needed in your life growing up and one I wasn't at the time. I wasn't a bad man. But I was a wanderer, a rough trap-per, and I knew that wasn't the best life for you," Derek admitted. "I regret not being in your life. Deeply so. And I'm getting on in years. I came to tell you I'm sorry. And the choice is yours if you want me in your life or not. I ain't going to force it."

Bryce's brows furrowed together. He chewed on his bottom lip, working it back and forth with his teeth. His head bounced around for a bit then he shrugged.

"Help me get this inside the house," Bryce stated.

Derek nodded, a slight hanging to his head. "All right."

He put on a mask of indifference as he helped carry the hutch inside for Jane. *Once I finish her roof, I'm done with Denver. I can't do this to my son or myself.*

# CHAPTER FIFTEEN

Jane watched Derek leave to take the wood back with a happiness in her she hadn't felt since Seth. Derek made her feel like a desirable woman, something she hadn't felt in a long time. She felt beautiful.

Happily, she moved about the house to begin scrubbing windows and floors. The floor was swept clean and cobwebs were gone. Grabbing a metal pail left behind by the previous tenants, she walked down to the well to get some water to scrub.

The fall sunshine brought some warmth to her body. Birds chirped merrily. The train whistled sharply announcing the arrival or departure of the latest locomotive.

Jane paused at the public well site, waiting for the other woman to get her fill of the water. One thing she loved about the Whitman Hotel was their own hand dug well. They were never short of water and did not have to walk very far to get it.

The woman moved on, taking her pails with her. Jane moved in, getting her water next. Sighing, she glanced over her shoulder to the house.

*I feel different*, she thought. *I'm no longer saddened by the loss of*

*Seth or having its weight harbingering on me. I'm at peace with myself and where I'm at. And I really like Derek. He's kind, attentive, endearing.* She smiled, turning back around to the pail of water.

Taking her load back up to the house, she set the sloshing water on the wooden floor.

"Knock-knock," Audrey called.

Her former employer and friend came inside her house with a beaming smile. Behind her, Kelly from laundry, with her bags stood at her door. The woman grinned, smiling in her clean yellow traveling suit. Kelly, even though younger than herself appeared older and worn out. The lines on her face gave way to a troubled life.

"Seems we are both off to different things," Kelly commented. "No more scrubbing for me and no more ordering for you," she teased with a smile.

"I will miss you," Jane said, giving Kelly a careful embrace as she didn't want to soil her friend's dress.

"I will miss you as well. I decided to go back home to Omaha to my parent's farm. They are getting on in years and maybe I can find myself a suitable husband," Kelly explained. Switching the luggage in her hands, she moved outside.

"You're going to find yourself a wonderful husband," Audrey encouraged.

Jane stood outside her front door in a semicircle with her friends. Jane smiled at herself. Not so long ago, she did not think she had any friends, believing all the people she interacted with were more colleagues than friends. How wrong she had been. These grand people had been her friends all along.

"Hello ladies," Elena Anderson said, approaching with her daughter. "Bryce is on his way to deliver your hutch. Ophelia and I needed to stretch our legs."

Audrey animatedly began talking to both Kelly and Elena about something she found most funny. Jane could only smirk. Her friend could weave a story so well a pine cone falling to the ground would be humorous.

Jane spied Derek and Harold coming up the road. His worn dark leather hat pulled down low over his eyes to keep the sun out. Harold brayed. As he came closer, Derek smiled at her and she grinned back, feeling the butterflies' somersault in her stomach.

"I'd best be off," Kelly announced. "I will miss you all."

"Yes," Jane agreed. "Cheers to new beginnings."

Derek's face peeked over the edge of her roof. Jane moved, stepping to the side. "I'm going to be pulling shingles ladies. You may want to head inside."

Jane and Audrey embraced Kelly one last time. Kelly turned on her heel to leave.

"Safe travels," Jane said, heading inside with Audrey right behind her.

"Thank you," Kelly replied, striding briskly down the road to the train station.

*Eliza is going to have to hire a few new people soon,* Jane thought. *Gladly, in a few more days, it is truly, not my issue.*

Jane held onto the door, waiting for Elena and Ophelia to come inside behind her. Elena had a hand over her face, speaking to Derek. Jane tried not to pay attention. Knowing this woman was married to his son, made her body shiver with nerves. She hoped Derek didn't mind the situation.

*How insensitive of me,* she admonished herself. *I told him earlier but I still feel so guilty. Oh dear! How he must be feeling about this right now! Poor Derek... What have I done?!*

Audrey's clicking heeled boots sounded behind her as the woman gushed over her new home and how cozy it felt. Jane smiled politely, as Elena and her child came inside.

"How lovely," Elena praised, holding onto Ophelia's hand.

"Thank you," Jane replied.

"Where is the hutch going to go? Have you decided yet?"

Jane's lips pursed together. "I was thinking here, on this wall," she said, pointing to the right side behind the door.

"I think that is very practical," Audrey agreed. "I would put it in the corner though. It would make your home seem larger."

Elena nodded.

"I like that idea," Jane approved, then looked around for a moment. "I apologize there is nowhere to sit. I'm headed to Leonard's and Verploeg's later to order a few items."

"Moving homes is taxing on the body and budget," Elena added, letting go of Ophelia's hand and stroking her daughter's soft blond head.

The door to her home opened with a click and a grunt. Bryce, walking backward and helped by Derek, brought in her hutch. Jane felt her body turn icy, watching the torment linger behind Derek's emerald eyes at the sight of his son.

"Where do you want it?" Bryce asked.

Jane pointed. "In this corner, angled out."

Bryce nodded, going to where she directed. Seamlessly, Bryce and Derek set down their sides exactly where she wanted the large piece. Bryce backed away, going around to the right to stand beside his wife and daughter.

The anger and bitterness toward Derek clung to his frame.

*What have I done*, she thought? *I have unintentionally hurt the man I'm interested in. But it is somewhat intentional as I knew Bryce would be here and I did not stop it or arrange something different.* Jane fumbled with her hands. Derek gave her a questioning look. Jane shoved her hands in her pockets. *Seth was right. Sometimes I have no forethought.*

"It looks lovely in that spot, Jane," Audrey began her lilting voice interrupting Jane's thoughts. Audrey glanced at the door and gave a tiny nod at Jane as she inched her way over, saying her goodbyes as she walked.

Jane would readily admit, Audrey had a sense for reading a room. Jane supposed spending years in upper class society would do that to a person.

"Thank you for coming by, Audrey," Jane said, moving to get the door.

"Absolutely. It was a pleasure to see you, Andersons," Audrey called out and hugged her. In a whisper only Jane could hear Audrey said, "See you tonight at the hotel. I hope this goes well."

Jane slightly lifted her chin in acknowledgement. "Thank you again, Audrey."

She shut the door behind the leaving woman, sucking in a deep breath in preparation of what was to come. Turning back around, Elena stood by her husband Bryce and their daughter situated herself in between her parents. Derek stood still by the hutch, deflated and arms down at his sides.

"Thank you for bringing it over so promptly," Jane said, breaking the eerie silence.

"Our pleasure," Elena replied. Lacing her fingers in with her husband's, she began, "We'd best be going. I still have to start supper."

"Before you go," Jane said, fumbling for the money in her dress pocket. She held out a few dollar notes totaling twenty dollars. "Will this suffice for payment for the hutch?"

Elena strode forward, taking the proffered money. "Yes. Thank you, Jane. We'd best be leaving. It was a pleasure to see you both again. Take care now." Elena made a rapid move for the door.

Bryce remained fixed in his position. "Mr. Bennett," Bryce's harsh voice rang out.

Jane jumped at the hard tone; sinking further into herself as the memory of her late husband's similar tone came flooding back to her. Jane hated Seth's aggravated condescending tone, especially when she interrupted his paperwork or ledgers. They were both educated people, yet Seth continually spoke down to her with a likeness to Bryce's grating tone.

"Do you have anything else to say?" Bryce prompted. "I'm not sure what to believe since Ma always said you didn't love me and you beat her."

Derek strode forward, shoulders rolled inward and hands in his pockets. "I have told you everything," he nodded, bowing his head and sucked in a deep breath. Bringing his head back up, his green eyes locked on his son. "A father's love for his child never changes with time or distance. I never laid a hand on Tara. I never laid a hand on any woman," Derek felt his throat thicken, tears stinging profusely behind his eyes, yet he refused to allow them to fall. "I love you, and whatever you decide, if you want anything to do with me or not, I will respect your decision."

"I believe I need to cancel coffee this afternoon," Bryce said stiffly. "I apologize for the inconvenience this may have caused you."

Taking Elena by the small of her back and Ophelia's hand in his own, Bryce immediately left her house. The door slamming shut made her eyes blink and her body jump as the noise echoed in her small home.

Derek stood opposite of her. She watched his jaw work back and forth a touch. His green eyes became glassy. Jane's hands clenched the inside fabric of her apron. Without a word, Derek strode toward her front door. Hand on the knob, he paused. The jostling tack of the team of horses sounded through the walls; announcing the departure of the Andersons.

"I'm going to finish your roof today," he said.

Before she could utter a response, he was out the door. Jane jumped as her door slammed again. All the chills in her body filled her from foot to head.

"What have I done?" she whispered aloud.

The cracking and creaking of Derek climbing the ladder to her roof made her feel enclosed and trapped. Taking off her apron, she set it on the hutch. The pail of water remained in the middle of the room but it could wait.

Double checking her money in her cloth sack, she strode out of her home. She didn't want to be near Derek knowing she caused his current grief. Nothing she would be able to say would fix the problem she caused. Her mother used to say – *there is nothing an apology and a hug can't fix.* She was certain something like this couldn't be fixed so easily. Derek was finishing her roof now out of promised obligation.

Peeking back over her shoulder, her eyes caught Derek on her roof briefly. His green eyes struck hers and immediately looked away. Jane sucked in a breath, turning to continue down the road to Leonard's Mercantile.

*After Leonard's I'm going to head to Verploeg's beds and furniture and order myself a bed to be delivered to my home, and a settee. I don't want to stay at the hotel longer than necessary.* Jane peeked over her shoulder again and sighed. *Maybe I'm meant to be a hermit with cats. All I know is, I don't ever want to see that desolate look on a man especially knowing I'm the one who caused it.*

# CHAPTER SIXTEEN

Derek finished removing the wooden shingles in record time. The work kept his mind busy and not on all the chaos that previously transpired. Any time he thought of it, he pushed it all back, focusing more on the task at hand. He didn't want to think about Jane or Bryce. He didn't want to think about anything. The emotions of the day tormented him enough, urging him to dwell and process it when he wasn't ready.

All the wooden shingles were so weathered and worn, the little pieces came right up. After he pulled the last piece off, he went inside Jane's home for the broom. Climbing back on the roof, he swept it clean. He didn't want debris getting caught underneath the metal.

He finished sweeping just as Jeffrey showed up with the metal roofing. With their quick casual greetings out of the way, Jeffrey began handing him up the metal to lay down. The process was fairly quick with everything fitting nicely and the few nails they needed for the metal and the roof. Derek was impressed with the easiness and efficiency of it all. Jeffrey was a kindly man, staying long enough to help put the metal sheeting on and secure it. With the two of them working together, it took them around an hour to finish.

"Tell Jane I'll be by the hotel tomorrow for payment," Jeffrey said from the buckboard wagon.

Derek held up a hand. "Will do," he replied, heading to get Harold.

He wasn't going to tell Jane. He was going to tell the lady at the front desk to tell Jane. Part of him was pleased Jane gave him the courtesy of telling him about the hutch and that his son would be along to deliver it. The other part irked him because she knew how sensitive it was for him. Mainly, it was his fault. He could have left beforehand, yet he didn't. His emotions were of his own making.

*It's her home, she can have over whoever she wants,* Derek admonished himself. *But damn, it hurt. And with my son storming out how he did, I can't handle it. I'm done with Denver. I was wrong for coming here.*

Gathering Harold's reins, he led him back down the road to the Whitman Hotel. He dropped his mule off with Ross at the stables for the night. Without a word to the stableman, he strode to the hotel.

He checked the roads, being sure to keep an eye out for the beautiful blond woman who captured his waking and sleeping attention. She wasn't around. Taking the stairs two at a time, he strode inside.

The young brown-haired woman was behind the front desk.

"Hello, Mr. Bennett," she greeted.

Derek paused. "Jeffrey from the mill will be by to see Jane tomorrow."

The woman blinked. "Absolutely," she said, breaking out of her stunned silence. "I will make a note to tell her."

He nodded. "Can I have the supper special up in my room... please."

"Yes. Do you care to know what it is?"

"No," he replied, already heading for the stairs.

Taking the stairs up at a tired and deliberate pace, he felt rather guilty for being abrupt with the young woman. He watched her cross from her desk toward the other side of the hotel.

"Sorry," he called down to her. "Been a rough day."

She paused mid-stride, offering a wan smile. "No worries, Mr. Bennett. Supper will be up to you shortly."

Derek tromped the rest of the way to his room. A note was stuck in between the door and frame. Grimacing he opened it to find the laundry order he sent down yesterday was completed and ready for him to pick up.

*Perfect timing,* he thought.

Opening the locked door, he was pleased to find his room untouched. Going to his rucksack, he began piling it full with the clothes he purchased. He left out Darcy's favorite dress, hiding it on a peg behind the door.

With Denver holding so many awful memories for him, he cared not to ever return to this town. *Back to Ogden Utah I go,* he decided. *I saw and met my son and that's good enough for me.*

He didn't outright blame Jane for the ending of his day. It stung him. Unintentional though it was by her, it hurt. Jane was a kind woman. Watching her face morph and change to what was happening lent insight to him. She felt guilty for what happened. Derek didn't blame her. Not really. None of it was really her fault. Seeing his son so often in the last few days was a blessing and a curse. He didn't know how else to explain to his son his reasons for doing what he did.

*And I don't dislike the woman,* he thought. *I'm fond of her. I can't rightly explain how I feel around her, sudden though it was. I blame Darcy, the afterlife meddling witchy woman.* Derek sighed, letting the long breath out for long as he could. *Denver just doesn't hold much for me. What I thought would make it my place, won't. Even Jane, staying here for her, I'm not sure would make me happy.*

With his bag mostly packed, he went down the stairs with the note that his clothes were readied. The young woman at the front desk took him around the back to where laundry was kept. Hanging on a line, his leather trapping clothes were cleaned and smelled nice. He slung them over his arm, heading back to his room where his promised supper awaited him.

*Come morning, I'm heading out of Denver. I'm leaving this all behind me. I can't hurt my son anymore and I don't want to hurt Jane.*

---

Before the color even struck the sky, Derek and Harold were on the road toward Black Hawk. He checked out, leaving a note to give all the extra monies to his son. As he always had and will continue to do, any extra would go to Bryce.

Harold brayed irritably. His mule never enjoyed early mornings; and neither did he if he could help it. He laughed humorously at himself. His profession often called for early mornings, yet he avoided them when possible. Today was one of those unavoidable early mornings. Getting out of Denver was a priority to him. He couldn't stand to say goodbye to his son or Jane.

Derek sighed. Already his heart hung heavily on his person. Leaving the final piece of Darcy behind sat well with him. Leaving Jane behind, did not.

Knowing Jane as little as he did and for only two days at that, he found himself immensely fond of her. She was direct, both in her emotions and in her voice. She didn't coddle anything and try as she might, she couldn't hide her emotions from him. She could wear a mask to hide it to the outside world, but to any person who knows people, she could not hide how she felt.

Derek kicked a rock along the road. Denver was already an hour behind him. He stopped in the middle of the road, gazing all around him at the rolling hills with grass swaying in the slight breeze. Colorado was a beautiful place. No matter where he happened to be in life, it called to him. All those years ago and even now, he couldn't shake Colorado from his blood.

*I can't shake Jane from my head.* He glanced over his shoulder, gazing back the way he came. He tilted his head back, staring at the sky. The dawn was already passed. The clouds overhead accumulated with rain but whether it fell would be anyone's guess. He sighed; taking his beaver hat off and raking his fingers through his hair. He stuck his hat back on. *Every time something became hard, I ran away. I didn't fight for Tara. I didn't fight for Bryce. I'm not fighting to have a relationship with Bryce. And now I'm not fighting for Jane either. I'm a cowardly man; always running away.*

Harold nudged him on the arm, whinnying shrilly and showing his teeth. Derek patted the cranky animal on the nose.

"Damnit Harold," Derek said to his mule. "Would you like a relationship?"

Harold stared at him wholly disinterested. The animal lowered his head to the ground, pulling up a tuft of grass.

"Well I would," Derek replied, tuning back around to Denver. "I'm done running Harold. You are going to get yourself a relationship and so am I."

Harold's ears moved back as he whinnied breathily again.

"It's not so bad," Derek admonished. "Just agree, and say 'yes dear,' You may find you like it." Derek laughed.

Going back felt better on him than leaving. Yesterday, all he wanted to do was run away like always. Seeing all he was about to leave behind, yet again, didn't sit well on him. He couldn't leave like that. He couldn't turn his back again on his blood, and on a woman, he was coming to know, and love.

He changed moods and directions faster than a bird in flight. He tended to leave and block out what he didn't like. His mother had been like that and he'd watched and learnt from an early age - don't like someone or something, leave because confronting it caused problems.

It shamed him to think how well he'd learned that lesson from his mother, the woman who'd taken him and ran from everything, including his father. He'd rather be like his father and model after him – a father never quits. His father never stopped looking or searching for him; finally getting to him in the heart of Kentucky, and taking him completely from her. His father never stopped.

Derek ran a hand over his face. *Fifty-two years of my life, I've been an idiot,* he thought, striding back to Denver. *I want to spend the rest of my allotted years, being a little wiser.* Derek glanced to the heavens, closing his eyes at the warm sunlight rays dousing him in warmth. *Thank you, Pa, for never quitting on me.*

# CHAPTER SEVENTEEN

J ane woke early to get to her house. She left an assortment of
money at the front desk with Eliza for when Jeffrey came by
for payment. She didn't rightly know how much the metal
would cost, so she left the payment for the cost of wood that was
supposed to be used.

*It has to be somewhere in between there,* she surmised. *Derek
mentioned it would be cheaper.*

Her heart sank at the thought of Derek. She hadn't seen him
since yesterday. He took his meal in his bedroom and got the
clothing Kelly finished cleaning before she left for Omaha. And
now, early this morning he left.

*And it's my fault he is gone,* she thought, feeling her heart
constrict. *I brought Bryce Anderson and his wife over, knowing how
painful it was for him and I did nothing... absolutely nothing.* She hung
her head, folding up the quilt on her bed. *Maybe I'm not ready for a
relationship after all. This just proves my lack of forethought Seth always
said I had.*

Jane sighed, stacking the quilt on top of her bed. She bought it
years ago when she first started, wanting something that was hers

and not the hotels. Now, she was happy it would be coming with her to her new house.

*I'm not going to blame myself for the incident at my home. I did nothing wrong. It's my home. It's my* happy *home. And I did tell Derek beforehand. He had a choice to come back later if it truly bothered him.*

Jane held the folded quilt in her arms. Ross waited outside around the back with a horse and a wagon to move her things over today. Leonard from the Mercantile would be sending up Clyde with her order later. Her suitcase full of dresses was already in the back of the wagon. All she needed to load now was this quilt and a crate of trinkets from her office. Her bed and settee would be delivered later today as well.

Setting her quilt on top of her crate, she picked it up. The crate comfortable in her hands. Her eyes gazed around, taking in the finality of her decision. Her heart soared eagerly, happy to have something that would always be hers – a home.

With a deep breath, she backed out of the room she'd called home for so many years. The bed lay stripped of the linen, ready to wash for the next occupant to reside. The window was open, allowing for fresh air to come wafting inside to remove her lemon verbena scent.

Turning on her heel, she strode out of her room. Taking a left out of the door, she went to the back of the hotel where the employees sat on break and where Ross waited. He stood beside the wagon, waiting patiently for her to gather her things. Gently, and without a word, Ross took her items from her and carefully put it in the back of the wagon.

Jane glanced over her shoulder again at the Whitman Hotel. Her home for over a decade was a wonderful time in her life. She met some great people and had great relationships. And what a great ending to being there as well; meeting Derek Bennett was a treasure, even if that treasure was lost to her forever.

*And I'm happy for the first time in years. I'm truly, genuinely happy,* she thought, letting out a breath and feeling her spirit soar with contentment. *I'm happy – whether by myself or with someone. I'm happy. It's taken me years to be this way, comfortable in who I am and forgiving myself for Seth and his death.*

Mary waddled up the pathway, hands on the back of her hips. "There you are Ross Montgomery. I was lookin' for you."

Jane smiled. Out of all the changes the year brought, Mary was certainly her most treasured. The woman was keen on a person, far more than most ever gave her credit for.

"I'm taking Jane to her new house up the road from us. I told you this mornin' hun."

Mary's face contorted into a moue. "Dammit, I forgot. I swear this child is eatin' my brain too," she laughed.

Ross strode over to her, giving Mary a quick peck on the cheek. "Would you like to come with us?"

Mary shook her head. "No. All this walkin' has made me gotta use the privy. I came to ask Jane somethin' real fast."

Jane grinned broadly, moving closer to the pregnant woman so she wouldn't have to waddle anymore. "What is it, Mary?"

Mary arched her back. "Ross and I, we got no one around. Seein's how you're the closest person to family we got, and we love you like blood," Mary paused, reaching out her hand to Ross.

Ross cleared his throat. "We were wondering if you would like to be our baby's grandmother?"

Jane sucked in a breath before all the air could escape her body. Tears peppered her eyes, stinging behind her lashes profusely and finally splattering across her cheeks. Tears poured out of her eyes like water from a pitcher.

*I'm a grandma,* she thought. *I'm a grandma!*

The three words she couldn't help but repeat in her mind had her blubbering. "I would love to," she finally choked out. "I love you both."

With one arm around Ross and the other kind of around Mary, Jane embraced them both. She held them against her, savoring this moment and committing it forever to memory.

*God knew what I needed long before I did and by goodness, I needed this,* Jane thought.

"All righty," Mary said, breaking the emotional silence, "I'm gonna burst worse than a spring thaw," she announced, waddling off. "I love you, Ross. See you at home."

Ross chortled. "I love you too, dear."

Jane clambered into the buckboard wagon with a smile; her heart so full to bursting. She wiped the remnants of tears from her eyes, sucking in a deep contented breath. Ross climbed in on the other side, taking the reins in his hands.

"Ready?" he asked. "This is a mighty big change for you."

He gazed at her thoughtfully, waiting for an answer. Concern lingered behind his gray eyes.

"I'm ready," she said with a smile. "And I will be fine. Besides you and Mary are my neighbors so if I need a cup of sugar I know where to go."

Ross grinned.

Seeming placated with a firm answer, Ross slapped the reins on the horse's back and took off down the road. The sun was reaching toward the middle of the morning. Jane surmised it was around nine.

The city bustled with activity. As Ross merged into the street, she spied Clyde marching up the road. Ross must have seen it as well, for he pulled off to the left-hand side and waited for the boy to catch up.

"Here Miss Jane," Clyde said with a toothy grin and a huff. "Here's all your pretty plates and cloth."

Ross dismounted from the wagon, putting the gate down in back. Taking the crate of dishware and cloth from the kid, Ross gently slid it into the wagon. Straw poked from the top of the crate and Jane was excited to carefully peel each piece out, wash it and begin using it.

"Thank you, Clyde," Jane replied.

The boy dipped his head and took off running toward Leonard's Mercantile. Ross shut the gate on the wagon, climbing back inside. He got the wagon going again toward her home.

Jane felt her body shiver and stomach roil with excited trepidation. She couldn't wait to fully be in her home but was also nervous about her first night alone. At the hotel she wasn't alone, someone was always one room over.

*It's gonna be fine,* she soothed herself. *Let's see... I need to scrub the floors and get two rugs. One for the sitting area and one for the bedroom.*

She made a mental note of all she wanted to accomplish today, starting with her bedroom and the bed and settee that was to be delivered later today from Verploeg's.

During her mental planning, Ross arrived at her quaint little home. He pulled up, right past her front door and stopped the team of horses, throwing the brake. He helped her down off the wagon, waiting to the side, until her feet were settled. Going around to the back of the wagon, he unlatched it, getting her crate of dishes.

Jane hurried around, unlocking the front door. "Thank you, Ross."

The man dipped his head, heading inside with the delicate load. "When you're ready and settled, Mary and I would like to come see you, if you're willing," Ross stated.

Jane grinned. "I would love that."

Ross set the crate down in the kitchen and headed back outside. Jane grabbed her crate with the quilt on top taking it into the bedroom. The house had a different smell to it. Instead of the damp odor of wood, it smelled like the crispness of fall.

Jane inhaled deeply, a contented smile spreading across her face. She closed her eyes at the entrance of her bedroom door, her shoulders rising and falling with her deep breath.

*Home,* she thought, eyes still closed as she relished the moment. *I'm happy to be home.* Opening her eyes, she walked farther into the bedroom, setting her crate to the side. A dresser, one she hadn't purchased, sat in the right-hand corner and to the right, in the middle of the wall was the window.

"Have a good day, Jane," Ross hollered.

"Thank you, Ross," she answered.

Before she got to ask him if he brought in the dresser, the door slammed shut and the jostling of the wagon reached her ears. Jane shrugged it off. She had to go to the mercantile again later today for supplies and figured she could stop by the hotel later to ask anyway.

Disregarding the dresser issue for now, she strode back out to the kitchen. Startled, she stopped in her tracks. Derek stood before her, cheeks reddened, hat in hand. The leather ensemble marking him a trapper adorned his body, bringing out the richness of his brown hair streaked with silver and the full emerald green of his eyes.

Derek set one of the crates from the back of the wagon down on the floor. He stepped aside and toward the door.

"Thank you for putting on my roof," Jane began. "You left before I got to thank you."

Derek shifted the hat from hand to hand. Looking down, his feet shuffled a bit. He cleared his throat, "You're welcome," his deep voice stated.

Jane stuck her hands in her apron pockets, whirling her fingers on the inside of the fabric. She could feel the prickliness of their conversation on her skin like a biting winter hail.

"I'm sorry," she blurted.

Derek shook his head. His steady level gaze meeting her eyes. "It's your home. And I have something I want to ask you."

Jane's brow furrowed. "What is it?"

Derek clenched his hat in his left hand, striding forward. He stood toe to toe with her. His stubbled face peered down at her. His green eyes taking in her appearance with a sparkle and an observance that made her heart shudder and pine for more.

Jane wasn't blind to him and his attention. She desired a relationship with him. Although she would never say it out loud to him or even to herself.

*He makes me feel so valued, seen as a woman,* she thought. *I really like him.*

She gazed up at him, inhaling his earthy pine scent. If nothing was to ever become of them, she wanted to commit this moment and his smell to memory to cherish. There was something about Derek Bennett that drew him to her more than a queen to a throne.

"I," he cleared his throat. "I was wondering if you knew if Jeffrey named his mule horse Darlene?"

Jane burst into laughter, the tension she felt simmering dissipated. Derek grinned broadly at her.

Shaking her head, "No, I did not."

Derek reached for her hand, taking it in his own. "Whenever things change, I have a tendency to run back to the pine tree covered hills and hide; to ignore it all until time passes long enough for me to forget. But this last time, something stopped me from running," he said pausing, rubbing his thumb over the back of her knuckles.

"Yes?" she prompted, her voice a mere squeak of a whisper.

"It was you," he said. "I feel something blooming between us... I want to know where it goes with your permission," he paused, putting a hand behind her back, and pulling her into an embrace.

Jane allowed it, having wondered for a long time what it would feel like to have a man wrap his arms around her again. She relished his quiet protectiveness, the well-muscled power of Derek. He held her for a moment, tight enough to be firm yet not overly so; a perfect combination of tenderness and brawn.

"So, I was wondering," he continued, whispering in her ear, "since Harold agreed to a relationship, would you like one too?"

Jane giggled softly, her arms wrapping around Derek's waist. "I believe I would."

Derek grinned. He pulled back his face a mere inch from hers. His lips hovering above her own.

"May I court you?" he asked.

Jane replied with a kiss to his lips.

# EPILOGUE

Snow fell. Already Denver was inches deep with the white flakes. Wagons had a hard time making it through some spots with the snow covering deep ruts and holes.

Derek waited patiently for Jane. Standing inside the church was warm and cozy. A fire crackled in the fireplace behind him. To his immediate left, his son Bryce and his family sat on the first row of benches on the right-hand side of the church. He was surprised Bryce came. After helping Bryce carry in Jane's hutch, he hadn't seen or spoken to his son. Derek wrote to him about the wedding, respecting the man's boundaries to remain distant, and invited him. Jane spoke to Elena when she spontaneously met her at Leonard's Mercantile about it. But in all his days, he didn't expect his son to be here.

Jane's friends from the hotel lined three rows of benches on the left-hand side of the church, smiling and waiting eagerly for Jane to emerge. He didn't realize how many people Jane knew over the years. Kelly came back from Omaha, selling her family's ranch and would be a permanent feature at the hotel. She was a nice woman. But she was one of many.

Jane hadn't wanted a wedding but at his insistence, she agreed.

He wanted to make it proper for her. Or as he put it – memorable for their advancing age.

Derek shifted from foot to foot, waiting to see Jane emerge. He checked his long wool coat, picking imaginary specks from it. His mop of brown hair, streaked with gray was slicked back and secured at the nape of his neck in a leather thong.

Reverend Kester put a hand on his shoulder. "I'm sure she'll be along shortly," he soothed. "The weather is probably causing the delay."

Derek peeked out a frosted glass window. "You're probably right," he replied with a sigh. "I've never been more anxious."

The Reverend stepped closer. "My ma used to say – when a soul or heart binds to another, this feeling of superior elation and tranquility battles with itself to set the people God chose to right," he finished with a grin. "I never knew what she meant until I met Brigette," he finished clapping him on the shoulder.

Derek's face twisted as his eyes narrowed and lips pursed. He thought he found forever love with Bryce's mother, Tara. Upon discovering her love would never be mutual, it broke his heart. He married Darcy shortly after Tara refused him again, not truly wanting to be alone. And Darcy being the sweet, even tempered woman she was, didn't mind him. Darcy never made his soul or heart feel how the Reverend described. He'd not felt that way until he met Jane.

The doors in the back of the church opened, giving way to a sight which took his breath away and made his heart stop. For a moment, he utterly forgot how to breathe.

The ivory colored dress hugged her frame, going straight down to the ground instead of coming out with a hoop skirt or whatever women wore. Her hair fell in perfect long blond ringlets to the middle of her back. She clutched a winter bouquet of dried flowers.

Everyone in the church turned and rose. Derek hardly noticed. His eyes were riveted to the woman who called his heart. Jane made her way to him slowly, almost like she was floating on her feet.

She came to him, standing opposite with a wide smile and tears in her eyes. Gently he brushed a tear falling from her eye with a sweep of his finger.

"You look stunning," he complimented.

"And you look handsome."

Reverend Kester droned on, speaking about love and quoting the Bible. He couldn't hear a word. His mind went blank, his heart surging with a mixture of complete elation of this woman's love and the utter tranquility of finding someone to spend the rest of his life with.

He spent so long, trying to find something, aching for something he didn't know he needed until he came here to Denver. How Darcy knew what he truly needed; he didn't know. And for a moment, he felt guilty for never fully loving her as she deserved. He loved her, but not in the way the good Reverend Kester described.

Jane made him feel this way. She made him feel like a decent man who can begin anew instead of one trapped in the past by mistakes.

Derek glanced over at his son, sitting in the front bench row. His usual long, drawn face in Derek's presence was now morphed into a smile. Whether for him or for Jane, he didn't rightly care. Having his son here to experience this moment with him was unforgettable. And Jane did this for him. This kind, amazing woman, brought his son to this church on the last most important day of his life.

"I love you," he mouthed to her.

Jane grinned. "I love you too."

Jane's eyes tore away from his, bringing him to the present. "I do," she whispered, her keen brown eyes locking with his.

His entire body stilled its movement. He felt swallowed like something reached out, consumed him completely and gobbled him whole. His heart burst against his ribcage thundering wildly at the love of Jane overpowering him. And he relished it.

"I do," he replied, not waiting for the Reverend to ask the question.

"All right then," Reverend Kester chuckled. "Kiss your bride."

Derek rested his forehead against hers, kissing her lightly on the lips. The few people in the church cheering made the entire building echo. Taking her hand, they descended the elevated platform to join the rest of the attendees.

Jane's former employer and her husband were the first to congratulate them, followed by all the others. His son, Elena and little Ophelia waited at the back for him. Breaking apart from his wife, he strode over to Bryce.

"Thank you for coming," Derek began. "It meant a lot to me that you're here."

Bryce nodded, proffering his hand. Derek took it. His son was a man of few words. He couldn't blame him. He would be the same if the shoe was on the other foot. It still grieved his heart. More than anything, he wanted to be on decent terms with his blood.

"Congratulations," Elena offered, embracing him.

"Thank you, Mrs. Anderson," Derek replied, smiling out of politeness.

Ophelia tucked herself in between her parents, still slowly coming around to him.

"I get it now... Dad," Bryce blurted.

Derek blinked. Shocked and stunned, he stood riveted to his spot. Jane came up from behind him and looped her arm in with his, giving him a squeeze.

Being brought back to the present, Derek replied, "Get what?"

Bryce nodded. "You saw me get to have a loving family with Tara and Travis and interrupting it, didn't sit well with you. You didn't want to hurt me by making me choose. You mentioned it before and I was too angry and... shocked to understand fully what you truly meant. It took me a while... I had to think about my own daughter," Bryce paused, putting a hand on Elena's stomach, "And our next child, to get it and for it to make sense emotionally. I forgive you."

Bryce pulled him in close, wrapping him in an embrace, he did not ever expect to get. "I forgive you," Bryce breathed. "I forgive you."

Derek clenched his eyes shut, giving his son a squeeze. Inhaling sharply, his nose betrayed him with sniffles. "Thank you." Derek wrapped his son in an embrace. Tears filtered into his eyes and tracked down his weather wrinkled face. Derek sniffed, pulling back from his son and resting both hands on his shoulders.

"You're a good man, Bryce. Better than me by far," Derek said, sucking in a deep breath in between sniffles. "I love you."

"I love you too, Dad," Bryce replied, looping an arm around Elena.

Derek grinned, blinking back tears as he looked at the wood paneled ceiling. Jane looped her arm in with Derek resting her head on his shoulder.

"You finally got your achin' part healed," Jane commented.

Derek sniffed, his gaze falling on her. Gently, she wiped away his tears with a soft finger, smiling broadly at him. Derek kissed her forehead.

"I got the love of my life on my arm and my achin' part fixed," Derek replied, resting his forehead against hers.

Jane sighed, breathing in deep. "As have I."

She clutched on his arm, holding him tight. Derek glanced to his left, something catching the corner of his eye. Through the unfrosted glass by the fireplace, he spotted a bird take off from the sill. Derek smiled, turning back around and kissing Jane on the top of her head.

# WHITMAN NOTES

A friend of mine and also the former editor to the Castre World Novel Series, and I were supposed to co-write these westerns together. She backed out to spear head some other awesome projects with some big authors. She has followed her own dream, done her own things, and slayed it all! I'm thrilled for her and all her incredible success.

My friend left me Audrey Whitman to finish and to do as I pleased. I left it all sitting on my computer for a while, thinking about what to do. I wanted to finish the westerns, but I also wanted to write an Urban Fantasy Romance.

Then, my husband's cousin messaged me, asking me for something clean with no bedroom fun. So, for her, I opened the western back up. Since my husband's cousin loved Audrey, I figured why not 5 more haha. (And maybe 6 more later...)

I wanted to give readers a chance to read something in my style without the tumble between the sheets my other series has. I'm happy I wrote these novellas. They were super fun to create and made me appreciate the era in American history and my ancestors more.

I'm kind of a weirdo and stickler about names. I create a

spreadsheet for names so I don't repeat anything because I don't want the characters to get confusing as the series continues; or for my readers to wonder what the heck happened to that particular character. But also, so I can create a diverse and interesting society of characters within the book itself.

To make it even more interesting, I look up what each name happens to mean. I use a website I love called – www.meaning-of-names.com – and I absolutely love it because it offers a varied range of names from region to country. I get all my names from this site.

If you're curious, here is what all the names in the Whitman Series Romance's happen to mean.

1.) Audrey Whitman – origin is English – meaning is Noble Strength

   a. Eugene Turner – origin is English – meaning is Well Born

   2.) Kayla Langmoore – origin is American – meaning is Beloved

   a. Benjamin Coleman – origin is Hebrew – meaning is Son of My Right Hand

   3.) Mary Lockburn – origin is Hebrew – meaning is Of the Sea or Bitter

   a. Ross Montgomery – origin is Scottish – meaning is Headland

   4.) Lena Jenkins – origin is Israeli – meaning is Illustrious

   a. Quint Morris – origin is French – meaning is Born Fifth

   5.) Natali Hawkins – origin is Italian – meaning is Born on Christmas

   a. Wyatt Pearson – origin is English – meaning is Guide

   6.) Jane McCarthy – origin is Hebrew – meaning is Gift from God

   a. Derek Bennett – origin is German – meaning is Gifted Ruler

. . .

The hardest part of creating this series was the history. So much was going on in the early 1880's when these novels took place. With the end of the Civil War in 1865, and the beginning of the huge railroad expansions in the early 1870's, I had to create a setting where there were railroads coming in and out of Denver, Colorado.

Not only that but also when the cattle era was still widely popular. During the mid-1880's a huge drought and famine hit the mid-western states; essentially ending the era of cattle and cattle drives for a period while everyone recovered from the losses.

But why Denver?

The simple answer is, it's a beautiful country. The more involved answer, stated to me by Lauren M., was tuberculosis was still on the rise in the big, dense cities. Those who suffered were told to change their climate, mostly by heading west to the country areas. The Whitman Hotel was supposed to get changed into a rehabilitation facility to assist those suffering from the affliction to live out the rest of their days. I did not wish to do that.

Not that it would be complicated but because of the medical side of it all. There aren't a lot of books on it and treatment was widely varied. Even though there are notes about how to treat those suffering from tuberculosis, not all readers would know what the heck I was talking about. Keeping the Whitman Hotel as the Hotel was the simplest way to complete the series without confusing the heck out of myself and you lol.

In this series, I tried to keep the prices and money out of the books. Coins were the most popular form of currency. Dollar notes, first printed by Benjamin Franklin in the 1760's – yes really – he owned a huge printing company – weren't really a thing that caught on yet. Dollar notes or 'greenbacks' as they were called due their backside being printed in green ink, were brought back into circulation more around 1862 to help fund the Civil War.

And because of the currency and variation for goods, in To Find A Whitman, I made an error about the cost of train travel. It was paid by a set amount of money based on the mileage from large town to town. Surprisingly, it wasn't cheap at all. From St,

Louis to Denver the travel would cost about $125.00, and to put that all into perspective, a cowhand or even those hired to work on the railroad made between $25-31.00 a month.

With the end of the To Bind A Heart, fur trapper Derek Bennett shouldn't have made as much as he did on pelts in the beginning of the story, but I wanted to give the old man his due. A bear pelt would sell for $5-8.00 depending on the quality. And trapping for fur significantly was on the decrease by then.

If I am forced to be biased, I love Mary Lockburn (Montgomery). She is so sweet, endearing and a forthright character. I loved creating her. She wasn't supposed to get her own book but looking back, it was my most favorite to create.

Well, there it all is. If you have any further questions or comments about this Whitman Series, please feel free to email me at – erickashanniak@gmail.com

Take care. I hope you had a grand western adventure.

# ACKNOWLEDGEMENT

Brittany G., my friend and editor, I appreciate and admire you more than words can say. You are a true friend and wonderful mentor. I'm beyond grateful to have a friend like you in my life and to have met you and know you. Brittany, you are such a wonderful person and mother. The world definitely needs more people like you. Thank you so much for everything! Thank you for being my friend.

Thank you, Amir L. for formatting this book for me and every other book I have thrown your way. You are such a patient, kind and wonderful person. I couldn't have done it without you. You are the bestest, bestest ever! I am so happy to know you.

Leslie L., and Stephanie K., thank you ladies very much for reading my madness, believing in me, and supporting me. You all mean more to me than words could ever express. I love you both so much.

·  ·  ·

Thank you, Lauren M. for your mentorship in all the Castre World Novels, your friendship and your kindness. Audrey Whitman, the characters, and everything you helped to build will forever hold an endearing place in my heart. Thank you for everything.

# ABOUT THE AUTHOR

E.A. (Ericka Ashlee) Shanniak is the author of the successful fantasy romance series – A Castre World Novel. She is hobbit-sized, barely reaching over five feet tall on a good day. When she wears her Georgia Romeo's not only does she gain an inch, she is then able to reach the kitchen cabinets. Ericka loves to write at her desk that her daughter's cat destroyed. Fortunately for everyone, she can see over it.

Ericka resides in a small town of Molalla, Oregon with her husband, two kids, dog and cat. The cat was her daughter's idea.

If you care to follow
FACEBOOK
AMAZON
INSTAGRAM

or at her Facebook group – Shanniak Shenanigans –

Made in the USA
Columbia, SC
20 April 2021